About the Author

I've been writing stories since I was seven years old. Then, they were in my best handwriting with a pencil. As a teenager I was given a typewriter as a present and I started banging out a couple of romantic, teenage novels and poems; I guess as a way of channelling all that excess, emotional energy.

Throughout my life and wherever I have travelled, I always seem to carry a notebook around with me and jot down observations about people and life, which sometimes I turn into stories as the mood takes me.

Flint and Kiffy

Phito Panayiotou

Flint and Kiffy

Olympia Publishers
London

www.olympiapublishers.com
OLYMPIA PAPERBACK EDITION

A CIP catalogue record for this title is
available from the British Library.

ISBN: 978-1-80074-054-9

This is a work of fiction.
Names, characters, places and incidents originate from the writer's imagination.
Any resemblance to actual persons, living or dead, is purely coincidental.

First Published in 2021

Olympia Publishers
Tallis House
2 Tallis Street
London
EC4Y 0AB

Printed in Great Britain

Close Encounter of the Train Type

"So, tell me again, how did you get to meet your old man?" asked Jonas, in a manner not designed to disguise the disdain he felt for such a situation.

She frowned as she gently rocked the buggy back and forth in the hope that her little bundle of joy that was her daughter, stayed fast asleep in the buggy. It was hard work being a mother.

"On a train," she said and added with irritation, "I told you that already, Jonas."

"Sorry Adrienne, I forgot," he said, not at all convinced. "How on the train? Did he ask you out? People don't just meet on a train randomly."

"It wasn't exactly random," she said, recalling the day that she confronted him. "It started with him staring at me."

"Staring at you? Do you mean he was ogling you, like how you say, with lust?" Jonas was teasing her.

"No, not exactly, it didn't start off like that. It was weird, not how people normally meet," she said, smiling as she recalled what had happened.

"I had just moved to Epsom and took the train into London to get to work. It was Monday morning. There's a train that goes straight into Victoria without my having to change. In order to get into work on time I had to get the 7.30 a.m. but it was always crowded and you know me, I hate the crowds. So, I looked into it and there's a train that leaves at 6.23 a.m.; an hour earlier and I decided that if I could haul myself out of bed, I would aim to get that one."

"Wow, that is early!" he said. "Not enough sleep for me."

"I know Jonas, it is the price I was prepared to pay for avoiding the morning rush into work. But at that time of the morning every minute, every second is precious, no time to waste on eating or putting on make-up. So, I pick up a coffee and a freshly baked croissant from the coffee shop on the platform and jump on the train. As the train is empty, I get to choose where I sit. I sat in this carriage and I just started to do my make-up. Nothing strange right? Then I noticed that this man, not very far away, looking up at me. And he did not move his eyes when I looked back at him!"

"I don't understand. What is wrong with a man looking at you, Adrienne? I do it with girls all the time," said Jonas.

"You don't know the English, Jonas. They never stare. If you try and catch someone's eye, they look away immediately. The English, they hate eye contact. But this man did not look away, he was staring at me!"

"You mean, he was looking you up and down? Don't blame him; you always looked so cute," said Jonas, putting his hand on her back. She looked at it as if it was something she would rather brush off and he removed it.

"I didn't know what to make of it, his expression was typically English, just blank. You would think when he got up and dressed for work, he had forgotten to put his emotions on. Anyway, this went on day after day, each time I put on my make-up, he would be staring at me with that cold, stiff stare. But if I had to guess, he didn't approve of me doing my make-up where he could see me. It was as if it was an affront to his eyes. I was so cross with him! But it also made me think, that maybe it was more than him trying to make me stop doing my make-up. Once or twice, I was sure he was looking at me like a man does, running his eyes up and down my body."

"So what did you do about it?" asked Jonas.

"I did what every girl would do in that situation!" she said, giggling.

"Which is?"

"I stuck my tongue out at him!"

"No! You did that? Wow! You are very funny Adrienne," said Jonas, chuckling. "Only you would do that. I don't know of any girl that would be brave enough to do it. And what did he say to that?"

"Nothing! Absolutely nothing. He looked around to see if anyone else noticed and no one did, so he stared at me and then looked back down at his iPad," said Adrienne. "I was so annoyed with him. I was so hoping he would react so we could have a good argument but instead, he stayed expressionless, deadpan, just like a corpse. Nothing at all. So I had to think of another way to get him to react. I was determined to have it out with this cold Englishman who kept looking at me every day, making me feel as if I was a piece of shit or a *putain*, a prostitute."

"What did you do?"

"I learned a few things on that train coming in to London. Firstly, everybody seems to have their preferred place to sit. Mine is with my back to the direction the train is going."

"Why? Don't you want to know where you are going?"

"Of course, I know where I am going, Jonas. But I prefer to face the other way and look back on where I have been, then I can enjoy it more. If you face forward you just get a quick glimpse of everything as the train passes it. But if you miss it there is no second chance," she explained.

"You are weird!"

"That's what he said too," she said, smiling.

"When did he say that?"

"Not for a while, not for some time, in fact. The second thing I learned about the early morning commuters is that they don't talk. Nobody talks to each other. It is the same people every day but no one says a 'good morning' or 'how was your weekend?' or anything like that. The most I have seen is one man nod to another, like in recognition that they are both on the same train in the same carriage and in the same seats they have been sitting in for maybe years and years. It is just like that. You get more noise from a corpse in a coffin. Even when someone has the audacity to make or receive a phone call or play some game on their phone, as soon as there is any noise, as if by some magic, they all look at that person and will them to stop. It is that stare the English do, I swear no one else does it. They stare at the person who is making the noise until they stop. No words, just stare! Even the foreigners who get on the train soon learn that you don't make a noise or there is hell to pay with those stares," she said laughing, gesticulating with her hand shaking from side to side.

"Heh, heh. I've noticed it too. And us Germans are supposed to be the conservative ones," said Jonas, laughing.

"The third thing you notice on my train is that there are two distinct types. The traditional worker types, like builders, decorators and those sorts of jobs, dressed in their overalls, clothes with paint splattered on them. Some of them carry their tools with them, big boxes with wheels, long poles for painting ceilings I imagine and so on. And some of them smell. Not bad on a Monday morning but by Wednesday or Thursday, most definitely *mauvaise odeur*. Then there are the professionals, city business types, smartly dressed, some casual business types and even teachers. I notice a couple of teachers like me, doing last minute marking on the train. Bah, don't know why they do that. They put so much effort into teaching the kids something and then undo all that by not taking the proper time to mark what they have done. Just a tick, tick, crossed line in red and a stupid comment just so that they're done by the time it takes for the train to get to their destination."

"And you never do that?" asked Jonas.

"Never! Kids deserve to have their homework properly looked at and to have constructive comments fed back. Not just a tick or a line put through it!"

"You are dedicated, Adrienne!"

"You mock me, Jonas?"

"No, just saying how passionate you are about teaching," he said, turning red with embarrassment. "Anyway, how was he dressed?"

"Very, very smart. Dark, pin-striped suit, white shirt, cuff links, silk patterned tie and a waist-coat," she said, recalling what an impression it had made on her.

"He wears a waist-coat? Very old fashioned."

"Actually, I think they are back in fashion but you are right, I haven't seen many men wearing them. Women do, including me sometimes, as a fashion accessory. So, he was as smart as you get. And I half expected him to have a brief case but surprisingly he didn't, just a shoulder bag. Leather one of course, not a man-made one like everyone else. And I noticed his mobile phone was inside a leather holder together with his season ticket. His shoes were classic brogues. And you should see the shine on them: perfect. I swear almost clear enough to see the reflection of your face in them."

"The classic, English gentleman then," said Jonas. "Most people who come into our showroom are young financiers and they dress in an open necked shirt, chinos and casual shoes and just carry a mobile phone and their credit card. They know what they want, they have received their bonus and they order a car there and then. But every now and again, you get someone who comes in dressed just how you describe your guy and they are super polite, super calm, hardly show any emotion nor create a fuss. Thirty minutes later they have bought themselves something like a Mercedes SLK Roadster, a one hundred-thousand-pound sports car and you would never have believed it."

"This guy has a sports car too but it's an old one and he worries about it breaking down so he hardly ever takes it out; keeps a plastic cover over it."

"You still haven't told me how you ended up talking to him," he reminded her.

"I sat in his seat."

"His seat? On a train? I didn't think you could claim your own seat on these short distance commuter trains," he said, not convinced.

"You can't but it is not like the Tube where people hop on and hop off. On these overland trains there is an unwritten etiquette about seating arrangements. Everyone has a favourite place where they sit. Regular commuters know this and will not sit in someone else's seat. It's as simple as that. If you sit in someone's favourite seat it is like committing a crime, like heresy, like you have insulted his mother or something. Maybe even worse. So I decided to do just that, I sat where I know he likes to sit just to annoy him. As I get on at Epsom and he gets on two stops later it's easy. Not only did I sit in his favourite place but I also took out my make-up. As the train pulled into Cheam, I could see him standing there, as expressionless as usual in his own dream world. I don't think he even knew I was in his seat until he got on and turned left. Then he stood there, not moving at all, like there was a barrier preventing him from going forward. I must admit I was both thrilled and cocked and ready for a fight but at the same time scared. I was thinking with so much knife crime around, how do I know he is not a closet killer?"

"Really? You saw him as a possible killer?" said Jonas, incredulously.

"Nah, he might kill someone by staring them to death but he would not lay a finger on them."

"So, how did he react to you taking his spot?"

"He didn't. So annoying! There I was spoiling for a fight and all he did was look at me. He just sat down opposite me, took out his tablet, punched in something and then started to read. I was so annoyed I had to tell myself to calm down otherwise I would smudge my make-up. Then I would see, in that cold stare of his, that psychologically he had the advantage over me."

"Looks like your plan to get back at him didn't work."

"Just a minute Jonas. I am Adrienne, I don't let guys defeat me like that," she said, holding up her fist. "If he was not going to react then I would make him!"

"How?"

"The next day I did the same, I sat in his favourite seat again! And still he didn't react, just sat opposite me again, opened up his tablet, punched in some numbers and then put his head down. But I don't give up that easily; I did it again on Wednesday and again on Thursday. It was becoming a matter of wills, who could hold out the longest before something was said."

"Some might say a bit childish," he said. "What did it get you?"

"What did it get me? A victory! Even if he didn't react outside, I knew inside how he would have liked to lean across and grab me by my jacket and throw me out of his seat."

"Really, Adrienne! I think now you exaggerate. So did you get your way? Did you have that fight?"

"No, not exactly. The next week I was ready for him again. One guy who gets on at the same time as him, was shaking his head at me in disapproval. But my antagonist was not there. He didn't show up. Nor the next day, in fact all week he was not there, so I couldn't fight him. I was so annoyed with him!"

"Perhaps he took a different train altogether?"

"I did think that and believe it or not by Friday when he hadn't shown up all that week, I was beginning to feel slightly guilty that I had driven him to do that."

"You are not as heartless as you paint yourself, Adrienne," said Jonas, teasing her.

"Of course I am not! I never made out I was. Being passionate is not heartless. I wouldn't want to hurt anyone, not even him. Anyway, my fear of having driven him away disappeared when the following week he showed up again. He must have been on holiday or something as he looked slightly tanned. Not a great tan! The tan the English get when they are exposed to the slightest bit of sun."

"Same again then?"

"Yes, I was sitting in his favourite seat when he got on. This time, he stood over me and huffed, making no attempt to hide his resentment. It was the first time he gave away any sign that he was irritated by what I was doing and inside I was smiling. But outside I was being more English than him; I totally kept a straight face!"

"Well done, Adrienne, you won!"

"Maybe!"

"What do you mean?"

"What will it take to get you to move from my seat?" he said, standing there.

"Excuse me?" I said. "You talking to me?"

"As you are the only person there, I think that it is self-evident that I am indeed talking to you. However, if we must play this game, I repeat, what will it take to get you to move from my seat?"

"So rude! So, did you fire all your anger and passion at him? All that you had been saving up for two weeks?"

"No, I did not," she said. "The thing is, I was taken aback at how lovely his voice is. I had been expecting a kind of shrill, whiney voice but instead it was a deep, manly voice, seductive, almost sexy you might say. So, even though he was being rude Jonas, I didn't let fly at him. Instead, I said that there was a price to pay for me to give up that seat."

"You said that? Wow! You expected him to pay you to move?"

"No, of course not. He huffed again, sat down in front of me and looked at me with that same cold stare. He then put his iPad on the table, making sure that I did not take up more than half of the table. He rummaged in his inside jacket pocket, took out a beautiful leather wallet and started to remove notes.

"Say when," he said. He started off with a fiver, then he took out a ten-pound note, then another one, then a twenty."

"What did you do?"

"Nothing! Just stared back at him. He counted out maybe fifty pounds before I stopped him by holding my hand up."

"Put your money away!" I said. "No amount of money will work."

“What will work?” he said calmly.

“I so loved his voice I wanted to hear it again. So I said dinner, after work!”

“Dinner?” he asked. “My dear girl, whatever do you mean?”

“Firstly, I am not your dear girl, Mister. And yes, dinner. You buy me dinner and you can have your seat back,” I said and oh my God, were my temples throbbing.

He didn’t say anything. You could tell he was thinking about it although, as usual, his face did not change one bit.

“When?” he said finally.

“This Friday.”

“Where?”

“Victoria. Wasabi, in the station. Five o’clock.”

“And you will let me have my seat back?”

I nodded.

“Fine! I agree. Victoria station outside Wasabi at five p.m.,” he said and then held his hand out. “Do I have your word?”

“You do,” I said. I took his hand — it felt warm. Not hot and not clammy just soothingly warm. I had expected it to be stone cold like the proud edifice that was his face. That little touch between us, it was quite disconcerting.

“How do I know you won’t break your word?” he said.

“You’ll have to trust me,” I said.

“Hmm, trust, overrated! Not legally enforceable,” he said, as much to himself as me. “And that’s how I met Flint, my old man, as you call him,” she said.

Wasabi

He arrived fifteen minutes earlier than their appointment so he could get the lay of the land and purposefully strode over to Wasabi. He was aware that it was a fast-food takeaway with a handful of tables outside, serving oriental type food but had never been tempted to try it.

There seemed to be a queue of people, patiently inching forward in a line to be served from the canteen-sized steel sinks filled with teriyaki chicken, sweet and sour chicken, fish pieces, noodles or rice. He peered into the shop and wrinkled his nose at the sight and smells emanating from these hot dishes. On the cold-chilled shelves, he noticed rows and rows of raw fish prepared and put into little bundles for people to choose and make up their own sushi takeaway boxes, as well as those that had been pre-packaged by the shop for people to just pick up and go. There was another queue for that which bypassed the queue waiting for hot food.

He stood outside and decided that there was nothing that he eyed that actually appealed to him. He had skipped lunch but the food in Wasabi had not stimulated his taste buds at all.

'Extraordinary as to why someone from a country that produces some of the finest cuisine would choose such a place to eat,' he told himself. 'Oh well, if it means I get my seat back, then it has served a purpose.'

He checked on his watch again and there were still ten minutes to go and when one of the tables outside became empty, he made a play for it, apologising as he squeezed past a couple of diners wolfing their noodles down, to claim it. He was about to put his shoulder bag on it, like planting a flag for Britain when he stopped himself as it was greasy and had spots of teriyaki and wasabi sauce dotted here and there. He stood up and gestured to one of the staff that it was dirty and they nodded they had understood. He stood waiting for someone to clean the table but no one seemed in a hurry to do that so he sat down in an upright position, holding his shoulder bag on his lap, waiting patiently for the man to clean the table.

The station was filling up rapidly as hundreds and hundreds of people began to come up from the bowels of the Tube and off the streets around Victoria station for the start of their commute home. It was Friday, the day everyone is keen to get home even more than any other day so that they could begin the weekend, those precious forty-eight hours when your life was yours to do as you wished. There seemed to be an air of urgency as a throng of people gathered around the indicator boards, some looking anxiously up and down searching for that bright orange set of words we call a timetable, that would show their train was going to be there and get them home.

He could see people straining every sinew in their muscles as they ran as fast their legs could carry them to make that train before it left them behind. He sneered as he watched one woman miss her train by seconds and then shout out 'it's not fair, they closed the doors early!' He would never do that. Rushing for a train was something he could never see himself doing.

'There is always another along in half an hour,' he told himself. 'Can't understand why people would go to that length to make that train, as if it was the last one on earth.'

Victoria station is also the gateway to Gatwick airport and he had more sympathy for a couple of bemused tourists who, with their written guides, were looking around from one end of the indicator boards to the other, trying to find that train that their guide tells them will take them there. He recalled the time when a young German lady tugged his sleeve and said to him, "Excuse me sir, my guide says there should be a train at 6.17 for Gatwick but I do not see it," she had said.

He smiled and explained to her that she needed to get the Brighton train and showed her the indicator, adding that Gatwick Airport was the first stop. She smiled and thanked him and he had been impressed by how polite she had been but even more so, by the quality of her English, albeit spoken with a strong German accent.

In exasperation at no one turning up to clean his table, he took out a tissue from his little sheaf of Kleenex, squirted alcohol hand gel on it and started to rub the table.

"Are you doing their job for them?" came a voice. It was her and he hated it that she had caught him doing that.

"Seems like they are too busy to come and clean it," he said, shrugging.

She put her bag down, strode up to one man and putting her arm around his, pointed to the table and said something quietly to him. He nodded and she smiled back and then squeezed her way back towards the table. It gave him precious few seconds to peer into her bag and he noticed a stack of school books.

"School teacher," he muttered and smiled to himself at the discovery. As she neared the table, he stood up until she sat down.

"Finally get to sit down," she sighed and cast him a friendly smile. He did not reciprocate.

"You look like someone who is in the waiting room at the dentist," she said. "Come on, cheer up! The weekend is here; that should make you happy."

He looked at her and said, "I only go to the dentists on rare occasions and usually I know what to expect, how much it is going to cost me, whether there will be some pain, whether a needle is going to be stuck into my jaw to numb it whilst lying on my back with a plastic bib around my chest and a hard plastic draining tube stuck under my tongue. I see no similarity with what I am doing here."

She smiled and then started giggling. "You are funny, you know that?" she said.

"My dear girl, I am not the slightest bit interested in what you think of me and I am certainly not here to entertain you. I am merely here to meet my end of the bargain we struck on the train, so, unless you have changed your mind and I can have my seat back without having to do this, can we please get on with it?"

She put her elbow on the table in front of him and held her hand open. "Give me money! I will choose what we will eat!"

"Actually, I am not that hungry, you eat and I will sit here," he said, as he put two twenty-pound notes in her hand.

"That was not our deal. It was for both of us to have dinner, not me eating whilst you stare at me, waiting to see if I drop food on me so you can be even more arrogant and rude than you usually are!"

"Fine then, you choose what you want me to eat!"

She was bristling with anger at his discourtesy towards her and she pushed her chair back hard as she stood up. She strode into the shop and looked at what was on offer. She too, wrinkled her nose up at the hot food but as she was fond of sushi and sashimi, she found the choice on the cold-chill shelves very appealing.

"Spoilt for choice but don't know what the Englishman likes. Should have asked him," she said out loud. "Bah he will eat what I put in front of him whether he likes it or not!" At the payment till, she asked for chopsticks instead of forks and also extra Wasabi sauce. "That should put some fire up his ass when I mix this into his food," she chuckled.

He watched her from afar, taking care not to stare for any length of time for fear of causing her to be suspicious that he was eyeing her up. He was cross with himself for having been distracted from his objective as he watched her make her way back to their table, holding the packages of food aloft which showed the form of her svelte figure and the curve of her chest to good effect.

He stood up, took the food off her and set it down gently on the table. She smiled. This was the second time he had got up for her and even though she had already labelled him as being stuffy and rude, she did nevertheless appreciate his good manners for having done that.

"A small tasty feast for us to get through!" she remarked.

He looked at the selection of raw salmon, raw tuna and various rolls of rice: some filled with avocado, some with prawns, some with crabmeat and others he did not even recognise. He counted out thirty pieces of neatly prepared small parcels of food and watched as she tore the sachets of wasabi sauce and dribbled it over the food.

"I wouldn't characterise what is here in front of us as the components that make up a tasty feast. Nevertheless, it is here and as per our agreement, this constitutes us having dinner together and I will eat it," he said and began by stripping the top of the wrapping to free up a set of chopsticks which he offered to her.

She pulled out the chopsticks and said, "Thank you," frowning in surprise at him having done that for her.

She was also frowning because she liked the sound of his voice; that same enticing voice she had heard on the train that led her to the spontaneous decision to find a way to talk to him again and the reason they were there, sitting opposite each other. 'Nice voice,' she reminded herself. 'Wouldn't mind hearing more of it again. Perhaps a fait accompli was possibly not the best way of doing that.'

The liberal sprinkling of wasabi over the fish did not have the desired effect, it had not fazed him at all. Indeed, she watched as he took one of the pieces of salmon, dipped it into sauce that had run onto his paper plate and then popped it into his mouth, without reacting to the hotness of the spice at all. It was not what she expected and not what she had wanted to see!

"I haven't introduced myself, how rude of me," she said. "I am Adrienne Kiff."

She held her hand out and he put down his chopsticks and shook it peremptorily but said nothing in response. It irritated her.

"And you are?" she asked.

"If you don't mind, I shall continue to be rude and not offer you my name," he said, looking up from his plate briefly before deftly taking up one of the rolls of rice and avocado wrapped in seaweed with his chopsticks and devouring it.

"Oh, why is that? Afraid I might stalk you?"

He put his chopsticks down, dabbed his mouth with the paper towel and looked at her.

"You're right, stupid of me. My name is Fred Flintstone, pleased to meet you," he said and he looked down again at the food in front of him, surveying what he might try next.

"Ha-ha, very funny, Englishman. In that case I shall call you Flint from now on. You are funny like Fred and your expression is as hard as flint so, yep, that name suits you perfectly," she said.

In spite of himself, he couldn't help smile; he admired the quickness of mind for thinking that up as a riposte.

He had just put down the chopsticks to have a sip of water when he found his plate being pulled away from him and being replaced by hers.

"Change!" she said and added by way of explanation, "that way we get to try a bit of everything."

"Erm, I am probably being dense but I do believe that was my dinner!" he said, throwing his paper towel on the table.

"Don't be such a, how you say it? A stick in the mud. Try something different, like sharing. Heaven forbid!" she teased. "You never know, you might even like it!"

"I don't usually mind sharing. It is the basis of Spanish tapas, Italian antipasto and Middle Eastern meze and I like all of these. Usually, I get asked first. In some circles, that is considered being polite," he said haughtily.

"Yes, but where would the fun be in that?" she said, as she started to tuck into what had once been his plate of food.

"Oh, I see, it is fun for you to make fun of me is it?"

"Could be, Flint. Yes, it is fun!"

"Don't call me by that ridiculous name," he demanded.

"It's the name you get until you tell me your real name, Flint. Besides it suits you," she said.

"Fine then, I shall call you Sushi from now on. Raw and not very agreeable," he said, chuckling.

"Wow! You actually showed an emotion, Flint. Oh my God, be careful you might bring on a heart attack."

He blew out air and looked straight into her eyes. It was unnerving her but she tried not to look away.

"As it happens, I am recovering from a heart attack," he said gravely.

'*Merde*!' she told herself.

Adrienne found herself blushing with embarrassment. There was a French word that came to mind. 'I think I have made a false step, a *faux pas*,' she told herself.

She looked up at him. The truculence that was present in her erstwhile tone was now gone. It was soft and conciliatory. "I am really sorry, Flint. I shouldn't have said that. I apologise," she said, blushing profusely.

Her discomfort was very evident and taking a sip of water and looking down at her food did not ameliorate that condition. She could not face looking at him after that revelation. She sensed that his eyes were upon her but she daren't look up. All around them there was the deafening noise and bustle as people departed and left the station but at their table it was the opposite. Complete silence and very little movement.

"You not eating then, Sushi?" he said. "What you gave me is actually quite edible. Good swap."

She looked up at him almost involuntarily ready to fire back a comment and then she checked herself. 'Best not to antagonise him. Don't want to bring on another heart attack, do I?' she told herself.

"That's good," she said. "Glad you like it."

"Variety is the spice of life. Isn't that what they say?" he said and she noticed that his mouth had changed from what had been a grimace to something resembling a smile. 'He's let me off the hook, I think,' she told herself.

"Nice to see you smile, suits you."

"Me? Smile? What for? Other than pull your leg and watch you squirm and blush like the beacon of a lighthouse as you apologised, what else is there to smile about?" he sniggered.

"I said I am sorry, about your heart attack, didn't I?" she pleaded.

"What heart attack?"

"Your heart attack," she said through furrowed eyebrows. He was grinning from ear to ear.

"I've never had a heart attack, Sushi," he said, smiling at her.

"You mean, you made me apologise to you, caused me anxiety and…"

"Made you blush," he interrupted her.

"Yes! And made me feel…"

"Awful?" he offered.

"Yes! And very upset that I…"

"Was putting your foot in it?"

"Yes! Will you stop helping me to say what I want to say!" she demanded.

"Hot cheeks! Lighting up the concourse. I think even that man serving on 'Delice de France' the other side of the concourse can see your cheeks glowing red with embarrassment!" he said laughingly, pointing across the way to the shop opposite platform eight.

"Flint, stop it, will you. Enough teasing!" she said firmly.

"So, you don't like it when you are on the receiving end of it, do you Sushi?" he said. "I am done; must say better than I thought it would be. I still don't understand why people would eat their fish raw. In the days before matches were invented, I suppose they had no choice but even now."

"So that was to get back at me?" she asked.

"Just playing your game, Sushi. I thought I did rather well, don't you?" he said nonchalantly. "By the way was there any change for me from this oriental fare?"

"There is, but I am keeping it, Flint," she said. "After that exercise in humiliation I am not giving you anything back. And you need to redeem yourself. What you just did was very ungentlemanly of you. Enjoying seeing me in distress was very ungentlemanly of you."

"I agree, it was," he said and shrugged. The deadpan face returned. "Does it really matter?"

"Does it matter? Yes! It does matter to me," she said, pointing at her chest. She was hurt and was trying to think quickly on her feet, of some way to get back at him. "I am not used to this type of poor behaviour."

"Not even amongst your pupils?"

"How did you…" she said and stopped herself. She looked at her shoulder bag that was gaping open. "Did you rummage through my bag?"

"I didn't need to," he said. "I admit that I peeked inside as it was left open as it is now. But I guessed, even before then, that your profession must be something like a teacher. Who else is that stressed early in the morning? I'm guessing you teach French, possibly another language too. You ooze stress out of every pore. You try and hide it well, you try to put on an air of sang-froid, a positive public face, bubbly and full of life.

Yet I feel sure that the reality is somewhat different. Oh yes, you dress well, in a manner only the French are good at and indeed, have the confidence to even attempt. You wear your hair with coiffured abandonment, a long fringe that falls over your eyes here and there in places. Your cheeks, notwithstanding that they are now flushed with anger, are thankfully devoid of the plasterwork that seems the norm among modern, younger women. Instead, they have a subtle rouge applied expertly on them, which enhances the natural look of your skin. I correct myself, except in one place, approximately two centimetres from your left cheek which suggests you are trying to conceal either a blemish or possibly a scar. Your lips which you are biting right now look real enough although I can't tell. Sadly, nowadays one can achieve the same effect by pumping in a toxin produced by the bacterium

Clostridium botulinum. The long, hooped earrings, I counted three connected hoops, are meant to contribute to an air of confidence but I suspect that in reality you would rather wear something more subtle. The beige trench coat on top of the flowery dress, green tights and brogue, flat shoes, work, and contributes to the overall picture. But isn't the reality that this is just a façade? Is it not Sushi?"

She sighed and her shoulders hunched. "Spanish," she said.

"I beg your pardon?"

"The other language I teach," she explained. "I teach French and Spanish in Westminster. I also teach classical piano and clarinet."

He said nothing; instead, he smiled to himself, "Good guess."

"I was right then, you were staring at me on the train. And Flint, don't for a moment think I didn't notice you ogling me when I was going to get our food and then again when I was bringing it back. And the only reason you know I wear green pantyhose is because you were staring at my legs — is that not so? Go on admit it! God! I feel as if I have just been undressed," she said. "Bastard!"

"My dear girl, as far as I know, my parents were married when I came forth into this world. The… Our women are known for being chaste and take their marriage vows seriously. Perhaps spreading ones loins may be a la mode in your country, where they are known for more liberal views on lifestyle but where I come from, it is not a done thing. But strange things do happen and perhaps I should make a note to myself to check again, you obviously know something about my background that I was not aware of," he said, with an air of disdain.

"You really are a horrible man, Flint," she said.

"Yes, I agree with you. So, shall we agree that I fulfilled my end of the bargain and shake hands on it and be done here?" he said, as he held out his hand.

She reached out her hand and then immediately withdrew it. "We're not done yet, Flint," she said.

"Oh dear, what now?" he said, rolling his eyes.

"You owe me a proper lunch for all the distress you've caused me. I haven't enjoyed this one bit!" she said.

"What? Are you insane! Why on earth would you want that? In any case, I do not recall in our agreement anything that included that the meal had to be pleasant or words to that effect," he said. "I have fulfilled my end of the bargain and it is now incumbent on you to do the same."

"It is implied when two people go to dinner that there is some expectation that it will be pleasant, at the very least not antagonistic and hostile."

He was about to reply with a riposte and he stopped himself. He recalled a saying attributed to Pubilius Syrus which one of his schoolteachers used to utter, often in times of altercation. 'You can accomplish by kindness what you cannot by force,' he reminded himself.

"Very well, what did you have in mind?" he said.

"Organico, in Epsom," she replied.

"Never heard of it."

"Yes, you have. I have seen you in there. You were there with another woman. Your wife? She looked very bored. What were you saying to her?"

"It was my sister!" he said.

"I'm not falling for that one, Flint. She did not look like a sister to me, more like someone who was after you," she teased. "Did you get to have sex with her?"

He sat up straight. "What an impertinent question!"

"Well did you?"

"Certainly not, she is a friend's wife," he protested.

"So? What was stopping you? Oh, I forgot, you don't do such things, remain chaste, take life very seriously. Nobody does that in leafy Surrey, right?"

"You are incorrigible!" he said.

"Maybe I am, maybe I am not. Either way you are taking me to lunch next weekend: Saturday, Organico, one o'clock. Deal?" She reached out her hand to him for a handshake.

"Deal."

"And Flint," she said.

"What?"

"You have to be pleasant to me or it does not count," she warned.

"Fine. I will put on my best manners for you," he said drily.

"That's not good enough, Flint. I don't want stiff, upper-class, cold manners. I said you had to be pleasant to me. I want warm, convivial conversation, with no acid remarks, no cynical comments or anything derogatory about my French background. Is that clear?" He nodded.

"Yes Sushi, it's crystal clear. I shall brush up on my convivial conversation; I am out of practice. Can we leave now?" he said, shaking her hand.

"Not yet," she said, pulling his extended hand so he was forced to sit once again.

"What now?"

"I don't like the nickname you chose for me. Sushi is not very nice. Either call me by my name, Adrienne or choose another more agreeable nickname."

He rolled his eyes in irritation and then said, "Adrienne Kiff, right?"

"Yes."

"Then I will call you Kiffy," he said.

"Kiffy? Hmm. Not sure I like that either but yes, you can call me Kiffy," she said and smiled. "Okay, let's go Flint. We don't want to miss our train."

At her insistence, they stopped by the Café Nero kiosk so she could get a skinny decaf latte. He ordered an English breakfast tea and she also had an almost croissant. He looked to her to pay for it from the money left over from the dinner but she shook her head and he touched his credit card discretely so she couldn't see his name.

They quickened their pace to get to the train which had just pulled in. She tried to pull him into the nearest carriage and explained that it suited her for when getting off at Epson station but he refused to go in. He told her that it did not suit him as he preferred the front of the train but for her to go there; that he wouldn't be offended and he wished her a safe journey home.

"I will come and sit at the front with you Flint but next time, you have to sit my end of the train," she said.

'Looks like I am going to have to put up with her all the way home. Oh joy,' he told himself.

"You don't have to, really. I tend to be unsociable on my way home: just stare out into space," he said, trying to shake her off. "If it's better for you to get in the other carriage, don't mind me, I most certainly won't be offended."

"No problem, I'll walk up with you this time," she said, batting away his slight. Inside she was boiling at his dismissive, rude, behaviour but outwardly she remained calm and friendly.

"First class," she noted, as they boarded the front carriage. "Is that why you like this carriage, Flint. You like to travel first class?"

"Yes, I do but not for the reason you might think," he said. "It is because even though anyone can sit here, the mere sign of 'First Class' intimidates people, so invariably they shun it. Which is great as it means most of the time, I have the table, the seat next to me and the two in front entirely free and at my disposal. Plenty of space. That's why I sit here, Kiffy."

"You crafty fox, Flint. But I like it," she said, as she sat down opposite him.

The train pulled out of Victoria moments later and he turned to look at the river as it came into view. The Thames flowed like an artery in the heart of London and it never ceased to thrill him as he watched its green-grey blood meander along the city, lined with an eclectic assortment of low and high-rise buildings from historic to the ultra-modern.

"Here, have a bite," he heard her say and looked around to find a half-eaten croissant staring at him.

The look on her face suggested that it would be futile to refuse her. 'Best to maintain the entente cordialle,' he told himself and took the smallest of bites.

"Thank you," he said and was relieved to see that it made her smile. Better than having her admonish him for some unintended slight in front of fellow commuters.

It had the desired effect and he felt relieved. She giggled and leant across to wipe the icing sugar off his cheek. He was embarrassed as her hand made contact with his cheek. It was a soft hand and what made him uncomfortable, was that it had thrilled him.

It seemed to relax both of them and they started to chat, where she did all the talking and he just listened. In the thirty minutes between Victoria and Cheam, as much as he was trying to ignore her, he had learned she had moved from Putney to Epsom and in the process bought her own apartment, as she put it 'for the first time', much to the chagrin of her parents who harboured hopes that she might set down roots where they lived in Normandy.

As she spoke, he was trying to piece together the sequence of events that had led to this point where a young and beautiful French woman was sitting opposite him, talking ten to the dozen as if they were long-lost friends. Part of him wanted to reach across, grab her by the scruff of her coat and ask her what her game was; what was she after. Yet as she talked, he was also drawn to her, a latter-day siren calling him and he felt he would need to act so as not to let doom befall him.

"Are you even listening to me?" she asked.

"Of course, hanging on your every word," he said, facetiously.

"What have I said?" she quizzed.

He repeated everything she had said back to her and she was miffed that he proved her wrong.

'Being a lawyer has its uses, even in these situations,' he told himself.

She continued her monologue and he made a point of looking at her directly. He was impressed when she let on that she was a teacher in Westminster School, one of the most elite public schools in the country. It was hard work but the pupils were very bright and willing to learn which was very satisfying for her as a teacher. In addition to academic teaching, she also volunteered to teach classical piano and clarinet to the younger boys, some of whom made it into one of the school orchestras.

"The next stop is where I get off," he said and rose to leave. He held his hand out. "Have a good weekend."

She stood up, taking his hand and leaned forward to kiss him on one cheek and then the other. "You too, Flint."

He took in her scent and found it very alluring.

She waved to him when he got off the train but he did not look back to see her do that. "Very nice, very manly aftershave," she said, smiling. "And Flint, don't forget our date!"

Looking

He parked his little Nissan Micra next to a brand-new Range Rover Evoque and smiled. "Always park next to a car that is much more expensive than yours. That way, you reduce the risk of someone opening their door and hitting you," his friend Andy had once said to him. Andy also drove a small car, a one-litre Ford Fiesta that was affectionately known as 'the lawnmower'. He had relentlessly teased him about how small the engine was. On a holiday in the Swiss Alps, Andy had admitted it had struggled to get up some of the steeper hills. He had offered to accompany him on one of his trips if only to get out and push if the need arose. Andy was single, like him. And, like him, had been single for some time. They were of similar age and in the last few years had become close friends. As he skirted along the grass edge of the car park heading towards his destination, he wondered what Andy would be doing on a Saturday morning.

"Probably enforced kiddy-minding his grandchildren. No doubt I will hear about it on Monday," he muttered, "if not on WhatsApp before then."

He had no such ties. There were no grandchildren and he had no responsibilities towards anyone, other than his cat, Philip, the fish in the pond and the birds he fed in his garden. Other than that, there were none.

He had time on his hands and he decided that he would pop into the charity shop to look for any curios that might serve as a birthday present for his father. In a few months, his father would be seventy-nine and he would be paying him a visit. Even at that age and having all the trappings of life that money could buy, his father was still an avid collector of all sorts of curios but it was becoming increasingly difficult to find something that might be to his taste. Searching for a gift for his father also served another purpose, that of keeping him calm before meeting up with her; something that he was expecting would end in sparks flying again in spite of their undertaking that it should be a pleasant lunch.

He found the concept of being pleasant, unreliable, as it had so many connotations and meant different things to different people. He tried to be polite, not rude and not ill-mannered and he considered that as being pleasant.

"Yes, but having good manners is not enough, old chum. You need to show that you are nice and good-natured and most of all, smile. If you smile, people think you are being pleasant," Andy had pointed out to him.

"What have I got to smile about?" he joked.

"Okay then, imagine pleasant things. Like eating your favourite cake, or watching Arsenal win the FA Cup," he teased.

As he left the shop with his purchases and walked along Epsom high street, he said to himself, 'Strudel, that's my favourite cake.' He tried to remember the last time he had eaten it. "Vienna," he said and smiled. "Nothing wrong with my memory."

As quickly as a faint smile came to him having recalled that seven years earlier, he had spent Christmas there, it did not last. He also remembered who he had spent it with and that made the smile vanish.

As he crossed the busy road that was the turn off for the A24 and skipped onto the pedestrianised area with the clock tower, he recalled having read that someone had once said that if you are pleasant until ten o'clock in the morning, then the rest of the day would take care of itself. Looking up at the clock face, it was gone midday and he had already been pleasant twice: once to pay the cleaning guy in the car park to wash and polish his car even though it hardly needed it and the second time, was to insist in the charity shop that he did not need any change from the notes he had handed over to them for his purchases. 'That should set me up nicely,' he told himself.

It was 12.30 p.m. when he arrived outside Organico, a small restaurant that is popular with those that are a little more concerned than the norm, about eating healthily. He had eaten there before, having bumped into Frances, a colleague from work; someone he had known back at the office but who he did not work with. They had chatted amiably enough but he had been wary of her as she had made rather obvious romantic overtures towards him in the past and he was on his guard and could not relax. It was easy for him to appear friendly, indeed it was part of what made him successful in his career. He could switch on an easy-going, languid manner and that seemed to have been misconstrued by Frances, as being a signal for her to indicate that she was not averse to their office relationship becoming more intimate outside of work. He had been embarrassed by that incident and managed to salvage the situation, citing the demands of his job which entailed variable hours and travel. It had been the perfect get out of jail free card. When he reflected on it afterwards, he felt that he must have been giving out the wrong signals and he chided himself for doing that. Now, in less than thirty minutes time, he was going to meet another woman, albeit this one did not have the added complication of being a work colleague. He reminded himself that whilst he would need to be friendly and convivial as per the agreement, he would maintain decorum and maintain emotional distance. He would be pleasant and cordial but still remain sufficiently aloof and distant, to mitigate against the risk of emotional attachment on her part or his, for that matter. This was purely a transactional arrangement for a specific purpose.

He looked at his watch; there was still twenty minutes to go but he decided to enter the restaurant anyway rather than wait outside. He could, in any case, secure the two seats closest to the window as two people got up to leave. The window seat was important to him, a bit like the window seat in an aeroplane; you could look out of it if you didn't want to look at what was around you. Also, as someone who valued his personal space, he preferred it as it meant that you had other diners adjacent to you on one side only. That arrangement was preferable as it minimised the risk of having two sets of people talking and guffawing loudly, distracting and spoiling his lunch. Finally, as a private man, it also reduced the number of potential people who might choose to listen in on his conversations with his fellow diner, in this case one Adrienne Kiff, his antagonistic, fellow train-traveller and today's lunch date.

Once again, he found himself looking in the direction of the restaurant staff to get them to clear away the plates and cups from the previous diners. A young lady smiled and made her way to his table, armed with a cloth and a spray gun.

"What a waste," he muttered, seeing her take away a plate half-full of food. "Eyes bigger than her appetite. So much food going to waste whilst people in the world are starving." He ordered a coffee and a glass of water whilst he waited for his sparring partner and fellow diner to appear.

'What am I doing here?' he asked himself. 'Wouldn't it have just been so much easier if I'd moved to a different seat on the train? All this palaver to secure my seat? It is not even mine. Maybe I should just move and be done with it. Or is it more than that? Is it a game I am playing or she is playing or we're both playing, where the rules are unwritten, haven't been set and are being made up as we go along? What strategy do I need to use for this second locking of horns?'

"Hey Flint! You are here after all. I wasn't at all sure you would be coming," she said pleasantly, as she stood in front of him.

He had not seen her enter as he had been looking down into his coffee cup and it threw him seeing her there. He stood up.

"Hello, Kiffy," he said awkwardly and then had to endure her version of *La Bise*, kissing him on both cheeks, her scent and the touch of her soft cheeks wreaking havoc with his senses.

In those few seconds before they sat down, he took in what she was wearing: a simple, open-necked cotton shirt with very faint stripes, sleeves rolled up to below her elbows, faded-blue jeans, held up by a black leather belt, which showed off her figure to good effect. His eyes followed the jeans down, from the slim waist, all the way until the jeans stopped a few inches above her ankles. On her feet, he noticed she wore black, high-heeled, suede shoes.

It was casual but worn with elegance.

'Why can't we British be like that?' he asked himself. 'If that had been an English girl, I was meeting she would be having fake blonde hair, be heavily made up, wearing jeans with tears in them and probably wearing trainers. Not the French, not her.'

"I'm glad you chose the window seats," she said, "away from noisy diners on both sides of us."

He smiled in recognising a kindred spirit. "Yes, I had considered that too."

They took turns to order their lunch and she chose a concoction of fresh fruit and vegetables which he wrinkled his nose up at.

"Try it," she said, offering her glass to him with a straw.

"I'd rather not, if you don't mind. Reminds me of the green water in the pond in my garden."

"Ha-ha. You are funny, Flint. You know a Diet Coke is not good for you. It has so many artificial things in it," she said. "But I guess you know that anyway. Who am I to tell you that?"

"You are right, it is not good for me," he acknowledged. "But wherever you are in the world, you know that the taste is going to be more or less the same. And those E numbers and whatever else they put into it, are reputed to help relieve an upset stomach."

"Is that true?"

He shrugged. "Might just be an urban myth."

There was a moment's silence but it was long enough for there to be an awkwardness between them that was in complete contrast to their previous meeting, which had been all fire.

"What's that you've got in that bag? My turn to be nosey," she said.

"Nothing much; it is a few odds and sods I got from one of the charity shops for my father's forthcoming birthday," he said casually.

"You don't strike me as someone who needs to buy things from charity shops, Flint, so I am guessing you like to find unusual things," she suggested.

"Yes. You are correct. I like browsing for things."

"Like that Café Crème cigar box? Does your father smoke?"

"No but it is the sort of thing he might collect," he explained.

"A Pentax camera without the lens, a metal tin with Ocean Queen coffee decoration on its sides and a book, what's this?" she said, pulling up the book and reading the spine. "*'Notre-Dame de Paris'* in French?"

"Yes, Father would like that," he said proudly.

"Your father reads in French? I am impressed," she said.

"No, not really, perhaps a little more than schoolboy standard but he is not an avid reader, except in the Queen's English. I got it as he likes leather-bound books. This one is in green and the ridged spine is in good condition. He still likes to show off, the old goat, so this will go down well with him," he said, smiling.

"Eccentric but I like your father. Do you take after him, Flint? Are you a little eccentric too?"

He was about to say something to the effect of he was unsure which of the two of them was more eccentric but chose not to respond. 'The quicker we get this over and done with, the better,' he told himself.

"So, how come I didn't see you on the train all week?" she asked, breaking the silence. She looked up at him as she forked up a mixture of spinach and beetroot leaves.

He watched her full lips part to let the food into her mouth and then close sensuously. "I, er, wasn't at my office," he said evasively. He was raking the couscous on his plate, trying to separate the pomegranate fruit which wasn't to his liking. He had ordered it without the pomegranate but she had insisted that he should try with it, the way north Africans eat it. This wasn't something that he thought worth fighting over so he had just shrugged and now he was just pushing it to the side, hiding it under salad leaves.

"You didn't say you would be on holiday. Did you go anywhere nice? You look slightly tanned, at least for an Englishman," she teased. "Sorry couldn't help saying that."

"I said I wasn't at my office; I didn't say I was on holiday," he corrected her. "Sometimes, often, my work takes me away from the office. This was one of those occasions."

"You didn't say what you do."

"That's correct, I didn't say."

"Come on, don't be like that, Flint. What work do you do?" she asked and then smiling quickly added, "wait, wait. Don't tell me, let me guess, if you don't mind."

He put his fork down. "Go ahead. How many chances am I to give you?"

"Three. Yes three, that should be sufficient for an intelligent person like me," she giggled.

"Three it is then."

"Hmm, accountant, banker or lawyer?"

"That's three guesses all in one go! What made you say that?"

"The way you dressed going to work. On the train. Dark suit, white shirt, double cuffs, shiny, black shoes."

"Am I to infer that you would regard being one of these professions as boring?"

"No. I just like the way you dress for going to work: very smart. French men dress smartly but not for business. They are good at dressing up for going out but you British are the experts for dressing for business. You look the part. You can tell that you ran an empire for hundreds of years. By the way, I meant to say, I do like the way you look today. Nice leather jacket and shirt. I would lose the sleeveless pullover and also change your black shoes to, say, tan-coloured leather but otherwise very cool and trendy," she said.

"Thanks for the critique," he said drily.

"Don't be like that, Flint. I was just saying you look handsome and with a few minor changes, could look even more handsome. You will have all the ladies running after you!" she ribbed him.

"I don't want all the ladies running after me, thank you very much. Not even one," he said flatly.

"All the boys then. You are gay, Flint? I am liberal, you don't have to be shy with me if you are. Just a shame if it was so as I think you are quite handsome, in that English gentleman sort of way."

He sniggered. "I am not gay. I neither want ladies nor men running after me," he said. "At the moment I have no interest in…"

"Sex?"

"That's not what I was going to say but since you bring it up, I have no interest in that department either and were I to be, for the avoidance of doubt, it would only be with a consenting, adult woman," he said.

"That's a pity, Flint. I was thinking after lunch we could have sex. Back to my place which is just fifteen minutes' walking distance from here," she said, giggling.

"Kiffy, I don't know whether you're saying provocative and outrageous things like that is designed to shock me but I can assure you that it is not working with me!"

"Come on, Flint, did having sex with me never cross your mind?" she teased.

"No!"

"No, not even once? I know you want me, Flint. So you might as well admit it," she persisted.

"You don't have a shred of evidence to support that assertion."

"Yeah, I do. Like all the time you were ogling me on the train, day after day. And don't say it's because you disapproved of me doing my make-up. I accept that might have been true on the first day but after that, it was just an excuse to ogle me, Flint. You kept looking at my hair, my chest and my legs too. I bet you could tell me what shoes I wore every day of that week. And what about in Victoria? At Wasabi, you described me in such detail and precision, you took my breath away. Here was a man who was looking at me. Really looking at me, not just my boobs. You were checking me out, Flint. And what about today?"

"What about today?" he said, frowning.

"When I came in and stood in front of you. When you stood up, your eyes were all over me. You were checking me out as much as I was checking you out. Admit it, Flint," she pressed him. "I'm not letting this go, so you may as well admit it."

He blew out through his nostrils and sat back in his chair, adjusting the cushion behind him which was no longer making him feel comfortable.

"It is nothing personal. It is a trait in me: I do tend to observe. I do tend to focus on detail. It actually helps in my line of work. Attention to detail is important."

"You're an accountant?"

"Nice try but you guessed wrong!"

"Banker? But I don't suppose their attention to detail is any good otherwise we wouldn't have had a banking crisis all those years ago. So, I am guessing you must be a lawyer, Flint."

"Correct," he said with a faint smile. "And before you ask, no I do not wear a wig and say 'm'lud', wearing those antiquated garments in a court of law. I am a commercial lawyer; as boring as they come!"

"What colour trainers do I have on?"

"You are not wearing trainers. You are wearing black, suede, high-heeled, pointed shoes."

"The brown belt holding up my jeans is it made of fabric or leather?"

"It is leather and it is black, not brown," he said precisely. "And you are not that skinny. I used to think French women survived on a diet of cigarettes and magazines but you have a hearty appetite which is a good thing. I would hazard a guess and say you are no more than a size ten. And since we last met in Victoria, you've been to the hairdresser and cut your hair, not by much. I estimate perhaps two centimetres? You've also changed from hooped earrings to half wedding rings. And you've changed the colour of your nails, which were a sort of burgundy colour when we met in Victoria and now, they are a bright red. But you are wearing the same perfume. Do I need to go on?" She looked at him in astonishment.

"Wow!"

"I just notice these things, don't take it personally," he explained dispassionately, as if he was giving evidence in a court of law.

"Hey! I was feeling flattered that you have taken such a close interest in me; I felt as if you were undressing me and it felt quite sensuous. That is, until you spoilt it by saying 'don't take it personally'. Now I feel quite insulted. Are you saying you don't find me attractive? That's not nice!" she said and her eyes began to water.

"Oh dear. Now you are mis-representing me. I did not say you are unattractive," he said defensively.

Whilst he was not convinced that the tears were genuine, but yet more of an act she was putting on for him, he was, nevertheless, feeling decidedly uncomfortable as the conversation was straying into areas he would rather not go. Intimate discussions were not his forte. The truth of it was that he found Adrienne very attractive, very charming. Her smile was very seductive, to die for. He felt her eyes were like sparkling jewels and her lips full and sensuous, the colour of a ripe peach. In fact, what he found quite alarming and disturbing of his erstwhile peace of mind, was that there was nothing about her he didn't like! He found her whole demeanour quite ravishing. Every part of her was oozing charm and he would have liked nothing better than to take her in his arms there and then and kiss her. But he reminded himself to keep his distance, emotional distance so as to avoid any attachment.

"Kiffy, you are indeed very attractive," he said matter of factly.

"Oh thanks! Nothing personal then?" she said.

"Actually, I see you as being beautiful, quite stunning. And it would be disingenuous of me to suggest otherwise," he said finally.

There was silence.

"But I also find you quite terrifying," he said.

"Me? Why?"

"I have yet to fathom what you are about, Kiffy. For instance, the directness and informality with someone you barely know. You would agree with me, would you not, that it is not every day that one gets invited to have sex with someone they barely know? So, whilst I am honoured and grateful, I have been invited to getting better acquainted with you shall we say; I ask myself 'why me'? What have I done to deserve this gift and wonderful privilege?"

"You make me sound like a tart! It's just two people getting together, that's all Flint," she said.

He was not convinced and a lack of explanation from her only served to reinforce his suspicion that there was an ulterior motive to this behaviour. But as yet, he had not determined what that might be. After their dinner in Victoria, he harboured suspicions that he was, perhaps, being set-up. But by whom and for what purpose, he was in the dark about and that irked him. On the flight over to finalise a contract negotiation with one of his clients, he'd tried to piece together what it was about Adrienne that brought out this feeling of mistrust, a feeling that it was not just random that she had started to travel on the same train as him and at the same time and that she did not provoke him as part of a pre-planned setup. Discretion would be the better part of valour but he was intrigued and discretion just flew out of the window.

"Sorry to be persistent but I would like an answer to my question, preferably an honest one. I repeat, why me? Why would you want to hang out with me, as they say in modern parlance? We are not exactly the same age for a start, are we?"

"True, you are a zillion years older than me!" she said light-heartedly.

"Quite! I am ancient and you are not. And let's not forget that culturally we are also miles apart, different, unalike, you are..."

"A charming Frenchwoman and you are a sullen, conservative, stuffy Englishman?"

"Quite! Although, I might have used the word reserved rather than stuffy and I am most certainly not sullen, unless provoked. So aside from being on the same train at the same time and getting off at Victoria, we have absolutely nothing in common!" he said finally.

"For all the reasons why we are so different, is the reason why I am attracted to you," she said in a playful tone. She reached across the table and put one hand over his. It was not difficult to keep his hand there as the warmth of her long, slim fingers glided over the back of his hand, thrilled him and threatened to undermine his otherwise up 'til now, calm composure.

"Flint, I am fed up of young men. Younger men are always flattering my ego or being silly and showing off and I am fed up with that. I am bored with people my age, especially men. I have been looking for something different;" she explained, "someone to challenge me."

"Challenge you? You mean like when we fight? You actually enjoy that? You picked a fight with me on the train to get my attention?"

She recalled how bruised she felt when she got home after their dinner in Victoria. She had managed to stay calm, even be civil and friendly on the homeward bound train afterwards. But as soon as she got home, she was fuming at his rude behaviour, leaving a trail of discarded clothes strewn across the floor as she undressed, until she reached the kitchen and pulled out a large wine glass, filling it to the rim from an already opened bottle of red wine. She sat on the stool by the breakfast bar in her underwear and downed the wine in one go, like someone who was quenching a thirst. But it did not quench her thirst it simply added to the fire she felt in her belly.

As she hit the shower, she was sponging herself hard, almost as if she wanted to wash him off from under her skin. Water from the overhead rain shower was supposed to be soothing. Instead, it felt as if someone was trying to drown her. It poured over her and around her, running down her face, her body, over each and every one of her curves which in the past she had found sensual, like some hidden lover caressing her. But not today. Not this time. All she could see was his face and it made her angry. But when she switched off the shower and padded her way back to her bedroom, she felt much better. It was like a tonic and it helped untie the knot in her stomach that had been there on the train all the way home. She felt as if she had just washed the day away. Sitting on her bed in her soft bathrobe and starting to dry herself, she found her skin was tingling. For an inexplicable reason, she found herself feeling alive and refreshed for the first time in a long while. Massaging in her night-time moisturising cream had a calming effect and the person in the mirror looking back at her was wearing a smile on her face. "Flint, what have you done to me?" she recalled saying to herself.

Now she was sitting in a restaurant with him, having coerced and cajoled him into it. In the past, an invitation from her would have had her fellow diner jumping for joy but not him and that was the attraction.

She giggled. "I must admit I did enjoy our little fight: so refreshing to meet someone who is not afraid to challenge me. I liked that in you, Flint. I am drawn to that type of person, who is not afraid to oppose me. But Flint, ease up on the stony, expressionless face. Like right now. It makes it difficult for me to read you. I don't know if you are in love with me or hate every second you are here with me. You don't send out enough signals about how you feel and that disconcerts me, Flint."

He said nothing but stared at her blankly.

"See what I mean? Look at that face," she said, holding her hand out in his direction as if pointing it out to a friend. "That's the face that I see on the train. That I saw in Victoria. Makes me angry and yet when you didn't show up, I found myself missing you!"

"Good heavens! Missing me? But why, my dear girl? I haven't done anything but antagonise you!"

"Flint," she said, leaning forward and lowering her voice, "what colour panties am I wearing?"

"That is an unfair question as there is no way I could observe your undergarments is there?"

"Okay then, Flint. Am I wearing panties or not?" she said, raising her eyebrows in a provocative way.

"The way you phrase that question is designed to lead me to believe that you are not wearing any," he said and shrugged. "If it is true, then that wouldn't surprise me; you are French and that type of behaviour is the norm for you, isn't it?"

"Wouldn't you like to come back to my flat and see for yourself, for the avoidance of doubt, as you would say?" she said, in a seductive voice.

He looked down at his watch. "Oh look, is that the time already? Really sorry Kiffy and I hate to break up this charming lunch that we've just had but I need to do some shopping and I'm running out of time."

Adrienne pulled a face. "Shall I come with you, Flint, help you to choose a pair of tan, leather shoes, perhaps?"

"So that I might look more handsome than I already am?" he laughed. "Tempting but no thanks. I have to do some food shopping. I don't normally shop in Epsom but as there is a Waitrose here, I can get a few things."

"Why don't I buy a few things too and cook for us? Since you don't want my body, perhaps you might want my cooking. I am an accomplished cook, Flint. And before you say it, not everyone who is French can cook."

"Thank you, that is a very kind offer and very tempting indeed but it has been a long week and I would rather just get home and put my feet up," he said. "Perhaps another time."

"Okay, Flint, have it your own way," she said and he saw her eyes misting up and it made him feel uncomfortable.

"Perhaps, if the invitation is still open, I can come for a cup of coffee. You French know how to make a cup of coffee," he said, smiling.

That brought the reaction he hoped he'd see; a smile on her face. "Okay, let's go," she said and locked her arm around his as they walked back to his car.

When they got to the car park, she looked around and he pointed at the gunmetal-grey Nissan Micra.

"That is yours?" she teased. "Flint, I was hoping it would be a Jaguar or a Range Rover, even a Mini, not a little Japanese car. That is not the car of an English gentleman."

"Well, I'll have you know that my little Micra always tops the reliability league for small cars and gets me from A to B in comfort, for all the use I make of it, thank you very much," he joked.

"Which one of these is yours, Kiffy? One of the penthouse apartments?" he asked, looking up at the new building in front of them, shaped like the sloping deck of a ship, set in landscape gardens approached through wrought iron, electric gates.

"On my teacher's salary? I wish. I was lucky to get this place. If it hadn't been for selling my apartment in Putney, I'd never have afforded it," she said.

"You left Putney to come to Epsom? Most people would have preferred to go the other way."

"I prefer the cleaner air here. Putney is polluted," she explained. He looked at her, raising an eyebrow in disbelief.

"Okay, I broke up with my boyfriend. We sold the flat there, a nice riverside apartment overlooking the Thames. My share enabled me to buy this place."

"I do apologise if it seemed I was prying," he said.

"It's okay, Flint. Not a problem. I'm fine with talking about it. It's fine to bring things out in the open sometime. You should try it."

"Not one for airing one's laundry in public," he said.

"Right, as we are not airing our laundry in public, Flint, then let's go to the flat, shall we?" she said. "Perhaps that's a more convivial place for you to air your laundry should you choose to do so, n'est pas?"

"Erm, before we proceed to your *maison*, can I just bring something up in case my poor brain forgets. We had an agreement that we would meet today. Actually, that is incorrect, it was an addendum to our previous agreement to have dinner in Victoria. Would you say that having had lunch with you, I have discharged my side of the agreement and that you release me from any further obligation?" he asked.

"Flint, don't spoil our lunch by being a lawyer!" she scoffed.

"I'm only saying in case we forget later that I have carried out our agreement to the letter, that's all," he said, as he followed her into the building. "Do you not agree, Kiffy?" There was no response from her as she pushed for the lift to arrive.

"I'm on the third floor."

"Qui tacet consentire videtur," he muttered.

"My silence does not mean I consent," she said. "I studied Latin at school, too, Flint. Catholic, all-girls school. It was required reading although in the nine years I was there I never did find a Roman to practice with, just nuns, nuns, nuns."

"Good school then," he said, as they entered the lift.

"Yes, it was, except for the constant reference to God. Perhaps that's why I became so wayward; an act of rebellion from my strict catholic schooling," she said, giggling.

"Is that why you've taken to chatting up old men?" It was his turn to tease.

"Maybe. What's your excuse then?"

"For what?" he said frowning.

"For being so stuffy and cold. Sorry I forgot, I should say reserved. Was it your public-school education? It was a public school you went to wasn't it, Flint? And don't try to tell me anything different as I teach in one so I can recognise the type."

"I have nothing to hide," he said. "But if my public-school background offends you then perhaps this coffee isn't such a great idea," he said, as they stood outside her front door.

"Flint, don't take yourself so seriously. I was just teasing you," she said, putting her hand on his arm. "Now come on in, I make the best coffee in this apartment building."

He was tempted to throw in a comment to the effect of 'had she tried everyone else's to come to that conclusion?' but he thought might be going a bit too far.

The Flat

Adrienne opened the door to an open-plan, lounge-come-dining room and kitchen combined. It was airy and spacious and ultra-modern. It had two tripod-like floor lights with the lamps pointing to the ceiling which itself had an array of miniature recessed lights. There was a modern, bright rug in front of a fireplace where a huge mirror hung. She walked over to where there were French doors which she opened out on to a large balcony. He followed her onto it.

"Quite agreeable flat you have, Kiffy," he said, as he leant on the balcony railing. "And pleasant views over the park. You chose well."

"It is a good view isn't it?" she said, standing next to him and leaning over too. "Reminds me of home, Flint. In France, where I grew up. Surrounded by greenery everywhere. Not parks, just farmland. But even this little view, brings back memories."

"Pleasant ones, I hope."

She shrugged, "Mostly. Yes, they were pleasant."

He thought she was going to say something more but she stopped herself. Instead, she looked at him and smiled before inching nearer to him, until their heads were almost touching. Then she leant across and kissed him.

It was not what he expected, at least not then. On the way over to her place he considered what might happen. Would it stop at just coffee? 'Probably not,' he told himself. And here he was, hadn't been in the apartment more than five minutes and they'd had their first kiss, albeit something he had nothing to do with, just being on the receiving end of.

"I'll get that coffee," she said, smiling sweetly and making a beeline for the kitchen before he had time to react.

He followed her into the kitchen. "I err brought these for you?" he said, handing her a box of chocolates. I had intended it to be a sort of peace offering but since I am here and it is customary to bring a gift to someone when you first visit their home, it is now a home visit gift as well."

"From Rococo Chocolates. Very nice. Very exclusive. Thank you. Very thoughtful of you, Flint," she said. She put down the metal espresso maker and, turning to him, she gave him a hug and planted a kiss on his cheek.

"You're welcome," he said awkwardly.

"That's twice I've kissed you," she teased. "Hope your heart can take it, Flint."

"My last ECG said it was better than average for a man of my age," he said.

She giggled and then said, "Is that your subtle way of saying that you want me to kiss you again, Flint?"

"I was merely stating the condition of my heart," he said.

"When was the last time you kissed a girl, Flint? No, don't answer, I don't want to know. Go and sit down in the living room, put on some music if you like and I'll bring the coffee."

He walked back to the living room and spied a turntable in one corner of the room with a selection of LPs on two shelves below it.

"Impressive," he said, as he ran his fingers through the LPs, pulling one out, noting it was Chopin and put it back. "Too depressing."

He found an old box-set of the Opera Carmen with a picture of Maria Callas on the front and he took it to the sofa to read.

The white, leather sofa was soft and he found himself sinking into it and try as he might, he found his eyes getting heavy and then he drifted off into a dreamworld of his youth. He dreamt about his early life, bucolic and happy few years, where life was sweet and he didn't have a care in the world. He recalled being taken for a walk by his grandfather, who wore his old breeches, waistcoat and deer stalker hat even in the height of summer. His favourite walk was when they ended up in a clearing in the woods near the house where a brook ran. He could hear his grandfather's voice as clear as if it was yesterday.

"Now, I do believe we are out of earshot of the adults my dear boy. So now we can strip down and sit down by the water's edge and paddle our feet." Then he would watch as his grandfather would be down to his long johns and vest and dipping his toe in the water, always pulling a face making a big thing about how cold it was, in order to make the boy laugh. "Come along young pup, off with your breeches and get yourself in this lovely water." And he would laugh heartily when the boy winced with pain and shout, "Grandpa! It hurts! Why does it hurt? It feels like I've been stung." After one or two minutes, as the water was too cold to stay in it any longer, they would sit on the soft, grassy bank and dry off, his grandfather would open up his knapsack and invariably he would get a sandwich and a banana and as a treat, they would share a packet of Maltesers.

"Hey, Flint," he heard a voice from afar, calling him.

He could feel his grandfather hugging him and running his fingers over his face and it made him feel warm and safe and contended.

"Flint?" the voice called him again and then he felt something touching his lips lightly and his nostrils suddenly filled with something sweet and pleasant smelling. The image in his mind was that of his grandfather smiling but his senses told him it was not him. He felt something heavy and oppressive weighing him down. He opened his eyes and she was there, sitting astride him.

"Kiffy!" he said, stiffening.

"You fell asleep, Flint. I don't usually have this effect on men. Poor Flinty, you must be tired. You looked so peaceful sitting there, I didn't have the heart to disturb you," she said and kissed him again and again. She chuckled as she lifted herself off his legs and sat down next to him.

"I do apologise; very rude of me to do that," he said and pointing to the boxed LPs he added, "I was just choosing some music and I must have nodded off."

"Maria Callas, playing Carmen, one of the best of all time," she said. "Yes, I love it. Composed by a Frenchman, George Bizet. That Carmen is a beautiful witch who torments poor Don Jose," she said.

"Do you model yourself on her, Kiffy?" he teased.

"If I did, does that make you my Don Jose, Flint? Does that mean we will have a tempestuous love affair and that you will knife me at some point in our relationship?"

He sniggered. "Funny, I would have said more like the other way round. I fancy the knife would more likely be in your hand, Kiffy. My only weapon is my tongue and my wits, and I fear they are no match for your full-on joie de vivre!"

"You brute, Flint! I feel like more inclined to throw this coffee in your face than put it into a cup," she said, holding the cafetiere up in a mock show of anger.

"Just like what Carmen might have done," he said, laughing. "I'll take my coffee please and preferably in a cup if that's okay with you!"

She poured out the coffee and handed him the cup. As he leant forward to take it, she kissed him again and this time he seemed to respond.

"Mmm, much better when it's not just me doing the work, Flint. Care to try that again?"

"Not right now. Quite like to have that coffee, see if it as good as you claim. Perhaps later."

"That's five times I've kissed you, Flint. You need to start number six."

'Oh dear, why did I agree to come back to her flat?' he was thinking as he smiled.

She poured out the coffee slowly and deliberately, her eyes not leaving his. His eyes were darting between hers and the cup, wondering how she was going to tell when the cup was full and not spilling out.

"Tell me how you take it, Flint," she said.

"Pardon?"

"Your coffee. Black or are you going to be very English and insist on milk?" she said.

"I don't have much of a choice, do I? If I choose to be English that will further diminish me in your eyes. If I choose not to have milk, you may see that as a sign of weakness that I am bowing to your will. Some might say 'damned if I do, damned if I don't'."

"Flint! It's only a coffee, don't make anything out of it. Don't assume that there is a hidden meaning behind what I say."

"In my line of work, assumptions are something we try to eliminate: they are unreliable, can be misconstrued and interpreted by either party as…"

She stopped him by putting her hand over his mouth.

"Ssh! This morning I told my neighbour I was seeing a friend for lunch and she said whoever it might be, that he was a lucky guy. Are you a lucky guy, being my lunch date, Flint?"

"You changed your clothes when I feel asleep," he said, looking her up and down.

"Changing the subject. Nice! Flint, do I make..."

"I've never been lucky, Kiffy. Never won any competition or raffle or lottery or anything like that. Luck, I find, is too random and therefore hostage to fortune so I never set any store by it," he said. "So, being here, I am inclined to believe is not down to luck or chance. And indeed, I feel the same about when we met, dinner in Victoria, lunch and now this. Luck? No, I don't think that this is luck but I would be very interested, indeed appreciative, if I was to learn what this is all about, Kiffy," he said resolutely.

"There is no hidden agenda if that is what is worrying you, Flint."

"With respect, Kiffy. I fear you are being economic with the truth. For a start, I would not be exaggerating were I to say again that I must be a good deal older than you, perhaps even old enough to be your father. Not so?"

"That you could never be, Flint. He is not English, he is warm and loving and not at all stiff like you," she said, bitingly.

"Perhaps, Kiffy, if it will not stunt conversation, we could refrain from quips and insults about my Englishness and the perceived defects in my character," he said.

She was about to riposte his rebuke when she thought better of it and kept her counsel. There was a moment of silence. Finally, she said, "Perhaps we could."

"Good! Now you were going to address my point of how is it I am lucky to be here? Notwithstanding the considerable age difference between us. I am fifty-two, Kiffy and if I had to hazard a guess you would be what, thirty?"

"Thirty-two."

"Twenty years. That is a huge age gap and with respect, I ask myself why a beautiful, young woman would wish to consort with a much older chap like me? Putting aside your eloquently spoken taunts about the flaws in my character and cultural traits."

"I thought we weren't going to talk about your character flaws and your Englishness," she giggled.

"Kiffy, as a lawyer I am good at focussing on a point and you are still not answering my question. I'll ask again, why me?"

She put down her coffee cup and stood up. She was looking at him with her hands on her hips. Her eyes were looking at him intensely as if deciding what she was going to do. "Shall I go?" he said awkwardly and shifted forward to sit on the edge of his seat.

"Flint, sit down," she said gently and at the same time, she took the coffee cup off him and put it down.

He sat back in his seat but there was no respite from not knowing what was going to happen next.

Adrienne moved gracefully to stand directly in front of him. If it was meant to intimidate him, it was working but he remained outwardly calm. Not changing one's demeanour was very important in contract negotiations, he had been told as a young lawyer.

'Give nothing away, especially in sticky situations', had been the message rammed home time and again. 'Not a twitch nor a blink nor a shrug. Modulate your breathing and to all intents and purposes appear unruffled; as normal as one can be. Don't let your guard down. Remember our clients expect the best contract and as commercial procurement lawyers, it is our obligation to achieve that. Movement of one facial muscle in a tough negotiation could cost our clients millions.'

This was feeling like one of those situations. There was no money at stake and he was the client and lawyer all rolled into one. It made him nervous, uneasy and edgy seeing her towering over him.

"I feel you have me at a disadvantage," he said, raising a half-hearted smile.

"Am I making you nervous, Flint?" she said as she leant down, pushing his legs together before sitting astride him, putting her arms around his neck. "Why is it that a girl can't just choose anyone who she wants to? How did you put it, 'to consort with', Flint? Why can't we do what we want to do regardless of any of society's conventions? Tell me why I have to consort with someone of my age, Flint? Why can't it just be, Flint? Why can't it just be that I found someone who I am interested in? You Flint, even taking into consideration the things we said we wouldn't talk about. Maybe because of them, who knows. Tell me why it is expected that I should follow convention? I know you like me, Flint. Don't bother to deny it. I have no agenda, Flint. This is not a set-up. I am not after your money, I have no ulterior motive. Flint, sometimes…"

"A cigar is just a cigar," he interrupted.

"Yes, Flint. And my neighbour was right. You are lucky. In the three months I have been in this apartment you are the first man to pass through my front door, whether you believe that or not. And you are lucky because you are going to be my boyfriend."

"I am?"

"Yes, Flint, you are," she whispered in his ear.

"Do I have a say in this?"

"No, Flint, you do not. It is my decision," she said.

He could feel her breathing along his neck and her scent was playing havoc with his senses. Her proximity was making it difficult for him to keep his composure and he was having to summon all his willpower and concentration to not give away any sign that he might actually be liking everything that she was doing. Her arms around his neck, her lips millimetres from his neck, her breathing caressing him, her long, silky, brown hair cascading all over him.

"How do you know I am not already married?" he said to deflect her.

Adrienne pulled a face. "Really? Does it matter, Flint?" She giggled. "You are here with me, not so? Doesn't concern me, I am not English. Oops! We said we wouldn't say horrible things, didn't we? Sorry for that."

"I am not married," he said. "Never have been."

She let go of his neck and sat back, upright, resting herself on his thighs.

"Am I heavy? I can get off you, if you like. I would rather not. I like sitting on you."

"Do I have a choice? It's fine, you can stay as you are. I am not used to having such a weight on me but not a problem. I don't mind," he said.

She gave him a playful poke. "Hey you should not be saying 'you are heavy' to a girl, Flint," she said. "But I forgive you. Maybe you are out of practice in how to talk to a girl. I don't suppose when you are dealing with contracts you can easily switch to boyfriend mode,"

"Yes, it is quite challenging," he nodded. "Quite challenging, filling the newly-appointed role as your boyfriend, Kiffy."

"You may not say it but I know that you find the idea of being my boyfriend, Flint, as you English say, very agreeable. The way you were able to describe me in detail is not just because you are a lawyer and attention to detail is important. I don't buy that. You watch me and I can see it in your eyes that you like what you see. Just now you called me a 'beautiful, young woman'. The way you said it made me tingle inside, Flint. It was said with passion and warmth and you didn't even realise it. If you were not interested in me, we wouldn't be playing tennis with words all the time, you would just ignore me. But you haven't ignored me once, Flint. So don't try to pretend the idea of you being my boyfriend is unappealing to you. I think you very much like that. Just think what you can boast to your friends. That you have a beautiful, intelligent, full of life, French woman as your girlfriend."

"Hot-blooded and tempestuous also come to mind," he said.

"Yes, and warm, and affectionate. I could go on but it would take all day and all night to describe to you why I am going to be the best girlfriend you will ever have. That's why you are lucky, Flint," she said. "What do you have to say about that, Englishman?"

She leant forward again and was inches from his face and her eyes had misted over. They looked at each other but nothing was said. She could feel his hand slowly, slowly running over her arm until it reached her neck and then it was on her cheek. He was caressing it and she responded by tilting her head so it was resting against his palm. Then he gently guided her head down until she was face-level with him. He hesitated briefly and she frowned. Then he kissed her. It was much deeper and lasted longer than she expected of him. Abruptly, he pulled away and sat up, pushing her onto the sofa beside him.

"I, er, must go, things to do, Kiffy. I need to buy those shoes you recommended," he said and stood up. "Remind me, what colour were they?"

She smiled. "You know what colour, Flint. Don't pretend you forgot. But good excuse. Be on your way."

"Thank you for the coffee," he said shyly, as he headed for her door.

"Flint?"

"Yes, Kiffy?"

"Number six was good."

"Number six?"

"Our sixth kiss. You helping made it so much better. It was lovely, a very nice kiss for someone who has been out of practice," she said and blew him a kiss.

"Thanks, I think that was a compliment," he chuckled.

"Flint, just had a thought," she said.

"What now, Kiffy?" he said, turning to her, front door open.

"You haven't by any chance got another French woman tucked away anywhere, have you?" she teased.

"Another one like you? I think that would be taking entente cordialle too far," he laughed. "There is nothing in that department to direct that Gallic temper of yours to. Goodbye, Kiffy."

She jumped up and ran for the door, pulling it open. "Flint! Wait. I'll walk down with you. I have to let you out anyway."

The lift was narrow and they were standing opposite each other, inches away. When the button for the ground floor lit up he gestured for her to go first. He followed her to where his car was parked. His heart skipped a beat when he saw a note tucked under the windscreen wiper.

'How did I manage to get a ticket on a private estate?' he asked himself, as he pulled off the document. He furrowed his eyebrows as he read it.

"'I don't mind you parking in my space but please ask next time'. Explanation? Is this not your parking space, Kiffy?"

"No, that's my neighbour's. The one who asked who was the lucky guy. Mine is occupied by my car, next to it," she explained.

"The red Fiat 500? Oh dear, I don't want to be the cause of any disharmony in the neighbourhood, Kiffy. Had I known, I would have parked outside the gates."

"Don't worry, Flint. She is a friend and I will invite her for a coffee and she will be fine. She doesn't have a car and she has told me many times I can use it for my guests." He got into his car and pressed the window down.

"Goodbye, Kiffy."

She leaned into his car and kissed him. "Hmm, number seven was okay but not as good as number six."

"You are incorrigible, Kiffy. Now please open the gates so I can catch the shops before they close."

"Flint, before you go. How about lunch tomorrow? Come round. I will cook for you. Something French."

"That is very kind, Kiffy. But I can't," he said.

"Date?"

"No, not a date. Just need time to…"

"Get used to having a girlfriend, Flint?"

"Yes, something like that."

"It's just for lunch, Flint. It's what girls do for their boyfriends. At least French girls do that, maybe not English girls who can't cook."

He was shaking his head and laughing.

"Come for lunch, Flint. Just lunch and sex too if you want it. That is optional. Having me as your dessert. You'd like that wouldn't you, Flint? Don't say anything, your eyes are eloquent enough. Okay, I will let you go."

"I'll see you on the train on Monday, Kiffy," he said and started to reverse when he abruptly braked. "Wait! Almost forgot. I won't be around much next week, if at all."

"You going away again, Flint?"

"Job."

"Can I ask where to?"

"Not at liberty to say. Commercial confidence."

"When will you be back?"

"Not sure, it depends."

"How will I contact you, Flint? Can I have your mobile number? I can send you sweet texts. Help you relax after a hard day doing lawyer stuff."

"I would rather not. My preference would be for you to let me have your mobile phone number," he said without explanation.

"Don't you trust me, Flint?" He shrugged.

"Okay, have it your way," she said and told him her phone number.

"Thank you," he said.

"Aren't you going to enter it into your phone?"

"I will do later. When I get home."

"Won't you forget it by then?"

"I won't forget it, Kiffy," he assured her.

"Will you send me a text or a greeting?"

"I wouldn't hold my breath; I am not very good at doing that. When

I am in contract reading mode, I focus one hundred percent on that," he explained. "Nothing personal. Just work."

"Hey! Don't say 'nothing personal', Flint. It is for me," she said and he noticed she was being tearful as she started to walk back towards the entrance to the apartment block.

"Oh dear, this is hard work," he told himself, as he put the car into 'Park' and lifted the handbrake up.

He got out of the car, leaving the engine running and walked briskly until he caught up with her.

"Kiffy," he said, as he pulled her arm. "I will call you. Not text but call you. Just need to work out the best time because of the time difference."

She smiled and he wiped away her tears with his handkerchief. It was blue with white spots. He put his hand under her chin and kissed her firmly.

She put her arms around his neck and kissed him back. "I make that number eight and nine," he joked.

"Yes, and getting better," she said, giggling. "Definitely getting better, Flint."

"Okay, now that entente cordialle has been restored, can I go now?" he said.

"Yes, Flint, you can go," she said smiling and as he started to turn. She pulled him back. "Hey Flint?"

"I really must go, Kiffy. I've got the engine running. Someone could come and pinch my car."

"A Nissan Micra? Maybe my cute little Fiat but not your car, Flint. It's an old people's car and they don't steal cars like that."

"Thank you for that. Right then, you hauled me back, what is it you were going to say?"

"Oh yes, I just figured why you were happy to take my mobile phone number but wouldn't give me yours. You can contact me but still keep your number private. But you realise, Flint that I won't be able to send you sweet texts and messages."

"As heart rending as it is, I shall have to cope," he joked.

"Flint, last thing, no more after this, promise. What's my mobile phone number?" she asked and was taken aback when he repeated it to her. “I’m impressed, Flint!”

When the electric gates opened for him, he wasn’t sure whether to be relieved he was finally out of there or sad that it signalled that he wasn’t going to see her for several days. As he turned into the busy main high street, he chuckled to himself recalling her words ‘I am going to be the best girlfriend you will ever have’.

“Maybe she is right. Scary. Me, having a girlfriend at my old age. And a French one. Seems absurd. Wonder how that would go down with the folks and the Wiltshire country set? Doubt it will last that long, have nothing to worry about.”

Contract

They had just boarded the plane and were shown straight towards the front. He noted the smile the stewardess had turned on as soon as she recognised the revenue-earning, business-class passengers.

"That's what you pay for when flying business-class: you get wider seats, wider smiles and extra friendliness," he muttered.

Right at the very front of the airplane, close enough to smell the captain's aftershave, one could expect the very best of service with the staff exuding warmth and hospitality but that was for the preserve of the first-class passengers and their client's budget did not extend to that.

As the flight was going to be more than seven hours long, it had been agreed that they would fly business-class, courtesy of their important client in one of the smaller Gulf states, who had authorised it. The client liaison man, Colonel Ibrahim, did not bat an eyelid when he had it put to him that for flights longer than six hours it was the custom to use business-class. The Colonel was completely relaxed and at ease about it and made no fuss, when it was put to him that travel was chargeable to the client's account. Colonel Ibrahim spoke as if it was a matter of personal honour when he intimated that it was perfectly proper for the legal team to travel in comfort. It was, he said, "what hospitable people do when they invite guests into their country."

He was relieved for the sake of the others that the cost of flying the team business-class was being met by the client. If it had to be borne by his company, only he, because of his seniority, would be permitted to fly business-class and it would have made for a different quality of travel for them. As one joker quipped, the rest of the team would be 'slumming it in sheep class'. For some partners in that situation, it might have felt a bit awkward having their colleagues sitting back in Economy but he had no such compunction or scruples about doing that.

'I've earned the right to sit here,' he would tell himself. 'All those years of grafting, burning the midnight oil, studying, improving myself and bringing in handsome fees for the firm have given me the right to sit here.'

Yet when he had set out, law was furthest from his mind, having shown no previous inclination in that direction. Indeed, at school his main interests were what were known as the arts: particularly world history, languages and literature. These were the subjects that he was fascinated by and he went on to study classics at university. After obtaining a first from Oxford, he went on to get his master's degree in Middle Eastern studies from the School of African and Oriental Studies, which not only immersed him in the history and cultures of that area, it had also included intensive studies of Arabic, Hebrew and Aramaic, the latter as an indulgence rather than because it might be of use. It is not widely spoken, with only a few pockets of people who still speak the language of Christ. Part of the course had entailed being based in the Middle East which at the time, his father had thought an extravagance but the patriarch of the family, his beloved grandfather, had insisted that the 'boy should be allowed to spread his wings', as he had put it. After his graduation and his return from the Middle East, he turned his attention to what had later become the second love of his life — law and he secured an internship at one of the prestigious city firms, courtesy of family connections, in order to do a one-year law conversion course. His father had been keen for him to pursue the path that would eventually make him a barrister and then be able to appear in the high courts but it was not what he had wanted. Instead, after his law course, he stayed on and became a career solicitor. He was a star learner and rose through the ranks quickly and with the benefit of languages, he was often sent abroad on important overseas cases. He had become one of the youngest partners in the firm's history and his father, after his initial disappointment at his son's refusal to go to the Bar, was enormously proud of him. The prestige of becoming a partner before he hit forty was immense, as was the pay packet but it had played havoc with his personal life and he paid a heavy price for that.

He opened his laptop, clicked on a spreadsheet and started to itemise the various costs that would go into presenting the client with an invoice at the end of their trip.

'Let me see,' he told himself as he started to type. 'Five thousand pounds for each member of the team to fly business class. Hotel, as we are billing for a five star one that we've used before, that will be eight hundred pounds for Sunday to Thursday, four nights per person.

Now to fees. The fees for our services are: six hundred pounds per hour for a senior consultant lawyer, me, three hundred pounds an hour for Gareth and Vincent, as lawyers and one hundred and fifty pounds an hour for Nicola, as legal administrative support. Now excel, be a sport and tot it up for me.'

They were a team of four and if everything went to plan, they would be on the last plane home on Thursday night and get back in time to go straight into work on Friday morning, stopping at Heathrow to have a shower and change.

As the plane took off from Heathrow Terminal 5, he was transferring the answer from the spreadsheet into a pro-forma invoice ready to serve to the client on Thursday, after the conclusion of their work.

"Not bad, including charges for the prep reading we have had to do in advance, that's one hundred and twenty thousand pounds of business on this trip. Not bad for reading and correcting contracts," he said to himself and smiled.

He was pleased with himself as he had advocated taking on this case with one of the senior partners. The firm that the client had normally dealt with had been approached first but had turned it down. Knowing this, the partners in his firm were wary but the fees were too tempting to turn down. In the partner conference to decide whether to take on this business, he pointed out that to do so would further cement their credentials as procurement legal experts in that part of the Middle East. They had established a reputation for attention to detail, being able to dissect a contract microscopically, homing in on areas of ambiguity, contradictory passages, unused terms and above all, the finances. And a large part of this well-deserved reputation was down to him. He was trusted to get the best results for his clients, as one such person put it driving through 'the most economically advantageous outcome'.

"Better drink up as much as you can on this flight, it's going to be very dry when we get there," he overhead Gareth say to Nicola.

This was her first trip and he could see that she was nervous. She looked across the aisle towards him for guidance and he gently shook his head and mouthed, "No."

Nicola unbuckled herself and leaned over towards him. "Why no drink?"

It wasn't a grumble, just a young person asking for advice and he recognised it as such. "Did you not get the little briefing pack that all newbies travelling to this part of the world get? Anyway, drink dehydrates you and in a hot country it can really affect your wellbeing. I know we will be going from air-conditioned hotel to air-conditioned offices but still, even that dries you out. The external temperature will be in the high forties and you will be required to wear an abaya on top of your clothes, all day. You did remember to pack it didn't you?"

"Yes, I did. It didn't cost as much as I thought it would, less than fifty pounds. When will I need to wear it? Is it when we get to their offices?"

"My dear, just before landing you will need to start wearing it otherwise it could offend local people and we don't want to do that, do we?"

"Really? All day?"

"Yes. Except when you are in your room and if we get invited, at the ambassador's reception which I believe is scheduled for Tuesday evening."

"Do I have to wear clothes underneath?"

"I beg your pardon? Nicola, tell me that you don't mean to say that you plan to be sans clothes under your abaya, not a good idea," he said, frowning his disapproval.

"No, of course not, silly!" she giggled. "I was thinking, like shorts and a t-shirt, not proper clothes."

"In that case, I don't see why not. Besides, who's going to know?" he smiled.

He rested his reading glasses on his forehead and closed his eyes. He was not sleeping as such, it was as much to let the others know that he was not to be disturbed. On a long flight he had his routine which started by pushing the button that changed his seat from upright to semi-prone. Then he would slip off his shoes, undo a couple of buttons of his shirt and then loosen his trouser belt. Finally, he would fluff up the pillow and close his eyes.

Although other colleagues who had been given similar work might wrinkle their nose and look at anything to do with that part of the world with condescension, these sort of trips to the Middle East were very much to his liking. They had features which played to his strengths: the need to scrutinise contracts, terms and conditions in detail, setting out payment terms, liquidated damages in the event of a breach of contract and the service agreements. The other aspect was the negotiations: eyeballing those on the other side, remaining poker-faced where necessary, assessing when to concede a point, when to remain steadfast and resolute. It was very much grist to the mill as far as he was concerned.

Unlike many of his colleagues who, if they had to go abroad for business, would try and wangle themselves a trip to one of the trendier places such as Paris, Amsterdam, Frankfurt or even New York, he preferred and indeed, he opted for deals in the Middle East. Aside from generating a regular flow of business for him and his Middle East specialist team, resulting in handsome bonuses all round, he enjoyed the fact that the work in the Middle East was less prescriptive and rule bound as it was in Europe and North America. There was less adherence to standard practice as laid down by the Office of the European Journal for example, which had defined steps and procedures from market testing through to contract completion, with specific rules governing cooling-off periods, telling losing bidders why they were unsuccessful. In the Middle East, you were kept on your toes, not because of being bound by rules but because it was not unheard of for the client to insist on last minute changes, throwing many hours of work up in the air, or the people from the client changed overnight without so much as a warning. Those sorts of unpredictable situations put everyone under enormous pressure and he soaked it up. He was not averse to having to work through the night, relishing the challenge of achieving such changes and still adhere to the timetable the client had first agreed.

But above all, what he liked, even enjoyed, was the fact that he could be completely emotionally detached. His credo was that to get the 'most economically advantageous outcome', one had to be: devoid of any emotion, to think only rationally, to take nothing personally and give nothing away about yourself. He felt a clear, logical, and prosaic approach, with emphasis on being focussed, on being clear thinking, his brain not being clogged up with emotion or feelings, would ultimately achieve his objective and secure the best contract for the client. It was what made him be at the pinnacle of his career.

He chided himself for being ill-disciplined to allow his mind to be diverted by, of all things, a French woman! He was cross with himself for recalling the previous weekend, for seeing an image of her face, her full of life eyes, those firm lips, her womanly scent and coquettish ways. Ten kisses. That's how many they had managed. She had said that she would be his girlfriend and that had made him smile, something he had not done for some time.

But thinking about her, he reminded himself, was not at all conducive to coherent and focussed thought and he took out his mobile and ceremoniously deleted her name from his list of contacts as the plane took off.

'At six grand a day for my fees, the client deserves to have my complete and undivided attention,' he told himself as the name 'Kiffy' disappeared from his phone.

Personal relationships interfered with his mental wellbeing and did not sit easy with him. Wading through legal contracts, picking out the important points and providing the client with sound advice is what made him a consummate professional. He felt ill at ease with personal contracts as they were founded on an emotional rather than rational level and that made them unreliable and for a very long time now, he had steered clear of them.

"For one thing, the obligations on each party are never clear, the terms and conditions of the contract are seldom known and you find yourself going into it blindly," he once told his friend Andy, who queried why he had chosen to be on his own for so long.

"I've been married twice and if the right woman came along, I would be married again and again. You don't even try, old chap," Andy had quipped.

"I have never been married. I know a bad contract when I see one and would never enter into one."

"Stop thinking of it as a contract and enjoy it," Andy said.

"But Andy, even when you are enjoying it, you are in fact in a contract. Okay it's not a legal contract, it is not enforceable but it is a contract between two people, at an emotional level. And that, my friend, makes it too unreliable for my liking. When you start chatting up one of your lady friends, take Anita for example, you are already in the early stages of a contract. You are at the procurement stage, call it market testing."

"Procuring? I'm not procuring anything! Blooming cheek!" said Andy, shaking his head.

"I don't mean you are buying anything but you are, subconsciously, procuring a service. And when you start to see Anita regularly and your relationship is on a more solid footing you are inadvertently entering into an emotional contract. Both parties, you and Anita, have in effect agreed to be bound by a contract, maybe not a piece of paper but the moment she says, 'I want to be with you' and you agree, she has made you an offer and when you have accepted it, Andy, you are in effect, in a contract. The scary bit about it is that neither of you know your rights and obligations under the contract, nor the terms and conditions: you have no *caveat emptor* to protect you in the event that what you thought you were getting out of it, turned out to be false, you are exposed to *ex-gratia* claims when she says you did or didn't do something that she expected you to do and most likely you were blissfully ignorant of, you will no doubt, also be expected to cough up liquidated damages in the form of paying for her in some way or another for the loss of something she had allegedly incurred in becoming your other half and the coup de grace is the use of a contractual term that is very rarely invoked but women invariably resort to."

Andy furrowed his eyebrows trying to guess what that might be. "What's that then?"

"*Force majeure* or 'Acts of God' to you and I. A woman will find some mysterious way of releasing herself from the obligation she has towards you, due to unforeseeable circumstances that prevent her from fulfilling her part of the contract, which just like acts of God, can never be predicted. And I hate to say it, a bit like how your two previous relationships ended, Andy," he said.

"So, I should call off seeing Anita then?"

"I'm just telling you what you're entering into, that's all. As your friend, as well as your lawyer."

"No wonder lawyers have high divorce rates!" said Andy. "So you don't see yourself being in a relationship then?"

"Seeing people's faces after their *decree absolute* reminds me why I should not get married. Not just marriage as an institution but relationships in general. Keeping it casual is good enough for me. No emotional contracts for me."

It was Monday morning and on his side of the table were Colonel Ibrahim, Colonel Faisal and their support staff, together with his legal team. Everyone was smartly dressed, all the men in suits, including the two colonels who he had never actually seen in military fatigues. Nicola wore an abaya, it was as modest as decorum required but he noted it showed her youthful, beautiful face to good effect.

Across the table were the firm that were expecting to sell their services to his client. The team of lawyers was bigger, their senior salesman was there too, even more smartly dressed than them and their support person, who was female, did not wear an abaya. Nicola looked across at him and he nodded in re-assurance.

Colonel Ibrahim opened the meeting, set the agenda and he then handed over to him.

"Gentlemen, we wish to table one hundred and eighty-six amendments to the contract. We have prepared these in the document we have set in front of you," he began and he was smiling. He had the floor and he was in his element.

Four days later, they were shaking hands with their hosts at the airport and saying their goodbyes.

"You did it again, my friend," said Colonel Ibrahim, who was beaming with happiness. "My government and I are very grateful for what you have achieved for us. You have saved us millions of dollars if these amendments go through and we will also get a much better service. *Shukran* [thank you], my friend."

"My dear Colonel, that is very kind of you to say so but we're the ones who should be grateful. After all, you have paid us a handsome sum of money for our services," he pointed out.

"You have earned every penny and more, my friend. I have a gift for you. But please do not open it here as it is just for you," he said and thrust a small package into his hand. It was done in the blink of an eye so that there was no time to arouse curiosity in the others.

"Colonel, I am very grateful to you. Is it likely to lead to any questions being raised about it when I pass through security?" he asked. The reason he now asked whenever he was being presented with any package that contained a gift, was he recalled one embarrassing trip when the gift was a beautiful, bejewelled, ceremonial knife. It was only ceremonial but it was still a knife and it had been confiscated.

"Hehe, no it is not a gun or a knife. Nothing to worry about, my friend. Just something you wear: cheap jewellery. Besides, my cousin is in charge of security checking and he knows to wave you and your party through," he laughed.

"Many thanks, again," he said and they shook hands firmly.

"When will you be back?"

"They have a lot to consider but I think they have accepted most of our points, *inshalla*. I expect to hear from their lead counsel sometime next week and then we'll pop over to finalise the contract, God willing. If we do, it will just be myself and Nicola in support. This was her first trip and she was very good; I am glad I took her along."

"I agree, she was very good, I could see her making the changes as we went along. Very impressive. You chose her well. Also, may I say I am very happy she was very respectful of our customs and faith. She was very modestly dressed unlike the other woman. I was angry to see her like that!"

"Our company prides itself on being sensitive to the laws, the culture and religious beliefs of our clients, Colonel. We aim not to cause you any offence," he assured him.

The colonel nodded his approval and was about to let him go when he pulled him back and said, "By the way, thank you once again for the Cadbury's chocolate and the Terry's chocolate orange, my two favourites. My children loved them too. That was very thoughtful of you."

"Then I shall endeavour to bring some more on my next trip," he said, smiling.

On the plane back he started to update his spreadsheet to show the payment made for one hundred and seventy-five thousand pounds in total. On a new workbook he was going to do a revenue projection for the follow-on work and then stopped.

"Never assume that," he scolded himself and he deleted the new worksheet and closed his laptop. He had seen it in others, forecasting returns for which there were no guarantees and then finding themselves falling flat on their faces, frantically trying to generate the shortfall they had predicted in their budgets.

There was a cough and he looked up to see Nicola sitting sideways to him and smiling. "Can I interrupt you?" she asked sweetly.

He leant towards her. "Yes, of course. What can I do for you Nicola?"

"I just wanted to say thank you," she said.

"Thank me? What for?" he looked puzzled.

"Firstly, for taking me on this trip. I know it raised a lot of eyebrows. I did hear whispers that others thought that they might have been given this opportunity ahead of me in the queue, on account of their experience," said Nicola.

"Nicola, you are here because you deserved to be and for no other reason. And you have acquitted yourself well. Colonel Ibrahim was most impressed, as was I. You need not to feel guilty that you jumped the queue. For one thing, we don't have such a thing and secondly, I chose you because your work back in London has been excellent."

"I'm surprised you noticed my work. Someone like you, a partner, doesn't get to talk to someone like me."

"I do get to see your work and I do have regular meetings with your line manager. It may surprise you to learn that I know all about everybody's work: what hours you keep, what other things you get involved in. I like to know what all the members of my team do."

"I suppose that's what makes you a great lawyer, your attention to everything," she said shyly.

"I try and leave nothing to chance, if it all possible."

"Anyway, thanks for giving me the opportunity," she said.

He noticed that she seemed hesitant and he asked, "Was there something else?"

"Yes, there was. I also wanted to thank you for looking after me throughout the trip. Like advising me about when to wear the abaya, when I didn't have to. Like when you helped me in the hotel sorting out the room when they gave me a smoking room instead of a non-smoking one. And at the ambassador's, you briefed me beforehand about how to behave, how to hold my drink, what to say, what not to say. Like stopping in our meetings and repeating technical jargon in case I did not get it. But also, simple things like making sure I drank lots of water and waiting to escort me when I went to the ladies, when all the others had gone ahead."

"It's my job, Nicola," he shrugged.

"No, it's more than that. You are a kind man," she said and leaned forward and kissed his cheek. "I feel safe with you, just like having my dad with me."

He chuckled, "Thank you, I think."

"Do you have any children? Sorry, I am being inquisitive."

"No, none. Never seemed to have the time to get around to thinking about children," he said wistfully.

'Ah, children, the product of a relationship,' he mused, as he recalled in the distant past, he had been cognisant from the outset that to pursue his career aspirations, required of him to be single-minded and determined. Something had to give. He recognised the folly of trying to form a long-term relationship alongside working towards making those aspirations become a reality and he pursued nothing that was more than temporary. Nothing that would require too much investment in his time and energy. But it was more than that, he doubted whether he had the emotional capacity in himself to form long-term relationships such as marriage or living with someone on anything more than was on a casual basis. The type of women he had dated on and off got that and it suited both parties. No emotional contract of sorts had ever been made and none was likely to either. That is until now.

"The Frenchwoman. Kiffy," he muttered and sipped his scotch.

"Pardon?" said Nicola, sitting up.

"Nothing. Just talking to myself," he said and closed his eyes, to make it clear that he was not interested in further conversation.

Cooking Up

On Friday morning he went into the office and into his weekly briefing where each partner shared with those around the table, their key business activity and outlined the plan for the following week. He was pleased to see appreciative nodding as he spoke and there was even the faintest of smiles from the three senior managing partners sat at the other end of the table to him. Building on that positive response, he let it be known that he had booked further significant business which would entail him returning to the Middle East for three weeks. It was to support another section of the Ministry of Interior, that was just starting negotiations to buy major sub-station equipment and they lacked the confidence to do the legal work themselves. He said that he would go alone for the first week to get it off the ground but he would need one of his team and a support person for the following two weeks. In answer to the question he knew that was uppermost in their minds, he said that including work that could be done back in the office, he was expecting fees somewhere in the region of three to four hundred thousand sterling. There were smiles all round and he was excused from having to stay for the rest of the meeting, so he could start to prepare for his forthcoming trip.

He called his team to a meeting, having already texted Gareth ahead as he left Heathrow Airport the previous evening and they gathered for him to outline the work to be done. He said as it was a longer trip, he was looking for volunteers and they were forthcoming, more than what was needed.

As he was about to board the plane on Sunday night, he texted a message to her. It was brief, to the point of sounding terse. '*Have to go on another trip, won't be back for 2–3 weeks*'.

The work had indeed taken longer than expected and it was Monday morning three weeks later, when he boarded the train at his usual time and was about to sit in his usual seat when he stopped in the aisle. She was there, sitting in his seat.

She looked up at him and smiled.

"You're back," she said but made no attempt to move.

He noted that she was not putting on her make-up and was pleased.

"Would you mind if I sat there?" he asked coldly. "As per our agreement."

"Don't be like that, Flint. I am settled in now. I wasn't expecting you. Let's start next Monday."

He huffed and sat opposite her. "When did you get back?"

"Last night, late."

"You look well, a little tired maybe but otherwise well. And less pasty-faced than usual. Another foreign trip has done you good, Flint," she teased.

"Are you well?" he said, looking directly at her. "You look well."

It was the eyes, greeny-blue, looking back at him that gnawed at his determination to remain cool and aloof. The half-open mouth and the way her hair fell, conspired to undermine the need for him to maintain decorum, to keep up the façade of the calm, collected professional that he used to good effect day in and day out.

"Your phone call. Oh my God, it happened in the middle of a staff meeting and it was so embarrassing. I had to leave the room to take it," she said, laughing.

"Whatever are you talking about? I did no such thing. I did not phone you," he said, looking perplexed.

"Exactly! You did not phone me, Flint. I am sure you said when you left my apartment you would call me. Did you not?"

"I did."

"Perhaps your phone was not working?" she said, looking to him for an explanation.

"It was, there was nothing wrong with my phone. It was working fine."

"I know, you forgot to put my number into your phone so you didn't have my number, so couldn't possibly ring me," she said.

"That is not correct. I did not forget to enter your number into my mobile phone. But it is correct to say that I could not ring you," he said, with just the faintest of smirks forming on his lips.

"Will you stop the puzzles and talk straight? God, you are so

English!"

"Very well then. I have had my bit of early morning fun. Actually, I was quite enjoying seeing you worked up again," he tittered. He was going to add 'I missed that' but he checked himself.

"You like to make me angry in the morning?"

"Yes, you become so French! Eyes are fiery, cheeks start to blush, your nostrils begin to flare, your chest begins to expand as you start to breathe more heavily, your knuckles turn white as you clutch your handbag tightly as if you are clinging to a life raft. And, last but not least, you are bouncing one leg over the other and by the way, kicking me, as you show your agitation."

She wrinkled her nose and poked her tongue out at him and it elicited a smile in him. A broad smile. She returned the smile.

"You don't miss a thing, do you?" she said calmly.

He wanted to say, 'I missed you' but found that he could not utter those words. "You changed your scent," he noted.

"Yes, I did. Do you like it?"

He shrugged. "I prefer the other one but it is of course for you to wear the perfume of your choice. Not for me to say."

"I'll wear the one you like when you come round for dinner next Saturday," she said smiling.

"Dinner? Saturday? I don't recall receiving such an invite and my having accepted it."

"Flint, I've just invited you. I will cook you something French! I know you like French cuisine. You probably have been to more French restaurants in London than I have, entertaining your clients. So bring some wine and a movie or two for us to watch, something with a decent storyline."

"Do I have a choice of what wine to bring?"

"White wine as we're having fish. I am making a popular dish from Normandy for you to try. And, Flint, none of your fashionable English wines. I know in blind tasting English white wines were rated as good as our wines but I don't accept that. Not yet; maybe in a hundred years' time!"

"Hmm, most independent experts would disagree with you but I shall bring a non-English wine, just to please you. I understand the Irish have just started to produce wine, perhaps one of theirs!" he chuckled.

"Ha-ha. And, Flint," she said, leaning forward and lowering her voice, she added, "bring your pjs too!"

"Oh? Am I staying all night? Sleepover is it?"

"Yes, you are. We can't be watching a film together and then you get up and leave me just like that. You'll stay. I'll make you Sunday morning breakfast too and then I'll let you go!"

"How about I cook breakfast? Perhaps an English breakfast!"

"With all that fat? No thank you. Traditional French breakfast!"

"What time did you want me round?"

"Early evening? What time do you eat? I usually eat around seven thirty. Come earlier but be warned I can be a demon in the kitchen."

He smiled. "No different to any other time," he murmured but inaudible to her above the noise of the train.

"Okay that's settled then," he said.

"Don't be late, Flint. I don't like late."

"I won't be late."

The train was slowing down as it entered Victoria station. They stood up to leave and he was aware of her close proximity as he stepped aside for her to pass him.

"By the way, you didn't say why you could not ring me," she said, as they walked along the platform.

"I didn't have your number."

"It doesn't make sense, Flint. You said that you entered the number into your mobile phone, didn't you?"

"Yes, then I deleted it."

"Why?"

"I didn't want to ring you."

"Why not? You said you would."

"When I am with a client, I like to be focussed on them and only them. They are paying for my time and I need to devote my time and energy to that."

"Not even to ring your girlfriend for a few minutes?"

"Ah, yes, on that specific point, we haven't yet established that you are the said girlfriend nor indeed, I your boyfriend for that matter, would you not agree?"

They went through the ticket barriers side by side. Once through she said, "Flint, that was not a nice thing to say!"

"I was attempting to make the point that at this stage I would characterise it as being aspirational, would you not agree?"

She smiled. "So does that mean you aspire to becoming my boyfriend, Flint?"

"I don't know. I haven't made up my mind."

"I hate you, Flint!" she said and started to walk away from him.

"Does that mean Saturday's dinner is called off?"

She stopped and turned round and walked close to him. So close he could feel her breath on him.

"Saturday, I will cook you dinner, Flint. You will see what a great girlfriend I am!" she said and kissed him, her lips firmly pressing on his and her hand around his neck, before letting him go and walking off briskly.

She had kissed him on the concourse of a busy and crowded train station in front of everybody and he was feeling embarrassed and awkward. But there was no denying that it had thrilled him. Stirred feelings in him. Feelings for her. It was not setting him up in the right frame of mind to go into the office and into a weekly de-briefing meeting with his team.

***

It was Saturday evening. He parked his car outside the apartment grounds and walked in, just as the electronic gates were about to close after one of the residents was driving away.

He took the lift up to the third floor and was standing outside her front door, rucksack on his back and a bunch of flowers in hand. He checked his watch.

"Seven twenty. Can't be accused of being too early or indeed late. Unfashionably on time," he muttered, then pressed his ear to the door.

He held his breath momentarily and listened to any tell-tale noise coming from within. Other than the one-time clatter of something metal falling onto a hard floor, followed by a shout of 'merde!' there was no other discernible noise that might give away her state of mind.

"What am I doing here?" he asked himself, not for the first time that day. "If I knock on this door and enter, what message am I sending? Is it a tacit admission that I do aspire to be her boyfriend? I haven't even yet had the gumption to consider that as a possibility. Would it not be an implicit signal, like an unwritten contract, that I was willingly accepting her as my girlfriend? Is this not getting ahead of ourselves? How do I know if she is *bona fide*, even? Thus far, I haven't had the inclination to use my contacts to carry out some background checks on her. Perhaps I should. What if she is the French equivalent of a 'care in the community' person, perhaps even someone with psychopathic tendencies? All it might take is for me to say or do something completely innocuous, that triggers some inner brain turmoil and she comes at me brandishing a kitchen knife. I bet she has one of those extra sharp French Sabatier ones and I am being carved up like a Sunday joint. Good thing I told Anca where I was going."

He raised his hand to press the bell. "What was that Latin phrase we used to shout out in school to give us courage, just before we were running out onto the pitch for a game of rugby against bigger and stronger opposition, '*audeces fortuna iuvat*'. Hmm, I do not see myself as particularly brave and the moment I press this doorbell I have stepped out of the shadow of the cautious and will be relying on good fortune to see me through."

He pressed the doorbell and waited for the recognisable sound of footsteps from within approaching the door. But there was no response. Part of him was telling him to turn around.

"Could be a bad sign," he muttered and he slowly turned around towards the corridor, as if to walk away. "May be not such a good idea after all."

He had an all-consuming desire to leave, as he felt the weight of the next steps he was about to take as soon as that door opened. There being no answer added weight to his desire just to disappear from there. Normally a rational man and not given to acts of impetuosity, yet, if it wasn't for his sense of fairness that she had gone to the trouble of inviting him and having cooked and that it would be rude to just walk away, he would have done precisely just that.

He went back to the door and pressed the doorbell again. "One last go, and then I'm off," he muttered.

There was no immediate response and then he heard a shout of, "Just a minute, Flint." He fiddled with his shirt and adjusted the buckle of his trouser belt, checked that his zipper was done up all the way and waited for the door to be opened. It wasn't so much opened as flung open, catching him unawares. And there she stood, beaming from ear to ear. Her hair was up in an untidy ponytail, flour on her cheek, wearing an apron, looking very much as if she was in the throes of cooking.

"Sorry to keep you waiting, Flint. I was at a crucial moment in my cooking," she said and kissed him, la bise style and then on the lips. It was a light peck and he wasn't sure whether he was relieved or disappointed.

Adrienne smiled sweetly and locking her arm with his, lead him inside. "How are you, Flint?"

"I am fine thanks," he said, trying to keep his poise.

"Come in, come in. I was expecting you to ring me so that I could let you in to park your car. Where is it by the way? How did you get in?"

He smiled. "I didn't want to risk being the cause of neighbourly disputes so I parked outside the grounds and I was fortunate that someone was driving out just as I walked up to the gate. And here I am."

"You're late," she said frowning.

"I am not late, you said seven thirty, I was here ten minutes early and there are still five more minutes before it is…"

She stopped him by kissing him again, draping her arms around his neck. "What am I wearing, Flint?" she teased, in between planting little kisses on his neck.

"You want me to tell you?"

"Yes, I do!"

"A white t-shirt. Plain, no pattern and feels like cotton. Black leggings and an ankle bracelet on your right foot, looks like silver but I could be wrong. Your toenails are painted red, same colour as your finger nails. You are wearing the same hooped earrings as when I first met you, and also, I notice that you kept to what you said you would do and put on the same scent as before. The one I liked."

"I put it on for you," she said, looking sweetly into his eyes.

"Thank you," he said, feeling very uncomfortable at their close proximity. So close that he could feel her warm breath on him. Holding on to the flowers with one hand and his rucksack in the other, he could do nothing to disentangle himself. He was entirely at her mercy.

"What else have you noticed about me, Flint?" she asked, her breathing so close to him it was making his skin tingle.

"You have your hair up in a ponytail, looks as if you might have added some colour to it. And on your left cheek there is some flour. Hmm, not sure whether that is coincidence or otherwise but it covers the little scratch on your cheek which you are very self-conscious of."

She pushed him back. "That's not a nice thing to say."

"You asked me what I noticed, so I told you."

"You could have said something sweeter than point out my scars, Flint," she said with displeasure. "Boyfriends are supposed to say nice things to their girlfriends, don't you know that, Flint?"

"I apologise, I shouldn't have said that," he said earnestly.

"Apology accepted, now say something nice about me," she said, still holding him in a loose embrace.

"I will but if you don't mind, can I just offload these things I am holding first. I brought them for you," he said and handed her the flowers.

"Chrysanthemums? They are very nice, Flint. I have never seen the flower heads individually wrapped like that. You didn't pick these up from a supermarket, more like an upmarket flower shop. *Merci beaucoup*, very thoughtful of you, Flint."

He rummaged through his rucksack and handed her a bottle of wine.

She looked at the label. "'Chablis Grand Cru Blanchot Raveneau (Domaine) 2016'. This is a very exclusive, fine wine Flint. I am impressed."

"I was going to bring an English white wine, probably just as good I might add but I thought the better of it in case…"

"I was angry with you and smashed it over your head?" she giggled.

"Yes, something like that. I also got something to have with the dessert," he said and handed her a second, smaller bottle of a honey-coloured, white wine.

"'Muscat de Beaumes de Venise 2015'," she said, reading the label. "Another fine wine. I shall put them both in the refrigerator to keep cool. Flint, I am touched, you have put some thought into choosing your wines.

Thank you."

"Actually, I have to confess that I bought the Chablis some time ago and never got around to drinking it. Waiting for the right moment," he said and immediately regretted it, as he realised how that could be read. For a man who was always careful with his choice of words, he was cross with himself for having made such an elementary error.

He was surprised that she hadn't picked up on it or chose to ignore what he had said. Either way, he was glad she did not press him on whether this was the right moment. He remembered ordering the wine over the internet with the intention of drinking it in convivial company, to celebrate landing a massive contract for his company. At just under two hundred euros, it was the most he had ever paid for a wine but he felt he had earned it having bagged six months' worth of fees for his team, by putting together a number of contracts for a Middle East client who was undertaking a massive, new civil construction.

"I have another gift for you but I would ask that you do not open it until later, much later," he said and handed her a gift-wrapped box.

"I wonder what this could be?" she said taking it, feeling the resistance from his hand as he did not let go. "Okay, later!"

He released the box and smiled.

They walked into the flat and she took his jacket off him and his rucksack and hung them on a peg in the hallway.

"Any more goodies in here?" she said, squeezing his rucksack.

"Yes. I brought along a couple of DVDs: you said you wanted to see a film. Perhaps we can watch one of them after dinner."

She kissed him lightly, running the back of her fingers along his cheek. His hands may have been free but she had him pinned to the wall, looking at him intently making him feel even more uncomfortable.

"Your scent."

"What did you say, Flint?"

"You asked what else I noticed about you. It's your scent, Kiffy. It is intoxicating," he said and when she opened her mouth to respond, he put his fingers on her lips to stop her. "And the leggings. They show off your lovely figure to great effect, curves in all the right places. And you have long, slim, elegant legs. I wasn't going to say it, as it felt a bit indelicate to do so but now I will. I do believe that beneath your leggings you are not wearing panties. At least not traditional ones. I think they call them a thong. I believe you are wearing one of those, at least that's what it looks like to me. Also, pardon me for saying so, you are not wearing a bra."

"How do you know? My apron covers my boobs," she said, putting her hands to her chest.

"When we embraced and I put a hand on your back, I could not feel a bra strap," he said, smiling sheepishly.

"So, you noticed that, did you?" she said, teasing him. "Well, you are correct. I am not wearing a bra. Does it offend you? Do you wish me to go and put one on?"

"Err, are you asking me to choose whether you wear a bra or not beneath your t-shirt?" he said.

"Yes, Flint. I am. You get to choose," she said, holding him closely once again.

"Leave it off," he whispered in her ear and then kissed her neck.

"Good because you would only have had to take it off later if I wore one," she whispered back in his ear. "And Flint, I didn't want you to be clumsy, how you English say it? All fingers and thumbs."

He kissed her and whispered in her ear, "I am well practiced in the art of removing bras, you needn't concern yourself on that front."

She giggled and returned his kiss. "Much better, Flint. Much better. Now I must see to my cooking. Come to the kitchen and pour us some wine or sit on the sofa, up to you."

He was flushed, with a mixture of embarrassment and excitement. The evening was already turning out differently to how he had imagined it would. It was feeling more like a rolling stone that couldn't be stopped. He had wanted to dictate the pace and direction. But it was she who had set the pace not him, being intimate from the very moment she had opened her front door. He had set out to be in control, to be in the driving seat but it was not working out that way. She had hijacked that. She had torn to shreds the pre-planning he had done to map out how the evening might develop, with romance developing quite late into the evening, if at all. The plan had been to keep his options open, stay slightly detached and maintain decorum, gradually relaxing, letting his guard down as the evening wore on if it appeared that the situation was conducive to romance. In his mind, romance was not just about sex but something that was cerebral as well as physical. And that was what required time to develop. Sex was too easy; he had not been in short supply of that but he wanted his mind to be seduced too, not just his loins. However, all plans had been blown apart. She had already laid it on thick with romantic overtures and gestures and far from cooling it, he had been a willing participant. It was contrary to his plans and expectations but what he was finding disconcerting, was that he had found it very much to his liking. She had lost none of her allure. She was as attractive and appealing as any woman he had previously met.

He left his shoes by the door in the rack next to hers, took the DVDs from his rucksack pocket and put them on the glass coffee table in the living room and followed his nose, until he was standing in the kitchen doorway, watching her. Following her into the kitchen he was finding it challenging to maintain his poise.

"Come in. It's not a big kitchen as you can see: designed for English people who don't like to cook, but it's okay," she said, as she tossed some cream into a saucepan.

"Cosy. Some people would call this cosy," he said, as he opened a bottle of wine she had on the side and filled a glass, sliding it across the workbench to her.

She glanced at the glass and looked at him. "Where's yours? Are you not drinking?"

"I thought I would have some with dinner and perhaps a drop of the dessert wine. I don't want to be over the limit, it would be irresponsible," he explained.

"You won't be over the limit when you leave," she said, smiling. "Go on, pour yourself a glass, it is not nice for me to be having a drink alone. It is not as posh as the Chablis you brought me but very drinkable."

He poured himself half a glass. 'Looks like I am to stay the night. So much for keeping my options open,' he smiled to himself.

"A votre sante, Kiffy," he said, holding his glass up. "Your good health, I believe."

"Very good, Flint. But that is very formal. You can say '*à la tienne*' to me, which is used in an informal situation. It is like saying 'cheers'. We are in an informal situation aren't we, Flint?"

He looked puzzled. "Yes, of course," he said and took a sip of the cool liquid. "Is that how you see it too?"

"Yes, I do. But for you, I am not sure. You seem nervous and on edge, even more cold and distant than usual."

"Really? You think that, in spite of our earlier greetings?"

"Flint, come on. That was me doing all the greeting. I practically had to force myself on you."

"But I kissed you," he protested.

"Yes, only after I did. You felt so stiff in my embrace."

"I was holding a rucksack and a bunch of flowers at the time."

"You do want to be here with me don't you, Flint? There isn't a little wife back home who is waiting for you and you are nervous being away from her too long?" she teased. "As I said to you before, I don't care if you are married, just don't want to feel as if the meter is running and my time with you is limited. That's all."

He chuckled. "Kiffy. If you are fishing for me to tell you if I am married, then let me remove that doubt from your mind. I am not married."

"Divorced?"

"No."

"Single?"

"Yes, Kiffy. Just single. Not widowed, not spoken for, no paramour, nobody," he said, with a hint of irritation in his voice.

"But Flint, you are fifty-two and you have never married. What's wrong with you?" she teased.

"It could be because I am cold and distant as some people have suggested. It could be that I am not good at being expressive and effusive, at hugging and embracing unrestrainedly and gushing in words as some people are and qualities that most women seem to admire and are drawn to," he said, shrugging his shoulders. "It could be any or all of that. Or it could be that I am holding out for the woman who is not looking for these qualities, who may prefer my austere self. Could be I'm searching for the Holy Grail of relationships. And maybe just like the Holy Grail, it exists in people's minds, a fanciful notion rather than something that is actually real. But I am merely speculating. Who knows? At the end of the day, I am who I am."

She giggled. "Yes, all things about you are true, Flint. But don't be so hard on yourself."

"Oh, thanks," he said, grimacing.

"But wait. You are expressive in other ways, Flint. It's your eyes."

"Pardon?"

"Flint, it's obvious to me that hugging and using pretty words doesn't come easily to you. It's a pity," she shrugged. "But Flint, you may not realise it but your eyes seduce me. Your eyes run all over my body like some unseen lover, Flint. You don't miss a thing about me, Flint. Your eyes are more eloquent than words, Flint. And I like that. I like that a lot."

He smiled weakly and sipped his wine. She glanced across to him and smiled sweetly, winking at him. It made him uncomfortable as he was finding her so enchanting and it would have been easy to unshackle himself from his hitherto restraint, reach over and pull her towards him. But he did not. He just stood there, leaning against the workbench, watching as she stirred the food, tasting it, adding more spices, tasting, the wooden spoon on her fulsome lips. He might have said that he was enjoying watching her be a domestic goddess but instead he kept his counsel. Sometimes, silence is more eloquent. In contract meetings it could be invaluable. It could send a message to the other party that you were unhappy, that they needed to do more for you. When he prepped his clients, he encouraged them to show restraint in speaking up. Colonel Ibrahim had once asked him, "But how will they know what we want?" He had said to the Colonel, "They will know, don't worry."

"Set the table, please Flint. Dinner is almost ready," she said and told him where to find plates and cutlery

He set about his task, glad that he could escape for a few minutes to have time to gather his thoughts. He put the place settings opposite each other on the glass table tucked away in the corner, first holding each item up and looking at it for any signs of stains or marks. Then each item was placed with deliberation, knives and forks, water and wine glasses perfectly aligned, symmetrical, like a mirror image. He stood back to admire his handiwork and then adjusted one of the wine glasses by a few millimetres and smiled.

"That's better," he told himself. He had seen it done hundreds of times and remembered how his mother had said how important it was to get these things right.

Tidiness. That was very important to her. Tidiness in the bedroom. Tidiness in the bathroom and most important of all, at the table. Everything had to be in its place, precisely. She would gently chastise an errant maid who might have slipped up by putting a spoon across the plate the wrong way around or the blade of a knife was facing outward instead of inwards as decorum required. An ordered table led to an ordered mind she would say. And he believed that. At least it had been drummed into him so many times as a young boy, that he did it automatically as if his mother was there standing over him, watching to ensure he lived up to the high standards she had taught him.

"Voila," she said, bringing in a large pot of steaming food to the table. "Marmite Diepppoise, a traditional fish stew from Normandy."

"Wow! Looks delicious. But can I ask an obvious question? Does it actually contain Marmite?"

"That horrible tasting black stuff you English love so much? Of course not. I am not sure why it is called that but I assure you it does not contain Marmite, just good fish, mussels, clams with cider, creme fraiche and spices."

"Smells amazing," he said.

She was about to start ladling the food on to plates, when she stopped herself. "Hey, Flint. Why did you put the plates like that?"

"Pardon?" he said with furrowed brows.

"Don't you want to sit near me? You've set the plates opposite each other. Nicer if we were nearer don't you think. Friends sit near each other, Flint. Move your plate to the side of mine, that is if you want to."

"I'd rather stay here, if you don't mind," he said. "It's because…"

"Suit yourself," she pouted.

"Let me explain," he said.

"You don't have to," she said dismissively.

He put his hand on hers, stopping her from putting food on his plate. "If you really want me to, I will move but first hear me out."

She huffed impatiently.

"If I sit to your side, it means I will be denying myself the pleasure of looking into your eyes directly. Those beautiful, beguiling and dazzling, intelligent, full of life eyes. It means I will not be able to watch every tiny movement your lips make as you speak, as you eat, as you fork up your food, as you smile. The sweetest smile of anyone I know. It means I will not be able to fully enjoy the wonderful contours of your face, your lovely cheekbones. If I sit by your side it would result in my only being able to see one of your hooped earrings sway as they touch your wonderful, long, elegant neck. It would mean I wouldn't be able to enjoy the movement of your chest as you breath in and out, as you say something you are passionate or emotional about. I would be missing out on all these things. That is why I would prefer to remain seated opposite you. But of course, as you are the host, I will comply with what you want me to do."

She was silent. He looked up and there were tears in her eyes. Once he realised that his hand was still on hers, he pulled it back. Decorum had to be maintained. He was feeling very embarrassed for having said what he had said. He felt he might have been more circumspect or said nothing at all. 'Perhaps I should have just done as she asked,' he said to himself.

Abruptly she pushed her chair back and stood up. She looked at him through misty eyes and walked around slowly to where he sat, her gaze never letting go of his. She walked behind him and pulled him in his chair backwards and then sat on his lap sideways, linking her arms around his neck.

"I thought you said you can't be expressive? That was very eloquent, Flint," she said softly and kissed him.

"I didn't say what I said to be eloquent, Kiffy. I was merely stating facts as I saw them. Everything I said is fact."

She kissed him again and then went back to her own seat. "Stay where you are, Flint. I like it where you are sitting. It's better than if you were by my side. Now let's eat," she said and ladled the hot steamy fish stew onto each of their plates. He poured out the wine he had brought, into each of their glasses.

"A la tienne," he said. "Did I get that right?"

"Yes, you did, pretty much," she said, raising her glass.

They clinked glasses and they started to eat. It was her turn to watch him and she was pleased to see that he was enjoying the food and was even dipping bread into the rich fish sauce.

"You left out one reason why you wanted to stay sitting opposite me,

Flint," she said, smirking.

"Oh?" he said. He stopped eating and looked up. 'Wonder what she has in mind now,' he was thinking.

"You liked to see whether my breasts show through my t-shirt now that I have removed my apron."

He tittered. "The thought hadn't entered my mind."

"Hmm, from the man who misses nothing! As if I believe you, Flint. But as you can see, I am not a big chested woman, so not much for your observant eyes to see. I can get away with not wearing a bra and nothing shows."

"Oh, I wouldn't say that," he said, before taking up a spoonful of the stew.

"Flint! Are you flirting with me?" she chuckled.

"I was merely…"

"Stating facts as you saw them," she said, finishing his sentence.

He laughed. It had lasted only a few seconds but she could see that, perhaps for the first time during the evening, he was beginning to relax in her presence. Some of the stiffness in his shoulders seemed to have softened, at least in her eyes.

When they had finished, he helped take the empty dishes and pot back to the kitchen. He watched as she rinsed each dish in turn before loading it into the dishwasher.

"I was going to say, please sit down and I will bring the dessert to the table but then I thought I didn't want to deny you staring, Flint. I felt your eyes all over my ass when I was bent over putting the plates in the dishwasher," she ribbed him.

He was standing there, leaning against the door with hands in his pockets.

"Guilty as charged," he said facetiously. "Best get back to my seat before I get into trouble."

He wandered over to the balcony and looked out. It was a balmy evening with just a gentle, soothing breeze blowing. 'What am I doing here?' he asked himself. 'I hardly know this girl. And she is so young, so much younger than me. But irresistible. Very irresistible. Can't help myself. This is crazy. This has nothing but disaster written all over it.'

On the hard floor he had not heard her steps until she was standing next to him on the balcony, leaning over the steel railings. “Hey! Are you okay, Flint?”

“Yes, thank you. I’m fine.”

“Sure?”

“Yes, why do you ask? Do I seem not okay to you?”

“It’s just that when you rang the door and I didn’t come straight away, you were going to disappear on me. When you rang a second time, I had to interrupt my cooking and rush to the door in case you left. I saw you on the CCTV camera in the hall. We all have access to it as a safety device. It was not a happy face I was seeing. It was the face of someone who looked as if they would rather be somewhere else. Is that how you felt, Flint?”

He could not hide the look of someone who is mortified. “I wasn’t sure whether you not answering the door, was a sign that this was not meant to be,” he confessed.

“Really? What is not meant to be?”

He shrugged. “Romance. I rarely indulge in romance, not out of lack of opportunity but out of choice. I seldom yield to it. I don’t do impulsive things. I find romance is too messy, too random and entails too much emotional investment. It requires of one a disproportionate amount of effort, for something that is intangible, unordered, has unpredictable outcomes and can leave you wretched and unfulfilled. So, I have tended to steer away from it. I am not good at romance, Kiffy, as you’ve already seen by my ineptitude to say the right thing by you. I am not a naturally romantic person. So when you didn’t answer the door immediately, it seemed the path of least resistance was to reconnect with my rational self and step back from it, about turn and go back home.”

She smiled and took him by the hand. “Flint, you are much better at romance than you think. Come on, let’s go inside and have dessert.”

They sat back at the table as she served a traditional rice pudding from Normandy. They hardly spoke, mostly just smiling at each other. There was a connection between them that did not require the spoken word.

“Have you ever been in love, Flint?” she asked gently.

“Big question. What’s your definition of love, just so that we are working from a common understanding,” he said.

"Ha-ha. Come on, you know what love is, Flint. Don't start wearing your lawyer hat again. I thought you left that on the peg with your jacket."

'Have I ever been in love?' he asked himself. He recalled the very first time he thought he was in love was when he was in the sixth form and for the very first time, girls were allowed. Up until then it was an exclusive, boys' public school. In his history class he had been paired with a girl, for studying purposes. Hattie. She had been shy and reserved at first but as she got to know him, they became friends. With time they were confidants and he was smitten and she seemed to like him as much as he liked her. And when February 14th came around, he sent her a Valentine's day card expressing his love and devotion to her, in his own words, not manufactured by the makers of the card. He watched from afar as she opened it and then instead of being enamoured of the heart-felt words he had uttered to her, baring his soul, she just giggled. He watched as she showed it to her friends, the card being passed around, causing amusement and mirth. He was heart-broken.

At university, it was Alison who he met through his interest in philosophy. They hit it off and for two years they had been inseparable. They talked about getting jobs in London so they could move in together. The future was mapped out. He was happily in love. That is until she told him after their finals, that she was going back to her boyfriend in her hometown of Romford in Essex.

It did not end there. In Amman, Jordan where he was there as part of his masters' degree in Middle Eastern studies, he worked in the offices of a UN development agency. There he met Abla, the technical coordinator. She had improved his Arabic no end and he had improved her English. Their friendship had developed quickly and from that they became secret lovers, carrying out a clandestine relationship even after he returned to the UK, meeting up in Rome, Athens and Beirut whenever she could find an excuse to be away. They were seeing each other whenever the opportunity arose for close on to three years. It was in Beirut on a balmy evening, sitting in a swanky waterfront bar and holding hands and sipping cocktails that she told him that it was going to be the last time they would be together. Through tearful eyes and professing her love for him, she said that she was about to become betrothed to a fellow

Jordanian. She explained that it was a decision she had lost a lot of sleep over but ultimately, better for both of them as she could only marry a Muslim man and she didn't want to pressure him into converting to Islam. She said that whilst she was not a religious person, she could not give up her faith because to do so would be to give up her family and she could not do that.

It had taken him a good many years to get over Abla and when it happened, it came out of the blue. Marianne was on the opposite side of the table in tough contract negotiations, being the lead counsel for an American firm doing business in London, trying to win a government contract. They had had several meetings to iron out detail to the satisfaction of both parties and in the process, often worked late nights, with discussions over the phone, by skype, email. Over the course of months, they both realised that there was a connection between them but they maintained their professional distance. When the contract was finally signed by both parties, he felt free to pursue Marianne on a social level. And, throwing caution to the wind, he fell in love with her and it seemed she was equally in love with him. In those days, he had an apartment in the newly fashionable Canary Wharf overlooking the Thames and she moved in with him. It seemed an idyllic existence to him, living with a loving and intellectually stimulating woman who doted on him and made him feel on top of the world. Everything had been going fine until they started to discuss children and the possibility of having them. They were both in their mid-thirties and he was receptive to the idea. Then she dropped a bombshell when she said she didn't want to bring her children up in London; it was too much pressure on a child. He said that he wouldn't mind moving out to the suburbs or even into the countryside as he could commute in. They were sitting in a coffee shop in the City when she asked him how he'd feel if they had their children nearer to her hometown. Edinburgh. He did not say no straight away, as that was not a way to negotiate with her. Instead, he had explored how he might commute, fly down on Sunday night and stay in London, fly back Thursday night and work from home on Fridays. He put that to her as an option of how it might work. Her response was to say she preferred for him to make the move north, to be a full-time father. She couched it in positive terms, a fresh opportunity, could start his own legal firm, dire need for his commercial expertise and so on. But he could see that he was being cornered and when he put it to her that his work and his career was built using London as a base and explained his reasons for not wanting to move to Scotland, he could tell from the blotches in her cheeks that their relationship was over. From that point on, he had decided that being in love was unreliable, detrimental and wasteful of his energy. He sold his apartment and made a handsome profit, moved out of the city and into a detached, suburban house only thirty minutes by train into London.

"No, I can't say I have ever been in love, Kiffy. A few flirtations but nothing that might damage the old ticker," he said, thumping his heart.

"You're not a good liar, Flint," she said. "But I won't press you on that."

"What about yourself, have you been in love, Kiffy?" he asked, as he stood up to take their empty dessert bowls.

"In love? But of course, many times. I am not a person who finds it natural to be on my own for a long time. We French, we live for being in love, don't you know? In France, if you go to Carrefour between the boucherie and boulangerie sections you can buy love. It comes in bottles, big shiny ones, to entice you. Nicely shaped, tapering at the top and standing very seductively. You buy one, take it home and put it on the shelf thinking you've bought something special. And eventually you taste it and you convince yourself it is not that bad. Not as good as you expected but not bad. The trouble is, when you next have a taste it is worse than before, bad by the third or fourth taste and you just want to put it in the recycle bin. Then you go to a different supermarket and you buy another love, shinier and more alluring than the last. You take it home and taste it and it is not as good as advertised. By the fourth go you begin to suspect that what is being sold as love perhaps does not come all shiny and exciting. But you give it one last chance and surprise, surprise the first taste is good. It makes you feel good — at last you have found the right one. That is until you come home because of a Tube strike and discover that someone else is tasting what is supposedly yours."

He stood there holding the plates. Her eyes had welled up. "That was my last boyfriend. I found him in bed with a woman he used to jog with. In my bed! This, this stranger. Can you believe it? I moved out. We sold the apartment and I am now here."

He put the plates gently back on the table and walked around to stand next to her chair. After a moment of hesitation, he put his hand on her shoulder for comfort. He recognised how walking in on her boyfriend would have a deleterious effect on her emotional wellbeing and he felt sorry for her. He loathed people like her last boyfriend who repaid love with perfidious behaviour. Giving her shoulder a little squeeze was awkward but it felt the right thing to do.

"Allow me to make you a cup of tea," he said gently.

She nodded. "Thanks, Flint. No milk please, I'm not English," she said, wiping away her tears.

He chuckled. "I never thought I would be glad to hear her insult my Englishness."

When he returned with two cups and set them down, she had the gift in front of her. "Can I open it now?" she asked excitedly.

"Yes, perhaps it will cheer you up. At least I hope it does. Remember Kiffy, it is the thought that counts. Not that I am trying to manage your expectations," he joked.

"Flint, whatever it may be, it is fine. You shouldn't have."

He chuckled and said to himself, 'in my experience when people say that they actually mean, I am very happy that you did.'

Adrienne untied the gold, braided ribbons and commented on how well it had been packed. "I'm afraid I had nothing to do with the fancy packing," he admitted.

"You wife did it, Flint?"

"You are insufferable, Kiffy! I don't know how many times I have to tell you before you believe me that I am not married."

"Just pulling your leg, Flint. You don't mind if I do that do you? It's the only time I manage to get an emotional response out of you, Flint," she said, giggling.

She wiggled the box, holding it up to her ear, listening for any noise that might give a clue as to what it might be.

"Here goes," she said and lifted the lid off the box. She pulled back the tissue paper. "Flint, you bought me clothes?"

He smiled. "I got it on my travels. When I went to see my client last week. Open it." She lifted the item of clothing out of the box until it was fully open.

"A dress?" She looked at him for an explanation.

"It is an abaya and is worn loosely, at least this one is. It is made of the finest silk, very fashionable in the Middle East, I am assured."

"You want me to dress like an Arab woman? You want me to hide myself from head to toe just in case anyone else looks at me, Flint?"

"An abaya looked like it could be a comfortable thing for you to wear around the house. This one only covers you up to your neck. In retrospect I might have got you a niqab or a burka, especially when you are being critical, at least it will muffle what you have to say. Just joking before you erupt with indignation," he said.

She leant across and kissed him. "Thank you," she said. "Now where are the DVDs you brought? Let's have our tea on the sofa and watch one of them."

He went to his rucksack and took out the two DVDs he had brought with him. He looked at the titles again and wondered whether, with hindsight, he might have brought something a bit more overtly romantic from his collection of DVDs. He had very few of what could be characterised as out and out romantic films. Two of these were classics, 'Casablanca' and 'To Have and Have Not' both starring one of his favourite actors, Humphrey Bogart. As both of these films contained romance throughout, albeit with fine acting and decent scripts, at the time when he was deciding, he did not wish to bring anything that might be suggestive of an intent to be romantic. Now, in retrospect, it seemed that the films he had chosen were a bit too sombre and humourless for the evening.

"It was difficult to choose, as you didn't state what type of films you like, so I brought along two that are a bit above the norm in terms of quality of script and acting," he said, handing them to her.

"'Paris, Texas' and 'The Secret in Their Eyes'," she read out loud. "Natassja Kinski. Oh, I like her, Flint. Let's watch this one first and if we still feel like it, we can watch the other one too," she said.

"Good choice," he said. "Excellent cinematography, and the soundtrack by Ry Cooder is very haunting."

"Come and sit next to me and put your feet up on the sofa and relax, Flint," she said sweetly. "Don't worry. I don't bite."

They settled into their respective ends of the sofa and she started the film. In the dim light of the room, he had nothing but the reflection of the television and the distant hall light to help him ascertain as to how she was reacting to the film. From time to time, he furtively turned to see how she was taking it, concerned that it might be too sad for her liking given the earlier conversation about love. But there was no discernible change in her demeanour. He felt relieved as emotion was already running high and he didn't want to exacerbate matters. She seemed very focussed on the screen and did not budge an inch. Just after the scene where they are playing an old super eight film with Cancion Mixtecan as background music, she hit the pause button.

"Just need to get a glass of water," she said. "Can I get you one, Flint?"

"Thank you."

His eye followed her movement into the kitchen and he thought he saw her wipe her eyes with the heel of her hand.

When she returned, she smiled and handed him the water. She waited until he had drunk it and sat down on the edge of the sofa.

"Very good film, Flint. Good choice."

"Are you sure you want to see it, Kiffy? It is not the happiest of films I could have chosen," he said gently.

She leant against him and kissed him. "Thank you, It's fine. You are very sweet."

She budged his legs. "Open. I want to sit near you. I want to be inside your arms, Flint," she whispered.

He leant against the corner of the sofa and she sat between his legs, leaning back on him, her head resting against his chest. She took each of his hands in hers and wrapped them around her waist.

"Much more comfortable now," she said, as she re-started the film.

The combined effect of her womanly scent and the nearness of her body to him, pressed as it was against him, felt exquisite and delightful and made it hard to concentrate on the film. She was irresistible. He so wanted to kiss her, to press his lips against hers. To saviour their taste, to feel her cheek against his. But passion such as this, was a step he was too afraid to take. His previous experience of romance had been an abject failure time and again and he had hardened himself against trying again.

It had left him too inhibited to be making the sort of move he so desperately wanted to make. To hug her and kiss her, to hold her tightly and whisper sweet things in her ear. Instead, he took deep breaths so that he could be intoxicated by her smell, as it wafted into his nostrils.

As the film progressed, he surmised that the heaving of her chest could be suggestive of more tears being shed. When the scene played out where Travis has reconnected with Jane, played by Natassja Kinski, his guess proved to be correct as she lifted up his hand and used it to wipe away her tears. He patted her other hand gently and planted a soft kiss on her head.

The film was nearing the end as Travis leaves, having told Jane where he had left their son, Hunter, for her to go to. It is a poignant and touching scene when Jane takes her young son whom she hasn't seen in years, in her arms. It was too much to watch and she was bawling her eyes out and burying her head in his chest.

"Sorry, bad choice of film," he said, as he stroked her hair.

Adrienne sat up and looked at him, her make-up smudged and tears rolling down her cheeks. He rummaged in his pocket to bring out a handkerchief and used it to dab her tears.

"You okay, Kiffy?" he said.

She took his hand and kissed it, her eyes never leaving his, before letting it go and standing up in front of him. She held her hand out and he took it, edging off the sofa until he was standing next to her. At that moment, he felt vulnerable to the intensity of her gaze on him. It was sublime in its sweetness. Her hair was a mess and her mascara had smudged yet she looked radiant and dazzling.

Nothing was said between them as she led him by the hand to her bedroom. No words needed to be said.

Breakfast and Beyond

It was just after dawn when he awoke. He looked across and she looked peaceful in her sleep. He was wide awake and his head was buzzing with the events of the previous evening which had culminated in unbridled lovemaking in the dead of night. Now, in the early light of the day, he lay awake thinking of the consequences of what had happened. If it had been a casual acquaintance, he would have just got up furtively and left.

'Can't just get dressed and leave,' he told himself. 'She'll kill me on the train next time. I at least owe her staying, maybe have breakfast together and then leave. Make it more dignified and not just a fling after a night out.'

He slid off the bed as quietly as he could and tiptoed naked into the hall to retrieve his rucksack, where he had his towel and spare clothes, before heading into her bathroom to take a shower and shave. He stopped every few minutes to check if he had woken her. In the walk-in shower he leant against the wall and let the warm water cascade over him. He lathered up his sponge and was about to soap himself down when he paused. He was about to wash her off him, her scent, her womanliness and he wasn't sure he wanted to do that. He wanted to let it linger a bit longer.

'Don't be so stupid,' he told himself and scrubbed his arms and body vigorously, washing her away and down the plughole, washing away the remembrance of the sweetness of laying in her arms, bodies entwined and falling asleep together, her body glued to his own, sweaty and heady with the aroma of lovemaking.

He found himself laughing as he remembered the frenetic and frantic rush to remove clothes as their passion got the better of them, getting tangled up and falling on the bed, almost ripping their clothes in the process. It was hurried and clumsy and not in any book on the art of lovemaking but it was what they both needed then, no finesse, just raw passion.

"Not exactly like the movies," he muttered. "Like right now, if this was Hollywood, she would be stripping off and sneaking into the shower with me and we would be having sex. But in real life, she is in her bed asleep and I get to finish my shower in peace. Sex and water don't mix."

He switched off the shower and listened for any noise emanating from the bedroom. There was none. As he dried himself off, he stopped for a moment and looked at himself in the steamy mirror.

"Was it sex or lovemaking?" he asked himself. "Did Kiffy and I have sex last night or did we make love? What is the distinction? Is it about whether we care about the person we have had sex with? Is that what makes it not sex but making love? Hmm, better not dwell on it too long, not good to over-analyse these things."

As he lathered up his face to shave, his mind kept flicking back to the night, to being woken up by the feel of her hand around his manhood and in the darkness, feeling her sliding over him and then sitting astride him, leaning down and kissing him, slowly, not hurried. Slowing him down, calming his passion, frustrating him in his desire for release, prolonging the ecstasy of wanting her until she was ready. Until she had reached her own climax and only then, did she ensure that his desire was replete. Lying over him, all over him, body on body.

"Sublime, no other way of describing that," he told himself.

He put on a t-shirt and shorts, as he would have done on any given Sunday and packed away his other clothes, smiling as he could still smell her scent on them.

Silently, he made his way into the kitchen and closed the door behind him. He set to work to clear up, smiling as he remembered making a half-hearted attempt to suggest that they wash up when she was leading him by the hand to her bedroom.

"Fool," he told himself, as he started to pack away what he could into the dishwasher, washed the pots and pans that did not fit in there and mopped down all the sides.

He put the kettle on and looked for coffee, grinning when he found a jar of instant coffee.

"So much for the French looking down on us with disdain for drinking Nescafe!" he muttered.

He was sitting on one of the low chairs on the balcony and catching up on the news. Domestic news left him cold. Too much about Brexit, yet another story about knife crimes, more about what we should eat and what we shouldn't eat, about house prices. Most of all he detested the interminable discussions and portents of a dire future for mankind as a result of global warming. He considered all of these types of stories that made up mainstream news to be dull and 'no news'. Whether it was the BBC, the ITN news network or Sky, they all seemed to carry the same news, the only difference being the channel's political leaning with the Beeb leaning towards what one of his American friends called the 'pinko' side.

He skipped to the 'Al Jazeera' news network on his mobile phone, a richly-funded Middle-Eastern news channel based in Doha with offices in London, America and Singapore. Aside from his interest in that part of the world, what he liked was the fact that they seemed to have reporters everywhere. There wasn't a part of the globe they didn't report on, diverse stories, be it a mudslide in South America, the Chinese in Egypt or how people were fairing in the Andaman Islands years after the Tsunami, when western news agencies had long ago lost interest.

The hard floors of the apartment did not give away that she was walking towards him and he did not notice her until she was there, standing in front of him. He looked up from his mobile phone. He noticed she was wearing the abaya, the sun showing off the gold embroidery against the white background to good effect. She looked great in it.

"Good morning, Flint," she said. "Glad you didn't wait for me to get up, I am not the world's earliest risers on a weekend."

She manoeuvred herself around his chair until she was standing next to him and then lowered herself on to his lap, sitting on him sideways. She kissed him.

"Did you sleep all right? I know I can be a fidget in bed, I hope I didn't disturb you," she said.

"No, you didn't, apart from that one time you woke me up in the middle of the night," he joked.

She poked him gently in the ribs. "You're not complaining are you, Flint?"

"No, Kiffy. Couldn't think of a better way of being woken up," he said and gave her a peck on the cheek.

She took his cup off him and sipped from it.

"Yuk, horrible," she said. "Let me make you a real coffee and breakfast."

"I'd be happy with just a coffee. No need to make breakfast, Kiffy," he said.

"I want to! And thanks for cleaning up, that was very kind of you," she said, as she disappeared into the kitchen.

A few minutes later she called him over and they sat on high stools in the kitchen eating the warm croissants she had made filled with smoked salmon and French cream cheese and sipping freshly made coffee. He was watching her every move, enjoying seeing her eat heartily. She watches him watching her. They are smiling but neither is saying anything.

She kissed him. "You know, it's crazy but I feel like a young girl on her first date. Flint. It's a nice feeling. Why do I feel like that, Flint?"

Flint shrugged. "I cannot say, perhaps it is because you hardly know me," he said, before taking a sip of the coffee. "Erm, about last night, Kiffy…"

Adrienne put her fingers to his mouth and quietly said, "Ssh," and then leant over to kiss him before standing up.

She swivelled his stool around until he was facing her. "By the way, I love the abaya. Where did you say you got it from?"

"I didn't. Let's just say it was in a swanky shop in a smart shopping mall somewhere in the Middle East. In any case, it looks really nice on you, Kiffy. It fits you better than you thought it would and certainly brings out your womanliness. Perhaps our Arab friends are right, a woman should be more covered up and that way we can use our imagination as to what is underneath."

"You don't have to use your imagination, Flint," she said and lifted the abaya off her and stood naked in front of him.

Stepping closer to him until she was in his arms, they kissed as his hand caressed her back. Flint hesitated before allowing himself the pleasure of letting his hands meander down until they were touching her bottom, stroking and kneading her cheeks.

Adrienne abruptly stood back and pulled him off the stool and taking him by the hand, she led him back into her bedroom. She gently pushed against his chest, forcing him to walk backwards until he sat on the bed.

Her eyes never left his as she pulled off his t-shirt. Unlike the previous evening, it was unhurried. She discarded the t-shirt, running the palms of her hands over his chest, through the thick, wiry hair, before gently pushing him again until he was lying flat onto the bed. She reached down and undid his belt before pulling off his shorts.

"Nice pants, Flint. Didn't notice them last night," she said, as she climbed over him.

"That's because you and I were…" He wasn't able to finish what he was going to say as her lips clamped over his own and her hair was covering his face.

"That's because we were making love, Flint," she whispered in his ear, before playfully biting it.

'So, it was making love, not sex,' he told himself. 'Time to do my duty as an Englishman and a gentleman.'

He lifted her off and having laid her down on the bed, he planted kiss after kiss on her face, her eyes, her nose, studiously avoiding her lips, making her want him to kiss her. And when he did, it was light pecks, not lingering. He wanted to tease her, like she had done to him in the middle of the night. He kissed his way down her body, slowly, slowly, taking his time, looking up, her eyes telling him to quicken his pace but he was not to be rushed. She could do nothing about it as he had her pinned down below him. His kisses were getting lower and lower, having already played havoc with each of her nipples which stood to attention in a passionate acknowledgement of what his tongue and lips had achieved. When he got to her most sensitive, erogenous zone between her legs she desperately lifted herself up in anticipation but he continued to tease, kissing down her thighs in turn, getting closer and closer. Teasing her.

"Flint! Please!" she said.

He was not to deny her any longer and he returned to the area that had given him so much pleasure the night before and stayed there until he could hear and see her cries of release, her hands holding his head there, her heels digging into his shoulders as she was in the throes of a deep and satisfying, orgasmic climax.

'Give yourself a pat on the back for a good job done, old chap,' he heard himself saying in his head.

"Flint, you are a great lover," she whispered in his ear as they lay side by side. "Didn't expect that from an Englishman. Are you sure you are English, Flint?"

'And it seems I get a pat on the back from her too,' he told himself. It was proving hard not to be smiling from ear to ear.

Half an hour later, as she lay fast asleep, he was getting dressed for the second time that morning, taking care not to wake her up. At that moment he just wanted to go home, no more sex, or lovemaking, no more passion, just to be left alone in his own world. To be in peace, like any other Sunday morning: time to read the news on Al Jazeera, time for watering his greenhouse plants and last but not least, feeding the animal life that depended on him: filling up the bird feeder for the small hungry birds that made his garden their home, scattering a seed mix on the grass for the bigger birds and the ground feeders and finally, throwing a handful of pellets into the pond for the Koi and other fish to gulp down. The most important of the animals dependent on him was his cat, Philip. But he wasn't concerned about him, he would have been taken care of by the one luxury he allowed himself, a live-in housekeeper, Anca.

As he gently accelerated away from the apartment block, most of all he was just looking forward to reading his book on the patio with not a care in the world. That would be something of a routine he enjoyed on any given spring weekend. But instead, as he headed home, he was carrying a self-inflicted weight on his shoulders, that of having started an intimate relationship with her.

"Oh, why did I let it get this far?" he chastised himself. "What happened to my self-control? I let the desire to have sex with her make me take leave of my senses. Now what a mess I have to sort out! Idiot."

Sitting in his garden, sipping tea, with Philip curled up on his lap, he was seething at his poor judgement which now had the hallmark of an entanglement that was in danger of disrupting what had otherwise been, a serene and predictable existence. Notwithstanding that it felt great and she had invigorated him and made his senses alive for the first time in very many a year, it was also a reminder writ large that all of his previous romances had started off well but they had ended up doomed to failure. He felt that the one he had just been seduced into had disaster written all over it. This woman was scary, the antithesis of the so-called gentler sex.

If he stayed with this romance, he knew that the French woman was going to be high maintenance, that this would be no lark in the park. It would require of him a level of emotional commitment that he was not sure he was even capable of giving, let alone wanting to give. As he sipped his coffee, he looked back on his life and aside from historical failed romances, he was very pleased with himself for having managed to get to the ripe old age of fifty-two, relatively unscathed. When he compared his life to some of the others in the office, struggling with the stresses of parenthood, with paying alimony to ex-partners, with the demands of marriages and relationships, he thanked his lucky stars that he had remained single and master of his own destiny. When others had to run home to make sure they did not miss little Johnny's recital, or take little Martha to swimming classes, or traipse round Ikea to buy some inane object they had absolutely no interest in, he felt fortune had smiled upon him. Blissfully free from all these responsibilities.

"I have made you a bacon sandwich," said Anca, putting a little plate and a bottle of brown sauce on the glass, round table next to him. "Do you want more tea?"

He thanked her. She was wearing one of his Che Guevara t-shirts he had gifted her. It was very long and loose on her and fitted more like a short dress. He smiled. He could not help eyeing the shapely curve of her bottom when he was sure she was not looking.

'It's been more than fifteen years since my last fruitless attempt at a relationship and since then life has been good,' he told himself, taking a bite out of the bacon sandwich. "It would be folly to contemplate starting a new relationship now."

Still, the memory of the last twenty-four hours was fresh in his mind and he could not deny that it had been more than just a good night out ending in a 'shag', as one of his friends had once crudely characterised his weekend with an office hottie. Adrienne was different and he did not want to disrespect her or cheapen what had been a connection between them at all levels. He acknowledged that there was something about her that was mesmerising, intoxicating and magnetic that was drawing him in, making him powerless to resist as much as he tried to.

"Getting out of this one won't be so easy, old chap. You need to do this in such a way that she doesn't feel that you've treated her like a whore. You must respect her feelings and find a way, with the utmost courtesy and sensitivity, to say that it was a mistake on your part. Apologise; women like that. Say sorry for giving out the wrong signals that you were available," he told himself, as a strategy was starting to take shape in his head.

"Is there anything else you want, Theo, I was planning to go out?" asked Anca. "Do you need your car? I was hoping to borrow it."

He smiled and wished her a good time.

"I would like it if you could roll back the last twenty-four hours, Anca," he said out loud, after he heard the front door slam shut.

***

He was calmness personified as the train was pulling into Cheam station on the following day and the start of a new week. In a matter of seconds, he would be meeting her on the train. He was pleased with himself as, by the time he had retired to sleep, he had worked out a strategy that he felt would have the greatest chance of success of all those he had considered. If it worked, it would cause him the minimum of embarrassment and her the least painful let down.

As he entered the carriage, he could see that she was already ensconced in her seat, opposite his favourite one.

"Hmm, if nothing else, I seem to have got my seat back," he said to himself.

Strategy one, which was dismissed early on in his consideration, had been to avoid making contact with her altogether, like changing carriage or even getting a later train.

That was struck off. Avoidance was never a good contract negotiation strategy and applied to human interaction, could lead to an even less reliable outcome.

She started to chat to him as soon as he sat down. It was polite conversation about nothing, classic commuter talk, for those that felt the need to say something.

He did not respond, just looked at her, making only the slightest of facial expressions to suggest he was listening, when in reality he had switched off and was thinking ahead to planning his team's next foray to the Middle East. There were preparations to be undertaken ahead of a big, new signing that could keep them busy for months.

"You sneaked out without saying anything," she said, in an accusing manner. "You didn't say goodbye or anything."

That brought him back to the present. "You were fast asleep and I didn't want to disturb you."

She raised a half smile, not entirely convinced. She wanted to ask him why he didn't wake her and say something sweet or phone her up later but she decided not to. Instead, she changed the subject to talk about forthcoming language exams she was preparing for her students. She explained how teachers were under pressure to deliver results as, in a public school where yearly fees are close to forty thousand pounds a year, parents had very high expectations for their children.

"I don't want to be rude but do you mind if we don't chat, I had wanted to do a bit of reading," he said and then looked back down at his tablet computer, open at a Kindle story.

"It's funny how you English sound so polite when you say 'I don't want to be rude', then you proceed to be just that. Don't you think that is funny, Flint?" she said, pulling a face.

He resisted the temptation to answer her back as he decided that would play into her hands, instead his gaze remained downwards. He was reading about the Sumerians and how they had been one of the first civilisations to start to cultivate lands and form communities and how they had probably introduced the first written word, albeit, looking nothing like today's languages. He kept reading the same words over and over again as he was aware that she was staring at him. A quick glance confirmed his suspicion. Her gaze was indeed fixed on him, her elbows were on the table and she was resting her head between her interlinked hands and staring straight ahead at him.

"Do you mind not staring at me?" he said coldly.

"Hey Flint, you didn't mind my looking at you like that when we were having sex," she said.

He fought hard against the discomfort of being reminded of that so openly. He was trying to stave off the onset of reddening of the cheeks: a sure indication of embarrassment, exacerbated by the thought that others may have heard her. She had not exactly whispered it. It was wilful in its intent. Glancing to his left and around he was relieved that no one was close by, but a sharp-eared, fellow commuter might have picked up enough words above the noise of the train to put two and two together and conclude that they were more than just fellow passengers.

To add to his unease and discomfort, he felt her foot touch his leg, trying to manoeuvre up his trouser leg. He frowned at her in disapproval but she just smiled back sweetly. She was enjoying making him squirm but she was not to know that whilst he disapproved, at the same time he found it thrilling, especially as the foot adeptly made its way until it was resting between his legs and caressing parts that would not normally get that kind of attention on a commute into London.

"Hey, Flint," she whispered, leaning forward. "Some people say that communication is eighty per cent non-verbal. I think I am getting a lot of non-verbal communication from you, especially from where my foot is resting."

He tried not to smile but she could see the corners of his mouth move. "You are insufferable," he whispered back.

"Hey Flint. I hear that's what posh Englishmen say when they like something. Is it true Flint? Am I being insufferable, making you desire me?"

He shook his head. "Kiffy, we are coming in to Victoria. Would you like to meet me after work for a coffee? Say five p.m. in front of the Leone cafe?" he asked.

"Coffee, not dinner?" she frowned.

"Coffee. No time for dinner, not tonight."

"Okay, coffee it is. And Flint?"

"Yes, Kiffy, what is it?"

"You know, it is okay to smile. English people do smile, Flint. I have seen them. Not very often, usually after a lot of alcohol but they can smile. And so can you, Flint. We spent a lovely Saturday together. What's that phrase you like to use so much, 'wouldn't you agree'?"

"Yes, I would agree."

"You could say it with a bit more feeling, Flint."

"It was indeed a very enjoyable weekend in convivial company. The best in a long while," he said earnestly.

"In that case, Flint, when you come on the train next time, instead of maintaining that hard English exterior, can you smile for me? After we part for the day you can go back to being English, cold and distant. That's fine by me," she teased.

As he strode to work, he smiled to himself. 'Hmm, not sure this strategy is working so well. Might need an addendum!'

At the appointed time, he stood outside the coffee shop and waited for her as commuters brushed by and around him, walking briskly on their way home. He went into the coffee shop and ordered himself an Americano and took it to one of the outside tables so he could keep an eye out for her. He had an inkling that she might not turn up and after fifteen minutes he texted her. "Are you delayed? Will wait until 5.30 then will board 17.41."

He also removed the block on her being able to see his phone number. He thought that she would like that. But there was no response one way or another and at precisely 5.30 p.m. he kept his promise and left to board the 17.41 which would take him home to Cheam.

"Just as well. Won't need to talk about my forthcoming trip away for the next few days."

At 9.45 p.m. accompanied by Nicola, he boarded the overnight flight that was taking him back to conclude the business on behalf of his Middle Eastern client. He was looking forward to meeting Colonel Ibrahim once again, who he considered to be a friend, a man of the world and deep thinker, as well as being a great host.

In the twilight of the evening as the plane took off, he felt that he had at the very least, physically and emotionally put distance between them.

"Fortuitous but perfect timing in many respects," he muttered to himself, too low for anyone to hear. He allowed himself a private, wry smile.

He looked across and Nicola was already in dream world, the flat bed fully opened out and earphones in place, listening to music. He could see that she must have nodded off as her phone was dangling down and he leaned across to put it on the table next to her. He sat up and looking around, there was no air hostess to help. He felt awkward but in the absence of anyone he took it upon himself to pull up Nicola's blanket to cover her, as it had fallen down and she was exposing a good deal of cleavage.

Amendments and Addendums

The final amendments to the contract took much longer than expected and he found himself working through the night to ensure all the changes were assessed and included, so that the signing ceremony could proceed as scheduled. He felt sorry for Nicola as it was the first time she had had to work through her weekend and without a break. Before they left Heathrow, she had assured her mother, who had quizzed her as to why there was only the two of them going, that it was all above board and that it would just be Tuesday to Friday and she would be back home on Friday night.

"Mum, don't worry about me, I am in safe hands. He is not like that, he's very protective of me and fusses over me as if I was his own daughter. Besides, I am a big girl now, I know how to look after myself."

She had smiled but it did not assuage her mother's concern about her daughter being left alone with an older, single man.

So when she rang her mum to tell her that they would be staying there for longer, working through the weekend and finishing up on Monday, with a signing ceremony on the Tuesday, she had demanded to speak to him.

"I can assure you, Mrs Burnett, your daughter is required. She is doing vital work but I cannot elaborate as to what that is as it would be in breach of client confidentiality. What I can say is that if all goes well, I can release Nicola on Monday, a day early as she doesn't have to stay for the signing ceremony, if she doesn't want to. I can get her on a Monday evening flight back."

Nicola was shaking her head and mouthing 'No' to him. He handed her the phone.

"Mum, I don't want to come back a day early. I want to stay for the signing ceremony, I have been putting in a lot of work into…" she paused, looking across to him and he shook his head. "Into this deal and I feel I have earned the right to be there. It will be fun and there will be lots of important people present."

Whatever was said had the desired effect and her mother was appeased. "Let's hope nothing else needs to change," he said, as they worked on. "Here's the deal, Nicola. If we finish this off ready for tomorrow morning, I will take you shopping so you can buy a frock for the ceremony. It will be at my expense, well maybe the client's, if I can swing it. One way or another we can go to one of those posh ladies' shops they have in the malls and get something."

She gave him a hug which left him embarrassed and then they carried on redrafting, coffee, a fridge full of juices, cold water and chocolate providing sustenance to keeping them going. The amendments were finished on time. They were exhausted but having checked and re-checked them, page turning over one thousand pages, he was satisfied and submitted them for approval. He hadn't realised that Nicola had laid down on his sofa and was fast asleep. The message came through that the revised contract had been acceptable to both parties, so the work was done. He sat back, his hands stretched out and linked behind his head. He couldn't help smiling with satisfaction.

"This is what I live for," he said, quietly smiling to himself.

As much as he wanted to rest, making good on the promise to take Nicola clothes shopping was his priority. Looking at how soundly she slept, he decided to let her rest for a while and quietly made his way to the bathroom to take a shower and change.

When he got back to the room, dried off and dressed in a casual shirt, and trousers, he sat on the single armchair and watched with curiosity, as Nicola slept.

"I wonder, if things had worked out with Abla or Marianne whether we would have had children and I could be looking at someone who would be of about my daughter's age," he mused. Then he thought of the responsibility that parenthood brings and said, "Perish the thought. Not for me."

It was nearing midday before Nicola awoke, only to leap up and berate him for letting her sleep too long, thereby denying her shopping time.

'There's me letting her catch up on her sleep and I get told off! Kids logic, for you!' he said to himself, shaking his head.

He ordered a security-cleared driver and he took them to one of the swanky shopping malls, bursting with all manner of western good and prominent amongst these, were shop after shop of designer clothes shops for women. Nicola was delighted, she was like the proverbial kid in a candy shop and he enjoyed seeing her get excited when she was trying on various expensive designer clothes but positively felt very uncomfortable when asked for his opinion. Eventually, it boiled down to a choice of two and the one she had plumbed for made him gulp as it was low cut at the front and exposing more than would be acceptable in this part of the world. He wanted to tell her that it was not suitable but he did not want to offend her.

"Nicola, as an early Christmas present for you, I would be happy for you to take both dresses but only if you agree to wear my favourite one," he said and he pointed to the other dress, which he deemed proper for the occasion.

Nicola was over the moon. She was getting two expensive dresses instead of one. He was pleased with himself as he had managed to solve the problem of the dress in a way that was sensitive to her feelings. In the past he would have just said no to the dress, without batting an eyelid or care how it was received.

"Perhaps Kiffy's influence has made me more sensitive after all," he chuckled.

The smile was short-lived. Thinking of Kiffy reminded him that he had left the UK without telling her and he could foresee a negative reaction from her once they met. The prospect of being on the receiving end of one of her diatribes, had put a dampener on what had been a very successful trip, earning the firm in excess of a quarter of a million pounds in fees and a generous personal bonus for him as a gift from Colonel Ibrahim. There was also an undertaking to engage the firm in some capacity and the Colonel would be coming to London to broker the next part of the Emir's grand plan, to prepare his country for when the oil ran out. The next few months had the makings of an exciting and challenging period in his career and he was relishing the prospect of taking it on.

The flight got into London late on Tuesday evening and as they exited out of the Arrivals door, Nicola rushed up to the two people who were waving exuberantly at her. He wished they had not shared a trolley as it became obvious who he was and as he unloaded her case, he could tell their eyes were upon him. When Nicola distracted them with copious hugs and kisses, he thought he could make his escape unnoticed. But it was Nicola who spotted him heading off and ran up to him, grabbing his arm.

"Hey, sneaking off, are you? Not even saying goodbye?" she teased.

"Goodbye Nicola, many thanks for your help. You've been absolutely brilliant and I will be saying so to your line manager when I get back," he said stiffly, offering his hand.

"Thank you," she said. "Thank you for my lovely dresses. I am going to be doing so much showing off to my friends but don't worry, nobody at work. But mostly, thank you for the opportunity to help me develop, to show what I can do."

He smiled and said she deserved the right to be there and had once again shown she was worthy of being given the opportunity.

He was about to turn for the exit when she pulled him down to give him a hug and a kiss on the cheek. "See you back in the office."

He did not want to look back but could clearly hear one of the parents asking, "Is that him? Rude bugger not saying hello!"

"Mum, don't say that, he is lovely. Such a nice man," was the last thing he heard, as he turned to the car park exit.

"Me? Lovely? Nice man? Must be the Middle Eastern sun has affected Nicola," he said.

On Wednesday morning, he decided to work from home and it was not until Thursday that he boarded his usual train and at the usual time. It was not looking good from the moment he noticed that his seat had been taken as the train came to a stop. Getting on, he looked across and indeed, there was someone occupying his favourite seat. It was Adrienne and she was not making any effort to make eye contact. He hesitated, undecided as to whether he should just go into the other half of the carriage, thereby avoiding any potential scene she might be minded to make. But as with contracts, he hated the idea of any appearance of avoidance of responsibility and decided against it. In any case, he guessed that she would have noticed him standing there and it would be too obvious that he would be trying to avoid her.

"Good morning, Kiffy," he said pleasantly. "A fine morning it is."

"Is it?" she said in a sullen tone.

He shrugged. If that was going to be how it was going to be then he would just take out his tablet and carry on reading about the Sumerians and their cuneiform way of writing on clay tablets. He was fascinated to read how trained scribes would punch out details on a clay tablet, everyday mundane things: deals between people, recording trades, the sale of an oxen, building of a house. Dull, mundane things but it had been the trigger for the start of the written language.

'Probably wrote out contracts and bills of sale in cuneiform to be preserved in clay. Wish I had the time to learn cuneiform,' he told himself. 'When I retire, I will devote myself to learning about the whole Sumerian culture, such fascinating people.'

"You been ill, Flint?"

"Not at all, what makes you suggest that?"

"You been on holiday then, somewhere warm by the look of your skin."

"No, I have not been on holiday, Kiffy. I have been working."

"Where?"

"I am not at liberty to confide in you. Nothing personal, client confidentiality. But I can tell you is that it was not here and that it was abroad."

"Your mobile not work out there, wherever you were? No signal?"

"It would work fine, as far as I can tell but I had it switched off."

"Why? Why would you give me your phone number and when I do send you messages you don't get them because you had switched your phone off!" she said and he could see she was trying hard not to raise her voice.

"Kiffy, I explained this to you once before. When I am on client business, I switch off my personal mobile phone. I am on the client's time and it is only right and proper that I only spend my time on their business. I do not make any personal phone calls, I do not receive any personal phone calls, nor texts, WhatsApp, emails or any other means of communication."

"So, if by some miracle I had found out where you were and I wanted to surprise you by turning up in your hotel, you would not talk to me? You would send me away, just like that?" she said, clicking her middle finger and thumb.

He smiled. “Firstly, my behaviour is not dictated or shaped by the possibility that miracles might happen. Miracles come under acts of God in contract legal terms and lawyers, including myself, hate them. So, in answer to your hypothetical situation, if you did just turn up at my hotel, I would indeed send you away. Just like that,” he said, imitating her.

Her eyes were welling up. “That’s not nice, Flint. You are English and cold and distant but I didn’t think you are cruel too. Just a simple phone call or text to say ‘hi’. Would your client really have objected?”

“My client would not have objected. In all probability he wouldn’t even be aware. But it is my personal standard, Kiffy. If I do it, then I would have to let all my team do that and then we would run the risk of losing focus. We would run the risk of missing some important aspect of what we are doing. In a contract, Kiffy, a wrong word in the wrong place, a full stop or a comma misplaced, a simple word such as should instead of must, best endeavours instead of reasonable endeavours, can be devastating. Everyday words used every day but in contract terms they can have a huge impact on the outcome, can cost millions if they are used incorrectly, to the detriment of the client. I cannot take that risk. I have never taken that risk. So I shut off my phone and insist my team do that too. There are exceptions of course, for instance, I allowed my assistant to phone her mum and tell her that we were going to be staying much longer.”

“So, you took a girl along and it was all right for her to use her mobile phone but you couldn’t use yours?”

“It was one time, only. I have a duty of care towards her as her team leader. I have a responsibility for her wellbeing.”

“Did you sleep with her too?”

He looked horrified. “I shan’t dignify that question with an answer.”

“So, you did. Answer me! You owe me that, Flint,” she said.

“I do not owe you an answer to that question or any other for that matter, that has anything to do with my professional life. I am not answerable to you on any aspect of my work, Kiffy and you should just accept that. That said, I will concede that I should have made more effort to make you aware that I was going to be away. I was going to tell you when we agreed that we would meet for a coffee but as I recall, you weren’t there. You did not show up. Doesn’t matter.”

"Wasn't my fault. It was..."

"I don't need an explanation, Kiffy. You do not need to justify your actions to *me*," he said, cutting her off and emphasising 'me'. "As I said, in retrospect I showed an error of judgement for not trying to phone you later to let you know I was going away. And for that and only for that, I apologise."

She was silent for a moment.

"How are you going to make it up to me?"

"Pardon?"

"Words are easy, Flint. For you it is part of your upbringing but I will use an English phrase. 'Actions speak louder than words', not so? So what will you do about putting right hurting me like that?"

"Cooking!"

"Cooking? What do you mean?"

"I am inviting you to my house this Saturday, if you are free. I will make dinner and then you can go if you wish or you can stay and we can watch the other film we didn't get to see, if you like," he suggested.

She smiled. "Ha-ha, I see. So, you can get me all emotional and then take advantage of me," she said, giggling.

"My recollection of the event is somewhat different to yours, Kiffy. My recollection of who took advantage of whom is not the same. I am inviting you to dinner by way of an apology, nothing else."

"Do I get Sunday breakfast too?" He chuckled. "You want it?"

"I do! And Sunday lunch and Sunday dinner." She giggled.

"You drive a hard bargain!" he said.

"I will make you hard too, if you want, Flint," she teased.

"Shh! Don't say things like that on the train! People might hear," he cautioned.

"What do you care?" she said, shrugging her shoulders.

"So, are we on for Saturday then? Yes or no?" he asked. "I would appreciate an answer now so that I can do my shopping tomorrow, I've got the day off."

She smiled and blew him a kiss. As the train pulled into Victoria and they stood up to leave, she kissed him. He tried to appear nonchalant about it but it was not working and she giggled her delight at having made him embarrassed.

***

It was Saturday morning. The sun was rising up in the sky. It was that time of day when the morning chill in the air has dissipated, as the heat of the rising sun was pushing it away. But the sun was not so high in the sky and the warmth it was radiating was not sufficiently intense to burn. The morning breeze that was blowing had enough power in its lungs, to make the trees gently sway but no more.

It was one of his favourite times of the day and at one of his favourite times of the year. Some characterise it as late spring, others early summer. But he liked to think of it as being that perfect time of the year when the combination of temperature, light, heat and colour are exactly right. It would only last just for a few weeks before summer proper kicked in, but in that time, it felt as if nature had contrived to create something idyllic. It was one that his grandfather had taught him to appreciate, when they would go for a walk together before the others had even got up for breakfast, putting on their wellingtons to take Willy and Barney the family Labradors, for their morning walk. He would learn to smell the morning air, the dew on the glistening grass and the bracken trodden underfoot, as they strolled through a stretch of woods on the estate.

"I want you to promise me something, my boy. When this becomes yours and someday it will, after I've popped my clogs and your father has become too old to manage it, please keep it. Don't be tempted to sell any part of it off to some seductive scheme dreamed up by a property developer. Hang on to it. If you want to be able to take these walks, through this lovely piece of England then I beg you to keep it in the family, so that you and your heirs and others that come after you, can enjoy the morning, away from the mad world that is out there."

And on this morning, he could just close his eyes and remember those walks as vividly as if they had happened yesterday. The early morning chorus of woodpecker, tits and blackbird and cooing wood pigeons that were frequent visitors to his garden, were music to his ears.

It was an ideal that soothed and caressed, like some unseen hands that were massaging away the aches in his body and mind, releasing stresses and strains, relaxing sinew and muscle, letting his mind relax and be at peace. In short, as he sat down at the little table on the patio in his garden, nature was in total harmony and he felt privileged to be a part of it, to witness it. He had traded in his Docklands apartment for this standalone house on a private road with half an acre of land and at this time of the year, it served as a bucolic reminder of those halcyon days spent with his grandfather as a young boy.

"Grandfather, you would have liked it here," he muttered to himself. "Not like our country manor but still a bit of leafy Surrey estate that is a smaller imitation. Alas grandfather, there is a part of your dream that I cannot promise to fulfil as I do not have any heirs and the responsibility will be for Bertie and his children to continue. I think your dream is in safe hands, grandfather, Bertie loves it on the manor."

Lost in his thoughts, he hadn't noticed that Anca had arrived with a tray of two coffees, a bowl of fruit, *The Times* and a small pillbox.

"Lovely morning, Theo, isn't it?" she said, smiling.

"Good morning. Sorry didn't see you coming, Anca," he said, taking his bare feet off the chair in front of him and setting them back on the ground.

"Still a little cold, don't you think?" she said, tightening her multi-coloured kimono around her. "Are you not cold too in that t-shirt and shorts?"

"Just fresh," he said. He noticed that she was wearing one of his Che Guevara t-shirts under the kimono and it made him smile. The t-shirt had come from one of his trips to Havana and the Kimono a gift from a long-absent friend, who had mistakenly believed he was still with Marianne.

Anca got up and went inside, only to return wearing a blanket which she sat on and wrapped around her. She picked up the magazine inside The Times, a section she knew he didn't like to read and was head down into it. She reached out for a fruit at the same time as he did and she pushed the grapes in his direction.

"You have the grapes, I don't like the pips. My generation like everything seedless," she said, cheekily.

'Feel as if I have a daughter staying with me,' he mused. 'Second time this week I have been alone in the company of a much younger woman. And later on, it will be yet another one and yet none of them are mine. Not Anca, not Nicola and not Adrienne.'

A quick glance at his watch told him he still had plenty of time to prepare for her visit. "Anca, you did change the sheets, didn't you?"

"Yes, Theo and the pillowcases and cleaned the floor in your room, which was so dusty, considering you've been away most of the week. And the bathroom and toilet too, everything is, wait, what's that phrase you taught me? 'Spick and span'. That's it. Don't worry, everything is spotless for when your lady friend comes," she giggled.

He looked at her sharply and said, "Lady friend? What makes you say that?"

"It is obvious, Theo. You don't normally go to this much trouble on a weekend. Normally you are relaxed and you read your paper and you don't ever ask me about your sheets or anything else. Usually when a man does that, must be because there is a woman involved. Am I right?" she teased.

"Yes, that is correct. But you concluded this because I asked you if you changed my sheets?"

"Yes, a woman can tell. That and a quick glance at your calendar in the kitchen," she said, chuckling.

He laughed. "You nearly had me convinced then."

"So, is she pretty?"

"Yes, she is."

"English?"

"No. What makes you ask?"

She shrugged. "I don't know. I got the impression that you would only like English girls. A nice, well dressed, well spoken, English girl. Not one to raise her voice, talks in a whisper in a restaurant, has very good manners and has been educated in one of those fancy girls private schools."

"No, she is not like that at all," he said, with a wistful smile as he thought of his encounters with Adrienne thus far. "She's not like that at all."

"She your girlfriend, Theo? Sorry for asking."

"Hmm, good question, Anca. No, I wouldn't say that she's my girlfriend," he said, scratching his chin. "Not yet, at any rate."

"Does she know that? Have you made it clear that, how you say it, as far as you are concerned, she is not your girlfriend?"

"Not, exactly. No, I haven't."

"So she is coming to your house thinking she is your girlfriend. But you don't feel the same about her? Is that, what's that word you taught me the other day, Theo? I really like it. Oh yes, I remember now. Is it an equitable arrangement?"

"Hey, I'm the lawyer here. I'm supposed to be asking the awkward questions," he said half-jokingly.

Anca held her arms up. "Sorry, just saying. Doesn't look good from her, what's that other word I learned, oh yes, her perspective."

"Wish I hadn't taught you these words, now you are using them back on me!" he said.

He picked up The Times, once again signalling that it was the end of the conversation. The points Anca had made needled him because they had hit home. As someone who prided himself on his sense of fairness and justice, it rankled that his behaviour with regard to Adrienne had not run true to those sentiments.

One of the first things he had learned from his friend and advisor on all things to do with Islam and sometime cool Imran, was that the key to making a good curry, is not to cheat on the ingredients. He had said, "Don't buy from the supermarket, full stop."

"You will forgive me, my friend, when I tell you the supermarkets supply curry ingredients for the English. No Pakistani or Indian fellow who enjoys his curries will send his wife to buy the essential ingredients from Sainsbury, Tesco or any supermarket for that matter. If you want to make a curry that is flavoursome, that will make your mouth and your nostrils come alive as you taste the spices and take in the aroma as it wafts up into your nose, then you need to go to your local Asian shop. There you will get authentic ingredients."

And, for the dish he had in mind that he had learned out in the Middle east, he wanted to ensure that he achieved as authentic a flavour as his cooking skills could achieve.

After breakfast, he took a trip to Tolworth where he was spoilt for choice with one after another Asian shops selling an abundancy of mouth-watering fruits, fresh vegetables and cooking ingredients, the like and range of which would never be found in a mainstream supermarket.

He bought plump heads of garlic, full of the pungent taste. He enjoyed snapping off a fresh piece of ginger from a bigger root, just like the Asian shoppers were doing. He bought cardamom in pods so that he could pound them open to release the sweet -melling seeds within: cumin and coriander seeds, fennel seeds. He resisted the temptation to buy tomatoes from Holland. They looked bright red and you could smell the vine to which they were attached but he knew better that the flavour was not up to the mark. As there was no other choice, he decided on using tinned Italian tomatoes. Reading down his shopping list he found each ingredient in turn, finishing with the flat bread, a tub of sour yoghurt and a bunch of fresh coriander. He checked his basket and looked around for anything else that he might need to replenish for his larder that was not needed for the recipe. He smiled when he spotted a couple of things that he knew Anca enjoyed. The first of the things was Guava Jam which came from the West Indies. He was partial to it himself and when Anca first saw him spread it on his toast she had wrinkled her nose up at it but when she tried it, she became an instant convert. But even better than that were the small bananas that could only be found in Asian shops. They were being sold still on their main stalk and he picked one up. As he cashed up his purchases, he smiled to himself. 'She's not even my daughter!'

When he got home, Anca helped him unload and beamed a smile from ear to ear when she saw the bananas, pulling one off the bunch and scoffing it there and then.

It was time to start his preparations and he laid out the ingredients: the packets of seeds near to the stone pestle and mortar ready to be pounded or ground, four plump garlic cloves skinned and ready for crushing, the ginger peeled and soon to be sliced into tiny pieces, sitting prettily alongside the garlic in a ramekin sized pot, decorated in a hand-painted blue mosaic of Palestinian origin, part of a set gifted to him from a grateful client, the nutmeg next to its grater, almonds and yoghurt set aside, the latter in an earthenware pot he had picked up in a souk. The fresh coriander had been meticulously washed by Anca as her contribution and by way of thanks for the bananas and Guava Jam.

He had already washed and cut the chicken into pieces, the recipe he was using had said use breast meat but he preferred thighs as he found that part of the chicken more succulent and more forgiving with timing. Thighs were more tolerant to timing, didn't dry up, as breasts could if overcooked. The tin of tomatoes he had poured into a glass bowl and augmented by generous spoonful of his sister's secret green tomato chutney which he had received a large glass jar of, to have in curries and pasta sauces or together with cheese, she had said. Blunt knives, Imran had once advised him were more dangerous than sharp ones for anyone planning to cut food, so he had ensured his were as sharp as his butcher's metal steel rod could hone them. He washed the blades then laid out the knives on the wooden chopping board that had been a gift from his other sister on one of her rare trips to his house.

The wok, in which he was going to cook everything, was already on the stove. The preparations to all intents and purposes were complete.

He was moving his finger across the workbench, mentally ticking off each ingredient in turn and smiled his satisfaction

"I think we're good to go," he said, nodding.

As he lifted the heavy stone pestle off the quartz workbench and positioned it onto the chopping board, ready for him to set about to start grinding the seeds, the doorbell rang. He looked up at the kitchen wall clock and it was showing just before five so he was relaxed as he wasn't expecting her for another two hours.

He was going to wait for Anca to answer it as she was always receiving parcels from Amazon, when he remembered that she had gone out for the evening, clubbing with her friends. He wiped his hands on his apron and went to see who was at the door. The house had two inner doors that opened out into a small vestibule with a vaulted ceiling. There were boots and shoes on an old wooden stand and just before the outer door, an old-fashioned brass stand, laden with umbrellas of all sizes.

When he opened the door, he was caught unawares as it was Adrienne. "Kiffy!" he said.

"I know I am early, Flint. I had finished all the homework that I had to mark, so I decided that I would come to you a little early. Hope you don't mind. I can help you cook," she said.

He stood there not moving, blocking the door, looking beyond her to the Fiat 500 parked in his drive. She had parked it right up behind his own, trapping it in.

'Hmm, symbolic,' he mused.

"Flint! Are you going to let me in? I know I am early, but I can't be standing here for the next two hours," she teased.

"Good God, I am forgetting my manners, of course. Come in, come in," he said and ushered her, touching her elbow.

She entered the hallway and turned around to kiss him, la bise style, then as before draped her arms around him and kissed him on the lips.

"Hey! Put your arms around me, Flint. Show me that you really want me to be here!"

He held his arms wide. "I would Kiffy, really pleased you are here but my hands probably smell of garlic and other spices," he explained and as if to make the point, he returned her kiss with one of his own, with just enough passion to keep her happy.

"Nice house, Flint. Only expensive lawyers can afford a house like this. My apartment can probably fit in your hallway. Are you an expensive lawyer, Flint?"

"Hire me as your lawyer then you'll find out," he joked. "In the meantime, would you like to come through into the kitchen, I can carry on cooking and I'll get you a drink."

He held his hand out but she took his arm instead as they passed the staircase in the centre of the hall. "I like garlic but I can smell it on your hands. Didn't know you could cook, Flint."

"I try. It relaxes me."

"You're not going to poison me are you, Flint?" she giggled as they entered the kitchen.

"It is tempting at times, Kiffy," he joked. "But not this time, at least not intentionally."

"Some kitchen," she said, matter of factly.

She walked around the room touching the work surfaces, opening and closing cupboards. She was unashamedly opening everything that was within reach, his American double fridge, looking inside his freezer and even going through his larder, changing the position of this can or that jar. She smiled when she saw the big jar of Marmite. She took it out and waved it at him.

"What a surprise," she said. "I would have been very surprised if this wasn't in your cupboard. Haven't seen any Branston pickle."

"It's in the fridge, half open. What's wrong with Marmite and Branston pickle? I have you know they are two of Britain's best inventions!" he said with mock hurt. "If these were ever to stop being made, it will be the end of the civilised world as we know it."

"Most of the world would disagree with you, Flint. Speaking of which, where do you stand on this Brexit nonsense?"

"Hmm, not my favourite subject to talk about. Here," he said, handing her a drink.

"Mojito? Are we having food from South America? What are you cooking for me, Flint? I don't see any beef around? Where are the parsnips and are you going to make your own Yorkshire Puddings or are you going to cheat and heat up ready-made, frozen ones?"

"I know you French call us *rosbif* but it may surprise you to learn that not many people actually have roast beef with Yorkshire Puddings nowadays. People are more health-conscious, concerned about the effect of eating red meat, any meat for that matter. Not one of my favourite dishes I have to say and as for the puds, can't stand them!"

"So what are you cooking? I see lots of spices and seeds, something North African then? A Tagine?" she said, as she perched on one of the white, leather, high stools on the island in the kitchen, opposite him, where she had a ring-side view, like in one of those restaurants where they cook in front of you.

He stopped what he was doing, went to a drawer and pulled out an apron, choosing a patterned one. She watched him open it out and head towards her.

"You're not going to get me to cook are you, Flint?" she said, as he approached her, holding it out.

He did not respond, instead walked behind her, carefully putting it over her head and tied it around her. He leant down as he did that and kissed along her neck. "This is just so that I don't accidently spill any of the spices on you, Kiffy."

"Or was it an excuse so that you could come up behind me and kiss me. You don't have to make up an excuse, Flint. You can kiss me anytime you want."

"It wasn't an excuse, Kiffy. It is true, I do not wish to risk staining your clothes. Kissing you was a natural reaction, how could I not? Seeing you there, your lovely neck exposed, it was just asking me to kiss it. That's all."

She chuckled. "I like that, Flint. You should do it more often! You may assume my neck is always asking you to kiss it. Not just my neck either. You need to learn to read body language, Flint. That's where you English are behind; you can read the words but not the body language."

'Hmm, I wonder how many contract negotiations I have won for clients over the years just on the basis of correctly reading the body language of the other side,' he mused.

"Anyway, no time for any more of that now, got to get on with cooking otherwise we will have to have a takeaway at this rate."

"You still haven't told me what you are cooking, Flint. I'm beginning to suspect that we are going to have just that, a takeaway. I don't mind, if that's what you want. Leaves more time for…" she said pausing and then added, raising her eyebrows, looking straight at him, "other things."

"Kabuli Chicken."

"What did you say, Flint?"

"I am cooking Kabuli Chicken. It is an Afghan dish, similar to a chicken curry, only the yoghurt and the almonds make it sweeter and it is less hot as there's no chillies in it. I am serving it with Afghan flat bread, not rice. And a salad. For dessert, I thought I would continue the theme and have made *Firnee*, which is a bit like rice pudding but without rice and *Muhallebi*, a favourite with the Lebanese. They are both in the fridge as they need to be served cold. And later on, *Paklava* to have with our coffee or tea. Might all turn out to be a disaster but I was struggling to decide what to cook. Wanted something different. How does that sound, Kiffy?"

"Never had any of these dishes, looking forward to it," she said. "Is that where you've been this last week, Flint? Afghanistan?"

He stopped pounding the seeds. "You know I am not going to tell you, Kiffy. Client…"

"Yes, yes, I know. Client confidentiality. You keep saying that. But I am your girlfriend, Flint. Surely you can tell me. Don't you trust me, Flint?" she said impatiently.

"Kiffy, you must stop saying you are my girlfriend thereby making me the boyfriend. Did we not agree that these were aspirational? Kiffy, even if you were to become my girlfriend, or my wife, or my consort or any other epithet that signifies that you and I are in a close, social relationship I would still not tell you. Client confidentiality, any confidentiality for that matter, only remains that way by not telling others about it. It's like keeping a secret. The same principle. It operates on a need-to-know basis and with due respect, Kiffy, you do not need to know. Nothing personal, just professional. And you should not infer that by my cooking Afghan food that I was in Kabul or any other part of Afghanistan last week, any more than cooking pasta would imply that I was in Italy or making a salad Niçoise implies I was in the south of France. I just wanted to please you, to be less English, as you might say and cook something different. And on the question of trust, I do not set great store by it. How many times have I heard, 'trust me', when in reality it is asking someone to betray a confidence that is not in their gift to give and requires no commitment on the part of the person saying 'trust me' to keep that confidence? Trust and confidentiality do not make good bed companions, at least not in my book."

"Flint, I hate you," she said and picked up a lemon and threw it at him, hitting him square in the chest.

He bent down and picked up the lemon, rolling it in his hand and holding it up to his nose to take in its refreshing essence.

"I was not in Afghanistan last week. I have been to Kabul before but not last week, I can tell you no more," he said quietly.

"Do you like me, Flint? Do you feel anything for me?" she said, her eyes pleading, hungry, looking to him for a morsel of acknowledgement that she meant something to him.

He looked straight back at her but his countenance was devoid of any expression. Deadpan, not a twitch or anything to give away how he felt. He blew out and then he spoke.

"You are wearing a striped, collarless shirt, the top four buttons are undone, the aim being to be provocative, showing just a hint of cleavage, enough for me to see that you are not wearing a bra, nice. I am sure that was meant as a tease so don't even pretend you forgot to do those buttons up. Your jeans are tight, could be mistaken for leggings they are that tight. They do the job they were intended for, which is showing off your lovely curves, especially your shapely bottom and I know that you know that I was looking at it as we walked into the kitchen. Today, you are not wearing your ankle bracelet and I do believe you have been for a pedicure as your toenails have been shaped and re-painted but clear, au naturelle. Your hair cascades down naturally at least, I am not an expert to know whether you've paid some hairdresser to make it look like that. The eye shadow you are using is very subtle and emphasises what enchanting eyes you have. You have worn two things the same as before, your hooped earrings and your scent. You know that I like both of these and you wanted me to enjoy them, as indeed, I am doing just that. You are smiling and angry and making the sort of comments you've made before but inside, you are in reality, quite tense and not relaxed at all. This is not home turf, you are in my house and in unfamiliar surroundings and that makes you less certain. Now, have I left anything off? Do I like you? Would I notice these things about you if I had no feelings for you? Would I bother to argue with you and risk a lemon being thrown at me? Luckily it was just that and not something sharper. Would I do that if you meant nothing to me?"

Her eyes had welled up and starting to sparkle. She was biting her lip in an effort to hold back her emotions as he walked around the cooking island and stood in front of her and taking hold of her stool, swivelled it around so that she was facing him. He lifted her chin up and wiped away the tears gently with the back of his hand. Then he kissed her lips, gently and with tenderness. It was just the once, then he swivelled her stool back and returned to his side of the cooking island.

"And as for you becoming my girlfriend, against my better judgement, the idea is growing on me," he joked. He looked up at her and it seemed to have the desired effect.

She started to smile once again. "I suppose I should be grateful I am getting a five-course meal out of you, Flint," she sighed.

He continued to pound the seeds, stopped and looked up. "Five courses? How so?"

"Yes, five. Let me see, a first course of a mojito, well made by the way, a little too much mint but good job. A second course of abuse following an innocent question, followed by a third course of sweet words, very sweet words. Then Afghanistani fourth and fifth courses.

God, I am such a lucky girl, almost a girlfriend!" she chuckled.

He winced in embarrassment and then added, "There is also an optional sixth course."

"Oh? What is that, Mr Flint?"

He walked around the island once again and bent down to whisper in her ear, "Passionate love-making. But it is as I say an optional course. Your choice."

As he straightened up, she pulled him back down by the apron. "I opt to have it, but I want the sixth course now!"

"Now?" he said and took her by the hand and led her up the stairs and into his bedroom.

Sometime later, having served up the optional sixth course, he returned to the kitchen. As he put his apron on once again to re-start his cooking, he couldn't help but smile.

"Oh well, who said you have to have all your courses in numerical order. Defies convention but who cares?" he muttered.

Having prepared everything before the unexpected turn of events earlier, he was pleased that blending, mixing the spices and yoghurt and then gently cooking the chicken in the combined mixture did not take long and he found himself only needing to stir in the cream, add some black pepper and coriander leaves before he was finished. Clearing away the preparation bowls and knives, he rummaged through a drawer full of napkins and tablecloths and pulled one out with a Provencal pattern, given to him by Bertie and his wife from one of their trips to the south of France. He spread it out on the patio table, together with plates, cutlery, water glasses, the napkins and a small citronella oil lamp. It would provide sufficient light to illuminate their food and also served to keep away biting insects. He stood back and looked at the place settings, making minor adjustments so that one place setting was the mirror of the other, as exactly as he could get it.

He nodded his approval as if he was judging someone else's effort rather than his own. "What do you think, mother? Have I left anything off? All it now needs is for her Highness to come down and we are good to go."

He sat on a garden lounger and glanced at his watch and smiled. Two hours earlier, they had skipped up the stairs and indulged in passionate lovemaking that was full of hunger and desire. It had been as someone put it, making you forget where you are, where you forget about time, where you do not care what others may think. You just indulge in the oldest of man's intimacies, made that much better when it is with someone who cares for you and for who you care for. It was that last aspect that he was contemplating and what that meant for him, when she appeared. She had not changed back into her clothes.

"You like?" she said walking towards him, stopping when she was standing next to his lounger,

He looked her up and down. "Wearing one of my work shirts, with one of my ties, and…" he paused to lift the shirt up, "and nothing underneath? Yes, as a matter of fact I do like."

He ran his hand up and around her leg until he was caressing her bottom but she pulled away.

"I'm hungry, feed me," she said.

Candles and Stars

She sat at the table and watched as he fetched a serving bowl full of the Kabuli chicken. It was steaming as he carefully placed it on a candle lit burner to keep warm. He returned with a tray which included flat bread wrapped in a napkin to keep warm, the salad heaped in the Palestinian blue decorated round bowl and a jug of iced water.

"I think that's about it," he said as he sat down. He looked around and then quickly moved his plate and cutlery so that he was to the side of her, remembering how she had wanted that back at her apartment.

She smiled. "You remembered."

He served the food and showed her how to scoop it up onto the Afghan flat bread and soon they were tucking in. He was pleased that she was eating heartily. He did not solicit a comment or flattery as to how the food was. The best compliment did not need any words, just food disappearing off the plate. It was eloquence enough. When she helped herself to a second spoonful and pulled off more bread, he was delighted. It had been worth the effort.

"This is nice. Dinner in the garden, on a nice table cloth with proper napkins, lit by a small lamp. Delicious food. Excellently prepared and laid out. Very romantic of you, Flint. So," she said and hesitated.

"If you say, so not English, it will be my turn to throw the lemon," he joked.

She giggled. "I was going to say, so considerate. You put a lot of thought into it. You could have just put on a roast and I would just assume that being a guy that's all you could manage. But I don't mind telling you, that it was a pleasant surprise, exceeded my expectations. I would never have considered you to be quite an accomplished cook."

"Marks out of ten?"

"For cooking or lovemaking?" she teased.

He sniggered. "For cooking, I daren't ask about the other."

"For cooking, I give you eight out of ten," she said.

"Good enough for me, wait 'til you try my dessert, perhaps I can go up a mark."

"Can we do dessert a little later? I am still digesting dinner. Show me around your garden, Flint."

"At night you can't see that much, other than what is lit up by the dim light of the solar lamps but we can take a stroll, help with digestion and all that," he said.

She took his arm and they walked down the stone stairs of the patio and into the garden proper, where she could discern the shape of tall trees and mature bushes laid out in a number of curves and beds of different height, stone walling giving the impression of there being islands of planting areas. The garden was very long, so long that she could not see the end of it, even with solar lights planted among the plants. Dotted around the garden randomly, she could see seating areas, set within clumps of plants so that they looked as if they were part of the landscape rather than sticking out prominently and being jarring to the eye.

"What's that noise, Flint? It sounds like running water. Do you have a stream in your garden?"

"No, it's a pond. That raised bed over there you can make out is a pond with a waterfall that trickles down into it. Can't claim credit for that, it was put there by the previous owner. I just extended the pond, so that the fish have more room to swim around in and frogs and toads can live there to their hearts' content. There is also a seat there where I sometimes like to take a book and a coffee to sit and read. Very relaxing, mentally. Walking further along, she noticed a small glass building in a black metal framework.

"Is that a greenhouse, Flint? Do you grow any of the salad things we have been eating tonight?"

He laughed. "Not a greenhouse, let me show you," he said and led her along a windy path and up to a wooden deck to the building. "This is my observatory, Kiffy."

He pressed a button and a red lamp came on, illuminating a very large telescope pointing skywards.

"I enjoy looking up at the heavens, there is so much to see and to marvel at. But alas, I don't seem to have as much time as I used to have to indulge my interest in astronomy. There was a time when I could sit here for hours and pick out well known objects like the Ring Nebula or the Andromeda Galaxy or a globular cluster in Hercules. But I don't get to spend as much time at home as I used to and even if I did, there is too much light pollution. Even in a neighbourhood such as this where the houses are detached and the land around them is substantial, you still get light pollution which makes it difficult to get good viewing light. My neighbour two doors along likes to play tennis in the evening and he floodlights his garden. Not great for me when I am trying to pick out some deep space object. In the winter it is better, as the sky is naturally darker and neighbours tend to spend less time outside. But it is cold."

"What do you see in the stars, Flint?" she asked, looking up at the sky.

"The vastness of the universe. Unexplored, beautiful, yet desolate and seemingly empty, so far away from us. Billions and billions of stars and no doubt with billions and billions of planets, probably some like our own, supporting all manner of life. Yet we know so little about these other worlds. We can only imagine what's out there and I don't think we will ever find out. Its awe inspiring to just stand and look up, don't you think?"

"You are quite a dreamer for a lawyer. Flint. I like it. And quite human when you relax and stop being a lawyer. I like that too," she said and planted a kiss on his cheek. "As for the stars, where I grew up we are not hampered by the city lights so you get a truly wonderful sky. It looks as if someone has taken a brush and painted lots and lots of little dots. That's what my grandmother used to tell me when I was growing up and as a little girl, I sort of believed her. Perhaps one day you and I can see that sky together. Now let's go and try those desserts of yours, my bare feet are getting cold."

"I'd pick you up but as svelte as you are, I don't think I could manage that," he joked.

"Give me a piggyback then. Come on Flint. Bend down, carry me on your back. Haven't had someone do that since I was a little girl."

"Oh dear, this is where I make a fool of myself. Why did I have to say that?" he murmured quietly, so she could not discern what he was saying.

She was laughing as she hoisted herself on to his back, wrapping her legs around his waist and her arms linked around his neck.

"Come on, let's get going," she said, digging her heels into his belly. "Flint, I am enjoying this."

"Can't say I feel the same. Would you mind letting up a bit holding me around the neck, I feel as if I am being strangled. You don't want me to pass out and drop you, do you Kiffy?" It took just a minute or so to get back to the patio but every step seemed an eternity. Every step was a reminder that in the space of a few weeks, the peace and tranquillity he would enjoy at this time of evening on a weekend when he was at home, had been completely transformed. He was laden with a woman on his back, a French one at that. He felt it was symbolic of a much bigger issue.

'The days of us putting one over on the French are well and truly over,' he chuckled to himself. 'The French are now riding us, we're the subjugated lot not the other way around. Look at me, a spirited Frenchwoman is treating me no better than a cart-horse. This is what the EU has done to us. Can't even be master of my own bit of England.'

When they reached the patio, he crouched down so she could slide off him. He was winded and out of breath and it took considerable effort and the use of the chair as a lever, to haul himself back up. She rewarded him with a kiss. It was a deep, passionate kiss and a hug. His arms went around her mechanically as he was worn out from the exertion.

'Note to self: must use the gym more often. Do weight training. Must get Anca to show me what to do.'

"Sit down, sweetie. Let me get the desserts. In the fridge you say?"

She kissed him again and strode back inside, dancing elegantly from one foot to the other on tiptoes, with the grace and elegance of a ballerina. He couldn't help looking at her and she turned around and waved a finger at him.

"Hey Flint," she said, as she ladled out the dessert into two small bowls. "I know you said I am not yet your girlfriend and I do not have a right to know but I need to ask you one question."

"Oh joy, what now?"

"The shoes in the hallway. I couldn't help seeing them as soon as you opened the front door. Next to the men's shoes, which I assume are yours, there were women's shoes. You have a woman living with you or someone who comes round?"

"What do you mean, living with me? It has connotations. For the avoidance of doubt, can you be clearer as to what you mean?"

"It's a simple question, Flint. Is there a woman living in this house?"

"Yes, there is."

"How old is she?"

"I am not at liberty to say," he said flatly.

"Is she younger than you?"

"Yes. Where are you going with this, Kiffy?"

"Are you having sex with her?"

"No!"

"Are you sure, Flint. You can tell me. I don't mind, really but I'd rather know, than find out later you are doing it behind my back."

"I think I would know if I am having sex with someone."

"Why do I feel you are being evasive with me, Flint? Why can't you just be straight and tell me what's going on? Why is a young woman living with you in your house?" she said angrily.

He took a deep breath. "If it will put a stop to this interrogation and put your suspicious, Gallic mind at rest then I will tell you about the young woman living in my house. Her name is Anca. She keeps house for me and looks after Philip my cat when I am away. In return, I let her stay rent-free. She is not here right now, not because I was trying to hide her away from you and by the way give me credit, if I had intended to do that then surely, I would have enough gumption to have removed her shoes from the porch! She is from Slovakia. Left there like a lot of young people to find work in a richer country. She chose Britain because, as difficult as it might be for you to accept, we were friendlier than the Germans and indeed than your fellow countrymen! She is struggling to make a living as a personal trainer and Pilates teacher. She was looking for a place to live around here because someone told her that there are a lot of middle-class housewives who regard personal trainers as part of their accoutrement, like their BMW and Audi four by fours. Not quite made it yet, she has a few regular clients but she is hard working and determined and I expect she will succeed in her endeavour. Why is she living with me? Simple, one weekend I over did it on gardening and strained my neck and shoulders, so I searched on Gumtree and she came up as the only person being free so I hired her, thinking that Pilates entailed massage too. I was mistaken but she said that she was trained as a masseuse and agreed to do me. We got talking and she told me she lived in a dump with five others, a horrible sounding place with dampness and rats. She asked if I had a spare room she could rent, as her clients were mostly in this area and she did not have a car. So, in a rare moment of humanity, I offered her a roof over her head in exchange for keeping my house, and looking after my cat and Pilates lessons and massages. We agreed, drew up a contract and that's as far as it goes, Kiffy. The contract makes no reference directly or implied to my receiving any sexual favours. I would not break such an agreement. That would be dishonourable of me, don't you think?"

"Yes, sorry for asking. I had to know, Flint. I may appear liberal and…"

"Flirty," he added.

"Yes, that too…"

"And forward," he teased.

"That too Flint."

"Coquettish!" he said, relentless in teasing her.

"Stop it Flint. What I am trying to say is that I am also a jealous woman. My last boyfriend was fucking another woman behind my back. I thought I was in a trusting relationship. Just me and him but it wasn't true. I left him. But I don't believe you are like that."

"No, Kiffy. I am not like that. The thought of you catching me with another woman strikes the fear of God in me, even if you are not my girlfriend and we haven't exactly discussed any terms on which any future relationship might progress. But be that as it may, I have everything I need here to satisfy my loins. Right here, sitting next to me, I don't need anyone else."

Adrienne smiled sweetly and pushing her chair back, she got up and bent down to kiss him, sitting astride him in the process.

"I am your girlfriend, Flint. I know it and I think you do too. You just need to admit it to yourself," she whispered in his ear, before nibbling his earlobe.

They kissed passionately and then she leant back, her eyes never leaving his for a moment as she undid button after button of the shirt she was wearing, until there were no more buttons to undo. She let the shirt fall off her shoulders and took his hands and put them on her breasts. He pulled her head down to kiss her tenderly, taking in her womanly scent. As he caressed her nipples, her hand snaked down between them and loosened his belt and then unzipped him to pull out his manhood. The kissing had had the desired effect and raising herself up she lowered herself on him and they threw caution to the wind as their bodies succumbed to the primeval power of raw lovemaking. In spite of the earlier exertion carrying her from the far end of the garden back to the patio, he had recovered his stamina and met her passion with his own, effortlessly. When it was all over, exhausted from the passion of making love, she lay in his arms on the steamer lounger. They were as naked as the day they were born. He was looking up at the stars and she was gently running her fingers through his, resting her head on his chest, nestled under his chin.

"Nine out of ten, Flint," she whispered.

"Pardon?"

"Your lovemaking: nine out of ten."

"I didn't know that I was being put to the test. I am glad you didn't tell me beforehand. I might have fluffed my lines. Anyway, can I ask why not a mark of ten?" he asked, squeezing her fingers.

She giggled. "I don't know. Maybe if I give you nine, you will keep trying to please me. But if I give you ten, you will get arrogant and take me for granted."

"I don't think I could ever do that, Kiffy. You wouldn't let me."

"What about for me? What mark would you give me?"

"Hmm, not sure," he teased. "Let me think about it."

"Hey! Flint, you are not supposed to say that to a girl. That's not nice," she said and pinched him.

"Ouch! What did you do that for?"

"You were being mean to me."

"No, I wasn't"!

"You just said you weren't sure. Did you not say that?"

"Yes, I did. But if you had let me finish and not interrupted, I was going to say I wasn't sure if it was an eleven out of ten or twelve out of ten."

"Really? That much?" she said, giggling.

"Yes, Kiffy. That much. I am sore from your lovemaking. My lips hurt, my you-know-what hurts. Seems like I had the sixth course twice!"

"On that note, I shall start the seventh course," she said and put her hand down on his manhood.

"Really, Kiffy no more. It will drop off."

"Coffee silly, not that," she said and then leaned down and kissed his cheek, before sitting up and pulling herself off him. He watched her as she put his shirt back on. The faint light from the solar lamps, showed off, to good effect, her graceful figure, the profile of her breasts and curvaceous bottom, stirring in him yet more desire.

"Down boy," he said, as he jumped out of the steamer and got dressed.

Sitting at the table and looking up at the night sky, he trained his eyes directly overhead. He smiled when he recognised the combination of three bright stars that formed the so-called Summer Triangle, signalling that summer had indeed arrived. Even though it was still only mid-May, he was pleased to see the three constellations whose prominent stars made up the Summer Triangle, appearing in the night sky directly overhead. It was somehow reassuring to see them there, every year, always there. Whenever he looked up at them, it reminded him that it was his grandfather who had taught him to look up at the stars. Recollecting the first time made him smile. He had been sent to his bed early for having been naughty. His grandfather had said he would ensure that the boy brushed his teeth and went straight to bed. At the time he was hurt, as his grandfather was his closest friend and confidante and he was surprised that he would act like that. Until, part way up the stairs, his grandfather winked at him and he knew it had just been a ploy. Instead of going to bed, his grandfather unlocked the door to the stone staircase that led to the roof for maintenance. They climbed up it and grandfather introduced him to the delights of the night sky. Holding his hand to prevent any mishap, his grandfather had pointed out the perfect right-angled triangle that was made by drawing an imaginary line between the three brightest stars from three constellations: the star Altair from the constellation of Aquila, the Eagle constellation, the star Vega in Lyra and the star Deneb in the constellation of Cygnus, the Swan.

Now, looking up at the sky, sadly obscured by so many city lights, he marvelled at the beauty of these three blue-white stars, twinkling like diamonds in the night sky. Timeless, every year, there to sooth and hearten in their commitment to grace the night sky. Of the three, he found Deneb the most fascinating of all, as it was reckoned to be some two hundred times bigger than the sun and some fifteen hundred light-years away.

"That means, I am seeing you as you were fifteen hundred years ago, my dear bright friend. It has taken that long for your faithful light to reach me. And I am grateful to you and Altair and Vega, for making me a happy man. Especially tonight. I made love to a French goddess under your shining light. I thank you."

"By the way, where is your housemate, Flint? Did you throw her out for the night as you didn't want her interrupting us?" she giggled. "I don't suppose it would have been fun having to suppress our lovemaking so that we wouldn't make too much noise. Or would you have loved for her to listen in. Where is her bedroom? Does it overlook where we did it? She's not upstairs is she, Flint?"

He laughed, "No Kiffy, she is not upstairs and I did not throw her out. Like any young person on a Saturday night, she is out clubbing with friends. She is out with another Slovakian girl, Lenka. I gave them a lift into Kingston where they are meeting up and going to a cheap bar for cocktails and then on to a club. That is as far as I know. I will be surprised if she is back before sunrise."

"How long has she been with you?"

"Nearly a year."

"What does a fifty-something man talk about with a twenty-something Slovakian woman?" she teased. "Or don't you do much talking?"

"Let me ask you this. How do you, a thirty-something woman, manage to find something to talk about with a fifty-year-old man?"

She shrugged. "I know but she's a physical trainer, not a teacher or someone, who spends a lot of time reading. Do you get on?"

"Yes, we do, now. It wasn't always like that. At the beginning it was awkward, her English was poor and I was not used to having someone stay with me so things would disproportionately irritate me. It was a lesson, perhaps a salutary reminder, that I have been alone for a long time. I did not like sharing my space with someone, be it two sets of toothbrushes, be it having her laundry mixed in with mine, be it eating together, having my things moved around. We had nothing in common and conversation was so limited I would sometimes go to my study just to have a bit of space and privacy and do my own thing. In the early days, it was only honour and a code of personal ethics that stopped me from tearing up the contract and sending her on her way. She hadn't done anything wrong. It was just me. But two things happened which were key moments in improving things. The first thing was when I found my favourite fountain pen out of its box and left open on my desk. I had said she could use it but I had told her so many times to put it back in its place. I got up and was striding, walking towards the living room and about to give her an angry ticking-off when I stopped. I thought I could hear a noise coming from within and I tiptoed as quietly as I could manage and put my ear to the door. I heard her talking to my cat Philip.

"I am lonely, Philip. You are my only friend," she said and I could hear her crying.

I backtracked and returned to my study. Instead, I looked up what movies were playing locally and I went back to invite her to go to the cinema with me. She was delighted. It was an awful movie but she enjoyed it."

"That was very nice of you, Flint. Very caring. I knew you had it in you, even if you are English," she said, cuddling him closer and kissing him. "And the second thing. You said there were two things that happened."

"Oh yes, the second thing was when I fell ill to a mysterious bug. Must have caught it on one of my various trips. Anyway, it knocked me for six and I was laid up at home. She nursed me, always made sure I drank lots of fluids, she changed my clothes and bedding when I was drenched with fever-like symptoms. She rang the GP on my behalf to discuss my condition, of course they gave her the standard line, it's a virus going round, keep him hydrated blah blah. She even made me some soup. Okay it wouldn't win any prizes but I appreciated her attempt. She even read to me, albeit as part of my helping her improve her English but she sat on a chair next to my bed and read to me until I fell asleep. I was touched by how much time she had devoted to me, without asking anything of me. So, those two things seemed to elevate our relationship from being purely functional to something better. So now we are a lot better around each other. We click more, we are both more relaxed with each other, she even gets my jokes now and again. And I no longer lock my bedroom door, for fear she is going to come in the middle of the night and slit my throat. Just joking, Kiffy. No, what I mean to say is that we have become natural with each other and if I had to characterise the relationship we have, it's one of friendship that spans the twenty-five plus years difference in our ages. I think she sees me something of a surrogate father. God knows why as I have never had children or been particularly exposed to them, except for the young people in my office and occasionally, my nephews and nieces. At any rate, I am content that she sees me in that way."

"So am I!" said Adrienne. "And I am very glad she won't be back until tomorrow. That way I have you all to myself for a few more hours. I want to know about your life, Flint. And don't tell me it is confidential please. You are not protecting a client's privacy."

"I don't mind telling you about my life," he shrugged, "not terribly exciting but sure, what do you want to know?"

"Tell me about your childhood, your family. And I will tell you about my family and the little girl who grew up to be me. But before we start, can you just hold off a minute?" She got up and disappeared back into the kitchen. When she returned it was with a plate of food, a piece of Afghan flat bread and a blanket.

"Love making always makes me hungry," she whispered. "Flint, let's sit on the steamer, it's cosier there."

He sat on the steamer and she sat on him, holding the plate of food and he covered them both with the blanket, a present from his grandfather from a trip to an Edinburgh woollen mill via a remote whiskey distillery for a few bottles of his favourite single malt. It was many years ago but touching the blanket always brought back happy memories.

"Okay, now you can begin, Flint. Tell me everything there is about you, growing up, where you lived, how you lived and so on."

"Honestly, Kiffy, my life is not that interesting but I know if I don't say something you will not let me be in peace so here goes. I was borne into the countryside, in the West Country. My early years were spent in green pastures, fresh air, tall swishing trees and brooks and streams; a far cry from London. My father was always busy running our estate: many acres of farmland with sheep, cows and pigs. My mother seemed to be busy producing children, at least that's how it seemed to me. I am the eldest and when I was the only one around, she doted on me and I felt very close to her. Alas, that did not last very long as, less than two years later, my brother popped out into this world. By the time I was four years old my mother gave birth to my sister. Two years later, my second sister was born. Needless to say, she did not have any time for me. I didn't feel jealous of my younger siblings getting more attention than me. In fact, that suited me down to the ground because by that time I had grown very close to my grandfather, Archie. So I didn't mind at all."

"So that made four of you? Only two in my family," she said.

"There was another child, my sister Hannah. But she didn't make it. Some sort of virus and the poor thing didn't make it to her first birthday. My mother was devastated at the time and it took her a long time to recover."

"Sorry to hear that, Flint."

He shrugged his shoulders. "It never really affected me; she was just a baby and I didn't have much to do with her. Archie was my playmate and he kept me occupied and away from my mother who needed space to make sense of Hannah's death. Grandfather was notionally head of the family but at sixty, he decided to pass that responsibility down to my father who was chomping at the bit to take over anyway, as any young man in his early thirties would be. Grandfather and I would go for long walks, at least as much as my little legs would manage. He showed me how to appreciate the countryside. I learned so much about nature from him: what grew in what season, the woodland flowers, how to recognise poisonous mushrooms and toadstools, to listen to the different birdsong, to look at frog spawn turn into tadpoles and then into adult frogs, to the sound of crickets in the summer. Grandfather was the font of all knowledge to me in those tender years. He was a great friend, my confidante — what secrets a young boy could have and most of all, he had my heart.

I remember the day my father called me into the drawing room, something he rarely did. I was worried about it and pulled my grandfather by the hand to come with me. As he had patted my shoulder and ruffled my hair, I was reassured that it was not because I had done something wrong. Yet father seemed a little agitated and was rambling on, talking about our family traditions and that these started from birth. He was telling me about character building, the need to acquire life skills and to start the journey of learning. I guessed that he must be talking about my going to school and I relaxed. There was a Church of England school in the village and I knew some of the children who attended it, so I was more than happy to be joining them. It was then that I learned what this early preparation for life meant. In my father's eyes preparation for life, the nurturement to a future life, to achieving one's potential was best served by sending me to preparatory school. He said it was a great school and I should feel privileged that they had accepted me. I was indeed proud to be going there. But the penny dropped, only when he said that he would try and come and see me from time to time. I looked at grandfather quizzically and that's when I found out that I was being sent away to a boarding school. I wouldn't get to see my grandfather at the end of the day after school. No, it was very many miles away and I would be sleeping there. I would be coming home only at the end of each term. So, that's where I spent my youth, from the age of five until I reached thirteen, Kiffy. You may find it hard to believe Kiffy but the day my father drove me to my school, I was devastated. I felt rejected and hurt. But I did not shed a tear. My grandfather said it was time I started the road to becoming a man and that meant accepting decisions I didn't much care for."

Flint waited for some reaction from Adrienne but it was not forthcoming. He held his breath for a moment and then smiled.

'She's fallen asleep,' he told himself and kissed her head to get a response but none was forthcoming.

He looked at his watch and it had turned midnight. "Can't sleep here all night," he muttered and gently lifted Adrienne into a sitting position.

"A little longer," she said in her half-asleep, half-awake state and tried to lie back down.

"Come on, bedtime," he whispered and lifted her up gently until she was standing upright, albeit leaning heavily on him.

For a second time that evening, he found himself carrying her on his back, this time from the patio, through the house and across the hall to the foot of the stairs.

'God, so many steps to climb,' he mused, as he put a tentative foot on the bottom rung. Looking over his shoulder, Adrienne seemed oblivious to his exertion. With every muscle strained and every sinew stretched, coupled with a strong determination and gritted teeth, he managed to climb the twenty-two steps up to the next floor and then across the galleried landing to his bedroom.

"I think I just completed the fourteenth labour of Hercules," he muttered, as he wavered as to how to put her down, resisting the temptation to just drop her on the bed. Instead, as gently as he could manage, he laid her down on one side of his bed and then fetched a t-shirt from his wardrobe to serve as a pyjama. He sat her up once again, pushed the shirt off her shoulders and managed to get the t-shirt on her, laying her back down onto the bed. It could not have come any sooner as his strength had just about given out. He sat on the edge of the bed panting heavily, his shoulders aching, his thigh and calf muscles feeling taut and strained.

"This is a job for Anca, tomorrow," he told himself.

Having partly recovered, he tiptoed back down, locked up and returned with water in one of those fancy thermos type bottles, a present from Anca. He set the downstairs alarm on from the wall unit and crept back into bed. Adrienne was fast asleep, laying on her side away from him, which was just as he liked it.

"Peace at last," he told himself. "I am so tired and achy. Feel like I have been digging my garden. Not cut out for this malarkey. Oh, for a return to having my own space and being on my own once again. Another twenty-four hours and back to normality."

Sleep did not come easily to him. There was a buzz ringing in his ears and his mind was whirring around too fast for him to just switch off and enter dream world. Reflecting on how the day had gone he felt that they had got on really well and that there had been something akin to romance going on. But the question that was undermining his attempt to see this as a positive step in their relationship, was whether in coming on strong, being uninhibited in her passion was Adrienne using sex to get something out of him? Did she have some ulterior motive in mind; perhaps even setting him up for something, as yet unknown but damaging to him, in some way yet to be determined? Had she really just appeared on his train that fateful morning, out of the blue? Had she planned all this out? If so, what was her motive?

'Don't be so suspicious,' he told himself. 'She's nothing like that. Just a bubbly, charming, tempestuous French woman.'

He fell asleep mentally exhausted, no nearer to having resolved the questions that were spinning around in his head.

But it was not to be the long sleep that his body and mind craved. It was not to be a sleep so that his body and his mind could repair itself and he could wake up refreshed. Instead, the harsh ring tone of his mobile phone jolted him less than two hours after he finally got to sleep and he was disorientated, knocking the phone onto the wooden floor in trying to answer it. He shot out of bed, picked the phone up and left the room to stand in the hallway.

He sat on the hall chair, a leather, Victorian, nursery chair which was a gift from one of his sisters when he moved in.

The voice on the phone was crying and babbling, making it difficult for him to understand, exacerbated by the sound of a lot of background noise. He tried to calm the person down but the crying continued loudly and he had to hold the phone away from his ear. Eventually the voice changed, it was another person speaking and he was at last able to find out what was going on. He closed the phone and went back to his bedroom as quietly as he could manage but Adrienne was awake and sitting up. "What's wrong? What's happened?" she asked, as she watched him go to his wardrobe.

"It's Anca. She is in hospital."

"Oh dear, was she in an accident?"

"No, apparently someone had spiked her drink in the club they were in. Not just her but her friend Lenka too. I must go and get her," he said as he dressed. "She's okay, I spoke to the nurse. She was sick and cramping and doubled up but she is better. They have given her fluids and re-hydrated her and they want to discharge her, but not alone. I will go and bring her home."

"What hospital is she in?"

"Kingston General, about twenty minutes away this time of night."

"I'll come with you, Flint. She may need help in the car whilst you are driving," said Adrienne, as she swung her legs out of bed.

The A & E department was full of people the worse for wear from drinks, drugs and fighting. Looking at the disparate bunch of people scattered across the waiting room, Adrienne felt as if it was like entering a warzone. When Flint pushed open the door into the A & E department, there were people holding bandages to their heads, arms; people staring into oblivion, minds befuddled with intoxication; people writhing in pain. She swallowed hard and tried not to look.

As they discharged Anca into his care, he noted that on the paper where it said 'Next of kin to contact' it was his name that was written there. It left a lump in his throat, thinking about all the young people who were leaving their families and their homes, in search of a better life, with no one to take care of them in situations like these.

An hour later, they arrived back at the house just as Anca retched and vomited on the drive. Adrienne helped her to drink some water and between them they led her inside; her legs so weak from the intoxicating effects of the drug some callous person had slipped into her drink. She was whimpering more than crying, holding on to him for dear life, ignoring the help from Adrienne.

For the third time, he clambered up the stairs with a woman on his back, Adrienne behind him in case Anca slipped off him and fell. Between them, they managed to get Anca to her bedroom and lay her down.

"Her clothes are wet with a combination of sick and God knows what else. We need to get her out of these clothes," he said and pulled Anca into a sitting position, resting against him and started to unzip her dress.

Adrienne intervened. "Flint, let me take over from here. You go make us a cup of coffee and I'll see to Anca."

He smiled. "Thank you for your help, Kiffy. Don't know what I would have done if you were not here."

"You would have undressed her yourself, Flint, you are pretty adept at taking women's clothes off them, I can vouch for that."

He chuckled and left them to it. When he returned with the coffee, Anca was sleeping on her side, peacefully. Adrienne had drawn up a low chair to sit near the bed.

"One of us needs to be with Anca for the next few hours as the nurse said. I am wide awake. I am happy to stay here with her Flint, you get some rest."

"I'm wide awake too. Lost my appetite for sleep," he said as he sipped his coffee. "Don't mind staying up on watch."

"Stay up together? She's dead to the world, exhausted poor thing," she said and reached over to pull a lock of hair away from her face. "I mopped her down with a wet towel as she smelt of vomit and I think she weed on herself too. She was oblivious to me washing her. The bastard who did this to her should be locked up for a long time."

"Kiffy. You have done everything a nurse would have done for her and probably more. I thank you."

"You are welcome, Flint. Never considered myself a nurse," she giggled.

"Oh, I don't know about that. I think a nurse's outfit would suit you!"

"Ha! You are being a naughty boy, Flint. You are thinking with your other head not the one that sits on your shoulders."

"I was not!" he said, pretending to feign innocence.

"By the way, Flint. How comes she has men's t-shirts in her wardrobes. When I was looking for a nightie to put on her, I couldn't find any. Just men's t-shirts, which I presume are yours? Hmm, what are they doing in there? Have you been spending time in this room despite what you told me earlier? Maybe the relationship is not just platonic after all," she giggled.

"Not guilty. You are right, she doesn't have a nightie but then there are lots of things she doesn't have. I said she could have some of my t-shirts. Around the house, she will sometimes wear one like a loose dress, especially on a warm day."

"Hmm and you wouldn't by any chance be looking at her?"

"I might, it is only natural but really, she is a kid as far as I am concerned," he said. "Unlike you."

He reached across and kissed her, lightly. "Feeling amorous again, are you?" she asked.

"No, just glad you are here right now, that's all. It's three thirty in the morning, Kiffy and I would have liked to have been in bed with you. No, it's not what you are thinking, just sleeping together. Sleeping, nothing else. But we have to look after Anca so sitting here with you is the next best thing."

Theo

In as much as they spent most of the night making sure that Anca did not suffer any further adverse effects, he could not sleep-in and he crept out of bed soon after dawn, leaving Adrienne in deep sleep. He popped his head into Anca's room and went close enough so he could listen to her breathing and he concluded that it sounded normal. He walked slowly down the stairs, holding onto the banister as his legs were still aching from the exertion of the night before, carrying two grown women up to bed.

Philip was there waiting for him. He knew the ritual: first his master cleans the bowl, emptying out any food left over from the previous evening and then he follows him to the utility room where he knew his master would have a juicy bowl of chopped up cat food for him to consume. No need to miaow loudly, they both knew the routine and it was the same, day in day out, except when his master was away and then he would miaow loudly at Anca, despite her taking over the role of feeding him and cuddling him whenever his master was out.

"Philip, old chap, looks like it's just you and me having breakfast," he said, stroking Philip as the cat wolfed down a tuna concoction. "I'm hungry too, so I'll leave you to it and make myself a nice bacon sandwich."

The sun was rising but there was still a chill in the air as he laid out a teapot with a cup and his bacon sandwich on the little table on his patio, with cushions for two chairs. The cat was running towards him.

"Yes, Philip, I got you a chair too. You won't have to climb on mine and be annoying. Now, sit there and be quiet; people are still sleeping."

One of the pleasures of life was breakfast on a Sunday morning, where he had the time to read a paper as he tucked into a bacon sandwich made with crusty bread and English country butter and washed down with a cup of strong, English Breakfast tea. And the best bit about it was that he would be undisturbed, no one to have to talk to, no one to grab sections of the paper off him. Sitting there with Philip next to him was as delightful a morning as he could ever wish for. In all his travels, staying in luxuriously appointed hotels, he could never get the same level of satisfaction as a simple breakfast in a quiet English garden, silent except for morning birdsong and the swishing of trees. He had just poured himself a second cup, and started to read the financial pages, pulling a face when the headlines were all doom and gloom about Brexit.

"This is getting so boring. Why can't they write about our successes instead of just regurgitating the same dire economic predictions and forecasts of recession and mass unemployment?"

It was mid-morning when Adrienne finally made an appearance, holding a cup of coffee. She was wearing one of his t-shirts.

"So, this is where you are hiding away from me," she said and leaned down to kiss him.

"I was about to make a fresh pot of tea," he said.

"Ah, you English, you think everyone wants to drink tea."

"Hey, don't knock it Kiffy; the British Empire was built on cups of tea," he laughed.

"That may be so but I prefer a coffee any time. Perhaps we French are more mature in our tastes than you English."

He was going to say, "Perhaps that's why you lost all your wars," but he checked himself. He did not want to provoke her this early in the morning.

"Explanation?" she asked, pointing to her t-shirt. "Somehow I don't see you as a left-wing socialist."

"Che Guevara? Yes, about that. A few years ago, I went to Havana for Christmas. It was 2009 and they were celebrating fifty years of the revolution. I arrived just after midnight but my baggage was stuck in Madrid. It took six days to get my bag sent to me. In the meantime, I had to buy clothes. I don't know about now, but in 2009 you didn't have much of a choice in Havana. So, I bought eight Che Guevara t-shirts to keep me going, all of different designs but as you can see, all very bright. I threw away the other clothes, horrible nylon stuff but kept these. Anca uses them for casual wear around the house and now you are doing the same."

"I like it."

"I suppose I'd better go up and check on her," he said.

"No need. She is up and having a shower. She'll be down soon, Flint. Or should I call you Theo?" she said, looking at him with her head tilted and giggling.

"Ah, you found out," he winced. "I suppose it had to happen sooner or later."

"Anca blurted it out asking for you. So, Theo is your name?"

"Yes, Kiffy, my name is Theodore, Theo for short," he said.

"Well, I am still going to call you Flint," she said. "Theodore, even Theo sounds too nice for you!"

Just then, Anca walked out into the garden with a bowl of fruit and a glass of milk. She too, was wearing one of his t-shirts. Adrienne looked her up and down disapprovingly and noted that the t-shirt barely covered her bottom, exposing her white knickers.

"Thank you for coming to get me last night, Theo. I didn't know who to turn to," she said. "It was horrible. And thank you for looking after me through the night."

She leaned down to hug him and planted a kiss on his cheek and then took a sip from his tea, before pushing a reluctant Philip off his seat and pulling it next to him.

"Not sure I could have done it without Adrienne's help. She came with me and also stayed up with me until we were sure you would be all right."

"And in case you were wondering how you got out of your party clothes, wet with vomit and God knows what else, it was me. It was I who undressed you, washed you and then put a t-shirt on you for you to sleep in. It was not Theo," said Adrienne.

Anca shrugged. "Thanks."

"How are you feeling, anyway?" he said, embarrassed at the awkwardness that had arisen.

"A little cold, and my stomach feels very delicate but otherwise okay," she said, taking the cold toast from his plate and dipping it into his tea.

"If you are cold, don't you think, you should wear something more substantial? Also, it's not very becoming for a young lady to be showing her knickers to an older man, don't you think?"

Anca looked at Theo as if to ask, 'Who is this woman? Thinks she can tell me what to do.'

"I don't know what you are suggesting but it's not like that between us, Adrienne. Theo does not mind how I dress and he does not look at me in that way. If he did, I would be very scared. He is just a very nice guy and the nearest thing I have to a father here in England. That's all it is, isn't it Theo?" she said and leaned across to kiss him on the cheek, as if to emphasise the point.

Theo nodded. "Yes, that is exactly how it is."

He could see from the frown on her face that Adrienne was not happy with that arrangement. She drank her coffee and put down her mug, hard on the glass table before getting up and going back into the house.

Anca and Theo looked at each other.

"Is that your girlfriend?" said Anca. "Seems, how you say it, highly strung."

"Just had a bad night, that's all. Didn't get much sleep looking after you."

"So why is she giving me so much trouble about what I wear?"

"Anca, I don't know, perhaps she feels threatened. In any case, maybe when she is around, don't wear these t-shirts without something around your waist to hide your underwear. Maybe one of the sarongs I bought you."

"But why, Theo? If it doesn't bother you, why should I change just for her? Unless you tell me, she is about to move in, in which case then of course, I will dress to please her. Is she about to move in, Theo?"

"No! Definitely not! She's not really my girlfriend, at least not yet. We are just finding our way, as you've just seen. But don't worry about it. And you are quite right, you must dress as you please, not what others think."

Adrienne re-emerged carrying a tray of food. "I see you got in some croissants and cheeses, French cheeses for me, Flint," she said and placed these on the table. "I had plans to make you bacon inside a croissant, a sort of fusion of British and French cuisine. But I couldn't wait so I made myself breakfast."

She cut open a croissant and put a knife full of Chaource soft cheese inside it, before taking a massive bite. "Mmm, this is so delicious and I feel quite hungry now. Here take a bite Flint," she said and held it up to his mouth.

'As much as I don't like French cheeses in the morning, if I don't bite this, I am going to cause a diplomatic incident,' he told himself and leant forward to accept the croissant. "Very nice," he said and quickly followed it with a gulp of tea.

Anca smiled secretly, batting her eyes at him.

He opened his newspaper, it was a signal that he just wanted to read undisturbed. "So, what's in the news, Flint?"

"Brexit!"

"Oh that. We haven't spoken about it yet, have we? How do you feel about it? Flint? Let me guess, you are a Remainer? After all, you have a French girlfriend and a girl from Slovakia living with you, it would be contradictory for you to be a Brexiteer. Not so? How did you vote in the referendum, Flint?"

He put his paper down. "It's my business and only my business as to how I voted."

"Come on, Flint, you do have an opinion, don't you?"

"Theo thinks that Britain should pull out of the EU," said Anca.

"Flint! No! Why?" said Adrienne, shocked that he would be pro-Brexit.

"Listen, Kiffy, I will explain my reasoning to you," he said and he could see Anca smile out of the corner of his eye.

"Whether we stayed in the EU or decided to go was left by politicians for once, to the whim of the British public in the form of a referendum. A referendum is a form of contract. The government had made an offer to us, the British public, to vote whether we stay in or out. It stipulated that it would discharge its obligation once it has acted upon the outcome. We, the British public, accepted that offer, so we now have the essential components of a contract. Not legally enforceable but it is a moral contract if you like and therefore, the government should make good on its contractual commitment. Unexpectedly and against all polling predictions, the British public voted to leave the EU. The government should therefore have made good on honouring their commitment to carry out the outcome of the referendum. No second referendum, no half way in or out, it has to be out."

"Brexiteers are racists!"

"I don't think so, Kiffy. You can't say nearly seventeen and half million Britons are racists, just because they voted to take back their sovereignty. People voted to free themselves from the eurocrats in Brussels; faceless people who tell us how powerful our hairdryers and vacuum cleaners should be. Who have a court that sometimes makes bizarre decisions which seem alien to people in Scunthorpe, in Derby and other towns. And on the subject of racism, I think we in Britain stand out well to scrutiny, don't you think? Who is better? The Polish? The Hungarians? Both of whom make monkey noises whenever black British play over there? Or your lot, the French who continue to treat six million immigrants from former north African colonies as second-class citizens."

"Britain will suffer if you were to leave. Is it not a big risk? All the big businesses are against leaving the EU, are they not?"

"Yes, a lot them who do business in the EU do wish for us to stay but that is not what the people voted for. Their wishes must be respected. Also, I am not convinced that if we left the EU that the world will come crashing down on us. Britain has proved in our history, a level of resilience in times of adversity that few other nations can come close to."

He got up, folded the paper under his arm and walked back inside the house, leaving Adrienne bemused.

"Where is he going? Is he cross?" Adrienne asked Anca.

"Don't take it the wrong way, Adrienne. Theo likes nothing better than to spend Sunday mornings reading the paper cover to cover. On his own, undisturbed. I'm sure he is in his study, sitting on his favourite armchair, feet up and already into the foreign news," said Anca. "Don't feel offended. He does that with me too and at first, I thought it was very rude of him but I know he just wants a bit of peace and quiet on his own. If you are going to be mistress of the house then I should spend some time with you, telling you how it works. You are moving in, aren't you?"

Adrienne shrugged and it made her wince to have to admit that he had not asked her to do just that.

"He will, I'm sure. You two seem to get on well but you need to relax more Adrienne."

"And you would know this," she said, cuttingly.

"Yes, I do actually. I am a trained masseuse and a Pilates instructor and I can see when someone is stressed. I can see it in you, from your face, your shoulders, the way your arms hang down. Why don't you let me give you a head and shoulder massage?"

"No! No thanks!" said Adrienne, curtly.

"Come on, you will feel so much better," said Anca, as she stood up and walked behind Adrienne.

Her fingers gently squeezing on her neck muscles made Adrienne wince. "Very tense. You are very tense, Adrienne."

Anca ran her fingers gently through Adrienne's scalp and there were more signs of pain. "I think we should take you to the treatment room and spend the next hour sorting out all these tight muscles and sinews. Come on, follow me," said Anca.

Adrienne looked at her and she could see that Anca was not going to take no for an answer and stood up to follow her, if for no other reason, than out of curiosity.

When they entered the so-called treatment room on the second floor, Adrienne was surprised to see a big room laid out with mats everywhere, the type you find in any public gym. In the corner, there was a full-size massage table already set up. Pilates equipment was in another area and there was also a variety of expensive looking gym equipment.

"What is it you French say, *voila*. The treatment room," said Anca. "It was here when I arrived although I persuaded Theo to give it a bit of a facelift and make it more modern. Adrienne, I will put fresh towels down and then I need for you to get on the table. Please take off Theo's t-shirt."

"Why do I need to do that?" said Adrienne. Her bashfulness surprised Anca.

"Adrienne, I need to use oil on you and we don't want the t-shirt to get dirty, do we? You are not wearing a bra so that's good, too. Makes my work easier."

Lying flat on the table, her head wedged in the hole, Adrienne began to feel the positive therapeutic effects of Anca's touch, albeit there were times when she had to grit her teeth as the pain seemed to penetrate all the way up her neck and into her head.

"So, tell me more about Theo. If at some point I get invited to stay here, I should know what's what, right?"

Anca squirted a few drops of the lavender infused almond oil and started to work it into her shoulder blades.

"Philip. Whatever else you might do, don't say anything bad about his cat, Philip. Theo and Philip are like best friends and they are very possessive of each other. It has taken me all these months for him to even allow me to stroke him."

"Is that Theo or Philip we are talking about?" Adrienne chuckled.

"Let me put your mind at rest, Adrienne. As Theo taught me to say, for the avoidance of doubt, I can categorically say that Theo and I have never had sex."

"So, you've never slept in his bed before?" Adrienne persisted.

"Actually, there was one time, maybe two. When we had that awful thunder and lightning earlier in the year. I thought the whole house was shaking and I was frightened. So I crept into Theo's room and asked him if I could sleep with him as I was scared. And that's all we did Adrienne, sleep. I felt safe. It was like sleeping in my parents' bed."

"Okay. I believe you, Anca" said Adrienne. "I er just wanted…"

"It's okay, you are a woman and you were feeling threatened by my presence but you have nothing to fear. I hope he does invite you to come and stay as it gets very lonely at times. When he is away on his business trips, it can be two, sometimes three weeks before I see him. I have my work, which helps, but it's just nice to come home to have someone to talk to, not just Philip."

"Does he tell you about his business trips, like where he goes?" Adrienne probed. Anca hesitated.

"Yes, he does. For one thing, I pick him up from the airport sometimes; especially when his flight gets in late. Also, in case of an emergency I am the main contact."

"He doesn't tell me anything. Just that he will be away and that he will see me on the train or something like that. Until this weekend, I didn't even know where he lived. I can see why he kept that quiet, not many people live on a private estate with electronic gates and immaculately kept gardens and stone columns for an entrance."

"Theo is a very private person," said Anca and then put her fingers through the elasticated waist of Adrienne's knickers."

She arched herself backwards until she was resting on her elbows. "What do you think you are doing?"

"I need to take these off so that I can start work on your glutes and hamstrings," said Anca, matter of factly and as if to emphasise the point she pressed her fingers on one of Adrienne's buttocks. "Like here, for instance."

It achieved the desired effect and Adrienne lay back down, burying her head in the massage table hole, as Anca removed her panties in one fell swoop.

"I can cover each side of you so that only one side is exposed if you are self-conscious," Anca suggested.

Adrienne shrugged. "As you've seen every bit of me, it is late for me to become demure, not so? Do you do this with Theo too?"

"Yes, Adrienne, I see him naked. Yes I have seen his penis too but for me it is just another part of his body. Is that okay with you? Do you want me to tell him in future you don't want him to be fully naked when I massage him?"

"That would be silly," Adrienne giggled. "You have seen his penis many more times than I have."

"Yes, but you and he, I assume, have a relationship so it is different, not so?"

"What else can you tell me about Theo? So far, I know that he loves his cat, he likes to spend Sunday mornings reading his paper in silence, he goes on foreign trips and he tells you where so that you can pick him up from the airport. What about family?"

"His parents live in the West Country, at least that's what he calls it. Seems like it must be quite a big house as his brother lives there too with his wife and children, so does one of his sisters with her husband and their kids and his youngest sister, who is divorced, she lives there too but I think she has an apartment in London and she has been to this house and stayed a few times."

"What's she like?"

"It's not for me to say, Adrienne. I'm sure Theo will tell you at some point."

"You are very loyal to him Anca, I admire that," she said, genuinely. "I don't suppose you can drop me a hint as to where his business takes him. I guess it is somewhere in the Middle East as he bought me an abaya as a gift once. But he never mentions any country specifically."

"It's not for me to say, Adrienne," Anca replied, remembering the non-disclosure agreement Theo had put into the contract with her. If at any time she was to give out any sensitive information about him — and a list was drawn up defining what that included, (she smiled remembering the phrase he had used, '*including but not limited to*') — then he was within his right to revoke the contract. Her English had not been very good back then, nearly a year ago but he patiently explained what it was about. The contract was for an initial period of two years with an option to extend by either party for a further two years. He explained, in response to her question as to why the contract had to say for how long, it was for her protection since not stipulating duration left her open to the whim of the employer, in her case, him. The contract went on to list all the services she would be required to perform, again with the phrase '*including but not limited to*'. And in return she would live rent free, all the food that she could eat, she could also drive his car when he did not need it and he would pay for two flights back home a year. He said that he was happy to pay for her to have an independent lawyer to check it over but she had just smiled and said she trusted him. The two terms and conditions that stood out above all else was the need for her to never disclose his business and personal travel and never disclose any significant aspect of his private life.

She tapped Adrienne on the bottom. "Right, time to turn over." Adrienne hesitated.

"Can I please have a towel around me?"

"Sure. But I will need to move it slightly when I massage your thighs and your adductor muscles." She handed Adrienne the towel, looking away.

"I like your slim body, Adrienne. You just need to tone your muscles a little with a training programme and you will not only be slim but your abdominals will feel tighter, your glutes too. You don't want a wiggly bum, do you? To avoid it, you need to start soon. Are you a member of a gym?"

"Gym? I am a teacher, I can't afford eighty to a hundred pounds a month for gym membership, especially as during the week I am marking papers and preparing for the next day."

"Why not come here and use our gym? I can guide you and for you, a special rate of forty pounds per month."

"You would charge me?"

"But of course, I have to make a living and believe you me that is very cheap. I normally charge seventy pounds an hour for the people around here."

"Tell me more about Theo, will you?"

"What is it you want to know?"

"Tell me everything you know about him, Anca, go on. I can keep a secret, if it means revealing anything he wouldn't be too proud for me to know."

"I cannot do that. You have to ask me a specific question and if I am able to answer I will. I am not free just to tell you anything and everything about him."

"I like you. Anca. At first, I wasn't sure about you but now I can see that we could even become friends. If I ever become mistress of this house, you can be assured that I will keep you on."

Anca sniggered. "Thank you, Adrienne, it is very kind of you. But for you to be aware, I have an agreement with Theo, a contract and only he can revoke it, no one else."

When they returned downstairs, Anca motioned for Adrienne to follow her. She tiptoed towards Theo's study and turned the door handle slowly, opening the door silently and just enough so she could peek inside. She motioned for Adrienne to look in, before closing the door.

"Theo is fast asleep with the cat sitting on him," said Adrienne, as they sat in the kitchen. Anca giggled.

"The two gentlemen of the house are taking their Sunday nap," she said.

"What happens now? When do we wake them? What am I saying, when do I wake him? Theo?" said Adrienne.

"Soon, he will be awake. Doesn't normally sleep for more than half an hour. Maybe as last night was a bad night a bit longer. But he has an important meeting here in the house later, so he knows he needs to be ready for that. In the meantime, I will prepare lunch. He said to make a simple roast, something English and traditional. So I better get on with that. Stay and chat if you like," said Anca.

"What meeting is this? He didn't tell me about it. I thought I had him all weekend?" Adrienne frowned.

"Neighbours. He is hosting a meeting of neighbours. I cannot tell you any more than that, sorry. But Theo did say that you will be staying for lunch and you are welcome to stay for the meeting too. It is up to you. Might be boring but at least you get to see Theo in action".

"In action? Is it a legal matter?"

"Not for me to say, Adrienne. Theo is the host, the main, hold on, let me try and remember the word he used," said Anca and then added, "oh yes, the main protagonists are the neighbours."

Adrienne took her hand and stroked it gently. "Anca, when I listen to you talk about Theo, it is not like someone who is talking about their employer. It is with pride and affection and even love. Are you in love with him?"

Anca blushed. "No, it is not like you think, Adrienne. I admire and love Theo as if he was a father to me, that is all. He is the father I would have liked to have had. He makes me laugh because he thinks he would be hopeless as a father, yet everything he does for me is what a father would do for his daughter. He has shown me kindness, understanding, and yes affection too, but not in any sexy way. You don't have to worry about that. My father was not like that. He treated my mother badly, taking out his frustrations on her. When he left us, it was like pressure had been lifted off from my mother and me and my brother and sister. It was a struggle but at least we did not have to deal with his shouting, his big anger and yes, his abuse too. Not like touching us but he scared us, constantly threatening and criticising. We could never do anything right. And my mother would not stand up to him and if he was not abusing us kids, he would take it out on her. I came here to make a living for myself and one day, God willing, I will return to my home town and buy my own little house and maybe if the right man is there, marry and have my own kids. I am very lucky that Theo found me as his masseuse and when I became his housekeeper, it was like I had won the lottery. But really what has made me feel that way is that in Theo, I feel as if I have the father that my real father never was. Of course, Theo can never be my father but he acts in a way that makes me feel comfortable, safe and I have someone who cares for me and who I can look to for help, for advice, to chat with, to have dinner with when he is around which is not much and even when he is asleep in the next room; I feel it is something that a father would do and it makes me feel warm inside. Sorry, I am probably not making much sense but it is how I feel about him. You have nothing to worry or be jealous about Adrienne; I do love Theo but not in a romantic way. More like he was my dad. I wish my dad had been like him."

Just then, the object of discussion popped his head into the kitchen.

"Who's for a cup of tea?" he said, as he sat next to Anca and took a sip from her tea-cup. The gesture was not lost on Adrienne and she felt a pang of jealousy as he had not sat next to her, instead of Anca. 'Not sure my father would be doing that,' she mused.

"I'll get it," said Adrienne.

Anca slid off the stool and disappeared into the larder, on the pretext that she would start to prepare lunch.

He was sitting on his own on a high stool and smiling. It was the first time he'd had two women in his house for some time, excluding his youngest sister, Suzannah, who would pop round from time to time whenever she was in town.

Neighbourly Relations

"Right then, you've both stated that you want to be here for this meeting, so I will need to brief you as to what this is about and also set out some ground rules. Are you both sitting comfortably?" said Theo.

They were in the living room with Adrienne sitting on the three-seater sofa, her legs tucked under her. Anca was stretched out on the two-seater and he sat upright in his armchair.

"So, here goes then. Four houses away lives Mr Khan with his wife and son. Mr Khan has submitted a planning application seeking permission to add a two-storey, front and back extension to the side of his house. The council has written to us all and this has had his direct neighbours up in arms."

"Why, Flint? What's it got to do with them? Why are they concerned about it?"

"A number of reasons, I suppose. Perhaps the possible impact on the look of the road, a suspicion as to his motives given that he already has an eight-bedroomed house and there are only three people living in it. Perhaps concern about the disruption, the noise and so on. Anyway, as the application stands, his plans would almost certainly be rejected by the council given the powerful group of people that are his neighbours, who will be lined up against him. Although they are vehemently opposed to his plans, at the same time, the neighbours are anxious not to cause ill-feeling and so are seeing whether there is a compromise solution that might be acceptable to Mr Khan and also address their concerns. They have tried to see him directly but thus far he has refused point blank. He has been curt and belligerent towards them. However, their persistence seems to have paid off and he has now agreed to meet them via an intermediary."

"You?" asked Adrienne.

"Yes. I was approached by one of the neighbours to see if I would be willing to act as a sort of peace broker, on the basis that as a lawyer and someone who is not directly affected, I might be acceptable to Mr

Khan. He did not object and so, in less than two hours' time, I will be hosting a meeting here, in this house, with all the interested parties involved, facilitating a discussion with a view to finding a way forward acceptable to all."

"Who are the neighbours?" asked Adrienne.

"Anca, you know them well, better than I do in fact. Do you mind briefing Adrienne? I need to make a couple of notes," said Theo.

Although she listened attentively, it rankled with Adrienne that he had delegated telling her to Anca.

"Happy to do that, Theo. Right then, Adrienne, here goes. So, to the left of Mr Khan's house as you look at it, lives Mr Donald and Mrs Becky Taylor. What is interesting is that Mr Taylor is a property developer and it is possible his objections may have something to do with his business, as much as his concern about the light and the impact on his house. Then, on the other side of Mr Khan lives Mr Kiril Stoikov and his wife Svetlana. He is, what's that phrase you taught me Theo? Something about his nose" she asked.

"Hard-nosed!"

"Oh yes, I like that phrase. Mr Stoikov is a hard-nosed, Bulgarian building contractor and again, I think maybe he has his own motives for not wanting Mr Khan to extend. I know his wife Svetlana; she is one of my clients. Very flamboyant. If she comes to this meeting you are in for, what's that phrase, wait. I have it. Oh yes, a visual spectacle!" said Anca, giggling.

"Is that it? Anyone else coming?" asked Adrienne.

"Yes. The Shah family. Mr and Mrs Beju Shah. He is the chief executive of his own software company. They live with his parents and their two children. I teach Pilates to Indira his wife and once a month I do personal training for her. Very modern family."

"So, if they all come and including the three of us, that is eleven in total. Where will you put everybody, Flint?"

"Might be twelve if the Khans bring their teenage son, too. The drawing room should fit us comfortably. It can hold up to sixteen people if we move a few sofas and chairs around. Which brings me nicely to talk about ground rules," said Theo, leaning forward.

"What do you mean by ground rules?" asked Anca.

"I think he is about to tell us how to behave." joked Adrienne.

"Don't laugh Kiffy, behaviour in this situation is extremely important. As is appearance. Let's start with that first as it is the easiest. Mr Khan is a religious man as far as I can fathom, so it is important we are sensitive to that. So Anca, you can't where that t-shirt as it shows off your bum. Wear a pair of trousers, but something loose fitting. Kiffy, can you change too?"

"You want me to go home and bring my abaya, Flint?" she giggled.

"No, of course not! But you can start by putting on a bra and also buttoning up your shirt all the way to the top!"

"Are you jealous that Mr Khan might fancy me and want me for his second wife, Flint?" she teased.

Anca giggled. "And me as his third?"

"This is no laughing matter. I am being serious!" he said. "It is a delicate matter and we do not need any distractions."

"So you agree then, Flint. That having two young ladies in your house, dressed as we are, is a distraction?" she teased.

"I repeat, this is not a laughing matter. Let's talk about behaviour. Your behaviour, both of you. Some points for you to adhere to. First and foremost, do not say anything unless I ask you to."

"What? Are you serious, Flint?"

"Yes, very serious. The neighbours know Anca and they know she lives here. I will convince them that you are about to move in too. But this is about the neighbours, not who lives in this house so your role is as observers, you have no role to play as participants. Equally, I must ask that you do not make any facial or body expressions that might suggest you approve or disapprove, agree or disagree, or have any feeling whatsoever about what is being said. That means no frowning, no rolling of the eyes, no smiling, no deep breathing, no nodding or shaking of the head. Deadpan. You need to appear emotionally dead."

"You are joking, Flint. You want us to be like statues?"

"Yes, you must not show any feeling that could be misinterpreted by anyone. Some strong views may be expressed and we must not react to them, no matter what our personal views are. Mr Khan or any of the neighbours, cannot read into your body language how you feel about what is being said. No matter what your personal feelings are, they must believe you are totally neutral about the whole thing; that you are not leaning towards one side or the other. I cannot emphasise that enough."

"You are English, it comes natural to you but I am French and it is normal for me to be expressive about how I feel. If someone says something I don't like, I might frown, as you say." He looked at her intently and then said acidly,

"If you believe that there is the possibility that you might be unable to refrain from doing that, then you should consider whether it would be better if you were in another room whilst this is going on, Kiffy. We are supposed to be neutral and I cannot risk you undermining that position. The neighbours can be emotional but we cannot. As I said, we must remain calm and emotionally detached."

There was silence. Anca was looking at the floor in embarrassment. Adrienne looked glum and then got up and left the room, slamming the door.

'Just showed me why she shouldn't be there,' he told himself. 'The petulance of a Frenchwoman I can do without!'

"I'll go and get changed," said Anca shyly.

***

The first to arrive were the Taylors and they happily acquiesced to Anca's polite request that they remove their shoes and leave them in the porch area. She offered them slippers, the type you get in hotels, as an alternative and then took them through to the drawing room where Theo was there to greet them, shaking hands with Donald, giving Becky Taylor a peck on each cheek and then offered them a choice of tea and coffee or a range of juices. He explained quietly that the lack of alcohol was out of deference to Mr Khan who was a devout Muslim.

The Stoikovs arrived next, Svetlana complaining that had she known that they would have to remove shoes she would have ensured her nails were perfectly manicured and painted. Anca smiled. "They're better than mine even after I have had them done."

She unwrapped the slippers and put them on, looking to Kiril for sympathy but he was too busy tapping away on his phone to notice. When they entered the drawing room, Theo greeted them in the same way as with the Taylors, ushering them towards the tea and coffee and soft drinks. The Taylors greeted them and soon they were talking amongst themselves in hushed tones.

Theo inwardly smiled. 'I think Donald has noticed too, as has Becky,' he told himself, in reference to the low-cut blouse that Svetlana was wearing which showed off her ample, silicone bosoms.

Beju and Indira Shah arrived next, dressed simply but elegantly and they made no fuss at all, showing themselves into the drawing room. Out of all his guests thus far, Theo liked the Shas the best, Beju was very helpful whenever he had a PC problem and Indira would sometimes bring round a plate of the most delicious samosas for him and Anca to gobble up.

Finally, some quarter of an hour after everyone else, Mr Khan arrived with his son Mohamed but without his wife. Mr Khan did not need to be asked to take off his shoes; he did it as a matter of course and was happy to walk barefoot into the house. He was wearing traditional Muslim white robes and a skull cap. In contrast, Mohamed was wearing a t-shirt with a New York City print and jeans with fashionable tears in them. He kicked off his expensive trainers and made chit chat with Anca. Had he been a little older, Theo felt sure that he would ask her out on a date and she would have gladly accepted.

Everyone was sat at their seats and with a beverage in their hands. Making an entrance, just as Theo was about to start, Adrienne helped herself to coffee and sat on the sofa next to him. Out of the corner of his eye, he noticed she had changed into a black dress which he recognised as one belonging to Anca. It was long, too long for her as Anca was taller and it reached down to her ankles. She had a silk scarf around her neck, which he recognised as one of his and to all intents and purposes she was completely covered up.

Adrienne looked around the room, expressionless as required, at the same time listening to Theo open the meeting in a calm manner, soothing to the ear, engendering a spirit of compromise, emphasising that the desired outcome was a win-win on all sides. There were nodding heads. Inwardly, she smiled.

'This is what he is good at,' she told herself. "Mrs Stoikov is especially taken in. I bet he could charm the panties off her, if he hasn't done so already."

"Theo, thank you for inviting us but I was just going to say, do we need everyone here to discuss what is a simple matter of my building plans?" said Mr Khan, gesticulating with a movement of his arm in an arc across the room.

"What are you suggesting, Mr Khan?" asked Theo politely.

"I was going to say, we could just discuss this amongst the men only. We do not need women to be present. I, for one, left my wife at home and I had expected the others would do the same."

The disdain in his voice did not endear him to any of the women in the room but he seemed oblivious to how he had riled them. Theo sneaked a glance to his side to see if there was any reaction from Adrienne but other than notice her grip the seat of the sofa tightly, to the extent her knuckles were turning white, she was otherwise the epitome of calmness.

"Mr Khan, I know you mean well and wish to get on with the discussion but the women in this room all have a keen interest in the outcome and I am sure you would agree, that it is their right to be here. I accept you may not have been expecting women to be present and if you want us to temporarily stop so you can bring your wife, or if you wish to send Mohamed to get her, I am sure everyone would be happy to wait."

"It will not be necessary to do that. I can represent my family," he said, proudly pointing to his chest.

Theo nodded and smiled.

"As far as I am concerned," said Mr Khan, putting his glass of orange juice down on the coffee table next to him and leaning forward in his armchair to a more commanding position, "I must be allowed to build my extension as shown in the plans. I have plenty of land on my property and I intend to use it. The extension is needed as I am bringing my family over from Pakistan and this is where they will live."

Theo looked around the room to gauge reaction. As expected, there were some worried faces. The Taylors made no attempt to hide their disapproval and Svetlana was shaking her head.

Theo thanked Mr Khan for making his position clear. He said that the neighbours were sympathetic to his wish to be together with his family but there was concern about the impact on them, of having this two-storey building in their vicinity.

"What impact is this? Can anyone tell me? Am I going to build on your land? You, Mr Taylor, what are you worried about? I said I would spend money and use the same expensive material as the rest of the house. You would hardly notice it. And what about you, Mr Stoikov? What is your concern? We all live in houses with plenty of land around them, so how is that impacting you? Or is it just because you do not want to see any more Pakistanis spoiling the neighbourhood, like weeds on the grass lawn?"

"Come now, Mr Khan. It is not like that at all," said Mr Taylor, calmly and politely.

"What is it then? I look around me and all I see is white faces and I think maybe it is racism that is against me, because I am an Asian and brown-skinned."

"Mr Khan, I object to being labelled a racist. You forget that you are not the only Asian in this room. I too am your neighbour and I share the concerns. It is none of my business but my wife and I don't understand why you would need such a huge extension, when you live in an eight-bedroomed house with just your wife and son!" said Mr Shah, raising his voice.

"You are Indian," said Mr Khan with contempt.

Before Theo could respond to calm the situation, Mohamed butted in. "Dad, it is not helpful to call people racists. They are our neighbours and they have been nothing but friendly towards our family."

Theo was relieved and praised Mr Khan for raising such a mature and wise son. The look Mr Khan gave his son was not lost on the people in the room. It looked as if he saw his son's interjection as an act of betrayal, rather than one of pride in him.

"Anyway, I still think the women should withdraw so that the men can get on with this business," said Mr Khan, changing the subject. "It is not a woman's place to be here. I am offended by seeing them expose their flesh. It is against Islam. It is against my religion. In Islam, women dress very modestly, not like this."

He was looking at Mrs Stoikov when he uttered those words and Theo was pleased to see that Kiril had taken his wife's hand as a means of restraining her. Svetlana looked as if she might have got up and punched Mr Khan on the nose. She was not the only one. Becky Taylor was shaking her head and even Anca, who had hitherto remained calm was on the edge of her seat.

"Now, now Mr Khan, I think we agreed that the women here are stakeholders in this discussion and have every right to stay. Did we not agree that? Also, let's be clear about the question of modesty. There are at least three religions represented in this room: Islam, Hinduism and Christianity. As far as I am aware, only Islam has a dress code. And having read the Quran, it does not explicitly state how males and females should dress. Would you not agree, Mr Khan?"

"You read the Quran?"

"Yes, at least twice. Behind you on the shelf, there is an English translation of the Quran," said Theo.

"English translation? I bet they took out some of the teachings of Mohamed, blessings be upon Him," said Mr Khan.

"Actually, I first read the Quran in Arabic, Mr Khan," said Theo and then spoke to Mr Khan in that language.

Mr Khan looked up in surprise but was still shaking his head.

"The Quran also preaches tolerance. It is the teachings of the prophet Mohamed, blessings be upon Him, Mr Khan."

That seemed to calm him down and there was a collective sigh of relief. Adrienne looked at Theo with pride. 'Well done, Flint,' she told herself.

Theo paused for a minute and then calmly stated that in his professional opinion, the plan for the extension had zero chance of getting through the council's planning department.

"Aside from the size and the aesthetic impact, when you purchased your house, your solicitor should have made you aware that there is a restrictive covenant on all the properties in this private road. This restricts you from extending or adding buildings to your house without the agreement of all the other property holders in this road," Theo announced.

He had remembered when he was buying his own house that his own solicitor had made him aware of it but he had thought nothing of it at the time. As a single man with an eight-bedroom house, it was not something that was of any concern to him at the time.

The announcement had taken Mr Khan by surprise. It was a bombshell and it was noticeable that a slight twitch above his left eye appeared but he remained silent. "I see you are all against me," said Mr Khan. "Even you, Theo."

"Not at all, Mr Khan. I merely stated the facts as they are. No more, no less," he said and turning to his son he added. "What's your view, Mohamed? How do you feel about this?"

"He does what I say!" said Mr Khan angrily, thumping his fist on the arm of the sofa.

"Dad! Stop it! I've had enough," said Mohamed. He took a deep breath.

'I fear, all hell is about to break loose,' said Theo to himself.

"He just wants to bring over a load of illiterate and backward Pakis to England. None of them speak English. Only one of them, a cousin, has a useful skill. He is a bricklayer. They all come from my dad's village. They haven't been anywhere before, not even Islamabad or Karachi, so London will blow their minds."

"Quiet boy!" Mr Khan shouted at his son. He proceeded to berate him in Urdu and threatened to cut-off funding for his medical degree if he continued to oppose his father. Theo intervened, praising Mr Khan for being an honourable, family man and stating that he admired how sincere Mr Khan was, in wanting to provide for the wellbeing of his relatives.

"Yes, but not mum's family. He won't let them come over. My granny is getting weak and needs full-time care but he won't have her in the house as she is on mum's side of the family. He is cruel."

"Don't listen to him. It is not true!" said Mr Khan and a further tirade in Urdu directed at his son followed.

"Mr Khan, can I just clarify something that was said earlier?" said Theo, remaining calm. "Is it right that there are just three of you living in your house?"

"Yes, what of it?"

"So, you have an eight bedroomed house and presumably, you use just two of them and please forgive me if it is intruding into your private affairs; are the remaining six bedrooms insufficient for your relatives? Your plan is for a four-bedroom extension and if it was to be approved, that would mean ten spare bedrooms. That would mean extra accommodation for anything between ten and upwards of twenty people."

"What of it?" said Mr Khan, evasively.

"I'll tell you. It is not about bringing over lots of relatives. It is just one family who are coming. The rest don't have passports and I very much doubt they would even get visas," said Mohamed. "Sorry dad, you're always telling me to be truthful so I shall. This is not about relatives. It is an investment. Dad has plans to split the house in two and sell one off."

Khan lost his patience with his son's revelations and reached across and grabbed him by the throat, yelling "Shut your mouth!"

Mr Shah was the quickest to jump up and pulled Mr Khan off his son. He was met with abuse in Urdu, to which he responded in kind. Mohamed was close to tears and excused himself from the room. The front door could be heard closing. He was gone.

There was a lot of talking between couples and if looks could kill, Mr Khan would be meeting his maker at that point.

"Time for a break I think," Theo whispered to Anca and she stood up and announced that there would be a five-minute break for people to stretch their legs and she was making fresh, hot drinks. Adrienne followed Anca out of the room and into the kitchen. Everyone stood up and Theo noted the body language exuded by each person. There was a spectrum of feelings, from exasperation to anger, most of it directed at Mr Khan. Theo gravitated towards Mr Khan and they chatted, seemingly on friendly terms, to the extent that Mr Khan patted him on the back.

Adrienne and Anca returned with one tray of drinks and another with an assortment of things to eat, including a variety of samosas both vegetable and meat, fish balls, cheese and spinach parcels in filo pastry, as well as buns, bite-sized cakes and chocolates. Once it was explained to him that the chicken and lamb samosas were made with Halal meat, Mr Khan tucked in and despite his earlier aversion to having ladies present, he congratulated them on their cooking. Anca did not let on that they had been bought from a specialist, Asian shop.

When everyone resumed their seats, Theo felt that the tension that had threatened to boil over had dissipated and there was now an air of calmness. It was the time to look forward. He reiterated that there was no chance that the extension would get approved and even if it did, the restricted covenant would render it dead in the water. Mr Khan grimaced but said nothing.

Theo let that sink in for a few seconds, as it was important that it was a red line and there was no going back to that.

"However, there is a possible way forward that might be to your advantage Mr Khan. Your neighbours want to do right by you and Mr Taylor, who as you know is a property developer and Mr Stoikov, who is a building contractor, have got together with a proposal."

"What proposal?" said Mr Khan, regarding them with suspicion.

"Hear them out, Mr Khan. You may like what they have to say. Over to you gentlemen," said Theo, nodding in their direction.

Mr Taylor was the first to speak, outlining his development of a large site in Greenwell, consisting of a number of two-bedroomed, three-bedroomed and four-bedroomed houses. Mr Stoikov was contracted to provide these and there were three show houses available for viewing. Mr Taylor let it be known that Mohamed had told him that Mr Khan had family living in Greenwell, in amongst a significant Asian community there, which included shops, restaurants, a mosque and a community centre. For people coming from abroad, it would be much easier to integrate there than in Cheam, where they would be stuck out in an area with no shops nearby, no buses and in an alien community.

"Kiril and I are prepared to offer you one of the three-bedroomed houses at cost price for your family, Mr Khan," said Mr Taylor, brightly.

"Why would you do that?" said Mr Khan.

Theo noted his demeanour had changed significantly. He no longer seemed so agitated and his shoulders had dropped.

"We do this out of friendship, Mr Khan. It is not because we do not want your family living here in Cheam. We were just thinking how we could be helpful. And if you only want to keep the property as an investment, then we have no problem with that. We would ask that you keep it for two years, so that other potential buyers don't get spooked into thinking there is something wrong with the house."

"And how much would such a house cost?" asked Mr Khan, in a more emollient tone and with the faintest of smiles.

"Can I ask gentlemen that you discuss the details amongst

yourselves at a later date and time? At this point I just want to establish whether the proposal is acceptable to all parties," said Theo.

"It is a really good offer," said Mr Taylor.

"Mr Khan?" asked Theo.

Mr Khan shrugged. "I suppose so."

"I need a more definitive answer, Mr Khan. Are you happy with Mr Taylor's and Mr Stoikov's proposal?"

"Yes. If the price is right."

"The price will be right, Mr Khan. Greenwell is not Cheam. Properties there are much more modest than they are here," said Mr Taylor.

"Okay. I accept your proposal," said Mr Khan and he smiled.

Theo looked at Adrienne. He did not smile but he allowed himself a squeeze of her hand. She returned the squeeze and entwined her fingers with his own.

After they had all left, everyone with smiles on their faces, Adrienne said, "Very impressed, Flint. I can see why you are a good lawyer. You remained calm throughout. I can now appreciate why you need to be so careful about what you say and how you look. I like the way you staged it, with an important break just as things were getting very heated up."

"A lot of preparations beforehand went into this meeting. Even the food Anca and I went scouring for, is genuine Asian food that would be acceptable to Mr Khan. As for the staging, it was important to establish in Mr Khan's mind that his plans were absolutely hopeless, that he had no chance of it ever materialising."

"You certainly did that. And his son's outburst was very helpful in achieving that," said Adrienne.

Theo looked at Anca and they smiled knowingly.

"What?" said Adrienne. "Are you two going to let me in on this?"

"It wasn't exactly spontaneous," said Theo, smirking. "Mohamed came to see me a few days ago and explained the situation. I merely encouraged him to speak up, admittedly not in those terms."

"Flint! You are so devious!"

"No, just prepared."

"And the proposal from Mr Taylor and Mr Stoikov, I suppose you knew about that too, Flint?"

"Yes, I did. We discussed it," he admitted.

"So you weren't impartial. You were not neutral, Flint!"

"I beg your pardon. I was completely impartial, Kiffy. Did you hear me take sides? Did I not stick to the facts? I merely facilitated the discussion; the neighbours did the rest."

"Do you think they will reach agreement?" asked Anca.

Theo replied, "D*um spiro spero*."

Anca looked towards Adrienne for an explanation. "While I breathe, I hope."

"Let's have a bite to eat and then I need to get packing," said Theo.

"Oh Flint, not going away again, are you? How long for?" asked Adrienne. She looked towards Anca for an explanation but none was forthcoming. She tiptoed out of the room before Adrienne could fire any questions at her.

"Hopefully, no more than two weeks," he said.

"In two weeks' time we have a school break for Whitsun and I was planning to go to visit my parents. I was going to invite you to come with me," she said, with a note of disappointment in her voice.

"To Normandy? I would like that. Should be back by then but Kiffy I…"

Adrienne grabbed him and kissed him. "Thank you, Flint. I was afraid you would turn me down."

"Just hold your horses, Kiffy. I said I should be back but I cannot promise that. If negotiations take longer, then I am afraid that takes precedence. You do understand that don't you, Kiffy?"

"Yes, of course. I get it. But I know you will try, Flint," she said and kissed him again and he hugged her. "I am so going to miss you whilst you are away."

"I will miss you too, Kiffy," he said, stroking her hair.

"Even though I am only your aspirational girlfriend?"

"Yes, even though you are only my aspirational girlfriend!"

"Pig!" she said, giggling.

"By the way, I should say thank you for remaining calm and collected in that discussion. Very self-controlled of you despite the, shall we say, provocations."

"It was hard keeping my mouth shut but I managed it. I don't know how you do it. Yes, I do, it's because you are English and it comes easy to you," she teased.

"I'll ignore that last remark. And well done for putting something modest on, although I recognise that as being Anca's dress."

"Don't worry, I will take it off before I leave!"

"I think you should take it off right now," he said, grinning.

"But Flint," she said and leaning forward and pulling him down, whispered, "I am not wearing anything underneath."

"Nothing?"

"Nothing!"

"Still think you should take it off, don't want any coffee or tea stains on it do we," he smirked.

"Or your stains, peut-etre?" she said.

He smiled and turned her around to face away from him so that he could unzip the dress.

"But Flint, what if Anca comes in?"

"So?"

"You know me, I don't mind if she sees us. I am quite liberated about these things. But you?"

"We shall have to take the risk, won't we," he said, as he lifted the dress over her head and discarded it on the sofa.

"What am I wearing, Flint?" she said, looking into his eyes.

"Just your hooped earrings, the scent that I like and a smile, Kiffy."

She melted into his arms and he led her by the hand to the nearest of the sofas. Anca was about to enter the room but the faintest of muffled noises emanating from within suggested she should not. A slight opening of the door confirmed that it was best that she should not and she back-pedalled to the living room.

Abla

Settling into his business-class seat, he smiled to himself. Outwardly there was no discernible change in his countenance lest that might be picked up by those closest to him: Gareth to his immediate left and Nicola across the aisle to his right. Gareth had volunteered to be going as, on top of the fees they would earn the company and help to enhance his own credentials for consideration to a more senior role, it was above all, a great way of getting out of half-term 'fatherly duties', as he called them. As for Nicola, she had been delighted to be told by her line manager that the client had specifically requested her, as word had got back to them that she was a very capable contract legal assistant. Theo was not disappointed to learn that either, as he was mentally pencilling her into his future plans to join the Middle East team on a more permanent basis and this engagement was building on her skills and experience. On top of that, there would be more fees coming in because as a matter of policy, the firm charged a premium for named individuals and the charge for her services would rise from fifteen hundred to seventeen hundred and fifty pounds per day. The slogan, 'every little bit helps', applied to legal fees as well as supermarket shopping. This trip, as short as it was, was important to the firm.

But the inward smile that they could have no inkling of, was unrelated to having them on board. There were two reasons why this particular engagement in the Middle East had piqued his interest above the other ones he had been engaged in of late. The first and foremost of these was a new line of business that had emerged within the Emirates. The trip, as short as it was, was important to the firm as the instigator was Rashid Qubaisi, a very senior and influential figure in government circles. Theo had met Mr Qubaisi several times on previous trips to the Middle East at conventions and they had chatted and got on well but this was the first time, that the firm had been engaged to work with him and his team. He was not underestimating the potential value of having such a client. If they managed to pull it off and the outcome was successful, it would not only expand the firm's portfolio but the brief provided, suggested that it could become a much longer engagement, potentially lasting several months with follow-on work. That suited him down to the ground as it aligned very much with his plans for the future, which were about the feasibility of establishing a semi-permanent base out there, with him running the office. What had hitherto been a blocker, was the need to generate sufficient volume of business, particularly repeat business to give it traction and justify the cost of setting it up. He had seen it as an exciting possibility, that would enable him to immerse himself in the cultures of the Gulf with which he had an affinity that went beyond the studies of his early years. As he sat re-reading the brief, he was trying not to give any visual indication to anyone around him that he was excited at that prospect.

He reminded himself that excitement in such matters was another unreliable feeing to have, since it coloured one's judgement which could lead to miscalculation and an undesirable outcome. Desirable, economically advantaged outcomes for his clients, for his firm and ultimately for him, was what the game was about.

The second reason why this trip was of interest to him above the norm, was something that he had almost missed at the foot of the brief, which had listed the roles and responsibilities. It had said that in the role of Assistant to the Project Head was to be one Abla Saleh, who he knew by her previous surname before she had married, as Abla Haddad. They had not met face-to-face for very many years. He had lost touch with her soon after they had parted; she to return to Jordan to marry a fellow countryman and he to start work with a prestigious City law firm. The impediments to them having more than a furtive relationship seemed insurmountable at the time. Whilst they parted still very much in love, it was in the recognition that, at most, they might be able to just keep an eye on what each of them was making of their lives. But that was easier said than done, not least because when they were in their twenties the technology to do that was in its infancy. E-mail had barely got going and was certainly not the worldwide tool that everyone takes for granted today. Writing would have been too risky. But there had been chance encounters over the years, either directly in regional conferences or through mutual acquaintances who might make passing casual reference about one to the other. So, notwithstanding that, he had not spoken to her for several years, Theo had learned that Abla had had two children and that she had returned to her work soon after they had started going to school; that her family had moved to one of the Gulf states as it was more lucrative than Jordan, a largely poor country, not having the benefit of sitting on a giant oil well like some of the other Arab states. And now, in less than twenty-four hours, he would be meeting her and for the next two weeks they would be working together. He would have to listen to her voice and look into her eyes. He wondered how he would react to seeing her once again. He was confident that the passage of time had deadened any erstwhile romantic notions. What was in the past had to stay in the past and he had to remain focussed on the business that was responsible for making it happen in the first place. It would be a professional interaction. The possibility of seeing Abla socially was a prospect that he wished to put into the far recesses of his mind, for fear it might reawaken feelings that had been dormant for over twenty years.

It was the end of the first day and he was back in his hotel in the luxurious suite that had been booked for him. Sitting on the plush sofa, wrapped in his white fluffy bathrobe, feet up on the low table, having a cup of tea, he was looking out on the Persian Gulf and pondering what it might be like to be doing that on a more permanent basis. The floor to ceiling windows afforded a panoramic view across the harbour and out into the sea, illuminated by the streaks of light from the brightly-lit, modern, tall buildings. The room was quiet and peaceful and he could begin to relax on his own. It was just as he liked it. He could see that if he lived there, then he would have more time to enjoy the Gulf and the richness of its cultures, rather than having to keep flying back and forth.

"I'm leading two lives," he told himself between sips of tea. "One which is out here, albeit with a different and distinct set of social rules and customs but ordered and focussed and predictable. I am in my element here. I am very comfortable with the set up here."

"And what of my other life back home. Home?" he scoffed. "And what is that exactly? My house? Is it my live-in housekeeper who is young enough to be my daughter? Is it the fiery Frenchwoman who insults me at every opportunity, who has latched on to me as the self-appointed girlfriend? Is it that or all of that or some combination of? God, what chaos! Two lives, one perfectly ordered and predictable and the other a mess. I'm suited to the former and yet I am thrilled by the very madness and anarchy that is the latter."

Gareth and Nicola had tried to persuade him to join them for drinks in the hotel bar but he had declined. He wanted to reflect on the first day of business. He had expected it to follow the usual pattern, when time can be taken up with introductions and preliminary work but not this time, they had made much more progress than he had expected. He was impressed by how much everyone seemed to be switched on, had read up on the material he had prepared and sent ahead and were quite clear about what they were trying to achieve. There was a certain sense of satisfaction that the advanced work that had been done back in London had paid off. If it continued at this rate of progress, then he could comfortably finish at the end of two weeks. That would enable him to keep an engagement, that of accompanying Adrienne to her home in Normandy for the Whitsun school break; if not for all of it, then certainly for some of it. The idea of spending an entire week together with her, staying on her parent's farm did not exactly thrill him.

Adrienne having characterised life on the farm as being fun had not sounded convincing and he had extracted a concession out of her that they would stay with her parents on their farm for just three nights and then drive back to Paris for the remainder of the holiday. In return, she was going to be able to show him off as her boyfriend; that was his concession. Negotiations had been successful.

As he padded over to the kitchen area and made himself a second cup of tea, he could hear a door slam and he recognised it as Nicola entering her room. It was adjacent to his and inter-connected with his own. As a result of a mix-up at the office, he had been booked into an executive suite but instead of being just for himself, it actually comprised of two adjoining rooms with a common sitting room and kitchenette. It had irritated him at the time, as he did not like to share but as the hotel was fully booked, he had no choice; preferring to share with Nicola rather than Gareth.

'If I share with Gareth, we will end up drinking and talking shop and setting the world to rights, all through the night,' he told himself. 'At least with Nicola, I can enjoy more easy-going conversation and I can relax.'

There was a knock on the door and a voice saying, "Theo, are you decent?"

"Come in Nicola," he said, smiling, as he tightened his over-sized bathrobe around him. 'There's a question which can have all sorts of connotations,' he thought. 'What is decency?'

Her hair was still wet and she was also wearing her hotel bathrobe and matching slippers on her feet, as she appeared through the inter-connecting door between their respective rooms and padded over to where he was sitting. She stood in front of the window and looked out.

"Great view!" she said. "I could stay here!"

He looked up, raising his eyebrows. "Could you?"

"Yes. So different from life back in England. And the Emirates is more relaxed than other countries around here. I don't have to wear an abaya for instance and alcohol is available, at least in the hotels."

"Yes, it is, in designated areas but we only partake in moderation," he said gently, as a reminder.

"Yes, which is why I am here and not downstairs with Gareth," she said sweetly. "Don't worry, Theo, I won't let you down. I will behave the part, I will dress the part as well as produce the highest quality work I can possible manage. You can rely upon me."

He smiled. "I know I can, Nicola. I would not have brought you out here, even if the client requested you by name, if I did not have confidence in you in all respects."

"If it didn't breach some sort of professional protocol, I would come over and hug you for saying that," she said.

"Best not," he said, trying to hide his embarrassment at the suggestion. "Neither of us is best attired for hugging, if you get my drift."

Nicola giggled. "Why Theo, am I making you uncomfortable? Do you want me to go back to my room and get changed into clothes? I can do if you want me to."

"Don't be silly, of course not," he said, trying to keep his cool.

"I am totally covered in this robe. You can't see anything, can you?" said Nicola, tightening the robe even more.

"No, you are fine Nicola," he said. He had wanted to say that when she was standing there facing towards the sea, her silhouette reminded him of Adrienne in some respects and he found himself thinking about her. He rebuked himself for even countenancing the notion that he might break his own self-imposed rules and text her.

"Theo, just wanted to let you know that the reason I felt I could come dressed just in my bathrobe, just as you are, is that I knew I could trust you. I feel that I am safe with you. I know that I can sleep with the interconnecting door between our rooms unlocked and I would have no worries. What I am trying to say Theo, I know that you are a true gentleman."

"Thank you, Nicola. I am touched. Not sure I can live up to the 'true gentleman' tag but you can relax. You are definitely safe with me. And if it makes you feel better to keep the door between us unlocked, I don't have a problem with that, as long as you tell me you are not a sleepwalking, axe woman!"

She giggled and sat down next to him. She leaned across and kissed his cheek. "Thanks."

"For nothing," he said.

"By the way, I must tell you," she said, as if about to announce a great revelation. "That woman has the hots for you. The one who sat diagonally across from you. Abla Sala."

"Saleh," he corrected her. "What makes you say that, Nicola? I hadn't noticed."

"Women, notice these things, Theo. She kept looking at you, not just when you were speaking. Little sideways glances. I think you've made a conquest, Theo," she teased.

"Me? I don't think so," he scoffed.

He wanted to say that at one time, Abla had been the love of his life and that it had taken him a long time to come to terms with not seeing her; to get over her. Even after he had read Abla was married, he had kept a little candle lit for her, notwithstanding the hopelessness of his feelings for her ever being requited.

"Can I ask you about something you said earlier?" he said, changing the subject. "You said you could stay here. As you've probably worked out for yourself, we have been successful in getting significant work out in the Middle East. If this work was to grow, it may reach the point where we might have to consider whether it would be viable to have an office out here, in one of the Gulf states. I have been giving it some thought for some time now and a team of three or four people could be based out here, perhaps for several months at a time or even longer, possibly as much as a twelve-month posting. It is hypothetical at the moment but were it to come to fruition would you want to be…"

"If you are asking if I would be interested, Theo," she said, enthusiastically interrupting him, "the answer is most definitely I would. Count me in."

He laughed. "Wow! Didn't need to work at persuading you then. Good to know," he said. "But it is early days yet so don't get too excited, Nicola. Also, it is not something to enter into lightly. I will be producing some guidelines and an FAQ for potential volunteers to consider, just to be sure they know what they are letting themselves in for."

She looked at him quizzically. "Such as?"

"For a start, you will be leaving your family, friends, boyfriend, etc behind you. That is quiet a big wrench."

"I don't have a boyfriend. And with my family we can skype and I am sure they would want to visit. It is not that far away. My parents go to New Zealand once a year to see my brother and that doesn't bother them."

"It can also get quite lonely. It doesn't bother me but social isolation can be hard to take. Mixing in with the local community, especially for a single girl, can be difficult."

"What do you mean?" she asked.

He explained as delicately as he could without scaring her, that Arab boys may consider a young, attractive, European girl as 'fair game'. He explained that European women had an undeserved reputation with having loose morals and willing to jump into bed with them and she may find herself on the receiving end of unsolicited attention, some boys may even pester them.

"Then I will come to you to protect me," she said and grabbed his arm.

"Of course, as a team we would root for each other. If we manage to win significant business here in the Emirates then we could open up here where there is a more relaxed and enlightened attitude towards women by the menfolk. Anyway, at the moment it is just a future aspiration, very much predicated on our ability to win more business; big business!"

She giggled.

"Care to share what is amusing you?" he said, looking across at her.

"You are funny, Theo. First you tell me about this possible opportunity that might come up and get me all excited and then tell me all the bad things that I might have to think about if and when we do open up an office over here."

"I was just thinking of your welfare. I have a duty of care towards you and Gareth so I thought I should appraise you of what to expect," he explained.

Nicola stood up and leaned down to kiss him on the cheek. "You do look out for me, Theo. Just like my dad. And just for that I will make you another cup of tea," she said, cheerfully.

The discussions had gone well, the legal sticking points in the proposal had been removed and Mr Qubaisi's team was relieved and happy that Theo's team had got them out of a sticky situation and they had got the result that they wanted. Theo's team had created a very positive impression and were praised for their legal and negotiating skills. After a celebratory dinner, Theo was taken aside by Rashid, thanked once again and then presented with a document to be read once back in the UK. He had also whispered that there was a personal gift for him waiting for his collection back at his hotel.

As the diners left their tables and gravitated towards the balcony looking out over the Gulf, Theo did not wish to follow and was glad to find himself standing alone in his own company.

'Another successful trip,' he told himself.

"A penny for your thoughts," a voice said, coming from behind him.

He turned around and she was standing there and smiling, a discrete distance apart, partially hidden from the views of prying eyes by the large, potted, palm trees.

"Abla!" he said quietly. "I was wondering where you had gone."

She emerged but still keeping her distance, her eyes sparkling in the sympathetic light thrown by the fronds of the palm trees.

"Why? Were you looking for me, Theo? You've been ignoring me all week," she said and he detected just a whiff of complaint in her voice.

Even when she might be uttering a complaint, Abla's voice had a richness and seductive quality that had not diminished in its power to draw him in, to wreak havoc with his senses.

"Yes. I was looking for you, Abla, hoping we could catch up. I have kept my distance from you during these discussions as it was important, we kept it on a professional basis," he explained.

"And now?" she asked.

"Now we can socialise, have a chat and talk about old times. Speaking of which, you remembered: 'A penny for your thoughts'."

"Yes. How could I forget? It was one of the first English phrases you taught me."

"How are things with you?"

"I'm fine. My kids have grown up and following their own dreams," she said proudly.

"And your husband? How is he?"

"My husband? He too is following his dreams but without me. We are divorced, Theo. We haven't shared a bed in two, nearly three years now. He has found another woman. Easy to do that for a man in the Middle East. Not easy for a woman to do the same. But don't feel sad for me as I am happy, very happy. For me, divorce is very liberating. I am free to do as I want, go where I want and without being hindered by having to follow what my husband wants to do!"

"I am pleased for you, Abla. Do you ever go back to…?"

"Beirut? Yes, I have been once or twice, stay at the same hotel as we did and go to the same bar and walk along the same boulevard. The hotel is smarter now and the bar has changed owner. I like going to Beirut; it is full of happy memories of when you and I were together," she said.

He nodded in agreement but remained silent.

"Perhaps one day, you and I could meet there, for old time's sake," she said.

"Maybe," he said equivocally.

Abla put her hand to her mouth. "Forgive me, Theo. I hadn't heard of any marriage on the grapevine and so I assumed you were still single. Of course, not if you are in a relationship."

He suggested that they sit on the sofas in the public area, so as to not arouse any suspicion as to whether anything untoward was going on between them. She sat on a two-seater and he sat on the single armchair at right angles and next to her. He explained the situation back in the UK, that he was still living alone apart from a live-in housekeeper but there was a woman on the scene, who had just appeared in his life. "Is she your girlfriend, Theo?"

"Abla, I don't rightly know. I am not even sure what the role of a girlfriend is supposed to be. It has certain connotations but ask two people what they think a girlfriend is and you will get different opinions for sure. This woman has come into my life out of the blue. I was not looking for a relationship and still I am not. We don't live together and we don't make plans together but we do see each other, now and again."

"Does she share your bed, Theo?" she asked, almost in a whisper.

"It would be an indelicate thing for me to respond. I sleep alone, normally, Abla."

"Hmm. Do you love her?"

"Hah! I knew that question would arise sooner or later," he said.

"Do you love her like you once loved me?" she persisted.

"Abla, I am a different man to what I was then. I have different expectations of life now, to what I had over twenty years go. The things that are important to me now are different and love is not one of them. I have not made a great success of love and have not courted for a very long time. It is too unreliable for me, makes disproportionate demands without any clear idea of whether it will yield the desired outcome. When love comes calling, I give it a wide berth and keep myself from becoming emotionally entangled in something, that is, at best, intangible and at worse, a nightmare.

"Does that mean you are not in love with her?"

"It is not a question I can answer despite your persistence in extracting one from me, Abla. In short, I don't really know her, not least because I spend so much time being away, out here in the Middle East."

"Perhaps you should move out here. You've always liked it here."

"True, I do. It would be a big move but I have been thinking about it of late."

That seemed to make her smile. It was the sweetest of smiles and he still found it captivating but he recognised that the intensity of the allure and enthralling effect that it once had on him, had diminished with time. Some twenty years earlier he felt sure that they would have made a beeline for his hotel. Now, they could just sit and smile, each in their own thoughts of what might have been and what had been lost.

"I will be passing through Jordan on my next trip and perhaps we can meet in Amman or Beirut if you like," he suggested.

"I'd like that, very much. Beirut. Amman is my hometown but let's make it Beirut." When the others returned, he stayed a few minutes and then excused himself to return to his hotel nearby. Gareth and Nicola were staying to keep up the British end and he whispered in his ear, for the former to keep an eye out for the latter. As he said his goodbyes to his clients, Nicola disengaged herself from the group that had gathered and trotted after him.

"I would like to come home with you, Theo," she said. "I'm tired and had enough."

"What is it with the younger generation? Don't seem to have the stamina for festivities," he teased. "I'm the older of the two of us Nicola, not you. Why are you not staying with the others?"

"Don't fancy it," she said.

Nicola reached out to take hold of his arm but he withdrew it immediately and she looked up at him confused and put out.

"Best not be seen walking too closely together. I know it is meant as a friendly gesture, Nicola but some people might get the wrong impression. I am just protecting your reputation, Nicola," he explained and her smile suggested it had had the desired effect.

Outside their rooms, she leaned over to him and kissed his cheek. "Thanks," she said.

"What for?"

"For just being you, Theo. My protector." He smiled and wished her goodnight.

In his room, he had dimmed all the lights but one and switched the TV channel to the Al Jazeera news channel. Instead of the English language version of the channel, he switched on the Arabic version and was pleased with himself that he could understand nearly everything that was being said, even if the announcer had a particularly strong accent. He recalled how, when he was with Abla, as much as she wanted to practice her English on him, he wanted to reinforce the intensive Arabic language lessons by practicing on her. They agreed to compromise by having some days where only English would be spoken and other days to converse solely in Arabic. It had caused nothing but mirth at first until such time as he had become sufficiently well-versed, that he could whisper sweet words of affection towards her.

After a few minutes, he tired of the bad news reports coming from around the world. Al Jazeera had a huge network of reporters that seemed to cover the entire globe: the Americas, Africa, Europe in particular and the Far East and they seemed to bring to the screen, nothing but doom and gloom. He did not want to hear about sad events that peoples of the world were enduring and he switched it off and went to bed.

It was just after midnight when his phone rang. In keeping with his strict adherence that personal calls should not interfere with business, he had only switched it on once he had returned to his room, having deemed that work for his clients had concluded.

The voice was instantly recognisable. "Monty, it's me," said the glum voice.

"Suzy! Good to hear from you, although the tone of your voice suggests all is not well with you. What's up little sister?"

"I'm in hospital. Don't worry. Nothing life threatening, just a little broken ankle and a few cuts here and there," she said lightly.

Suzy then, in a nonchalant manner, outlined that she had been hit by a car having absentmindedly crossed the road, without looking in the right direction. She said thankfully it was slow-moving traffic and it was no more than a tap but it was enough to get her into hospital where she was calling from.

"Suzy, hold on a second. Did I hear you correctly? Did you say you were looking in the wrong direction? Where exactly were you?"

There was a momentary pause and then she answered. "In Brussels, came to meet up with a friend. After I left my friend's house and as it was a pleasant afternoon, I thought I would walk to the station to get the Eurostar train back to England. I was crossing the road and stupidly looked right instead of left. Just slipped my mind that they drive on the opposite side of the road to us and I got hit by a Volkswagen Polo. I would have preferred it to be a posher car like a Beamer or a Merc but hey, you can't be choosy about who knocks you over," she said facetiously. "And here I am Monty, laid up in a fine Belgique hospital. Must cost a bomb to stay here but luckily, I had my EHIC card on me and flashed it at them.

Anyway, they've patched me up and the duty doctor has said that they will keep me in tonight for observation as my head hit the ground but I will be discharged tomorrow and then I can go. I don't think I am going to be very mobile. Aside from my broken ankle, my hips are already feeling sore from falling on to the hard road, so I don't think I can get on that train without some assistance. I know it's asking a lot, but…"

"Don't worry little sis, I will come and get you and we can go home on the Eurostar together."

She blew him a kiss down the phone. "Monty, I knew I could rely on you. I haven't told mum or dad, nor do I intend to, at least not yet and not before I get back to London. I don't want to get the lecture from Mum," she said.

He hung up, having agreed that he would text her with his travel details, so she could know the approximate time to expect him. Jumping out of bed, he noticed there was a shaft of light under the inter-connecting door between his room and Nicola's.

'Not my business,' he told himself, refraining from speculating as to what she was up to and with whom.

He sat at the desk in his boxer shorts and t-shirt and powered up his laptop. There was a tap on the door and Nicola popped her head round.

"Can't sleep either?" she asked.

"Not exactly but as you are also awake, you couldn't put the kettle on and make us some tea, could you Nicola?"

She smiled and entered the room, wearing just a sleep vest and panties and padded over to the kitchenette area. "I'm thirsty too; must be the rich food we ate earlier," she said. His eyes followed her lithesome movements, admiring the youthful curves of her body and he rebuked himself.

'Stop it,' he told himself, quickly averting his eyes.

He was surprised to see that there were a few seats available on a number of early morning flights to Brussels but there were none that would get him there directly, thereby adding to his journey. The best flight he could find left at 9.00 a.m. and would take a total of nine hours and included a stopover in Munich. He booked it and texted Suzy the details, signing off as 'Monty' with a smiley emoji. Monty was the name he used instead of Theo, as it was a reference to his middle name,

Montague. It was Suzy who first coined the epithet Monty and she was the only one who used it and only when talking between them. It became his call-sign for Suzy.

Nicola joined him at the table with two cups of tea together with a small box of individually wrapped chocolates, that the hotel had left for them. Theo informed her that he was having to fly back early as there was an urgent family matter to attend to. He tried not to look but as he was speaking to her, he could not help but notice that the sleep vest she was wearing was quite revealing and he felt embarrassed.

'I don't think she realises that the air conditioning is making her chest more distinct,' he told himself, as he stood up and looked around; but not at her.

"By all means, you and Gareth enjoy your stay here, we are paid up for tomorrow and your flights back are not until the morning after. Plenty of time to sight-see and relax," he said.

He saw what he was looking for and returned to the table, putting a sofa wrap around Nicola's shoulders, draping it over her.

"Thanks," she smiled. "You must have read my mind that I was starting to feel cold."

"Yes, something like that," he said, uncomfortably.

"Oh my God, just realised," she said and went bright red with embarrassment.

He patted her arm in reassurance. "Don't worry, secret safe with me." She kissed his cheek.

"My hero, once again."

After Nicola returned to her room, he did something he had never done before; he sent a WhatsApp message to Adrienne. It took him longer to construct than writing a paragraph of legal speak in a contract. The words did not logically flow, exacerbated by him analysing what import might be attached to each of them by her. After several attempts he was satisfied and hit the send button.

At the other receiving end, Adrienne was surprised to be getting a message from him and smiled. That is, until she read the message.

"Kiffy, hope you are well. An urgent family matter has come up. Unable to join you at start of visit to your parents. Send me details of itinerary and will see if feasible to meet you there or in Paris."

She was sitting on the balcony of her flat with Anca, who she had invited over for a meal with her. Anca could see that the smile that had been previously worn on her face as they swapped anecdotes about humorous moments in their lives, had turned into a scowl.

"Flint, you are infuriating," she read out loud, when he stonewalled her in response to the question of what the family matter was. His response of '*I am not at liberty to discuss*' had not gone down well with Adrienne.

"Bad news?"

"This man drives me crazy!" she said, holding her arms out. "He says he can't come with me to see my parents as he has an urgent family matter. Sounds like an excuse to me. I must admit I was a little surprised when he agreed so easily. I thought, perhaps he has changed, but it was just his way to stall me, to give him time to think up a good excuse!"

"Maybe it is not like that. Maybe there is an 'urgent family matter' after all," Anca said, shrugging her shoulders. "I have not known Theo to lie, at least not to me."

Adrienne looked at her with pleading eyes. "Anca, could you text him and find out please?"

Anca twisted uncomfortably in her seat as she was being put in a position between her host and burgeoning friend in Adrienne and her employer and mentor, who had put a roof over her head and given her succour at a time of great need. Then she remembered something that he had once told her, that in a complicated situation always try to break it down to the simplest components. She smiled to herself, the response was obvious.

"Adrienne, I would really like to be helpful but even if I was to text Theo and he was to tell me, I am contractually bound not to reveal what he has said," she said with relief. 'That is my 'get out if jail free card' as Theo once called it,' she reminded herself. Adrienne knew it would be futile to persist and gritted her teeth. She admired Anca's loyalty to him as much as it was frustrating not to know and it only fed her anger with him.

As much as she wanted to scold him, she realised it was futile and just responded that she hoped the family matter was not serious and would be resolved in time for him to join her. She added her family's address and 'xxx' at the end and sent it off. She re-read his message and pulled a face when she noticed he had not sent any emoji or a sign of affection towards her.

Anca was leaving as she said she had an early morning client who liked to go running with her. She felt a pang of guilt as although what she said was true, the reason for leaving was as much to avoid any further potentially embarrassing outbursts from Adrienne, as wanting to be fresh for a morning run.

When she returned to clear away the coffee cups, Adrienne was surprised to see a further message from him. It was short, very short but it put a smile back on her face. It simply said, '*Thanks, x*'. That single letter word, between the 'w' and the 'y', sent by him meant a lot to her and she went to bed much happier for having received it.

On the following morning, an early mist over the airport delayed Theo's flight by an hour and he arrived in Brussels at 5.00 p.m. He texted Suzy that he was going to check them into a hotel for the night near the station and that he had also bought two tickets on the Eurostar train the following day and to round off a busy day, he was able to purchase a wheelchair to be make it easier for her to get about in. Her response had tickled him in that in addition to thanking him profusely, her main concern had been whether he had obtained first-class tickets on the Eurostar for their passage back to England. When he had confirmed that he had, she said, "Big kiss to you Monty, you have style. Bertie would have booked us into freight-class."

Twenty-four hours later they had arrived back in London. He had texted Anca that he was on his way, that he was bringing Suzy with him for dinner, that she would be staying for a while and to open up one of the unused bedrooms in the annex attached to the house.

When they got into the black cab at Kings Cross, he gave the address as his house. Suzy half-heartedly suggested that she could be dropped off in Holland Park where she kept an apartment but Theo would have nothing of it. She needed assistance for the next few days until she was well enough to hobble around. By the evening, they were back in his house and she was ensconced on her brother's sofa, foot up on a pouf and with Anca fussing over her.

"Is this the urgent family matter?" she asked Theo.

He nodded. "Ask her to tell you all the gory details. Suzy loves telling a yarn, don't you little sis?"

"Hey, it hurts!" she said, wiggling her foot around and holding up her bandaged arm.

"Don't let her boss you around, Anca," he said, taking her to one side. "You know Suzy, she will take advantage of any kindness."

"I don't mind Theo, honest," said Anca, smiling. "I like Suzy, she makes me laugh,"

As he climbed the stairs with weary legs, he could hear giggles and laughter coming from the room and it made him smile. Even with a serious injury like that, which would be very painful and would keep her off her feet for some six weeks and require physiotherapy and cuts and bruises over her body which would also hurt, Suzy was still able to hold court and put on a good show. He was pleased that she was staying with him, albeit because of unfortunate circumstances. Suzy was the most frequent visitor to his house, every two or three months she would fly in and at short notice say she was coming round to see him. He liked that spontaneity in her; she was the complete opposite to him, like his alter ego. In contrast, other members of his family, like his brother or other sister would rarely venture outside Wiltshire. They much preferred to stay in the country and ventured up only for business or some theatre production that would not be doing the rounds of the provinces. They would make him aware and they would meet up for dinner or drinks and on those occasions where they couldn't or didn't want to try and get back at night, they would accept his invitation to stay with him.

The warm water of the shower was very welcome. The overhead shower rained down on him, its soothing drops of water helping to gently wash away the aches and tension of the last two days. Instead of his usual two-minutes in and out shower, he lingered for much longer, playing back the day's proceedings, from the successful business conducted, meeting Abla after a break of nearly a quarter of a century and the rescue of his sister. But the last thought he had was what might be the scene in the Kiff household, hundreds of miles away in the Normandy countryside. He expected that Mr and Mrs Kiff would be none too pleased that their guest and their daughter's beau was absent from her side. They would no doubt feel slighted. He expected that and it was, he told himself, a perfectly natural reaction. But what irked him was that he had, through no fault of his own or anyone's for that matter, let Adrienne down. Yes, it could not be helped but he was not given to make promises that he could not keep.

"There'll be hell to play when she gets back," he thought.

He was sitting on his bed and in a contemplative mood. He had read the document given to him by Rashid Qubaisi and it was good news, very good news. Yet, instead of being really pleased in that it was looking like a significant step forward towards realising his ambition to move to the Middle East and the Persian Gulf, he felt somewhat deflated. It was a strange feeling and he did not readily understand why he was not feeling elated.

There was a gentle knock on the door and at his beckoning, Anca entered.

"Theo, how about I give you a massage? You look as if you need one," she said kindly. "Come on, lie down."

He needed no persuasion, lying face down on his bed and letting Anca's hands work their magic on him.

As she kneaded his back and shoulders, Anca said, "You know she loves you."

"Suzy? Of course. She and I are very close."

"Not Suzy, I meant Adrienne. She loves you, Theo," said Anca.

"Oh," he said but did not elaborate and Anca did not push him. She was loyal to him. It was obvious that he did not want to talk about it and that being so, it was not her place to probe any more. She had wanted to let him know that whilst he was away, she had got to know Adrienne. They had spent time together, cooking, drinking and going for walks in the park and they seemed to hit it off. She wanted to tell him that he came up as a topic of conversation all the time. She wanted to tell him that even as Adrienne was saying unflattering things about him, she would also tell Anca that he was always on her mind and that she missed him. She wanted to tell him that they had become closer and she had become fond of Adrienne and didn't want to see her hurt. But she uttered none of these words.

'Ah Theo, if only you knew,' she said silently.

By the end of the following day, Theo had arranged for a

professional helper to assist Suzy and made several appointments for her to see a physiotherapist to begin her rehabilitation.

"Theo, if you want to meet up with Adrienne, I am here to look after and entertain Suzy," Anca suggested.

He looked at her quizzically. "She told me," Anca explained.

He smiled wryly. "Is there anything she did not tell you?"

The WhatsApp message was simple. '*Family matter being managed. Can we still meet in Paris?*'

He was sitting in his office and reading through Rashid's proposal carefully, making notes and highlighting parts that might need clarification. A quick glance at his personal phone, showed two blue ticks next to his message. Adrienne had read the message. But there was no response from her. As he picked out the salient points from the proposal that he would present to the board, he glanced at his phone from time to time to see if there had been any response, even a negative one.

An hour later, it was time to go to the board and there was still no response from her. He shrugged. "No time to ponder on the whys and wherefores of the behaviour of others. It serves no purpose to try and second guess them," he muttered, as he walked briskly to the main boardroom.

Nicola was watching from her desk and the body language seemed to be very positive. He was sitting at the head of the table next to the chairman and there were many affirmative nods.

"So gentlemen, in conclusion I feel that this proposal from Mr Qubaisi is worthy of serious consideration and it is my recommendation that we enter into discussion with him and his representatives with a view to signing contracts by October.

"That's just four months away, Theo, can we move that fast?" was one of the questions from around the table.

"How much did you say the value was?"

He answered both questions and others with confidence, having anticipated and planned for these. He allowed himself the slightest of smiles as the board heartily endorsed his recommendation, topped by the chairman, a man not given to public displays of emotion, patting his shoulder after the others had trotted out of the room wearing big smiles.

"In thirty minutes, I have managed to outline a complex proposal to a group of level-headed individuals and persuaded them to back me and commit to my recommendation. Ten people, all of whom brook no nonsense, listened to what I propose with cold, dispassionate focus, all sold on what I had to say. I managed that with relative ease. Why can't I do that with matters outside of work?" he asked himself, as he returned to his desk to find that there had been no response to his message.

Back home, Suzy had started her rehabilitation and was in relative comfort and content. Philip had taken a shine to her and was ensconced on her lap as she stretched out on the sofa. She was reading a book when Theo poked his head around the door to announce his arrival. He could hear thumping above him and looked up.

"Exercising," she confirmed. He nodded.

"Monty, whilst she is not here, I wanted to ask if you and Anca are an item. I know she keeps house for you and she is young enough probably to be your daughter."

"For God's sake Suzy, I'm more than twenty-five years older than her."

"Yes, yes, I know all that Monty, she told me. But there is a definite spark between the two of you. Hey, as a liberated woman, with two ex-husbands I see no problem with the age difference if that is who you want as a life partner. Funny thing is, I had assumed that in recent years you had signed up to being a life member of the bachelor club. Bertie would like that very much if it stayed that way as he would have a much stronger case to usurp you as head of the family next year when dad hits eighty. But it would tickle me if you and Anca did become an item. Can you imagine the look on his face when you announced it! You must ensure I am there when you do that!" she said laughing, shaking to the point it was hurting her sides and she had to stop.

"I can assure you, that there is nothing going on between Anca and me, Suzy. I am, after all, her employer. We are close, as you have already observed and she is much more than just an employee, I consider Anca a friend and to an extent, a confidante. I see her more like the daughter that I never had and she sees me like a surrogate father. So very much a father-daughter type of relationship, no more than that. I would not be taking Anca to any family gathering to wind up Bertie or provide you with sport, for that matter. So, behave yourself and please, no mischief making."

"Who would you be taking to the next family gathering, which by the way, is just a few weeks away. Dad's birthday."

He stopped to think. At one time he had toyed with the idea of asking Adrienne to accompany him. Introducing her to his family would certainly put the cat amongst the pigeons. But what made him hesitant and chary about doing that was the real possibility of it being misconstrued by Adrienne as showing some sort of intent towards her. He was not yet sure as to whether he wanted to be taking any step that might ratchet up what he had going with her, if at all. Indeed, with the Rashid proposal looking very much like becoming a reality and seeing the prospect of a move to the Persian Gulf also getting nearer to becoming a reality, Theo was seeing having a relationship as being irrational. It would also be unfair to be misleading someone into thinking there was future in it, when clearly there was not. Yet, in the private recesses of his mind, he could admit that if it was going to be anyone that he would wish to introduce to the family it would be Adrienne.

"Currently there is no one who I will be taking to dad's birthday, Suzy," he said, trying not to display any sign of being resigned to the fact.

"Monty, it's me. Suzy, your little sister who you are talking to. Come on, beneath that veneer of calmness, I can see you are a troubled soul. Tell me, who is this person that is making you agitated?" she said and patted the sofa for him to sit next to her.

He looked up at the ceiling and the noise was still discernible, albeit it had changed. He explained that he had been seeing someone on and off but that it was not on solid ground and his business taking him to the Middle East had not helped. He was, in any case, feeling unsure as to whether to carry on or stop it altogether. He did not want to be making commitments and he acknowledged the unfairness of leading her on when it was futile. Better to end it before it got too far. He had not figured her or any other woman for that matter in his long-term plans.

"Oh dear, you are in a bit of a pickle, aren't you?" she said, as she took his hand in hers. "I'm afraid I can offer no advice, Monty. As you know, my life has not been a rip-roaring success when it comes to human relationships. Seems like you and I are destined to remain singletons for some time yet. Although between you and me I am very taken by the graphics designer, who has moved into the flat next to mine. We're having drinks next week, so wish me luck."

It made him chuckle.

Tears

It was Monday and he was boarding his early morning train with an air of calmness and poise. But that was no more than a disguise to hide the trepidation he felt at the possibility of being harangued by Adrienne, in full view of every commuter in that part of the carriage, so as to cause him maximum embarrassment. As he boarded the train, he steeled himself against the ominous prospect of being at the receiving end of her shrewish behaviour.

He looked into the carriage and he was relieved to see that she was not sitting in his seat, although he would have preferred it if she was not ensconced directly opposite him. He had no choice but to face her.

"Don't be ridiculous old chap, just act normal, after all you have done nothing wrong," he told himself.

"Good morning Kiffy," he said. "How are you keeping? You are looking well and rested," he said, smiling.

"I am, thank you," she replied.

Her terse reply did not bode well and he felt any further comment might just be stoking whatever fire was already in her belly. His strategy was to remain unflappable and good-natured and not respond to any provocation or goading. To get to the end of the journey without being on the receiving end of any tirade or outburst was his aim. He could be patient.

'As Saint Augustine once said, 'Patience is the companion of wisdom',' he told himself, 'and I for one deem it wise to remain silent. This will be the longest thirty-three-minute journey I am making for more years than I can remember.'

As was his usual habit, Theo switched on his electronic tablet and launched Kindle so he could continue to read his current favourite subject, the history of the Sumerians. It fascinated him to read about one of the earliest recorded cultures that could be recognised as a civilisation, rather than just being bands of people hunting and gathering food together. It enthralled him to learn about their transition to modern man and recognisable community living with laws and rules they had formulated so that they function as a society, written down by paid experts whose sole job was to record transactions, laws, the accounts of traders, the history of the people and all done on clay tablets.

When he next looked up, the train was pulling into Clapham Junction and he dared hope that the journey would finish without incident.

'Just five more minutes to go and I will have escaped unscathed,' he told himself. 'Just three hundred seconds to go and then I can make my escape and I am off the hook.'

The train seemed to take an agonisingly long time before it lethargically pulled away from Clapham Junction. But much to his relief, as it began to accelerate, he could see the iconic, refurbished chimneys of Battersea Power station, now a sprawling development of luxury accommodation. Not wishing to risk making eye-contact with Adrienne, he continued to read about Sumerians although the words seemed to have been written in a different language, as he was finding himself reading the same sentence over and over again.

When at last there was an announcement that they would shortly be arriving at London Victoria, he began to relax from the tension that had been dogging him throughout the journey. In fact, as the train slowed in its approach to the platform to end their journey, Theo felt sufficiently confident after packing away his tablet to want to wish Adrienne a nice day, at the start of a new term following the Whitsun break.

In his determination not to make any eye contact whatsoever, it was not until he was actually about to leave the train that Theo looked up to speak to her and that was when he saw that tears were running down her cheeks. She was quietly whimpering, her eyes red from crying and cheeks flushed with emotion. It came as a shock to see her crying like that and he felt his stomach tighten. Yet to the outside world, he was the model of calm behaviour. Despite the sight of a visibly emotional woman in front of him, he remained steadfastly calm and collected.

As others left the carriage and hurried on their way to work, he was left alone with her, feeling acutely uncomfortable with the situation but doing his best not to show it.

He was inclined to stay in his seat as if it was a haven, a place of emotional safety but convention dictated that he should do something, a gesture that acknowledged that there was an upset person and that they needed comforting. He slid out of his seat awkwardly and shuffled next to Adrienne, gingerly putting his arm around her, only resting it on her shoulder once he was sure that it would not be met by a negative reaction.

"You are upset," he said and winced at saying such a crass thing. She looked at him abruptly and said sarcastically,

"Oh, you noticed?"

"Sorry I was too absorbed in my book," he said, meekly.

"Do you even care that I am upset?" she said, through teary eyes.

"Yes, of course, I do," he said and tried to pull her closer to him but she was resisting.

"Care to hazard a guess as to what might have caused me to be upset?"

"I would rather not hazard a guess and listen to you telling me instead. And, may I suggest we get off the train before it starts to leave once again. Let's go to Leon's and have a sit down and talk," he suggested, warmly.

She looked around to see people had started to board the train. "Come on," he said, squeezing her shoulder.

He stood up and offered his hand and she took it, much to his relief. It felt good to feel her hand in his and he gently squeezed it affectionately.

She chose a table that looked out onto the concourse, with its cavernous interior held up by a pair of soaring, Victorian, wrought-iron columns. The people traffic was increasing as train after train pulled in and workers from all parts of southern England from Kent in the east, Sussex in the south and even as far as Hampshire in the west, all converging on Victoria in transit to their jobs in London and thereabouts. Thousands and thousands of them. Yet, as she waited for him to bring coffee and watched them pass by Leon's, Adrienne felt deflated. Instead of feeling refreshed and revitalised from having had a week's rest away from the frenetic pace of teaching in one of the most demanding schools in the country, she felt dispirited and out of sorts. Anyone walking near her table would see someone looking glum and down, and looking as if she would rather be elsewhere.

"There. I don't know if you had any time for breakfast beforehand so I also got some croissants and avocado on wholemeal toast. That seems to be popular with people nowadays and being old-fashioned, a bacon roll for me," he said, as he put down the tray of food and drinks.

He placed a coffee in front of her. It was black, as he remembered that was how she took it. She took a sip of the bitter, hot liquid but remained silent.

"Shall I start, Kiffy? Let me repeat first what I said earlier, I do care for you." Adrienne sneered at that.

"Yes, yes I get it you are upset with me and you're probably thinking that I am just saying that to appease you. But you know me well enough by now to know that I only say what I mean. I am not given to petty words. I have missed you this last week and I am very disappointed we did not meet in Paris. You may not believe me but I spent a considerable amount of time and energy to ensure that I could get to Paris so we could be together."

"You did not come to Normandy with me though, did you?" she said, accusingly.

"That could not be helped as my text indicated," he reminded her.

"How convenient for this urgent family matter to coincide with going with me to meet my parents. Do you know how hurtful that was? Do you know how humiliating that was to turn up to my parents' place without my boyfriend, someone who they had been looking forward to meeting and having to tell them that you were not going to show."

"Did you not tell them about my text?"

"Yes, I did but they were no more convinced that it wasn't a pretext so that you would not be coming than I was. Flint, why didn't you just be honest and say you did not want to come with me when I invited you. I would not have been happy but I could have respected that. Instead, you did not show up inventing a, what is that lovely English phrase, 'a cock and bull story', about an urgent family matter which has miraculously been resolved. You are and I will use a legal term, so you can better understand how I feel, guilty as charged!"

He shook his head and pondered how to respond to a wounding remark that he knew in his heart not to be true. He muttered quietly, "*actus non facit reum nisi mens sit rea.*"

"What did you say?" she said, accusingly. "Are you saying

something rude about me?"

"No, not all. It wasn't meant for your ears. It's just a legal term which means that an act does not make a person guilty unless the mind should be guilty. So in my case, as the defendant, I am guilty of missing your trip to see your parents, I accept that. Guilty as charged as you say. But my mind was not guilty; it had not been my intention to do so, just unfortunate circumstances," he said earnestly.

Before she could respond he put his hand up and said firmly, "Hear me out." He then went on to explain what had happened, leaving nothing out.

There were tears in her eyes. "You could have saved me a lot of sadness if you only you had told me this, Flint. You could have stopped me from hating you all this time. You could have stopped my parents for berating me for having a cold-hearted Englishman for a boyfriend," she said but there was just a hint of her tone softening.

"Is that what they said? And did you not defend me?"

"No, I agreed with them!" she said and there was the faintest of smiles as she said that. "Well, that is what you are, Flint. Cold and unfeeling, emotionally impotent, unable to say just a few crumbs of comfort, a word of explanation that might make all the difference."

He was finding it difficult to remain stoic in the face of her attack on his character. "I did state why I could not make it," he insisted. "Was that not enough for you to trust me?"

"No, it was not! Flint, why couldn't you just say Suzy got hit by a car and that she was in hospital and you were going to her assistance?"

"Because it was not in my gift to do that, Kiffy."

"What do you mean?"

"When Suzy told me what had happened to her, she did not give her consent for me to pass on that information to anybody else at the time. Indeed, our parents still do not know that she has been injured in a car accident."

"Couldn't you just tell me? Could you not trust me?" she said, pointing to herself.

"I'm afraid not, Kiffy. A confidence is only a confidence if it is not passed on. If I told you, I would be betraying that confidence and therefore a trust. Confidence and trust are of paramount importance in that situation. Do you not see that?"

"No, I don't! You and your family are so secretive! No wonder England has the best secret service in the world; you are all born to it. It comes naturally to you all," she said, smiling.

She picked up a croissant and started to munch on it. It made him happy to see her do that.

'Light at the end of the tunnel as far as hostilities go. Armistice,' he told himself.

The cold bacon roll was tasting a lot better than it did earlier. She seemed to be back to her chatty self and he dared to lift her hand up and kiss it.

"Kiffy, I need to get to my office as I have an important management briefing to attend. But in the spirit of glasnost, I can tell you that I am flying out on Sunday night and that I will be gone for two to three weeks."

"Again? The Arabs see you more than I do or do you have an Arab girlfriend out there, Flint?"

"We are trying to conclude a piece of business for a client before the start of Ramadan when everything grinds to a halt for a month. It is in a deeply religious country and they observe fasting and praying throughout Ramadan, when it makes doing business nigh on impossible then."

"Okay, I suppose you must go, it's your job," she said, sadly. "Perhaps I should move there and that way I'll get to see more of you."

"I don't think you'd like it there, Kiffy. It would not fit in with your, how can I put it, bubbly personality. For a start, you could not wear that blouse, which by the way the top button has come undone and you are exposing, erm, aspects of your chest. You would not be allowed to walk anywhere alone and you and I could not be seen together as we are not married to each other nor are we members of the same family. We would get arrested and there would be a good chance of one or both of us getting whipped for offending public decency."

"Do you want me to button up, Flint?"

"It is not for me to say, it is up to you," he shrugged.

"Stop being such a cold Englishman and tell me how you feel about me exposing my chest!"

"Button up!" he said, raising his voice and then added in a more moderated voice, "Must go or I'll be late."

He bent down and kissed her on the cheek and rushed off before she had time to react.

Adrienne was smiling again, finished her coffee and croissant and bit into his half-eaten bacon roll and spat it out. "Why do the English believe it is okay to put a pig between two slices of bread like that!"

As she headed for the exit to the street, she received a WhatsApp message from him.

'*Forgot. Meant to invite you round for dinner tonight. I'll rustle up something for us.*'

She grinned from ear to ear. '*Prefer you come to my flat and I'll cook something instead. Have brought back some lovely French food from Normandy. Xxx*'

'*Okay, look forward to it. X*' came the reply.

"Even in his text he is mean with his kisses. Just the one, couldn't do two or three. Not Flint, just the one," she chortled with delight. "At least I will have him all to myself again."

For the next three days he was a daily visitor to her flat but did not stay the night on any of those days, nether was he invited to do that. Instead, after dinner, as the days were now longer and the sun did not set until well into the late evening, they went for walks. The first walk felt the most awkward for him as she insisted on holding hands and, as they passed other walkers also out enjoying the balmy evening, he was acutely conscious of what they might be thinking, seeing an obviously much older man holding hands with a very much younger woman; a stunningly beautiful woman at that. If he had been in their shoes, he might even have concluded that an old man was with a lady of the night which he had hired for the evening. Adrienne was not exactly dressed modestly either. Going braless and wearing just a thin, white, cotton t-shirt and loose-fitting shorts that showed off her long, slim legs, now tanned after a week in Normandy, further drew attention to them. Inasmuch as he was the beneficiary of being in the company of French womanhood, he was not enamoured at being the subject of the idle curiosity of passers-by. The occasional looks, with just the briefest of eyes upon them before it became too obvious, which Adrienne seemed oblivious too, made him uneasy and even embarrassed.

'If it is going to be like this just walking down the street, what might it become if this became more serious. We would be like performers in a circus. Clowns to be laughed at?'

"Penny for your thoughts, Flint," she said, as they sat in one of the outside tables of a coffee shop.

"Nothing really," he said, wistfully.

"Come on Flint, stop being so middle-class English and tell me how you feel. It's good for the…"

"A dirty, old man," he blurted out.

"Pardon?"

"It might be construed by an independent observer that I am behaving not unlike a dirty, old man who is taking his squeeze out on a date." he said.

"What is a squeeze, Flint? I have not heard of that expression before."

"A squeeze is a girl who is not one's girlfriend but he is in a sexual relationship with that person. Given the obvious age difference between us and that you are ravishingly attractive and how can I put it, dressed in a certain way that is most alluring, someone might conclude that."

She was silent for a moment. "Hmm, well most of that is true, Flint. Is it not? You are much older and we are in sexual relationship. But the difference is I am your girlfriend, at least, what was it you said? Aspiring to become your girlfriend," she giggled. "As to what I am wearing, well it is a warm evening and I am a free Frenchwoman and at liberty to dress how I please. Isn't it ironic that in this country if you wear summer clothes it attracts attention and some people will label you as being a slut, or as you put it, someone's 'squeeze'? And if you decide to cover from head to foot, you also attract attention and someone puts a 'terrorist' label on you. I am sorry if it makes you feel uncomfortable, Flint. Do you want me to dress differently, Flint? Is that it? Shall I wear a longer pair of shorts or trousers even and maybe a sweatshirt on top of my t-shirt?"

He chuckled. "One of the things I missed last week, one of many things, is listening to you when you talk about something with rousing passion."

"Speaking of passion, what about sex with me? Did you miss that too or was someone taking care of this for you?" she said, putting her hand under the table and for the briefest of moments running her fingers up his leg and on his crotch.

"Kiffy! For heaven's sake this is a public place," he said, looking around to see if anyone had noticed them.

She giggled her delight at seeing his awkwardness.

"Whilst I remember," he said, recovering his poise, "I was planning to go down to Bournemouth this weekend for a short break before flying out. Thinking of leaving Friday after work and returning Sunday afternoon. I was wondering whether you would like to join me. That is if you have no other plans or commitments."

Adrienne looked at him in that coquettish, suggestive way that he just knew she was about to say something designed to embarrass him.

"Flint, are you inviting me to have a dirty weekend away with you? Brighton would be better for that. It is famous for it!"

He stiffened. Sitting up straight and putting his coffee cup down, he looked at her but did not wish to react, not least because it was said loud enough for one of the two young women at the next table, to glance in their direction and smile.

"Oh look, is it that time already? It's getting late and I have a few things I want to go over before I turn in," he said and pushed his chair backwards.

"Okay, if that's what you want," she said, miffed at the dismissive way he had decided to end their evening. She stood up and started walking away.

The girl who had listened to Adrienne's comment, now watched him tuck his chair back under the table and turn to follow her. They made brief eye contact and he couldn't help but say quietly, "it's not like that."

"Better run after her," she said, giggling.

Theo quickened his pace and caught up with Adrienne who appeared not to have noticed his presence. He walked alongside her and tried to catch her eye but she was having nothing of it, purposefully turning as if to look at the shop windows so that he could be left in no doubt that she was choosing to ignore him. In fact, all the way to the gated-entrance of her apartment block she chose to look away from him.

'St Augustine, are you sure I am being wise for being patient with putting up with this puerile behaviour? If it is then, I can tell you that my patience is wearing thin,' he told himself.

She punched in the numbers for the side door to open and was about to enter, when he grabbed her arm and pulled her towards him. She tried to resist as he kissed her but he persevered and his lips made contact with hers. She tried to pull away but he held her head and kissed her firmly.

She raised her hand up to his chest and was about to push him away when he stopped kissing her and loosened his hold.

"Enough of this play flighting, Kiffy. I'm going to Bournemouth for a little break. I am inviting you to join me. No wait. I would be very happy if you would accompany me but if you don't want…"

"Brighton. I prefer Brighton," she said.

"Well, I am going to Bournemouth. Not Brighton," he said firmly.

"There's more things to do in Brighton," she explained.

"Look Kiffy. I'm sorry to say this but the location is not up for negotiation. I am going to Bournemouth, not Brighton. I'm staying at the Highcliffe Hotel. Before you say anything disparaging about it, I am aware that the Hilton is more modern and swankier but the Highcliffe is more traditional and cosier and quiet, almost to the point where some may consider it boring. But I like it. I have booked a room which overlooks the bay and the sea beyond. It is very relaxing to just sit in an armchair by the window, with a cup of tea in one hand and a book in the other. It appeals to someone of my generation but is not for all."

She was silent for a moment and looked at him intently, wearing a scowl. He was losing patience and was about to turn away when she said, "Okay," and smiled.

He nodded. "Great. I'll pick you up, say around six. Goodnight, Kiffy."

"Thank you for inviting me, Flint. It was very thoughtful," she said in a conciliatory tone and kissed him on the cheek.

My pleasure, Kiffy."

"No, that's to come," she said giggling.

"Kiffy, you are incorrigible."

"You don't want that, Flint? I can be a stuck-up English woman, Flint? I can pretend to be like that all weekend, if you want," she teased. "Do you want that, Flint?"

In answer, he put his hands around her slim waist and yanked her nearer to him, until she could feel his breath on her face and his eyes were meeting hers. She did not resist as he kissed her once again. This time, her sensuous lips were responding to the touch of his own with equal feeling.

"No. I would prefer you to be the passionate, charming, fiery Frenchwoman that you are," he whispered in her ear. "Now I've got to take off. See you on the train."

"Hey Flint, you don't fancy a warm up tonight?" she giggled.

He laughed, got into his little Micra and quickly drove off before he succumbed to the temptation on offer from her, that was standing there waving him off.

On Friday, as Adrienne did not have any teaching classes after lunch, they agreed to set out early to avoid the Friday night rush out of town and at two o'clock he was parked outside her apartment block, waiting for her to come down. It was a warm and bright afternoon and the sky was clear except for a few high-altitude, thin clouds.

"Kiffy!" he called out, waving to her when he saw her looking around for him.

She was dressed in a pair of jeans and a white t-shirt with thin horizontal blue stripes. "As charming as ever," he muttered quietly. "Oh Kiffy, you do know how to drive me wild."

"Wow! A new car, Flint? What's happened to the Micra, Did you sell it?" she said, kissing him. She walked around the open-topped silver blue sports car that he was leaning against.

"No, the Micra is in the garage. I decided as it is a lovely day and we are going for a country drive, I would take out this little friend of mine. Do you like it?" he said, running his hand along the sleek body.

"Yes, très chic. Very cool, indeed but I don't recognise it. What is it?" she said smiling.

"It is a 1961 Austin Healey. I bought it some years ago off a friend who bought it as an investment but decided not to keep it in the end. Stays in the garage most of the time. I don't use it around town; there is no point as the Micra is a perfect run-around for that. But today, as the forecast is for good weather, rather than be cooped up in the Micra, I thought you might like to be driven down to Bournemouth, with the hood down and wind in the hair. Could make for a pleasant drive. What do you think?"

"Could be even more pleasant if you would let me drive it. Can I, Flint?" she asked sweetly, putting her arm around him.

"Ha-ha, Anca has also asked the same thing and I will say the same thing to you as I said to her. Which is I would let you but you are not insured on it."

"Never mind, it will still be fun sitting in it," she said, as she dropped her bag on the back seat next to his and made her way round to the passenger seat, running her fingers along the body, caressing the smooth finish. Theo ran around quickly and opened the car door for her. She blew him a kiss which turned into a real one, when he reached across for the car seat belt to strap her in.

"Mmm, you're wearing my favourite perfume," he noted, as he kissed her neck.

"But of course," she said.

As they drove off, he said, "I have to confess, I don't like anyone but me to drive this car, insurance has nothing whatsoever to do with it. It is mine and I don't like to share it."

"I knew that, Flint. I could see it in your eyes that this was your baby and no charming French woman, not even the Queen of England would be allowed to drive it!" she giggled. "And don't think I was fooled by you coming around to open the door for me. You were just afraid that I might slam it. Not so?"

"Correct," he said, relieved that his confession about the car had been taken in good spirit.

"So English! A middle-class, privately-educated schoolboy, no way would you want to share," she teased him, stroking the back of his head as they got on to the motorway.

"That's right, Kiffy. I don't like to share certain things. That goes for women too, Kiffy. What's mine is mine in that regard too," he said. "Don't like to share a woman."

"Am I your woman then, Flint? I thought I was only, what was that wonderful term for me you used, your aspirational girlfriend? Has something changed?" she giggled.

"Sorry, didn't hear a word you said, Kiffy. Must be the wind, all this open-topped driving; I forgot about the noise," he laughed.

“Ha-ha, very funny Englishman!” she said but did not press him on it, as she was quietly pleased.

‘For the first time he has referred to me as his woman,’ she told herself. ‘Not his girlfriend, but his woman. Hmm, progress. Flint you don’t know how happy that makes me.’

A Dirty Weekend

The hotel that Theo had in mind was not the most modern or luxurious but its position high up on a cliff had great appeal. When he wanted somewhere quiet, away from the buzz of the City or the heat of the Middle East, the Highcliffe hotel, away from busy roads, overlooking the sea was a respite; a tonic for the overworked senses. At the Highcliffe, there would not be any rowdy parties going on, it did not attract that kind of clientele and when he could spare the time, he would book a short break here and come down, with the minimum of packing in an old, leather holdall and a couple of books to read. Any time of the year, even when it was cold and windy, rain pelting down on the large windows, he would sit there and wile away the hours on his own. It was a world away from contracts and procurements, tenders and bids. Here there was no need for legal professional privilege.

Some two hours later they had pulled up into the car park of the Highcliffe Hotel. He looked around and found a space well away from any people carrier or cheap car, whose owner might carelessly fling the door open and damage the paintwork on his beloved AH as he called it.

"Blenkinsop. Until now I didn't know that was your surname," she said, as they got into the lift. "So, you signed us in as Mr and Mrs Theodore Blenkinsop. Why did you do that? Why not as we are?"

"It raises less questions. Easier if people think we are a married couple," he said lamely.

"And you think she believed you?"

He shrugged.

"It was the look on her face, Flint. She tried not to show it, very subtle but she could see that you are much older than me and the look was saying, I know what you are up to."

"Do you care?"

"I guess I don't, otherwise I wouldn't be here. Flint, are you not worried that people might see you as an old man with his tart!"

"Kiffy. In matters of human relationships, I try not to guess what other people are thinking about me. I am only master of my own thoughts and nobody else's. I am here for a short break and with the person I would like most to be with me doing just that. What other people think, I do not give a jot for. Does that work for you? If you are having cold feet about it, then we can go back downstairs and I can book another, separate room for you," he said, as he took the plastic swipe card from his pocket outside their bedroom door.

She smiled at him, took the card from his hand and swiped the door open. He pressed down the handle and gestured for her to proceed.

"Oh, wow. A suite. And what a view," she said, walking to the windows and looking out on to the calm waters of the English Channel, glistening in the early, evening sun. "Flint, this is a great choice and I can see why you just like to sit here and read your book. It is a beautiful view."

"Glad you like it, Kiffy. As I said, it is cosy, not too ostentatious and it does have that view. I have stayed in the best hotels in Brighton and none have this view, not even the Grand. And as we are high up, there is no passing traffic and no noise. Peaceful and quiet," he said and walked up until he was right behind her, pressing himself against her.

He leaned down and kissed her neck, before his hand slipped around her waist and she felt the belt of her trousers being undone and the zip being pulled down.

"Flint! What are you doing?" she said quietly.

"About that dirty weekend. I thought we might make a start on it before we go out to dinner," he whispered in her ear, as he dropped her trousers down to her ankles and then unzipped himself.

"Flint, you naughty boy. Is this what a respectable Englishman should be doing?" she said.

Reaching behind her, she took hold of his manhood and positioned it to where its owner wanted it to go and then felt its stiffness as it slowly entered her. She stayed leaning on the window as they made love, tenderly at first and then more urgently as their passions rose.

"We really are dirty," she said, as an hour later they were sitting in a fish restaurant and tucking into their starter course of scallops.

"You wanted it that way, Kiffy. I did say we should shower first but you said you were too hungry to spend time in the shower!" he laughed.

"I didn't know you were going to take me like that. I thought that it was going to be an end of evening thing, Flint," she said.

"Ssh, quieter please," he said. "Sorry, I don't know what got into me. I just saw you like that, irresistible and I er…"

"Hey Flint, don't apologise," she interrupted. "I liked it. I loved it. Still making me tingle. Such raw passion, never knew you had it in you, Flint. So…"

"I know what you are going to say, 'so not English'!"

"Actually, I was going to say that it was so unexpected but lovely. I felt very close to you," she said and then leaning over whispered, "in spite of the fact that all I could see was the waves ebbing and flowing as you were making love to me. It was very sensuous!"

When the main course came, Adrienne expertly took the lobster apart as she talked about her holiday with her parents, about the farm and how it was part of the local community and so on. He listened attentively to what she had to say, enjoying the animated and detailed way she described everything, gesticulating and pulling faces in turn. He couldn't help but laugh and smile.

'Perhaps I could take her with me,' he mused.

After dinner, they decided to go for a walk along the promenade. He suggested in the opposite direction to the pier and explained that on a Friday night it would be quite noisy.

"Let's walk down to the beach, Flint. Come on let's take our shoes off and walk by the water's edge," said Adrienne. She did not wait for his response, pulled off her sandals and skipped off the boardwalk and onto the sand.

Theo removed his socks, folding and tucking them into his trouser pocket, before following her with some trepidation down to the water. The waves gently lapped the shore and there was minimal splashing. The water felt cool and refreshing and was illuminated by the lights of the promenade and the now distance pier lights.

After a few minutes, they returned hand in hand back to the promenade walk, washing their feet in a beach shower put there for that purpose.

"That was lovely wasn't it, Flint?"

"Yes, it was, not as cold as I thought it was going to be. Felt good.

Was worried that you might fall in and then I would have to rescue you," he joked.

"Might have to give me mouth-to-mouth resuscitation, hey Flint. How is your mouth-to-mouth resuscitation?"

"Don't know, I think I might need some practice."

"Care to practice on me?" she said and pulled him against a retaining wall and kissed him passionately, unrestrained and with not a care in the world if anyone was watching.

Out of the corner of his eye and some distance afar off, Theo could make out the shape of figures heading in their direction and gently tried to disentangle himself from her arms, which held him around the neck tightly. They managed to straighten up just in time as the figures became a couple, with a dog in tow. Strolling passed them, the elderly lady wished them a 'good evening'. Theo did not want to make eye contact and he made a pretence of pointing to an object out to sea.

"You're going to get us into trouble, if you pounce on me like that, Kiffy. Best left to the privacy of our bedroom, I think. Don't want to be done for public indecency, do we?"

"Quelle rabat-joie!" she said, giggling as she twirled on the spot, arms out like a ballerina.

"Meaning?" he asked.

Adrienne took hold of his hand and kissed it. "Flint, don't be such a, what's that English phrase? Oh yes, a stick in the mud!"

"Hmm, maybe I am. But I value my career and I would hate to put that in jeopardy for a bit of public hanky-panky. As a lawyer, I don't think I could argue in front of a magistrate that I was ignorant of the law."

"Flint, sometimes you have to take a risk in order to embrace life, to enjoy what you enjoy, when you want to. And if it is passion, seize the moment, don't wait to get back to the seclusion of a hotel bedroom as the moment will be lost. Take off that English upper-class yoke that sits on your shoulders and unburden yourself. Be free. Enjoy the freedom of not having to live by everyone else's rules. Unburden yourself of what convention expects of you. Let yourself go now and again."

"Isn't being here with a young woman some twenty years younger than me, freeing myself from that yoke as you put it? Isn't sharing my bed with a woman young enough to be my daughter, not bucking convention? Or am I missing something?"

"Yes, it is Flint and don't you feel better for having a young woman share your bed?" she teased.

It was a question said light-heartedly but it was food for thought. It had rankled on more than one occasion on the drive down, as to how he would feel about eyes upon him being with a younger woman. He did not like to draw attention to himself and as much as he wanted to be with Adrienne from the moment they had checked in, he could not shake off the feeling of awkwardness and embarrassment at how their liaison might be perceived.

"Do you want to go back to the hotel?" she asked.

"I am not in a hurry to go back," he said, shrugging. "We can stroll further along this promenade. There's a small road with a great view at the top, that winds up the hill and we can take that route back to the hotel if you like. Or we can just turn around and go back. Whichever you want."

"Let's be adventurous and go on, Flint. Forwards is always better. Going back the way we came is familiar and boring, no excitement in doing that is there?"

By the time they had reached the gap in the cliff front, the sun was setting on the horizon and he was relieved as it gave him some cover from prying eyes that would look in their direction, especially as Adrienne was being playful and drawing attention to them.

They stopped to watch the sun slowly disappear and go into hiding, signalling that the day was over and it was the start of darkness.

Taking her hand, Theo led Adrienne to the little map that showed where they were and he pointed out the path they would have to take to return to the hotel. The hill road was steeper than Adrienne had expected and after initially marching ahead, her steps became more laboured and ponderous and he could see by the soft glow of the street light that she was becoming out of breath.

"Not too far to go now," he said reassuringly, as he put his arm around her, taking the strain off her.

"Flint, I'm tired," she moaned. "Can't walk anymore!"

With a combination of encouragement and cajoling and a promise of running a bath for her when they got back, he managed to get Adrienne to climb a set of steps that led to a short-cut, across the gardens at the top where the ground was level and the going easier. It pepped her up and she was able to walk on her own unaided, even skipping to the railings where there was a gap in the vegetation and she could look out to sea from this elevated position.

"It's beautiful here, Flint," she said. "It was worth coming this way even if my lungs nearly burst with exhaustion. Wow! What a view! From this high up you can see for miles and miles into the distance. It is lovely. Very romantic with the moonlight. Very impressed, Flint."

"Not such a stick in the mud, then. What did you call me, a joyless rabbit!" he said, pinning her to the railing and kissing her deeply, his hands snaking into her jeans, finding their way to the smooth cheeks of her bottom, pressing her to him in a hungry passionate embrace, before letting her go.

Adrienne was breathless with desire for him and couldn't understand why he stopped abruptly.

"Flint?" she said, looking to him for an explanation.

"We stiff, upper-class English folk call it the starter. And like all good starters it is a taster for the main course," he said, laughing.

"Main course?"

"Yes, that's back at the hotel. None of this two-minute, flash fry, Ryan Air, EasyJet sex that you French are good at. We go for the long haul, not rushed, enjoyment of the finest England has to offer," he said proudly and kissed Adrienne one more time, before linking his arm with hers and leading her in the direction of the hotel.

Just as they were clearing the railings, she abruptly twirled out of his arm and reached out to cling to one, holding it tightly as if her life depended on it.

Theo was taken aback and muttered to himself, "What now?"

"I'm not sure I want to go back and receive British Airways love-making, Flint. After all, not many people like BA, always coming bottom for the service they provide," she said. Theo wasn't sure whether this was yet another tease and she was just feigning or she was taunting him. Either way, it was too dark to tell by looking at the expression on Adrienne's face and the tone in her voice had not given away any clue either.

He shook his head and sat on the park bench opposite. 'Too old to play these games, and at this rate, we may as well go straight into breakfast when we get back,' he told himself.

He could discern her walking towards him and then lean down as if to kiss him and just as he was craning his neck and puckering his lips, she pulled away. "Race you back," she said and then she was off.

"For one who is supposedly tired, there's some speed in those lovely, long legs!" he called, as he trotted off after her.

Back in their hotel room, he lay on the bed as she started to undress. "Hey! Stop ogling me, Flint. Get up. You promised to run me a bath."

"I did, didn't I?" he said and jumping off the bed, reaching for her, unable to resist the temptation to caress her bottom as he walked past her to the bathroom.

As the bath slowly filled up, he looked at himself in the mirror, examining his chin for any tell-tale signs of stubble.

'What are you doing here, Theodore?' he asked himself but he did not have time to consider that question, as Adrienne walked in, naked as the day she was born and pressed herself against his back, looking at him in the mirror, her long, dark hair in contrast to his short, greying mop.

"Ever thought of shaving this?" she said, reaching around him to his manhood.

"No, certainly not!

"Rabat-joie!" she giggled.

"It's too high maintenance. All I hear from women who have done it, is that it itches and needs constant attention and who am I to disagree?" he explained.

"Seen any totally naked ones then have you, Flint?" she teased, as she started to stroke him.

He turned around to face her. "In recent memory, only yours, Kiffy," he said. "Looks like it could do with a shave."

As he put his hand down to confirm his observation, she brushed his hand away and lowered herself into the bath.

"Hey Flint, come into the bath with me, sit in front and I will wash you," she gestured with a soapy sponge.

He had always regarded washing himself a strictly private matter and not one to be shared and he hesitated before trudging towards the bath. "Are you sure? Perhaps I can go first and then leave you to it. I won't take long, just a few minutes at most."

"Come on in, Flint. You need to wash and I want to soak. There is only one bath in here, so get in with me and then you can go so I can relax in peace," she explained.

In a thrice, Theo was washed and out, wrapped in a hotel bathrobe, lying under the covers of the bed and flicking through the various TV channels until he came to his favourite channel, Al Jazeera news. He turned the volume right down until it was barely audible so that he could be alerted to when Adrienne was going to enter the room and could quickly switch to another channel. He was in no doubt she would see him in a poor light, if she caught him watching news whilst on a romantic weekend away. He was loathed to give her ammunition to fire yet another unflattering epithet at him. He hardly bothered with TV, yet watching the news, particularly world news, was one of the few categories of broadcasting that he could watch with interest. News, live news and world news in particular, be it illegal logging in the Amazon, or a sad tale of exploitation in

Africa, tensions in the Middle East or the fractious complexities of US foreign relations, it was engaging and engrossing as far as he was concerned. "Gourmet food for the mind," he'd once told a friend.

When Adrienne emerged from the bathroom, the TV was switched off and there was not a sound in the room save for the air conditioner above. Complete silence. Theo was sitting propped up with several pillows, a book open on his lap, but as far as she could tell he was already in the world of dreams.

"Hmm, so much for long haul love making," she sighed, hands on hips as she stood next to the bed. "Maybe I am too tired anyway."

But she smiled with contentment as just having him be with her was making her feel as close to his body and soul, as that of making love itself.

Adrienne knelt up on the bed and took the book away, frowning when she read the cover, 'Sumerian Mythology'. 'Clever boy but not exactly bedtime reading,' she mused. She switched off all the lights and tiptoed back to bed, standing over it and looking at Theo for any signs of movement. Other than his chest gently moving up and down, he was perfectly still.

"Flint, everyone is telling me it's insane and in truth, I don't even know why myself but whatever the reason, I am madly in love you," she said in a whisper and she leaned across to plant a peck on his cheek.

She climbed into bed and gently nudged him until he had slid down and was lying on his side facing her, very much asleep. Adrienne ran her lips over his and then twisted and turned her body until she was lying in a spoon position next to him, taking his arm gently and draping it around her. She could feel his breath on her. It was gentle and warm and Adrienne smiled.

"For the avoidance of doubt, you are sleeping next to your girlfriend," she whispered and taking his hand, she interlocked her fingers with his.

It was in the early hours of the following morning when Theo awoke suddenly, momentarily feeling disoriented. Looking at Adrienne, curled up in the foetal position next to him, he was in two minds as whether to risk disturbing her with a kiss. He decided against it and instead, slipped out of bed and walked barefoot over to the window, pulling the curtains just wide enough apart so that he could look out. The sun had not yet climbed above the horizon but what was left of the waning moon provided sufficient light to illuminate the sea in front of him. It was no better than a torch light whose batteries were running low but it created, what looked like, a blue grey film above the surface of the water, smooth and silky. He nodded his appreciation of the scene painted by nature for him to enjoy. Turning back to the bed, he was minded to take his book and sit by the window and read. But then he looked at the beautiful, naked woman lying in his bed. It was no contest, the book could wait.

Cuddling up next to Adrienne, he started to plant little kiss after little kiss on her face, her nose, her lips. His hands were not idle, finding their way down her warm body, teasing her nipples until she opened her eyes.

"Flint! What are you doing?" she said, sleepily.

"Making good on the statement I made earlier," he whispered in her ear.

"What time is it?" she yawned, as she stretched her arms out and around his neck.

"Time to make love," he said, gently pushing her onto her back.

Theo pulled her arms up and above her head, holding them there as he smothered her with kiss after kiss, deep and passionate. When he let her go, he was already kissing his way down her neck and then inching lower and lower until his lips were running over where his fingertips had just been. He lingered there, flicking his tongue over each nipple in turn. It had the desired effect as he could feel hands on his head, fingers ruffling his hair. Then he felt a gently push on his head. Words were unnecessary, he knew what she wanted and he started to kiss his way slowly, teasingly slowly downwards.

They made it to breakfast just in time before the buffet was about to close. Adrienne spoke to the chef sweetly and he was persuaded to make her an omelette. Theo looked on in admiration. 'How easily she can turn on that charm that men find so irresistible. How I find it irresistible,' he laughed, as he loaded crispy bacon, sausages and fried eggs onto his plate.

They sat away from the boisterous noise coming from families and their young children that were already there having their breakfast. A little boy kneeled up on his chair and was looking back at them. He caught Adrienne's eye and she waved to him, which elicited a show of his dinosaur toy for her to see. When she smiled in acknowledgement, he beamed a chubby-faced smile back at her.

"I think I have a new admirer," she said, "pity he is only three or four years old."

"One of your many, I'm sure. I bet those pubescent school boys at Westminster, are attracted to you too," he remarked.

"Jealous, Flint?"

"No. Should I be?"

"Are you asking me if I am being faithful to you, Flint?"

He put his knife and fork down for a moment and said quietly, "Look, what you do in your private life is up to you. I don't have any call on you."

"So, if I was to have sex with someone else you wouldn't mind? Is that what you are saying, Flint?" she said, trying to contain her rising anger.

"I did not say that. But we have not really talked about, how can I put it, the boundaries in our social relationship," he said, awkwardly.

"Boundaries. What sort of bullshit is that?" she said, angrily. "Why don't you stop being so uptight, middle-class English and ask me straight if I am fucking anyone else. That's what you really want to know isn't it, Flint? You are so infuriating!" she said and got up to leave.

He looked around and aside from an elderly couple, who briefly looked up and then away in good manners, no one else seemed to have noticed.

"Good bacon," he said as he got up, swigged the last drop of tea in his cup and left to go back to the room. She was not there.

Theo put on his jacket and took hers with him. She was standing there outside, looking out to the sea. He walked up to her and put her jacket around her shoulders. Standing next to her, he could see her eyes had shed tears and he was irritated with himself for having made her upset.

"I apologise for my inappropriate language at breakfast," he said and put his arm around her shoulder.

She shook it off as she turned to him. "Just because I am French and open and friendly and smile when someone smiles at me, all the things you are not, do you take me to be a whore!" she said, fiercely.

"No, of course not," he said, as he tried to wipe away her tears with his handkerchief.

She resisted at first but he persisted and she allowed him to do it

"You do not know me, Flint. Despite what you might think, I do not sleep around. If I am your girlfriend then I am with you and only you. But of course, I am not yet your girlfriend, am I? What is it you called it? Oh yes, 'aspirational'. Another bullshit expression of yours, which is your way of telling me you haven't made up your mind about me. Perhaps this is a good time to talk about it," she said, as they started walking down the hill towards the promenade.

"It?"

"Yes, 'it', our relationship. Flint. We have been dating now for three months? Maybe longer and yet I don't really know where I stand with you. Wait, let me finish," she said, putting her fingers over his mouth as he attempted to say something. "On Sunday you go off on one of your secret trips for three weeks. I don't know where you are going, I cannot contact you at all, my life is like it's on hold while you go off and do your thing. I don't like it but I accept it. But when you come back, you and I are going to have a conversation. You will need to tell me where I stand with you, no ambiguity, no circumspection, just an honest and open talk about us. Don't say anything now, think about it. Put your lawyer's mind to it and come back with either 'yes, Adrienne, I want to be with you' or 'no, Adrienne, it was fun but that's it'. No English, middle-class bullshit, just straight talking."

He nodded as they walked on in silence. "I would mind," he said.

"What?"

"You asked if I would mind if you were sleeping with anyone else. I would mind. I would mind very much," he said. "Just thought I would make it clear for the…"

"Avoidance of any doubt," she said, finishing his sentence and laughed sardonically. "Well, I suppose, that's telling me something of how you feel about me, Flint."

The walk down the hill was done pretty much in silence, except for the one time when a small group of Chinese tourists politely asked them to take a photograph with the sea as the backdrop.

"Perhaps each of us should learn the Mandarin word for smile, so we can use it when they ask us to take photographs," he said, lightly.

"Perhaps you need to teach yourself to smile first before asking others to do it," she said, cuttingly.

"Perhaps I should, Kiffy," he said, glumly. "Perhaps I can get a book on it from WH Smith's, can you recommend one? Or even better, perhaps you can give me one-to-one tuition in the art of smiling, seeing as you are a master of it."

Adrienne was about to hit out and then changed her mind. Instead, she turned and walked on, leaving him behind.

Theo kicked a pebble over the edge of the cliff in irritation, banging his fist on the metal railing. 'I'm too old for these games,' he told himself. 'This is not working. Perhaps a weekend away with her was a mistake. Perhaps this is a sobering glimpse of what the future would be like if we ever considered being together; one fight after another. I think I have just about had my fill of tempestuous and fiery charm. I don't need this, living on tenterhooks all the time, wondering when the next insult is going to be coming at me. Still, if the deal comes through, I'll be off to the

Emirates and all this will just be a dream. Maybe, for now I should just bide my time, keep her at arms' length, let it whither on the proverbial vine. Maybe, I should just do that.'

Yet, even as he was saying that he knew that it was not what he wanted. Despite her temper tantrums and the countless insults about his heritage, he knew he was hooked, like a junkie who can't stop, even though the highs are short-lived and the side-effects are unpleasant. Like a junkie, he did not want to give her up. He couldn't, she was the one exciting thing in an otherwise sterile and numb social existence, focussed solely on his career and the drive to be at the top of his profession.

Theo paused briefly to train his pocket binoculars on the oil exploration rig out at sea in the distance. "Progress," he muttered, disapprovingly. When he turned towards the hill, he could see that Adrienne had already reached the bottom and was walking towards the pier. He pondered whether to follow her or just wander back to the hotel. Wandering back had a greater appeal and he would have liked to do nothing better than just that. Just to be able to sit in his hotel room, order up a pot of tea and read his book, preferably alone and undisturbed. That would have been perfect. But he was only too aware that she would see such an act at the very least as being typical of him, English and unfeeling and at worst, a deliberate slight. He did not wish to leave to chance how she might react and so he strolled down the hill.

As he set foot on the boardwalk at the start of the pier, he could see her in the distance, sitting down on one of the many wooden benches that line the pier, one slim leg across the other, looking out to sea, seemingly content with the world. Whilst he had felt a sense of aggrievement at the unfairness of the way she had lashed out at him, it was with a sense of trepidation as to what lay ahead for him, as he gingerly walked in her direction, looking down between the gaps in the floorboards, watching the greyish green sea water ebb and flow beneath. The sense of injustice reminded him of the one and only time he had ever been found in violation of school rules. He recalled something his tutor had once uttered when he had been summoned to explain a serious charge of sneaking in alcohol into his quarters. He had protested his innocence, certain that another boy had stashed it in his trunk.

"I am inclined to believe you, young Blenkinsop; drink is not your vice, for sure. But the principal will not accept that we do not have a culprit. So, I am saying to you *'nolo contendere'*, accept the punishment without admitting guilt."

'Perhaps I should do just that. If a cold shoulder and aggression is her punishment for my transgression, then so be it, nolo contendere,' he told himself as he neared her.

Adrienne was wearing sunglasses and looking away from him, far out to sea, her hair blowing in the gentle wind, obscuring her face. He could see that she was on the receiving end of many an admiring glance, mainly from men but occasionally from women too, as they strolled past her. It made him smile. She was a naturally attractive woman, oozing so much charm and not someone you ignore. Two thousand years earlier, she most certainly would have made a man launch a thousand ships to get her back to him.

He sat himself next to her but left a gap between them, the symbolism of doing that not lost on him.

"I know you're there, Flint," she said without looking at him.

"Really? I thought I did quite a good job of being very quiet," he said. "Trying to be as inconspicuous as possible. Trying to melt into the background, so you won't tell me off again," he joked.

"Here, have a doughnut and get over it," she said, thrusting a paper bag at his stomach, her attention still turned away from him.

"I don't eat doughnuts, don't like them," he said. "Surprised you do."

"I had two and it's upset my stomach," she said.

"So, you thought you'd give them to me so they can upset my stomach too?"

He thought he detected the first sign of a smile. It was faint, very faint but craning his neck, he thought he could see the corner of her mouth turn up.

He opened the bag and looked inside. "Did you add anything to flavour the doughnuts you left me, like…"

"Poison?"

"Exactly, my thoughts," he joked.

"Now why would I do that? Who else am I going to torment?" she said and there was a clear lightening of her tone.

"Still, for the avoidance of doubt, I think I will let the gulls have them," he said and stood up, throwing pieces of each doughnut into the air. As if on cue, swooping, hungry birds caught the sweet offerings before they hit the water and flew off before other birds could steal from them.

"What I like about you, Flint, is how trusting you are," she said, shaking her head.

"Trust is not a virtue with which I am imbued liberally, perhaps a sprinkling at best. I do not trust people who say 'trust me' as it has no basis of a solid foundation. When someone says 'trust me', in my mind it is akin to asking me to have blind faith and I have never set any store by that. The ability to trust is, in my book, a virtue whose importance is exaggerated," he said, as he sat down next to her, still maintaining the gap between them.

"So, you don't trust me? Full of charming thoughts about me today, Flint. You are on top form," she said, badgering him.

"You misrepresent me yet again but I do not wish to argue with you, Kiffy. We could sit here on this charming pier, take in the sun and sea breeze and discuss the sins and virtues of mankind, mine in particular, all day. But my preference is not to do that, as stimulating as it would be to hear one misrepresentation of me after another," he said and stood up.

"What is your preference, Flint?" she said, with just a hint of a quiver in her voice.

"I am going back to the hotel. I am going to sit in one of those armchairs by the window. I am going to order up a pot of tea and sit and read my book. That is what I am going to do, Kiffy."

"What now? All day? That's boring."

"It isn't for me but I can appreciate that it can be for others, so I would like to suggest something cultural. There is a decent art gallery in Bournemouth called Russell-Cotes Art Gallery & Museum. I've marked it out on the map the hotel gave me, very easy way to find it. They have quite a good selection of art from a collection started in late Victorian Times," he said, handing her a paper map folded open with the route indicated.

"You not coming with me then?"

"I'm afraid not. I seem to have stressed you today with anything and everything I have said and I don't want to risk adding to that by coming with you. I think you will enjoy it far more alone, without me. We can meet up later for afternoon tea and or dinner, whichever you prefer, just send me a text and let me know what you want to do. See you later, Kiffy," he said and kissed her lightly, his lips barely making contact with her own.

He turned and left in a hurry, his temples throbbing, his heart racing.

"Audentes fortuna iuvat," he muttered, as he made haste. "I sincerely hope good fortune does come my way, because if I have overplayed my hand, she could be on the next train back to London."

By the time he made his way up the hill and was standing outside the front gates of the hotel, he was physically exhausted from the exertion and out of breath. Yet, as his heart began to beat less fast and his breathing returned to normal, he felt a strange sense of elation. He had spoken his mind, not in measured terms, not in the precise language of the lawyer but just lashing out. He had allowed himself to get angry, to get emotional, to speak his mind without regard to the consequences and it felt refreshing. He dared to admit to himself that it had felt good.

"Maybe fortune will favour the bold and maybe it will not but either way, I'm glad I did it," he said and then skipped up to the front door of the hotel and even, and he was in such high spirits, instead of taking the lift, walked up the stairs to his room, taking two steps at a time, something he rarely did.

No sooner had he got there and he was kicking off his shoes in any direction and flinging his jacket on the bed, the sleeves turning inside out in his rush to strip himself of it.

'Decadent. So not me,' he mused, 'but so delicious to do it.'

He sat by the room phone and picked out an apple and pear crumble to have brought up to his room, together with a pot of English Breakfast tea. He waited for it to arrive, giving the waitress an over-generous tip when she set down his order on the table by the window. When she had left the room, he plonked himself down into one of the two armchairs that faced the window and broke off a small piece of the crumble with his fingers and stuffed it into his mouth. It felt good. When he was sure that the tea had brewed, he poured it out, watching the golden-brown liquid as it left the pot and filled his cup up. He poured a dash of milk and stirred. Leaning forward, he took in the aroma of the hot liquid and sighed. He took the cup in its saucer up to his chest and sipped the tea, grinning with happiness from ear to ear. It tasted so good, going down slowly, warming his innards, soothing and calming his otherwise frazzled brain.

'Can life be any better?' he asked himself, as he opened his book at his home-made bookmark: a folded envelope from one of the hotels he had once stayed in. He had kept it as it was made from an unusually heavy weight of paper embossed with the hotel's logo. He had picked a light read from his bookcase at home, in preference to his more intellectually demanding read about the Sumerian culture. Sholem Aleichem's humorous tale of *Tevye the Dairyman* was just the sort of story he wanted to read on a relaxing weekend.

After the first chapter, he stopped to finish his tea and then forked up another piece of cake before pouring out a second cup. He set the cup down and leaned forward to pull the other armchair closer, so that he could stretch out and use it as a footrest.

The second cup of tea was downed quickly and he reluctantly got up to order another pot to be sent up to his room. "Must be the bacon and sausages; very salty," he said aloud. "Nice though. That's something I miss when I go away to the Middle East, the lack of a proper English breakfast."

When the second pot of tea arrived, he wanted to savour this one and put a clean towel over it after the waitress left to keep it warm. He settled down again and was soon enjoying reading about Tevye's tale of woe at the hands of his relatives. He found himself laughing aloud heartily, something he hadn't done for a while. It felt good to let himself go, to not have to worry about what others might think; to not have to consider his comportment or behave in a way that might give anything away, like in the great game of contract negotiations where the slightest twitch can reveal how one was thinking and influence the outcome. As a lawyer, one had to maintain control at all times, emotion just clouded one's judgement and led to compromised thinking. As one of his university tutors had once said quoting Aristotle, "'Law is reason, free from passion'." Over the passage of time, he had perfected the skill of doing just that, reason over passion, remaining emotionless over getting emotional. It worked for him.

The tell-tale buzz of the door, indicating that someone was about to enter the room, jolted him back to the present from being immersed in the lives of Tevye and Golde in tsarist Russia. At first, he thought it might just be housekeeping and as he was dressed and not in any compromised position, he stayed calm and relaxed, continuing to drink his tea and read. But when the door opened and it became clear it was not housekeeping, he found himself tensing, the sinews in his legs straining and the look of laughter was, in an instant, wiped from his face.

"Hi," said Adrienne. He looked briefly.

"Hi."

"Decided not to go to the art gallery."

"Oh?" he said, trying not to show his disappointment that she was back so soon and interrupting what otherwise would have been a peaceful time spent alone.

She looked around the room and saw that his jacket was lying untidily on the bed, one shoe across the room, the sole leaning against a wall, while the other one could not even be seen. 'Not like him to be so untidy,' she thought.

"Having tea by the window, as you said you would," she remarked as she walked in, setting her bag down and taking off her jacket.

"Yes. Very peaceful. Having a cup of tea and cake. Fresh pot if you want some," he offered but she shook her head. "Can't vouch for the coffee here but if you want some, I can order it up."

"No thanks. I'm fine."

There was silence and he decided it was best if he turned to his book again, although it was meant as a gesture rather than he was actually reading it. The pleasure of the book could not be derived with her in the room, hovering.

"What you reading?" she said, now standing over him.

"Oh, just some light comedy, set in a small village in pre-revolutionary Russian," he said.

"Oh, okay," she said and then looked for somewhere to sit down but Theo had his feet up on the other armchair and was about to bring them down to make way when she added, "Don't worry, you can leave your feet there, it's fine."

He could tell that she wanted to say something and reluctantly he bookmarked the page he was on and closed it. He went to sip his tea but she took the saucer and cup off him and set it down on the table.

"Can we talk?" she said and without an invite, lowered herself until she was sitting on his thighs, sideways on.

Notwithstanding the unexpected turn of events, Theo resumed his customary cool and collected self. The earlier outburst was a one-off, confined to history. He was now back in control of his emotions and nothing she was about to say was going to rile him or engender any uncontrolled response from him.

"I haven't come back for a fight," she said, calmly looking into his eyes whilst he did his best to avoid hers.

"No?"

"No. Flint, please look at me. I came here to say I am sorry for the way I treated you this morning."

Theo did not react, remaining deadpan, giving nothing away.

"When I thought about it, I realised that I was such a bitch to you this morning and I deeply regret it," she said. "I don't know why I did it, maybe I'm just being hormonal although I hate using that as an excuse. I am sorry if I embarrassed you at breakfast and I am sorry I said a hurtful thing when you took a photo of the Chinoise and I am sorry for what happened at the pier. I shouldn't have done any of that."

Theo remained completely inert, unresponsive to her unprecedented apology. "Flint, please say something. You must hate me," she said, desperately.

He sighed deeply.

"You accused me of treating you like a whore," he said, "and lashed out at me in a public place."

"I know I was wrong, I should never have done that. I shouldn't have said it."

"I made a joke about saying 'smile' in Mandarin Chinese and you attacked me."

"Sorry."

"You offered me your uneaten doughnuts saying they upset your stomach, thereby implying you wouldn't mind if they upset mine and then you accused me of not trusting you."

By now her eyes were welling up.

"For the record and the avoidance of doubt, I have never treated you like a whore, I have never mistrusted you and I have never, to my recollection, ever lashed out at you in public and caused you embarrassment. And no, I do not hate you. I'm English, we do not do hate in a hurry, we reserve that for a select few. You being a tempestuous, fiery…"

"Hot-blooded," she offered.

"Volatile, unstable…"

"Loving," she added.

"Wild and unpredictable…"

"Yes, I am, that," she agreed.

"Jealous…"

"That too."

"Frenchwoman…"

"Indeed, I am that and cannot change."

"Does not remotely qualify you for me to hate you. It is not an emotion I have ever used and, God willing will never have to," he said.

She took his hand and kissed it. "I'm sorry, Flint. Please forgive me."

As she held his hand against her cheek, he thought about whether he was willing to do that, let bygones be bygones as it were. He recalled in Roman history, Cicero had once stated that nothing was so praiseworthy, nothing so clearly showed a great and noble soul, as being ready to forgive. But that had been in reference to his enemies and she was not that. And in more modern times, he remembered that Mahatma Gandhi had said, 'Forgiveness is the attribute of the strong'. But he didn't feel that applied either. These were two great men, philosophising about worldly issues. Was this just a petty squabble between them that had just got out of hand? Was this her way of showing irritation at his inability to be clear about their relationship? Was it he who should, in fact, be entreating her to forgive him?

"Let's just forget about it," he said finally, taking her hand in his and kissing it to reassure her. It appeared to work as there was an instantaneous relaxation in her face and the faintest of smiles had returned.

"Thank you, Flint," she whispered and kissed him lightly.

"Now, I have a favour to ask," he said.

"Oh?" she asked and then quickly added, "Anything. What is it?"

"Will you move off my legs, they are getting numb? I don't mind you sitting on me, just move a bit otherwise the first time I get up I am just going to fall on the floor in a heap," he joked.

Adrienne giggled. "Flint, are you saying I am too heavy? Do you want me to lose weight?"

"No, not at all, I like you just the way you are, perfect," he said, eyeing her up and down as she stood up. "Just rein in some of the volatility and insults is all I ask, Kiffy." Adrienne knelt next to him and said, "Flint, I promise you, from now on, I will not say anything horrible to you. No outbursts, no volatility, nothing."

"Stop it! You don't need to make such a promise," he said and encouraged her to get up off her knees.

"I want to. I am being serious."

"For a start, you wouldn't be able to keep such a promise," he said, as he pulled her to sit on his lap across the armchair, kissing her as she leant her head against him. "I can say with a degree of certainty that by the time we get back home, you will have broken your promise, possibly more than once even."

"Flint! I can keep a promise!"

"I don't want you to make or keep such a promise!" he said.

"Why not?" she said, nudging him in the chest with her elbow.

"Because my dear Frenchwoman, I would rather know how you feel when you feel and it be out in the open rather than have you bottling it up," he explained. "That works better for me."

She smiled. "Okay, just for you Englishman," she said, turning his head towards her and kissing him deeply.

"Besides, as perverse as this sounds, part of the attraction is that raw, hot-blooded passion."

"Really?"

"Hey, that doesn't give you license to insult me as and when you like, Kiffy. What you did this morning is not something I will forget any time soon. But at the same time, don't hide from me how you feel about things, that's worse; much worse."

Adrienne wiggled herself around until she was sitting astride his lap.

He watched her fingers as she undid button after button of her shirt, slowly and deliberately and then peeled it off before theatrically holding it up and letting it drop to the floor. As she looked seductively into his eyes, she lowered the straps of her thin vest to reveal her nakedness. Theo brazenly stared at her bare breasts, unabashed and unflinching in his gaze, nor did he get distracted as she started to unbutton her jeans. His eyes travelled from hers down to her breasts and back up again, the entrancing smile adding to his desire for her.

Lifting herself off him to remove her jeans, Adrienne then sat back once again astride him, leaning forward to embrace him passionately, kissing him all over his face until she found his mouth as hungry for her as she was for him. She gently bit his lip and then pulled back before he could react. Her hands wasted no time undoing the buttons of his shirt one by one and then pulling him forward forcefully, so that she could push the shirt off his back. She ran her hands through the tufts of hair on his chest, before leaning forward so her breasts were crushed against his chest.

"Kiffy," he said, between kiss after kiss. "If this is an act of contrition on your part, whilst it is most welcome, my willing participation should not in any way be construed as forgiveness for…"

"Shut up, Flint," she said and planted her mouth over his to make sure no more words were uttered by either of them.

Two hours later, dressed in his bathrobe, Theo resumed his seat by the window and once again opened his book to read about Tevye, the poor dairyman and his bucolic life at the time of the Tsar in Russia. He could hear Adrienne singing in the bathroom as she bathed. Whilst sated, recollections of the intensity of their lovemaking were still fresh in his mind and it distracted him to the point that he was having to re-read the same page before it sunk in.

"I'm hungry," said Adrienne, when she emerged wrapped in a bath towel.

"Me too. Let's get dressed and go out to eat. It's our last night here," he suggested, closing his book.

"Flint, I'm tired. If you don't mind, can we just order up some room service and just, how do you say it, slob out here in our room?"

"Tired? But you haven't done anything, Kiffy. Weren't you the one who was telling me we should have gone to Brighton as it has more nightlife?"

"I changed my mind, I like it here. Can't be bothered to get changed into clothes. Can we just stay here and just do nothing?" she pleaded.

"Nothing?"

"Not exactly nothing," she said, dropping her towel and sitting naked on him. "I was thinking, we could just order up some food, probably rubbish English food, heh, heh." She kissed him, just the lightest of pecks.

"It's actually Brasserie Blanc, I think, carrying the name of that famous English chef Raymond White, not so?" he giggled.

"Then we read our books," she said, planting another peck.

"Then?"

"Then, if you are lucky I might…" she said, whispering the rest in his ear so quietly that were it not for her licking his earlobe, he might not have guessed what she had in mind for him.

Theo grinned. "My dessert?" Adrienne nodded.

"And what's your dessert?"

Adrienne whispered her answer in his ear.

"But Kiffy, I could not enjoy my dessert until I knew that you had enjoyed yours first," he said, kissing her. "I'm English and over here it is customary and indeed considered good manners, for a lady to come first. You don't have that back in the land of the Gauls?"

"Who is insulting who now," she said laughing, as they started to playfight, trying not to guffaw as he tickled her.

"Not insulting Kiffy, just pointing out cultural differences," he said, pinching her bottom.

"I like our cultural differences," she said, leaning forward and biting his earlobe, "And for once I am happy to concede that you English are right, at least as far as who gets their dessert first."

Several hours later, after they had had their dinner and 'dessert' and after much persuasion and cajoling, Adrienne got dressed for a walk with Theo.

"I don't want to walk down that hill, it's too steep," she whined, as they left the hotel. "Can we go somewhere else?"

Theo suggested following the path that ran along the top of the hill where it was level and where they could still enjoy the vista of the calm sea ahead and below them. They walked hand-in-hand, stopping now and again to admire the view, listening to the gentle ebb and flow of the sea as it kissed the shoreline, just discernible in the faint light of the waning moon above and the dim lighting of the promenade below.

"I concede, there is something enchanting about Bournemouth, not as vibrant as Brighton but I do like it," said Adrienne, as they leaned over railings. "It is not as beautiful as my village in Normandy, of course…"

"Of course, *mais naturalement*, being in France it would have to be more beautiful," he teased.

"Shut up, Flint. I'm trying to say something nice about Bournemouth," she said, pushing against him. "I was going to say I am glad you brought me here."

"Are you?"

"Yes. Maybe could have done with less melodrama earlier today but still it has been good for us to spend time together. Not often we get to do that. During the week with school for me and you working long hours, we don't even get the weekends with you being away so much. So this has been great, don't you think so, Flint?"

Theo put his arm around her and squeezed it, trapping her against the railing. "Yes. Can't think of anyone else I would rather spend a weekend in Bournemouth with," he said.

She giggled. "I thought you were about to say dirty weekend in Bournemouth," she said.

"It may have crossed my mind but I thought it might be a bit unseemly. I had not planned it on that basis. Still, as you've brought it up, as dirty weekends go, I wouldn't say it was *that* dirty," he joked as he kissed her.

"Flint! What are you saying? How many times have we done it?"

"Who's counting!"

"You really are a naughty man," she said, before putting her hand down between them and unzipping him to rummage inside his pants.

"Not another fry-up for you today, Flint. For breakfast you are going to have something lighter: croissants, cheese, fruit and some yoghurt. Stay there and I'll get it for both of us," she said. It was seven thirty on Sunday morning and they were in the restaurant about to have breakfast, before heading off so he could get back in time, pick up his bag and then catch his flight out, which was due to leave London early afternoon.

He watched as Adrienne spoke to the chef. It was clear from her animated expression that she was disapproving of the croissants on display and then she was pointing at the cheeses and pulling a face in response to whatever he had said.

He smiled, admiring the passionate way in which she engaged the beleaguered chef, arms gesticulating expansively, her expressions changing from a frown to a smile, to one of looking perplexed, to a coquettish smile, ending with a gently squeeze of his arm. She returned with a variety of cheeses, ham and two bananas.

"No croissants? I'm gutted!" he teased.

"That very nice chef says he will heat up fresh ones for us," she smiled.

"Did he have any choice in the matter?" he joked.

"Flint! I was nice to him. Anyway, he will bring them over to us, if you want to wait. If not, there is sourdough bread to have with cheese and ham but I have to tell you, these cheeses are not good. Somerset brie? Whoever heard of English brie? It is good for, maybe, you English but my mother wouldn't feed it to the chickens and the Roquefort is not mature enough for my liking," she said.

Theo chuckled. "If your mother wouldn't eat that brie, then I will refuse to eat it in solidarity with your mother, Kiffy. And as the Roquefort is not mature for your liking, then I will also refuse to eat that too in solidarity with you. That leaves the ham. Ham as you know is made of pork, as is bacon, not much difference, one is cured and the other is smoked. There are also no croissants to hand either. The prima facie evidence as it stands, does not support the case for a lighter breakfast, as you call it. So, through having no other choice and for no other reason, I propose to have crispy bacon, on sourdough bread, with sliced tomato. And, if I can persuade the chef, although I don't propose to squeeze his arm or flirt with him and get a piece of lettuce and a bit of mayo out of him, I will be having a classic BLT."

Adrienne looked at him scowling and then started to laugh. "Flint, now I know why you are a great lawyer. You manage to twist things around to do what you want to do. Okay chérie, go ahead; I won't stop you."

He kissed her cheek. "Can I make you one too? No? You don't know what you're missing," he said, as he slid across the booth to get up. He pushed the banana she had put in front of him towards her.

"I have one," she said.

"Have mine too, seems like it's the only thing you're going to get to eat, this morning," he said, as he rose up.

She pulled him back down and whispered in his ear, "I had your one last night or have you forgotten already."

Theo looked around to see if anyone nearby had heard. "Now, who is being naughty!" He returned, laden with a plate of crispy bacon, sliced tomatoes, lettuce and small dish of mayonnaise with his sliced bread. The grin he was beaming at he, was replaced with a scowl, as he could see that the chef had been and Adrienne was smugly tucking into a hot croissant.

"Hmm, that chef fancies you for sure," he said, putting his plate down.

"Flint, before you sit down, can you get me a knife please? I seem to have forgotten mine," she said.

When he returned from the cutlery counter with a knife, he noticed that some of the bacon, a leaf of lettuce and a slice of tomato was missing from his plate and the spoon in the mayonnaise looked as if it had been used. Adrienne held up her croissant, stuffed with the BLT ingredients from his plate.

"Mmm, nice BLT," she giggled. "It is the best. A fusion of French and English cuisine!"

"Why do I feel as if I've been had!" he laughed.

On the return journey, Adrienne was quiet despite his attempts at conversation. When they left the motorway and the sign for Epsom appeared, he said, "Do you want to come back with me for a cup of coffee? I have plenty of time."

"No, just take me home, if you don't mind," she said quietly.

"Sure?"

She nodded and he thought he detected a whimper. Arriving at her flat, he got out to take her bag to the door.

"It's okay, no need to come up; you've got a plane to catch," she said through tearful eyes.

"Kiffy, I'll only be gone for three weeks," he said, holding her against him and stroking her hair.

"Only," she said. "It's a long time, Flint, especially as I won't even get to talk to you during that time, not even text. I know, I know. You have your reasons and I respect them but that doesn't mean that I like it."

"I will be back, Kiffy and we will be able to spend more time together. Ramadan is starting shortly when everything slows right down and also your school term finishes. I will take some time off and we can be together for longer than just a weekend. I promise, I will do that," he said, trying to lift her spirits.

She had wanted to say that she wanted him ali the time, not just for weekends or holidays but she could not bring herself to do that.

"Okay, Flint. Sounds good. Have a safe journey and I'll see you when you get back," she said and reached up to kiss him, before turning towards the entrance to the block of flats. Her departure had left him with a strange feeling in the pit of his stomach. It was one of emptiness and it caught him by surprise.

"Must be feeling hungry," he said to himself dismissively.

When he returned back home, Anca was not there but his bag was waiting for him in the hall. A quick rummage confirmed that she had packed everything he asked for. Looking at his watch, he had time for a cup of tea. But as he put the kettle on to heat up some water, he flipped the switch off. He changed his mind as he felt sure that it would not taste right. The reason for that was less than three miles away, lying fully clothed on her bed and sobbing her eyes out.

Middle East

Colonel Ibrahim had greeted him with his usual friendly manner but Theo thought he could detect an edge to his voice and that concerned him. So much so, that when they were alone and away from others, he asked him if there was anything wrong.

"My friend, I can tell you that this is most probably the last time that you and I are going to be working together. After Ramadan, it is God's will that I am to be reassigned to another project. I will no longer be living here. I will be moving to another city altogether."

"If it is not betraying a confidence Colonel, can I ask why that is?"

"It is, as you say in English, that there is a new broom and he is making a clean sweep, putting his own people that he trusts in place. All of us are going, including the director. So we must work hard and conclude our business before Ramadan, including arranging payment for your services. Please, we must get our teams to work around the clock, if necessary, to complete the contract and get it signed off. There is as they say, no time to waste, starting with a working lunch today. After you check into your hotel and freshen up, our driver will come and pick you up and we can make a start."

"We will be ready Colonel and we will work our hardest with your team to ensure that the work gets done. I will tell my team about the urgency but nothing else about what might happen in the future."

The colonel beamed. "Thank you, my friend. I know we will make this a success."

Theo told his team that it was imperative to complete the work before Ramadan and to expect to have to work long hours to make it happen. As a sweetener, he said that there would be a bonus for each of them and for every day they worked through the night, they would be granted a day off when they got back up to a maximum of the five days the firm allowed.

"What makes it that urgent Theo, if you don't mind me asking?" asked Gareth.

"They would like it all completed before the start of Ramadan," he said.

They looked unconvinced and he added, "There is more to it than just that but I am not yet at liberty to say. We just need to do our job, do it as well as we always do, meet the client's expectations, get paid and return for a well-earned rest. So, let's get cracking, unpack, have a shower and a rest and see you back in the hotel lobby, say in an hour.

And one more thing, just a gentle reminder to switch personal phones off please. If you want to receive calls from family and friends then text them that they should leave a message for you with reception. We cannot be distracted during this very important engagement."

The work began at pace, with Colonel Ibrahim introducing his team; most of whom they recognised from previous occasions when they had worked together. There was one new person, who introduced himself as Mohamed. The sideways twitch of the face that the Colonel made looking at Theo, made him concerned as to who this person might be. Given the earlier conversation, he was minded to conclude that the new broom had already established itself in the shape of one of its own, embedded into the team to watch and report back. A so-called 'plant' as it were. His suspicion was further aroused when in the short five-minute break for tea, Mohamed had left the room to stretch his legs and the Colonel gestured with his head towards the door, raising his eyebrows. Theo nodded his understanding. He was not going to tell the team to be on the lookout for this man as he did not want any change of behaviour that might alert Mohamed that they were onto him. Indeed, as the day progressed, it was very evident that the Colonel too had not informed his team and everyone acted naturally. Whatever his furtive role was, Mohamed was a willing and knowledgeable participant and the furrowed brow that he wore at the start of the proceedings had all but disappeared by the end of the day. In previous visits, Colonel Ibrahim would have invited them all to dinner but on this occasion, there was work to be done and no time to waste. Colonel Ibrahim and Theo agreed that it would be more efficient if they split the work, Theo's team to concentrate where they could do best, in reviewing the contract terms, whilst the Colonel's team would lead on reviewing the responses from the two short-listed companies to the contract tender documents he had sent out.

"Okay all, can I start by saying well done. Very good progress made today. The Colonel's idea to start early has been vindicated and we are in a good position. Our objective for tonight is to make a first pass run through the contract proposal being made by the French company. It is very wordy and has all sorts of conditions and stipulations. We'll divide the sections up between the two of us, Gareth."

He proceeded to outline how Gareth would work with Emma, his graduate assistant on one set of clauses, whilst Theo, with support from Nicola would scrutinise the financial terms.

"Right, just two more things to say. Firstly, although we told the Colonel we would work through the night, I don't believe it is necessary and besides, if we are tired, we won't be as sharp as we need to be tomorrow. So, unless anyone feels otherwise, let's all stop at midnight," he said.

Looking around, everyone nodded their agreement.

"The other thing relates to Emma and Nicola. Strictly speaking, we are offending local sensibilities by the two of you being in my suite as men and women who are unrelated cannot be in the same hotel room, hence why there is a women-only floor in our hotel. So we have to be careful. We do need to escort you back to your rooms when we stop at midnight but we have to exercise absolute discretion. Although this hotel is a bit more relaxed than others we have stayed in, nevertheless it would be embarrassing and damaging to the firm's reputation if it got out that women were staying in our rooms however above board that it was. So Gareth, when you go back to your suite with Emma, do not put your room lights on until your curtains are closed.

After Gareth and Emma had left, Theo turned to the paper version of the contract that was to be reviewed whilst Nicola opened it on her laptop switching 'tracked changes' on. They worked through line by line, Nicola adding comments in the margin where something needed clarification, making changes where the language was loose and putting red lines through clauses that Theo regarded as unacceptable. He looked at his watch and they had worked non-stop for two solid hours.

"Shall we have a little break?" Nicola suggested

"Yes, why not!" said Theo, smiling and stretching his arms out. "Fifteen?"

Nicola pulled a face. "Can we negotiate? Could we possibly make it thirty minutes? It will give me time to have a shower and in return I will make us a cup of tea."

"Shower? You're not planning to go down to your room are you, Nicola?"

"Actually, I was hoping a kind gentleman might let me use his," she said sweetly. "And as I said, I will make a cup of tea in return."

"Hmm, okay, although I do feel you have outwitted me in this negotiation," he joked.

"For the avoidance of doubt, Theo, I think you are a sweety," she said and planted a kiss on his cheek.

"Softy, more like but please don't tell anyone, otherwise everyone will be taking advantage of me, not just you!"

Nicola returned wearing his bathrobe and holding two cups of steaming tea. "Made it with ten minutes to spare. So, as I am ahead of schedule, can we have our tea before we make a start please?"

Theo laughed. "Okay, as we are ahead of schedule, let's do that."

Nicola chose to sit on the sofa, legs tucked under her rather than resume her seat back at the table. She patted the seat next to her.

"I think I will take mine up here," said Theo awkwardly. Nicola giggled.

"You needn't be afraid, Theo. I don't bite."

"It's not you that I fear, Nicola. As you know, aside from your great professional ability, in a social context I see the profile of our relationship as being the father-daughter kind. I merely wish to continue to keep thinking of it in that way."

Nicola smiled. "I think what you are telling me, Theo, is that you might actually find me attractive. It's okay to say that, really. You don't need to be circumspect. A girl likes to hear compliments like that even if it comes from a much older person. You've always behaved impeccably towards me and I feel very safe with you. I could never run a shower in Gareth's room or get into his bathrobe and sit there with not a stitch on underneath. But with you, knowing that you see yourself as more of a father figure, I can do that without fear. And that is a compliment to you."

Theo nodded. "Okay, lets drink up and get back to work. We can squeeze in another couple of hours before the witching hour is upon us."

By the third day, they had established that there were many loopholes in the draft contract the French company had submitted as part of their bid and Theo recommended that they send it back with a list of questions and counter proposals. Colonel Ibrahim agreed and asked his team to draft a cover letter, setting out the questions and returning the contract with the tracked changes that had been made. Everyone agreed that it was the right course of action.

"Actually, with respect Colonel Ibrahim, I humbly disagree," said Mohamed. He was the epitome of modesty, averting his eyes out of respect for the Colonel's seniority in standing, yet the tone of his voice suggested that he was not to be ignored.

Everyone turned towards him and the Colonel in particular, raised his eyebrows by way of asking for an explanation.

"I have taken it upon myself to look through the contract that they propose and whilst I can see there are a few loose ends to tie up, it is, on the whole, a fair one and it would be very beneficial if we proceeded with them. Let's not spend any more time on this. My recommendation differs from that of our English friends. It is my belief that we can shorten this long process and invite them in, sit around the table and conclude the contract, making one or two amendments 'for the avoidance of doubt', as Theo might say."

The Colonel took a deep breath, trying not to show his displeasure that he had been openly disobeyed and in such a public manner. He had said to everybody in his team that if they had any concerns, to raise them first with him and then if need be there would be a discussion on the team and a consensus reached. Mohamed had openly undermined his position.

"My friend," said the Colonel with disdain, "of course, as a team, we are all free to express our opinions and yours is as valid as anyone else's. It is good that we have a challenge so let's hear in detail why you think we should stop the tender process and move to award the contract to this company. Does everyone want to hear what Mohamed has to say?"

Mohamed began, with hesitation, less certain of himself now that his analysis was under scrutiny by everyone in the room. He projected onto a big screen the contract and pointing out item by item all the positive aspects of it. When he finished, Colonel Ibrahim congratulated him on a clear and articulate presentation and then said they would have a thirty-minute break to give time to the London team to consider his points and then Theo would be invited to comment on it. Everyone stepped out of the room except the Colonel, who nodded to Theo to stay behind too.

"My friend, you do not need to tell me that if we accepted this contract it would be disastrous. I don't know whether he wants it to be that way so that I get blamed and so it acts as a good excuse for getting rid of me, or as seems more likely," he said pausing and gesticulated with his hand.

"Taking a baksheesh, a back hander?"

"Exactly!" said the Colonel.

"What do you want me to do, Colonel?" asked Theo.

"Just present it as it is my friend. Tell it straight. Do not be afraid to contradict him where he is wrong."

"He might not take too kindly to that. It could end up with him losing face. Would it not be better if we discussed this with him in private?" said Theo, voicing his concern.

'No! I want the team to see that. I want the team to see that I am a strong leader and not afraid to put him in his place. You challenging his analysis adds weight to that. The team respect you and your team."

When they returned, Nicola had prepared a copy of Mohamed's presentation and annotated where they thought he was incorrect in his analysis.

"Everything all right?" she asked.

"It has got complicated Nicola but regrettably, I am not at liberty to give you any more detail than that," he sighed.

Whilst they waited for everybody to enter, Theo considered how far he should go to support Colonel Ibrahim. Whilst they had a great working relationship and the firm had benefited substantially with the amount of business put their way, he faced a dilemma. If it was true that Mohamed represented the interests of the 'new broom', it would not be prudent to be upsetting him/ After all, future business might depend on having established at least a working relationship with him. The dilemma was how to be supportive of the Colonel, a trusted business associate, yet not kill off any prospect of a future line of business.

'I think I should just stick to my principles and do what I am paid for: what is good for the client. It is the honest thing to do,' he told himself and felt better for it.

Theo cleared his throat and started by repeating his thanks to Mohamed for having used his initiative to review the contract independently. He also said it was refreshing to hear an alternative viewpoint and thanked him for putting forward a challenge to their findings.

"But before we go into the detail, first and foremost, the key test in my mind, is whether the contract would be beneficial to you as the future clients of this company. As lawyers, when considering this type of service-based contract on your behalf, we ask ourselves is the contract likely to lead to, 'the most economically advantageous outcome?' It doesn't matter if there are other positive aspects to the deal but it must pass this test above all other considerations, otherwise it is a bad contract. After careful analysis, our conclusion is that the contract, as it stands, fails that test," he said and paused, waiting for a reaction.

Colonel Ibrahim allowed himself the slightest hint of a smile. There were faint nods from all the others on his team, except one. Mohamed remained stone-faced.

"The second test I apply to each contract is one of fairness. By that what I mean is, whether one party is unduly advantaged at the expense of the other. Ideally, we should be aiming for a win-win outcome, where both parties have benefited from it. The client feels that they are getting what they wanted and at a fair price and the supplier feels that they are well-rewarded for the goods or services they are supplying. That makes for the best outcome for the duration of the contract, especially a long one such as the one being proposed. Having examined the terms of this contract, our conclusion is that it fails the fairness test too, since it heavily favours the supplier; in this case, the French company bidding for the work, at the expense of the client i.e., yourselves."

"I did say that the contract needed a few changes before we can sign it," Mohamed pointed out, trying not to sound defensive but the body language said it all.

"Okay, let's discuss that very point," said Theo. He looked across to Gareth who handed him a wedge of paper. "We would challenge the assertion that it needs only a few changes. We have itemised and documented no less than two hundred and seventy-six material changes that will need to be made to this contract, before we feel it will become fit for purpose.

The Colonel asked, "Can you explain what you mean by 'material changes'?"

"In this context we are referring to explicit clauses that we feel are sufficiently significant that not to change these, would produce a sub-optimal and unsatisfactory contract with potentially undesirable side effects and therefore, be detrimental to you. To not make these changes could expose you to financial cost, not only upfront but further downstream and for the duration of the contract. Other material changes that are required include conditions on which support and service will be undertaken, that are currently extremely restrictive and limits the responsibility of the company and therefore would give you an inferior service. It may not be their intent but if you had to go to court to hold them to account, their lawyers would easily be able to show that the commitment was within the terms of the contract."

The picture that he had painted was dire and it was clear the contract had to be changed. Mohamed was not comfortable but cheered up when Theo suggested that he could temporarily join his team to review all two hundred and seventy-six changes that were put forward for amendment.

After another break in proceedings, Colonel Ibrahim took Theo by the arm and said, with a note of pleasure in the tone of his voice, "My friend I am very grateful to you. Your team have done a great job in flushing out the inadequacies in this contract. Thank you."

"It is what you pay us for, Colonel," said Theo.

"And I must also congratulate you on solving another problem for me. Mohamed. What's that English phrase, 'keep your friends close and your enemies closer still'," he said, chuckling.

Theo smiled faintly as he was concerned as to what impact this was going to have. He was certain that Mohamed was at the very least reporting back to his paymasters and may even be tipping off the French company bidding for the work, especially if the Colonel's view that he was taking bribes proved to be true. At the very least, he was wary of him.

They had agreed that the team would split into two, with Gareth and Emma working with Mohamed to go through the changes and clarifications that were needed and Theo would work with Nicola and another seconded person from the Colonel's team on the other company bidding for the work; an Italian consortium of prestigious names. A quick reading of the terms set out by the consortium had suggested to Theo that this was potentially a better deal and he felt more predisposed to them than the other proposal; but as always, the devil was very much in the detail. He took Nicola aside and offered her the opportunity to take the lead on checking out each of the five member companies that made up the consortium, carrying out financial and other checks on them. Nicola was over the moon at this elevation in her responsibilities, as it demonstrated a level of trust in her abilities and she hugged and kissed Theo, much to his embarrassment. He urged her to call upon the team back in London to support her, to do the running around and use their business contacts to build up a picture of each firm. Theo was assigned Faisal, a young, graduate lawyer who was just finding his feet and was new to the world of procurement and commercial contracts. He was self-motivated and enthusiastic.

"Very quick to learn and keen as mustard," he reported back to Colonel Ibrahim after the end of the day.

The Colonel smiled. "Good. I am very pleased as he is my brother's son: my nephew." After dinner, back at the hotel, they agreed the same arrangement as before: Gareth working with Emma and Theo with Nicola, going through the terms and conditions as laid out in the tender documents submitted by the Italian consortium.

"Gareth and Emma, if you concentrate on the key terms for support and service, acceptance criteria and warranty, Nicola and I will review the financials as well run through the intelligence report Nicola has put together, to assess the viability of each member making up the consortium. As before, let's stop at midnight. If any of you do find yourself getting tired before then, please do stop. Tiredness leads to impaired judgement and concentration and it's better to stop. We're okay as far as time is concerned. I don't anticipate that we will finish early; it will take the full three weeks but I am not expecting it to drift into a fourth week. Finally, one last thing, you will be aware of how Mohamed feels about this tender process. He had made up his mind that the French company was the one to award the contract to. But it is our duty to the client to review both bids equally and fairly, by the rules set out in the tender proposal. And in the interest of fairness, please try not to do a comparison of one bid versus the other. We only assess what has been put in front of us, nothing else. The comparison and scoring will be done later."

Theo ended by thanking them for the work they had done thus far and wished them a good night's sleep. "Nicola, see you in an hour?" he called, as she was leaving his room.

"Sure, just going to take a shower and be straight back down with my laptop. Won't take an hour," she smiled.

"Erm, can I ask a favour? When you do come down for us to resume, can you be wearing some clothes under your bathrobe," said Theo, awkwardly.

Nicola giggled. "Sleep vest and panties okay?"

"Of course, thanks Nicola," he said, relieved that his request had not caused any offence.

"I'm sorry if I embarrassed you, Theo," she said earnestly.

"It's not that so much, as me making sure that I think of myself as a father-like figure when it comes to you," he said.

Nicola smiled and then disappeared.

"And continuing to think of you in that way," he muttered after the door shut.

When she returned, Nicola was wrapped up in the hotel bathrobe, holding it closed at the neckline. They started immediately and worked through the economic intelligence reports that she had compiled on each of the consortia members. She explained each in turn, enthusiastically and in precise language, explaining where she had concerns. All the consortia members checked out bar one and she drew attention to where the weakness was but stating that, as this company had a minor role and not be delivering a core service, the risk was minimal. When she finished, Theo looked at her and smiled. "What? Is something wrong, Theo?" she asked, anxious that he might have found an error in her assessment.

"No, not at all. I am very impressed Nicola. Very thorough, very coherent and persuasive arguments put forward. You've done a fine job," he said and patted her arm and immediately withdrew, for fear of it being mistaken for affection; which left her confused.

She suggested they paused for a cup of tea. Theo got up and started to do stretching exercises that Anca had taught him, to alleviate the tightness in his neck and shoulders. His favourite she had called the 'dumb waiter' and entailed turning the neck in the opposite direction to the direction of turning his arm, with the elbow prised against the waist. Nicola looked on from the kitchen area. "Good idea!" she called above the noise of the kettle heating up the water.

"Would you be offended if I took off my dressing gown? I am wearing a t-shirt and lounge shorts," said Theo.

"Don't be silly, of course not, go ahead. I was going to suggest it as this room is so warm even with the air conditioning on but I didn't want to spook you," she confided. Theo dropped the gown on to the back of the sofa and continued with his exercises. When Nicola returned with the tea, Theo was looking ruddy faced from the exertion. "Theo! You have a hole in your t-shirt. It looks so tatty. Can't believe I'm looking at a partner lawyer wearing a t-shirt that is fit for the bin," she teased.

"I know. You are quite right. The bin is where it belongs but it is my favourite one and I don't want to throw it away. It has almost racked up as many air miles as I have," he joked. "The funny thing is that the hole came from a cigarette burn and it wasn't even mine but a friend's and I didn't even notice that the ash he flicked had landed on it, until it was too late."

They sat back at the desk and Nicola opened the Italian consortium's tender response documents, in tracked change mode, for changes and comments to be recorded as they had done for the French proposal and for the next hour, they worked non-stop. There were as many questions and comments as there had been in the other proposal but what was emerging was that other than two so-called 'show-stoppers', the amendments were of a minor nature and easily fixable with co-operation. They stopped for a five minute 'pee- break' as Nicola described it, and on her return, she asked if she too could remove her bathrobe as she was feeling warm. Theo swallowed hard and nodded.

"Don't worry, Theo I'm not naked underneath," she giggled and undid the tight knot she had made, that had kept the bathrobe wrapped around her.

She was wearing a white bedroom vest with fine straps that led to a pretty lacy design at the chest. Although it was loose fitting and opaque, it did nothing to conceal the shape of her breasts beneath. The vest stopped at the waist and Theo tried not to notice the figure-hugging panties. In another time, in another age, he might have said 'a sight for sore eyes' but in the present moment, it served only to remind him that he missed Adrienne.

"Am I decent?"

"Pardon?" he said, his reverie of the weekend in Bournemouth being disturbed.

"Am I okay or do you want me to cover up again?" said Nicola, doing a playful turn for him.

"Don't be silly!" he said and added, "Come on, let's drink up and do another hour then call it a day."

When Nicola's phone alarm rang an hour later, they had made substantial inroads into the contract and the financial picture had become much clearer; so much so that when Theo stretched out his arms, it was in satisfaction. At the very least, from a financial point of view, the consortium was looking good. He closed his eyes. In the background, he could hear Nicola rinsing the cups and putting them on the sink drainer. Having been hunched over papers it had stiffened his neck, to the point of irritation and he started to do his dumb waiter stretches again.

"Here, let me help," said Nicola, as she put her hands around his shoulders.

Theo hadn't heard her approach him and it took him by surprise to find her hands around his neck and her body pressed against his back. Before he could object, she had started to knead and massage him and any resolve he might have had to tell her to stop disappeared, as the soothing effect of the nature of the touch was having the desired effect on his neck.

"I do this for my mum when she gets a stiff neck," she explained. "Seems to work for her."

"It is also working for me, too," he said, "but I feel I have worked you enough today and maybe you should be heading off to bed."

"It's okay, I don't mind. A couple of more minutes and you'll soon be right as rain, then you can escort me back to my room," she said.

It seemed like a very long two minutes when she finally pronounced that she was done and he accompanied her back to her room, taking care that no one saw them.

'Thank God, she is back in her room and I can now relax,' he thought. 'Working this closely takes its toll on one's nerves. Maybe I should look to move Nicola to work with Gareth. Maybe not, she has done nothing to be ashamed of and neither have I. Don't be so stupid, Theo. It is all innocent and above board.'

He wasn't sure whether he was convinced by his own argument, as by the end of the massage he was not feeling very father-like towards Nicola.

By the end of the second week, they had managed to get through both proposals and had responded back to both sides with questions and clarifications. It was decided that everyone would have the Saturday off, as the first of the video conferences would not be taking place until Sunday morning: the start of the new week. Faisal was delighted to be invited by his uncle to show Theo's team around and he took Gareth, Emma and Nicola to a souk, whilst Theo stayed behind with Colonel Ibrahim, accepting an invitation to have lunch with him. They had driven out of town, which was breaking with security protocol that the Foreign and Commonwealth Office had drummed into all business-people working out there but he was not concerned, as he had complete trust in the Colonel. If he had a concern, it was the way their driver comc security guard, weaved his way in and out of other cars, people walking along the street and at one time, coming within a hair's breadth of hitting a camel. As they left the densely populated area of the vast city, the roads began to clear and they headed out into more open countryside, stretching out as far as the eye could see either side of the motorway. It seemed a world without end, devoid of vegetation and any signs of human habitation; seemingly empty except for a few low-lying buildings, bathed in a sandstone, golden-hue by the sunlight. Looking into the distance, the light was shimmering with intensity even before the sun had reached its zenith. This was no place to be wandering around and there were no signs of human presence anywhere to be seen.

The car pulled up in front of a modest, traditional country house fringed with tall palms, which provided welcome shade.

"Welcome to my humble home," said Colonel Ibrahim. "It is here that I come when I want a break from the madness that is living in a big town with millions of people. I am a country boy at heart and this is where I belong. Here I can stop being Colonel Ibrahim and just be a simple man, in a simple house, living simply."

He led the way through the front door, held open by a bare-footed, wizened old man dressed in traditional Arab clothes, bowing respectfully as they entered in turn after having removed their shoes and leaving them under a little ceramic cover made for that purpose. Copying Colonel Ibrahim, Theo also removed his socks and then padded after him, trying not to wince from the shock of the heat underfoot, taking care not to put the soles of his feet fully down onto the hot flagstone across the entrance as the Colonel had done.

'Western feet are not made for this kind of environment,' he mused.

In contrast to the harsh brightness and heat of the outside, inside it was much cooler and the light was more sympathetic. It was devoid of any furnishings except for an old, tall, wooden table with crossed-legs on the side against a whitewashed wall, on which there was nothing except a string of juicy-looking, golden-yellow, fresh dates lying in a glazed, blue-mosaic bowl. As Theo's eyes adjusted to the softer light, he could see nothing but a hazy shaft of light at the far end, under what seemed like further doors. He also took in the sweet and pleasant aroma of flowers not dissimilar to jasmine but he could not tell where it emanated from, as there was no obvious presence of flowers in the room. Behind them, the old man closed and bolted the door and then ran ahead to open a set of double doors, richly carved in a dark wood, aged and cracked with ornate, wrought iron handles, which he pulled down and then flung aside to open up to a lush, courtyard garden.

Theo smiled. "How delightful," he said.

"My own Garden of Eden," said the Colonel proudly. "I can tell you when I planted each of my beautiful trees."

They walked around the courtyard, which had various fruit bearing trees on all four sides, not just tall palms but there were also: orange and lemon trees, in blossom, contributing to the divine sweet smell, pomegranate and bananas, the wide leaves of the latter helping to keep the harsh sun at bay. But the thing that stood out the most, was the giant, three-tiered fountain in the middle, water cascading from the topmost tier to the next one down and the third tier, into a circular pool where fish swam among the water lilies and other marginal plants. The sound of the water dropping from one level to the other was soothing to the ear. The Colonel took a handful of water and poured it over his face, inviting Theo to do the same, who was admiring the carved, stone masonry.

"I had this especially imported from Italy," he explained. "My dear wife fell in love with it when we were in Rome and she was out sightseeing whilst I was at a conference."

The old man returned, pushing a trolley with two large bowls of water and towels for them to wash before dinner. Once again, Theo copied his host, washing his hands up to his elbows and then pouring water on to each of his feet and then using the towel to dry off.

"Come, let's go and eat," said the Colonel and they headed towards one corner of the courtyard which was covered by a white sail held up by ropes, to make it not unlike the shape of a Bedouin type tent. Beneath it were patterned rugs and large, well-padded cushions with gold braiding. There were no chairs or any other items of furniture. The old man gestured for them to sit. Colonel Ibrahim was first as was fitting for his status and he sat effortlessly cross-legged. In contrast to the swift and elegant movement with which the Colonel had moved from a standing to a sitting position, Theo looked ungainly in first kneeling down and then twisting around so that he landed with a thud onto the thick rug.

The old man served them a delicious *kapsa*, a spicy chicken and rice dish, with a flat bread with which to scoop up the food from a shared bowl. This was not the first time Theo had eaten in this fashion and he had no hang-ups about sharing from a communal bowl or using his fingers if need be, although he preferred to scoop up with the flat bread. He was hungry and he kept pace with the Colonel in spooning up handfuls of food. The Colonel was pleased that his guest ate heartily and started to talk about how he had been brought up in such a rural environment, away from the bustle of the city. He had been the first of his family to reject a farming existence and he was initially looked down upon as someone who shirked hard work. But when he graduated and returned in his uniform, there was nothing but pride in his achievements. A country boy had made it.

"But this country boy may have outlived his usefulness to the new regime, the new broom and I may be retired early or moved to another less important job, far away from the seat of power. Either way, I am relaxed about it. Yes, my pride will take a knock but it does not matter. Out here in the desert my pride means nothing. I came from the desert and I can return to the desert. I thank Allah that he has given me two fine sons and they are both settled with their own families. I even have grandchildren so I have served my purpose in life."

"When do you think you will find out what they have in mind for you?"

"Soon, maybe in a few weeks, maybe after Ramadan," he shrugged. "I might just make my own decision and quit. My wife has long departed this world giving birth to our second son. It was Allah's will that she should go to Paradise early. I have never taken another wife, so I have no one who depends upon me except that old man," he said, pointing his head in the direction of the figure sweeping the unripe fruit from the date palms that had fallen into the garden.

"The old man who met us at the door and has cooked for us?" asked Theo, looking to the Colonel to elaborate.

"Yes, him. He is my father!" he said matter of factly, as he took a plump date from the bowl of fruit laid before them. "You are shocked, no? Why do I treat my father as if he was a servant? It is his choice, my friend. He likes to fuss over me as if I was still a child. It gives him a purpose in life. He is seventy-eight soon to be seventy-nine but he says if he just sits down and has servants, then he will surely die."

"Colonel, you won't believe this but my father is shortly to be seventy-nine also; his birthday is coming up in four weeks' time. There are many people helping him out as our farm is too big for one person, but he still works as hard now as when he was a young man and he does not wish to stop. It gives him a purpose, as you say."

"We are the same, are we not? Where would we be without our purpose? Allah has blessed me with two sons, and every time when I say my prayers, I give thanks to Him. But that is not enough. A man needs something to strive for in his life, beyond his duty to Allah."

Theo nodded in agreement but he did not count himself amongst those who Allah had blessed with children. Indeed, he had never felt strong enough or felt the need to have children. Marianne was the only person with whom he had ever contemplated having them and it was at her instigation. There was never a strong desire to become a father throughout his life. Sometimes he might have a whimsical notion of what life might have been like had he had his own family, especially at random times when he was waiting for a train or at the airport and he might observe a family: mother, father and two children interacting. He might let his mind wonder what it might have been like to have his own but just as quickly, that would go. 'Not for me,' he would tell himself.

Tempting Offers

The first of the video conferences was with the French company who gave a very polished performance. If Theo had doubted the extent of Mohamed's involvement with the company beforehand, the tell-tale subtle signs of recognition between them left him in no doubt that, at the very least, he had been in contact with them. Indeed, as their presentation progressed, Theo detected an air of arrogance about them that suggested that they thought the deal was in the bag. Whilst they had answered most of the points that had been raised, they made it clear that they would not budge on certain key deliverables and did not seem at all concerned that they might be marked down for that. After the end of the conference with the French company, the team got together to verify and confirm the accuracy of what they had heard and then to update their records, with a view to replay their record back to the French for confirmation.

The video conference with the Italian consortium followed. Shortly after Colonel Ibrahim had opened the video conference, barely had the introductions been completed when technical issues at the Italian end occurred causing a loss of picture. Unbeknown to the Italians, the sound was still online and they could be heard arguing amongst themselves in animated tones. Even though nobody knew what they were saying, it caused a good deal of mirth and amusement just listening to it. Their senior salesman rang the Colonel and apologised profusely and he was granted an hour to sort things out.

In the break, Theo left the room to answer a call from Abla that had been left as a voice mail for him. He sat in a corner of the ante room attached to the video conference room. She had left him a message on his business phone that there was something which she wanted to discuss with him. As the message was on his business phone, he felt obliged to take it.

He rang her and after an exchange of pleasantries, she said "Theo, I just wanted you to know that on Friday I am flying out to Beirut."

"Are you?" he said in his usual non-committal, deadpan tone.

"Yes, staying at the Cedar Palace hotel. The one we…"

"Stayed in," he interrupted.

"You remembered. How time flies. Seems only yesterday. Anyway, I thought, if you were able to get away, we could…' she paused.

He could detect uncertainty and anxiety in the breathing down the phone. "Meet up?" he suggested.

"Yes, and perhaps we can take a stroll along Martyr's Square. You were always very passionate about what it commemorated. I liked that about you."

"Very pleasant to walk along there, at least then. Some say it is choked with traffic nowadays," he added.

"And end up in Cafe Younes and have a strong cup of coffee and a bite to eat."

"Our favourite place," said Theo.

"Just a few days, perhaps a weekend if you can get away."

"And re-live old times, Abla?"

"That would be nice, wouldn't it, Theo?" she said but the inflexion in her voice did nothing to disguise that it was as an appeal, rather than just two old friends catching up. Theo hesitated. It was an attractive proposition to spend a weekend with Abla; just the two of them, perhaps re-kindling a romance of yesteryear. A romance that had ended so abruptly with her announcement that she had been compelled by family pressure to marry a fellow Jordanian. He recalled how close they had been, how inseparable they had been; how in his mind she was the woman of his dreams and he had contemplated proposing marriage to her. Could it be re-started? Could it work, second time around. "Theo?"

"Abla, I…" he hesitated.

"You don't want to go with me, do you?"

"Abla, had you asked me that twenty-five years ago, I would have got onto the airline and booked my ticket straight away. But now…"

"But now?"

He breathed out, sighing as he was finding it difficult trying to speak to her without being face to face, without being able to look into those dark, hypnotic, eyes and full lips, parted slightly as they would take in what he was about to say.

"Abla, the thing is, Beirut no longer has the same appeal as it once did. Beirut is now just another town for me. And the Cedar Palace hotel where you and I once stayed is now just another hotel and Cafe Younes is just another coffee shop."

"I understand. I had to ask, Theo," she said apologetically. "I just wanted to let you know that if you wanted to, I would want that too, that's all."

"Still friends, right?"

"Of course, Theo. Hopefully we will be working together in the not-too-distant future. Rashid wants this to happen. We just need to make sure the details suit both sides."

"Thanks, Abla," he said, with some relief.

"One question, Theo, if I may. Is there someone else?"

Theo hesitated as the image of Adrienne came up. He smiled at the thought that she would be scratching his eyes out if she even knew that he was talking to an ex-girlfriend, let alone contemplating spending a weekend with her. Aside from thinking of every kind of rude epithet she could to shout at him, she would be very hurt and he could not do that to her.

"Yes, there is," he admitted, as much to himself as to Abla.

"Lucky girl," she said. "I made a mistake of letting go of you twenty-five years ago. I hope for her sake she does not make the same mistake. I must go now before I make more of a fool of myself than I already have. Hope to see you in the Emirates soon. Bye Theo."

The phone went dead. He sat there looking glum and deflated, having made Abla sad again twenty-five years later. But he had no time to dwell on the phone conversation he had just had, as Nicola came rushing out to inform him that the Italians were back online and he was to return.

Despite creating a not very flattering initial impression with their technical breakdown, the Italians acquitted themselves well in their presentation, having a very good grasp of what their client was trying to achieve, answering nearly all the points that had been raised with them. They were also honest and apologetic about not being able to meet a highly desirable requirement without incurring significant extra cost but would be prepared to meet their client half-way in cost sharing. This admission and their proposal went down well with the Colonel's team and it earned them brownie points for their honesty. Even Mohamed was gracious in the post-conference discussion that ensued.

Colonel Ibrahim said, as they had all the information to hand, it was time for the next stage to proceed which was to formally score both bids against the criteria that had been set out in the tender documents. To ensure even-handedness, he announced that Theo's team were appointed to collate individual scores and to act as moderators, questioning any score which was out of kilter with the rest. He cautioned against discussing amongst themselves each of their scores, it was to be done in secret. He also cautioned against a natural inclination to compare the two bids, item by item, each was to be assessed and scored on its own merits.

Nicola had prepared scoresheets for each member of the Colonel's team, already pre-populated with drop down menus and validation rules to make it easier for those completing the scoring. Gareth was appointed as lead moderator with Emma in support and the Colonel would be responsible for taking the outcome forward, supported by Theo, who would apply the changes in the contract for the winning bid, with Nicola holding the pen for the final version that would be sent out to the winner for ratification. The Colonel said that this would be the model of assessing bids going forward with full auditability, transparency and conducted fairly, with everything above board. He paused. It was less than a second but the sideways glance he cast in Mohamed's direction let him know beyond any doubt, that he was not going to brook any attempt to influence the outcome of the scoring. Mohamed remained deadpan, giving nothing away.

The scoring proceeded at pace and by the middle of the third week it was nearing the end of this phase of the procurement. Individual scoring had been completed and Gareth was busy moderating the scores to ensure that the final scores were not skewed in any way. As each score was confirmed, Nicola entered it into the master sheet which then calculated and accumulated each bidder's final tally. She was entrusted not to reveal to anyone how the scores were progressing and to ensure that each tally was kept secret, she password protected her spreadsheet, with the password kept in the safe in her room. No one, not even Theo, was allowed to know it.

It was Wednesday night and they had returned to the hotel. Theo was in his hotel suite, re-reading parts of the contract that he had amended but he was finding it difficult to concentrate. He pushed the lid of his fountain pen until it clicked closed and then put it down. It had been a gift from his father. "Every lawyer has one of these or people don't take you seriously," he had said. He picked up the Mont Blanc pen, blew warm air onto the gold handle and polished it against his t-shirt. He was not satisfied with the result and stood up and walked around the room looking for something to polish it with. Pacing up and down, pen in hand, he was lost in thought, polishing it having been forgotten about. What was distracting him was not the need to put a shine on his pen but his personal phone, sitting there switched off for the best part of three weeks, dead to all communication. On more than one occasion he had been tempted to break his own rules on the use of personal phones, one time going as far as switching it on, before reason returned and he switched it off.

Theo looked at his watch. "Hmm, three hours behind, wonder what she is up to? Probably having dinner," he guessed. He sat on the sofa so that his eyeline was out of view of the phone which sat behind the contract on the table.

"Would it be that bad if I just rang to say hi?" Theo muttered, trying to justify to himself why once was probably okay.

He was still having this internal debate as he slid to the edge of the sofa and heaving himself up to get to a standing position, leaning forward as he did so, the way Anca had taught him to reduce the strain on his back. He was now standing and looking at the phone on the table. It would have been so easy to reach for it and ring her. Who would know?

"A rule is a rule" he said, slapping his side just before slumping back down. He berated himself for his weakness and for lacking backbone for even contemplating doing so. Back in England, Adrienne had made a simple pasta dish and phoned Anca to join her for dinner. She had not wanted to eat alone. It gave her too much time to think about the future, about him and it was making her sad and she did not want to feel sad.

"You miss him, don't you?" said Anca, in between wolfing down a forkful of linguine. Adrienne looked up from her plate, frowning.

"Don't you?" she said.

"Yes, of course. The house is empty without him. Philip misses him too. They are buddies. Theo is his favourite lap to sit on," said Anca and then putting her fork down added, "but neither Philip nor I miss Theo the way that you do Adrienne."

"I don't miss him!" she burst out. "I hate him!"

Anca was taken aback by the vehemence of her pronouncement and sad for her friend, as she saw tears forming in her eyes.

"I hate that he is away so much. I hate that I don't get to see him every day. I hate that I don't get to talk to him every day. I hate that he is not here to fight with, to laugh with, to make love with," she said. "I hate him, I do."

"Adrienne, you don't really hate Theo, do you?"

"No," she said quietly.

"You love him, don't you?"

Adrienne nodded. Anca reached across the table and squeezed her hand. She felt for Adrienne. But when she had said that she did not miss Theo in the same way as her, in her deepest thoughts she knew she was being disingenuous. As much as she didn't want to see her friend sad, she had to admit she also felt for herself. Despite willing herself to think of Theo only as a father-figure, deep in her heart she harboured her own feelings of love for him. She knew it was ridiculous and irrational to think of him in that way. She knew that it was absurd to even think that there might just be a chance for her. 'Don't be crazy Anca, he is old enough to be your father,' she would tell herself. At times, when it pre-occupied her to the point of distraction, she tried to convince herself that she was mistaking gratitude for love.

"I know he has a rule that he never answers his personal phone but have you tried phoning him, Adrienne?"

"What's the point? He won't answer it; he made that clear. He told me off last time, telling me how when he was with a client, he was one hundred percent focussed on them," she said, in a defeated tone.

"Why not just leave him a message? He will pick it up, I know he will, even if it is only at the airport on his way out of the country."

"You think so? I'm not so sure," she said, plaintively.

"I know so. I always get a message to confirm his travel plans so he will inevitably see that there is a message from you," she said, trying to sound positive for her friend. "Come on. Send it now whilst I clear up."

Adrienne prided herself on her ability to write eloquently, even in English: not her native tongue but constructing a message to show him how she felt at that moment, was proving much more difficult than she thought it would be. Conveying the strength and depth of feeling and putting them into an otherwise sterile, two-dimensional text message was taking a lot longer than the few seconds with which a normal text would be keyed-in and then sent on its merry way.

Anca had set the coffee down and tried to peer over Adrienne's shoulder.

"I'm fighting with the simplest of words. Struggling to put everything down that I want to say. I want him to understand that I want him to be here not there and not doing a good job of it," she said, in exasperation. She threw her phone on the sofa. "Let me drink my coffee and maybe that will clear my head."

"Can I?" said Anca, picking up her phone,

Adrienne nodded, "Please do Anca, you can do a better job of it than me for sure!"

"I'm lucky because my English is not very good so I have to make my messages simple. Why not just use a few words? Your message is too long, Adrienne. Theo will not want to read such a long message; I know what he is like."

"What do you suggest?"

"Can I change it?"

"Yes, anything is going to be better than my long, boring message; not that he will read it," she said forlornly.

Anca backspaced all that Adrienne had written, making her frown as she saw each of her words disappear. Her words of feeling were slowly being erased. The symbolism was not lost on her. All of the message was now purged, obliterated and had disappeared into the ether. Anca paused and thought about her own feelings for Theo.

She keyed in the message that she would have liked to tell him from herself and then handed the phone back to Adrienne. "It is a simple message but he will read it," she said.

Adrienne read it to herself. It said,

'Miss you. Love you. Come back soon.'

She was pleased with it and leaned forward to kiss Anca on each cheek. "Thanks, Anca. I feel you are like the younger sister I didn't have."

She re-read it one last time and then hit the 'send' button.

***

Theo was still undecided as to whether to switch his personal phone on. He got as far as holding it, lightly as if it was a hot potato, when there was a knock at his door. He quickly put the phone down like a naughty school boy who is attempting to hide the apple he had stolen from a school friend's bag and answered the door.

It was a bare-footed Nicola in her bathrobe and laptop under her arm. "We've finished," she said excitedly. "The results are all in."

Theo beamed his delight. "Come in, come in," he said.

"I've emailed the spreadsheet to Colonel Ibrahim as agreed and he has scheduled a meeting for 9.00 a.m. tomorrow," she said.

"Sit down, sit down. Let me make us a cup of tea before we jump into it," he said, hardly able to contain his excitement at wanting to know the outcome. "As the saying goes Nicola, 'good news can wait, bad news will refuse to leave'. A cup of tea can make the former even sweeter and the latter more palatable."

'Phew! So glad I didn't phone Kiffy. Imagine being caught red-handed by none other than Nicola to whom I should be setting an example,' he told himself, as he put the kettle on to boil and tea-bags in the cups.

When he returned, he was holding two cups and watching them every step of the way, concentrating on not wobbling and spilling the tea over the polished, tiled floor. Setting them down on the table gently, he looked up to see that Nicola had removed her bathrobe and was sitting at the desk in just her underwear, laptop on and open at the master spreadsheet that displayed the aggregated scores for each bidder.

But Theo was not looking at the spreadsheet as he put coasters under each cup so as not to mark the tabletop. He could not help but notice that Nicola's vest was shorter than the previous one, much shorter, exposing a good deal of her midriff at one end and cut lower at the top, displaying much more of her cleavage. He chose to ignore it as best he could but it was a reminder of the hunger he felt, the need for the warm body of a woman, one a few thousand miles away, who would by now be teasing him for staring at her breasts, if not asking him to describe what she was wearing.

"So, what have we got here?" he asked as he sat down, trying to concentrate on the screen and the outcome of three weeks' worth of the combined effort of twelve people. It was nearly midnight and by his reckoning, Adrienne might be sitting up in bed reading, wearing just a thin, sleeveless vest, if anything, propped up by lots of pillows, deeply immersed in one of her many books on philosophy or a biography of some famous Frenchman, which he would tease her about. 'Never heard of him,' he would say. "These are the results after moderation, Theo and weighted as per the agreed formulae," Nicola stated, as she clicked on different sections for each bidder, explaining in detail how the formulae she had put into the spreadsheet was able to automatically update the value entered in each cell, according to the criteria set out.

As she sat back, oozing pride at her achievement, sipping her tea, Theo set to work at the laptop, checking through each of the scores and the formulae behind them, to ensure there were no spurious results that could skew the aggregated score in favour of one bidder over the other. Nicola stepped away from the table, cup in hand and walked over to the window and looked out onto the busy, bustling streets below, illuminated by the unsympathetic, harsh lights of the tall buildings that had become the feature of the business area of the city.

'Wouldn't be my first-choice to be living here,' she told herself. 'Just steel and glass everywhere, cars whizzing up and down the roads, honking horns even at this late hour and that's aside from women not having the same rights as men."

Theo sneaked a look towards Nicola now and again when he was sure she was facing away from him, admiring the exposed curves of her bottom.

'Now, if I had been more father-like in my mind, I would have sent her back to her room to change into something more modest,' he mused. 'But as an employer, I have no right to do that as she is not breaking any dress code that we have back in the office. Besides, as Gareth might say, she does have a rather peachy bum. Stop it Theo! Concentrate on the spreadsheet!'

Half an hour later, having pronounced himself happy that it was correct and could stand up to scrutiny and challenge, he emailed Colonel Ibrahim to confirm that the results stood as they were and that he was prepared to sign them off. As always, he headed the email, 'legal professional privilege', thereby protecting the Colonel from their exchanges ever having to be disclosed.

Theo stood up and stretched his arms out as Anca had taught him.

"Done," he said and joined Nicola, standing next to the window. He took a sip of the tea but it had gone stone cold and he flinched.

"I'll make us a fresh one in celebration," said Nicola, smiling.

As Nicola turned around, Theo averted his eyes having glimpsed her breasts through the thin material of her underwear which barely concealed what lay beneath it. Having walked past him, he noted her panties were not too dissimilar to what Adrienne might wear, being lacy and of the French knicker-type, loose and worn high, exposing a lot of flesh. He swallowed hard and looked away.

"Theo, stop looking at my bum," she joked as she walked towards the kitchen.

"I wasn't," he said, weakly.

"Yeah, you were ogling me. It's okay, you're a guy, you can't help it," she called back. "But that's as far as it goes. No further!"

Theo smirked. "Whatever I say might incriminate me. Besides it's not my fault you come dressed pretty much bereft of any clothing whatsoever."

Nicola chuckled. "I don't mind, really. It's okay Theo, no need for you to be embarrassed." When Nicola returned, they stood opposite each other, awkwardly sipping tea.

"If you were my boyfriend, I'd take this off right now," she said quietly, pointing to her vest.

Theo smiled. "If I was twenty-five years younger, I would have liked to have been your boyfriend, Nicola. But I am not. Old enough to be your father as you remind me from time to time."

Nicola put her cup down and hugged him, planting a kiss on his cheek. "And I would have taken it off myself," he whispered in her ear.

Nicola stood back and looked at him. 'Was he joking or what?' she thought.

"Do you want to see me naked, Theo? You can if you want to. Look but not touch and it is our secret," she said, provocatively.

Theo nodded. "Look but not touch; our secret."

Nicola stepped back and turned herself away from him, facing the window. She slowly lifted up the sleep vest over her head. For the first time ever, he was now seeing her naked back and he noted the lack of a tell-tale bra-strap tan line.

'God, perhaps this is not such a good idea,' he told himself and turned his head away. But the temptation to see her naked breasts was muddying his judgement and he did not resist it.

When she turned around to face him, Nicola was covering her breasts shyly with her sleep vest. She looked into his eyes for some reaction and let it drop, exposing her naked breasts to his view for the first time. It had been several years since she had stood like that in front of a man. It had been her one-time boyfriend who she had ditched soon after university, having had enough of his ego-centric behaviour.

Theo's eyes hungrily roved all over the youthful firmness and curve of her breasts, before staring at her nipples which stood out, pink and pronounced. Nicola was blushing profusely. She followed the direction of his gaze which seemed to wander further down to her midriff but didn't linger, moving quickly back up to her eyes. The message was loud and clear and putting her thumbs into the elastic, she pulled her panties down, letting them drop to her ankles and then stepping out of them.

What previously had been hidden and left to his imagination was now exposed to his view, waxed naked except for a small triangular tuft of hair.

"Beautiful," he said quietly, looking up into her eyes.

"Your turn?" she said, her eyes not leaving his.

"Pardon?"

"It's only fair, Theo. Remember what you taught me, the best outcome is fairness to both sides. So in the interest of fairness, I think you should do the same."

Theo removed his t-shirt and then hesitated. "Perhaps I should keep my bedroom shorts on," he said, indicating the prominent bulge with his eyes.

Nicola did not flinch or avert her eyes from his. "Off," she said. "Take them off, Theo." Theo was in two minds but as she pointed out, it was only fair that he should expose himself as much as she had done and he dropped his shorts and stood naked before her.

"Nice," she said, admiring the erection he was sporting. "Not circumcised."

"No, apparently father thought it was a grotesque habit to mutilate young boys, as he put it," he explained.

"Do you want me to touch it?" she asked, looking at him, searching his eyes for guidance.

"What happened to look but don't touch?"

Nicola shrugged. "I know I said that but if you want to, I do too."

"Nicola, you don't know how much I want you right now," he said and before he could finish what he wanted to say about not taking things too far, she flung herself into his arms.

They hugged and kissed passionately and held each other tightly.

"Theo, you can have me, I am yours," she whispered in his ear, before biting his lobe.

"I would so love to do that my darling girl, but I can't," he said kissing her gently. "It's not fair on you and..."

"Theo, I want you," she pleaded and reached down for his manhood.

As thrilling as it felt having a woman's hand there, he gently removed it, putting it back up on to his chest.

"Nicola, we've been out here for three weeks working in close proximity and feelings can start to develop. But if we make love — and I do so hunger for you and it would be the easiest thing to do right now — it would also be a step too far," he said, kissing her lightly, feeling her warm flesh against his, fighting against his primeval instinct to possess her.

Nicola nodded and planted a kiss on his neck, allowing herself one last touch. "Frustrating, but you are right," she said and gently pulled back.

"I'm sure you can take care of it yourself," he joked.

"I can but not the same, is it?" she tittered, as she dropped down on to the sofa. "What about you, Theo?"

"Me?"

"Yes," she said, looking down at his erection. "Why don't we take care of it together."

"Pardon?"

"Play with it and I'll do the same," she said, her suggestive tone and fingers roaming down to her sensitive spot, only served to undermine his determination to end it there.

"You mean…?"

"Yes, Theo. You know, look but don't touch."

"You want to watch me…?" he hesitated, unable to bring himself to say it.

Nicola nodded, "and you can watch me!"

Theo was rooted to the spot, unable to decide for himself what to do. 'I know I should just pull my shorts back on and walk away but I can't find the willpower to do that. I am entranced by some latter-day vixen,' he told himself.

"You haven't forgotten how to do it, have you Theo?" she teased. "Want me to show you?"

Theo abruptly took a step back. "Erm no, I haven't forgotten but it is not something that I do regularly," he admitted. "And before you say it, nothing to do with age. Just not something that I indulge in."

"I do it all the time, it's healthy to do that," she said, playing with herself which did nothing to diminish his desire for her.

"I'd not heard that," said Theo, sitting himself on the arm of the sofa, having strategically draped his vest around his waist to try and maintain some decorum.

"Want me to do it for you, Theo?"

He did not answer but the look in his eyes and the state of his manhood was eloquence enough and Nicola kneeled up in front of him, her eyes not leaving his. She shuffled forward on her knees, stretching up to kiss him passionately whilst her hand reached down between them. She was touching him where he would not. Soft and warm fingers around him, caressing and squeezing, making him shudder with lust for her.

But Nicola had her own urgent needs and letting go of him, she took his hand and directed it to where she wanted it. He left his hand there motionless, just savouring the moment of the intimacy of his touch on her most private of places. Her furrowed eyebrows told him that he had to do more and as he started to work his finger, the smile returning. Nicola cast all modesty aside as she rocked back and forth along his fingers, as she reached out and held on to his manhood as if she was hanging on for dear life. Her breathing was getting faster and more ragged as his caressing was having the desired effect and before long, she shuddered to a climax, collapsing on him, her weight pushing him back on the sofa so she was lying on top of him, completely drained.

As she lay in his arms, in a strange sort of way he felt protective towards her. She was completely in his trust, vulnerable yet feeling safe enough to just be lying there in his arms. Nothing was said between them. He gently caressed her head as it rested on his chest and he kissed the top of it.

In a few minutes, it was clear from the deep and regular breathing sounds that Nicola had fallen asleep on him and he reached for the robe on the back of the sofa and covered them.

Theo smiled to himself. "I think I have achieved a sort of *virgo intacto*, not by being in any way virtuous but through my one-time lover falling asleep on me," he said drily. "Frustrated but at least nothing of any substance has happened to me. Must be Kiffy casting a spell to stop it going any further."

Winners and Losers

There was a hubbub around the table whilst everyone waited for Colonel Ibrahim to make his entrance and announce the results of the tender. It was to be the culmination of many months of hard work to get the tender out and that had been followed up by a gruelling assessment, to eliminate all but two of the bidders to ensure that they ended up with the right products supplied by the right bidder. And now, at the end of three weeks of intensive evaluation of the two short-listed bids, one from France and one from Italy, today there was going to be an announcement of the winner and the mood was one of excitement and expectation.

Colonel Ibrahim came into the room wearing a crisp, newly-ironed uniform, razor sharp at the edges, shoes gleaming with high polish. Everyone fell silent, their eyes following him around the room to the head of the table, laying down his laptop that held the results. His countenance gave nothing away as he greeted them, looking around the room to each in turn, thanking them for the contribution to make it happen.

"My friends, before we look at the results I wanted to state once again how proud I am, of what a great collaborative effort this has been and a model of how procurements must be done in the future," he said and then paused.

He looked around the room once again and there were nods in agreement. "Would you not agree, Mohamed?" he said abruptly, turning towards him in a fixed grimace.

Mohamed smiled meekly.

"When you report back to your masters, Mohamed, I hope you will have the good grace to tell them how thorough and open we have been, throughout this process."

Mohamed looked up, all eyes were upon him as until that point, he was not aware that the Colonel had known about him being a 'plant' for the new regime. He was clearly embarrassed but tried to maintain his composure when he wanted nothing better to do than lash out.

"Now, if you recall, in our tender documents we stated in the section on how marks would be awarded, splitting them between quality and price, with sixty percent assigned for quality and forty percent to price. You all scored each bid on its quality and myself and Theo evaluated the pricing, taking into account the initial cost and the downstream cost of ownership for the ten-year duration of the contract. I can now reveal that the French bid won on price, being significantly lower than the Italian bid."

There were surprised murmurs around the room as it sunk in. It was not what had been expected or hoped for. Out of the corner of his eye, the Colonel saw Mohamed trying to disguise his glee at the outcome, with just a barely perceptible tightening of his fist. But the gesture, whilst insignificant, was not lost on either Colonel Ibrahim or on Theo. "Now let's turn to the results for quality in which you all took part, either as scorers or as moderators. On quality, I can report that the Italian bid was significantly higher than that of the French bid, coming very close to meeting our requirements as stated in the tender documents."

There were smiles all round except for in one corner, where Mohamed remained expressionless.

Colonel Ibrahim was a master of suspense, waiting whilst the information sunk in and nodded for Faisal to switch on the overhead projector that he had plugged his laptop into. "Now to the overall score which is obtained by combining the score for pricing with the score for quality for each bidder," he said, pausing once again, whilst Faisal called up the spreadsheet with the summary of each bidder's score.

"As you can see from the charts my friends, when you combine the scores, the Italian consortium has won by a big margin, with an overall score of seventy-eight percent against a French score of sixty-seven percent. Therefore, I declare the Italian consortium as winners and the French bidder as the loser. I will be making an announcement to that effect."

Mohamed could contain himself no longer and stood up.

"My dear Colonel, how can you say that? The French company is so much cheaper. We should be giving the contract to them."

"You are correct, Mohamed, the French bid is cheaper but as you can see, we would not be getting what we want. Of course, we cannot ignore price but what is more important is getting what we want. Would you buy a camel with three legs just because it is cheaper?"

There were titters around the room but this did not deter Mohamed. He was determined to press his case.

"With respect, Colonel Ibrahim, it is not our decision to make. We should just report our findings to our sponsors and let them decide which is more important."

The room became suddenly quiet. You could hear a pin drop. The team averted their eyes at the obvious slight and blatant attempt to undermine and diminish their leader's position.

Colonel Ibrahim was seething but outwardly he was calmness personified.

"Mister Al-Houdi, you are right. It is not our decision to make," he said nonchalantly, to everyone's surprise.

Mohamed allowed himself a smile bordering on a smug grin and sat down.

'I wouldn't pat myself on the back just yet,' thought Theo, looking at his self-satisfied demeanour.

"It is not our decision to make, Mr Al-Houdi," he repeated, only this time the timbre in his voice had changed subtly to one of foreboding which was not lost on Mohamed. The smile on his face was disappearing as fast as it had formed.

"It is my decision and mine alone. Not you, Mr Al-Houdi, nor anyone else. I decide. Your role has been to participate in evaluating bids as part of a team and you have done that magnificently and I thank you for it. But it is not your role, Mr Al-Houdi, to tell me what to do; just remember that!"

He was silent for a moment to gauge reaction around the room. There were broad smiles except for one, who bit his lip and seemed to shrink into his seat.

"For your information my friends," he said, his voice changing back to that of the amiable Colonel before Mohamed's open challenge, "the next stage is for Theo to prepare a final draft contract and send it to the Italians after I have informed them that they have won. We will then have a formal signing ceremony. As the value of the contract does not exceed one hundred million, I am empowered to sign the contract myself which

I fully intend to do.

One last thing before I let you all go: I shall be pleased to invite you to dinner tonight to thank you for all your efforts. My secretary will advise you of where and at what time." After the Colonel called a close to proceedings, Theo advised his team that, as they had finished a day ahead of schedule, if they wanted to get back home earlier, he would be happy to put up the extra cost of changing their tickets. He said he was planning to do just that himself, flying out on the Friday rather than wait until Saturday. He was not surprised when they all said they would change their flights too, and leave earlier. Whilst there were reforms in the offing, the kingdom was not yet a place where you could just idle away the hours, especially for the two women in the team.

The second thing Theo advised them of was that the Colonel had told him that there would be a government dignitary at the dinner and it would be formal, so everyone had to be suited and booted.

When they were dropped off by their cab driver back to the hotel, he took Nicola aside. "Just a little reminder, Nicola, that our hosts are very sensitive to modesty as you know," he said awkwardly.

Nicola giggles. "Of course. Only you get to see my charms, Theo!"

"Er yes, good. See you later," he said uncomfortably, a flashback of their evening together earlier in the week coming to the fore.

The dinner was a sumptuous affair, graced by the special guest that Colonel Ibrahim had invited, a senior official at the Ministry. Theo did not know him but surmised that he must be of royal descent, probably a prince. His accent was a dead giveaway, a cut-glass English one honed on the playing fields of Eton or Harrow, he guessed. The speech he gave was polished, thanking his host and the team for the hard work and excellent outturn. He said that the splendid work had earned each of them a role in the new special projects ministry that was being set up as part of the drive to modernise and, with the script he was reading from, he pointed at the Colonel and stated he was pleased to announce that Colonel Ibrahim would head up this new team. Everyone clapped their approval.

A notable absentee from the dinner was Mohamed. It was clear he had not been expected to attend as there was no evidence that a place setting had been set out for him.

"No retirement or consignment away from the city for you then, Colonel. My congratulations," said Theo at the end of the evening.

Colonel Ibrahim thanked him for his support and for the diligence and skill of his team which had impressed senior people in the regime, for the open and even-handedness, seeing it as a model for future contracts.

"And Mohamed?"

"That one?" he said, sneeringly. "He is clever but not as clever as he thinks he is."

"He has quite a big bite, Colonel. I'd watch myself if I were you," said Theo.

Colonel Ibrahim laughed. "No, he doesn't have a big bite, my friend. In fact, he just barks out loudly. Does a wolf run away just because a dog barks? I am a wolf and that dog does not scare me at all."

Theo looked at him for explanation of what that meant.

The Colonel moved closer and said, "It will be a long time before he enjoys the comfort of his home again."

"Meaning?"

"Theo, my friend, you have just two eyes but I have sixteen."

He then went on to explain that his 'eyes' had been watching Mohamed from the very beginning that he had joined the team and had taken incriminating pictures of him meeting representatives of the French company in Rome. That had implicated him in collusion but they did not immediately confront him with that.

"Shall we say, we acquired his bank details and it showed a significant deposit on his account? Through a family member, we were able to trace where the money came from," he beamed.

"How did he react when you confronted him with the evidence?" asked Theo.

"Mohamed made it easy for us by signing a confession of his wrong-doing and asked for mercy, which we will of course show him," said the Colonel.

The chuckle suggested otherwise.

"What will happen to him now, Colonel? If you don't mind my asking?"

"Put it this way, my friend. When he returns to normal life, he will have lost that puppy fat around his belly and maybe his beard will have a few grey hairs in it."

Theo nodded.

"Look, he played the game and lost. Today the Italians won, my team won, you won, I won. The French lost and so did Mohamed. There are always winners just as there are always losers."

Back in the hotel, Theo handed sealed envelopes to each of the team, telling them it was a bonus from him to thank them for their hard work, revealing that they had earned the firm close to half a million pounds in fees. What he did not reveal to them was the that the money had actually come from Colonel Ibrahim to him as a personal gift by way of thanking him for his role in contributing to the Colonel's success. He told Theo that he would be a friend for life and was always welcome to visit him for another taste of desert life, sitting under the canopy and sharing a dish of rice.

The money had been left for him in an embossed envelope inside an ornately decorated, black, wooden box inlaid with gold and lacquered to a highly polished finish that Theo had spotted at the Colonel's house in the desert. Opening the envelope, Theo was staggered to find fifty thousand dollars inside, with a thank you note written in Arabic, as he knew Theo could read it. Although the gift was intended solely for him, without a shadow of doubt in his mind, Theo felt that they had all earned it and therefore decided that it should be shared, so he distributed it according to each person's contribution. By far the most important contribution had come from Gareth and he set aside fifteen thousand dollars for him, six thousand to Nicola and three thousand to Emma, commensurate with each of their roles; keeping the bulk for himself. The money was welcome and he had no compunction about taking it. He was not known to decline any gift. 'Would never wish to insult my client by refusing their token of gratitude,' he would tell himself.

Sitting back, hands entwined on the back of his head. 'Another job done,' he told himself with satisfaction. In all the years he had been in professional practice, he prided himself on never having come out worse for his client; never failed to have achieved the outcome they wanted. His clients were always the winners. It was a source of immense pride in having an unblemished record of success, with only one other partner in the firm having achieved that. But he did not relax.

He recalled being told by one of the other partners after another success, "Don't rest on your laurels, Theo. There is still time for you to drop the ball. I did it when I was seconded to the Treasury, losing them four million in settlement to an aggrieved bidder in a defunct procurement. Still haunts me."

Theo did not rest on his laurels. He had once told a young intern: never to cruise, never to assume, always treat each case as if it is your first. That served as his doctrine for success. Whilst the gift was most welcome and chalking up another success was also gratifying, what gave him the most satisfaction was being recognised for his ability and skill so as to achieve a desired outcome for the client. That made him most proud, above all.

In Flagrante Delicto

It was all over and time to go home. Although he could have packed in the morning, Theo preferred not to leave it to the day of travel. As a practiced hand at this, he folded each of his newly-washed shirts mechanically into piles ready to go into the suitcase, followed by trousers and then underwear, leaving nothing but what was needed for the journey in the morning. His suits were in their zip-up bags and ready to go into his suit holder. All that was left were toiletries which would be a last-minute thing. He threw a folded t-shirt on his pillow when he was ready for bed and walked back into the living room in just his pants. He wanted to look outside at the city at night for one last time. The double glazing made it eerily silent.

"As much as I like the people I have worked with, I don't think I could live here," he said aloud as he stared out. "Too big. Too many people and probably not the place to be in whilst these reforms are taking place. Much prefer the calmer waters of the Emirates." As he looked into the distance, he realised that he missed home and by that he meant he missed her: Kiffy.

"Not the sort of place for you, Kiffy. I can just see you here arguing with anyone and everyone and either ending up receiving lashes in prison for offending local sensitivities or starting a people's revolution like your brethren of yesteryear," he said, laughing to himself. "Oh Kiffy, I do miss you."

He paced around the room from one corner to the other where he had a grandstand view of the intersection of two roads, cars racing across, not stopping or slowing down not even for red light. It seemed that everyone was in a hurry and it was a miracle he did not witness a crash. Colonel Ibrahim had said they had one of the worst records in the world for road crashes. He explained that it was not because they were such bad drivers but more to do with the average driver having total belief in that their fate was in the hands of Allah and if He willed it, then they would live. It was like watching one of those scary movies and it made him shudder at the risk of a multiple pile of cars right before his eyes.

"Right then, one last check before I sit myself down with a cup of tea and catch up on the news," he said, turning away from the window. He went from room to room, checking every nook and cranny, every cupboard and drawer in his bedroom, leaving the office area to last. In doing that, he opened the drawer in the desk they had been using and found clothing neatly folded in it. It was Nicola's underwear, exactly as he had left it. He remembered he had put it there to be away from prying eyes, especially from the housekeeping staff. Although in this hotel they had a reputation for being customer- friendly and it had been known for them to turn the occasional blind eye, when one of the guests had sneaked a female into his room, he had not wanted to take a chance. There was always the possibility of a member of staff being offended at the sight of female underwear in a man's room so he had put these in a neat pile into the drawer, before he left to go to work the morning after Nicola had spent the night in his room. Now it needed to be returned. He did not wish to push his luck too far and cause an incident on the very last day in the country. It was time to return the underwear to its rightful owner. Looking at his watch, he thought Nicola might still be up. He was about to text her to come and get it but decided to phone instead.

'Hmm, best not do that,' he told himself. 'Text can incriminate me and who's to say Colonel Ibrahim's 'eyes' might not intercept the message.'

There was a gentle knock on the door. Looking through the spyhole at the bug-eyed view of the world the other side of his room, he saw Nicola smiling at him.

He opened the door and gestured for her to enter, his eyes stealing a quick look as she walked in, barefooted, wrapped in her hotel bathrobe and with a towel worn like a turban around her wet hair.

"Sorry, just finished packing and had a shower. Didn't have time to dry my hair, before you called," she said. "Can I use your bathroom to do that, Theo?"

He nodded. "Go ahead," he said and couldn't help ogle her lithesome figure from behind as she eased the bathrobe off before she reached the bathroom door.

"Oh dear. I think she is teasing me again," he muttered. "Best act normally."

His thoughts turned to Adrienne and he smiled to himself. 'Just like Kiffy, does. Wonder what she is up to this Friday night? Alone? Wish I was there with her.' he thought wistfully.

When Nicola re-appeared, she looked flushed from the heat of the hair dryer but the thing he noticed the most was that the bathrobe was now worn distinctly loose and he could not help eying a good deal of cleavage and naked flesh. He resisted the temptation to stare at her breasts or lower still, maintaining eye contact. Instead, it was Nicola who seemed to be doing the staring and it made him feel a mixture of discomfort and thrill. Adrienne would make him feel that way too when she wanted to stare and she would do it quite unashamedly. Nicola was slightly more furtive but it was clear that she was checking him out. He realised that he was standing in front of her in just his bedroom shorts.

"I packed everything except what I need for the journey," he explained. "Shall I go and put something on?"

"No need, Theo. Not as if I haven't seen you in your undies before," Nicola tittered.

"I was having one last search of the room, making sure I hadn't left anything behind when I looked in the desk drawer and found your, er underwear," he explained. "I must have put it away for safe keeping."

Nicola smiled. "Thanks, Theo."

Theo put the underwear on the desk, with the frilly knickers on top. There was an awkward silence as they both looked at it and then back at each other. No words were exchanged and it was brief but the frisson of the moment was not lost on either of them.

"Right then, I'll make us a cup of tea and then must get to bed as we have a long journey back," said Theo.

Nicola jumped up from sitting on the arm of the sofa. "No, let me get it," she said, blushing as she turned towards the kitchen area.

On her return with the two cups, Theo glanced up briefly and he could not help but notice that the rope that tied the bathrobe together was even looser than before, exposing yet more flesh, especially the curve of her breasts and he had to look away for fear of the effect it might have on him, dressed only in bedroom shorts.

"Before I forget, there is a couple of things I wanted to say," said

Nicola, positioned with her back against the work-table, whilst Theo sat on the sofa, legs crossed. Whether it was intended or not, Nicola's bathrobe had further inched apart and Theo was finding it increasingly challenging to concentrate on what she was saying. It was beginning to play havoc with his senses.

"Oh?" he said, trying not to look anywhere but his teacup.

"Firstly, I wanted to thank you for my bonus. When I opened the envelope, I was gobsmacked. The first thing that came to mind was that it must be some kind of mistake."

"It was no mistake, Nicola, you earned it. I've taken you away from your family, your friends and put you to work extremely long hours in not exactly the most female-friendly environment. And you have produced work of the highest order. Your attention to detail has been phenomenal," he said, earnestly.

"Six thousand dollars! That will pay for a few things," she laughed. "For a start I can ditch the old TV my mum gave me for a new Samsung Smart TV and the kettle I've had since uni is going and I'm treating myself to a new Dualit one. And when I replace my old lumpy bed with a new one, like one of those with the memory foam, I hope I will finally get some restful sleep," she said, rattling off a list without a pause for breath. "But most of all, I can now afford to take a few weeks off and see my sister in Australia. Thank you, Theo. This bonus will make that happen."

Theo smiled. "I'm happy for you, Nicola. No thanks required. Like I said, you earned it through your dedication and skill. It is not something I do as a matter of course but everyone on the team, including those back in the UK who helped, is down for a company bonus. This one is above that and comes from me. What I would ask is that you do not discuss the actual amount as not everyone will be getting the same amount — as you would expect."

"Mum's the word. Your secret is safe with me," she said, putting her fingers across her mouth.

Theo nodded his acknowledgement and thanks. He took a sip of tea and managed to sneak a further look at her charms.

"And the second thing?" he asked.

Nicola put her cup down on the desk, and looked at him directly.

"Second thing?" she asked quizzically.

"You said there were two things you wanted to say. The first was the bonus. Was there a second thing?"

"Oh yes," she said and she started to blush. "The second thing is the matter of my underwear."

"Your underwear?" he said, looking at the said items next to her on the table.

"Yes, those," she said, glancing down at them. "You see, I've packed all my clothes and my suitcase is crammed full with the souvenirs I bought in the souk. I can't be bothered to open it up again just to put these two things in there."

"You want me to dispose of them?" he said.

Nicola grinned. "Or you can keep them, if you want," she said, looking at him to gauge his reaction.

Theo gave nothing away. His expression was deadpan as he stood up, put the empty teacup on the desk and ignoring her, walked towards the window at the far end of his room, above the crossroads where cars were still hurtling past even at this late hour. Images of Adrienne were interspersed with images of the young lady in his room, when two days earlier he had seen her naked as the day she was born. When her luscious body was pressed against his own and his fingers had been in her most intimate of places. He turned around and leant against the window. He was now facing her.

"Do you not want to wear them in bed? Wouldn't want you to get cold," he said flatly. Nicola walked up to him.

"I don't wear clothes in bed. I sleep naked, Theo," she said in a sensual voice. "I don't have anything underneath this bathrobe, Theo. You can look for yourself if you don't believe me."

She was standing inches away from him and waited. Looking into his eyes, willing him to make the next move. Theo remained still and for a moment she thought she had misunderstood the charged atmosphere between them and she started to blush. "Have I got this wrong," she told herself.

She didn't have to wait long to find out. Theo's eye contact never wavered, as he slipped the loose robe off her shoulders and she stood naked before him once again. He allowed his eyes to wander from the crown of her head, to her sensuous lips, slightly parted in anticipation and longing for a kiss from him, tracing a line down her throat, pink with anticipation, to her breasts, then looking up into her eyes again which were smiling warmly, encouraging him to go on, to look further. Even though he was only looking, she felt as if he was undressing her and it thrilled her. It did not go unnoticed, as Theo's eyes fixed on her breasts, noticing that her nipples were already swollen with expectation. His eyes lingered just for a moment but it was long enough to see Nicola's chest heaving and her breath beginning to get a little faster, with the expectation of excitement to come.

Theo's eyes started to wander unashamedly further down, admiring how flat her stomach was and then further down still, until he came to her pubic area. He was somewhat surprised to find the absence of any hair. The tuft that had been there previously had disappeared, the skin smooth, with no tell-tale signs it had ever been there. He looked back up into Nicola's eyes.

"Your eyes have not deceived you, Theo. I shaved it right off. Decided on a new look. Probably regret it as it will need…"

"Regular maintenance?" he offered with a chuckle.

Nicola giggled. "Never heard it called that before but yes, regular maintenance as you put it. You like?"

"Are you asking me if I like the look of it?" he said, looking back down.

"Yes, I am. Or do you prefer it as it was? Just interested, from a man's point of view," she teased.

As Theo accepted her invitation to look at her nether region, he recalled a similar conversation with Adrienne. He had said at the time he liked it being naked, devoid of hair and he had even volunteered that he found it sexier. She had replied in no uncertain terms that it was not nice if it was completely bereft of hair and levelled one of her many cultural observations at him.

"But you are English, Flint and everybody knows how kinky the English are: so, you would like me to wax it completely," she said.

He had frowned, throwing his arms up at having given an open opinion which had been turned against him.

"I tell you what. If you do yours Flint, I'll do mine." He had politely refused.

"Strictly from a man's point of view? I think I would prefer it with just a tuft on top. But I don't really mind, both work for me," he said, cognisant of the way his body was reacting to the sight before him.

At the same time as finding it thrilling and exciting to be give license to gawp at her naked glory, he found having a conversation with Nicola about his preference on how her privates were coiffured somewhat incongruous.

Nicola giggled. "Funnily enough, I was expecting you to say you preferred me completely bare."

He chortled. "You're not the first to say that. I don't really have a preference, Nicola. It looks divine either way. You look divine, like some ancient Greek siren, that lured men to smash their ships onto rocks."

"Am I luring you then, Theo?" she said seductively, looking down at the prominent bulge in his shorts.

He nodded and that seemed to act as a cue for her to close the short distance between them and press herself against him. They held each other tightly, enjoying the primeval feelings one gets from the closeness of two human bodies coming together. The kissing was passionate but unhurried, savoured, not rushed and bruising as it had been before. Each kiss was to be enjoyed, sensuous, delicious and breathless, every nerve in each other's lips alive with passion.

Nicola felt Theo's hands wander down until he was gently caressing the cheeks of her bottom, sending pulses through her as his fingers touched the firm flesh. Gently prizing herself out of Theo's embrace, Nicola stood just far enough apart from him so that she could look directly into his eyes once again, wanting to see his reaction as her hand slipped down between them and snaked inside his shorts. Theo tried to stay steadfastly still, hands by his side, resisting the temptation to reach out and touch her. But his face did nothing to hide how much he was enjoying the gentle caress at her hands, eyes half-closed, looking into the unknown, eyebrows furrowed, his mouth opening and closing, biting his bottom lip. Nicola smiled. There was no need for him to say anything as to how he felt, she could see that for herself. Seeing the excitement she had engendered, of being in control using the primordial gifts that nature had given her, added to her own pleasure. It was power that any woman has over any man.

But Theo could not stay still any longer and instinctively his hands found their way around her once again, one hand moving between them, caressing and kneading and slid down from her breasts seductively, until his fingers were hovering above her intimate area, touching her where there once had been a tuft of hair.

"Smooth, very smooth," he said quietly.

Nicola kissed her way up to his ear and whispered, "When I was shaving, I was thinking about your welfare, Theo. Making it smoother for you. Against your face," she said and licked his earlobe before pulling back.

"Nicola, you are incorrigible, young lady," he said, as he gently took her hand in his and into his bedroom.

Theo sat her on the edge of the bed and stood between her open legs. She reached for him, continuing the erotic ministrations she had started earlier, smiling as the caressing had the same effect as earlier. As much as he was enjoying the pleasure and delight of Nicola's touch, the image that appeared before him was not of Nicola but of Adrienne. In his mind's eye, the person who was at that very moment driving him wild with hedonistic desire with playful kisses of his manhood, was not Nicola but Adrienne. It was her eyes he was looking into, not Nicola's. It was Adrienne's sensual mouth that was wreaking havoc, not Nicola's. As he stroked her hair, Nicola was not to know that he was thinking of none other than the tempestuous French woman who was thousands of miles away.

Abruptly Theo pulled back. Nicola frowned until he bent down and kissed her before pushing her back on to the bed until she was lying flat. Nicola used her heels to quickly push herself up the bed and held her arms out. "I want you," she said.

Theo climbed over and between her legs, leaning down once again to kiss her passionately, kissing his way down to her breasts. She reached between them to take his manhood but he stopped her before she put it where nature intended. Instead, he continued his erotic kissing, teasing her breasts and then meandering further down until he had reached the point where previously there had been a small triangular landing strip, as one of his casual girlfriends had called it. He paused to feel the smoothness on his chin, before millimetre by millimetre the tip of his tongue trailed further down.

"Please Theo, now," Nicola demanded, desperate for relief from the intensity of sexual feeling that was running right through every fibre of her body, every bit of her feeling super-sensitised.

It did not take long to bring about in Nicola the culmination of their lovemaking. All it took was a few seconds of flicking his tongue over her sensitive spot and she was bucking wildly, like a bronco horse, holding his head down, wanting to enjoy every thrill, every electric shock that went through her as she reached a shattering climax, moaning aloud, barely able to breathe.

"Oh Kiffy, I hope you enjoyed that," he muttered but Nicola was too self-absorbed, wrapped up in the blanket of a climactic release, every cell in her body tingling with pleasure to notice what he had said.

Nicola was exhausted and she closed her eyes. Theo rolled the bedcovers on to her and quietly left the room to take his second shower of the evening, before heading for the living room, content that he had made her happy. He chuckled. Nicola had not only won a bonus from him but also two nights of pleasure. He had won a huge bonus from Colonel Ibrahim but lost out both times with Nicola.

'Perhaps I was always destined to lose when it comes to matters of love,' he told himself. 'But then again, this doesn't exactly fit into that bracket does it?'

Sitting on the sofa, bath towel around him, he reached for his mobile phone for something he had wanted to do all day but had been frustrated with one thing or another getting in the way. He was going to call her. Looking at his watch, it was after two in the morning.

"Hmm, three hours behind, so eleven o'clock back in England. Kiffy will be fast asleep, not a night owl like me," he muttered. "Best not wake her, she will only give me an earful of abuse."

Theo turned on his phone, if only to see her name come up as a WhatsApp contact. And there it was, a message from Kiffy, waiting for him. He read it. He re-read it and it left a small lump in his throat. He wasn't easily given to emotion and he wasn't sure what the cause of it was but he felt sad. He typed out a response and fired it off. Then fired off another message just to add 'x x x' which he had forgotten in his first message. Having done that, he followed it up with a message to Anca, who answered it within a minute.

"A night owl, like me, I knew she would be up," he said.

They sorted out the details for her to pick him up at the appointed time from Heathrow Terminal 5. He also asked Anca to let Adrienne know that he was going to call her but figured she would be asleep.

Anca's next message was not one he had wanted to read. It said,

'Adrienne not asleep, sitting here with me. Got your message. She is cross with you.' "Oh dear, looks like I'm in the dog-house once again," he said aloud. "Still, that's normal for her."

He closed his phone and walked over to the window once again. Traffic had lessened but there were still plenty of cars racing up and down, including some that were in the so-called hyper-car bracket, each costing more than what his firm had earned in fees for three weeks of toil. Soon it would be too hot and they would be shipping their cars off to Europe, mostly London, where they would flaunt their opulence by revving them up for everyone to see from Kensington High Street through to Piccadilly and up to Hyde Park Corner and Park Lane and back again. He smiled.

"Good for the economy and all that," he muttered.

He was entranced by the number of close misses he witnessed, so much so that he hadn't noticed that Nicola had woken until she pressed her warm, naked body against his back, snaking her arms around him.

"Nicola!" he said. "I thought you were fast asleep. I didn't wake you, did I?" he said, turning around so that he was cuddling her in his arms.

"I slept like a baby, after we, er I. You know what," she said, kissing him gently.

"Come on, let's get you back to bed," he said and led her to the bedroom, pulling back the cover for her to get into.

"Stay with me," she said, not letting go of his hand until he climbed into bed and lay next to her on his back.

"That's much nicer," said Nicola as she cuddled up.

He was wary of any attempt on her part to re-kindle the flames of passion of a few hours earlier but she seemed disinclined, much to his relief. Other than a hand wandering down to his waist, all was calm, and in a few minutes, they feel asleep in each other's arms.

At the airport as they went through immigration, Theo was met by Colonel Ibrahim, who took him to the executive lounge reserved for the highest calibre of VIPs and they drank tea together.

"I am here in my new role as head of the special projects team. I will be quick, as I know you have to catch your flight back to London. As you know Theo, soon it will be Ramadan when we stop business and concentrate on our devotion to Allah. So, I give you this assignment to be completed by the end of Ramadan in thirty days' time," he said, handing him a sealed envelope.

"May I ask what it is?"

"You may ask but I will not tell you. Don't worry: it is nothing illegal or anything that will get you into trouble. But I do have high hopes it will meet with your approval. When you have relaxed, in a day or two, open it and read. Do not contact me as I will be observing Ramadan away from the city and back at my place. I bid you a safe journey, may Allah protect you."

They shook hands and the Colonel left. Theo was intrigued but just put the envelope into the inside pocket of his jacket and got up to join the others.

Home

Before they left through the Arrivals gate of the airport and went into the public area, Theo's team waited for each other until all four of them were together. There were hugs and goodbyes all round. Emma was the first to leave, in a hurry to get the train and then Gareth, as his wife was urging him to go quickly so that she could avoid incurring a bigger parking fee.

Theo was left with Nicola alone.

"Just wanted to say, one more time, well done, Nicola. You have been a great asset and when I next see your line manager, I will report back to her to that effect."

"Thanks, Theo. Much appreciated," she said, smiling.

"Also, you look very tired so I would like to suggest that you take a couple of days off to recuperate. We don't want you to fall ill, do we?" said Theo, putting his hand on her arm.

Nicola leaned up and whispered, "It was you who drained me, Theo. Last night was heaven!"

She giggled and then kissed him on the cheek, adding, "And I'm wearing what you nearly forgot to give back."

The Arrivals door opened automatically as people exited from having collected their bags and he could see Adrienne waiting for him, leaning against the rail.

"Oh dear," he said.

"What's up?" asked Nicola.

"'*Morituri te salutant*' would be a good way of putting it," he joked. "The person I am meeting is cross with me."

"Girlfriend?"

"Sort of. I would like her to become that, if she doesn't kill me first," he laughed.

Nicola giggled. "Anyway, before we part, just wanted to say it has been great working closely with you in the last three weeks. Learnt a lot from you and from Gareth and well, the evenings were fun too!" she said.

"You were a star, Nicola, pleasure having you on the trip," he said, smiling. "Best not to hug and no kisses either once we go through these doors. As I recall, the last time your parents were none too pleased to see us do that, even if it was totally innocent and I doubt if the person waiting for me will be too pleased either."

Nicola blew him a kiss and then walked to the far end of the exit, left her bag and then ran up to her mother.

Theo waited until Nicola was clear and away before he emerged through the doors. Being late at night, the crowd waiting for the newly-arrived passengers was small, mainly cab drivers with blank, expressionless faces holding up hand-written placards. He headed towards where she was standing, smiling and waving to her, although his gestures were not reciprocated. But he was prepared for such a reception and had already decided that he would not lose his composure, not get perturbed in any way. No matter what treatment she metred out, Theo was determined to remain cool. His outward demeanour was the epitome of calmness, giving a good impression of typical English insouciance. Yet inside, having been pre-warned by Anca as to what to expect, the nearer he got, the more he began to find it challenging keeping up that appearance. Adrienne was rooted to the spot, smiling weakly at best, her eyes following him as he wheeled his case around the barrier and then back towards where she was standing. He could see from her face that she was starting to show tension, her eyebrows knitted, the slightly open lips and the white knuckles gripping the steel rail like a vice; he should be aware and ready for a hostile reception.

"'*Audentes fortuna iuvat*'," he told himself, "May fortune indeed fall kindly on me, as I do not feel very bold right now!"

As he approached her Theo found himself smiling and relaxed as a single clear vision came to him as to what he had to do. Instead of his normal guarded approach, Theo threw all caution to the wind and decided a pre-emptive strike was what was needed and before she had time to react, he grabbed Adrienne around the waist, hungrily kissing her and hugging her so tightly she could hardly breathe.

"I missed you, Kiffy," he whispered in her ear and then, holding her head in his hands, kissed her with passion and abandon, oblivious and not caring a jot if anyone was watching them.

Adrienne had been preparing to pour forth a vociferous stream of complaints for his welcome, the magnitude of which developed with each stage of his flight, getting stronger when the plane landed and grew as the baggage was deemed to be in the hall. She was ready and cocked but she had barely opened her mouth before he had attacked her! It was not what she was expecting and it had totally taken her by surprise. When he let go, she was flushed and short of breath but he had achieved his aim. Adrienne was wearing a smile.

"Wow!" she said, looking around her. She found herself in the unusual position of being embarrassed at the so very public display of affection from him.

"You took my breath away, Flint," she said, her cheeks still burning.

"I've been wanting to do that for some time," he said. "Oh Kiffy, you don't know how much I missed you and I am not articulate enough to tell you."

"Oh, I wouldn't say that, Flint. What you just did was articulate enough," she said, smiling warmly, taking his arm and locking it with hers as they headed back towards the car park.

"Anca? Is she not here?" he asked.

"Luckily she wasn't," she giggled. "She is getting the car for us."

They took the lift to the Drop-Off point where Anca was waiting for them with his car. She got out of the car and ran around, almost jumping into his arms.

"Seems like I'm not the only one who is happy to see him again," Adrienne said to herself, reflecting on whether running up to him with a sweet embrace as Anca had done, might have served her better, rather than standing cold and aloof, ready to pounce with complaints.

"Couldn't have asked for a better reception," he joked, as he squeezed his bag into the boot. "Perhaps I should stay away like this more often!"

"Don't you dare, Flint," said Adrienne and blew him a kiss as he sat on the back seat.

"Okay, let's head home," he said. "And tell me, what have you guys been up to whilst I have been away?"

As each of the women talked about what they had been doing, he found the soothing sound of their voices lulling him and he felt his eyes getting heavier and heavier until they were shut closed completely.

"I think Theo has fallen asleep on us," Anca whispered, looking in her rear-view mirror.

"You missed him a lot, didn't you?" asked Adrienne. But her tone suggested it was more of a statement than a question.

"Yes. I did," she happily acknowledged, checking in her mirror that Theo was still sleeping. "It gets lonely when he is not there, just me and Philip. Sometimes my friend Lenka comes over to keep me company. Theo doesn't mind. And it has been great when you've been round too."

"No other visitors?"

"No, not very often. My mother came and stayed with us twice, that was great. She said I should marry Theo, even though she is younger than him but that would be crazy and also, he doesn't see me in that way! I'm like a daughter to him, no more than that."

The question Adrienne really wanted to ask was whether Anca was in love with him but she resisted the temptation. She did not want to hear what she already had an inkling of and that the young lady whom she had grown to like, was also a potential love rival for the man who sat peacefully sleeping behind them.

"His sister, Suzy, who you've met comes by from time to time, usually just turns up and usually after something has gone wrong in her life," she joked.

"What about the rest of his family, have any of them come to see him?"

"His brother, I can't remember his name, as I have only met him once. He was very British, very snobby. He was looking down at me, so different to Theo. But apart from him, I have never met his parents."

"Friends?"

"There's a guy who phones up about once a month and they go to the local pub, usually on a Saturday afternoon. Theo says it is the perfect time for older men to go as the kids who crowd it don't come out until much later, so it's quiet and they can talk and drink in peace. He doesn't stay very long, I get a call to pick him up maybe two hours later, maybe two and half, but no more."

"What about girlfriends? Have there been any of those coming around? Has Theo talked of any girlfriend?"

Anca looked across at her friend. "Adrienne, you know that if I knew anything, I would not be at liberty to talk about it," she said. "Also, if you know Theo, he is a very private person so he wouldn't tell me about things like that."

Adrienne pulled a face.

"Only those visitors that I have already mentioned to you, I am personally aware of coming to his house," she said, patting Adrienne's knee.

Anca glanced at her friend who mouthed 'thank you'.

"Why don't you move in, Adrienne? It would be great to have your company," Anca suggested.

"I can't," she replied.

"Can I ask why not? You want to don't you?"

"He hasn't asked me," Adrienne sighed.

"Do you want me to ask him?"

"No! Please don't. If he wants me to, he can do it himself."

Theo awoke just as the electric gates to the house opened and Anca pulled up in front of the house.

"Must have dozed off," he yawned. "So nice to be coming home to a cooler climate, where I can sleep without air conditioning or cars whizzing past, driving like crazy." As Anca fiddled with her mobile to unset the alarm, he noticed that Adrienne was turning towards her car.

"Kiffy? You're not thinking of going, are you?" he said, taking her arm.

"I came to the airport. Maybe you might just want to have a relaxing weekend without me around you just yet," she said quietly.

"Kiffy, I meant it when I said I missed you; I won't relax unless you are here. Don't go. Please, I want you to stay," he said and started pulling her away from her car and towards the house. "I don't want my girlfriend to be going back to her place."

Adrienne smiled. "Girlfriend?" she said, as they entered the hall.

"Yes."

"Not aspirational?"

"Not aspirational. Girlfriend. That is if you think I am fit to be your boyfriend," he said, grinning.

"Hmm, let me think about that," she said and then pulled him in for a kiss. "You know I came to the airport to be cross with you. But you took my anger away in one breath and I am glad you did. It is not good for me to be angry with you. It is bad for my health," she laughed.

"Not good for me either, always gives me a headache," he joked.

Anca re-appeared to say goodnight, kissing both of them and then went up the stairs two at a time.

"The energy of youth," he commented.

"How's your energy, Flint?" she asked, putting her hand down to his crotch.

"Tired. Just want to get out of these clothes, take a shower and go to bed," he said, stretching his arms out.

Adrienne fell into his arms. "So good to have you back, Flint."

"Good to be back," he said gently holding her.

"Coming up or do you want to stay down until I've unpacked and showered?"

"You go up," she said. "Need a glass of water."

As he unpacked his suitcase, Theo remembered that he had a sealed letter from Colonel Ibrahim. He reached into the inner pocket of his jacket that he had already hung up in the wardrobe and found it. He was about to open it when he changed his mind.

"If it is good news, it will be even better in the morning," he told himself. "If it is bad news, then reading it at midnight, will only make me sleepless."

Having finished unpacking, he stripped off and walked into the wet room attached to the bedroom. Normally, he would use the smaller shower head to wash, but on this occasion, he wanted to feel the warmth and soothing action of the big, overhead, rain shower and he pushed the button for it to come on, walking in when the light stopped flashing, indicating it had reached the temperature he had set it to. He poured an over-generous amount of body gel onto his sponge, squeezing it until the soap had lathered up and put the gel back in the niche in the wall. He was about to start washing himself when a hand took it off him.

"Here, let me do that," said the voice and even above the noise of the powerful, rain shower he knew who it was. Even if she was behind him and he could not see her, he knew who it was. He recognised the warm body pressed against him. As Adrienne started to gently wash his shoulders, he became aroused. He began to hunger for her but more than anything else, the pervading feeling was one of being comfortable, of being warm and safe knowing that she was there with him and he knew that what he wanted was for her to be with him.

Adrienne continued with her ministrations, getting more and more sensual as she dropped the sponge and continued with her hands. Reaching around his waist, she smiled.

"I see not all of you is tired," she said.

"Guilty as charged," he said and then turned to face her, reaching his hand down between them as the rainwater poured over both of them.

"What's this?" he said through the water.

"I shaved it, for you, Flint," she said.

Theo started to laugh. It was silent, not for her ears as he recalled the last person who had done that for him.

"For me? Or for you?" he joked.

"For both of us," she giggled.

Theo pulled her into his arms, his fingers working their way between her legs. "Is it wet because of the water or…"

"Shh. Let's get out of here and you'll find out," she said, pushing the button to stop the shower and then kissing him deeply.

Taking him by the hand, she led him out of the shower, putting a towel around both of them, drying him off first. But he was impatient for her and pulled her into a passionate embrace, before gently pushing her back onto the bed. He was kneeling down and starting to kiss his way up her legs, the image of Nicola briefly flashing up. Unlike Nicola, there was no English reserve, Adrienne was writhing, demanding of him to give her pleasure with his tongue, crying out when it made contact with her most sensitive of area. Her orgasm came very quickly but her hunger was not yet satiated. Pulling him up, for the first time ever in their lovemaking, she was talking dirty to him and it seemed to add to his arousal.

"Fuck me, Flint. Fuck me now," she demanded.

He needed no persuasion. His needs were as hungry as hers. In the three weeks he had been away, circumstances had contrived to leave him frustrated and he was very much in need of sex. With Nicola, despite her willingness to go all the way, he could not. It wasn't especially because he thought it was a step too far for them to take, or for any moral reason, it was just because the only person he wanted to have sex with, to make love to, was right there in his bed. There was no one else he wanted to be in his arms.

It was Sunday morning and he was sitting in his shorts and t-shirt in the bright conservatory reading his newspaper, feet in walking socks, up on the small pouf, which he shared with Anca who sat adjacent to him in her Che Guevara t-shirt and pants, wearing another pair of his walking socks, reading the world news whilst he trawled through the financial pages. Earlier, he had crept out of the bedroom leaving Adrienne fast asleep. He stopped to look back at her, before he closed the bedroom door as quietly as he could manage.

"Sleeps like an angel, makes love like a siren, if only she could curb that sometime acid tongue of hers and she would make the perfect…" he stopped himself. The thought had sent a shiver through him.

Theo looked up from his paper and touched Anca's hand. "There was something I wanted for us to talk about, Anca," he said.

She put her paper down. "Yes, Theo?"

"It's about Adrienne," he said and hesitated.

"Yes?"

"I want to ask her to come and live with me. But before I do that, I wanted to discuss with you how you feel about it."

"You want me to leave?"

"No! Why would I want that? Aside from the fact that this is your home, Anca, you are very important to me, you have become a part of my life. You are like the daughter I have never had and I would never ask you to leave," he said, holding her hand.

There were tears welling up in Anca's eyes and she kissed his hand.

"I was worried that you were going to ask me to go," she said.

"Come here, don't be silly," he said and she got off her chair and sat on his lap, leaning her head on his shoulder. He patted her back for reassurance. "Anca, I sometimes wish I had been your father. Even though we are not biologically related, I want you to know, I feel for you as if I was your father."

"Thank you, Theo. I love this place. I love you," she said and then added quickly, "that is, I love you as if you were my dad."

"So how do you feel about Adrienne coming to stay with us, assuming she will accept?"

"I'd love it!" she said enthusiastically. "Adrienne and I get on really well. We spent a lot of time together when you were away. She says she sees me like her little sister."

"Hmm, I'm afraid I don't see her that way," he joked.

"Theo, I am one hundred percent with you to invite her to come and live here."

"To be clear, I am not expecting you to run after her, like you do for me. That is not part of our contract. However, if you do want to, then I am happy to increase your allowance to reflect that and add it to the contract as a formal change. But only if you want to," he stressed.

She got off him and sat on the pouf, taking his feet and resting them on her. "I don't really do that much for you, Theo. You're hardly ever here. Apart from running you to the station and back in the morning, to the airport, a bit of cooking when you're not taking me to a restaurant or us having a take-away, I do your laundry, massage you once a week, and Pilates twice a week and that's about it. Do you want me to do the same for Adrienne?"

"The same for her, I guess. Not sure about the massage, she's never said anything about that but maybe some gym training for her."

"No problem, you don't have to pay me any more. You're generous enough as it is," she said.

"No, it would be changing the terms of the contract, which by the way I also wanted to discuss with you and this is as good a time as any. I was going to ask you, how would you feel about extending it for five years instead of two with an option for a further five years? And, subject to Adrienne agreeing to move in, an additional five hundred pounds per month?"

"Wow! That's very generous, Theo. You pay me two thousand a month already, I eat and live rent-free, I drive your car more often than you do, whenever I need anything you buy it for me, really I don't need any more money from you."

"My dear, it is what any father would do for his daughter and I want you to think about investing it. Investing in your future, maybe think about having your own Pilates and fitness studio or something like that.

And as for the contract, as much as I think of you as a daughter, it is for your protection. You never know, one day Adrienne might hit me over the head and it turns me into a psycho who becomes mean to you," he joked.

"I doubt that. But thanks. Thanks Theo," she said and leaned forward to kiss him.

He couldn't help notice her shapely, naked breasts as she did that and quickly looked away.

"Last thing from me and I want an honest opinion from you, even if I don't like it," he said.

"What is it, Theo?"

"Do you think I am too old to have a girlfriend as young as Adrienne?"

"Of course not!"

"Even if she is twenty years younger than me?"

"Theo, age is not important. I know Adrienne loves you and she is not put off by you being that much older, so why should you be?"

Theo smiled. "Thank you, Anca."

"Right then, I'll make you a fresh cup of tea and then I need to get dressed and get going. I have two clients this morning. One wants me to run with her up by Epsom Downs and the other has a gym in her house and we are having a workout with her and her daughter. Another two hundred in the bank. Investment in my studio, Theo. I like that idea," she said and then added, "Can I take the car?"

Theo smiled. "Yes, of course. And don't forget to let me know…"

"Where I'm going for my safety? It's already in your phone as a text," she said and kissed him on the head as she skipped to the kitchen.

Drinking his tea after Anca had left to go to her clients, Theo had his tablet on his lap and was looking up the value of one of the funds he had invested money in. He smiled when he saw that in the three weeks he had been away, in spite of the volatility in the market with the uncertainty over Brexit, the America-China trade spat, Iran and Saudi Arabia fighting a proxy war in the Yemen, the fund had gone up in value. He closed his tablet and then his eyes, in satisfaction. Money was working for him, both in his investments but also in the fees generated out in the Middle East. As a partner, he would be entitled to a significant return on the half million pounds worth of business generated from his last trip. Career wise, all was well, the future was looking very rosy. Theo thought he heard a noise somewhere behind him but did not look up, attributing it to his cat, Philip, who had repeatedly miaowed his complaint to his master for not being around for him to jump onto his lap. Then he felt arms around him and then a kiss on the nape of his neck, from behind his seat.

"Good morning to you, Kiffy," he said, as she walked around his armchair and on to his lap. "Sleep well?"

"Eventually," she said and then whispered. "Someone kept me awake for quite a long time late last night."

She was wearing one of his t-shirts which hung loose and he pulled it down by the neck so he could see inside.

"Hey, stop that," she whispered, her eyes pointing in the direction of the kitchen.

"You don't need to whisper, Anca is out with a client," he said, putting his hand under the t-shirt and fondling her breast.

She jumped up and out of his reach. "I'm hungry," she said. "What have you got in the fridge that is edible for me, Flint?"

"Eggs, bacon, cheese, the finest English cheddar and Marmalade, prime English marmalade, albeit made with Seville oranges. And there is fine country bread and scones with Cornish cream if you fancy it. Not a croissant in sight," he joked.

"Ha-ha, I shall have to suffer," she said, as she traipsed off to the kitchen.

She returned with a tray of a coffee pot, toast, marmalade, cheddar cheese, a couple of poached eggs and half an avocado.

"Good heavens, that's enough to feed a family of four," he joked.

"I'm hungry. Seem to want to eat more nowadays. Must be all the stress you're causing me, leaving me alone for so long. Besides, it's not all for me, it's for you too," she said.

"I'm sure as soon as you see me eating, you'll get jealous and want some and start to steal my toast, so I made extra."

"Can't stand poached eggs, rest assured I won't pinch those. Not overly fond of avocado on toast either. But I would be grateful for a buttered toast with a bit of marmalade smeared over it when you make yours," he said, picking up his tablet and setting it on the table.

"What's that? Playing computer games on a Sunday morning, Flint? Didn't think you liked that sort of thing. I thought you liked to play more adult games," she teased.

"You're quite right, Kiffy, not computer games. Just checking out my finances. Haven't looked at them for three weeks. Need to make sure I can put bread on the table," he joked.

"Hmm. Never heard of a lawyer going hungry, Flint."

"Well, I've got mouths to feed, Kiffy. Anca, me, Philip. And maybe even a fourth," he said, as he sat up straight, putting his toast onto the pouf.

"Fourth?"

"Yes, a fourth," he said.

"And who might that be?"

"You, Kiffy," he said, looking at her straight in the eyes.

"Me? What are you saying, Flint?" she said, trying to contain the nervous excitement that was starting to bubble up in the pit of her stomach.

"Kiffy, you and I have been seeing each other on and off for several weeks now…"

"More like four months," she interrupted, "but carry on."

"That long? At any rate you and I have been having a relationship of sorts, have we not? We have been seeing each other sometimes after work for a few hours, mostly on weekends work permitting and even went down to Bournemouth for a…"

"Dirty weekend," she interrupted.

"The conventional term for our social liaison is I believe, dating. Yes, we've been dating. Anyway, whatever you call it, the thing is I was wondering whether you would like to move in with me, Kiffy. Live here, in this house," he said and was irritated with himself for not being as lucid as he would have liked.

"So you can have sex on tap, is that it?" she giggled.

"That too," he laughed and then added in a more serious tone, "but mostly because I have become very fond of you, Kiffy and I miss you when I am not with you. I may not phone you, text you or anything of the kind but that doesn't mean I don't think about you when I'm not with you, because I do. I know you hate it when I am away but my job is my job and I go where it takes me; I can't help that. But when I am here, then I don't want to have to try and catch you on the train or for a few hours stolen here and there. It would make me very happy if you came to live with me."

He looked up and saw that there were tears in her eyes. "You know I love you, Flint."

"Does that mean you will live with me?"

"Yes. I will come and live with you," she said, wiping her tears on the t-shirt and, getting up, she sat back on his lap and he hugged her, planting little kisses on her face.

"From today? We can load up what you need when Anca returns with the car," he suggested.

"What's going to happen with Anca?" she asked.

"She is staying."

"How do you know if she wants to?"

"I asked her this morning and she is cool about the whole thing. In fact, she is looking forward to you being here," he said, cheerfully.

She sat up straight. "You discussed my moving in with her before talking with me?" she said, accusingly.

"Yes. And she is happy to look after you too, including giving you Pilates instruction twice a week and a massage too, if you want it. And I will increase her allowance in recognition of her extra responsibilities; although she did not want the money."

"Wow! All this discussed this morning whilst I was asleep. You were pretty sure of yourself that I would say yes. Typical! English arrogance!" she said and jumped off him.

"Kiffy?" he said, bemused as to what was happening.

He was holding his hands out as she left the room, "What have I done wrong?" he said, looking at Philip who was grooming himself on the other armchair, watching his master. "I don't understand women, Philip. Maybe my parents should have cut my balls off like we had done to you, that way I would have no interest in them and life would be so much easier. Fancy swapping places, old chum? You get to be a human and I get to be a cat. Life would be so much easier and more pleasant. Freedom to come and go, eat when I want to, sleep when and where I want to, sit on a comfortable sofa looking out at the world. Hey, what I wouldn't give to be in your shoes, or should I say, your paws, Philip."

He was about to get up and find out where Adrienne had got to when she returned with a cup of tea and with three strips of bacon on a slice of toast.

"I suppose if I am going to live here, I better earn my keep," she giggled. "Would sir like some more tea, toast and a fried pig on it?"

He laughed. "Perhaps I should buy you a French Maid's outfit, Kiffy. Hmm, can envisage you in that."

"Don't be naughty, Flint!"

"You had me fooled. I thought you had gone off in one of your Gallic huffs," he said, as he bit into the toast.

"I was mildly annoyed," she admitted, "You should have asked me first. But then I thought about it and you were being kind and thoughtful towards Anca, who is my friend, so I am happy."

"Phew!"

"But Flint, for the avoidance of doubt, to use one of your favourite phrases, don't think for a moment I will not speak my mind just because I'm living in your house. I'm still…"

"I didn't for a moment think you'd change, Kiffy. Don't want you to change. As a wise man once said, 'be yourself, everyone else is taken'."

"And another thing, we're adding croissants to the weekly shop and decent coffee, not what you have in the larder here."

"No problem, just tell Anca and she will get whatever you want."

"And another thing, speaking of Anca, can you tell her to wear a bra under her t-shirt when she is walking around the house," said Adrienne, taking a bite out of his toast with the bacon on top.

"I don't see you wearing a bra, Kiffy," he said, quietly smiling to himself when he saw the bacon disappear into her mouth.

"Yes, but I don't have big breasts like Anca."

"Hadn't noticed."

"Liar, you don't miss a thing, Flint. And your t-shirt that she wears. It doesn't really cover her derriere either. You can see her knickers and the shape of it. Tell her to change that, too."

"Kiffy, I can't tell her to start wearing a bra or to hide her knickers. This is her home. She feels safe dressing the way she does and I wouldn't want her to start to feel uncomfortable around me, or you for that matter."

He noticed that she had taken another bite out of the toast she had brought for him. "And she sees you naked when she massages you."

"Yes, of course. You want me to cover up, wear a t-shirt and shorts, perhaps?"

"Flint! Are you making fun of me?"

"No Kiffy but I like it that you are jealous, even if you have nothing to be jealous about," he assured her.

"And these shorts of yours," she said, tugging at them.

"What's wrong with my shorts? They are high-quality, lounge shorts from Debenhams."

"They are revealing."

"What? They are black, Kiffy. What can they reveal?" he asked.

She hesitated and then said, "They show the shape. The shape of your dick."

He laughed. "Only when I'm hard and trust me, I've never been that in front of Anca." Adrienne pulled a face, before taking another bite at the toast, discarding the end crust. "Kiffy, all this time when you haven't been in my house, nothing improper has ever occurred between Anca and myself. Do you think we are going to start now that you're moving in?"

She thought about it and then shrugged. "Perhaps not but I will be watching you and if I see anything, I will cut it off, Flint. I'm a fiery French woman and..."

"Yes, yes. I know. If you ever see me misbehaving towards Anca then I will give you the scissors to do as you see fit."

The knitted eyebrows disappeared and turned into a smile and then a giggle and then a little laugh. She was happy and leaned over to kiss him passionately, allowing him the pleasure of staring down her loose t-shirt at her breasts and further down. He reached out and touched her.

"Still smooth," he said.

"Yes, it is. You should take advantage of it," she said, kissing him.

"Now about these lounge shorts. What did you say you can see?"

She sat back. "Look! You are bulging out. If Anca walked in right now she would know straight away that you have an erection."

"So what if she did? I'm sure she would turn around and leave discretely," he said. "Now you were saying about the shorts."

Adrienne leaned forward again and touched him through his shorts.

"Perhaps we should remove the evidence," she said, as she knelt in front of him.

After they had showered once again and changed, Theo cajoled her into going for a walk with him. "Just round the block," he said. "By the way, did you know we have mice in the house," he said.

"Mice? Where? How do they get in? I hate them. Disgusting animals. They poo and wee, everywhere," she said with distaste.

"They're only in the conservatory," he said, trying not to show any mirth on his face.

"Really? Where Flint?" she said, tugging on his arm.

"On my plate. Did you not see them, they ate my toast and bacon too? At least I think it must have been mice; just left me the crust," he said, starting to laugh.

"Pig!"

"Pig is exactly what you ate, Kiffy. Nice, British pig growing naturally in the Wiltshire countryside. Sliced and cured and made into the finest bacon. Loved watching you devour my bacon and toast."

"I was hungry!"

"Kiffy, I can see you and I are going to get along just fine," he said.

When Anca returned, they had lunch which Adrienne had cooked: a rack of lamb with rosemary, French style as she proudly pointed out. Anca volunteered to help Adrienne pack and move in. So, whilst the two gentlemen of the house as Anca referred to Theo and Philip, slept on the sofa, they drove the Micra back to Adrienne's flat. She had decided only to pack her immediate things, which included smart clothes for the last week of the summer school term, after which she could be more relaxed in what she wore. Together with her laptop, her iPad and a few personal things, ten pairs of shoes which Adrienne insisted was the absolute minimum she needed, they managed to squeeze everything into the back of the car.

"See you next week, for a drink," she told her orchid that sat proudly on the windowsill in her kitchen.

Two hours later, they were back. They could hear voices coming from the living room. Anca put her ear to the door and listened in.

"I think it's one of our neighbours but can't make out who it is," she whispered.

They tiptoed in and out of the house, bringing Adrienne's things into the hall, before carrying them up the stairs.

"Problem?" Adrienne asked, after she heard the door close and saw a man wearing traditional Muslim clothes, head down, walking up the drive.

"No, nothing like that," he said, patting the sofa for her to sit next to him. "That was Mr Khan. He is leaving and going back home to Pakistan. Had enough. Sold the house to a cousin who has been wanting to move into the area for some time. I don't think Mr Khan did him any favours; forced him to pay the full market value."

"Really? He would have made a lot of money."

"Wasn't always like that. He was telling me what life was like when he left Pakistan to come over to England. The only job he could get was as a London bus driver, despite his skills as a builder. He and his wife, who worked in an East End sweat shop as a seamstress for pittance, scrimped and saved until they could get their own house. He said it was awful but in time they fixed it up. Being a builder, he was able to do a lot of it himself."

"Is that how he made his money? As a builder, buying and selling old houses," she asked tucking her feet under his thigh as she leant back in her seat.

"I thought that might be the case too but actually, he made his money in meat. As a devout Muslim, Mr Khan only wanted to eat meat prepared in the Halal way as prescribed in the Quran. But finding a Halal butcher wasn't easy; the nearest one was a bus-ride away. So, Mr Khan used the little money he and his wife had saved and found a derelict shop, did it up and opened the first Halal butchers in his area. It was an instant success. Everyone, be it Pakistani, or Bangladeshi, basically any Muslim in the area would come to his butchers. Soon, he had enough money to open another one and then another, wherever there was a large Muslim community which did not have a Halal butcher. With the money, he was able to move out of his modest home into something a bit better and bigger but he kept the old house and rented it out to students, convenient for those who were studying in St Mary's colleague, which is part of London University. As much as the butchers shops were a success, he was finding it hard work trying to keep on top of them, scattered as they were across London, from Greenford in the West to Mile End in East London. So, he sold the retail shops and opened a wholesale Halal meat business instead and it has since become one of the biggest Halal meat suppliers in the south."

"And now he wants to sell and leave?"

"He has sold up everything, Kiffy. His businesses, his houses, everything. He says he is going back home to Pakistan. Back home to be with his family and spend the remainder of his days there, living a quiet life for as long as Allah wills him to be on Earth. So, Mister Khan came to say goodbye, to wish me good fortune in my life and invited me to his home in Pakistan, a mini paradise the way he described it."

Country Matters

It was a week after Adrienne had moved in with him and the summer school term at Westminster school was over. Theo had mentioned that his father's birthday was coming up in a fortnight's time and it was customary for the family to get together for a few days to celebrate it. He asked Adrienne if she would accompany him to it, although he would understand if she did not want to. Having initially said she had felt awkward about going, encouraged by Anca she changed her mind and said of course she would be glad to go but was concerned the clothes she had would not go down well with the West Country set. She had also gone through his wardrobe and had concluded with horror that none of his clothes were suitable either. There was only one thing for it: to fly to Paris and buy new clothes! Despite his protests that there were perfectly good clothes shops in London, she was insistent and he acquiesced. A whole week without quarrelling had been somewhat of a novelty and he wanted nothing more than for it to stay that way. So, on the very first Monday after school closed, they flew into Charles De Gaulle airport, for two days of shopping in Paris. She had wanted to go via Eurostar as she felt train travel was more romantic but he wanted to fly and she did not push it.

"Kiffy, tell me again why we have to come to Paris to buy clothes when there are perfectly good clothes shops in London where, by the way, people from all over the world come to buy the most fashionable brands they have ever heard of?" he asked, as they strode past the Arc De Triomphe, with hardly a glimpse upwards and turned down towards the Champs Elysée.

"Flint, we've been through this already. We can't go to your father's birthday celebration next week with the clothes that you've got in your wardrobe. Mine, maybe I could get by with but yours, definitely not," she said and the tone suggested this was not a matter up for discussion.

"There's nothing wrong with my clothes. They are very smart. No-one has ever complained about my clothes. Besides, it's my parents —

they don't look at what I wear and we're only going to be there a few days."

"Flint, one last time. You are going with me, not so? And what you wear is a reflection of me. Yes, you do wear smart clothes but they are all work-like clothes and don't be offended, what's the English word, oh yes, plain!"

"Plain?"

"Okay, maybe not plain. How about conservative? Flint, I want you to look modern and wear fashionable clothes and we have come to the most fashionable city in the world. You will look really cool when we go to visit your parents, trust me."

"Why I need to do that, I don't understand but I won't argue. Okay, can I at least ask one small favour?"

"I won't say yes and I won't say no, until you tell me what it is," she teased.

"Can we get my clothes shopping done first and then I disappear to the Louvre whilst you are doing yours?"

She thought about it and then smiled her assent.

"This credit card of yours is going to get warm by the end of the day, Flint," she giggled. They were back on the plane the following morning after breakfast, suitcases heavier with the best that Paris could offer for the well-heeled, his credit card white-hot from the exertion.

They had left the motorway and travelling down narrower 'A' type roads and then onto more country lanes. The twists and bends in these narrower roads had the effect of waking Adrienne up.

"Where are we?" she said, yawning.

"Not long to go now, Kiffy. A few more miles and we will be there," he replied. "Just in time for afternoon tea."

Adrienne sat up and craned her neck to look out onto the verdant fields either side of them but it was impossible to see, as the hedgerows were too high.

"I'm afraid these roads do get a bit narrower as we get nearer and it's difficult to see around bends. I might have to brake hard if there is a car coming in the opposite direction," he warned.

"You're not going to kill me, now that I am officially your girlfriend are you, Flint?" she joked.

"It did cross my mind but I thought London would be a better place as there are so many more people, the loss of one more, especially a fiery Frenchwoman would probably go unnoticed," he said, laughing. "Don't worry Kiffy. This time of day there won't be many cars around, maybe the odd tractor and a rabbit or two scurrying across the road."

"And it's quite bumpy too," she said, holding the door handle tightly.

"Yes, it is. I'll go more slowly to reduce that but nothing I can do about it, as it's the roots of the trees not to mention the suspension of this old car. I don't think when Austin built it, they meant it for it to be used on windy and bumpy country roads," he explained.

"Maybe you need to trade it in for a new one, Flint. I like the Jaguar F-Pace; very cool design. Must have been done by a Frenchman," she teased.

"Actually, he was British, a Scot, I believe. Anyway, what do I need a big car like that for? My little Micra does everything for me around town and this classic British sports car, designed by an Englishman I might add, serves me well on longer trips like this," he retorted.

Some quarter of an hour later, he slowed right down, almost to a halt, turning into an even narrower road between two newly-painted, white fences. The road seemed to have been cut through a wood and it became suddenly darker as the dense foliage all but filtered out the bright sunlight. It felt much cooler and Adrienne lifted her jacket back up over her shoulders. At one bend, he had to stop the car to push aside a fallen branch that was blocking the way.

"Where are you taking me, Flint? Doesn't look like anyone has been down this road for ages. It is a bit scary," she said, looking to him for reassurance.

"Nothing to worry about, Kiffy. The tree must have fallen sometime today. This road gets used every day, so someone would have noticed it. We're nearly there," he said, patting her leg for re-assurance.

Ahead of them, there was a shaft of light indicating that the wooded lane was finally opening out. Soon, they were back into a sunny day, the change of darkness to brightness making each of them squint, Adrienne dropping her sunglasses down from her hair.

"Flint, when you said your parents have a house in the country, you did not say anything about how big it is. Mon Dieu! It is huge! In France, the name we give to a house looking like this is 'chateau'," said Adrienne, as a large country estate came into view.

Theo shrugged. "It is still only a house, Kiffy."

"Some house. How many people must live in it? Apart from your mother and father, your brother and his wife also live there right? And how many children?"

"Three."

"Big house for just seven people to live in."

"It's not just them. My other sister and her husband and two children also live there. Only Suzy and I do not live at home," he explained. "Eleven members of the family. When my grandparents were alive that would have been two more. So, although it is as big as a chateau as you call it, it is well-occupied. And of course, there are rooms for guests coming down, like us for example. No one has to give up their rooms for us."

"Hey Flint, will your parents be expecting us to sleep in separate rooms? Are they going to be okay with me sharing your bed?"

"It is not Victorian times you know!"

"It's just that you English are weird about these things. I don't mind sleeping in a separate room to protect my virtue," she giggled and then added, "I like the idea of you sneaking into my room in the middle of the night and taking advantage of me."

Theo sniggered. "It is more likely that it will be the other way around, Kiffy. I'm the one who will be fighting you off, I think."

"So, your mother is responsible for this house and everyone who lives in it. I can't imagine that she looks after everybody does she? Do you have lots of servants and maids? And maybe a gardener, too? Wow, Flint, posh family living in a posh house. Is your father some sort of Lord too? Is it like Downton Abbey?" she teased.

"My father is not a Lord, just a gentleman farmer. Yes, we are quite a big family but most of the children, have either been packed off to boarding school or are at university and just come home at the end of term. But you are correct in surmising it takes a lot of people to run the estate. There are many helpers. Mrs Chalfont is the house manager and she has a team working under her. Don't know how many. Mrs Chalfont has her own cottage as do the head gardener and the farm manager. There are also groundsmen, others who look after the horses and farming folk but most do not live on the estate. They live nearby or in the village. Anything else you want to know?"

"Just like Downton Abbey," she teased.

"Having never watched it, I can't comment. All I can say is that Josiah Hall is a working farm, as you will find out shortly," he said, as the road ended, replaced by a wide, gravel path, bordered by well-kept lawns, which meandered its way to the front of the house.

"What did you call it? What hall?"

"Josiah, named after the person who built it, Josiah Blenkinsop, during the reign of George IV. It was originally called Josiah's House but someone along the way had it renamed to Josiah Hall. Not sure why or when, you will have to ask my mother about that."

"Old family? When was the reign of George IV?"

"I think he was king in around 1820, didn't last very long, I don't think. Again, ask my mother, she does the grand tour for the tourists and guests."

"That would be at the time of the return to royalty for France. Louise XVIII. He didn't last very long either. And he had to stop Napoleon trying to take over for the second time. Well, well, you are indeed a country gentleman, Flint. I am impressed. And one day you will be the head of all this?"

"In theory, next year when my father reaches eighty and he officially retires, I become head of the family," he said matter-of-factly.

"So you will be the new lord, Flint. Wow! And I shall be your humble servant and you can ravish me any time you want, my lord," she said, giggling.

"Okay, we're about to come to the house, behave yourself please, Kiffy," he said.

"Yes, your lordship," she teased.

Even from a distance they could clearly see there was a hive of activity going on with people coming and going, heading down a path towards a building at the far end and to the side of the house.

"What's going on, Flint? What's that house next to your house that everyone seems to be going to?"

"It's preparations for my father's birthday. Everyone gets invited, all the estate workers, their families, local dignitaries, like the vicar, the mayor and so on. It is an annual event that everyone looks forward to and gets to enjoy. There will be a barbeque, including a hog roast and there will be music and drinking and all-night revelry, if you like. It's too big to host in the house so we use the barn, the building you saw and a marquee is put up joining on to it but you can't see it from here. Everyone will be busy preparing and being overseen by my mother so if she sounds a bit brusque when we meet her, it is just the stress of it all. She is normally quite affable."

They pulled up to the side of the house where a number of cars were already parked. Theo recognised Bertie's Land Rover and Suzy's Jaguar sports car and he parked next to them, where spaces were reserved for immediate family members. They walked around to the front of the house, Adrienne feeling nervous and holding on to Theo's arm. The wide, oak doors under the huge, stone-arched entrance to the house were open as people came and went but one of the servants waited for them, took their weekender bags and led them into the hall.

"Is it okay for me to say wow!" Adrienne whispered in his ear.

"Welcome sir, miss. Mrs Blenkinsop sends her apologies for not being here in person to greet you. I am instructed to tell you that you will be in the Blue Room on the second floor, sir," said the servant politely.

"Thanks, Joseph."

He took their luggage and they followed him up the wide galleried staircase, adorned with paintings of different gentlemen, who Adrienne surmised were previous residents of the house.

"Blenkinsops?" she asked Theo, quietly.

"Yes, miss. From Josiah Blenkinsop, the person who built this house, to the present, Mister Aubrey himself as we go up the stairs," said Joseph, overhearing her.

They had reached the Blue Room and when Joseph opened the door, it made Theo smile. The décor had not changed much since he had left Josiah Hall. Except for the thick curtains, hanging heavily and tied back and a new bedspread, glancing around, it felt as if he had gone back to the time of his youth. The antique rug was still underfoot, faded from years of exposure to the sun and worn from the patter of feet on it. The burgundy red, Queen Anne armchair still sat there proudly, the leather had cracked in places, next to his favourite window, facing out, exactly where his grandfather would sit and read him stories. The stone fireplace looked as if it had not been used for a long time but the stains of burnt wood on the back were still recognisable. The Blue Room, his room, was where he had grown up and contemplated what dreams might come.

"Yes, just like Downton Abbey," said Adrienne, lying back on the four-poster bed. "Are you sure it wasn't filmed here, Flint?"

"As I said, I have never seen Downton Abbey and I haven't a clue where it was filmed, except I am pretty sure it wasn't filmed here. I am sure my mother would regard it as common to allow a film crew into her house," he said, as he sat on the edge of the bed, imagining the look of horror on his mother's face if a TV film producer approached her to make such an opera.

He pulled one of the heavy curtains tight against the wall and looked out of the window onto the ornamental gardens below, kept in immaculate condition by two full-time gardeners under the supervision of the head gardener, who in turn was answerable to his mother. Long ago, she had decided that the immediate grounds around the house, the landscaping, the rose garden and two ponds, one for lilies and the other shared between koi fish and whatever amphibians chose to live in there, were her responsibility and no one was going to question that. As a child, he recalled that she had admonished him for floating the wooden boat he had made on the lily pond, describing it as an 'eyesore'.

"I have unpacked our bags, your Lordship and I have changed my clothes," said Adrienne, as she silently crept up behind Theo and pressed herself against him, her arms snaking around his waist.

Theo turned around and Adrienne pushed him down onto the Queen Anne armchair and stood before him naked.

"Is there anything I can do for your lordship?" she said, turning on a sweet, innocent-sounding, voice.

"Anything?" he asked, looking into her eyes.

"Anything, your lordship," she giggled.

He smiled. No words were needed as she knelt down in front of him and started to undo his shoelaces, taking off a shoe at a time, slowly and deliberately, her eyes never leaving his. Then came the socks, tossing them over her shoulder. He remembered them being bought in a fancy man's tailors in Paris, at an eye-watering price and now they were being discarded just like any other cheap, Marks and Spencer socks made in India or some such place.

When she pulled his trousers off, Adrienne smiled. The object of her desire was already bulging in his pants, there was no denying that she was making Theo excited and that excited her too.

Adrienne ran her hands up each thigh, allowing her nails to rake over his skin lightly. It was the finest of feathery touches, just enough to tantalise. Theo was squirming in his seat, she was tormenting him and it felt like torture. And he liked it. Having reached the top of his thighs, her hands were starting to stray inwards. Abruptly, Adrienne halted her ministrations and sat back on her haunches.

"Shall I stop, Flint, I mean your lordship?" she said.

"It is only good manners to finish what you started," he replied, trying to keep up a façade of indifference.

But no sooner had she pulled down his pants and started to play with him when there was a knock on the door. Theo leapt up like a gazelle being chased by a pride lion, pulling his pants on in the process and Adrienne, as quick as a flash, jumped on the bed and under the covers.

Theo ran to the door and poked his head around it, keeping his body hidden behind the door.

"Mrs Blenkinsop, that is your mother," said Joseph, remembering there was more than one on the estate if you included Bertie's wife, "has asked if you and your friend would like to take afternoon tea with her. She will be in the Italian garden, sir."

"Thanks, Joseph. We'd be delighted. If you could let mother know, please," said Theo and as Joseph was about to leave, he added, "And Joseph, she is not just any friend, she is my girlfriend, and her name is Adrienne."

Joseph nodded. "Very good, sir. I will let your mother know that you and the, and Miss Adrienne will be joining her for tea."

When he had closed the door, Adrienne started to laugh. "That was close, Flint. Too close. I think we should wait until the night before we fool around again."

"Coitus interruptus," he laughed. "Still, we have a few minutes before we have to rush down."

He pulled his pants off and jumped into bed next to Adrienne and started to caress her but she pushed his hand away. "No Flint! You know how I go all red and flushed when we make love. Your mother will know what we have been doing. I will be too embarrassed. Save it for later," she said and sat up. "Now let's get dressed."

"Spoilsport," he said and tried to pull her down but she stayed out of his reach.

When they had washed and put on fresh clothes, they walked hand in hand down two sets of stairs, peering over the balustrading, seeing many tops of heads going back and forth. It looked like an aerial view of a multi-level motorway, with people going in different directions.

The Italian garden was so-called because many years earlier, Theo's grandfather, Archibald Blenkinsop, had taken a holiday in Italy and fell in love with a statue in the garden of the villa he had rented and entreated the owner to part with it. Many millions of lira later, he had succeeded and had it shipped back home, much to the horror of his wife, Theo's grandmother. Nobody knew where to put it exactly until one of the stable lads had joked that it needed its own garden around it. And, as Theo and Adrienne walked down a path and through an opening of a cropped hedge of yew trees, they could see the result of that flippant remark made fifty years earlier. They feasted their eyes on a beautiful, circular, sunken garden, in the centre of which was the statue of a child being held by its mother, water trickling around it and into a pond where lilies and marginal plants were bursting with flower.

At the far end of the garden at ground level, it was laid out with six seasoned, teak, garden chairs, padded with thickly-stuffed cushions on which to sit, a long table, covered with a white linen cloth atop which sat a variety of cakes and tea things, all under a canopy to protect from the intensity of the summer sun. It was here that Beatrix Blenkinsop, head of the household and Theo's mother sat. As they got nearer, Adrienne began to get nervous and squeezed Theo's hand instinctively.

"Don't worry, she doesn't bite," he whispered reassuringly.

As they reached the table, Beatrix rose from her chair as Theo introduced Adrienne. She greeted each of them in turn, first kissing her son and then Adrienne. She ushered them to sit, motioning for Adrienne to sit next to her.

"Theodore rang to tell me he was coming and asked me if he could bring his girlfriend. I had no idea he even had one; he keeps his private life very private, my son," she said, holding her arms out. "That said, I was very pleased for him that he did have a girlfriend and of course, I was very happy that he was bringing her to his home. And now that I've met you in person, I am enchanted my dear. Welcome to our family home."

"Thank you, Mrs Blenkinsop, I am happy to be here. I hope, Fl… I mean Theo said positive things about me," said Adrienne, trying to hide her nervousness.

"Please, let's not be so formal, call me Trixie, everybody else does. I never used to like it. My mother brought us up to address people by their full names but now that I am an old woman, I like Trixie; makes me feel young again," she said and took Adrienne's hand into her own. "I hope you can stay for a few days, my dear, so I can get to know you. This is such a male dominated place, other than my daughter Constance and Mrs Chalfont, there is no other woman to talk to."

Theo was about to add, 'and Arabella too' but checked himself. Bertie's choice of wife was not one his mother had approved of, albeit she came from a well-to-do family. In all the years that he had known Arabella, he had never seen his mother warm to her, always polite but there was a gulf between them. Yet, as Theo watched the body language between the two women, much like he might do at a contract negotiation, the signs were positive. Soon, Adrienne and his mother were talking ten to the dozen and he found himself able to relax and enjoy the country air and reminisce about the happy times he had spent here in his early youth, especially the time spent in the company of his grandfather, Archie. As a young boy, he had looked up to Archie, who was not only his grandfather and the person who he doted on but also his playmate, his actual father being too busy running around building up the farm.

Joseph arrived to inform his mother that Mrs Chalfont needed her in the house and she stood up, apologising for having to leave them.

"On second thoughts, Theodore you won't mind if I steal Adrienne away from you for an hour or so, would you?" she said and then, holding her hand out added, "Come my dear, let me show you around, Theodore can manage on his own, can't you darling?"

Theo smiled, comfortable that he could leave them alone together without being anxious as to how they would get on. He finished the last of the cakes on the table and then got up to wander around the grounds, giving a wide berth to the barn and the marquee which were a hive of activity preparing for his father's birthday bash the following day. He hadn't seen his father for several months and yet he did not feel an especial longing to go and seek him out. 'I'll see him at tonight's dinner, no need to interrupt the preparations,' he told himself.

Passing by the stables, he saw giggling young girls grooming the horses enthusiastically. Part of the legacy of Josiah Blenkinsop was to offer local children, in return for mucking out the stables and grooming the horses, a chance to ride on the estate for an hour or so, supervised by one of the stable hands. The family owned eight horses and often the weekends and school holidays were busy with children riding. Theo was not a keen horse rider, in fact he flatly refused to ride one, explaining that he would not wish to subjugate another species for his pleasure. When he first made his feelings public, his father and his brother Bertie were saddled and mounted and were impatiently waiting for him to do the same.

"How odd," was all his father could say, when he announced how he felt about riding. Bertie, didn't say anything, just sniggered his disdain.

Taking yet another winding path, Theo walked towards where he could hear the sound of someone shouting. It made him smile as he recognised the voice belonging to his sister Suzy. Through another hedge he came to a tennis court where there was a game going on between his other sister, Constance and Arabella, Bertie's wife. Suzy was sitting upright on a wooden garden bench, padded with thick blue cushions and acting as umpire, the walking stick beside her a reminder that she had yet to fully recover from her accident in Brussels. Constance blew him a kiss and Arabella waved with her tennis racket.

"Hey sis, how are you?" he said, leaning down to kiss Suzy before sitting next to her.

"Monty, my saviour and hero," she said, giving him a hearty hug. "Come and watch Wiltshire's answer to the Wimbledon ladies final. What they lack in skill they make up for in enthusiasm and determination, especially our sister-in-law. Arabella is very competitive as you see. And not afraid to grunt Maria Sharapova style either."

He laughed. "Good to see you, Suzy," he said, putting his arm around her. "How's your leg doing? I saw your car earlier, surprised you could drive here."

"Ssh, shouldn't really be doing that but I wasn't going to get the train here and then ask dad to send a car for me, was I?"

"Good to see Connie stand up for herself," he said, as he watched the two women walk up to the net and argue over a point. "Time for you to do your job, little sis."

"I think it's actually Arabella's point but I'm going to call it in favour of our sister just to annoy her," she said quietly.

Theo laughed. "I think I'll leave you to it. I'm going to find Adrienne. Mother decided to take her away with her when we were having tea."

"You brought her here? So, does that mean Adrienne is now your official girlfriend?" He nodded.

"Well done, Monty! When we met, you were still prevaricating. What made you change your mind and decide?"

He shrugged. "Can't say I know myself. It's just that I like being with Adrienne more than I like not being with her."

"Monty, you're in love!"

"Oh, for goodness sake! Why do women have to bring up the dreaded 'L' word? I wish I'd never told you."

"Monty, you're in love," Suzy repeated, giggling. "Go on, admit it."

"I admit nothing!"

"Bertie will not be pleased. You know our brother is pushing dad to bypass you and let him take over next year when dad hits eighty. With you having a girlfriend, that will most definitely put his nose out of joint."

"I am not concerned about it," he said, nonchalantly.

"Watch your back, Theo. Bertie is a determined man," she warned.

"Right! On that note, I had better go and find Adrienne to parade her under his nose and see what happens! I'll see you tonight at supper," he said, kissing her and waving goodbye to the others.

"Your mother is really cool, Flint," said Adrienne, catching up with him later in the day.

"I told you, nothing to worry about."

"She is so friendly and open and so unlike you, Flint. I am guessing you must take after your father," she teased.

"Mother is the customer-facing part of our tourist business and they all love her."

"Tourist business?"

"Yes, in addition to being a farm, we have diversified. Josiah Hall also offers holiday breaks for those who wish to see what it's like to live on a country estate. My sister Connie runs it. Does very well, attracting foreigners, mostly Americans and increasingly Chinese, even some of your countrymen. The high point of any visit is when they get invited to spend the evening having supper in the main part of the house with my mother and father who put on a good show, my mother especially. She oozes affability and the guests, especially the Americans, go home feeling they have had the honour of meeting English royalty and, needless to say, we don't disabuse them of that."

"I'm impressed, business-minded farmers; wish my parents were more like that. My father just likes to farm, even though where we live is the quintessential rolling hills of Normandy and ideal for bringing in tourists, especially British tourists who like all that. But he won't do it, too conservative," she moaned.

"We've had to diversify in order to survive, Kiffy. You cannot run an estate like this purely on the proceeds of the farm, it barely makes a profit. The tourist business and hosting weddings generates the most revenue by far. I know Bertie is always looking at ways to bring in more business and from what I see of the accounts, he has met with success. Anyway, enough about our business, how did you get on with my mother? You said she was cool?"

Adrienne told him that his mother introduced her to Mrs Chalfont, a formidable character who ran the household like a captain of a ship, never barking orders but with a firm modulated voice that commanded respect and obedience. From there, his mother had taken Adrienne through to the vast kitchen where there were staff preparing different dishes to be consumed at the birthday party: all manner of cakes, pies and terrines. The smell of freshly baked bread permeated throughout. In the adjoining room, the rotund head chef had the meat laid out and was butchering a whole lamb carcass, next to several trays of chickens he had already prepared for the barbeque. Next to him, a young lad was putting chunks of beef through a mince-making machine, collecting it as it came out and passing it over to another person, who was mixing it with spices and herbs and then pressing the mixture into moulds to make burgers. Adrienne said that there must have been at least fifty or more burgers already stacked up.

Leaving the kitchen, they headed out the back where a truck had pulled up and people had started to unload barrels of beer and cider and crates of wine. Adrienne said that his mother was able to rattle off what they were supposed to deliver without even having to refer to a list. Adrienne had been very impressed by her.

"And the way your mother walked so fast, I had to almost run to keep up with her, Flint," she said. "It was, as you say in English, a whistle-stop tour of the preparations for your father's birthday party. Your mother said she will show me around the house when there is more time and she can relax, maybe not until after the party. I think she is excited by the party. She said it was the one time of the year when the whole family, including aunties and uncles, cousins and friends all got together. I asked how many people but she said she didn't think it was that many."

Theo laughed. "Not that many, hey? At least one hundred and maybe as many as one hundred and fifty, from little children taking their first steps to my great auntie, Harriet, who's coy about her age but we reckon she is in her nineties."

"Wow! That's as many people as live in my village!" she said, laughing.

They were walking back towards the house, when a tall man with a thick-mop of grey hair and wearing an open-necked shirt, riding breeches and knee-length, leather boots beckoned to them.

"Who's that?" asked Adrienne quietly.

"That is my father," said Theo flatly.

The man quickened his pace and for someone who was about to celebrate his 79th birthday, Adrienne was impressed with his spritely jaunt as he approached, holding his arms out to greet them.

"My dear boy, so good to see you again," he said, embracing his son, slapping him on the back. "And who is this charming young lady?"

He took Adrienne's hand and kissed it, much to her embarrassment, as Theo introduced her.

"Please don't call me Mister Blenkinsop. Aubrey is my name, we are informal here at Josiah Hall. Delighted you could come my dear, I know it's a bit of a drive down here from London. Come let me show you around, I'm sure Theo won't mind, will you son?"

He did not wait for an answer and for the second time that day, Adrienne found herself being whisked off to another part of the estate with Theo's father, who put one arm around her as he pointed in the distance towards the barn where the preparations were taking place.

Theo shrugged and continued on, back into the house and then up the stairs heading towards the Blue Room where he had spent much of his early youth. When he was up on the first landing, he looked down the stairs and along the balustrading where his grandfather had secretly taught him how to ride it down to the bottom like a slide. The first few times he had been scared and his grandfather had held his hand for most of the way down but as he grew in confidence, he was soon whizzing down of his own volition, followed by his grandfather who enjoyed it as much as he had done. They had been caught out only the once by Mrs Chalfont's predecessor, who happened to be crossing the hall and did nothing to hide her displeasure at their boyish behaviour. He was worried that he would get into trouble but his grandfather had said a quiet reassuring word. "Don't worry my lad, I'll sort it." Whatever his grandfather had whispered in her ear seemed to placate her and no more was heard of it. He had meant to ask what he had said but was so relieved that she was not going to tell on him, that he had ran up the stairs and into his room for the rest of the day.

"I wonder if I can still do it," he thought, as he lifted one leg over the handrail and sat on it holding on to the stair spindles. He had that same feeling of unease as he had felt the first time but at the same time, he felt the presence of his grandfather and let go. He hurtled down the highly-polished oak and landed at the foot of the stairs in a matter of seconds, stopping himself in time before he would have bashed into the bottom newel post, a huge stout piece of carved oak that would have brought a tear to his eye had he made contact with it. As he dismounted,

Arabella was walking across the hall, tennis racquet in hand and looking at him, frowning.

"Still up to your boyish games, are you Theo?" she said, smiling.

"One day I'll grow up," he said, dismounting carefully.

He could see that she was sweaty from the exertion of playing tennis. There was something earthy about seeing a woman with dark patches under her armpits and between her breasts and he could not help but stare which made her redden with embarrassment.

"Theo, behave yourself," she said half-heartedly.

"What?" he feigned ignorance.

"You're staring at my breasts. Have you no shame?" she joked.

"Arabella! How can you say that? You're my brother's wife! I would never do that," he said smirking. "How are you anyway? Did you defeat my sister?"

She grinned.

"Oh dear, hope Connie is not going to be in a foul mood at supper tonight," he joked. "You should have let her win, Arabella. She is a sore loser."

"Why should I? You Blenkinsops win at everything, so a small victory for me every now and again, even if it is only at tennis, is good for the soul!"

"Whose soul?"

"Mine, actually!" she giggled. "Now if you don't mind, delighted as I am to see you, I need to go upstairs and have a shower. I don't suppose I can walk up without you looking up my skirt, can I?"

"Certainly not, what colour knickers have you got on today?" he said, knowing too well that she was actually inviting him to look.

"Not telling!" she said as she left him and strode up, taking two steps at a time.

"They're white!" he shouted after her and he could hear her giggle in response.

Although Arabella was not particularly well-liked by the others, he was not averse to her company and felt sorry for her. Yes, she could be standoffish and aloof, even haughty at times but he put that down to being a sort of front she put on as a defence, against the lack of warmth she felt she was getting from the family. The first time he had met her was when his father had thrown an informal party to celebrate Bertie's forthcoming betrothal to her. He had come down for the weekend more out of a sense of duty than anything else but when he met her, he was quite taken aback.

"The lucky sod! How did Bertie manage to capture the heart of such a fine-looking woman?" had been his first thought. At the time he felt quite troubled and the reason for that was that he found himself being envious of Bertie, to the point of being jealous! Arabella was accomplished, well-spoken, very well read on the arts and current affairs and much travelled, it seemed. In short, quite a breath of fresh air in the otherwise stolid and unadventurous world that was country life. The impact was immediate and everyone seemed to take to her. In some respects, seeing the way his parents had reacted to Adrienne reminded him of those early days of her arrival at Josiah Hall. But farming life and rearing two children were clearly not enough for her and she made no secret of being bored, especially when her children were old enough to be packed off to boarding school. She had once confided in him that she missed having her children around, if only because it was a distraction from supporting Bertie to manage the estate.

"Nowadays, one of the few pleasures in my life, Theo, are little trips into Bath and Bristol where I can re-learn and reacquaint myself with what it's like to be a townie," she said. "As a town girl, I feel more at ease surrounded by people, cars, noise and shops; more so than the peace and serenity of the countryside. I'm sure too much fresh air is as bad as not having any, Theo."

With that confession, he had wondered whether to alert his brother, if only to recognise that yearning in his wife and perhaps take time off now and again and perhaps go with her or even further afield. But it was said in confidence and as a lawyer, he could not betray that.

Theo reached the Blue Room but decided not to enter, instead he followed the landing around and up another set of stairs, to somewhere he had not been in a long time: the attic floor. He remembered that the attic, which ran the entire length of the house, was divided into four rooms, two of which had been bedrooms, although he had no idea what they were used for now. When he reached the attic level, somewhat out of breath from the exertion, he headed for the darker, far end of the corridor, the wide floorboards creaking underfoot. It brought back memories of night-time, secret rendezvous with his grandfather, tiptoeing in their pyjamas to explore further up. When he reached the room he was looking for, he halted and gently knocked on the door in case it was being occupied. But there was no discernible sound from within and as he turned the brass doorknob, it opened into a bright but airless room, stale and stuffy from not having been used for a long time. He walked in, taking care not to bang his head on the sloping ceiling and looked for a narrow doorway. It was there, in the middle, innocent-looking, paint fading and peeling in one or two places and without a hint of what lay behind it. It looked that it could be no more than a door to a fitted wardrobe. But Theo knew different and he went straight to it, dusting the handle before turning it. The door was a little stiff but it eventually gave way after a few attempts and a whoosh of fresh air came rushing into the room, along with dust. Theo waited for this to settle and then took a tentative step up, testing it for sturdiness, before taking another and then a third, stopping briefly to crane his neck and peer out. He smiled. Two more steps up and he was now level with the roof and took a foot gingerly onto it. Satisfied that it wasn't going to give way from his weight, he took one final step and stood straight up, the late afternoon sun still bright enough to make him squint. There was a refreshing breeze as he carefully made his way along the roof, leaning his body against the tiled, sloping roof as his grandfather had taught him to do many years earlier. This was the first time he had ventured up onto the roof, for well over twenty-five years, when he had sat alongside his grandfather, then in his mid-seventies and confessed his love for an Arab girl. He had let on that the relationship was looking like it was doomed to failure as she was from a devout Muslim family and they would not countenance her marrying a Christian.

"I don't suppose there is any chance that she would consider becoming a Christian?" He shook his head.

"Oh dear, you are in a pickle, my dear boy," he had said, as they shared a flask of coffee laced with the finest Cuban rum or Havana grape juice as it was euphemistically referred to. "But you must decide for yourself what needs to be done, no one else can do that for you."

Abla had decided for both of them by marrying one of her own countrymen.

Looking down from the roof, he had a grandstand view of the party preparations and there were so many people involved it was looking like the army had bivouacked on one of the fields. He walked around as far as the roofing line would allow him and leaned over a parapet wall, where he could just make out his father near the marquee, in his element directing operations for his own birthday celebration.

"The old goat loves it! Sure to be a rum do tomorrow," he said and looking skywards added, "Looks like the weather is going to be kind to the partygoers this year."

When he returned back down to look for Adrienne as she might be looking for him, he saw that she was in the scullery with Connie and Arabella drinking freshly-made lemonade and eating strawberries.

"Hey, big brother, come and join us," said his sister, waving him in as he stood at the door.

"I wouldn't want to disturb," he said, as he ventured in and stood next to Adrienne. She handed him her drink and he downed it in one go.

"It's okay, we're not having a girly conversation if that's what you are thinking. Just chatting about Brexit and what impact it will have on the business. Never did hear where you stand on the subject, Theo," Connie probed.

"And you won't," he said. "I need to wash and get ready for supper. I'm sure it will come up tonight one way or another. But for the record, I did not vote in the referendum. See you all tonight."

He watched the bemused look on Connie's face, mirrored by Arabella and he smiled. Adrienne just frowned and stood up.

"Wait, I'm coming too," she said, thanking her hosts for their delightful company. "Hey Flint, you didn't vote?" she asked, as they walked up the stairs.

"No, I did not."

"Why? Did you not feel the weight of responsibility? Did you not think it was important to participate? I am surprised that someone as intelligent as you would not do so, Flint," she said.

He shrugged his indifference.

"What does it matter if I voted or not? Look what's happened since. The wishes of nearly seventeen and a half million people are being ignored because a group of barely six hundred and fifty strong, wise men and women parliamentarians, think they know better. Would it have made any difference if it was eighteen million or twenty million in favour of leaving the EU? No, because the MPs say they know better and maybe they do but that is not what the referendum, what the people, said they wanted."

"So, you knew it would turn out that way and decided not to vote; I don't think so?" she said in disbelief.

"No, Kiffy. Of course, I did not know it was going to turn out that way; I left my crystal ball at home the day I had to cast my vote!"

"Flint, don't be sarcastic with me. I am asking you a perfectly simple question which requires a perfectly simple answer. If you don't want to answer just say so. I respect that you want to be private about it but don't treat me like a kid!"

They had arrived outside the Blue Room and he unlocked it with a big, brass key and opened the door for her to enter first but she stood in the doorway and blocked him from entering. "Are you going to tell me why you didn't vote or did you vote and this is just your clever way of stopping people from asking how you voted?"

"Kiffy, come on. Let me get past, I need to jump in the shower."

She stood her ground and lifted her foot up and rested it against the architrave blocking his entry altogether.

"Flint, if you are going to sleep in my bed tonight and not on the floor, you'll have to answer my question first."

"Kiffy! That is *my* bed. That is the pillow on which I rested my head on for the first eleven years of my life."

"And if you want to make it eleven years and a day, then tell me why you did not vote," she insisted.

"Kiffy, using sex as a weapon to get me to bend to your will is cheap and beneath you. I will not do that. The floor it is."

She scoffed at his petulant refusal to answer her. "You English make such a big deal of democracy, of the sense of fair play, of having your say and yet, given the opportunity to exercise that, surprisingly, you choose not to. I wish you hadn't told me you did not vote, Flint. But now that you have, I am intrigued as to why not. Theodore Blenkinsop does not do flamboyant gestures; everything is measured, so there must have been a reason for you not to vote, so don't be so stubborn Flint and tell me!" she said, exasperated by his refusal to answer her.

She removed her foot and let him enter. He sat on the armchair and started to undress. "It is correct to say it is a simple question. Why did I not vote? But to answer is not so simple. On the surface, to vote was straightforward, just choose: stay in the EU or be out. But in my mind at least, before I could decide I needed to understand what were the possible consequences of either scenario. Just before the referendum we were being bombarded by both sides; a lot of hot air and rhetoric being spat out: on the television, over the internet, on the radio and in the newspapers; information overload you might say. Both sides espousing the reasons why I should choose one in preference to the other," he said and paused whilst he bent down to pull off his shoes and socks and put them neatly to the side of the armchair.

"With all that information you couldn't make up your mind? You weren't going to vote out and use the money for the NHS and close up the borders to foreigners or stay in and as a big player, help the EU shape its future, or whatever the arguments were."

"That's just it. What were the arguments on both sides? What would enable me to make an informed decision? So, to help that, I asked myself what the compelling reasons were to stay in the EU and I could not think of one. Similarly, I also asked myself what the compelling reasons were to leave the EU and again, I could not think of one either. I asked others, experts in finance, friends in the civil service, thinking they might have some insight that I had not been able to garner for myself. Over many weeks, I came to the conclusion that the arguments on both sides were largely emotive. I have spent my career putting together contracts acting on facts and measurable outcomes. In the referendum build up, both were in short supply and I came to the stark conclusion that I had insufficient information for me to make up my mind with any degree of certainty as to why I would cast my vote one way or another."

"So you decided not to vote."

"Correct," he said and finished undressing. He walked naked to the old armoire, smiled when the familiar smell of beeswax wafted into his nostrils and grabbed two towels, throwing one in Adrienne's direction. He padded barefoot to the door, his towel draped over his shoulder.

"Flint, where are you going?"

He laughed. "Kiffy, in case you hadn't realised, this is an old house, built nearly two hundred years before en suite bathrooms were invented. I have to use one of the bathrooms across the hall."

"Wait, wait for me, I'll come with you," she said and stripped off, leaving her clothes in a pile and walked up close behind him.

"You know, Flint, so far every one of your family that I have met has been really nice, friendly, open and so sweet to me. Your mother and father especially but also your two sisters and Arabella, your sister-in-law. Everyone has been charming to me. I haven't met your brother Bertie yet but I'm sure that he will be nice too," she said, as she lay soaking in the Victorian-style, roll-top bath whilst he showered.

"Yes, that's my family, all smiles. Friendly, especially to Johnny foreigner," he teased.

"So different to you. Are you sure you are part of this family? Perhaps you should have a DNA test Flint, in case you are not really a Blenkinsop. Maybe you were adopted." It was her turn to tease.

"Maybe I was but that does not explain why they are friendly. After all, we English are cold and unfeeling and never express our emotions: not so," he said, splashing water on her face when he got out of the shower.

"Perhaps they're not English? Flint, maybe they are French," she laughed.

It elicited a response from him. He reached out to scoop up some water to splash her with but she was too quick for him, dunking her head under the water.

"Ha-ha," she said when she emerged. "Now, do my back for me. Wash my back for me, Flint."

"Hmm, let's negotiate," he said, sitting on the edge of the bath and running his hand over her breasts, teasing each nipple in turn.

"What are you after, Flint?" she smiled.

"I am willing to soap your back, but…"

"But?"

"You've got to finish what you started earlier," he said.

"Who's using sex as a weapon now?" she teased.

"Not looking much like a weapon at the moment," he laughed. "But I am quite certain you can remedy that."

She giggled. "Okay but wash my back first."

"Oh no, as a lawyer I like to deal in certainty. Me first!"

The message from Joseph was that supper was to be served in the main dining room but first, everyone was to meet in the drawing room for pre-dinner drinks. Dress code was to be informal but his mother had requested that this did not extend to wearing jeans or trainers. Despite his protestations, Adrienne insisted that they put on the clothes they had bought in Paris and picked out a pair of trousers and a shirt for Theo and had chosen a sleeveless, wrap around, low-cut, floral, summer dress for herself.

"Flint, how do I look?" she asked, doing a twirl.

"Hmm," he said, sounding unconvinced.

"Flint! Stop looking at my breasts and tell me what you think!"

"That's just it. If you go downstairs dressed like that, all the men will be staring at your chest. It's too revealing, Kiffy. Can't you pull that wrap around a little more?"

Adrienne giggled. "Are you jealous, Flint?"

"When we were in Paris, Kiffy, you said what I wore is a reflection of you. The same applies the other way around. What you wear is a reflection of me and I would please ask that you cover up a little," he pleaded.

"Okay, Flint, I will. I am happy that you are jealous and you don't want other men to be ogling me," she said, as she untied the waist band and pulled the dress tighter so that the front showed less cleavage. "Anyway, I have small breasts, no one would have noticed, Flint but have you seen your sister-in-law's? They are very big and she doesn't hide them, does she?"

"That is different. You are with me, Kiffy. Cannot comment on Arabella; that is for Bertie to deal with."

When they entered the drawing room, everyone seemed to have already gathered, clumped into little groups. Adrienne mentally counted twelve people, including five of whom she had not met before. Although the dress code had been advertised by Joseph as casual, her eye for fashion told her that it was anything but noting many classic and expensive English country-wear. She felt vindicated by her insistence that they dress smartly and squeezed Theo's hand and he smiled at her smugness.

Beatrix, having spotted them out of the corner of her eye, left her little group and made a beeline for them, kissing and hugging both, before taking Adrienne by the hand and leading her away.

"Come, my dear. Let me introduce you to other members of the Blenkinsop clan that you may not have met today," she said.

Theo's natural inclination was to gravitate towards the two men propped up against the stone fireplace, his brother Cuthbert and his brother-in-law and Connie's husband, Hugo. But remembering previous such gatherings, he found their company tedious and boring to the extreme as they seemed to mainly want to talk about the estate and ways in which they could do this and do that.

The alternate bunch he had as a choice to attach himself to, were the trio of women sitting one end of the room, legs crossed, long dresses and showing lots of flesh that were his two sisters and his sister-in-law, or the group with his father holding court, captivating an audience of his grandchildren, with his eloquent storytelling.

Theo was reluctantly making his way towards the two men, when he saw that his mother was heading in the same direction with Adrienne and turned instead towards the trio of women.

"Thank you, mother. Owe you one," he muttered under his breath.

"Lucky escape there, Theo," said Suzy, as he sat down opposite the three ladies in a single armchair, running his fingers over the well-worn leather.

"Whatever do you mean?" he said, feigning misunderstanding.

"Come now, Theo, don't pretend. I know you. Talking country matters with Bertie and Hugo, no offence to you Connie or you Arabella, is not exactly a turn-on for a much-travelled, city lawyer.

"Suzy, I am sure you are misrepresenting me; I was heading towards the boys. Just did not want to interrupt mother introducing Adrienne to all and sundry," he joked.

"You may not admit it, Theo but from where we were sitting, the glum look turned to a beaming smile when you saw your chance of escape," said Connie. "Don't blame you, I do remind my sweet hubby not to talk shop when we are in company but as soon as he and Bertie get together, they switch right back."

Theo took a glass from the side, filled it with Madeira and then offered it out to the ladies, trying not to stare at the substantial cleavage that Arabella was showing when he leaned down to fill her cup up. It made him smile when he remembered Adrienne's earlier comment.

"So, if country-matters doesn't turn you on, what does, Theo?" she asked.

"Pardon?" he asked, stalling for time.

"Can't you tell? He's enraptured by the French *Oh la là* lady, flirting with your husband I think Arabella," Suzy teased.

"Suzy! Have you had too much to drink already?" he said, in a disapproving manner.

"Pain relief for my gammy leg, my dear brother," she replied.

"Dad has found a willing audience for his stories of old. I swear each time it's never the same yarn that he spins," said Connie, pointing her cheek to where her father stood.

"You should have been here a little earlier, Theo, when mother politely threw out Gerry and Rupert for coming to dinner wearing t-shirts, jeans and trainers: standard university wear for you and I. But mother wouldn't stand for it and invited them to return when they were properly attired," said Suzy.

"I did warn Gerry," said Arabella, "but he insisted his grandmother would understand. So humiliating!"

"Mine was the same, Arabella. I told Rupert but he wouldn't have it. Don't worry; no reflection on either of us. Mother knows students can be rebellious," said Connie, patting her hand.

"Were you ever rebellious, Theo?" asked Arabella, as she crossed one leg over the other, pointing her immaculately manicured foot at him.

"Me? Never. I never had to be. When I was very young, mother was too busy bringing up Bertie and then Connie and then Suzy. Each of you were a handful for mother. I spent most of my time keeping well out of the way."

"Grandad Archie was his playmate. Those two were inseparable," Connie explained.

"Only until I went to Charterhouse. After that, it was straight to university so I did not get to see much of my grandfather except during non-term time. No time to be rebellious."

"Why did you leave the estate?" asked Arabella.

"Good question. One day I will think of an erudite answer and tell you. Now, if you will excuse me ladies, I should circulate. Bertie and Hugo, here I come," he said and rose from his armchair.

But it was too late for him to join them. Dinner was announced as being served and as tradition had it, the parents led the way and then Theo accompanied by Adrienne were next, the heir apparent.

"What's for dinner? I'm starving," Adrienne whispered.

"Nothing fancy, just a simple roast for tonight, I think," he smiled.

Family

The light was fading in the distance, the sun having already set, when they closed the backdoor of the house and set off on an evening stroll around the grounds. The walk was meant to work off some of the largesse that had been supper. Suzy had suggested the need to do that after the after-dinner brandies and ports but there were no takers other than Theo and Adrienne. It was therefore just the three of them that were strolling down the windy path that skirted the Italian garden and down a gentle gradient towards the walled, rose garden. Suzy was holding onto Theo's arm on the one side, her other hand firmly gripping her trusty walking stick and Adrienne was doing the same on his other side. It was a mild evening and one to be enjoyed not rushed. Birdsong could still be heard in the trees.

"I'm stuffed," said Suzy. "If it wasn't for this leg, I think I would love to run down to the woods all along the track and around the lake and back again."

"I feel very full, too," said Adrienne, rubbing her stomach. "I don't understand how everybody else can just go to bed. I have too much food inside me to be able to do that."

"Ah you see, Adrienne, they are country folk. We are not. They rise early, they get to bed early. You, me and Monty are city folk, we rise early and get to bed late."

"Monty? You have another name?" she asked, turning to Theo.

"Oops! Sorry Monty," said Suzy, putting her hand to her mouth. "Oh well it is out now. Shall I enlighten Adrienne or do you want to?"

"Go ahead, you seem to be doing a good job of it yourself," he said drily.

"Theodore Montague Josiah Blenkinsop, son of Aubrey Gerald Benedict Blenkinsop! Montague was our mother's great-uncle whom she was very fond of and well, Josiah as you know, was the founding member of this family. Only I get to call him Monty, Adrienne, so I beg you not to betray this confidence."

"Of course. Your secret is safe with me, Monty," she giggled. "I have my own name for him but as his lordship might say, I am not at liberty to discuss this with you."

Theo laughed. "Yes, you are not and if you do, you're walking all the way back to London, *Adrienne*!" he said, emphasising her name.

The path levelled out and split into two. Suzy indicated with her stick for them to take a left turn as it followed the stream that ran through the grounds of the estate, before meandering back up to the right side of the house. Although it was summer, with the volume of rain they had received during May and June, the stream was flowing freely instead of just being a gentle trickle, fast enough for it to be heard cascading over the rocks in the water.

"Is it true what Bertie told me? That all the meat we've just eaten, including the lamb, the poussins, quails and even the ducks are all grown on the estate." asked Adrienne.

"Yes, it is. And the pork we are having as a hog roast tomorrow too and not just that: the burgers, the sausages, everything else that you will see on the barbecue, came from the estate. All organically fed and free range," said Suzy proudly. "No chemicals or hormones have been used in growing any of the Josiah Hall meat. All the animals get to roam freely, the pigs live outside and the chickens can scratch and forage like they should, not be kept inside where they never get to see any daylight. The ducks live in and around the chickens and sometimes like to wander down to the stream. We also grow our own vegetables so virtually everything we ate tonight was produced right here on the estate, including the fruit that went into the apple pies and the rhubarb crumble. If you are interested, get Mrs Chalfont to show you her preserves larder. There is every type of pickle, jam and chutney you can think of and honey from our own bees. She is very proud of it and would be delighted to show you, for sure."

They reached the point where the path was now turning back up towards the house and stopped briefly. In the distance, they could see the lights of Mrs Chalfont's lodge and the head gardener's cottage porchlight. They could also discern the faint glow of Bertie's hall-light but otherwise it was dark everywhere, the only illumination coming from the house itself.

"It is so peaceful here; reminds me of my home back in Normandy," said Adrienne wistfully.

"It is: maybe too quiet for me. I am used to the buzz of Holland Park right up until the early hours of the morning. London traffic weirdly lulls me to sleep. This silence is too noisy for me. I can hear noises in my head instead of outside it and that freaks me out," said Suzy.

When they were back in their bedroom, Theo sat down in the armchair, and sipped on the tea that he brought up from the kitchen. "I was thinking tomorrow we could walk the stream down to the lake, if you like, Kiffy. The party guests will probably not start arriving until around midday and the party proper does not get going until the afternoon, so plenty of time to wander around."

"Maybe. Feeling tired so don't necessarily want to be going too far otherwise I will be too tired to dance with you, Flint. You know, all this time, we haven't danced once."

"We've danced around the bedroom a few times," he quipped.

"Very funny!" she said and taking his cup off him, manoeuvred herself so that she sat down on him and put her arm around him. "I like your family, Flint. I think I like your mother the most. She doesn't put on airs and graces. Her no-nonsense, down-to-earth approach is great. I like the way she cuts someone down to size, including your father, when they start being pompous or arrogant. I like Suzy too, she is a lot like me from what I can tell. You should invite her round more."

"She is great, isn't she? What did you make of Connie?"

"She's okay," Adrienne shrugged. "She is very quiet and I get the impression she is in awe of Hugo, although I don't know why. Your mother told me that Connie is the brains behind the tourist business, Hugo just fronts it. The Americans, especially the women, are apparently taken in and swoon at all the charm and demeanour he puts on for them."

"Were you taken in by it?"

"No, not at all and neither is your mother, who according to Suzy, once described him as a pretentious popinjay in the way he behaves when middle-aged American women are booked in. Had to look up what 'popinjay' meant on my phone and it made me laugh."

"Hugo is just fleecing them of their money in the nicest possible way. It is theatre and the tourists are his audience. As I am one of the beneficiaries of the income we get from the tourist business, I can't complain. Can I ask who did you like the least, if you don't mind saying, Kiffy?" he asked. "I am just curious and will not be offended."

"You probably won't be surprised if I say, it is your brother. I mean, he is okay, really. Just found him a little bit superficial. Pleasant and courteous and said the right thing but really not that interesting, except when we talked about the farm and then he seemed to come alive."

Theo nodded. "That's my brother. Get him talking about his organically-grown broccoli and cauliflowers and his eyes light up! He is most definitely a country boy!"

"But what really surprised me, Flint, was that nobody, not Hugo, not even Bertie, was stuck up! Nobody displayed any of that classic, upper-middle-class English snobbishness, or egotism that I was expecting to see. No one was aloof or distant towards me. Basically, everyone was friendly. I was horrified, so not what I expected!"

"Shocking! We have a reputation to keep up! Don't go telling anyone we are actually friendly, it will be the end of the British Empire as we know it."

"Ha-ha, the British Empire was lost a long time ago, Flint," she said, kissing his nose.

"Perhaps that's the reason why we lost it. We got too friendly instead of being aloof and supercilious. It behoves me to fight a rear-guard action and maintain that reserve, that coldness and rebuild the empire," he said.

"You are doing just fine yo…" she stopped herself.

"You were going to say?"

"No! I will not say. I promised myself that I will try and stop being rude to you."

"Kiffy, you know that is impossible for you to refrain from doing that. It would be more challenging than the twelve labours of Hercules combined. Zut alors!" he teased.

She thought about it and then giggled. "Maybe you're right. Maybe only whilst we are staying here then."

He tickled her. "That's my girl!"

"Am I your girl, Flint?" she said, kissing along his neck.

"Would you be sitting here on my lap if you were not that?" he said and tried to reach under her t-shirt but she stopped his hand and sat upright.

"Flint, next year your father will be eighty years old and you will become head of this family. You won't be sleeping in this room any more. You will be moving out of the Blue Room and moving into the master bedroom, that is unless of course, your brother Bertie steals it from, what's that English phrase? From right under your nose."

"You are not the first to suggest that but I do not believe Bertie is like that. He is not that ambitious."

"So far, what I am hearing is that Bertie might well be and even if he isn't, his wife is," she warned. "From what I've seen of Arabella so far, and admittedly it has only been a few hours, I can tell she is very status conscious and she is very ambitious for Bertie."

"Really? I did not get that impression."

"That's because you were mesmerised by her femininity!"

"Her femininity?"

"Do I have to spell it out? Her big breasts. I saw your eyes, the way they undressed her when you were pouring our drinks. That sultry, seductive smile. I am sure she does that for effect."

"Really? I do not think so, Kiffy."

"Flint, in French we have a phrase for women like Arabella: *Cherchez la femme.* Do you know what that means?"

"Beware of the woman behind the man, right?"

"Yes, and in Arabella's case that is very true. She sees herself as being queen of this place one day with Bertie beside her, although the way she was flirting with you so openly, disrespecting me by the way, I don't think she would mind if it was with you."

"Kiffy, you have nothing to fear on that front," he reassured her.

"It's you I fear for, Flint. Your birth right could be taken away from you if you are not careful."

"Kiffy, if he wants it that bad, let him have it. Let's face it, I am never going to be living here, am I? My career is miles away from here, in the dizzy lights of London and the stifling heat of the Middle East. I do not see myself, I have never seen myself, as a country gent. Bertie is cognisant of that, as are my parents. Maybe as a little boy when Grandfather Archie was around, I might have had childhood dreams about this place but not anymore, not really."

"Flint, it may surprise you to know that your mother not only expects you to become the head of the family next year but she told me that she is not keen for Bertie to take over whilst she is living."

"Really? She confided that in you?"

Adrienne nodded. "Yes, when she was showing me around the house. We were walking up the stairs and she was giving me a little history of each of the previous Blenkinsops whose pictures hang on the wall. She said that next year, when you take on the role as head of the family, she will be very happy to see your portrait hanging up there too."

"Oh dear, not sure that strikes an accord with my own plans which certainly do not call for my giving up my career as a lawyer and heading up a country estate, for which I am not suited to. Did mother elaborate as to why she doesn't want Bertie to take over? After all, he practically runs the place now."

"She didn't say but maybe you can talk to her about it."

"Anyway, enough about Bertie. As you say, he is not that interesting to be talking about," he said, feigning a yawn. "It is late, let's go to bed."

"A little bit longer; I'm still feeling a bit full."

"What you need is to do some more exercise," he said, pulling off her t-shirt.

"Did you mean sexercise?" she giggled.

"You must have read my mind, Kiffy!" he said, as one of his hands traced a line to her breast.

She held it there, stopping him from going further. "Hey Flint, would you prefer if I had big breasts like Arabella?"

"Kiffy, I like you just as you are, the whole package as it is," he said, kissing her. "Very diplomatically put Flint but really, you don't mind that my breasts are small?"

"No, I don't mind!"

"Pig!"

"What?"

"You should say that you like them just as they are, not you don't mind them being small," she said, reaching down and pulling his manhood.

"Ouch!" he said wincing. "Kiffy, I do like your breasts as they are, honestly. But what I like most about them is they are yours and they belong to you. And I was going to say this to you but have yet to get around to it and that is, tonight you were the most beautiful of all the women, the most elegant and the most charming."

"Hmm, you know how to get round me, don't you?" she said and kissed him.

"Did it work?"

She freed his hand to continue its exploration.

The Day After

Beatrix was sitting in the morning room, dressed in her robe, sipping tea and looking out as the sun was rising over the treeline in the distance. It was the day after her husband's birthday party. She seemed to be wrapped up in her own thoughts and did not hear Theo enter the room. As he poured himself a cup of coffee from the machine on the sideboard, the clatter of china woke Beatrix from her reverie.

"Morning Mother — didn't mean to startle you," he said. He cast his eye over the range of items laid out for breakfast, wrinkling his nose. From under a napkin, he spotted croissants and smiled.

"Theodore! Come and join me," she beckoned. "Looks like it's just the two of us."

He padded over to where his mother was sitting, holding a tray laden with tea, croissants, yoghurt and strawberries."

"Adrienne joining us?" she asked

"Not just yet. When I crept out of the room, she was fast asleep."

"She must be worn out, poor thing. I think just about everyone asked her to dance and I don't think she turned anyone down, not even the grandchildren. Very charming, young lady."

"Yes, I did not get to dance much with her, that's for sure, there was always someone ahead of me in the queue. Still, I got to dance with you, Mother."

"Charming! You make it sound as if your mother was second choice. Not very gracious, Theodore," she remarked.

"I did not mean it like that, Mother," he said, taking her hand in his. "What I meant was that it is not often that I get a chance to have you to myself. As the hostess, you are forever running here and there making sure the party is running smoothly, so catching you whilst you paused to take a breath was lovely. You are a great dancer, knock the spots off everyone else," he said, hoping he had assuaged her feelings of slight.

It elicited a smile from her and he felt comfortable enough to compliment her further. "I must say Mother, you do know how to throw a party. Everything was great, the music, the food, the flowers, the way the barn was adorned was particularly excellent, everyone commented on it. Can I book you in for my sixtieth birthday party in eight years' time?"

"If I am still alive and I have the energy, then of course I will be glad to do that for you," she said, putting her hand on top of his. "Such events take a lot of planning, a lot of organising, months in the making and I have had many a sleepless night ensuring I left nothing to chance. And I do believe it was a success," she said proudly. "Of course, next year when your father reaches eighty it will be an even more a special birthday and I have already started to sketch out an outline plan in my little notebook."

Theo bent down and kissed her on the cheek.

"Wow! What's got into you, Theodore? You're not normally this affectionate," she said, turning towards him. "You're normally more of a cold fish!"

He pulled a face and she added, "I am pulling your leg, my dear boy. Just took me by surprise, that's all. None of my children were very affectionate towards me, not you, certainly not Cuthbert nor Constance, all except Suzanne who was very much a clingy, mummy's girl until she left for school. I sometimes wonder when Aubrey sent the boys in this family off to Charterhouse and the girls off to Cheltenham Ladies College, whether it was such a good thing. When you all came back you were like strangers to me. Perhaps I should have been more insistent that you went to a good, local school rather than board far away from us."

"It was to make men of us, as I recall Father saying," he said, without a trace of the resentment and bitterness that he had felt throughout his teens.

"Be that as it may, I think the price we paid may have been that we lost something of the bond that exists between parents and children. Still, that is all in the past, let's talk about the present," she said, taking a croissant from his tray. "Tell me about Adrienne."

"Adrienne? What do you want to know?"

"What are your intentions towards her?"

"Intentions?"

"Theodore, stop pretending to be obtuse. You are a very intelligent man, probably the most intelligent living Blenkinsop and you know exactly what I mean. But for the avoidance of doubt as you might say, I'll spell it out for you. Where does Adrienne fit in with your plans? You must be serious about her, otherwise you would not have brought her down to visit."

"I haven't made any plans, at least not regarding Adrienne," he said honestly.

"What! Then why have you brought her into my house, introduced her to the family if you intend to just…" she paused and then added, "If she is just a plaything for you that you will get rid of when you tire of her."

"Mother! Adrienne is not a plaything for me," Theo corrected her and realised he had raised his voice and winced. "Sorry I should not have shouted."

"Forgive my intrusion, Theodore. I am not asking you to be indiscrete. I am your mother; I am naturally concerned. I will say no more on the matter."

He was silent, drinking his coffee, gathering his thoughts. His mother's question had hit a raw nerve, as it was a question he had been asking himself increasingly in recent times and he had yet to formulate a coherent answer and that irked him. For someone whose life revolved around the strict corridors of legal language, of contracts, of procurements and tenders, a relationship was uncertain ground and came with unpredictable outcomes, obfuscated by emotion and feelings. He was wary of control slipping away from him, of getting in too deep and unable to pull out. It was also complicated by his long-term desire to move out to the Middle East; something he had yet to share with anyone. And, as if that wasn't a sufficient hurdle, his parents expectations that he would do his duty and take up his position in the family when the time came, further exacerbated the situation.

"I am very fond of Adrienne," he said finally.

"Fond?"

"Yes, Mother, fond of her. She has recently moved in with me at my request," he said. "But I am taking it one stage at a time."

"Whatever does that mean? I never understand it when people say that. How long have you known Adrienne?"

"Several months, on and off."

"On and off? What does that mean exactly. Theodore, I don't wish to rebuke you but I do wish you would stop talking in riddles," said Beatrix, showing signs of losing patience with her son.

"It's complicated because, as you know, I spend a good deal of time away from home working in the Middle East. So, the relationship has, in many respects, not developed or matured as much as it might have, had work not kept me away. But as Adrienne has moved in and as it is now Ramadan in the Muslim world and work slows down, I have taken the opportunity to book quite a lot of holiday to be able to spend more time with her," he explained.

His mother smiled. "So, forgive me if I appear to be labouring a point, are your intentions towards her serious?"

Theo hated being put on the spot like that. It made him feel as if he was a witness in a dispatch box and being interrogated by a hostile lawyer.

"It would seem that way," he said quietly.

"Good boy, I do like Adrienne and I think she is good for you, Theodore. I think you may have met the right woman for you, for the first time in your life. She looks like wife material to me," she teased.

"Mother! Please do not go saying that to anybody, I beg of you. It is too early to be thinking about marriage. I am not even sure I want to take myself a wife. I implore you not to share your thoughts with anyone, not even father. As I said, I am very fond of Adrienne but that is as far as it goes."

"Theodore, you do know she is in love with you?" she said.

"Did she tell you that?"

"She did not but as a woman, I can tell. And I am also reasonably sure that you are in love with her!" she said, laughing.

"Oh, for goodness sake! It's absurd, there is absolutely no basis for you making that statement," he insisted.

"Theodore, I may be old but I haven't lost my marbles yet. You may not admit it to yourself but you love Adrienne as much as I think she loves you. My dear, it is a fine thing for a man to love a woman and in Adrienne, I am certain that love will be returned even more than your own."

"She may not have told you but Adrienne is only thirty-two, that makes her twenty years younger than me, Mother. Does the age difference not concern you?"

"You are in fine fettle, are you not?"

"Yes, as far as I know."

"Well then, you have nothing to worry about, Theodore. Anyway, I have arranged to go horse riding with your good lady this morning so I will probe more on your behalf."

"Horse riding?" he said, frowning.

"Yes, I know, you disapprove of subjugating horses for our pleasure. Be that as it may I am taking Adrienne horse riding with me. It's a beautiful morning and seeing the estate on horseback is very pleasant. You will have to find something to do to amuse yourself, Theodore. Perhaps some tennis with Constance or Arabella if either of them show their faces"

"Actually, I am going fishing," he announced.

"Fishing? I have never seen you show the slightest interest in that particular sport."

"Bertie invited me to go fishing with him, so fishing it is. I am off to change and then wander over to his house."

"Wonderful; my two sons spending time together, what could please a mother more? But Theodore, please do not drown poor Cuthbert in the stream, will you?" she joked.

"From what I am hearing Mother, it is more likely to be the other way around. Your dear son has designs on my birth right."

"Well, it is up to you to not let him take it from you, Theodore. I am not interfering."

Fishing with Bertie

Theo took the winding path, lined with lavender and hebes in full bloom. It led to Bertie's house, a four-bedroomed lodge on the estate set beside the stream, surrounded by a well-kept hedge of dense yew, affording protection from prying eyes. And Bertie was indeed a private man. Whilst happy to engage with all and sundry in managing the day-to-day running of the estate, he was more taciturn and introverted outside that role, preferring his own company. He liked nothing better than to walk for an hour or two around the estate with Henry, his dapple-coated, pointer gun dog, or finding a quiet stretch along the stream and engaging in the battle of man versus fish.

Although many a young lady would have given her right arm to be his wife and become part of Josiah Hall, he had instead been taken in by Arabella, who he met at a country fare. A good deal of the attraction was that she was precisely the opposite to all the girls in his social circle of country girls. Arabella was urbane, polished and oozed sophistication. Bertie was smitten. Whilst lacking in the genteel manners of her circle of male admirers, she was nevertheless, drawn to the handsome rugged man who wanted nothing more than for her to become his wife. He was not debonair or suave in any way but she found that part of his charm and when he asked her to marry him, barely three months after they had met, she was flattered, feeling something akin to love towards him and accepted his proposal. Children followed soon after, first Clementine, who Arabella had named after her grandmother, then Gerald, who he named in honour of his father, whose second name it was and the third and last child, a boy they name Rupert. Now, at the age of forty-eight, he was contented with his lot in life, as much as anyone could be. All was well, that is except in his relationship with his wife. The so-called honeymoon period lasted until after the birth of Rupert when she told him she'd had enough of procreating, did not want any more children and intended to become sterilised so that he could not browbeat her into changing her mind at some point in the future. It had come something of a shock to Bertie as he had always wanted to have four children and he begged her to reconsider but she put it to him bluntly, that the allure of being a Blenkinsop breeding machine had lost its attraction and she wanted to refocus her life more on herself. When she stubbornly refused to listen to his entreaties for one more child, he wanted to hit the roof in frustration but it was not his way. He remembered what his mother had once told him. 'Blenkinsops do not row, they discuss and resolve.' He had tried in vain to dissuade her but Arabella was adamant and backed up her determination, by a thinly veiled threat of returning to her home in Bristol, if he did not acquiesce to her wishes. He was defeated and paid for Arabella to have the discreet procedure in a private hospital in London, far away from any inquisitive eyes. But Bertie was cheerful by nature and he put it behind him and got on with the important job of making sure that Josiah Hall would continue to stay in the family for many years to come, through his hard work and diligence. Things were also looking up in his relationship with Arabella, since the weight and expectation of having children had been lifted off her shoulders and they began to function more like a couple than they had done for some time. Indeed, when he revealed to her his plans to usurp Theo in his role as head of the family and assume that role for himself, she reverted to being a very supportive wife once again and life became much more tolerable.

When Theo reached the small garden gate that was the gap in the hedge of yew trees, he called out for his brother and waited. As there was no response, he decided to walk around the side and look for him. He entered the garden via the side wall, ducking the overhanging wisteria which was still in bloom, hanging down like bunches of purple grapes. He called out for Bertie as he looked around but there was no response once again and he ventured further in.

"He's down in the back, getting his rods and nets together," said a voice, hidden from view.

He craned his neck to see where she was and then averted his eyes. "Sorry, I didn't realise you were, er, sunbathing, Arabella," he said, trying not to look at her naked breasts, as she lay in just her bikini bottoms on a sun lounger.

"It's okay Theo. Please come and have a seat and wait for him," she said, making no attempt to cover up.

"Perhaps, I can go and look for him," he suggested.

"I wouldn't if I were you. That shed is his private Aladdin's cave and no one, not I nor any of the staff, can go anywhere near it. Come and have a drink with me. Can I pour you one of these healthy concoctions or some iced lemonade?"

Theo sat on one of the high-backed, steamer chairs at an angle. He felt very uncomfortable sitting there in the knowledge that his brother might appear at any moment now and may not be too understanding seeing him there next to his half-naked wife. Theo put his sunglasses on, not only because the bright sun was making him squint but also to hide his embarrassment at seeing his sister-in-law lying prone not three feet away, her fulsome breasts on show and her long legs splayed out, her lower garment leaving very little to the imagination.

"Do you want me to cover up?"

"Pardon?"

"I can see you are very agitated seeing me in my sunbathing attire and if it will make you feel more comfortable, I can throw a towel over me," she offered.

"Er, it's your home, Arabella, you must do as you please," he shrugged, as if he did not care one way or another. In truth, he would have much preferred for her to have put on a robe on, or even better, for him to have got up and left but that would have been seen as a weakness, that she had had that effect on him and so he chose to sit there as if it was the most perfectly ordinary thing for him to be doing.

"If I was doing as I pleased, Theo, I would be lying here au naturelle, as nature intended but I don't want to shock you, do I?" she teased. "In fact, I was planning to do just that before you came."

He shrugged. "As I said, this is your home and you must do as you please, Arabella," he said, reverting to his usual deadpan voice of a lawyer.

As Arabella was also wearing sunglasses, he could not tell from her expression what she was thinking or what she intended to do in response but he did not have to wait long, as Arabella drew up her legs until her heels were pressed against her body and then untied the strings to her bikini bottoms. From where he was sitting, Theo could not see anything other than the side of her leg nearest to him and it irked him to realise she was playing with him and that it was having the desired effect. Arabella faced him but as each of them was hidden behind sunglasses, neither could tell what the other one was thinking. It felt like it was as if they were playing a game of chicken; who would react first and he was resolute in not being the first to do so, not moving an inch. To do so could be construed that he was being affected by her and he did not want to give her the satisfaction of knowing that. Whilst her gaze remained fixed on him, Arabella, slowly started to lower her legs, deliberately starting with the one furthest away from Theo, tantalising him, so that he could not yet get a glimpse of what his mind was already actively imagining was there. But he was not to find out as the bang of a shed door closing alerted him to the presence of Bertie nearby and he left in a hurry, via the side entrance and went to look for him.

'Lucky escape!' he told himself, as he quickened his pace to set some distance between him and Arabella.

Soon he came across his brother and together they set off with their rods, live worms in a box and foldable stools over their shoulders. Bertie also carried a thermos flask of tea and a knapsack of sandwiches and cakes for lunch, that Arabella had prepared for them.

It took nearly an hour of walking along a path beside the stream, before they came to a bend where the water flowed more gently and Bertie pointed to a little clearing close to a weeping willow, its long sinewy branches overhanging the banks and dipping into the water.

"Here's the spot," said Bertie. "It's ideal. The fish like the shade, makes them feel safe."

"Until we harpoon them," said Theo, noting the frown of disapproval of his comment on his brother's face.

Theo opened his folding stool and slumped down into it as Bertie methodically set out the two fishing rod bags and box of live bait to one side and then laid a tartan blanket on top onto which he put two metal, tea mugs, the flask and the knapsack of goodies for them to enjoy later.

"Looks like you're a practiced hand at this, Bertie," said Theo.

"Oh yes, love fishing. Love the challenge of it," he said. From the inner pocket of his gillet, he pulled out a hip flask and joked, "To keep out the cold."

Bertie then threw the smaller of the rod bags to Theo, unzipped his own and started to assemble his rod. In a minute, he was ready to bait it and looked across to his brother who seemed to be struggling with attaching the reel to the rod.

Bertie reached across and put it together for him. "Out of practice, old chap," he said, his face smirking at his brother's ineptitude.

The note of criticism in his voice did not go undetected but Theo chose not to react.

"Here, put one of these on your hook, fish love them. Careful not to stab yourself," said Bertie, thrusting the box of live wriggling worms under Theo's nose.

Theo looked down at the worms, squirming and writhing. He took one in the palm of his hand and watched as it wriggled and stretched, trying this way and that to get away. It felt cold to the touch. He realised that he could not bring himself to stab the helpless worm.

"Squeamish, Theo?"

"Just psyching myself up to impale this poor creature," he said. "Why do we do it, Bertie?"

"I thought that would be bloody obvious! How else will we catch a fish, silly sausage?" he said and grabbed the fishing line and hook off Theo impatiently, added, "Here, let me do it!"

"No, please don't do that, Bertie. Not for me at least," said Theo, pulling his rod back before his brother had a chance to hook the worm. "Never really understood why we spear a poor worm onto a hook and then launch it into the water in the hope that a passing fish sees it and gulps it down, and in the process, lodges the spike in its mouth."

"And if we are quick enough, we reel it in with our rods, hopefully," said Bertie, laughing. "And then, being the good anglers that we are, we throw it back into the stream for someone else to have a go."

"That's just it, Bertie. I do not get it," said Theo, reeling his line all the way in, carefully removing the barbed hook at the end.

"What don't you get, Theo?"

"We kill an innocent worm, injure and distress a fish and we do this not because we are hungry and need to eat but just for our pleasure. Our pleasure comes at a price of the death of a worm and the injury of a fish. That's what I don't get."

Bertie looked at his brother and frowned. "It is only a worm, Theo.

And as for the fish, everyone knows how stupid they are!"

"All the same, I would rather you did not bait my rod, Bertie. Never was that keen on fishing. But you go ahead. I'll just sit back and enjoy the lovely view before my eyes."

"Suit yourself," Bertie huffed and stood up, launching his line ostentatiously, looking back to see his brother's reaction which was not forthcoming.

Despite the tasty morsel on offer, the fish were not yet hungry enough to be tempted and after a minute or so, Bertie sat back down on his stool, pegging his rod against its V-shaped rest. Theo reached over to the thermos flask and poured out two teas, handing one to Bertie.

"My being here isn't about fishing, at least not for fish, is it Bertie?" he said, as he took a sip from his metal cup.

"What do you mean?"

"You and I never went fishing together before today. As I recall, it was something you enjoyed doing on your own. What's on your mind, Bertie?"

"Perhaps it's long overdue, us spending time together," he said, sounding unconvincing.

"I see you wish to be circumspect, so I will make it easier for you, Bertie. I think you want to discuss the estate and what is to become of it once father reaches his eightieth birthday, not so?"

"Now that you mention it, then, yes I am more than a little curious as to what plans you have for the estate under your stewardship?" he said cautiously.

"I will be honest with you Bertie. I have been very busy with my work and not given it much thought. Father's birthday has brought it home to me that it is only a year away when I take up my role and that I need to focus on making the transition from him to me smooth. I am interested to hear what you would do if you were in my position, Bertie?"

Bertie shrugged. "Not for me to say really as I am not in your position."

"Okay, as you are being coy about this Bertie, then I will be blunt with you. I am given to understand that you wish for father to bypass me and for the estate to pass straight to you. Is that the case or have I been misinformed?"

"You have not been misinformed. I will lay my cards on the table then, Theo. I do think I am better suited and better qualified to be head of this estate. I know every aspect of it. I live and breathe it every day of my life, I've raised three children here and I belong to this life. You are, by any reckoning, an excellent city lawyer. Your life is in the city, not here. You spend very little time in the country and have never shown any interest in running the farm, nor the tourist business or the weekend wedding reception business. In as much as I know very little about the practice of law, you know very little about the practice of running a country estate. I know what makes it tick. I fear under your stewardship the estate will quickly fall apart and we may end up losing it. It's nothing personal, dear brother but I have invested a lot of my life here and have a lot at stake and I don't want to let you ruin it."

"So, you see it as your responsibility to, how should I put it, usurp my birth right, in order to ensure, if I have understood you correctly, the survival of the Blenkinsop legacy?"

"Indeed, my duty and I hope not but if necessary, I will seek to petition the courts in order to achieve that, if I cannot persuade you to step aside," he said, solemnly.

"Bertie, it sounds very noble of you. Your willingness to go to that extent to ensure that there will be Blenkinsops on this estate for generations to come could indeed be perceived as the actions of a decent and moral man. On the other hand, it could be seen as no more than the tawdry action of a nakedly, ambitious man, who will not let a little thing like his brother's birth right get in his way. Hmm, I wonder what a high court judge would say to that? Might I take it you have already engaged a firm of solicitors?"

"No, not yet. I wanted to hear what you had to say, first. I wanted to see if you could be persuaded to step aside for me."

"As we are laying our cards on the table, let me be straight with you. I have no intention of stepping aside for you. For the avoidance of any doubt, you may have as to my resolve, let me be clear. I will not be giving up my birth right to you and I hope it will not come to it but if necessary, I will fight you in the courts to ensure that never happens. And on that subject, I have actually consulted a retired judge, a friend of mine of many years and somewhat of an expert in matters of property rights and inheritance. Her legal opinion is that you have very little, if any chance, of success as the law is most definitely on my side. My lack of experience in country matters is not in itself a good enough reason for the courts to agree with your petition that I would be unsuitable to the role, not least because, when all is said and done, I could hire a professional person to run it on my behalf."

Bertie was shaking his head in disagreement. "It would be a disaster."

"Be that as it may, it would be my disaster, Bertie!" he said impatiently but added in a more emollient tone, "but it does not have to be that way. I am a practical man and I would concede my credentials for running this estate do not stand up to scrutiny. You have done a magnificent job of managing the estate and everyone, including myself is very grateful to you, Bertie."

"I don't need your gratitude, thank you very much, Theo," he said, bitterly.

"I agree, you do not, so I have a proposition for you," said Theo. "Let's have a snort of what's in that flask and a bite of these delicious looking smoked salmon sandwiches that your good wife prepared for us and I will run through my plan."

By the time Theo had explained what his future plans were, Bertie's countenance having started off being glum and despondent, metamorphosed into one of a bright mood and cheerful disposition to the point of a smile from ear to ear.

"Does that make you happy now, Bertie?"

"Yes it does, very much so," he said and offered his hand. "Let's shake on it."

Theo took his hand but added, "A handshake is good, Bertie but for the avoidance of doubt, I will draft a document for both of us to sign as our agreement."

Bertie laughed out loud, "You and your avoidance of doubt. I would have accepted your word, Theo."

"Alas, even in families, it is always better to get things written down, Bertie. As I said, for the avoidance of doubt!" he chuckled.

Riding

When Adrienne awoke, she found the note from Theo reminding her that he was going fishing with Bertie and that she was spending the morning with his mother. After a good night's sleep, she felt refreshed and ready to start her day. Sitting up in bed and stretching her arms out, she smiled as she recalled the enjoyment and merry making of the night before. It was now mid-morning and the sun was desperately trying to penetrate the thick curtains of the room, to no avail.

"Looks so bright outside, must let the light in," she said, as she lifted herself off the bed. The hardness of the wooden floor was a reminder of how much dancing she had done, the tender soles of her feet still feeling sore.

'I think I overdid it,' she told herself, as she put on a robe and tiptoed across the hall to the bathroom, toiletries bag under her arm.

Sometime later, having soaked her feet in the scented bath salts she found in the wall cabinet with the etched glass mirrored door, Adrienne felt rejuvenated and emerged dressed, and on her way down to meet up with Theo's mother. She found her immersed in the Sunday Times crossword, sitting cross-legged with her feet up on a stool. Her thick, silvery hair was tied back in a bun and Adrienne noted that she was wearing jodhpurs and riding boots, a reminder that Beatrix had offered to take her riding: 'the best way to see the estate' as she had put it.

Adrienne greeted Beatrix with a kiss to each cheek and then helped herself to a coffee and yoghurt and to her amusement, she also found a warm croissant under a cloth. Beatrix found it pleasing to see Adrienne eating so heartily and reading the headlines, belying the perception that French women only lived on cigarettes and magazines.

"What shall we do today?" asked Adrienne, after returning with a second croissant which she lavished with a spread of thick-cut orange marmalade.

"I understand you are returning to London this evening."

"Yes. Theo wants to get back; he has some business to attend to," she said, crunching through her croissant.

"My dear, I wish you could stay a few days longer. Hardly had the time to have had a good natter and now you will be off. We have been remiss as hosts in not showing you round the estate properly, and today I thought a nice long walk would have been a good way of doing that. It would have been a good stretch of the legs. But if my son says he has to get back then who am I to press him to stay? I am only his mother. I see so little of him and well, time is moving on," she said wistfully. "Perhaps another time."

"I'd like that very much," said Adrienne, earnestly.

"And you could stay much longer, spend more time here, not just three days. Still, it is a glorious day and let's not waste it. We do, after all, have the rest of this morning and the afternoon before you and Theodore depart. So when you are done with breakfast my dear, I was going to suggest you and I go for a ride together. So much more pleasant to see the beautiful countryside from high up on horseback. You do ride don't you, Adrienne?"

"Oh yes. Not for a while but I have ridden a horse before," said Adrienne, cheerfully.

"Good! In that case, whilst you finish your breakfast, I'll let one of the stable boys know to saddle up two horses," said Beatrix warmly.

When Beatrix left the room, Adrienne's smile evaporated. She did not much care for riding or walking anywhere far that morning but did not want to risk upsetting her host, who had shown nothing but friendliness towards her.

With breakfast out of the way and having changed from her dress into a pair of fitted jeans and walking boots as make-do riding clothes, Adrienne met Beatrix at the bottom of the stairs.

"Are you going to be comfortable in those?" asked Beatrix, looking at her attire. "Perhaps I should have provided you with more suitable attire. Would you like me to send for Mrs Chalfont to fit you out?"

"Thank you but I am comfortable with what I am wearing," said Adrienne, as they headed out of the door.

They were following the path in the direction of the paddocks and Beatrix told Adrienne something of its history, from when it first housed no more than Josiah's Arab stallion and two Shire horses, that were used as beasts of burden pulling carts laden with farm produce to market, to its peak in the late nineteenth century when as many as twenty horses were housed there, to the present where they were mainly used for tourism and giving children riding lessons.

They had reached the point in the path where it split in two, one sloping up and to the right and leading towards the paddocks and the other meandering down a gentle slope towards the gardens. To Adrienne's surprise, Beatrix unexpectedly stopped and took her hands into hers.

"My dear, you do look rather weary, if you don't mind my saying so. Perhaps riding might not be such a good idea after all," she said, with a look of concern.

Adrienne nodded. "Do you mind? I'm sorry, I am tired."

"Don't be silly! Of course I don't mind. We can ride together another time, perhaps on your next visit. Poor you, why didn't you say so?"

Adrienne shrugged in embarrassment but relieved that she did not have to go horse riding.

"Can we walk down to the rose garden? It's not too far and I love it there," she suggested.

"Perfect. This time of the year, with the roses in full bloom, it is my favourite of all the gardens. Let's head for that shall we and I'll send for Joseph to bring us some refreshments?" said Beatrix, tapping out a text into her phone. "Come along, hold on to my arm and we can hold each other up. I hate to admit it but my old legs are feeling a little leaden too."

"My feet still ache from all the dancing," said Adrienne.

"Mine too. Must educate Aubrey not to throw me about the dance floor. I am not as spritely as I used to be."

A few minutes later, they arrived at the rose garden and sat in the steamer chairs under a summer awning that kept the bright sun at bay. Joseph arrived soon after with a pitcher of a lemonade concoction and a platter of two cakes.

"That looks lovely," said Adrienne, sitting up. "What is in it?"

"It is lemonade made with freshly squeezed lemons, slivers of apples, ginger and mint leaves in it, Miss," said Joseph, as he poured out two tall glasses. "And we have two cakes, baked this morning. One is a Jamaican ginger cake: Master Theodore's favourite when he was a young boy and the other a mixed-fruit cake."

After Joseph had poured out two glasses, at Adrienne's request, cut slices of ginger cake for her. Beatrix smiled at him and nodded her thanks, before glancing in the direction of cushions in the other steamer chairs. Joseph nodded his understanding and picked one up.

"If you will permit me, Miss," he said and placed the cushion behind Adrienne's back. She thanked him and looked at Beatrix who blinked her appreciation.

Adrienne did not hesitate to tuck into the ginger cake, wanting to taste what made it her boyfriend's childhood favourite.

"When he was four or five, cannot remember exactly, Theodore aided and abetted by his grandfather, would sneak into the scullery and help himself to whatever cake happened to be around and squirrel it out before anyone could notice. Then one day, he left a little note in his best handwriting, 'Please can you make Jamaican ginger cake, I love it'. When Mrs Chalfont's predecessor brought it to my attention, it made me chuckle and I had it framed and put up on the wall there. So whenever Theodore is coming down, Mrs Chalfont makes a point of getting the cook to make Jamaican ginger cake. Same recipe, nothing changed."

Adrienne giggled, "I can see why he likes it, tastes great."

"Adrienne, I'm sorry for pushing riding onto you earlier. If you had said that you were not keen, I wouldn't have been offended," said Beatrix.

"I didn't fancy getting on a horse," she explained.

"Has my son been filling your head with that nonsense about humans not having a right to subjugate other animals like horses for our pleasure?"

Adrienne giggled. "He has mentioned it. But that did not put me off. Today I was just not feeling up to it. I am not as confident as I once was and was scared at the prospect of hoisting myself up so high, I guess," she explained.

She could tell from the expression on Beatrix' face that she had not sounded very convincing. Beatrix poured each of them another glass of the lemonade and then looked at Adrienne, intently making her feel uncomfortable.

"My dear, you will pardon the impertinence of what I am about to say but are you with child?"

"Pardon?"

"Adrienne, are you pregnant?"

"What makes you say that?"

"My dear, I have been a mother to four, actually five, children. Admittedly it was a long time ago but I do recognise the signs," said Beatrix.

Adrienne hesitated, taking a long sip of her cool drink. She took a deep breath and then nodded.

"Is it Theodore's?" She nodded again. "Is he aware of it?"

"No, I haven't told him," she confessed.

"You are planning to have the child, aren't you?"

"Yes, of course."

Beatrix turned her body more towards Adrienne and said, "Don't you think you should tell him?"

"I will do, just need to pick the right moment," said Adrienne, nervously. "I'm terrified of telling him."

Beatrix raised an eyebrow. "Are you now? Am I given to understand then that it was unplanned?"

Adrienne pulled a face. "You could say that."

"Oh dear," said Beatrix, "it will come as something of a surprise, if not a shock to my son then."

"That's what terrifies me, I am not sure how he will react," said Adrienne, fighting back the tears.

"I am sure Theodore will rally round and be supportive once he reconciles himself to being a father at the age of fifty-two. But best to tell him sooner rather than later before it becomes obvious," she said, looking down at Adrienne's stomach.

"Does it show that much?"

"Yes, if you know what you are looking for. You are slim my dear and can easily conceal it, although I had an inkling at supper the other night. You were, of course, immaculately dressed but I thought I could just make out the tell-tale bump. I noticed you were very careful not to drink any alcohol except for one glass of wine which you nursed right through to the end of dessert and that further added fuel to my belief that you might be pregnant. At Aubrey's party, although you hardly stopped dancing you hardly touched any drink, not the punch, not even the champagne where we toasted his continued good health. This morning confirmed it. You didn't want to ride as you were afraid that if you fell off the horse it could hurt your baby, not so?"

Adrienne nodded. "I was scared."

"Understandable, my dear," said Beatrix and patted her leg for reassurance. "How much into your pregnancy are you? I would hazard a guess and say less than three months?"

"Two months, give or take a week."

"Then I suggest you tell Theodore as soon as possible when you get back, before he works it out for himself. Far better coming from you," said Beatrix. "Don't let it upset yourself."

Adrienne agreed.

Beatrix chuckled. "I know one person who will not be happy: Bertie!"

It was early evening when they were ready to set off back to London. Aubrey finally made an appearance having spent most of the morning in his bedroom nursing the mother of all hangovers, as he put it. He was still unsteady on his feet as he hugged them both goodbye. Beatrix embraced each of them in turn.

"You will take care of Adrienne, Theodore, won't you? I do like her. I like her very much, indeed," she said quietly in his ear. Theo also noticed that his mother whispered something in Adrienne's ear but he could not discern what it was.

"Mrs Chalfont has packed a hamper of some of the estate's produce for you to take back," said Beatrix, handing a wicker box to Theo. "Hope you can squeeze it into the tiny boot of your car alongside your luggage. When are you going to get yourself a more practical car, Theodore?"

"I have a Nissan Micra back in London, Mother. It gets me from A to B quite nicely," he said.

"But that is so…"

"Little?" Adrienne giggled.

"Yes, quite right, my dear. Something more suitable for…" she said, hesitating. She had been about to say 'a family' and stopped herself.

"Mrs Chalfont's hampers?" he offered.

"I was going to say, something bigger. Something, more suited for travelling on the motorway and these country roads in comfort and safety."

When they drove off, Beatrix waved and muttered, "Phew! Nearly let the cat out of the bag."

"What was that darling?" said Aubrey.

Beatrix sidled up to her husband and put her arm around his waist. "Do you think they look like a couple, Aubrey?"

"Yes, very much so. I like her, Trixie. I think she is good for him," he said. "There is definite, what's that thing they call it nowadays?"

"Chemistry. Yes, I agree with you. Do you think there was chemistry between us when we met all those years ago, Aubrey?"

"Oh yes. Fireworks Trixie!" he said and hugged his wife closely.

"Aubrey, you do know how to say the right thing to a girl, don't you?" she said and lightly kissed his cheek. "Pity you reek of alcohol and cigars."

As they left the country roads, the sun was much lower on the horizon and set off Adrienne's hair, giving it a fiery, red hue. Theo glanced across at her and smiled.

"You do look extraordinarily beautiful, Kiffy," he said.

She smiled but said nothing. The next time he glanced at her he noticed that her eyes had welled up.

"Kiffy? What's wrong? Are you unwell?" he asked, slowing the car down. "I'm fine, Flint," she said and wiped her tears with the palm of her hand.

"People do not normally shed tears if they are fine, Kiffy. If I have done something to your dislike please spit it out. I can take it, Lord knows it won't be the first time, will it?" said Theo.

"You haven't done anything wrong, Flint," she said.

"Kiffy, you don't have to hold your tongue. Be as rude to me as you like, you know you enjoy making sport of me."

"Am I that bad?" she giggled.

"Yes, that's part of your appeal," he joked.

"I'm just happy, Flint. These are tears of happiness, Flint. French girls express their emotions, not like stuck-up English girls. We don't have a stiff upper lip, not genetically possible in a French girl," she said, laughing.

"Good try, Kiffy but I don't buy it. There is something on your mind but I will not press you," he said.

The tone in his voice chilled her. "How did fishing with your brother go?" she asked, changing the subject to stop him pressing any further. Adrienne feared an interrogation.

"Changing subject. Good one. It went as I expected it to," he said.

"Meaning?"

"Kiffy, you may have already garnered an impression that Bertie and I are not that close as brothers. Never have been. Different outlook on just about every aspect of life."

"The body language between you says as much, very lovey-dovey," she said, wryly.

"Quite. So, when Bertie invited me to go fishing with him, I was under no illusion as to his motives: that of fishing as to what my intentions were towards the estate. He admitted that he felt that he was more suited to succeeding Father than I am."

"Told you, Flint. He wants your birth right!"

Theo went on to explain that Bertie had threatened legal action but Theo had dissuaded him from doing that.

"So, you made him an offer that he could not refuse, Godfather style?" she chuckled.

"Nooo. Why should I hurt a poor horse just to get Bertie around to my way of thinking? Just used friendly persuasion to get him to see that his attempt would be fruitless and that my proposal would be more beneficial to him," he said, with a hint of smugness.

"My clever lawyer," she said, stroking his head. "Remind me, if I ever need a lawyer, I should engage you, Flint!"

"And what about you and Mother, Kiffy? How did you get on with Trixie?"

"I think we hit it off all right. No embarrassing moments. Did she say anything to you about me? I saw her whispering in your ear."

"Told me she liked you," he said.

"Is that all?"

"Said to take care of you. And with that in mind, when we get home I shall do exactly that!"

"Flint! That is so naughty. You shouldn't say things like that to me. Disrespectful!" she giggled.

Practice to Deceive

They had been back a week from having spent three days visiting Josiah Hall and celebrating his father's birthday. Theo looked back on it with a certain sense of fulfilment and achievement, having successfully persuaded his brother not to make a bid to oust him on their father's eightieth birthday, in a year's time. It may have taken ceding some of his income from the estate to Bertie but Theo felt it was a price worth paying, and in some respects, he felt that he had earned it in any case, given the hard work he put into it on a daily basis. Having notarised the agreement in a signed document, he was content that he need not have any anxiety about what the future held in that direction.

But what had surprised and pleased him, going far beyond his expectations, was how well Adrienne had hit it off with different members of the family, most especially his mother. As the host, he had no doubt that Beatrix would be her usual friendly and companionable self towards Adrienne but he felt that it went beyond that. In the space of just a few days, Adrienne and his mother seemed to have established something of a bond between them and he found that comforting to see.

As Adrienne was arranging the roses she had cut from the garden into a tall, storage-jar type of vase, the scent reminded her of the rose garden in Josiah Hall where she sat enjoying a beautiful morning with Beatrix, sipping lemonade and eating Jamaican ginger cake. It gave her a warm feeling and when she let her mind stray, conjuring up images of possibilities, it left her breathless of what might be. She dared not think of it.

It was Saturday afternoon, and Theo was preparing for his next trip to the Middle East, flying out on the next Sunday night. On the surface, all seemed well. There were positive signs that Adrienne was settling in, like adding subtle feminine touches here and there, finding scented candles in the bathrooms and seeing fresh flowers throughout the house. It made him smile with satisfaction and to an extent, feel more relaxed about her staying there, not least because in asking her to live with him he had felt uneasy about the possible impact on his personal freedom. He had been anxious not to have to make any significant compromise, not to lose his personal 'space', or be dictated to about how he dressed, what he ate, what times he kept. But thus far, Adrienne had been the perfect housemate and as an added bonus, was clearly getting on very well with Anca; something he had also been anxious about.

Packing his papers into the document case he was taking with him, reminded Theo that the purpose of part of the journey was to further the establishment of a permanent office in the Emirates with him as its head. It was the next stage in making his vision of moving to the Middle East, specifically to the Persian Gulf, taking what had hitherto been a young man's dream and making it become a reality. It was tantalising close. He estimated it would take anything between six to eight months from the moment the contract was signed, to get up and running. The contract had been through several revisions already and thus far, there had not been any insurmountable impediments for it to be signed but he could not take it for granted. Rashid was just as keen as he was for this to proceed and as long as he remained in charge of his department, it would happen, he had assured Theo. If everything went well, Theo anticipated that by late summer, the contract would be ready for signing and then the work to establish the office and look into housing could begin. And whenever he paused to map out the impact of the move, the question that was always there at the back of his mind would come to the fore and keep him awake, as he had yet to consider what the possible answers to it could be. The question that kept going round in circles in his mind, was what to do about Adrienne. Would she accept being in a long-distant relationship with him? Would she be willing to give up her job and move out there with him, far away from her family and friends? Would he need to consider the most drastic of outcomes, the darkest of his thoughts, which was to end the relationship before he got in too deep? He felt that whilst no contract had yet been signed, then he had time to consider what to do and he would therefore let things between him and Adrienne carry on as normal. It was July and the most optimistic of timetables would have Rashid signing by the end of September: three whole months before he had to decide what to do. In the meantime, his strategy was to say nothing to Adrienne, to do nothing, just carry on as normal.

As Adrienne was on her summer leave from school, she was happy to have Anca for company when the latter wasn't with a client or in a class. In previous years, she would have bolted to her parents' farm, interspersed with a holiday, boyfriend in tow, ten days of nothing but partying, somewhere where the clubs and nightlife would be loud and non-stop. Here in a quiet suburb of Surrey, life was more sedate and she preferred it that way. For the first time in a long while, she felt she did not have to rush about. She could enjoy a book and not be interrupted and in a luxurious setting, where one could be private and not have to listen to what was going on either side of you. All was well, at least on the surface. Sitting on a lounger in the conservatory, she was trying to make inroads into a book lent to her by a fellow schoolteacher and friend, *The Bondmaid* by Pearl S. Buck, the first American woman to win the Nobel Prize for literature. She was not getting very far, reading passages over and over again. It was not that the book engendered slow progress but she was distracted by the thing that was being played over and over again in her mind — how and when to tell him. She recalled the advice Beatrix had given her: "*I suggest you tell Theodore as soon as possible... before he works it out for himself. Far better coming from you.*" He was about to head off for another business trip that would take him away for some two to three weeks and if she waited until when he returned, she would be some twelve weeks gone by then. Although Beatrix noticed it, she hardly showed any visible sign and she could delay telling him until then. There was no hurry, she kept telling herself.

The object of her thoughts appeared, carrying a tray with a coffee pot and a platter of things to eat.

"I was getting a bit peckish and I thought you might be too, Kiffy," he said pleasantly, putting the tray down on the coffee table next to her. "There are cheeses, pickles and ham and pork pies from Mrs Chalfont's hamper. I'm afraid I've made a bit of a mess carving slices of ham, Anca is better at it than I am. I've also toasted some of that nice sourdough bread and cut up some avocado, too. Brewed coffee for you and tea for me. Barring the avocado, this might be described as a typical ploughman's lunch. Used to be a very common thing to be served in English pubs but nowadays seems to have disappeared off the menu."

"Why thank you, Flint. I'm impressed. Never thought you were that domesticated. And waiting on me, wow! Can you go back and come in again so that I can film it to show Anca. She won't believe you did all this," she said, laughing.

"Tease as much as you like, Kiffy but you are about to enjoy a quintessentially English lunch, not a gooey French cream cheese in sight and no smelly saucisson, or rock-hard baguettes that penetrate the roof of your mouth like a fishing hook. And served up by a modest English country gent, not a snooty French waiter with his nose six thousand feet above sea level."

"Ha, ha! Very funny, Flint. I like it when you are funny," she said and pulled him down for a kiss.

"That's me, regular comedian. Now tuck in, before it gets cold," he said.

"But Flint, everything is already cold. This is like a cold buffet, n'est pas?"

"See, there's another advantage to English luncheon, you can eat it cold!"

Adrienne watched as Theo cut a thick slice of hard, cheddar-like, cheese onto his bread and then spread a teaspoon of onion chutney on top. She watched as he chomped into it and decided to copy him, only she put the chutney on the bread first and a thin sliver of cheese on top. Theo paused from wolfing down his food to watch Adrienne take her first bite, smiling as she nodded her approval.

"Kiffy, I'll make you an English woman yet," he said.

"No! Never! You want me to be a typical, stuck-up, middle-class English girl, who speaks as if her lips are glued at the corners and she can't open her mouth? Is that what you want me to be, Flint? Like Arabella?"

He smirked, "That would be funny, wouldn't it? You pretending to be like Arabella." His mind cast back to the unexpected delight of seeing Arabella sunbathing nude, her curvaceous body before him to behold.

"Flint, I am not changing and I don't think you would really like me to change, not so?"

"Yes, I would not wish to change you in any way," he said and kissed her. "Well maybe to get you to drink tea with milk!"

When they had their fill, Theo poured himself another cup of tea and sat back. He looked at his watch.

"We seem to have a couple of hours before Anca gets back, what shall we do, Kiffy?" he said smiling.

"Flint, it's too soon. We've only just eaten and I couldn't. Maybe later," she pleaded.

Theo laughed. "I didn't actually have sex in mind, Kiffy. Not up for it just now. I was thinking more of a cosy fireside chat, sort of thing. You know, put our feet up and contemplate life and the pursuit of happiness and all that."

"Oh? What do you want to talk about?" she asked nervously.

"Just a general chat about this and that," he said.

"Like what?"

"For instance, it may be my misreading of the situation but since we've got back, it seems to me that you've not been your usual, chirpy and bubbly self. At first, I put it down to the possibility of it being just tiredness from the trip but that doesn't really explain it. You have been doing your best to disguise it but there have been odd times when your guard has dropped and I see a woman who is pensive, pondering, things on her mind. I would very much like it, if you could talk to me about what it is, Kiffy."

"Maybe it is because of tiredness?" she said, shrugging her shoulders.

"I think not," he disagreed. "More to it than that, Kiffy."

"What do you mean? How have I been different, Flint? We have spent all week together, haven't we? We've been going for walks, going to the theatre, making love every day; I'm not sure what you mean," she said. She was aware that he had subtly changed his posture as she spoke, sitting more upright and the jokey countenance had all but vanished. The smiley man in the pub eating a ploughman's lunch had been transformed back into the lawyer. It unnerved her, as this was not going to be a cosy fireside chat; far from it.

"Kiffy, are you trying to throw me off scent? There is something on your mind and I think it would be better if we talked about it. You're normally very open about how you feel, why the silence now?"

Adrienne shook her head. He took her hand. He could see that she was biting her lip, trying to fight back tears that were threatening to pour out.

"Flint, I love you and you know that, don't you? I have never felt that way about another man before, never felt this close, even with my ex-boyfriend who I lived with for three years. You are twenty years older than me, have stuck-up English ways, can be infuriating and often without emotion and you do make me cry, look at me now for instance. But you also make me laugh and you stimulate my mind and challenge me like nobody other. You can be tender and caring not just with me but with Anca and others around you. You are the man of my dreams and I didn't know what that meant until I met you. In short, Flint, I love you with all my heart," said Adrienne and the first of the tears started to roll down her face.

It was his turn to feel uncomfortable but he was determined to show no outward sign of it. Other than grip his seat tightly, he did not move and he remained expressionless.

"Say something, Flint."

"I will, in due course. I am waiting as I sense there is more you wish to say," he said. She threw him a glance. He was not making it easy for her and she resented him. "Flint, do you love me?"

"We get along, do we not?"

"That's not an answer, Flint. Do you love me?"

"Would I ask you to come and live with me if I didn't?"

"For goodness sake, Flint. It is a simple question. Why can't you just give me a simple answer? Do you love me?" she said, raising her voice.

"The question is not simple, Kiffy and neither is the answer. Before you shout at me, hear me out," he said pausing, waiting until her sobbing had died down. "Kiffy, I have had two previous attempts at what is conventionally called love and each ended in failure, so you will forgive me if I do not subscribe to the concept. The word 'love' is overused and has different meaning for different people. It lacks clarity and purpose, can be set off like a firework and just like a firework it is gone in the blink of an eye. So, what does it mean to love and why does it have to be said, in order for it to exist? People say the 'L' word all the time, it gets banded about so much and with such levity, it has become a bit of a hackneyed phrase. It has, in my view, lost its import, if it ever had any. Some people, maybe most, express it sincerely but what of those people who prefer not to say it but show it, by deed or action? What about those that believe that love can better be expressed in two people sharing values, sharing experiences, wanting to be with each other, missing each other when one is not there, admiring each other from near and afar, admiring their passion, their anger, their laughter. Their warmth, a kiss here, a kiss there, being in the same house, not tied together twenty-four seven, just knowing there is someone to come back to at the end of the day, knowing someone is thinking about you. In short, having a bond with someone that is beyond the social interaction that one has with others. It is my contention that this is what you and I are building. It is not yet complete and so to call it love seems premature. When I said, in evidence to support my case, that we get along and that you are living with me, I did not intend for that to sound glib. This is a very big step for me. I have been a single man for a very long time Kiffy, you must understand that. But that said, of all the people in the world who I might wish to share my life with, to be with, to be my soul mate, my friend and my lover, then I wish for no other than you, Kiffy. Does that answer your question?

"Yes, it does," she said, almost in a whisper. "I love you even more for saying that."

"Does that get me off the hook?" he joked.

"It helps but I'm afraid not," she said, raising a half smile which he was not sure how to interpret.

"There is more?"

"Yes, there is," she said and taking a deep breath added, "Flint, what would you say is the ultimate expression of love between two people?"

"Pardon?"

"You know what I mean. I told you that I love you and you told me that you love me, at least in your own special way, you said as much. The question is, what is the ultimate expression of that love?"

He had to think on his feet. "Marriage? Is this what this is all about, Kiffy?"

"Marriage? No, it is not about marriage, Flint. Whoever said marriage is the ultimate expression of love! How many people get married and before they catch their breath, they are heading for the divorce courts. Marriage can be a positive thing and even in today's throw-away society it is supposed to cement relationships but it is not necessarily *the* ultimate expression of love is it?"

"Don't get me wrong, I have thought about it, Kiffy. It's just a little early. There are a lot of things going on in my business life at the moment that will shape the future and I have not had time to consider where marriage fits into that, if at all."

"Oh, that's comforting to know, fitting marriage into your future plans. Where does it come on the priority list, Flint? Somewhere near the bottom I imagine," she said and started crying again.

"Kiffy, don't be like that. I just need time, let things follow their natural course, don't be in a rush," he said, trying to remain calm.

"You don't know how true your words are, Flint," she laughed sardonically. "Things are taking their natural course more than you know it."

"Kiffy, I'm afraid you've lost me. You are talking in riddles and maybe I am slow of wit today but I do not have a clue what you are talking about. I would appreciate it if you just spit it out and say what you want to say. Be brave and…"

"I'm pregnant!" she cried, interrupting him.

"You're what?" Theo said, astounded at her declaration.

"You heard right, Flint. If things follow their natural course, you are going to become a father to this baby that I am carrying," she said, patting her stomach.

For the first time in as long as he could remember, Theo found himself speechless. No words would come out in a coherent way and he kept his mouth firmly shut. The shock of digesting what she had just told him was being replaced by one of indignation and outrage. He felt that he had been tricked, that he had been made a fool of and that she had lied to him. He could not stop himself from thinking that this had been a ruse all along to get herself pregnant and then lay a claim to his money. All the initial suspicions as to why it had been him that she had chosen for a boyfriend that he had put to bed, now came to the fore. The penny had dropped. He had been hoodwinked into believing a thirty-something young woman could actually be attracted to a fifty-something older man. All the protestations about love and sex had just been a means to an end. When he analysed the facts of the situation, more than anything else, he was very disappointed in himself. He had let his guard down, let himself be taken along for a ride, failing to apply even the most basic of prudence that in his profession as a lawyer, he would have exercised as a matter of course. He was intensely irritated with himself for showing such poor judgement. He had let himself be carried away without so much as a smidgeon of suspicion that this might not just be a simple romance. And what a romance. Now he recognised it for what it was: a tawdry paperback of trashy emotion where two people meet and fall in love, overcome cultural and social barriers and live happily ever after. The loneliness of being away in the Middle East had coloured his judgement and here he was, sitting opposite a woman who had just announced, to all intents and purposes, that she had tricked him into fathering a child. His mind was a whir of disjointed thoughts, buzzing and spinning around in his head. Dark thoughts as he began to question whether in fact it was even his. What if she was already pregnant when he met her? They had only been together, whatever that meant, for less than three months so could it be she had already been carrying someone else's seed? Is she even pregnant now? Where is the 'bump'? He cannot see any noticeable sign that she actually is pregnant. Perhaps she is mistaken and that she has just missed her menstrual cycle. Surely, she would have checked with one of those blue stripy tests that they advertise on the TV, before blurting out that she was pregnant. Then he recalled that she had pointedly said that *he* was going to be a father which suggests that she had confirmed that. He dismissed the possibility that it was not his. She was too intelligent and knew him too well not to expect that he would be demanding a DNA test as proof when the child was born. Accepting that he had been duped and was now facing fatherhood, what of the consequences? Was he to pay her off and then throw her out? And what about his plans and dream to live out in the Middle East? What about his reputation out there? In an Islamic world, it would reflect very badly on him on having fathered a child outside of marriage. It could even affect his business dealings. Everything he had worked for to try and make that dream a reality, was now in jeopardy. When all was said and done, he was in the soup, made, stirred and served up by the woman sitting next to him. But the lawyer in his head reminded him to keep a cool head and do nothing irrational. He needed to think, to consider, to review what had been said and weigh up what his options were, the pros and cons of each so as to arrive at, if not an economically advantageous outcome, at least to salvage the situation and come up with an outcome he could live with. It sent a chill down his spine.

Theo could not trust himself not to say something that might enflame the situation and stood up and walked towards the French doors, holding on to the handles to steady himself as he felt light-headed.

"Flint, say something," she said gently, as she padded over to him and put her hand on his arm, gently squeezing it.

"Was it an accident?"

"No."

"So you deceived me then," he said accusingly.

"Yes, I did," she admitted. "I stopped taking birth control once I knew you were the right man for me."

He sniggered in disbelief. "The right man to be the father of the child you wanted to have," he scoffed with disdain.

"Yes, Flint. You are probably thinking that I planned the whole thing, that I deliberately set out to entrap you. But that is so not true, Flint. I didn't ask my boyfriend to sleep with another woman. I didn't know that when I broke up with him that I would end up in Epsom. I didn't know that I would be on the same train as you and at the same time. I didn't know that you would be so precious about your stupid seat on the train. I did not know that I was going to fall in love with you, so quickly, so deeply. I didn't know that you, a horrible, rude, cold and haughty Englishman would have that impact on my life, that you would be the thing that was missing in my life. From that point on, I stopped taking birth control and let nature take its course," she said, matter-of-factly. "It seemed perfectly natural to surrender to the fate that nature had in mind for me."

"Fate, huh? Don't you think I had a right to be involved in any decision to have a child or not?" he said and twisted away from her, so that she was no longer touching his arm.

He was looking out into the garden through the glass, his face close enough so that his breath briefly misted it up before the sun evaporated it away. He felt it was symbolic of the way the relationship had gone thus far, warm words that settled for a while and then evaporated away, as reality kicked in.

"Maybe," she shrugged. "But I was a woman in love Flint, what was I supposed to do? Sit opposite you at the table and negotiate if and when we would have a baby together and risk you dissuading me from having your child?"

"I get that you wanted a child, Kiffy. Crystal clear!" he said, with a note of impatience in his voice. "Be that as it may, do you not agree that I had a right to choose if I wanted a child or not?"

"If you wanted that choice, Flint, then you should have used condoms! That would give you the ultimate choice but you chose not to use them!"

"I assumed that as you did not say anything that you were on the pill," he said and winced as it sounded so naïve.

"You know what they say about people who assume, Flint."

"Yes, and you've certainly made an ass of me!"

"Really? Is that what you think, Flint? God willing, I am giving you the most beautiful gift a woman can give a man, bringing a new child into this world. An heir for you, Flint, something that will be your legacy. There will be a part of you that will live on. Isn't that…"

"Spare me the philosophical side effect of your duplicity, Kiffy," he said dismissively. "The fact is you are expecting a child as a result of a deception. You are going to have my child and I had no say in it."

"Would it have made any difference to you if I had said I wanted us to have a child?"

"It would at the least have given me a chance to consider the possibility. And I do not know how I might have reacted to that. I hadn't given it any thought. I am a man in my fifties and contemplating fatherhood for the first time, when others of my age have fully grown-up children. It is not a responsibility I expected to have to bear."

"Listen, you don't have to do anything at all, Flint," said Adrienne, pulling his arm again so that he was forced to look at her.

"Pardon?"

"Flint, you can carry on living your life as before, I am more than happy to bring up our baby on my own. In getting pregnant, I had considered that as a possibility. In fact, I kinda predicted that a stuck-up Englishman would behave exactly as you are behaving now. Whilst you were fucking me every day, life was cool and you were very happy, even invited me into your home to live with you, no doubt to have sex on tap!"

The last comment riled him and he grabbed her firmly by the arms and shook her. "That's a flagrant misrepresentation! I would never do that and you know it," he retorted angrily.

"Okay, I'm sorry I said that. I know you did not do it for that reason," she said. "But as I said, I am not worried about becoming a single mum. Nowadays, there are so many single mothers that there is no social stigma attached to being one. I can carry on teaching and have a nanny to look after my child until she is old enough to go to school."

"She?"

"Yes, the baby is a girl."

"How pregnant are you?"

"Eleven weeks, maybe twelve, not sure. I am due to give birth in mid-December or thereabouts."

"I never had an inkling," he said, as much to himself as to her. "It is not obvious, doesn't show at all."

"It does, if you look carefully," she said and smiled, as she lifted up her t-shirt to show him. "Look, Flint."

Theo glanced at her abdomen but the look was vacuous and blank, completely devoid of any expression that might reveal how he felt. He moved back to a lounger and dropped down into it. From where she stood, leaning against the French doors, Adrienne saw a man leaning forward with his head in his hands. He cut something of a forlorn, lonely figure and she felt sorry for him. She had hoped that he would take her announcement more positively and with hindsight, she was thinking that perhaps she might have laid the groundwork beforehand, prepared him for it rather than just blurting it out as she had done.

Adrienne walked slowly back to where he sat and kneeling in front of him, lifted his head up, searching for some sign from him as to how he felt but the mask of detachment and reserve was not to be penetrated. She rose up off her knees and manoeuvred herself to sit on his lap, leaning against him.

"Flint, I know it is not what you expected and this has come as a shock to you," she said and put her fingers to his mouth to stop him reacting. "But you will be a good papa, I know it in my heart. You have nothing to fear. And I will be a good mama and together we can bring up our child with love and happiness. She will be a Blenkinsop and a Kiff, half of you in her and half of me in her."

She crooked her little finger and hooked it around his but there was no response from him.

"I'm too old to be a father, Kiffy and I am hardly ever here, as you so often point out. And, if anything, it will get worse as I am going to be spending more time in the Middle East. What father role can I be playing if I am not here? What sort of relationship will I have with the child? Just a stranger who pops in and says hello from time to time," he said.

"We'll manage, Flint," she said, trying to reassure him.

"I am not sure about me managing, I doubt that I am cut out for fatherhood at this stage of my life."

"Flint, I love you and this baby is proof of that. But I don't want you to be unhappy. I now realise that having this baby has left you displeased, so I am happy to move back to my apartment and bring her up on my own, if you do not want to be a part of it. You need not be involved in her upbringing and you can come and see her whenever you want to," she said, stroking and kissing his hair.

Adrienne was softly crying and wiping away her tears with the end of the t-shirt. She was about to slide off and away from him, when he caught her hand and held it tightly.

"Don't go. Stay," he said, almost in a whisper. "It is not what I want."

Adrienne started to sob and collapsed into his arms. "Oh Flint, my love," she said and she hugged him tightly, her head pressed against his.

The lovemaking that followed was intense and frantic, clothes cast aside; bodies entwined. There was no finesse or gentle build-up, just raw passion which exploded in the intensity of emotional and physical release, leaving both of them exhausted. And that is how Anca found them, naked and asleep on the lounger, Adrienne draped over Theo. She tiptoed backwards until she was at the door and then closed it behind her, as quietly as she could manage.

She smiled. "Someone's been having fun whilst I have been with my clients."

Later in the evening, as the sun was lower in the sky and now more of a golden-orange globe, Theo was walking around the garden on his own, secateurs in hand, ready to dead-head any roses that had finished or to clip an overgrowing Choise here or a Robin there or flick a beetle off the lavender that cascaded over a crescent-shaped, dry stone wall. He had planted the lavender to attract bees and at the height of flowering, there were so many bees clinging to every stem that he had nicknamed it the 'bee hotel'. As much as he enjoyed gardening, he rarely had an opportunity to do anything substantial, employing a local retired man to manage it for him. Jack had been with Theo for many years and understood what he liked and disliked better than anyone else. It was no accident that the garden had a profusion of flowers that would attract insects, or trees that would bear berries for wintering birds to feed on. Anyone looking in the garden shed would see nothing but organic fertilisers and only natural compounds to combat insects and other pests. Theo would not have it any other way, despite Jack's protests that they were losing a higher percentage of flower buds and vegetables as a result. In return for this strict adherence to everything being organic and animal friendly, Jack was given pretty much free-reign. One of Theo's favourite aspects that Jack had created for him, was a secret garden within a dense area of evergreen bushes and slow growing conifers that acted as a perfect screen. It was where he could enjoy peace and quiet, unobserved and away from any wind that might be blowing. And it was here that Theo headed, following the windy path, that started at one end of the crescent of lavender and was made of old recycled bricks with wide gaps, allowing for moss and grass to grow in between. It was bordered with dry stone walling on either side which the ever-resourceful Jack had made from salvaging old paving blocks. The path opened out into an area big enough for an old-fashioned park garden bench which Theo had bought from a reclamation yard. It had been lovingly restored by Jack to near its original condition, with the poignant message from a woman in memory of her loved one still clearly visible on the cross piece.

Theo sat on the bench, warmed up by the sun and looked back towards the house, largely obscured by the smoke bush and Japanese maple in front of him and the dense foliage of the bay tree to his right. It was a great place to sit and contemplate life and he closed his eyes to do just that, his other senses heightened so he could feel the gentle breeze on his skin, hear the tweeting of birds and smell the lavender as it wafted in his direction.

He had not been there for more than a few minutes when the snap of a twig underfoot disturbed his reverie and he opened his eyes. Anca was nearby and approaching. She had learned that he would sometimes disappear and if he was not in his workshop, then the next place she would look for him was the secret garden.

He smiled when she came into view.

"Sorry to disturb you, Theo, just to remind you that I am out with Lenka tonight," she said and sat next to him.

"Yes, I remember," he said. "Double date wasn't it?"

"Yes. Two boys we met on Tinder."

"You will be careful, won't you? And please leave me the details of where you are going," he said.

"Already done, I've texted you which club and its address," she said.

"And use my uber account to come home."

"Thank you," she said and leant over to give him a hug and a kiss. "You always want to look after me, don't you?"

He shrugged. "Of course."

"Other than my mother, you are the person who I am most close to," she said.

"I am here for you, Anca," he said, earnestly.

"Right then, I better get ready," she said, standing up.

"Already? But it's only eight o'clock: a bit early isn't it? I thought clubs do not kick into life until nearer midnight."

"Theo, you should know by now a girl needs a minimum of two hours to beautify herself. I've got to have a bath, shave my legs, shave…" she stopped herself as she realised, she was reading aloud a mental list and giving him too much intimate information. "Anyway, it takes time."

"Er, before you go off, can I ask you a question?"

"Yes, of course, anything," she said and sat back down next to him once again.

"It is rather intimate and I apologise in advance and please do not take offence. I ask only because I care for you," he said, nervously.

"Theo, don't worry, you can ask me anything, honestly. I won't get offended," she assured him.

"Okay, here goes. Are you on birth control?"

"Is that it? No, I am not. I am afraid of what the chemicals will do to my body. Also, I would never have sex with a boy I didn't know who did not use a condom. No condom, then they can forget it. Even oral sex, they have to wear a condom, I don't want to risk getting some disease. That wasn't so hard, was it?"

"Thank you, Anca. I am sorry for intruding. I just wanted you to be safe and also not risk an unwanted pregnancy."

"Not much chance of that, Theo. I haven't had sex for a long time. Haven't found the right boy to do it with!" she joked.

"I am sure you will," he said.

"Was there anything else?"

"Just one minor thing, something that Kiffy, I mean Adrienne seems to be bothered about," he said. "It is a bit awkward and once again, I apologise in advance for bringing it up."

"Theo, go on just come out with it. As I said, I won't be offended."

"It's about your breasts."

"Pardon?"

"Adrienne thinks you should wear a bra around the house, under your t-shirt, for example."

"Really? She said that?"

He nodded. "She thinks they, I mean it, is a distraction for me," he said, trying to hide his embarrassment at having brought up such a delicate subject.

Anca giggled. "And are they? Do you find my breasts a distraction, Theo?"

"No, I cannot say that I do. Obviously, I am aware that you walk around without a bra but it does not stop me from doing the Sunday Times crossword," he joked.

"Do you want me to put on a bra, Theo?"

"It is entirely your choice, Anca. This is your home and I have always wanted you to be as natural and do as you please. It is not for me to decide that," he said.

"Really? What if I wanted to walk naked around the house?"

"It would not bother me in the slightest but I am sure Adrienne would have something to say about that. I think you could expect to be on the receiving end of quite a few choice French words," he chuckled.

"Don't worry. It's not going to happen. But I would like you to choose for me whether I wear a bra or not around the house, Theo. If you are offended, then of course, I will start to do that."

"No, I am not offended, Anca. If you want to go around bra-less that's fine by me."

"Great, thank you," she said, bending down to kiss him, slowly and deliberately so that he could look down her t-shirt.

Theo could not resist looking and she smiled when they made eye contact. "It's okay to look, Theo. I don't mind," she whispered in his ear.

"I should not have done, I apologise."

"Theo, it's fine, there is nothing to be sorry about. You can look at me if you want to, it doesn't change anything," she said.

"Sorry," he said once again and looked down.

"Theo," said Anca. In a jiffy, she had pulled off her t-shirt and was standing in front of him in just her knickers. "You can look, Theo. No need for you to be, what's that word you taught me, furtive. I think that is correct, isn't it?"

"Anca! Put them away. If Adrienne saw me looking at you like that she would go crazy!"

Anca frowned as she put her t-shirt back on. "Sometimes I don't understand people. Earlier, when I came back home, I walked into the sunroom and you were both lying naked, fast asleep. I did not think that was anything bad, just two people enjoying each other after having had sex. The most natural thing between a man and a woman. You looked so beautiful like that together."

"Still, Adrienne would not be so understanding if she saw me looking at your naked breasts," he said.

"She doesn't mind that I see you naked when I massage you?"

"I think she does but accepts it," he said.

"Okay, I had better go and get ready," she said and turning around, flashed him her breasts one more time. "Look, Theo."

He shook his head. "Be off with you."

Aftermath

The following morning, Theo was sitting in the sunroom reading the Sunday paper with Philip on his lap pawing at it to get his master's attention. He ignored the cat, skipped over the incessant coverage of Brexit and switched to foreign news to glean anything on the Middle East that he hadn't already read elsewhere, ahead of his trip later that day. There was nothing of note. Even though Ramadan had ended, nothing of any note seemed to have happened that was newsworthy in the Times and even Al Jazeera did not report any new regional developments or breakout of violence, not even in Yemen where Iran and Saudi Arabia were fighting a proxy war to cement their own brand of Islam.

He folded the paper and discarded it as he stared out into the garden. It was early morning and beautifully quiet except for the familiar sound of robins, who were tweeting their sweet songs instead of flying out in search of food. Adrienne was still fast asleep, seemingly happier now that the stress of keeping her pregnancy secret had disappeared. As for himself, he had had somewhat of a restless night and heard Anca and Lenka trying to tiptoe quietly up the stairs, suppressing giggles when one of them stumbled judging by the noise. He had looked at his watch and it read 4.45 a.m. He had barely caught a couple of hours sleep as he wrestled with trying to dissect the consequences of Adrienne's revelation. Now, in the light of the early morning, knowing what to do was no clearer than it had been throughout the night. He was going to be a father, trapped into it and it irked him. It was happening whether he liked it or not. In a few months' time he would be staring at a new human being, forever tied to him in one way or another. It was going to change the complexion of his lifestyle, socially and professionally. These were incontrovertible facts. Adrienne, in delivering to him an unwanted child could also drive a coach and horses through his dream of moving out to the Middle East. But what irked him above all else, was that he had lost control of the situation. He was being carried along by the tide of events and he did not like that exposure. This is not how he conducted his life.

Theo was standing by the French doors sipping his tea and looking at a squirrel that was determined to reach the food on the bird feeder, hanging on the end of a long, thin thread. It was causing the feeder to sway as it tried to slide its way down, dropping to the grass time and time again, thwarted in its attempt to get at the prize offering.

He felt like the squirrel, inching nearer and nearer to his dream and then being frustrated by factors outside his control.

"Get a grip, Theodore," he muttered. "Get back control of your life."

Lost in his thoughts, he was unaware that the source of his discord had entered the room until she was curling her arms around him, resting her head on his neck.

"Good morning, Flint," she said sweetly. "You got up early."

"You know me, up with the larks, Kiffy," he said. "Read my paper and had a cup of tea, before the day starts proper."

"And what shall we do before I take you to the airport tonight?"

He looked at his watch. "I'll start by making breakfast for us. It's that time already and my stomach is grumbling," he said and extricated himself from her arms.

"Wait! Let me make it," she said pleasantly. "What would you like?"

He shrugged. "Don't mind. Toast and something to have with it. Is that okay?"

"Coming up," she said and grabbed him as he sat back at the table, bending down to kiss him on the neck. "And Flint, I just wanted to say, I love you, Mr Blenkinsop."

Despite the intensity of their lovemaking, in the sobriety of the next morning, Theo felt they had lost something following Adrienne's pronouncement of her pregnancy. Yesterday, her arms around him, hugging him tightly as he thrust into her, was intense, electric and made him feel very close to her; that he could not do without her. This morning, her arms around him did nothing, left him cold and indifferent. If her words of 'I love you' were meant to reassure him, they failed in that purpose. At that point in time, he wished that he could fast forward the day so that he could be boarding the plane to Abu Dhabi, away from here, away from her. Time. He needed time to be apart so he could think what to do next. The strategy that had been forming in his head was one of containment or damage limitation: how to make the most of a bad situation, to recover and go forward.

He remembered a phrase attributed to Hannibal, the famous Carthaginian general, '*aut viam inveniam aut faciam*'. 'I will certainly find a way or make one!' he told himself.

Adrienne returned carrying a tray of breakfast things. He was inclined to stay sitting and let her struggle with it but he could not do that and got up to help her. He wondered whether it was years of breeding and good manners or because he still cared for her and wanted to help her. 'Do not really know which it is,' he told himself.

Adrienne served up omelettes and toasted bread with cherry tomatoes and poured him out a cup of tea. He eyed everything up and cut a slice of the omelette.

"You like?"

"Spicy but I like it," he said, taking another bite.

"Tabasco. I drizzled some into the eggs as I was beating them, gives it a bit of a kick. If you are looking for the bacon, that's also in the omelette and there are mushrooms too."

"Very nice, Kiffy. Thanks. Should keep me going all day until I eat on the flight tonight," he said.

"Tell me again, how long you will be gone, Flint?" she asked.

"Up to three weeks but more like two. Maybe a week in the Emirates, a few days in Jordan and a couple of days in Lebanon," he replied.

"It is a long time. You can't tell me what you will be doing?"

He paused, putting his fork down. "I cannot tell you any of the commercial details, you know that. But in the spirit of *glasnost*, I can tell you that the trip to the Emirates is part of an on-going discussion to establish closer ties between my firm and the client. I will be flying into Abu Dhabi. In Jordan I am making good on a favour I promised a friend, to help one of the farming communities there. I will be in Amman. I am aiming to be in and out in three or four days at most, after all it is *pro bono* work so no money in it either for myself or my firm," he pronounced. "Just goodwill and friendship. I know, it is hard to believe that lawyers actually do some work for altruistic reasons sometimes, isn't it?"

"Yes, you could say that. If God came down and told me a lawyer is working for nothing, not sure I would believe Him," she joked.

"It is a favour and by definition, it does not cost the recipient of the favour anything."

"Who is this person who has so persuaded you to work for nothing? Or is it a secret?"

"No, it's not a secret. Her name is Abla Saleh."

"Friend or girlfriend, Flint?" she asked, raising her eyebrows.

"I think we have already established that you are the girlfriend, Kiffy," he huffed.

"Am I? Am I still your girlfriend, Flint? You seem a little distant this morning."

"Oh? What makes you say that?" he said, furrowing his eyebrows.

"You seemed to want to pull away from me when I came to hug you. You've never done that before. You don't know how that hurt, Flint."

"I was just going to make breakfast, Kiffy," he said but made no attempt to sound convincing.

"Okay, let me believe that to be true but so far, since we've had our chat, I have not seen you smile, not even once. I'm not imagining it, Flint."

He was sitting opposite her and she was looking directly at him. She was so beautiful and so desirable and yet he found himself resenting her.

"What have I got to smile about exactly?" he said finally. "Twenty-four hours ago, my life had a different perspective to what it has now and I am still trying to work out in my mind what the impact is of…"

"An unwanted child?"

"I didn't say that."

"You've as good as said that, Flint," she said and her eyes started to well up once again. "I know I deceived you and I wish to God that I hadn't, seeing how you have reacted. But having a child enriches lives, does it not? And, if for no other reason than for your peace of mind, the sooner you accept that you are going to become a father the better it will be."

"On the subject of the child, for the avoidance of doubt, I would like a paternity test done as soon as the baby is born," he demanded.

Adrienne sneered at his stipulation. "I expected nothing less from you, Flint. For the avoidance of your doubt, even though it is a shitty thing to be asking for, I agree. And so that this does not continue to poison your mind about me, we will organise a test just as soon as you get back. We don't have to wait until the baby is born. I've done some checking on-line and it can be done non-invasively, just needs a blood sample from both of us. That way we can move on with our lives and start to think about the baby's future, if you even want to do that," said Adrienne, bitterly.

"Is that all it takes? What about a sample from the child? I do not wish to put it at risk. I can wait," he said.

"Apparently I carry the baby's DNA in my bloodstream and they can tell with ninety-eight percent certainty from that. Is that a good enough test of my fidelity, Flint?"

"That's fine," he said and winced.

"Sure? No doubt that lawyer brain of yours will be thinking that there's still a two percent chance that the baby I'm carrying might not be yours. You do only get ninety-eight percent certainty that I have not been fucking someone else, Flint. Will you be able to sleep peacefully knowing that? Being such a slut, I might have slept with someone else."

"Kiffy, I know you are not like that, have never thought that. It is nothing personal."

"Nothing personal! Flint, do you even realise what you're saying?"

"Kiffy, in order to move forward I have to remove any doubt. In my professional life, one needs to deal in the elimination of doubt, of uncertainty. It is the basis of going forward. With certainty comes a solid foundation on which to build and this applies to one's private life, would you not agree, Kiffy?"

"Yes, totally agree, Flint. But we would still have had a solid foundation if you just believed in me, if you just trusted me, would *you* not agree?"

"Trust? Huh. In my experience, trust, just like any other emotion-based virtue, never quite lives up to its intent. I prefer to deal with reality, Kiffy; the tangible in preference to the ethereal which is founded on emotional entanglement and is itself unreliable."

"Maybe that's why you are fifty-two years old and you haven't yet had a relationship that's lasted," she spat out acrimoniously and immediately regretted saying it. "Flint, I'm sorry, that was a cruel thing for me to say. I take it back. I didn't mean it, Flint. It was just said in the heat of the moment, to wound you. Please forgive me."

Theo shrugged. "I am pretty certain that you did mean it, Kiffy. It is my experience that people do actually mean what they say in the so-called 'heat of the moment'. Quite logical really, when you think about it. In that moment, a person will have involuntarily let their guard down and what would normally restrain them from saying what they mean has been set free and it pours out *exactly* how they mean it. But have no fear. I am not offended, Kiffy. You may be right. I probably am naturally mistrustful. But at the end of the day, I am who I am and I am not going to change," he said. He had wanted to add, 'take it or leave it' but he was not having his 'heat of the moment' instance and he restrained himself.

Adrienne got up out of her chair and walked around the table to Theo. She pushed his leg to the side so that she could sit on him. She hugged him tightly and then sat back taking his face in her hands.

"Listen to me, Flint. I love you just the way you are. I wouldn't want to change you in any way. You are the complete deal for me, everything I have ever wanted in a man. Which is why I wanted to…"

"Have my child?" he interrupted.

"Yes, exactly. Having a baby is not something a woman does lightly, you know. I am going to be carrying this child, our child, for nine months. My body will be contorted and misshaped. There will be days when I will be exhausted, when I won't get any sleep. Soon, none of my clothes will fit me; I will be even more moody than I am now."

"Heaven forbid. Is that even possible?" he chuckled and put his arm around her waist.

She drew comfort from feeling that contact. It meant more to her than any words he might utter. She kissed him.

"Flint, my point is, I would not go through all of this if I didn't love you, whether you believe that or not."

He sighed deeply. "I believe you. I do. But the manner of how it came about is much more difficult to accept as it involves deception; something I had never expected that of you."

"Flint, you are everything to me. If you really want me to, as much as it will be very sad and difficult to accept, I would be willing to terminate this pregnancy," Adrienne said, earnestly.

"What? Absolutely not. It is a living being, Kiffy, how can you say that? She is more than four centimetres long. She has hands and feet, fingers and toes and ears on a big head."

"Just like her father," she giggled through tears. "You have been reading up, I see."

"As I could not sleep, I decided to do some research," he shrugged. "There is an awful lot I do not know."

"Yes, my darling. You will learn; we will learn together," she said and kissed him again. "And Flint, I know you will be a great father."

"Time will tell. For now, my ambition is much more modest; to read and understand what this means even if I may not be happy with the manner in which this baby was conceived."

"Oh? I thought you enjoyed the manner of it very much!" she chuckled.

"What I meant was, well you know what I meant. I was going to say, I am, if nothing else, a practical man and dwelling on what happened and how, whilst it rankles, serves no purpose. That does not mean that I am forgiving your deception, Kiffy, however well-intentioned. But I wish for me, for us to move on, to consider the future."

"I love you for saying that, Flint," said Adrienne, using his t-shirt to wipe her tears away and then lifted it off his head altogether.

She stood up and pulled her sleep shirt off and then knelt in front of him, pulling his shorts off, before straddling him, kissing him passionately.

"I want you, Flint. Fuck me," she whispered in his ear.

She guided his manhood where she wanted it and started to gently rock back and forth on him.

They had not heard Anca walk into the room.

"Hey! Stop it you two," she said through sleepy eyes. "Can you keep your hands off each other long enough so I can have my breakfast? I'm so hungry."

Adrienne giggled and hugged Theo tightly. "I'm making love to the best man in the world," she said.

"Don't mind me," said Anca, picking at Theo's unfinished toast.

Adrienne got off Theo and walked out unashamedly staying naked. "I think I'll go and take a shower."

"Sorry for interrupting your lovemaking, Theo," she giggled, when Adrienne had left the room.

"Oh that; I do apologise, Anca. We should not have carried on like that."

Later in the evening, Adrienne drove him to Heathrow Terminal 5. He had intended to take a cab but she insisted on driving him so they could spend another hour or so together.

"Flint, as you're going to be away, I thought I would visit my parents for a couple of weeks and return when you are on your way back," she said, as they walked up to the business-class bag-drop off. "I might also stop off in Paris to see an old university friend along the way too."

"That's cool. I will let you know when I arrive in Beirut. I only plan to be there for a couple of days."

"Is that pro bono work too?"

"No, meeting an old friend and before you ask, yes, it is an old girlfriend," he revealed.

"Oh? How old?"

"Do you mean how old is she or how long ago was she my girlfriend?" he teased.

"Flint!"

He chuckled. "She was my girlfriend when we were in our twenties."

"Was it serious?"

"We thought so at the time but it could never be. It was doomed to failure from the start but neither of us wanted to call it out for what it was. Family impediments, you might say."

"She didn't fall for your stuck-up, English, middle-class aloofness that I fell for then?" she giggled.

"Yes, could be that, doesn't seem to work on everyone, much to my chagrin, Kiffy. Or it could be that she was a Muslim and there was zero chance of her marrying someone outside her faith."

"Oh, I see. You didn't love her enough to convert?"

"Everyone has their limits," he said. "She married a fellow countryman and that was that."

"So, if I had been a Muslim, you would not have wanted me for a girlfriend?"

"A bit of an academic, hypothetical question, is it not? The fact is, you are not a Muslim so there is no religious impediment. Cultural? Oh

Yes! As you know, we English have been disliking the French and vice versa for very many years, centuries in fact, probably since we whipped your asses, as the Americans say, at the battle of Agincourt," he teased.

"Ha-ha! But your daughter is going to be half-French. How will you cope with that, Flint?"

"I know. I will just have to brainwash her from the moment she is born, make sure all her nappies and sleepy things or whatever they are called are draped in the Union Jack!"

"Flint, I like it when you tease me. I like it very much when you are funny. That is the English part of you that I absolutely adore!" she said and kissed him.

"You don't seem to mind my genes either," he joked.

"I love your genes! Will make me a perfect baby!"

"Okay, enough of this banter, I need to go and catch my flight," he said, looking at the indicator board above him. "Listen Kiffy, after I get back I was thinking we could go to Amsterdam for a couple of days."

"Amsterdam? I have never been there. Why Amsterdam?" she asked.

"I have a friend over there that I have not seen in ages and I said I would pop over and see him after my trip. Two, maybe three days at the most. And Amsterdam is lovely this time of the year."

"Great. I will be ready," she said and hugged him at the entrance to the VIP security gate. "Flint, I am so going to miss you, especially as you won't even read any of my texts or send me any."

"Look, you know how I feel about doing that, Kiffy. But if you are unwell and really need me then of course, get in touch. Anca has my work phone number for emergency use."

"You trust Anca with it but not me, your girlfriend?"

"That is correct."

"Pig! I hate you, Englishman," she said and then pulling him closer whispered, "But I love you really. Now go and woo those Arabs and come back to me."

The Gulf of Persia

"Can you go over what we want to achieve on this trip, one more time please Theo?" said Nicola, once they were airborne.

He looked around and most of the business-class seats were empty. Once he was satisfied that no-one was within earshot, he gestured for Nicola to sit across from him on the complimentary seat that came with the individual business class booths.

Nicola sat on the edge of the small seat so he wouldn't have to talk loudly, laptop in hand.

"Password protected?" She nodded. "Always."

"With the new fifteen-character regime that our security department has demanded?"

"Oh yes. I told you what it was, remember?"

"Er no, forgotten it," he admitted. "Tell me again."

Nicola leaned forward and whispered the password in his ear. Her scent reminded him of the last time she had been that close to him.

"Right, got it," he said and he was relieved she was sitting back across from him once again. The proximity was too close, dangerously close and likely to lead to reactions he would rather not have.

"So, to why we are going. As you know, there is a deal on the table which, all being well, would lead to the establishment of an office out there from which we could serve our clients and others in the neighbourhood."

"You haven't forgotten to include me in consideration for one of the jobs, have you Theo?"

"Not, at all. I have in my mind, already picked the team and I do know you want to be a part of it, Nicola and I would be happy to have you onboard. We have yet to work out the arrangements before we can put out formal letters to those that we have in mind. We are working through these with HR."

"Arrangements? What do you mean, if you don't mind my asking?"

"Everything that will be affected. For example, we would need to consider whether to back-fill those people who will be gone from the London Office. We also need to sort out the terms and conditions for those staff who will be leaving their homes to spend three years away. Everything: from salary, accommodation, benefits and so on. But all these are academic until we have actually signed the contract with Mr Rashid Qubaisi and we are still some way off from doing that."

"Hence the trip this week?"

"Yes, that's correct. There are some important points we need to work on before we can be happy with the deal. We will not be able to sort all of these out on one trip but there are four key points that I would like to progress on. The first of these is to write into the contract, favourable payment terms. We want to establish as far as possible that we get paid upfront."

"All of it?'

"Ideally and that would be our opening position. But I doubt that they would agree to that so I would settle for fifty percent on contract signing and then twenty-five percent each subsequent year in advance. That would ensure that we recover our costs and are not left high and dry, in the event that they decided to dispense with our services. Whilst this may not be high risk, for the avoidance of doubt, we would like to stipulate that in the payment terms part of the contract, so can you annotate your notes to that effect, please Nicola."

"Done."

"The next thing, which also relates to the payment terms is to agree how we manage currency fluctuations. Our client wants to pay us in dollars but as you know, the pound frequently wobbles against the dollar, which would suit us now but may not do so at some point in the future when it rebounds. So, in order to protect us from currency volatility, we would wish to build in a maximum variance factor whereby if this was exceeded, the value of the contract payments change to reflect that."

"What did you have in mind, Theo?"

"I've taken advice from our accountants and they suggest two things: firstly, fix the rate at contract signing at the LIBOR rate then prevailing and then change the value if the dollar-pound exchange rate changes by plus or minus ten percent either way."

"LIBOR? I should know this. Wait, don't tell me. It's the London

Interbank Offer Rate, published daily. Is that correct?" she said, smiling.

"Yes, it is correct. It is used globally so no reason why they should not accept it.

The third item that I would wish to resolve is the matter of membership of the team. The client is insisting that one of theirs is on the team and runs the local office. You may remember her: Abla Saleh."

"Yes, I do remember her, Theo. Isn't she the small pretty one who had the hots for you?" she giggled.

"Hmm, it is just your conjecture, Nicola that she was having the hots for me, as you put it but yes, it is her."

"She is nice from what I remember and very sharp. Wouldn't it be good to have her on board?"

"Possibly. But it would rather complicate things, would it not? For instance, she is not a company employee and there may be things we might want to discuss that are commercial privilege and not for her ears.

The fourth item is to remove the clause from the proposed contract that ties us to work exclusively for our client. This is not company policy and we see this, in any case, as an opportunity to grow our regional business in the Middle East. I have a proposal here from Colonel Ibrahim and I would like to take that forward alongside the work we will be doing for Rashid. We should be free to conduct business with other clients whilst out there. At the moment, the contract does not allow for that possibility. It is too constraining."

"Do you think they will accept our revisions?"

"Possibly. May take some time and several attempts and it will need sensitive handling. We may have to acquiesce on other less important points if only to appear to be compromising and not just wanting our own way through and through. But I am looking for a positive outcome."

"When do you think we will be in a position to sign contracts?"

"Hard to tell. On the plus side, we do not have to worry about OJEU rules as it's outside Europe, which can hold things up but we are in the Middle East and the path to decision making is not always clear. So, in answer to your question, Nicola, my best guess is three months. Where are we now? End of July — so work that out."

"Octoberish?"

"Yes, thereabouts."

They had agreed beforehand, to keeping the number of people involved to a minimum and to concentrate on the major items only. Theo was to be the only legal representative from the firm. As Nicola had left them with a positive impression the last time she had been in the Emirates, it was agreed that she would act as official recorder of what was said. For his part, on the first day, Rashid Qubaisi once again introduced Abla as his assistant and project manager whose role was to oversee the contract through to sign-off. Rashid had said that her remit was to remove any obstacles to making it happen. He said his vision was to have the office up and running from January 2020, as there were important projects coming up and he wanted Theo and his team to be on-site and ready to start by then.

Theo was uncomfortable with Abla being so closely involved, prior to contract sign-off and felt her presence could compromise negotiations give their prior relationship; albeit something that had happened more than twenty-five, nearly thirty years earlier. He could not admit a conflict of interest to Rashid, which at the very least would be a source of humiliation to Abla and she had done nothing to him to deserve that. At worse, it could put the whole deal at risk as it could well be taken as being an insult to Islam. He decided that the best ploy was to keep quiet about it altogether.

At the end of the first day, he was satisfied with progress as they had resolved the easiest of issues, agreeing the terms of the currency fluctuation; indeed, Rashid had gone as far as suggesting a five percent variation in the dollar-sterling rate would trigger a cost change to the terms and Theo thought it would probably be acceptable.

Putting his feet up on the sofa, he was thinking ahead to all the things that needed to happen if they were able to achieve an October or even earlier contract signing. He felt that the timetable for getting the office up and running was ambitious and that February to March 2020 was a more likely target but that didn't mean they couldn't bring people over and have them housed in hotels if necessary. He fired off a message to his contact in the HR department to ask for a progress update for the arrangements and benefits, for the staff who would be committing to a three-year contract away from home in the Emirates. It was just as he started to look at possible accommodation when he stopped abruptly. The search engine had asked him the simplest of questions, 'How many bedrooms?' It got him thinking about the future, his future and the people around him. At contract signing, Adrienne would be six months pregnant. By the time the office was supposed to be up and running, the child would be born and already a month old.

He had not considered how that would work. Would he visit every few months, trying to maintain a long-distant relationship? One of the gripes that he had had as a child was being sent away to a boarding school, away from his family and friends. And here he was considering doing the same thing. The baby was yet to be borne and remained an abstract concept. But he knew once it was out into the world and a real living being, it would be difficult to ignore that he was a father, a parent and with responsibility towards the child and indeed its mother.

And what about Anca — what was he to do about her? He had a responsibility towards her too.

He changed the search criterion from one bedroom to four plus, if only to see what was available, he told himself.

It was then that Nicola knocked on the inter-connecting door and entered.

"I'm making myself a cup of tea, would you like one too, Theo?" she said sweetly.

"Would love one, thanks," Theo replied, grateful for the distraction, as thinking about accommodation and the future was causing him some anxiety.

He looked across to the kitchen area where Nicola was humming a song and clattering teacups and saucers noisily. It cheered him up to listen to her. He sneaked a stare at her long, shapely legs. 'Behave yourself, Theo,' he told himself.

After a few minutes, Nicola made her way to where he was sitting, a tray with two cups of tea and Swiss individually-wrapped chocolates in hand, a gift from Rashid. As she was putting the tray on the coffee table, Theo couldn't help sneaking a further look and found himself trying to discern as to whether she was wearing anything under the nightie.

"Caught you looking, Theo," she giggled.

"I was not. I was just checking if I should help you with the tea tray in case it fell," he said weakly.

"Yeah, you were, I could feel your eyes roving all over me," she said. "It's okay, you can look but…"

"Not touch?" he offered.

She giggled again. "You haven't forgotten, then."

"If anyone forgot, as I recall, it was you not I. Forgetting to take your knickers back with you," he teased.

"Hmm, my recollection is slightly different, Theo. Like: you kept them for yourself until you realised that if you took them home with you, there would have been some explaining to do to your girlfriend," she teased.

"Well, you had better keep them on then, for the avoidance of any doubt!"

"They're on. I'm wearing them now, Theo. Look," said Nicola, as she lifted up her nightie. Theo glanced at them and then back at her.

"Hmm, yes, well done. Keep them on," he said, clearing his throat.

"Don't worry, Theo. They are staying on," she said and adding provocatively, "but any time you change your mind…"

Part of him wanted to do just that, to tell her to remove them. He just could not help his senses being heightened by her youthful curves and seductive manner and it would have been so easy to just let the flirtation take its course. Nicola was undoubtedly very attractive and she had made it clear, in not so many words, that she was making herself available to him. He was quite cross with himself for showing weakness in the face of such temptation.

"Perhaps I too, should have wax put in my ears or tied to a mast," he said out loud, recalling Ulysses' journey in the Odyssey, after Nicola had returned to the kitchen area to make a fresh cup of tea.

But whilst every fibre in his body had wanted Nicola, what had ultimately acted as an unseen restraint was something that had hitherto been quite alien to him. What he acknowledged and it even irritated him at times knowing it but was becoming increasingly a factor in all his thinking, colouring his judgement, disturbing his otherwise tranquillity and freedom to do as he pleased, was a feeling that it was not right to do so. Whereas the last time it was easy to cavort with Nicola, now that the relationship with Adrienne was on a more even keel and there was a child involved, he felt that he had to behave. At least that's what he told himself.

Seeing that her initial attempt at playfulness had been turned down, Nicola turned to work. "What's on the agenda for tomorrow, Theo?"

"Tomorrow could be sticky as we are going to be discussing payment terms, specifically staged payments."

"You said earlier that ideally we want all the fees upfront," she said.

"That's right, on contract sign-off but we would settle for fifty percent if we can swing it."

"And what is the value of the contract, four million wasn't it?"

"Per year, Nicola! Twelve million in total for the three-year term," Theo corrected her.

"Twelve million up front; that's a lot of money," she noted.

"As I said, we'd settle for half that up front and then two further payments at the end of the first year and at the end of the second year."

"We will be making a lot of money."

"Indeed, we will, Nicola. But remember it is not just the few of us who will be here that are involved. These fees reflect the cost of all those back in the office supporting us. We do have a lot of mouths to feed."

Theo's prediction that there would be some push-back from Rashid came true. He had taken the time to explain the rationale behind the payment terms, stating his case calmly and coolly. The nods coming from Rashid and Abla had suggested that they were not averse to the idea. But there was something about their body language that had concerned him; something was not right. It therefore came as no surprise that Rashid wanted to modify the payment terms so that he would pay a maximum of fifty percent at contract sign-off. Indeed, he was quietly pleased with himself for having predicted it. But what he had not expected was when Rashid went further and indicated that his preference was that this initial payment would be paid in two instalments instead of one, four million dollars immediately and two million dollars once the office was up and running. It had surprised Theo that Rashid would become hard-nosed about payment, having not previously given any sign or indication that money was any issue. His department had very deep pockets, so it seemed uncharacteristic to be holding back what for him, would have been a very modest amount. The furtive smile on Abla's face was the clue he was looking for as to the possible cause.

"Cherchez la femme', as they say,' he told himself, when they started to pack up at the end of the day to reconvene on the point the following morning.

As Theo and Nicola were about to leave, Abla approached them, gesturing.

"Theo, I was thinking if you do not have any plans for the evening, I was going to invite you and Nicola to come and have dinner with me," she said pleasantly.

He thought for a moment and said, "I have a bit of work to do, given the way the day turned out but sure. We would be glad to join you for dinner. If you give us the address of the restaurant, Nicola and I will be there."

"Actually, I was inviting you to come to my place for dinner."

"That's very kind of you Abla. Are you sure? You must be as tired as we are after the hectic day we've had."

"It's fine. Theo, I will be glad of the company. I have a very breezy apartment overlooking the harbour and we can eat on the terrace."

"It's a deal. Thanks," he said.

Abla left, having texted her address.

Back at the hotel, Theo had just finished taking a shower and was sitting at the table with his laptop firing off an email to the management team on the progress of the contract talks. He also asked HR to expedite completion of the proposed terms and conditions for staff who agree to work in the new office.

He was casting his eye over the numbers once the initial payment was cut into two, with only three million pounds secured at contract signing. Whilst it was adequate, it carried a greater degree of risk as the firm would be making financial commitments to rent office space, accommodation for at least three members of staff, hire staff to back-fill and other expenses even before they got started. If the deal was scuppered for whatever reason before they actually got started, they would have been left with financial commitments to then have to extricate themselves from. Even if they were successful in doing that, Theo was concerned that the time wasted might have otherwise been spent more fruitfully, building up the business with other clients.

"Hmm, not good enough. Must raise this with Abla when we see her later," he said out loud.

"What was that Theo?" said Nicola, as she came into the room.

Theo glanced up and noticed she too was only wearing her bath towel. It was tight around her body. He swallowed hard, trying not to think of the exposed cleavage only a short distance away from him.

"I was just running over the payment terms if we agree to do as Rashid has requested and I have to say I am not thrilled by it. Puts us under pressure to get the office up and running sooner rather than later. Not as easy as it sounds as, even if we can bring the contract signing forward, we need to find: office space to rent, accommodation to buy or rent, whichever is cheaper, hire staff to back-fill those coming out here and of course, let's not forget, we need to give those staff time to make their own arrangements, for example, to rent out houses and so on."

"You don't have to worry about me, I'm only renting," said Nicola, leaning over him and peering at the spreadsheet Theo had opened. "Wow, seven hundred and twenty thousand pounds for accommodation and three hundred and twenty thousand pounds for office rental. That's a lot of money. Why so much?"

"Prices in Abu Dhabi are not cheap, these are estimates that the office back home has asked us to assume for cost purposes, three-year rentals. So you see, if we only get three million upfront, one million alone would have already been committed just on rental agreements, even before we would have set foot in the Persian Gulf!"

"What will we do?"

"Get it changed!"

"How? What if Rashid digs his heels in?"

"We won't wait until tomorrow to find out. I will be working on Abla to get him to change his mind tonight when we go around for dinner," he said.

Nicola giggled. "You won't want me there then," she said.

"Huh? What do you mean?"

"Didn't you say she was an ex-girlfriend, Theo? If so, then you'll want to work your charm on her," she giggled. "I think I might just get in the way unless she is pretty broad-minded."

"Hmm, my charm, if I have any, will have to work without me

sleeping with her if that is what you are insinuating, Nicola."

"But that would be more fun, wouldn't it, Theo? Who's going to know? Sacrificing yourself for the good of the company. There are worse things you could do for the company."

It had crossed Theo's mind that Abla may have had an ulterior motive behind the invitation to dinner but if he had to speculate as to what that might be, he erred towards a direct order from Rashid to be his eyes and ears, rather than as a precursor to re-kindle a romance long dead. Theo felt that as he had made that clear the last time that he and Abla had met and there was no reason to suggest that she was still trying to do just that.

"Would you?" Nicola asked.

"Would I what?"

"Sleep with Abla, if it meant she could influence Rashid to meet our payment term demands?"

"I am certain that it would not come to that," he said.

"But if it did? If sleeping with Abla was the only way that she would do it, would you not sleep with her, Theo?"

"I prefer not to think about it," he said.

"I was going to flirt with you, Theo but you may need to save all your strength to use it on Abla tonight!" she teased.

"You, cheeky monkey!" he said and pulled the towel off her.

"Theo!"

"Oops! Apologies, I should not have done that," he said, sheepishly.

"You are naughty, Theo," said Nicola, putting her hand to her mouth.

He noticed that she made no attempt to cover up and as bold as brass, stared at her nakedness.

"I see that you are the same as last time we were, er…" he stuttered, looking down at her nether regions.

"You mean shaved? I think you liked me being shaved before didn't you, Theo?"

"I seem to recall you asking me which I preferred and I said that I didn't mind, maybe a little tuft?"

Nicola was standing next to him, leaning against the table. "I think you told me you liked the smoothness against your face," she said, relentless in teasing him.

"I said that? Doesn't sound like me at all," he said, shaking his head nonchalantly.

"Theo!"

As Theo paid the taxi, he could see that the address that Abla had given was a modern, luxurious block of apartments overlooking the harbour as she had said. He looked around and up at the modern concrete and glass building, counting at least ten storeys before giving up to follow the path towards the entrance, illuminated by sympathetically placed lighting. He could see that the gardens either side of the path and further along had been landscaped expertly, immaculately kept and looking very lush. The smell of wet earth was pervading, suggesting that the plants had only just been watered, as is the custom in hot countries, to minimise evaporation.

Theo pondered what it might be like to live there, a place to come back to at the end of the day. Although it felt cooler now, he was under no illusion as to what to expect during the day when the ferocious sun would be beating down. Even under the shade of the numerous palms growing in clumps around the grounds, the tallest of which lofted all the way up to the sixth storey of the building, it would still be uncomfortably warm to live there. It was a sobering consideration to have to factor into his plans to live out there, should the deal currently on the table go through.

Before he entered the building, he stopped to look around once again. There were advantages to renting an apartment over a house. For one thing, the security was going to better, as evidenced by the electric gates to stop cars from entering the grounds. Further security could be ensured if you lived high up the block as Abla did, you at least had some chance of escape even if would-be intruders got into the building. The amenities in some of the managed apartments he had seen in brochures also had communal gyms and a swimming pool and even coffee shops, making the overall experience much better. But as someone who had been borne in the country, he had always valued space around him as a must, in consideration of where to live. No matter how luxurious an apartment, it did not meet that requirement. The idea of being hemmed in, of choosing to live next to neighbours no further distant than the thickness of the brickwork of the adjoining wall, was not at all to his liking. And, as much as he admired the handiwork of the landscaper in Abla's apartment block, he would prefer something less contrived, less formal and with his own stamp on it. His place would have to have some greenery in it, a place where he could sit outside with his cup of tea in the coolest part of the day, hearing birdsong and feeling a slight breeze, even if it was coming off the Persian Gulf. He had long-ago concluded that he would have to rent or buy a house, if he was going to want to live there for any amount of time.

The stern-looking uniformed concierge had received confirmation from Abla that Theo was a bona fide visitor and he was buzzed in and directed to the lift. Theo glanced at the holstered pistol the man was carrying, slung from his waistband. It was a reminder of the sign of the times and it gave him no comfort or made him feel safer seeing that.

The luxurious theme extended to the lobby, with marble and porcelain tiles everywhere, original abstract art adorned the walls and huge stone vases with plumes of flowers sat atop semi-circular tables, pressed up against the walls of the corridor. This was glitz. The lifts were in keeping with their surroundings, with bevelled mirrors on all four walls etched with floral decorations on two of them and polished gold handrails and floor buttons.

"Must cost a fortune to own or rent one of these apartments," Theo mused out loud, as he exited the lift into a wide lobby with just four doors leading off a central area with an Islamic eight-pointed star floor design and a table with yet more fresh flowers in a vase on it.

He rang the doorbell and waited, looking away from the spyhole towards the flowers. "Never understand the purpose of putting decorations in corridors. People spend so little time there, at most a minute, waiting for a lift. What a waste," he muttered in disapproval.

He heard the click of a lock and then she was standing there, smiling and looking radiant in a traditional, red embroidered dress. The smile was the same as it had always been and save for a few strands of grey hair and the hint of lines on her forehead, she was the same Abla that had been the love of his life a quarter of a century earlier.

"Theo! Welcome, come in, come in," she said. "Nicola? Is she not coming?" He explained that Nicola was feeling unwell and had sent her apologies.

"Did you make her unwell so we could be alone?" she teased.

"Abla! It is naughty of you to suggest that. Nicola is genuinely unwell, feeling nauseous. These are for you," he said, as he handed her a box of desserts that had been recommended to him from the hotel to bring to someone who invites you to dinner.

"Baklava and maamoul? Very nice. Thank you, Theo," she said, opening up the box of dainty pastries.

"Pour us some wine, will you? It is Lebanese, from the Bekaa valley. You remember that area don't you, Theo? We spent one holiday there helping to harvest the grapes."

"Yes, I do remember it. It was hard work but fun," he said, as he poured out two glasses.

He put her glass down next to where she was busy stirring a pot and stood back, leaning against the kitchen door.

"Smells good," he said.

"Me or my cooking?" she quipped.

"Both. Very nice scent you have on. And the smell of whatever you are cooking is divine. What are we having?"

"Chicken Machboos. It is a spicy chicken and rice dish from Bahrain that I learnt how to make when I was there a couple of years ago."

"You have travelled a lot haven't you, Abla?"

"Yes, mostly in recent times. After my husband left me and the children had flown the nest, there seemed to be no reason to restrict myself to a life in Amman. There seemed to be plenty of opportunities all over the Middle East for an educated Arab woman, even for a divorced Jordanian one like me!" she said, laughing.

Abla had laid out the table on the balcony with a view over the sea. He noticed that she had removed the third, place setting and put the two that were left closer together, so that they would be sitting adjacent, rather than opposite each other. They were to eat in a traditional style, the food served in a communal dish for them to share, the food in the middle and Arab flat bread in pieces around it. Abla pointed to the bathroom where he could wash his hands and she followed him.

"Let me," she said, taking his hands into a towel she held out, gently drying them, as she looked into his eyes.

Not a word was spoken as she slowly rubbed the cloth over his palms, over and around his fingers and up to his wrists, her eyes fixed on his, her sensuous lips slightly apart. He didn't know what to say, hypnotised, like something out of a tale from The Arabian Nights.

"Thank you. I am famished, Abla. Can't wait to sample your cooking," he said, breaking the spell as he pulled his hands away and stepped past her and out of the bathroom.

Theo sat at the table waiting for Abla to return from the kitchen.

'Phew! Close thing. Must be more on my guard, cannot afford to relax,' he told himself. 'On the other hand.'

He recalled what Nicola had said earlier in the hotel and smiled: 'there are worse things you could do for the company.'

"That's a nice smile. Are you feeling happy, Theo?" asked Abla, as she put down a large, oval dish between them. "Okay, let's eat."

She gestured for him to make a start, demonstrating how it should be eaten, by scooping up food onto the flat bread with his hands. He had wanted to bring up the subject of the contract but he remembered that etiquette in Arab circles frowned upon talking when eating. He also reminded himself that no matter how hungry he was, it was also important to leave some food on the plate so as not to invite times of famine.

When their hunger had been repleted, they stood up and looked over the balcony into the distance, enjoying the gentle breeze of the Persian Gulf coming into the harbour, gently swaying the palms nearby.

Theo decided that the time was now about right to bring up the subject of the contract. But being direct was not the way to do things in this part of the world. It was considered impolite.

Leaning sideways towards Abla, he kissed her on the cheek. "Thank you, that was delicious," he said.

"For nothing," she said. "It is a pity that your colleague did not feel well enough to join us. I hope it is nothing serious, her illness."

"Oh Nicola? You need not worry about her, Abla. She will be all right in the morning," he said, dismissively.

"Perhaps she just wanted us to be alone. To enjoy each other's company. She must know that you and I are old…"

"Friends. Yes, I told her that," he said, interrupting.

"Is that what you told her, that we were old friends? Truthfully,

Theo?"

"Not exactly. I told her that at one time you and I were lovers," he said. Abla smiled.

"And now?"

"Now?"

Abla took his hand in hers and led him into a darker, unlit part of the balcony and kissed him lightly, looking into his eyes for confirmation that it was what he wanted too. Theo returned the kiss. It did not last long but what it said pleased her and she kissed him again, reaching up to put her arms around his neck and press herself against him. They hugged and kissed again and then parted.

"Theo, we are going to be working together for a few years if this contract goes through, you know that," she said, as they returned to the balcony. "You will need somewhere to stay. Why not here? I have a spare bedroom; that is if you want to."

He tried to remain expressionless, hiding his excitement as she had given him a way in to bring up his concerns about the contract.

"I fear we are some way off yet, Abla. I am not doing any forward planning yet."

"Why is that, Theo? There is not much disagreement between us. We have made great progress, don't you think?"

Theo decided to play his cards straight and explained that having the upfront payment, in effect reduced by fifty percent, albeit until the office was off the ground, could be problematic. He highlighted the risk to the company in making a large commitment in renting office and staff accommodation for three years without having secured the funds in advance. He said that it was not what he had expected but stopped short of pointing the finger in her direction as the cause of it.

Abla smiled and said that if it made him happy then she would talk to Rashid to have that clause removed. When Theo smiled, she took his hand and kissed it.

"We shall soon be in a position for us to sign contracts, Theo, *Insha Allah*," she said, positively.

"Do you think we will need the hand of God to make it happen, Abla?" he said, holding her hand in his and kissing the back of it as she had done with his.

"We are ultimately all in His hands, Theo. But He wills it for it to happen, of that I am sure. But you have to accept that one of us will be head of the office."

"Who will that be, Abla? If it is not asking you to betray a confidence," he said, deciding to take the risk and be direct.

Abla smiled. "It is me, of course. When I said we will be working together, I meant that I will be running your office for you. Of course, I will not be telling you how to do your job but I will: plan and prepare the pipeline of work, seek to make sure you talk to the right people, smooth away any problems and push along any delays. Don't worry, Theo, I will help you and together as a team, we will make this work," she said.

"*Insha Allah*," he repeated.

"It will make me very happy, *habibi*," she said and once again pulled Theo closer to her for a kiss.

It was a searching kiss and he returned it with passion, breaking off only after Abla dropped her hands from around his neck to entwine her fingers with his, which had been gently caressing her lower back. In the darkness of the night sky, she led him back inside. There was nothing hurried, no frantic movement or rush as hand in hand, they walked towards her bedroom.

They were at the bedroom door and they kissed passionately again and going beyond that door, there was going to be a point of no return. They both knew it. She wanted him to decide for the both of them, to take the lead.

"Abla, it would be the easiest of things for me to go through that door. But I should not do that," he said.

"So, go through the door, Theo. You know you want to. This says you want to," said Abla, putting her hand on the bulge in his trousers as she gently nipped his earlobe.

"It does, very much so," he said, as they kissed. "But I must not do that. I cannot do that."

"Why, Theo? Is it that girl you have back in England?"

"No, yes, maybe."

"She is there, I am here for you, right now," she said, as she snaked her hand inside the zipper of his trousers. "Your stiffness won't wait until you get back there, Theo."

"Abla, you don't know how much I want you right now. But I have to think beyond what I want right now. I have to think to the time after we sign the contract and we are working together. Abla, it would be very difficult for us to be both lovers and also working together every day," he said and put his hand over hers and removed it from his trousers.

Abla sighed. "As always, you are the wise one of the two of us."

"I am not wise. But I do have to consider the future of us continuing to see each other, Abla, not as lovers but as the best and closest of friends. It is possible I might even make a permanent move out here and you will be the friend I turn to and I hope our friendship will become lifelong."

"Can I be your friend with benefits?" said Abla, joking. "But you already have one of those, not so? Is she going to come out here with you?"

He held his hands open and shrugged. "Honestly, I don't know, Abla."

"Have you even asked her?"

"No. It is not clear in my mind what I want to do. It would be a big thing to ask someone to move out here."

"Theo, as much as I would like it for you to move out here alone, it would be unfair on her not to ask her to join you. If she is sweet on you she deserves that, don't you think?"

"Now who is the wise one?" he said and kissed her cheek.

"Okay, Mr Blenkinsop, it is midnight and time for you to go," she said and took his hand into hers and walked away from her room, closing the door behind her.

That room was now closed to him for the time being.

In less than a quarter of an hour, the taxi pulled up in front of his hotel and Theo went up to his room feeling pleased with himself. If Abla followed through with her promise, then the contract would be changed back to how he wanted the payment terms to be. And, just as importantly, he had not succumbed to the temptation of Abla's bed. As much as he wanted her, yearned for her, it would only have complicated his life with two lovers: one back home and one out in the Middle East.

'East is East and West is West but the twain could well meet in this day of mass communication and easy travel. Oh no, not for me,' he told himself, when he kicked off his clothes.

Theo quietly tiptoed towards the interconnecting doors and looked at the bottom of them for any indication as to whether Nicola was still up. He had wanted to tell her what had happened and was disappointed that there was no sign of light. He went to his bathroom to wash once again. He did not need to wash as such but standing under the shower and letting the water run down and over him, he felt it was a symbolic way to wash Abla away and out of his system, once and for all.

Dropping his towel into the bath, he walked into the bedroom and walked towards his bed, turned on the side lamp and was about to get into bed when he saw that Nicola was already in it and smiling up at him.

"Nicola! What are you doing in my bed?"

"Didn't feel well, felt safer in your bed," she said, looking at his nakedness which he did nothing to hide.

"Are you still unwell?" he asked.

"A little. Nothing a little TLC won't remedy," she said, pulling back the sheet and inviting him to join her.

Theo shook his head and switching the side lamp off, he slid into bed alongside her. "Are you sure you are all right," he asked again.

"I think I am in need of an injection," she giggled, her hand straying down to his fast-reacting manhood.

"An injection? What sort?"

"Yes, one of these. Did you use it on Abla?"

"My injection?"

"Yes. Did you get her to agree to change the contract back?"

"Yes! A good result!" he said with satisfaction.

"Well done, Theo. You do have a very persuasive injection!" she teased.

"Did not need to use it, you will be pleased to hear. A persuasive tongue was all that was needed!"

"Mmm, yes, I remember how persuasive your tongue was the last time we were in the Middle East together," she said, stroking him.

"You do?"

"Yes, very persuasive," she said, kissing him. "But I now want to try this injection," she said.

"Perhaps you could make a closer inspection of it first."

"Perhaps I could," said Nicola and started to kiss her way down his body.

Theo lay back, his arms resting on the back of his head as Nicola got to work, teasing and caressing his other head. He was content, as provided that Abla kept her word, an obstacle to concluding the deal was looking as if it was going to be removed. That would be one step nearer to the realisation of his dream: the big move out to the Middle East. He was lost in a daydream of what the future might hold. In musing and dreaming of what might lay ahead, he hadn't taken notice of Nicola having stopped her ministrations and was now kneeling up and sitting across him, until she leaned forward and kissed him passionately. It brought him back to the present. As alluring as Nicola was, he would have much preferred if Adrianne was now rubbing herself against his thighs but she was far away and he had a pressing need of fulfilment.

"Poor you Theo, went there with the prospect of getting laid and came back, no doubt feeling very frustrated," said Nicola and raising herself up, she took his manhood and gently lowered herself on to him.

Theo could not suppress a whimper of satisfaction as Nicola started to gently ride him. It felt so good to be inside her, to feel the warmth and tightness around his girth. It was heavenly and he did not think he would be able to last very long. Then he went rigid and stopped. He sat up suddenly and putting his hands around Nicola's bottom, tried to stop her from riding him.

"Nicola, wait a second," he said.

"What is it, Theo?" she said, kissing him passionately, rising up again and pushing his hands away.

"Wait, just a sec. I should be wearing a condom. I'm afraid I did not bring one," he said.

"I haven't got one either," said Nicola. "But it's okay, Theo. Just pull out in time."

"No, no. We have to stop. I cannot trust myself to do that. And what if I leak? I don't want to risk getting you pregnant. That would be foolhardy and very irresponsible of me."

"It will be all right, Theo. Don't worry. I'm sure I passed my most fertile period and besides I can get a morning-after pill."

"No, Nicola, please I would rather not risk it," he said and gently lifted her off him.

"Oh Theo, I so want you, I was so close," she said.

He held her in his arms and kissed her, starting from the top of her head and working his way down until his lips and tongue found the spot which had given her so much pleasure the previous time, caressing her, enjoying hearing the whimpers and moans but his mind was not on Nicola, not even on Abla. As he gave her pleasure, Theo was imagining that he was giving pleasure to the French woman who was sharing his life back in England. And if there was a reason for him not to make love to Abla, above all else it was because he only wanted to make love to Kiffy.

Nicola lay in Theo's arms, satisfied with the attention he had given her young body, still tingling from the assault it had received from him.

"You are a great lover, old man," she told him, as she leant across his body.

"I don't know about that but I do know my way around a woman's body," he said, kissing her forehead.

"You most certainly do," said Nicola, as she started to fondle him, feeling pleased with herself as it started to respond.

Theo bit his lip as he felt her kiss her way down sensuously. It took only a matter of a couple of minutes before he was nearing the point of no return.

"Nicola," he whispered but she did not move until his passion was totally spent. Nicola kissed her way up his body and he reached to the side and pulled a tissue from its box and gave it to her.

"No need, Theo," she whispered in his ear, before kissing him gently.

It was nearly two in the morning before they finally went to sleep, naked in each other's arms.

The following day, Abla was good for her word and Rashid announced that the payment terms would remain as was. But to hurry the deal along, he offered an additional bonus of five hundred thousand dollars as an incentive if the new office could be up and running by the beginning of January. He explained that it was necessary to be ready earlier as he was anticipating a clutch of new enterprises entering the procurement stage and would need the expertise provided by Theo's team. He also announced that Abla would be his programme manager going forward and would be working alongside Theo's team. Her first task was to help find suitable offices.

"*Masha' Allah,*" said Theo, shaking her hand. "And my thanks to you for making it happen."

"I can do more for you, Theo. I can find nice apartments for you and your team to live in. I can organise a local estate agent of mine who is an expert in helping Westerners relocate to the Emirates. Whatever your needs, just come to Abla, I will do my best to ensure your stay here is a pleasant one."

The negotiations had gone extremely well, much better than he had anticipated and they managed to finish all but a small number of minor points within the week. It seemed that all that was now needed was to compile the various revisions that had been made and consolidate these into a new version of the contract and then to re-submit the latest version to all parties to approve. Nicola was responsible for making the changes as she held the master copy and she would do that on her return to the UK. In the meantime, the minor points that needed ironing out could be done via email rather than in face-to-face talks.

"Whatever your needs, just come to Abla," Nicola said, mimicking Abla's voice back in the hotel. "Did you hear that, Theo? She is willing to take care of *all* your needs. Perhaps you'd better get in a supply of condoms!"

"Ha-ha. Very droll, Nicola. Tomorrow we head off to the next port of call, so you had better get packing."

"Done that! As we've had dinner tonight, I've just left out my clothes to travel in and of course, what I'm wearing now," she said, pointing to her night vest and loose panties.

"Better organised than I am. I still need to pack so I will be a while," he said, walking towards his bedroom.

"Need a hand?"

"To pack?"

"Theo! Now who is being naughty," she giggled.

"Me?" he feigned innocence.

"Hey Theo. Do they sell condoms in Jordan?" she teased.

"Amman is a big town, I am sure they do," he said and disappeared into his room, closing the door behind him.

Theo finished his packing in no time and then took a hot shower. It was soothing to feel the water gently cascaded over him, like a mistress wrapping her arms around him in a loving embrace. There were many things on his mind, the first and foremost of which was to decide what and when to tell Adrienne of his plans and how she fitted into them, if at all. But it wasn't just about Adrienne anymore, there was a child involved and it complicated matters. He clenched his fist and banged it against the shower wall.

"Perhaps I should have used condoms then, not now when it is too late," he muttered sullenly.

But when Theo sat down on the edge of his bed, as much as he was cross at the situation, he had found himself in, he acknowledged that, notwithstanding the unconventional manner in which they had met and the ensuing battles days afterwards, Adrienne was the best thing that had happened to him in many a year.

He looked at his phone on the side table and reached for it, hesitating before typing out a simple message to her, '*I miss you*'. He quickly pressed the send button for fear that his rational ego might kick in and make him change his mind.

When Theo re-entered the living room, he found Nicola asleep, resplendent in her naked beauty on the sofa.

"Looks like Aphrodite doth repose," he said quietly, as he sat down on the sofa across from her, his eyes roving all over her, from head to toes and back again. There was something quiet erotic in being able to stare at Nicola freely, to be able to take in what nature had endowed her with. It awakened in him a desire to possess her; a want and need that Adrienne was not able to satisfy, that could not wait. He leant down and kissed Nicola gently. It was a feathery kiss, just enough to wake her.

Nicola opened her eyes and smiled. She recognised the look of desire in his eyes and welcomed him into her arms. He pulled her up and they headed for the bedroom. Nicola pulled him on to her, as they embraced passionately. It was frantic and hurried and when she reached for him to enter her, there was no objection, the need for a condom was forgotten about in that moment.

With her legs entwined around him, meeting his thrusts, he could not last long and when she sensed that his climax was approaching, she whispered, "Come inside me, I want you to."

It was like an alarm bell had gone off in Theo's head and woke him from his dream that he was making love to Adrienne. He pulled out just in time to spill his seed on her stomach, lying on top of her in exhaustion.

The three-and-a-half-hour flight to Amman was comfortable, if not luxurious, as they travelled economy-class.

"Amman is not like Abu Dhabi, Nicola. Unfortunately for the Jordanians, they are not sitting on top of oil wells like some of the other Arab states, so money is a lot tighter. They are to an extent, dependent on foreign aid to exist. But Amman is very charming and the people are friendly and welcoming. There is considerably less of the opulence you have been seeing all this week but it is still lovely."

When they arrived at the airport, Theo checked his personal phone. There was a WhatsApp message waiting for him from Adrienne. When he read it, he tried to resist a lump that was forming in his throat. It was not working. He re-read it. It was a salutary reminder that he belonged to her and the child she was carrying. In that moment, he would have dearly liked to turn around and just get back on the plane and head back to be with her. As they passed through customs, he re-played the words in his head.

'*I miss you very much. The bump misses you too. Come back to me.*'

The taxi pulled up in front of a building of modest height. Theo spoke to the driver in Arabic to confirm the address and then tipped him generously.

"This is home for the next four days," he said, as they wheeled their bags towards the entrance.

"It doesn't look like a hotel," Nicola noted.

"That's because it is not a hotel but a furnished apartment," he explained.

"Does that mean we are sharing one bed, Theo?" she teased.

He shrugged. "As desirable as that might be, I am given to understand that there are two bedrooms, a kitchen, a lounge and even a balcony with a built-in barbeque, not that we will be sizzling any meat, other than ourselves whilst we are here."

When they arrived in the apartment, a quick look around confirmed it was well- appointed but modest in keeping with his budget.

"Will not win any prizes for décor and I wouldn't say that the furniture is to my taste but overall, not a bad buy," he said, nodding his approval.

"Can we run through the plan of action please, Theo?"

"Let's get unpacked, take a shower if you want and then I'll go through the briefing with you."

Nicola nodded and headed off to the nearest of the bedrooms and then out again and looked at the second one.

"Theo, one room has a king-sized double and the other has two singles. I don't suppose you would be amenable to flipping a coin for the double?" she joked.

"You are quite right, Nicola. I am not amenable to that. He who pays gets to choose so I am afraid you get the two singles," he said, laughing.

"Maybe. I was thinking if I play my cards right, I may well end up in the double-bed, Theo," she giggled.

"Right, enough of this banter, let's get unpacking and start working," he said, marching into the bigger of the two rooms with the double-bed.

It was late afternoon and the sun was still fierce, so Theo decided to keep the balcony doors closed and run the air-conditioning instead.

'Air-con has got to be one of the best of man's inventions,' he said to himself, as he opened up his document case with the briefing papers and paper contract, which he had annotated with points of concern.

Nicola appeared with a towel wrapped around her. He noticed her hair was still dripping wet.

"Had to have a shower as I was feeling sticky," she apologised.

"I was planning for us to go out to dinner, later. We may have a kitchen but we do not have anything to eat," he pointed out.

"Don't worry, Theo. I can be ready in ten minutes," she said, sitting next to him at the table, her scent wafting over and into his nostrils.

"Okay, let's start the briefing," he said, clearing his throat, trying not to be distracted by her perfume which brought back memories of the previous evening. "We have been asked to help a local community in their dealings with a major European supermarket chain. Our client is a small cooperative of farmers who are trying to break into the lucrative European food market by exporting some of the produce that their farms grow."

"What are they exporting?" she asked.

Theo looked up and could not help but notice that the towel was becoming loose and there was more cleavage on show than before. It was only a matter of a few millimetres but it was having an effect on his concentration. He willed himself to look back down at his notes, even if he knew them off by heart.

"They are hoping to sell beans, the French green type, strawberries and tomatoes; all high value items in the winter months when Europe does not grow its own. It is actually quite a competitive market they are hoping to break into as the Kenyans, Egyptians and Moroccans are already established there. But they seem to have got this supermarket chain interested and its agricultural produce buyer has paid the cooperative a visit and the outcome has been that a specimen contract was put on the table for them to sign.

And that is where we come in. They cannot afford to hire lawyers to read it and negotiate with the company and they want to be sure that they are getting a fair price and that there are no clauses in there that might trip them up."

"How did they know about our firm?"

"Abla asked me as a favour to help them."

"Abla, as in the lady who we've been meeting all week?"

"Correct."

"Will she be there?"

"Not expecting her. I've already made contact, having spoken to the head of the cooperative, a Mr Karam Dirani, so can't see why she would be needed," he said. The towel had slipped a little further down and now the top of her breasts were visible.

"So, just the two of us. How many of them?" asked Nicola.

"Not sure. We'll find out tomorrow when we meet them in their office in downtown Amman," he said, as he reached out and pulled the towel back up again.

Nicola looked at him for an explanation. "Em, it was slipping down."

"So, the plan of action is for me to go through the points that need to be clarified. I have annotated the paper version of the contract, highlighting in yellow the points that need clarifying and in red those that definitely need changing. Really sorry, Nicola but I did not make any amendments to the electronic version. Seemed easier to do it with highlighting pens. You have the contract in your Inbox, the password is your first and second name, with zeros replacing the Os and ones replacing the Ls."

"Okay, I'll get on to it right away. Should be done in a couple of hours. I'll also put tracked changes on the document and also make a separate log of all the changes that are needed in Excel, ready for your perusal."

"Great, in the meantime I thought I would pop out and do a bit of shopping so we can have tea and a few breakfast things. You'll be all right on your own, won't you?"

Nicola nodded without looking up as she set about creating a new version of the contract in which to apply the proposed amendments and changes.

When Theo returned with several shopping bags, Nicola was about to tell him that it was taking longer than expected and was going to suggest they did not go out to eat, until she noticed two pizzas popping out of one shopping bag. "Thinks of everything," she muttered to herself.

It was late into the evening when Nicola finished. Theo in the meantime had made a salad and heated up the pizzas, cutting them into quarters and drizzling each of them with local olive oil and a chilli sauce. Over dinner, he read through the work that Nicola had done in transposing his handwritten amendments into the contract and then producing the log with the page and section references. She had also added a couple of questions she had thought about that he had not considered and he congratulated her.

"Very impressed, Nicola. Not one error and your questions were quite astute. Well done."

"I'm not just a pretty face you know!" she said proudly.

"I know," he acknowledged.

"What's that phrase you sometimes use, Theo? I know my onions!"

"You most certainly do. And I know when I am tired, so I think I will take a shower and then go to bed and suggest you do the same as we have an early start tomorrow."

When Theo showered and walked into his bedroom, Nicola was already in the bed and under the covers.

"Before you say anything Theo, I just want to sleep with you," she said.

"That is what I am afraid of," he joked.

"Just sleep, not sex, Theo. We're in a strange land and in a strange place and I would sleep better if I was next to you," she explained.

When he slipped into the bed, he was tense, waiting for something to happen but nothing did, except that Nicola had fallen asleep lying next to him, her legs up in a foetal position and she was holding his arm. He was relieved, recognising that his willpower to resist might have been found wanting if she had started to get amorous.

When they arrived at the cooperative, they were met by Mr Dirani who introduced a number of people involved in the enterprise and last but not least, stepping forward from the back of the crowd was none other than Abla Saleh.

"I believe you already know our project coordinator," said Mr Dirani.

"Hello, Theo," said Abla, shaking hands formally.

"I was not expecting to see you here," he remarked.

Abla shrugged her shoulders. "I have to work, Theo. I don't have anyone to pay for my apartment or put bread on the table. The job in the Emirates just pays me a small retainer until the office is operational. It is not enough."

"So, you're getting paid for helping the cooperative out but we're not. I thought you said they were poor," he said, smiling.

"Yes. They are just a group of peasant farmers who have decided for once in their lives to look up from the dirt and try and better themselves. They were looking for someone who can organise them and I offered my services. They can afford me as I am on very modest, Jordanian wages. What they can't afford but desperately need, is an international expert lawyer to help them cut a good deal with the supermarket. You are a kind man Theo, which is why you are here."

"We English are famous for being suckers for the underdog," he said.

They worked on the contract for three long days, holding a daily conference call with the supermarket buyer who, after initially trying to play hardball, softened his tone when he realised that they were no pushovers. By the fourth day, they had reached a position where the cooperative would get a premium market price for its produce and in addition, could choose to sell anything surplus to other supermarkets, something which had been a sticking point.

"I knew if anybody could, that you would do it," said Abla, at the celebratory dinner on the last night. "Thank you for helping my people, Theo. We Jordanians are a poor nation and we need all the help we can get. If this venture comes off, we are hoping it will encourage others to turn to the land; especially the younger generation, who are all leaving the farms to work in the cities."

"It was very rewarding, maybe not in monetary terms but in putting together something that is fairer to the people who will be toiling the land and putting most of the effort into producing these fine beans and strawberries. Shame we will not be seeing these in England."

"Who knows? If it succeeds, maybe one day one of your supermarket chains might come and look at what we have to offer."

After the final speech by Mr Dirani, it was time to leave and Theo took Abla aside.

"About meeting up in Beirut, Abla. I'm afraid I will not be able to make it. I have to get back."

"The girlfriend?" He nodded.

"She is a lucky girl," she said and kissed him on the cheek. "When shall I see you again?"

"Hopefully not too long into the future as we have a contract to finish and then we will need to start looking for offices and accommodation. I would like to take you up on your offer to help us do just that."

Abla smiled, "My pleasure."

When they got back to the apartment, Nicola turned to Theo and asked, "What did Abla mean by 'my pleasure'? Sorry, couldn't help overhearing that," she said, smiling.

"Nothing. Just a figure of speech, referring to helping us find suitable accommodation in anticipation of the contract being signed.

"I see. Speaking of pleasure then, as this is our last night and I've worked so hard and without any break whatsoever, I was thinking…"

"You want a night on the town?"

"Actually, I was thinking of pleasure, right here, in this apartment."

Theo chuckled. "You were, were you?"

"Yes, got to make use of this," she said and held up a pack of condoms.

"Where did you get that from?"

"Bribed the Sri Lankan cleaning lady. Cost me ten dinars."

"That's eleven pounds. Nicola you have been robbed!" he joked.

"Yeah, I know and I can't even claim it on expenses. This pro bono work is proving rather costly," she said, laughing.

"Yes, it is," he smirked.

"So, better make use of it, don't you think?" she said, waving the packet around and slipping off her evening dress and then her underwear. "What are you waiting for?"

It was dark outside and the evening traffic had died down when Theo got up and tiptoed to the bathroom for a shower, washing away the remnants of lovemaking. Drying himself off, he poked his head around the door and could see that Nicola was still lying where she had curled up next to him, fast asleep.

He padded over to the living room, opened the double doors onto the balcony and immediately felt the night air. It was warm, much warmer than the air conditioning but very pleasant on his naked skin as he leant over the steel railings of the balcony wall. The tall palms were casting shadows, looking like men on stilts and there was a fragrance reminiscent of white, summer jasmine. Not a soul was about, the only noise was coming from crickets and the occasional cicada that had been disturbed by something unseen.

Looking at his watch, Theo calculated that with Britain being two hours behind and France being ahead, then the time in Normandy would only be an hour behind the time in Amman. He walked back in to get his personal phone and then returned to the balcony, sitting down on one of the steel and leather chairs, his naked buttocks surprised that it had not yet cooled down, emanating heat even at the late hour.

He flicked on WhatsApp and sent a message to Adrienne, to say he had cancelled his trip to Beirut and would be back two days earlier.

"Perhaps I should have added a few terms of affection," he muttered after he had sent it. "Oh well, too late now."

Putting his feet up on the coffee table, Theo reflected with some satisfaction on how well the fortnight had gone. The contract looked more than likely to be signed sooner rather than later; he would be that much nearer to realising his dream and he had helped a bunch of Jordanian farmers realise their dream too. All in all, it had been a success. And the next stage of his plan, all being well, would be taking shape in the next few weeks. Switching his phone on again, he went to one of his bookmarked sights, read through the article he was interested in and watched a short video clip.

"Six centimetres long, digestive system starting to work, bone marrow beginning to make white blood cells," he read out loud. "Quite amazing at how in just twelve weeks, what was once just a clump of cells is a miniature person."

His thoughts were interrupted by the sound of a clatter of cups from the kitchen, followed by a kettle being filled up. He was pleased that Nicola had remembered to use bottled water not from the tap even if they had been advised that it was okay to drink. A few minutes later, she walked out onto the balcony carrying two cups of tea, wearing the t-shirt that he slept in. Including Anca and Adrienne, that made three women who wore his t-shirts.

Nicola handed Theo the tea and sat down next to him. "Just remember to give it back, before we leave," he said.

"The t-shirt? You can have it now, Theo. Its warmer here than in your bedroom," said Nicola and before he could react, she lifted it off, exposing her nakedness.

In the darkness of the night, he could just about make out the shape of her curves and it stirred his interest, although he tried not to do anything that suggested that, holding his teacup and saucer strategically.

"When we get back, I'll finish making the amendments in the contract and then hand it over to Gemma if that's okay, Theo. I'm planning to taking some annual leave," she said.

"Good, you deserve it. Going anywhere nice?"

"I have an auntie who lives in Ronda, in Spain and I thought I would spend a week there with her. We just hang out together, she's great fun. Then when the kids have gone back to school, a friend and I are planning to spend a week on a Greek Island."

"Oh? Which one?"

"She had wanted to go to Mykonos but it's too much in your face for me, so we compromised on Kefalonia, a bit more peaceful and we can swim and sunbathe."

"Nice, very nice, rest your weary bones and all that," he said.

"Hey! My bones are not that weary. We will be going clubbing most nights!"

"Pardon me. Of course, your generation have a lot more stamina than people of mine," he said.

"Oh, I don't know about that. You did okay, Theo," she teased and then added, "for an old man!"

"Thanks, Nicola. I think that was a compliment."

Nicola put her cup down and stood up in front of him, before lowering herself on to his lap.

"Do you think you can manage one more time or is this thing worn out?" she whispered in his ear, before her hand snaked down between them.

The Royal Jordanian flight back to London took just under six hours following a slight delay and they arrived in a wet and dreary London. As agreed beforehand, Nicola went on ahead and when she was clear away with her parents, Theo appeared to a cheerfully waving Anca.

When he was past the barrier, she ran up to him and gave him a big hug.

"I missed you, Theo. With Adrienne in Normandy, it has just been me and Philip in the house. I have even been pleased to see the cleaning lady and the gardener," she said.

"I missed you too, Anca," he said, putting a reassuring arm around her waist.

"How did it go this time? Was it successful? Did it turn out the way you expected?" Theo smiled when he thought about it.

"Lots to tell you but not now as I am tired. Later."

"Oh, nearly forgot. Congratulations on your news, Theo," she said excitedly, as she pushed a ten-pound note into the car parking ticket machine.

"News?"

"You know, becoming a father. Adrienne told me. How wonderful is that! You must be delighted."

"Perhaps a bit early to characterise it as being delighted. More like: I'm getting used to the idea, Anca."

Flawless Blue White

The two days before Adrienne was due to arrive gave Theo time to consider what to do next in his life. In his professional life, things were becoming much clearer as the contract was becoming a reality. Soon, he would be signing an agreement that would mean he would be committing himself and a small team to working in Abu Dhabi for three years. Abla had already started sending him brochures of potential office spaces and apartments to rent, including a huge penthouse apartment several floors above where her own was. That one went straight into the bin as he could see complications in living that close to an ex-girlfriend and colleague. Abla had also suggested that he could share an apartment with Nicola but he also ruled that out. What happened on the trip he saw as the last fling before he committed himself to Adrienne and only Adrienne. Nicola had been a joy to be with and to share his bed at night but that was that.

But in his private life, more thinking had to be done. Above all, he was acutely aware that he needed to make Adrienne aware of his plans and he was not at all sure what he wanted to do, let alone tell her about it. He was even less sure as to how she might react to each of the options that were bouncing around in his head.

"Time to make a list," he said to himself as he sat in his office at home. Whenever there was something of import, he had found it helpful to just put down thoughts as they came out of his head in a random list and then develop these from there. He would add lines and arrows where things on the list related or one thing depended on another; add sequences here and there if it made sense to and strike off any item on the list that was looking like a non-starter or heading down a blind alley. At the end of all that, more often than not something tangible would emerge to point the way forward, even if this was not what he might have expected when he first started off.

Such an undertaking was worthy of choosing the best tools at hand and to that end, he opened his desk drawer and took out his favourite notepad and his favourite pen. The A4-sized notepad was unlined and made of a heavy weight paper. He hated lined paper. It reminded him too much of school. It was too constrictive when he just wanted to sketch out ideas. He did not want to be channelled into equally spaced lines. It was like caging his words. The fountain pen his father had gifted him, had a perfect weight to it and he liked the smell of the ink as it soaked into the paper. The best thing about it, was the fact that it forced you to write much slower than with a ballpoint pen; gave you time to think and consider before committing to paper.

The first of the options he wrote down, he crossed out immediately. Leaving Adrienne was not an option he even wanted to consider. Time had moved on and in spite of himself; and he did not even know when it started, he had come to want to be with her. And of course, there was the child. 'To leave her, to leave them both, would be cruel. It is not what I want,' he told himself.

The second option was not to live permanently out in the Emirates but to commute, coming back to England monthly to see Adrienne and their child. That would be possible, there were those that did just that. The distance was a challenge as it would take seven hours each way to fly back and forth. With Skype for daily chats and catch up, it would not be as lonely as not seeing each other. But he had doubts as to whether a long-distance relationship like that was sustainable for three years. And whilst he did not have any paternal instincts, he wanted to feature in the child's early life. Being some three thousand miles away would make that nigh on impossible.

The next option to consider would mean the biggest upheaval of all, which was to get Adrienne to move out there with him. And he would include Anca if she wanted to go too. But it would mean asking Adrienne to move out to a part of the world that was alien to her, completely different culturally, where the climate was roasting for the most part of the year, dry and inhospitable, well away from her family and where she would not know anybody. But others had done it and Abu Dhabi had a large expatriate community with schools, western-style entertainment, restaurants and a lovely coastline. If it had been just the two of them, it might have been feasible but with a young child it added a complication.

After an hour of deliberation, there was no obvious answer staring out at him and he closed his notebook.

‘Return to it later when I’ve cleared my head,’ he told himself, as he stood up and stretched.

He was no nearer to a solution when Adrienne returned two days later. They hugged. It was the first time in nearly three weeks and he was certain of one thing, that he could not envisage living without her.

“Miss me, Flint?” she said, smiling as they cuddled up next to each other on the sofa.

“Yes, very much so. Glad you are back, Kiffy. I see the bump has grown quite a lot in only three weeks,” he said, looking at her stomach.

“Yes, it has. Do you want to touch it?” she said and took his hand and put it on her. “Inside here is your daughter, Flint.”

“Six centimetres long!” he declared.

“Yes, getting bigger all the time. Soon I will need new clothes as everything is beginning to feel a little tighter. Perhaps we can stop off in Paris and look for something,” she said.

“But we are going to Amsterdam in two days’ time, Kiffy. I feel sure that they will have suitable clothes there?”

“Ah, what do the Dutch know about fashion?” she said dismissively. “You don’t want me to look like some shapeless bag of flour, do you Flint!”

“Okay, on our way back then. I think there is a train that runs between the two cities,” he said,

“It does, I checked. Takes just three and a half hours,” she said and giggled when he rolled his eyes. “Have to plan ahead, Flint. Also, we need a bigger car. Neither my little Fiat nor your Micra is suitable for a family with a child. It needs to be able to have a child seat and a boot big enough for a buggy.”

“Not for a while, surely?”

“Delivery times can be several months, Flint. I checked,” she said, smiling.

“Let me guess, you have even researched which car would be most suitable?” Adrienne grinned.

“Flint, I know how patriotic you are. How passionate about being British and all that.”

“Hmm, I fear my Englishness is about to be used against me,” he laughed. “Okay, spit it out, which car did you have in mind.”

"I want the Jaguar iPace," she said.

"Heard of the F-Pace but I do not recall there being an iPace."

"It's a good family car, Flint, with lots of safety features. And also, it is very green as it is totally electric. We have to think of the environment, Flint. You want your daughter to be riding around in a car that does not pollute, don't you?"

Theo laughed. "Okay, I get it, you want to drive a big, flashy Jag. How much is this battery on four wheels going to cost?"

"How much did you say you charge your clients a day, for your services, Flint?"

"I didn't say. Let me guess, is it fifty thousand?"

Adrienne pointed her eyes upwards.

"More?"

She whispered the figure in his ear and then kissed his cheek. "Flint, for that you get happiness, safety and you will also be happy knowing that you are not contributing to the air pollution."

"Fine, go ahead, buy it. At least it is not some gaudy, over-complicated, French car designed for lunatics or a Teutonic Billy Wizz car with suspension made of concrete."

"Ha-ha, for once I agree with you, Flint. Anca and I were thinking of popping into the showroom tomorrow morning. Do you want to come?"

"I see, you were that certain that I would acquiesce, were you?"

"I was certain of two things, Flint," she said, looking lovingly into his eyes. "Firstly, that you are not mean when it comes to money and secondly, the most important thing of all, I was certain that you love me."

"You know how to get around me, Kiffy, don't you?" he said, laughing.

"Do I?" she said and then moved off the sofa to sit astride him. "I missed you, Flint."

For the next hour she showed him how much she had missed him. Their lovemaking was sensual and comforting and unrushed; two bodies entwined, caressing and touching.

"You know when I am much bigger, we won't be able to make love face to face, Flint. We will have to do it from behind," she whispered in his ear.

"Hmm, never thought about that. Perhaps we should get some practice in beforehand," he said quietly and lifted her off him.

***

They had just walked past the magnificent Royal Palace and Adrienne could not resist teasing Theo that it looked more stylish than Buckingham Palace. For once he agreed, much to her surprise. Although, Theo countered, that if you asked a hundred random people to name a palace, ninety-eight would probably answer Buckingham Palace. It was said without any weight or pride which was most unusual for him. Adrienne felt that he had something on his mind. He'd seemed distracted ever since they landed but she did not quiz him as to what it was. It was their first day in Amsterdam and she was enjoying just being with him.

'Truly, silence is golden,' she told herself.

"Hey, Flint, the *Bloemenmarkt* is just ahead of us, let's go there next. I have never been to a floating flower market before."

"Sure," he shrugged, showing not the slightest bit of interest in seeing the famous flower stalls sitting on floating barges that had been a feature of Amsterdam for over one hundred and fifty years.

As they neared the flower market, Theo tugged on her hand gently. "Kiffy, about the child and its status in relation to us," he said and there was an edge to his voice that she did not know what to make of. She could feel her pulse rising as it stirred up old feelings of uncertainty in her.

"The child? You mean our child to be, don't you Flint?"

"Yes. About that child, our child. It will be born illegitimate," he said.

"Nobody cares nowadays, Flint. There is no social stigma with it at all. I wouldn't worry about it," she assured him.

"I understand that, Lord knows it seems to be so common nowadays that nobody bats an eyelid. But I do not condone or endorse such a modern way of living."

"You don't?"

"No, I do not. Also, from a legal point of view, illegitimate children are at a disadvantage when it comes to things like inheritance, for example. And in the playground, children can say hurtful things, even in a public school, perhaps even more so where in the lower social strata it might be considered the norm. In short, I would not wish for the child, our child to be born illegitimate."

Adrienne yanked on Theo' s hand so that they stopped in the street. "Flint, wait a minute," she said and she was finding it difficult to stop her heart from fluttering. "I think you are asking me to marry you. Is that right?"

"Indeed, I am," he said and smiled.

"Hmm, let me think about it," she said and taking a leaf out of his book, tried to remain deadpan, even though inside she was thrilled beyond belief.

It was not what he expected and it threw him. They resumed their walk, in silence.

"Kiffy, sorry to press you but is there any chance that you can decide in the next fifteen minutes?"

"Wow! Why so quickly?"

"It is just that we will be meeting my friend Arne in fifteen minutes. Arne is a diamond jeweller, and I had arranged for us to meet him. I thought you might want to choose an engagement ring," he said.

"Engagement ring? Flint, it sounds like you were pretty sure of yourself that I would agree to marry you?" she teased, trying hard to contain her excitement.

"I was pretty sure that I wanted you to be my wife. And I was hoping that you felt the same way."

She yanked his hand again to a halt. "Yes, I am pretty sure that I want to be your wife, Flint," she said, smiling.

He looked relieved and said, "Thank You."

Adrienne yanked his hand again. "But Flint, I want you to ask me properly," she demanded.

"What do you mean?"

"Ask me to marry you."

"I thought I did," he said, frowning.

"Properly!" she giggled.

"Very well. Do I need to get down on bended knee, too?"

"No, I've never liked that, so undignified. You are not begging me

Flint, just asking me to be your life partner."

"Kiffy, will you marry me and be my wife?"

"And tell me why you want me to become your wife?" she pressed him, grinning from ear to ear.

"What do you mean? I explained that already, did I not?"

"Yes, Flint. You did. To ensure our child is not born a bastard. But what else? Tell me why you want to marry *me*," she insisted, enjoying seeing him squirm. "Go on, you can do it. I want you to say it. Try it. It's very liberating, you know."

"Really, Kiffy? I've never found it so. Quite the contrary, makes one a prisoner of sorts, does it not?" he said, kissing her.

"Flint, just say it," she whispered in his ear.

"And if I do, you will consent to marry me?" She nodded.

"Kiffy, I love you and would be very happy if you agree to marry me," he said. "There, I said it!"

"Flint, I do agree to become your wife. I want to be your wife with all my heart because I love you," she said and kissed him deeply.

"Okay, can we get going now or we will be late?" he said, taking her hand.

She chuckled. "See, the world didn't come to a stop because you told me that you love me," she ribbed him.

"Oh, I don't know about that. I am sure the sun stopped moving and did you see those birds take flight. May well be the start of the end of the world, at least as we know it," he joked.

"It is as you know it, Flint. It will be a whole new world, a bright new world with a wife and daughter and all before Christmas. How about that!"

Arne Heyden was a respected diamond dealer who owned a first-floor workshop behind an unobtrusive shop front, with a few of his designs on display. It was, in many respects, off the tourist track and he liked it that way as he was not interested in window shoppers, just those with a serious intent to buy. When Theo buzzed him that they had arrived, he personally came down, wearing his apron and an Ajax football cap and greeted them heartily, placing Adrienne's hand between his.

"Come upstairs to my humble workshop, my dear," he said and led them up a short flight of stairs to an airy room, where there were four people beavering away intensely, barely glancing up from their intricate work.

Arne introduced them in turn, explaining the role of each, from diamond polishing, melting gold or mounting the diamonds into rings. Finally, he led them into a smaller room, decked out with comfortable leather chairs facing a table made of yew inlaid with green leather and gold trim. From his antique cupboard with leaded-light doors, Arne took out a large, black, leather-covered box and sat it down on the table, so gently, it looked as if there were eggs inside and he was afraid of breaking one of them. There was a bit of a showman about him, slumping in his chair and then mopping his brow in an exaggerated way as if he was relieved that nothing untoward had happened. Theo smiled, watching his old friend at play, glancing sideways at Adrienne who was not sure what to make of his behaviour. Abruptly, he lifted himself up using the table as leverage and walked over to the cupboard once again.

"May I offer you a drink?" he said, politely turning to Adrienne. "I'm afraid I only have Scotch or Schnapps."

Adrienne declined but Theo accepted the Scotch. He poured himself a Scotch too and then downed it in one go.

"Now, this is how it works," he said. "Inside this box, well I won't tell you what is inside, you will soon find out. Anyway, in a minute I will leave the room for fifteen to twenty minutes. During that time, you choose three or four items from the box and when I return, we will talk about them and then you can decide which of these items you wish to choose."

"Items?" asked Adrienne, looking from Arne to Theo for an explanation.

"You'll find out the moment I leave the room," he said, grinning and then bowed before leaving the room and closing the door behind him.

Adrienne looked to Theo as to what was supposed to happen and he reached across the desk and turned the large box around so that the brass lock was facing them. He handed her the ornate key that fitted the lock and said, "Over to you now, Kiffy."

Adrienne took the key and slowly and carefully inserted it into the lock, turning it anticlockwise until she felt the spring mechanism release.

"Open it," said Theo.

"You do it, Flint," she said.

Theo lifted the top part of the box as wide as the hinges and the brass sides would allow, to reveal row upon row of diamonds, sparkling like the Christmas lights one finds on any high street.

"Diamonds! Wow!" said Adrienne, putting her hand to her mouth in surprise. "I was expecting to see engagement rings."

"Choose, Kiffy. You can have any one of these diamond solitaires. When you have chosen, Arne will take a look at them and give you his professional opinion about cut and quality and then you get to choose a ring for his guys to mount it."

"Wow! These all look fantastic, Flint. I don't mind any of them, they all look brilliant. You choose for me."

Theo insisted that as she was going to be wearing it, she had to choose the one that took her fancy the most. As Arne had predicted, she could not make up her mind, singling out four possible stones that she set aside. When he returned, Arne looked at each of the stones Adrienne had chosen in turn, examining them under an eyepiece he pulled out from his waistcoat pocket. He explained to her that they were all classified as flawless blue-white but ultimately, it was how the diamond sparkled at different angles that gave it the allure. He took out a small torch and patiently showed Adrienne how each stone sparkled as it was turned around in the professional tweezer-like prong he gave her with which to hold the diamond up. Theo sat back, crossing one leg over the other, sipping his Scotch and amused himself, watching as Adrienne flipped from choosing between one diamond and another, returning to one of those that she had discarded, before finally deciding. He topped up his glass as the next stage was for her to choose a ring and a mounting for the diamond to sit on. Once again, Arne patiently showed her different types and she decided surprisingly quickly, accepting his recommendation on the claw design, but insisting on 22-carat yellow-gold in preference to his suggestion that white-gold had become more fashionable.

An hour later, they returned to the workshop and Adrienne ran up the stairs ahead of both of them, Arne winking to his friend. "Good choice, Theo," he whispered.

"In the diamond or the girl?"

"Both!" he said. "What's the story?"

"As I told you on the phone, Arne, we've been seeing each other for some time and decided the time was right to get married."

"How long did you say you've been seeing her?"

"I didn't."

"Last time we spoke you didn't even mention you had a permanent girlfriend. How do you say it in English? Oh yes, was it a whirlwind romance!"

"Something like that," said Theo, not elaborating.

"And the Arab girl you were very fond of when we were out in the Middle East?"

"She is out of the picture."

When they got to his office, one of the workers passed Arne a small box with the ring inside. Arne handed it to his friend and said, "This is your job, Theo. Good luck, old chap, as you say in English."

Theo gave the box to Adrienne and said, "Kiffy, as a celebration of us taking the next step on the journey together and of course, as a mark of my wanting to be with you, I give you this ring to wear for me."

Adrienne took the box and opened it, her eyes lighting up.

"It is even more beautiful now that it is set in the ring," she said.

"Allow me," said Theo and taking the ring out of its box, he placed it on her finger.

It fitted snugly and sparkled in the room light to good effect as Adrienne moved her hand this way and that way. The tears started to well up as she hugged Theo and whispered in his ear, "I love you and I will wear this ring as a symbol of that love for you."

"You have a very fine ring, young lady," said Arne. "And now, I have to drag your fiancé away for five minutes to sort out the paperwork. Please excuse us."

Outside the room, the two men shook hands. "Forty-five, right?" asked Theo.

"Yes, discounted for an old friend. You won't find a better diamond in Amsterdam." Theo took out an envelope and handed it to Arne.

"Theo! You've been carrying forty-five thousand dollars in your pocket all this time? That's crazy, if I may say so. I was expecting to have to go to the bank and arrange a bank transfer. As a tourist, you run the risk of being mugged and you could have lost it all."

Theo shrugged. "It seemed a good idea at the time. But possibly, on reflection, not so wise when you look at it like that. Anyway, it's done now."

When they had left, with a promise from Arne to meet up in London when he travelled there on his next visit, they strolled along the street, Theo warning Adrienne of the need not to be overtly showing off her ring but she was unable to resist sneaking a look at it. It was impossible not to.

Theo handed her a piece of paper. "Kiffy, here is the certificate that goes with your engagement ring. It states that this is a 2.2-carat F1 diamond and a 22-carat gold ring. You need to keep it somewhere safe, for insurance purposes, just in case. In fact, we need to get it separately insured as an individual item."

"It is wonderful, thank you, Flint. Can I ask how much I should insure it for?" He laughed.

"Kiffy, are you fishing for how much it cost?"

She giggled, "Will you tell me?"

"I am going to be a tight-lipped Englishman and not tell you," he said.

"Not so tight-lipped that you can't kiss your fiancée," she said and leaned over and kissed him.

In Amsterdam, nobody looked, nobody cared, the kiss was just between them. "I want to go back to the hotel," said Adrienne.

"Tired, already?"

"No, I want to celebrate," she said, smiling. If there was any doubt in his mind as to what she had in mind, the squeeze on his hand was a signal for him to hurry up and drink his coffee. Theo paid the bill and they left. He waved down a cab; there was no time to be wasted for what they had in mind.

The Delights of Amsterdam

The Amsterdam Red Light District is famous the world over and on the top ten things to see in every tourist's list and Adrienne was no exception.

"Flint, I want to go," she said, after he had tried to dissuade her. "You can't come to Amsterdam and not go there. I want to see the women who sit in the windows so that people can choose them. I want to go to one of the erotic museums; there are at least three of them there. And maybe we can go to Casa Rosso; I've read all about it."

"Kiffy, Casa Rosso is not a night club or cabaret, it is a live sex show," said Theo, trying to put her off.

"So? I've never seen one before. I want to see it, just once, Flint."

"I have an alternate suggestion, why don't we do our own sex show? Why do we want to see others doing it?"

"We can do that too, later, when we come back, but let's go and see it," said Adrienne, refusing to be discouraged by his reluctance.

"I have been to one of these places before," he said. "It is not remotely erotic, Kiffy. Far from it. A bored, out-of-her-head housewife-type with an equally bored-looking man go on stage for a few minutes, do it and then leave. There is no eroticism about it at all. It's as erotic as doing your shopping in Tesco's or Sainsburys."

"You're just saying that to put me off," she said. "They have sex on the stage, don't they?"

"Yes, Kiffy they do."

"So, the man must get hard otherwise they couldn't do it, right? So, at least he must be getting excited, no?"

"I really would prefer not to go to the Casa Rosso, Kiffy," he said and she could see that he was uncomfortable with them going there.

"Ah Englishman, you are so prudish, so narrow-minded and puritanical about sex. I'm not asking if we can go on stage and do it with them, just to see, even if it is, as you say, five minutes. What's wrong with that?"

They had arrived on Oudezijds Achterburgwal amongst the throngs of tourists who were already there walking up and down, taking selfies, popping in and out of peep shows, bars and pubs. It was a balmy night and they walked hand in hand along the road with one of the many canals running through it. Adrienne's attention was drawn to the sex workers who plied their trade from windows and she pulled Theo's hand to take a closer look. Tourists were standing in front of one window that featured three scantily-clad women. They were taking selfies, to the annoyance of the occupants who were being prevented from showing their wares for genuine punters.

"Ever been inside one of these, Flint?" she giggled.

"No."

"Do you want to?"

"Pardon?"

"I don't mind, if you want to try it. Really. I give you permission to go inside, if you want to. I'm not stuck up about these things like you are."

"Thanks, but no thanks. I am not remotely interested, Kiffy."

"Flint, you are not interested in fucking one of these beautiful women? Why not? I said you can do it and sincerely, I wouldn't mind at all. Honestly. We're here in the city of sex and we are not yet married so feel free to do it. Do something wild but remember, once we are married no more for you."

"That is very considerate of you, Kiffy but I really do not have a craving to indulge in sex with one of them right now, or indeed ever," he said.

"Too tawdry for you, my stuffy Englishman?" she teased.

"Not at all and I do not sit in judgement on those that ply their trade that way or on those who go and make use of what is on offer. It is just not me. Never has been," he said. Theo was resigned to having to do something so as not to appear stuffy and strait-laced and agreed to go to Casa Rosso.

After the show, Adrienne was quiet and contemplative and he did not press her as to what she thought of it. In the show itself, he had noticed during one of the acts she had actually looked away from the stage, squeamish when a woman was performing acts with various objects.

In bed that night she said, "You were right about them looking bored, Flint. And I didn't like the man and woman who were having sex at all. Such expressionless faces. So many tattoos and piercings, why do they do that. Do they think it is erotic?"

"I did warn you beforehand, Kiffy. Although they call it an erotic sex show, it is not remotely erotic and I would even hesitate to call it a show. It is not the slightest bit sexy, but hey, if we as tourists decide to go in there, then it keeps several people in jobs."

"Looked so cold and unfeeling," she said, as she cuddled up to him.

"Yes, nothing has changed since I was there with a group of friends many years ago."

"Flint, let me ask you something. It's something we never talk about. Seeing those people there and the women in the windows, is there any, like, fantasies you've always wanted to do?"

"I beg your pardon? What do you mean, Kiffy?"

"You know, like something you've always wanted to try but never got around to it?"

"Where is this coming from, Kiffy?" he said, turning towards her, furrowing his eyebrows with suspicion.

"I was just thinking, since we are here, in a city where anything goes, if there was something you wanted to do, I would be happy to go along with it. Just once and then never again. I won't be judgemental in any way, you can count on that, Flint. Anything you want. Just tell me what it is."

"I get to choose something that I have always wanted to do? That may be sitting in the darkest recesses of my mind and never acted on?"

"Yes, exactly. Once in your lifetime and never to be repeated again."

"And if I wished to act upon this fantasy, can I also infer that you too would also have such a once in a lifetime type of choice?"

"But of course, it is only fair, Flint."

"But what if I was averse to your choice. What if I didn't like it at all, do I get to veto it?"

"How would that be fair?"

"Thank you but all things considered, I don't think I can do that, without knowing what your choice would be, Kiffy. I am not that brave. Your choice might be something that I would totally abhor."

"Like what?"

"Like you wanting to sleep with another man, for instance. I could never accept it, even if it was as you put it, 'once in a lifetime'. No, sorry, no deal and you can call me every name under the sun, I will not agree to that," he said adamantly.

"You are so prim and proper!" she complained. "But for your peace of mind, I do not want to sleep with another man. I only want you, Flint and no other man, so you can relax about that."

"What do you want then, Kiffy?"

"You tell me the fantasy you want to act out, first," Adrienne insisted.

"What if you find my choice distasteful? What if you don't like my fantasy?"

"Then I have a right of veto too!"

"Two women," he blurted out.

"You want to fuck two women?"

"No, not me. I want to watch two women having sex on our bed. Here, in our hotel," said Theo, trying to mask the embarrassment he felt in confiding something that he had never spoken to anyone about before. "You asked, so I've told you."

"You want to watch two women having sex on our bed? Is that it?" asked Adrienne, looking at him and smiling. "I'm okay with that, Flint. I'm sure it will be a lot more erotic than the two women having sex at the Casa Rosso."

"Kiffy wait. I have not finished. It is not just two random women. For my fantasy to come true, I would want one of the women to be you," he said nervously. "That is, if you do not find that prospect abhorrent."

"Me? You want to watch me making out with another woman?" she said. He could not make out whether her tone was mocking him or jeering at his sexual proclivity and it made him feel uncomfortable. He was hesitant about saying anything more and was waiting to hear Adrienne's reaction.

"Look, if you do not find that appealing, that's fine, Kiffy. This was your idea in any case. Trust me, I will not lose any sleep over it."

"Flint, I'd love to do that," she whispered in his ear and then elaborated as to what she would do for him with the other woman. She was delighted to see that it was having the desired effect.

"What will you be doing whilst I am having sex with another woman? Just watching?" she giggled. "Maybe playing?"

"Maybe," he said and she was enjoying seeing him redden with embarrassment.

"Would you sit in that armchair or be watching more closely?" she continued enjoying seeing him squirm.

Theo shrugged. "I really don't know. You have just sprung this on me and I haven't given it any thought as to what exactly might happen."

"I want you to start off just watching from afar, Flint. I want you sitting on the sofa and then come up on to the bed, to be near and watch more closely."

"Ring side seat as it were," he joked.

"Yes, right where the action is!"

"And, dare I ask what is your fantasy, Kiffy? Before you say what it is, just to manage your kinky expectations, I need to tell you upfront that I am not into peeing, I do not want to be tied, or beaten up, or whipped or humiliated in any shape or form. Neither do I want to beat you up or slap you, or do anything violent towards you nor have any sex toys pushed up my butt and last but not least, no food either."

Adrienne giggled. "Quite a list of things we can't do, Flint. Don't worry, I don't like any of those either."

"That is a relief to hear you say that, Kiffy. I know how kinky you French can be and I wanted to avoid any misunderstandings. That said and reserving the right to change my mind, I am open to anything else, so go ahead, what it is you fantasise about?"

"Two things. Firstly, I want to watch you do it with another woman," said Adrienne, matter of factly.

"You do?"

"Yes, on the bed and I want to be next to you, watching as you fuck her. I want to watch and film it as you take her."

"Film it? Not sure about that," he said and he began to get suspicious as to her motives for wanting to film him. For a fleeting moment, he could see it being shown in the divorce courts how he had been unfaithful and that she would try and take him to the cleaners. First a pregnancy and then the film and he would be destroyed.

"It's so we can watch it again in the privacy of our own home when we get back," she explained. "Nothing to worry about, Flint. I've done it before. It's fun."

"Hmm, not sure about this, Kiffy. If it ever got into the wrong hands, it would not only be humiliating beyond belief, it could also ruin my career and everything I have worked for." She thought about it for a moment and then nodded.

"You're probably right, Flint. Scrap that idea, it can stay in our heads."

"Good girl," he said, relieved. He did not relish having to refuse her wish. "What was the second thing?"

"Pardon?"

"You said there were two things, Kiffy. The first of these was watching me sleep with another woman and the second thing?"

"I want to shave you!" she said, giggling.

"Do I need a shave? I thought I was smooth enough. But if you think it is a bit rough, I can do that myself, no need for you to shave me."

Adrienne was laughing. "Not on your chin, silly. Flint, I want to shave you down below."

"What? Please say you are just kidding, right?"

"No, I do. I want to see you smooth there, I heard that it is the trendy thing for men to do."

"Hmm, I am not very trendy in that respect, Kiffy. And I quite like having pubes, keeps me warm in winter. But I am a man of my word and if you want to do that, then I will do it to please you. But be careful, for heaven's sake, I do not want to be rushed to Amsterdam's A&E hospital haemorrhaging my life away."

"Flint, I will be very gentle with you. This is safe in my hands," she said, fondling him through his trousers.

Adrienne joined him in the bathroom and set about her work, whilst he gritted his teeth for fear of her cutting him. He could not watch as the razor divested him of hair around his nether regions and it did not feel at all trendy.

"Feels really weird," he said, after she had finished.

Adrienne took control and said she would find a suitable escort from the internet to join them whilst he took a shower. She vetoed him having a say in which girl they would hire on the basis that if she was going to do it with a woman, it had to be with someone she would be comfortable with. Theo handed over his credit card details and walked into the shower.

'What am I letting myself in for?' he asked himself, as the water pulsed down and over him. 'Is this going to be a night of unadulterated passion or just some elaborate ruse to trap me in some way and then blackmail me?'

A vision of him receiving a brown envelope with photographs showing him having sex with another woman, together with a demand for a huge sum of money flashed up. It was like watching a nightmare image of him having to hand over a wedge of money to Adrienne and her accomplice, a chain-smoking, tattooed Frenchman wearing a beret and striped, blue t-shirt and she was saying coolly, "For the avoidance of doubt, I will be back for more to pay for your bastard child."

'Stop it, Theo. You've been watching too many crime films!' he told himself, as he switched off the shower and stepped out of the cubicle to dry off. He looked at himself in the mirror, his eyes looking at his nether regions. "Weird."

When he entered the room, Adrienne had already changed into the hotel bathrobe and was sitting up in bed, wrapped up in it up to her neck. She was wearing what he imagined to be red stockings but he could not tell for sure as she kept herself completely hidden. She had also laid out some clothes for him to wear on the bed and told him to put them on.

"Dress up? You want me to dress up again? Why?"

"Just do it for me, Flint. Please," she said pouting. "She will be here soon."

Theo shrugged and put on the trousers and shirt she wanted him to wear. "That soon? But you didn't show me what she looks like, this girl you have chosen, Kiffy," he complained. "What if I am not enamoured with her looks?"

"Oh, you will like her, trust me. She is beautiful and I am sure she is your type," she said, smiling.

"Hot-blooded French woman, is she?"

"Ha-ha. Nicely said, Flint but not like me at all. But don't worry, you'll like her, I can guarantee that. And she does everything you would want her to do, at least according to her profile."

"Oh? Like what, for instance?" he asked.

"Well, her profile lists all the things she does and all the things she doesn't do. For instance, she does OWO, CIM, COB, FFM, Anal. Okay, apart from anal, I didn't actually know what those acronyms meant but I looked them up and you won't be disappointed. But sex itself is with a condom and I checked with her that she is bringing them."

Theo laughed. "Yes, we would not want to risk another pregnancy, would we?"

"It's not the pregnancy you should be worried about, Flint. It would be getting a horrible disease."

He remembered the night of passion with Nicola and it made him shiver.

The gentle knock on the door signalled her arrival and Adrienne gesticulated for Theo to sit in the armchair as agreed and keep his eyes closed until she gave him the go-ahead to look. She looked through the spy hole and then opened the door. There was a brief exchange of quiet words and then footsteps leading into the room.

"You can look now, Flint," said Adrienne.

Theo opened his eyes to find a curvaceous blonde standing in front of him next to Adrienne, dressed in a skimpy blouse, short leather skirt and high-heeled, patent leather shoes. She was immaculately coiffured. Theo just sat there, mouth agape, staring.

"Hi, my name is Anca," said the woman in a Dutch accent. "I am here to have fun with both of you. It is not often I get a couple as a client and I am really happy about it. You are Theo, no?"

"Anca? Your name is Anca?" he said, taking her extended hand in his. "You look extraordinarily like someone I know."

"That's the point, Flint. For tonight, we get to play with Anca. You get to fantasise that it is the Anca you know."

"You do look so much like her. The likeness is uncanny," he said, looking up in disbelief at the woman who was just starting to embrace his fiancée.

"Enjoy your fantasy coming true, my darling," said Adrienne, turning her head to receive Anca's searching lips, meeting them with her own in a passionate kiss which sent Theo's temperature through the roof and signals to every fibre in his body.

Adrienne was playing her part to the full, not at all fazed by having a stranger caress and play with her body from head to toe. She was a willing participant, there was no doubt about that and inasmuch as this was living out Theo's fantasy, he could see that she was deriving as much pleasure from it as he was by watching them.

"Take your clothes off," she mouthed to him and indicated with her hand what she wanted him to be doing whilst watching her and the girl.

Theo stripped off and sat back down, enthralled at the show playing out in front of him.

"Oh Anca, I so want you," said Adrienne sensuously, glancing over at Theo as she kissed her way down the girl, caressing her nipples with the lightest of touches. She looked up and beckoned for him to get closer as she started to kiss her way further down the girl's stomach.

"Tell me what you want me to do, Flint," she said, hovering over the girl's abdomen.

"You know what I want," he said.

"Tell me!"

"Lick her. Lick Anca!" he said and could hardly contain himself as he watched, inches away as Adrienne started to carry out his demand, his fantasy.

Theo climbed on to the bed and Adrienne looked up to see that, for the first time, she was witnessing another woman hold the manhood of the man she loved. Secretly, she had been worried that in spite of her bravado about sex she might feel a tinge of jealousy in allowing another woman to touch her man but when it came to it, she felt nothing but the sensuous eroticism of the moment.

She was not to be left out and caressed her way up the girl and then they were kissing once again deeply, bodies interlocking, hands exploring each other. Adrienne moaned loudly, partly out of the sheer joy arising from what fingers were doing between her legs and partly for the enjoyment and pleasure of the man whose fantasy was being played out.

Theo sat back on his haunches and enjoyed the sight, resisting the almost overpowering primaeval need to satisfy his carnal desire to penetrate a woman, both women, Adrienne and Anca, one after the other, at the same time, any way and every way.

When Adrienne sat across her face he couldn't hold back anymore and knelt his way up next to her and kissed her passionately until she was in the throes of an intense orgasm and she grasped his hand, hanging on for dear life. Anca continued caressing her until Adrienne slumped onto the bed, Theo lying next to her.

The girl disappeared into the bathroom and Theo could hear the shower being turned on.

"Don't worry, we've got her for the night, Flint. She's just freshening up for you," she said, as he kissed her tenderly.

"Did you enjoy that, my sweet?"

Theo nodded. "Hated every moment of it," he joked and added, "can't you tell." Adrienne giggled.

"I loved it too, so sensual, so sexy. Only a woman knows what a woman really likes," she said.

"I enjoyed watching you enjoy yourself," he said.

"And I could see that you were enjoying watching me go down on her, on Anca weren't you?" she said, kissing him.

Theo nodded. "Yes, I did. Very much so."

When the girl returned to the room, she crawled on to the bed on the other side of Theo so that he was wedged between the two women. He was facing Adrienne but the girl pulled him around to face her and then they were embracing and entwining bodies, hands exploring. Adrienne sat back on the bed to watch her lover making love to another woman, watching as she caressed him, encouraging her to do more. Theo was trying to be patient, to relax and take it slowly but Adrienne could see that his need was too urgent and popped a condom on him and watched as he slipped his manhood into the girl.

"Fuck her, fuck Anca," she said, urging him on as she caressed herself in time with his thrusts.

Theo needed no encouragement, nature was taking its course. His fear that this was some ruse to expose him to blackmail and extortion was parked for now, forgotten as he enjoyed being in the arms of the girl that, were it not for her accent and the more rounded face, could well have been the Anca he knew.

In the early hours of the morning, Adrienne watched as the girl slipped out of bed between them and started to get dressed. She got up too and smiled, being met with yet another sensuous kiss.

"You are so lovely. Thank you," she whispered.

"You are lovely too, Adrienne. And your husband is a nice man, very gentle and it is obvious he loves you very much. You are a lucky girl."

They kissed one more time and then she left. Adrienne stood with her back against the door and smiled to herself. It had been one of the most thrilling and sensual times in her life, made even more so because it was done with the participation of the man she loved. The man who was lying in her bed fast asleep.

Nuptials

"Kiffy, how do you feel about getting married soon?" asked Theo.

It was Sunday morning a few days after they had returned from Amsterdam. They had just finished breakfast and he heard the door close as Anca left to go on her morning jog.

"How soon did you have in mind, Flint? We've only just got engaged," she pointed out.

"Well, it has just turned August, how about early to mid-September?"

"Wow! That is only a few weeks away, but sure. Let's do it. Just registry, I don't want a church ceremony, Flint," she said decidedly.

"Is that because you would not wish to love, honour and obey me?" he chuckled.

"Love and honour, yes. Obey, never! I would never do that for any man, not even you, Flint!" she said. "And I will bring my daughter up to be the same."

"I don't have a problem with that. And a registry suits me too, Kiffy," he said and then laughed. "My mother will no doubt be disappointed that we are not getting married in the village church with the vicar, who is also a family friend, carrying out the ceremony. But if we were to have the reception in Josiah Hall, that will ameliorate her hurt feelings and she will be very much in her element planning for it."

"In your parents' home? Mm, Flint, I don't really want anything fancy if that's okay with you. Just a simple gathering of close family and friends. My parents and my brother on my side and a couple of friends. If it was as late as mid-September, not sure how that would work out as that would be during school term time. I have to be back at work on the Monday and so do those of my friends who are also teachers."

"It is doable, Kiffy, even for your friends. We can have the reception on Saturday and they can leave on Sunday. And as for yourself, are you not able to get special dispensation and have a day off to get married?"

"Maybe; it is not something I have ever had to ask about until now."

"Is there anyone you can phone, even now to find out?"

"You really are in a hurry to get married aren't you, Flint? Ours must be the shortest engagement on record!" she chuckled.

"I have never believed in long engagements, Kiffy. I have never really understood what the point is of being engaged for months and months, or in some cases even years. Once you become engaged, are you not signalling an intent to get married? Having a long engagement is like saying you are not sure and the passage of time will help you to become sure? Is that what an engagement is supposed to be about, to become sure? Besides, as someone once said, a long engagement is fraught with danger as you might find things out about the person you are engaged to that might make you change your mind!" he said, laughing.

"Hmm, not sure I agree with that, Flint. But you need not be anxious about me. I don't think there is anything about me or my past, that could make you change your mind."

"That is very comforting to hear, Kiffy," said Theo and then added quickly, "not that I had expected there to be anything."

"What about you, Flint? Is there anything in your past that I should know about, that might make me change my mind about marrying you?"

Theo shrugged his shoulders. "Nothing that I am aware of."

"No hidden girlfriend?"

"Nope."

"Boyfriend?"

Theo snorted with laughter. "No!"

"Sure? I know what you English are like, all prim and proper and stuck up but under the surface, very kinky."

"Kiffy, let me assure you, I do not have a hidden girlfriend nor a hidden boyfriend and my vices are no worse than any other person's."

"I believe you, Flint. Just wanted to hear it from your lips. As you said, it is comforting to hear," she said, smiling.

"Thank you," he nodded.

"You are a little kinky, Flint, like fantasising about watching me and Anca making love and then having both of us," she teased. "Like letting me shave you down below!"

"Kiffy, that is not fair. That was in Amsterdam and it was you who initiated bringing our fantasies out into the open, was it not? All I said was I fantasised about seeing you with another woman. I did not say Anca, specifically. And it was you, I might add, who chose a girl who looked like Anca and even arranged for her to pretend her name was Anca. I had nothing to do with that," he protested. "Nor did I want my pubic hair shaved. I went along with it because I felt if I did not agree to that, you would no doubt just come up with yet another comment about how unadventurous I am!"

"I like you clean shaven there, nice and smooth to the touch!" she said, reaching out and patting his shorts. "You should keep it that way for me. Looks and feels very sexy, Flint."

"No way, I regret doing it already. Now that the hair is starting to grow back, it feels so itchy! And I would not trust myself with trying to shave down there. Anyway, none of these things were of my doing, Kiffy and you know it."

"I know, I know. I was just teasing you, Flint. It was my idea to have the girl be with us and to act as her being Anca. And it was my idea to shave you," she acknowledged.

"Why did you do that Kiffy? Was it to test me?"

"Truth?"

"That would be good."

"In my mind, I find the idea of making love with Anca very erotic. And watching you with that woman, I was imagining watching you with Anca," she admitted.

"Really?"

Adrienne nodded. "It was very erotic for me."

"Why?"

"I don't know, it just was," she said with a shrug. "Would you do it if I said you could and Anca was willing?"

"No!"

"Why not?"

"It would only complicate things," he answered.

"Bastard!" Adrienne retorted, sticking her tongue out.

"What have I said now?"

"I expected you to say that I was enough for you, Flint, not that it would complicate matters. All men are bastards. You just think with your dicks!" she said in mock anger.

"Every ninety seconds, apparently!" he joked. "But seriously, one of you is enough for me and I apologise, I should have just said that."

"That's better! But for the avoidance of doubt, as you would say Flint, I am never going to allow you to do that. You do not have a license to fuck Anca, ever!"

Theo laughed. "Kiffy, there is no need for you to fret! You have nothing to worry about. I do not see the real Anca in the way that we acted out with the escort lady in Amsterdam."

"Hmm, may be. Don't tell me you didn't notice she was not wearing anything under her jogging leggings this morning."

"Was she not? Really? I hadn't noticed," he said, feigning ignorance. He had found it was safer to pretend than to admit it to Adrienne. "Well, it is her home, Kiffy and she should be comfortable with what she wears. Look at me, I am not wearing anything under my shorts."

"Hey Flint, want to hear a confession? When I see Anca walking around like that, I remember what we did in Amsterdam with the pretend one and it makes me tingle everywhere," she said.

"Everywhere?"

"Yes. I shouldn't be telling you this but I couldn't help it. Must be my hormones changing as the baby grows, makes all my senses super sensitive."

"You know Anca noticed my nakedness bereft of pubic hair yesterday when she was giving me my Saturday massage," he said.

"What did she say?" said Adrienne, looking up from her magazine.

"She said it was nice. Wanted to know where I had it done. I told her you did it for me."

"What did she say to that?"

"She giggled at first and then proceeded to tell me something that came somewhat of a surprise, Kiffy."

"Oh? What was that?" said Adrienne and he noticed that her cheeks were just starting to flush.

"She told me that she had helped to shave you down there. That you had asked her to."

"Yes, I did. Not an easy thing to do on your own and I did not want to go to one of these so-called beauty parlours that do not have a clue how to do it properly and rip your skin off, pouring hot wax onto you.

Besides, not sure you can get one that does it all."

"So Anca shaved all your bits?"

"Yes, she did."

"So, she must have touched you down there?"

"Yes, of course. How else could she do it."

"And would I be correct in saying that it turned you on, watching her do it?"

"You want me to say that it did, is that it? Yes, Flint. It did turn me on. There, now you know."

"Hmm, now everything is falling into place. So, in Amsterdam, let me speculate for a moment," he said, putting his hand up to stop Adrienne interrupting him. "If my fantasy had not been to see you making out with another woman but had been, somewhat more vanilla and just for me to have sex with another woman, then I am surmising that your fantasy would not have been fulfilled to see me in action as you stated at the time. Your fantasy would in fact have been for you to make it with another woman. Is that not correct?"

Adrienne was blushing furiously as she nodded. "Yes."

"And in choosing an escort that looked the spitting image of Anca and by the way my credit card bill came through, fifteen hundred euros for the girl, you were in fact satisfying your fantasy to have sex with Anca; is that not correct too?"

"Yes, it's true, I was," she admitted.

Theo smiled, smugly nodding to himself for having caught her out.

"By the look of this thing sticking up, you like the idea of that, don't you?" said Adrienne, putting her hand on the bulge in his shorts.

"Maybe but can I ask you one further question and please, I want a straight answer. And let me remind you, we said we would be open about things we have done in the past."

"What is it you want to know, Flint?" she said, throwing one of the cushions from the armchair in front of her before kneeling down and facing him.

"When Anca was shaving you down there, you said that it was turning you on watching her do it. Was there anything else?"

"What do you mean?" she said, running her fingers delicately over the bulge in his lounge shorts once again.

"You know what I mean, Kiffy. But for the avoidance of doubt, Anca's fingers must have made contact with your skin, however unintentional it was?"

Adrienne shrugged. "Might have done."

"Okay, sixty-four-thousand-dollar question, as they say, Kiffy. Did Anca touch you, not just accidently as part of shaving you down there?"

Adrienne was quiet for a brief moment and then nodded. "How?"

"With her fingers."

"Did she use her tongue too, like the pretend Anca did in Amsterdam?"

"No! No way! But she did caress me with her fingers, on my clit and I encouraged her to put them inside me too. So now you know, Flint," she confessed and breathed out like a weight had been lifted off her shoulders.

"Oh my God," he said, his bulge now bursting to be released into the open.

Adrienne pulled at Theo's shorts and he lifted himself up so she could take them off completely.

"Did she make you…?"

"Yes, Flint, she did and I had a wonderful orgasm. And, before you ask, no I did not touch her. I was too wrapped up in what she was doing to me. We never spoke about it, not a word to each other, I just kissed her on the cheek by way of saying thank you. Honestly, if she had turned her head and we kissed properly I don't know if it would have stopped at that. But she didn't and that was the end of that."

"Wow. Wish I was there to watch," he said.

"You were, kind of. Not exactly Anca herself but nevertheless you enjoyed me and her. And Flint, just for the record, I did enjoy watching you fucking that girl when we were in Amsterdam, I really did. That was as much of my fantasy as my being with Anca."

"It was great, a pure delight and I would be lying if I said I didn't enjoy it too," he said. "Did you get up to anything else with Anca or was that a one-off?"

"It was just the once. Sorry Flint, there is no more to add."

"Would you do the same again if she was minded to do the same?"

"I don't know, it will depend at the time. I don't know why it went that way, it just did. No rational explanation as you might say. Are you annoyed? Do you want me to stop?"

"No, I am not annoyed, Kiffy. But I am mindful of Anca feeling put under pressure to do it," he warned.

"You are protective of Anca but you have nothing to fear. It was she who initiated it. I think she felt sorry for me as you were away. She enjoyed pleasing me, Flint. I did not force her to do it."

"Lucky you," he said.

"Flint, do you want her to do the same for you?"

"Pardon?"

"Play with you like I'm doing right now," said Adrienne.

"Are you testing me again, Kiffy?"

"No, seriously. If you want her to play with you I don't mind but only that and I mean only that, Flint. No more."

"Kiffy, this is crazy. No, I do not want to mess around with Anca," he said but as Adrienne continued to caress his manhood, it was Anca's hand that he was imagining on it and it made his climax that much stronger letting his mind drift to thinking about her doing it.

By the middle of August, whilst Theo was back in the Emirates, Adrienne, assisted by Anca, Beatrix, her future mother-in-law and his sister Suzy managed to book the registry wedding date and send out invitations to a reception at Josiah Hall, for the third Saturday of September. At Theo's request, the civic ceremony at the registry office would be kept to a minimum of people. He had asked Suzy to be his witness and Anca was thrilled to be asked to be Adrienne's witness.

Beatrix was delighted to be asked to help and volunteered to arrange the reception. She even drove up to London for a few days and stayed in Theo's house, together with Suzy who also moved in temporarily to help with the planning. Adrienne was happy for Beatrix to take the lead, she was clearly in her element, her only stipulation being that the reception should be low key and have some element of Frenchness about it, in honour of her parents and brother who would be coming over.

"My dear, we will make your family feel at home. Language will not be a problem as we all speak a reasonable amount of French in the family; Suzanne and Theodore in particular are fluent. And even Mrs Chalfont speaks passable French too. Call it one of the benefits of running Josiah

Hall as a weekend tourist destination. We do get a lot of French visitors who want the Downton Abbey experience so we have all brushed up on our French and Spanish too. We are even able to utter a few words of greeting to our Russian and Chinese visitors."

Even though she did not want a church wedding, Adrienne acquiesced to Beatrix' suggestion that the family vicar, who also baptised Theo, would say a blessing at the reception. Over the course of a few days, everything was planned with almost military precision: from the flowers, the music, the table arrangements and the menu, which was a hybrid of French and English cuisine. The beef for the Chateaubriand was coming from the estate. Beatrix chose the English white wine for the fish course and Adrienne chose the French Red wines that would be served with the Chateaubriand. The cheeses would be a selection of both French and English, celebrating the best of both with French dessert wine. There would also be apple pie and custard and chocolate eclairs with coffee. Adrienne was pleased with the proposal.

Mrs Chalfont came up for the day with Arabella, who used the planning of the reception as a pretext to get away and do some shopping in London.

"Haven't been up to Theo's house in years. He does like to live well, doesn't he?" said Arabella when she was in the kitchen with Adrienne, on the pretext of helping her to make sandwiches and snacks for the planning group.

"He works hard for it," said Adrienne, trying to hide her irritation.

"Nice Jaguar in the drive too, I noticed."

"Yes, he got it for me," she said proudly, and in a way, designed to instil jealousy in Arabella. It had worked.

"I guess you will soon become mistress of this house, too," Arabella observed.

"I do not need to wait until I marry Theo to feel like that, Arabella. He is very loving towards me and makes me feel I am already mistress of the house."

Anca came in to help and she could see there was a bit of tension in the air and ushered Adrienne out to the conservatory to join the others and she would take over.

Beatrix could see the strain on Adrienne's face, took her hand and suggested they stroll in the garden. Adrienne relayed the conversation with Arabella to her which elicited a warm hug.

"Don't take any notice, my dear. Arabella is just a little jealous. Not just about the house, also your engagement ring, especially the way Theo took you to Amsterdam to buy it, very romantic and of course, the car. Theodore was always more stylish than Cuthbert, who was more, shall we say, prosaic in his outlook, preferring the functional to the sublime. He is not mean with money, just has a different outlook on how to spend it than Theodore. And coming here is a reminder for Arabella of how much she gave up in order to marry into a country-living family. That's all. Cheer up," she said and kissed Adrienne on the cheek.

"I'm sorry, I must be hormonal. I blame this baby," said Adrienne, stroking her swelling abdomen.

"My dear, I just want to say something and I will do it here so I do not embarrass you in front of the others. Even though I have not known you for very long, I am certain that you will make a good wife for my son. You are the person who will make Theodore very happy. Indeed, I saw it then, when you came down to Josiah Hall. I knew he had made a good catch. Adrienne, I am delighted to welcome you into the Blenkinsop family."

"Thank you for saying that. It means a lot to me. Mrs Blenkinsop, you are a wonderful person," said Adrienne, squeezing her hand.

"Adrienne, please call me Trixie. I really do prefer it. Mrs Blenkinsop just reminds me of how old I am. And soon you are going to make me a grandmother yet again and I love it," she said, smiling, "and you must teach your child to call me Granny Trixie."

Adrienne giggled as they walked arm in arm back into the house. By the end of the third day, the planning was complete. Adrienne begged them to stay an extra night as she wanted to invite them all to dinner at her favourite French restaurant by way of a thank you. The night was a success, everyone was relaxed and enjoying themselves but what topped the evening for Adrienne, was Arabella standing up and making a little speech, welcoming her into the family, giving her an engagement present of a fine Waterford crystal bowl, followed by a hug and kiss. She whispered into Adrienne's ear, "Sorry for being a bitch to you."

"And perhaps your husband-to-be can have a word with my husband about how to woo a girl," she said, giggling. "I'm fed up of that Land Rover Discovery." She rubbed her bottom in mock pain that had everyone smiling and clapping. She had lost none of her city girl polish.

Adrienne smiled and looked over to Beatrix who winked at her.

The next day, everyone left and in the evening, Adrienne left to go to the airport to pick up Theo. She had wanted to go alone but Anca insisted that she go with her, under orders from Theo.

This time there was no hesitancy when he appeared out of the Exit door, running up to him and hugging and kissing him much to his embarrassment.

"Wow! That was some welcome. Missed me?"

"Not really, had to put on a good show, practice for when I am your wife, Flint," she giggled.

"So, what have you been up to?" he asked, as they walked arm in arm to where Anca was waiting with the car.

Adrienne told him about all the details, leaving nothing out, speaking so fast that she made herself out of breath. Theo hugged her and they kissed.

"Just think, Flint, in three weeks' time we're going to be married!" she said, excitedly.

"Oh my God, Is it too late for me to change my mind," he teased.

"I will kill you if you do, Flint!" she said, yanking his hand.

"It is usual for a femme fatale to wait until after they get married, Kiffy," he joked.

"I don't want your money, Flint. I want your body and soul," she said.

"And I want yours," he said and whispered in her ear, "especially now that you are developing breasts!"

"Naughty! You should have been here the last few days; Arabella came up and stayed with us. She was certainly not shy showing them to us all. Even bigger than Anca's and you know how much you like looking at them, Theo!"

"Kiffy, you are incorrigible!"

Adrienne laughed. "Me? So what did you do in Abu Dhabi. Did you fuck your Arab girl, Flint?"

"I tried. But shocking as it may sound, she resisted my attentions! I chased her up and down the harbour wearing nothing but my Union Jack underpants and a smile but to no avail. That old charm did not seem to work on her."

"Flint!"

"Kiffy, stop referring to her as my Arab girl. For the record, she was my girlfriend nearly thirty years ago. Secondly, we did not in any way have contact other than being in the same room discussing important business, which I might add is close to fruition and puts a roof over our heads and pays for the expensive car you brow beat me to buy for you."

"Oh, by the way, that expensive car was delivered whilst you were away. Apparently, its intended owner withdrew his order and as we said we wanted one in a hurry, they let us have his order."

"Really? They just let you drive it away?"

"Yes, once Anca paid the balance. But then you know that, right, as she would have asked for your approval. Stupid me! Anyway, I drove it here! It's brilliant."

Theo laughed. "Glad you like it Kiffy. Just remember to keep its battery charged up, otherwise you'll be calling the AA to give you a tow!"

When they got to the car, Anca jumped out and gave him a welcoming hug and a kiss. "What do you think?" she said, pointing to the gleaming white car in front of him.

"Nice car, battery powered just like my toothbrush," he shrugged. "Modern and dizzy with technology but I much prefer my little Micra around town and my good old fashioned British sports car for the open road."

"This toothbrush will hold all of us and the baby," said Adrienne.

Anca got into the driver's seat and Adrienne sat next to her as Theo wanted to stretch out in the back after a long journey. Within minutes, he was fast asleep.

"His lordship looks worn out," said Adrienne quietly. "I know it is his living that pays for things like this luxury car we're in but I worry about him spending so much time on aeroplanes. Can't be good for him."

"Perhaps if he manages to get this business he has been working on, then he can spend less time out there," said Anca, trying to be reassuring for her friend.

"Do you think so, Anca? I get the impression that he enjoys being out there. Not to be away from us but the whole culture. I know he studied out in the Middle East when he was much younger and he even had an Arab girlfriend."

"Abla?"

"You know about her?" said Adrienne, surprised that he had confided in Anca about her.

"Yes, we've chatted about her in the past but that part of his life was over long before you came on the scene. Adrienne, you have nothing to worry about," she said, patting her leg. "Anyway, I can't complain about him being away so much now that I have you for company. Also, he gives me his air miles, or Avios, or whatever they are called and I get to fly home four times a year for free!"

"He is very generous, isn't he?" said Adrienne, fingering her engagement ring.

"Very kind. He is a very nice man, Adrienne. You have made a good catch."

Adrienne thought she detected an element of wistful sadness in Anca's voice as she said that, reinforcing her feeling that Anca saw in Theo more than just a surrogate-type, father figure.

When they returned, Anca went up to the gym for her nightly workout which gave Adrienne and Theo time to spend on their own. He had washed and changed into his lounge shorts and t-shirts and they sat out in the conservatory, the doors open as the weather was balmy with not the slightest of breezes blowing.

"You know, Flint, in three weeks' time, I will become your wife and in living here permanently, I've been thinking about what to do with my flat."

"What did you have in mind?"

"I don't want to sell it. I want to keep it. But it seems silly for it to remain empty. So I thought I would redecorate it, maybe just re-paint it. Doesn't need anything else as it is new and in good condition and then rent it out. It will help to pay for my mortgage. What do you think?"

"I think it is a good idea to keep it. Property is always a sound investment. And I also think you should rent it. But I have an idea that I want to put to you and I suppose this is as good a time as any to bring it up."

"Idea? What idea, Flint?" she asked, furrowing her eyebrows.

"Kiffy, I have drawn up what is known as a pre-nuptial agreement for you to consider. As part of that agreement, I am proposing that I pay off your mortgage as soon as we get married, so that you own your property outright."

"Thank you for offering to do that, Flint. That is very generous of you. But tell me why we need a pre-nuptial agreement. I thought that was something that they only do in American movies? Is it even real?"

"Oh yes, it is real Kiffy. Certainly, in America it is quite normal and it has become increasingly so, here in England."

"But why do we need one, Flint?"

"It is to protect you and the baby," he said.

"Protect me? How does it protect me, Flint? In case you die whilst you are out in the Middle East somewhere? Or is it to protect your wealth from your wife? Isn't that why a man draws up a pre-nuptial agreement; to stop his wife getting his money if they divorce? Is that what you are worried about, that this whole thing is a charade, a plan by me to seize everything you've got?"

"I assure you there is no need for you to be so suspicious, Kiffy. It is not like that. The document that I will give for you to consider, sets out the terms by which our assets, not just yours, will be divided in the unlikely event that our marriage terminates. By having everything set out in a document, it means, in such a scenario, you would not have to go to court to fight for what is rightfully yours, thereby protecting you. Once you have read it and are happy with it, we both sign it and it becomes the future financial settlement between us. Hopefully our marriage will last forever, in my case until my dying day and we could get married and assume everything will be okay. But sometimes, even with the best intentions, it does not work out that way and divorces can be bitter and acrimonious and only the lawyers get to win. Would it not better and I am going to use my favourite phrase here, for the avoidance of doubt, that we have it set down and in the unlikely event of a divorce, it is clear and unambiguous as to what the terms of the divorce settlement are?"

"Okay, Flint. I understand what you want to do. Give me the document and I'll sign it. Unlike you, I trust you," she said tearfully.

"Kiffy, I do not want you to sign it just like that. I am happy to pay for you to receive independent legal counsel to satisfy yourself that the terms are fair to you. I have drawn up a list of lawyers who specialise in this sort of thing and please contact one of them to go through this agreement with you."

A week later, having sent the document to her appointed counsel, Adrienne found herself sitting in a plush office, being served coffee in a fine bone china cup and sitting adjacent to a lawyer. She was feeling agitated and irritated that she was being put in a position of having to consult a lawyer just a few weeks before her wedding.

"His lordship insisted on it. He would have it no other way," she told Anca, who had offered to go with her.

The lawyer introduced herself as Danielle Williams, a senior lawyer in the firm and an expert in the matter of pre-nuptial agreements. Adrienne did not like her handshake which was limp and moist but liked her overall demeanour, especially the contrasting steely face, framed by a tight fringe, ice-cold blue eyes and thin lips that managed to grimace a smile. It gave her assurance that this woman was not going to allow any man to mess with her clients.

"I'm here now and it seems really weird," said Adrienne, taking a sip of the coffee and grimacing as it offended her taste buds.

"How so, Miss Kiff?" said the lawyer.

"Well, instead of getting excited about my forthcoming wedding, I am here talking to you about what would happen in the event of it ending up in divorce! Not something that occurred to me to be thinking about right now. Scared the life out of me when Theo, that is my future husband said that he wanted us to have a pre-nuptial agreement."

The lawyer smiled faintly and said, "Let me assure you Miss Kiff, that having read the detail within the proposal Mr Blenkinsop has put forward, you have nothing to fear."

"Oh, why is that?"

"The proposal is complex and there are many conditions attached which are term-based but I am pleased to tell you that it is a fair agreement and I would not hesitate in recommending that you accept it. It is unusual in that it is the norm for rich people to want to get away with the minimum they are legally required to hand over in any settlement but Mr Blenkinsop has been very generous. It is a long document and I shall not bother you with some of the standard legal parts. You will be interested in the specific terms, which by the way include what happens in the event of death of either party.

"Okay, let me make a start. The proposal is in many parts starting with what happens once you get married. It then has a section which deals with provision for children that you may have between you. There is also a section that deals with the division of assets in the event of divorce. And the final section proposes how the assets should be divided in the event of his death."

Miss Williams looked up from her iPad at Adrienne, who was sitting there grim-faced. She took a sip of water to clear her throat and then continued. "Right, let me go over the first section, which deals with what happens at the start of the marriage. Mr Blenkinsop proposes that at the point of marriage, each person keeps their own assets prior to that date, in other words what's yours is yours and what's his is his. That is par for the course. However, he does explicit state that he will pay off any mortgage you have on your apartment. Were you aware of that?"

Adrienne nodded. "He said he would."

"In addition to paying off the mortgage, Mr Blenkinsop also proposes to deposit the sum of one hundred thousand pounds into an account of your choice. If you need any help with how to invest that money, I can put you in touch with a very good investment manager."

"Wait, he wants to give me one hundred thousand pounds?" Adrienne asked and her eyes were beginning to well-up, which made the lawyer uncomfortable.

"It would seem so, Miss Kiff. There are other generous provisions and I will go through each of them with you."

Adrienne was not to be rushed and asked questions on every aspect of the proposal, where the condition appeared unclear and demanded that it was changed. She could hear the author of the proposal in her head saying 'for the avoidance of doubt'. The lawyer found herself having to make copious comments in the documents to reflect her client's wishes.

When it came to the provisions for the education of the children they might have, Adrienne smiled and was happy to see that Theo had left open the door that they might have more children. But at the same time, there were two clauses in the proposal that she was unhappy with and demanded that they be changed. The first of these was that he had set a maximum of two children that he was prepared to provide generously for, thereby setting a limit on the future of any family size. She had in the past thought that her family was too small, her mother and father both being the only children from their respective families. As a result, she did not have any uncles or aunties and she had felt as a young child that she had missed out.

"Mr Blenkinsop is not intimating he will not provide for any children, were you to have more than two, Miss Kiff. He is just stating that the generous financial provision would not extend beyond the first two. From the size of the provision and given children are in school for some fifteen years, he is clearly envisaging private school education for the first two children."

"But only for two children!"

"That is correct."

Adrienne huffed her disapproval. "And why do the children have to be educated in England!"

"Mr Blenkinsop is stating he will only make such provision as we've discussed if the children are educated in England up to and including university level, where he will pay their school fees too. That does not prevent their education continuing in France, for example but that he would stop those payments in that event."

Nearly three hours later they came to the end of the document, having been through every aspect of it in minute detail.

"Before we discuss what you have found out about his personal wealth, can I have something to eat? I'm hungry," she said, causing Miss Williams to blush and phone through for her secretary to pop out and buy a selection of sandwiches from the local deli. She also offered to get more coffee but Adrienne declined. "You English don't know how to make good coffee," she quipped. "Oops, I shouldn't have said that. I apologise."

For the first time, it raised a genuine smile in Miss Williams. "I'm not English, so I am not offended. I know what you mean, you have such fine coffees in France and Spain but somehow we seem to lack the ability to achieve the same smoothness, even if the raw coffee beans come from the same place!"

After they had eaten, Miss Williams outlined Theo's wealth from what could be determined from a combination of public records and estimates based on an understanding of what someone at partner-level of seniority can expect to earn in fees. There was also his share of the income from Josiah Hall but the accounts only showed the gross income, not how it was split up.

"In summary, we believe your intended spouse has estimated visible assets to the value of between fifteen to twenty million pounds and potentially another five to ten million in off-shore trusts. I stress these are estimates based on the information we could glean from a number of sources and are, at best, indicative figures."

"So, my romantic husband-to-be, who is always thinking of my welfare, is just looking to protect his vast wealth in all this, is he not, Miss Williams?" said Adrienne, tears running down her face.

"Miss Kiff, I cannot comment on that. But what I can say is that it is a fair agreement and as good as one might expect to obtain in front of a judge presiding in a family divorce court and some are known to be less generous. But it is for you to advise us how you would like to proceed. We have been retained by Mr Blenkinsop to do as you wish."

"I will sign the paper as it is. Scrap all the things I said I want changed," she said, wiping away her tears. "I am not marrying Theo for his money and I am happy with what he says in the agreement."

Three weeks later, now some five months pregnant, Miss Adrienne Kiff became Mrs Adrienne Blenkinsop at Epsom Registry Office and left it, all smiles, wearing his wedding ring which he had especially commissioned and engraved with her name on it. In her Louis Vuitton clutch bag, was the certificate that stated for anyone to know that she was now a married woman and she was over the moon about it. She thought she felt movement inside her, like a gentle kick or turn from the baby, now much more mobile than a week earlier and it left her with a warm feeling of contentment. She felt as if the baby was giving her approval.

It was a bright, sunny day as Anca drove Adrienne, Suzy and Theo in the 'Toothbrush' as the all-electric Jaguar became known, to a restaurant in Tadworth, to mark the occasion. In keeping with the low-key theme, he did not alert the restaurant beforehand and they enjoyed a peaceful lunch, with a bottle of red wine, mainly drunk by Anca and Suzy as he would not allow his new wife to have more than half a glass as she wanted to drive back and was also concerned for the baby.

"Why, Flint, it is okay to have a couple of glasses of wine," she assured him.

"Be that as it may, I do not want my child to start getting used to alcohol from now. She will have plenty of time when she gets much older!"

Adrienne found it heart-warming that Theo had taken such an interest in the unborn child's welfare; far exceeding her expectations.

'Perhaps I shouldn't wait too long to try for another one,' she told herself.

"Well, what does it feel like to be married, dear brother?" asked Suzy, as they arrived back at the house in the afternoon and walked arm in arm in the garden.

"Truthfully? Has not quite sunk in yet. Suzy. If you had asked me if I had any plans to get married just a few months ago, I would have said you were off your head. And here I am, tied to another human being and soon to become a father."

"I do love Adrienne and I believe she is good for you, Monty. Makes you think about planting roots, all good stuff, keeping your end of the Blenkinsop bloodline going. But would you have married Adrienne if a baby was not on its way? I thought you were done with permanent relationships after Marianne."

Theo shrugged. "Who knows, Suzy? Maybe, possibly, probably, eventually, yes, I would have married Adrienne. We get on very well," he said.

"Pardon me for saying this, Monty. But I am your favourite little sister and drawing on that to take liberties with my next comment. But what you've just said doesn't sound like someone who is, as they say, madly in *lurve*," she teased.

"The L word, as you know, is banned from my lips. But if I had to use it with anyone in mind, it would be her," he said, looking back towards the house. "That tempestuous, fiery French woman who is looking back at me with the sweetest of smiles and who is wholly and totally committed to me. That's something with future in it, is it not, Suzy?"

"Time will tell Brother and I wish you well, Monty. Truly, I do. You've worked hard to get to where you are and with Adrienne by your side, your life is much more complete."

"*Tantum tempus narrabo* as you say," he agreed, as they started to walk back towards the house.

"I won't ask you what you two were talking about as it sounds like I am a nagging wife and I have only been a wife for a few hours," said Adrienne, laughing.

"Good heavens, things are looking up, already. In the past she would not have held back," joked Theo.

"Would you like some tea, dear husband?" she joked. "And how about dessert, French dessert from a new coffee shop in the village. The chef is French, speaks to me in French and serves French food and coffee you can actually drink!"

"Yes, but he is in England, in an English village and he is paying English taxes to Her Majesty the Queen and most, if not all, his customers are probably English," said Theo.

"I might even get a job there, serving people so at least I can talk to a civilised Frenchman," she said, poking her tongue out at him.

"Stop it you two! I feel as if I am living with two kids," Anca giggled.

"He is a big, English kid!" said Adrienne, as she snaked her arm around Theo and kissed him. "Flint, I felt the baby kick me today. I think she is happy for me."

"Right then, let's have some tea before these two become too lovey-dovey and give me indigestion," said Suzy, reaching for a cup. "To more important matters of the state, when are your parents coming over, Adrienne? The reception is only three days away. We need to be going down to Josiah Hall soon to get ready."

Adrienne seemed unconcerned. "Maybe tomorrow. It depends. My father is arranging for someone to manage the farm whilst he is over here and it is not easy, as the people around there have their own farms to look after."

That night, after Suzy had left and Anca retired to her room, Theo queried her parents' arrival and Adrienne cut him short. "I don't want to talk about it, Flint!" she said.

The sharpness of her response surprised him but he chose not to press her. Instead, he excused himself to read over documents in preparation for his forthcoming trip to Abu Dhabi, immediately after the reception.

"Well, what do you think, Philip? I am now a married man," he said, stroking his cat as it jumped up onto his lap, putting its paws on the table, looking as if he was studying the screen of the laptop. "Philip, you do not know how lucky you are. Life is so much easier being a cat. Want to swap for a little while? How about you be the husband and I will be the cat."

A few minutes later, Adrienne popped her head around the door and entered the study. She walked slowly up to Theo, looking glum. She stood next to him, prompting him to close his laptop.

"Sorry, commercial confidentiality," he said, when he noticed the frown on her face.

"Can't even show your wife?"

Theo shook his head. "No, I am afraid I cannot do that."

Adrienne was rocking backwards and forwards on the edge of the table, her back towards it in contemplative thought. The cat was eyeing her every movement, content to be sitting on his master's lap.

"I'm sorry for earlier, for snapping at you, Flint," she said finally.

"Forget it, Kiffy," he shrugged and took her hand by way of reassurance.

"About my parents," she said and he could see in her demeanour someone who was dealing with some inner torment.

"It is okay, Kiffy. If you do not wish to talk it is not a problem. I will be meeting them soon. It is not important that I know their travel arrangements."

"That's just it," she said and her eyes were filling with tears. "They might not be coming."

"Oh? Really? What makes you say that? Has something befallen them? Is someone ill?" asked Theo and seeing Adrienne very upset, pushed Philip off his lap and pulled her down to sit on him, hugging her and stroking her hair.

"I wish it was something like that, Flint. But I am afraid it is nothing to do with illness," she said and buried her head in his neck.

When she stopped crying and whimpering, Adrienne sat up and took a deep breath, as Theo wiped away her tears and patted her hand, smiling reassuringly. "When you are ready, there is something you want to say to me, Kiffy. I can see it is causing you much angst but is it not better to let it out?"

She nodded. "Can we go next door? Somewhere more comfortable, I want to sit on a sofa and put my feet up."

When they were in the living room and sitting next to each other, her feet raised on a cushion on his lap, Adrienne was ready to talk.

"Flint, we haven't really talked about my parents and my relationship with them, have we? If you had come with me when I went in May you, as the very observant person that you are, might have seen a little of what it is like. What you might have witnessed is a little friction between myself and my parents, particularly between myself and my mother. We are not very close. It has been like that for a very long time, from when I left home at eighteen to go to university. I was not the easiest of kids for a parent to bring up. I was a rebellious brat. I admit that."

Theo smiled, "Why am I not surprised to hear that?"

"I admit that and what made me look even worse in their eyes, was that my brother is not like me at all. Complete opposite of me. He's like a saint in comparison to me. I fought with my parents on anything and everything you can think of. I hated living on the farm. It was like an open-air prison for me and as soon as I could, I escaped to Paris where I studied. When I finished my studies, I had hoped they would come to Paris to see me graduating but they could not; the farm demanded all of their time. I hated that farm, so coming to England was an easy thing for me to do. In all the years I have been here, my parents have not come to see me even once. Of course, I go to see them, at the end of each term, Christmas, Easter, the summer, sometimes half-term too. In recent years, we have mellowed so we do not fight. I would go so far as to say we have a pleasant time together. But I know deep down I have been a disappointment to them. Left the farm, left the country, a string of failed romances, reached the age of thirty-two and had nothing to show for it. And on my last trip to see them just before we went to Amsterdam, I went there as a pregnant, unmarried woman. My mother was not happy to see me like that at all. Her words to me were, 'You know how to make a mess of your life, don't you Adrienne? Why can't you get anything right?

Good girls get married first and then have their children after'. I told her I was in a relationship but that meant nothing. Of course, I didn't know you were going to ask me to marry you then. Your timing was off, Flint."

"Would it have made any difference if I had asked you to marry me before you went to see them?"

"Probably not. Anyway, when I told them that I was getting married, my mother seemed to be pleased for me. She said the priest in the village would marry us and they could hold the reception in the hall behind the church. When I told her I did not want a church service, she was not happy. When I told her that I was getting married in England she was cross and when I told her that my husband was an Englishman, she saw it as the ultimate act of betrayal. She said, "They tell us there are four hundred thousand French people living in England, could I not find one amongst them to marry?"

"Oh dear, so I am not exactly flavour of the month for your mother. Did you tell her that I do speak French?"

"I didn't know that you did until your mother told me. Anyway, I doubt if that would have helped. She wished me well to be fair. My father was sad that I didn't marry a Frenchman but he was more forthcoming in congratulating me and asked when the wedding was. He was not happy about the timing, asking why I hadn't chosen a date later in the year, in the winter time when they had more time on their hands, rather than at peak harvest time. In their eyes, it was yet another example of my thoughtlessness, of being inconsiderate and only thinking about me, not others. And it hurt me to hear that. It made me reflect, to look at myself and I was thinking that maybe they are right. Maybe I have spent all my life only thinking about me."

"They are incorrect, Kiffy. From what you say and what I have personally observed, you care very much about your parents and you do think about them. If you did not care for them, why would you go back home three or four times a year? It is not exactly down the road, is it? You see more of your parents than I see of mine. So does that mean your parents are not coming to the reception?"

"Your guess is as good as mine," said Adrienne, holding her hands out. "What about your brother, what does he have to say about this?"

"My brother and I are quite close despite the difference in character and I am sure he will try and find a way to come, even if he has to leave his wife and kids behind."

"Can he influence your parents to do the same and come? Could he not put it to them to overlook that their daughter is marrying an Englishman and in England and make a point that that they should be there for her?"

"I don't think so. My brother wouldn't do anything to antagonise our parents. After all, he has to live with them and he doesn't want any trouble. He is like my father; just wants to keep the peace."

"Kiffy, I would very much like to speak to your brother if I may."

"Why? What good will that do?"

"Please let me have his phone number and I will give him a ring in the morning, as it's too late now. He sounds like a reasonable man and I will talk to him. And in French, that will impress him if nothing else."

At 10 a.m., French time, Monsieur Gabriel Kiff took a call from his brother-in-law whilst he was in the barn carrying out maintenance work on his tractor. He was taken by surprise but did not put the phone down when Theo introduced himself in perfect French, albeit with an English accent. After some thirty minutes of polite and friendly exchanges, the call ended and as far as Theo could make out, they had left on good terms.

Against her better instinct, Adrienne agreed to go down with Suzy and Anca two days before the reception to get ready, whilst Theo stayed behind to meet her brother and bring him down.

Two days later, on a sunny day in the Wiltshire countryside, Adrienne found herself standing under a white canopy adorned with heavily scented roses and carnations and climbing jasmine, lovingly decorated, courtesy of her mother-in-law, Beatrix. She stood nervously waiting with Theo to her right, holding her hand. He could sense the anxiety she was feeling and squeezed her hand gently by way of reassurance, smiling when he caught her eye.

They were standing in front of the vicar, the portly, white-haired Reverend Frederick Higgs, who was leaning towards Beatrix to better hear her whispering in his ear. Theo noticed he had placed a finger in the Bible from where he would be reading the blessing. Even though she was already a married woman, Adrienne was finding the event with so many eyes on her daunting and she was hanging on to Theo's arm for dear life.

"You look absolutely radiant, Kiffy," said Theo.

"Do I, Flint? Do I really?"

She found the warm smile and the pressure on her hand more assuring than any words that could be uttered. Here was the man whom she loved, whom she had committed to body and soul and she felt assured and drew comfort from having him there.

Behind Adrienne, there were whispers and then she could hear shuffling going on, as the Reverend called everyone to order. She looked to the side where Anca stood and blew her a kiss. Anca smiled sweetly and then indicated with a movement of her head for Adrienne to look behind her. She furrowed her eyebrows, not understanding and Anca repeated the gesture, and Adrienne turned her head out of curiosity. To say it was a surprise would be an understatement for standing in the front two rows of chairs behind her that had been laid out for guests, were her mother and father, her brother and his wife and their three children. She looked up at Theo who smiled. She was fighting back the tears as Reverend Higgs, in his best schoolboy French, began the blessing, repeating it in English as he went along, growing in confidence as he progressed through it. By the end of the blessing, Adrienne was overjoyed and overcome with emotion and cried her eyes out. There were hugs and kisses from everybody and the one that meant the most to her was the one from her mother.

"I'm so sorry I hurt you over the years, Mother," she whispered in Madame Kiff's ear.

"It is all forgotten," she said in French. "Your husband is old, you didn't tell me that, naughty girl. But he is also a very charming man and I like him. We had a long chat in the car coming down. Speaks very good French!"

Adrienne, having kissed her way through everyone including her little nephew and nieces, then went back to Beatrix and gave her the biggest hug of all, thanking her profusely not only for the reception but for also being her friend.

"I love you, Trixie," she said, earnestly.

"I feel the same way about you, my dear," said Beatrix and then took her hand. "Now let's go circulate before I make a fool of myself and start shedding tears."

Much to their surprise, Mr and Mrs Kiff found that most people were reasonably conversant in French and they were able to relax and feel welcome, far more so than when they first set off.

"How did you manage to swing that, Monty?" asked Suzy, as she pulled her brother away from Bertie. "Adrienne had let on that she was not expecting her family to come and well, here they are and apparently even enjoying themselves."

"I appealed to them through the brother," said Theo.

"Is that all? I didn't get the impression that they would be swayed by just persuasive argument alone. Come on, Monty, it's me. Tell me what it took."

Theo was in two minds whether to say anything, but a gentle nudge from his youngest and favourite sister led him to open up. "Persuasive argument and electronic banking, Suzy."

"Meaning?"

"Fifty thousand euros deposited into her brother's bank account, enough to get him a new tractor and fifty thousand euros deposited into her parents' bank account and five thousand to hire workers to mind the farm for two days. But that is for your ears only."

"Wow! That was *very* generous, Monty."

"It was very important to Adrienne. She would have been devasted if her parents had not been there. Now, she is the happiest woman in Josiah Hall."

"You really do love her, don't you Monty?" she said, admiringly.

"I told you before Suzy, I have never liked that word. Misused, overused and seldom backed up by deeds that show evidence of it."

Suzy kissed Theo's cheek. "Monty, why couldn't I have met someone like you to marry, Brother?"

He looked across to watch his wife dancing with her father and she looked content and that made him content. The reception had gone well.

Planning For The Future

On his return to Abu Dhabi, a week after the reception, the contract was ready for signing. At a formal ceremony, which Abla attended in her capacity as the future Portfolio Manager, Rashid signed two documents and Theo did the same on behalf of the firm, keeping one copy for himself which he handed over to Nicola for safe keeping.

Abla congratulated him and said she looked forward to them working together. He noticed her handshake was warm and friendly but was concerned if anyone noticed that it was perhaps longer than it needed to have been. She also handed over a leather attaché case stuffed with brochures, containing information for potential places to rent or buy office space and personal accommodation for those that would be spending three years in Abu Dhabi.

When they returned to London, he had received a message that a transfer of six million pounds was received by international bank transfer to Theo's firm, which pleased the other partners and they all went out for celebratory drinks. For tax purposes, Theo opted not to take his cut out of the fee, instead choosing to wait for the new financial year to kick in when he would be out of the UK and therefore not liable to pay any tax on his earnings.

The interviews for the positions in Abu Dhabi were arranged in London and conducted by a board which consisted of Theo, another senior partner in the firm familiar with the pressure on running overseas teams and a senior member of HR. There was never any real doubt as to the outcome, with Gareth invited to join Theo as the senior lawyer working with him and Nicola was appointed to the position of being Theo's assistant. She was delighted when she got the letter from HR confirming that she had been successful and bought Theo a bottle of champagne by way of saying thank you. Theo declined it, asking that it be shared amongst the back-office team instead, making some excuses about having an ulcer.

'Best not take it home,' he told himself.

Interviews were conducted the following day in which the successful applicants had to sign away their lives for the next three years. Gareth had read the papers HR had sent him thoroughly and was content to sign as is. At the end of the three-year period, he would have earned more than six hundred and fifty thousand pounds in fees alone and would be living in luxurious accommodation with his wife and young children, paid for out of the contract.

"Nicola, make no mistake this *will* be a tough assignment. You've had a taster of it in coming with me over the last few months to secure this line of business but each time, we've had a respite coming back every week or so. This is a three-year commitment. Of course, you will still have your annual leave but you won't be able to pop back home for a weekend, if you're feeling homesick," Theo cautioned.

They were sat in his office and he was going over the papers HR had sent her, line by line. She had requested the meeting to make sure she fully appreciated what she was about to be signing up to.

"Theo, I am really looking forward to it. This is a fantastic opportunity for me. I will be learning a lot working alongside you and Gareth and Abla. The knowledge and experience I will be gaining I could never get just being in our London office. And, well, I'd be lying if I said the money is not a big motivator too. Based on the HR terms and conditions of my appointment, I stand to earn over two hundred thousand, a small fortune for me, Theo. Unless I go crazy and spend it all, that should enable me to put down a big deposit for me to buy my first house when I get back! I'm really excited about it, Theo."

"Great. Any concern, or issue that you think of, don't hesitate to let me know and I'll see if I can fix it."

"There is one issue but I am pretty sure you won't be able to fix it."

"Oh, what might that be?"

Nicola bent down and whispered it in his ear.

"That I cannot do, must not do. I am now a married man so all that goes too, I'm afraid," he replied.

"I know, I was just teasing you," she giggled.

Having secured signed commitments from both Gareth and Nicola, Theo left the office grinning from ear to ear. "One more thing I can now tick off in making the dream a reality," he said. "Persian Gulf, here I come!"

On the train ride back home, he was recalling all the changes that had happened in his life in recent weeks and mentally ticked up September as having been a great success. A few months earlier he had been a single man, in an on-off relationship of sorts with a tempestuous French woman and commuting back and forth to the Middle East, picking up pieces of work here and there with a hope that one day, he might make a living out there. In what seemed like condensing what for some people might take a decade or more in years to achieve, he had become a married man with a child on the way. It made him smile when he thought of the unusual way it had all arrived at. And much to his surprise, the resentment towards Adrienne he thought that he would harbour for having tricked him had not lingered, had not consumed him. Indeed, it had quickly evaporated as he turned to making the best of what had been a very unsatisfactory situation, he had found himself in. And now, it actually felt comfortable and the most natural thing to be married to Adrienne, like he had fulfilled some prophesy. It was a warm feeling.

Having initially viewed the prospect of fatherhood when Adrienne had first announced to him her pregnancy, as having nothing but disaster written all over it, alarmed at the possibility of it derailing his future plans, Theo had since reconciled himself to becoming a father. From wanting nothing to do with it, he now had a bookmark saved on his browser that took him straight to a baby's development, where he read up on the progress of growth week by week. Anyone looking at his browser's search history, would see after world news, it was the most visited website that he clicked on.

"Let me see, so the baby is around twenty-three or twenty-four weeks old. What does the website say about her development?" he muttered to himself one evening as he read the article. He was smiling to himself as he marvelled at what was happening.

He glanced up to see that Adrienne was coming towards him with a bundle under her arm and wearing a glum face. She smiled weakly as she approached, which did not bode well and he clicked off the website he had just been looking at.

"When were you planning to tell me, Flint?" she said, dropping the bundle of brochures in front of him.

"It is only an option I am considering, Kiffy."

"Option? You're planning to live in Abu Dhabi and it is just an option? Really?" she said incredulously. "Looking at properties to buy doesn't look like just an option to me. Looks like you've already made up your mind. I'm not stupid, Flint."

"I repeat, it is just an option. And, to be clear, this option is not just about my living out there, Kiffy. It is about us and what is best for us. It is one of a number of options, which I am looking into for…"

"Us?" said Adrienne interrupting him, angrily. She picked up one of the brochures and thumbed through it, stopping at one of the pages with green sticky dividers. "So these properties with your writing on the side saying 'interested in, please look into it for me', is just an option? Really?"

"Yes, that is correct."

"Sounds like you've already made up your mind, Flint," she said accusingly, as her eyes welled up with tears. "Are you planning to leave me, Flint? Is that it?"

"Absolutely not!" he said, emphatically.

"Not sure I can believe you, Flint. These tell me that you are planning to buy a house in Abu Dhabi and I am completely in the dark about it. I only get to find out because these glossy brochures slipped out of your bag that was on the study table. Flint, I'm your wife, don't you think I should know about this?"

"I was going to tell you when I had all the facts at my disposal, Kiffy. I have not told you thus far as I did not want to cause you any anxiety about what was happening by not being in full possession of information, that would enable me to answer any questions that you might have had."

"So, hiding it from me was about not causing me anxiety? Listen to yourself, Flint, does that even sound normal? Does it sound like the words of someone who thinks about nothing but himself!"

The words hurt as he knew that there was an element of truth in what she had said.

"It is possible but I hope not. It was my intent to minimise any stress to you. To do that, I needed to have more information. The starting point for that is getting certainty on what the work future might look like. I now have that. The next thing I needed to do was to consider what that meant for me, for us and how it would affect our lives…"

"Wait! Stop there! You've lost me already. What work? Is this something that relates to all these trips back and forth to the Emirates?"

"Yes. I would not be betraying any commercial confidence if I told you that I have won a massive contract for my company with a major client in Abu Dhabi. It is a three-year contract. Arising from this work and other opportunities that have come our way, we have decided, indeed the client has demanded it, that we set up an office there manned by four people and a couple of local hires."

"And you are one of those four people, I take it?"

"Correct. I am in fact heading it up at the request of the client. It is a massive opportunity for me, Kiffy. As you know I love the Middle East and to be working out there is a dream come true," he said and she could see how his face lit up when he said that.

"And what about me? What about our child. What about us, Flint? Did you think about that too?"

"Of course I did, I have. It is the thing that I have spent most time on, reconciling the fulfilment of my life's dream with my responsibility towards you. Hence, why I have been looking at how we can make this work."

"And how is that?"

"It goes without saying that I cannot be in two places at the same time but one option is for me to commute. I can work in Abu Dhabi and once a month come back for a long weekend, perhaps Thursday to Monday. I am sure I can swing that with the client. It is not as if I will be out of contact. In between, we can Skype every day."

"I don't like that option at all," she said, cutting him off.

"I do not disagree with you, Kiffy. It is far from ideal which is why I have been exploring the idea of us moving out there, to Abu Dhabi. I have been looking at potential properties that would be suitable for a family. Did you get a chance to look at any of them?"

"No, I was too angry with you. Hurt that you were doing this behind my back."

"At any rate, there are some fine, western-style properties in very nice residential areas, where expatriates tend to live. There are good facilities, entertainment, restaurants, a lovely clean beach for us to go down to with the baby; everything you could possibly want.

Also, I was thinking about what you might do out there beyond caring for the baby. I was thinking that, if you fancy it, you could also give private French and Spanish lessons. There is a demand for that and apparently there are very few people qualified or offering such tuition.

And being there it is convenient for Dubai, just down the road. Cairo is just three hours flying time away, Beirut, Jerusalem, Amman not much more. This will be a convenient and great opportunity to see all the wonderful historic places in what is the cradle of modern civilisation. Kiffy, I can show you the places of my youth, places which are really interesting, vibrant cultures that belie the western image of backward, intolerant extremists."

"Thought of everything then? What about the house?"

"We can keep it going as we need somewhere to come back to when we fancy a break and of course during Ramadan when things tend to grind to a halt. Not renting it out, Kiffy."

"And Anca? What about her future.? I love her and I don't want to throw her out on the street."

"I would like her to come with us. My research tells me there is a dearth of Pilates and physical trainers in Abu Dhabi and I was thinking of buying or renting a place for Anca to turn into a fitness and Pilates studio and run it. Perhaps her friend Lenka might want to come out too."

"And what about someone to help me?"

"A combination of Anca and we would also have a housemaid and cleaner and gardener."

"Thought of everything, haven't you, Flint? What about my happiness? Away from my family, who I have only recently reconciled with and I will be gone. And what about my friends, I will surely lose those too. And culture? I moved to London not just to get a job but because it is the most culturally-rich city in the world. Now you want to move me to a cultural backwater. I don't like this option either. I don't want to go. And I don't want you to go. Why can't you send someone else?"

"Aside from fulfilling my life's dream to work in the Middle East and everything I have worked for, the client has demanded it. Indeed, my being based in Abu Dhabi is written into the contract, so I have to go. It is only for three years, Kiffy and I am sure you will find it very enriching."

"I don't know, Flint. You are asking me to give up a lot. I've been your wife for less than a month and have hardly enjoyed spending any time with you and you want to disappear. It's not fair, Flint," she said, openly crying.

"Kiffy, I am not disappearing and on the point of spending time together, if you are out there with me, you will get to see me every day. I will not have to work long hours. I will not be flying off to other places like I do now so you will see much more of me and so will the baby too. It is a great opportunity for us, Kiffy."

"For you maybe, and I understand that. But I will end up being alone, isolated, in a strange country with strange customs. How will I fit into that?"

"And coming to London, you didn't find us strange, weird, odd, cold, culturally a world away from Normandy and indeed Paris for that matter!"

"True. And you being the strangest, weirdest, oddest, coldest person I have ever met," she said but the half smile heartened him.

"You wouldn't have me any other way, my little, passionate, fiery French woman," he said.

"I hate you Englishman!" she said and pushed herself up slowly and sat on his lap.

"God, you're getting heavier," he said, nuzzling her.

"It's this baby of yours. It has made me fat; my ankles are swelling up and…"

"Your boobs too!" he said, putting his hand on her chest.

"And now you are going to bring her up as a little Arab girl!"

"No, she will be brought up as an English girl, culturally enriched by living in an Arab land."

"She will be brought up as a French girl!"

"Kiffy, I am truly sorry that I made you sad and angry but I could not say anything until the deal was signed."

"You could have told me of the possibility, Flint. I am a big girl, I can handle uncertainty. I think you have been living the bachelor life too long and not used to sharing stress and uncertainty with others. As a lawyer, you want to be reassuring to your clients, I get that. But you can share your worries and uncertainties with me, you know that. I want you to. I want to be there for you as much as you are there for me."

"Then will you come with me to Abu Dhabi?"

Adrienne smiled. "Yes, I will. I put us first, Flint. I know you want it badly. When you talk about the Middle East your eyes light up like a child in a candy shop. I would be a bitch to deny you your life's dream and I am not that."

Theo laughed and was about to say something when she put her fingers to his lips. "But I get to choose the house we're going to live in."

Theo smiled. "Kiffy, notwithstanding you are pregnant and I imagine in some discomfort but how about flying out there with me to see for yourself what Abu Dhabi is like? It should reassure you."

"No, I don't want to risk it. I will look at these brochures and choose from here, I trust to your judgement. Actually, I would like for you to take Anca with you and show her. I trust her to give me the woman's view. There are things men don't think about that are important to a woman!"

"I'm not sure I know what you mean but sure, let's do that."

"And Flint, for the avoidance of doubt, you going alone with Anca to Abu Dhabi does not mean you get to fuck her!"

"Kiffy! Whose idea was it to send Anca out with me?"

"Yes, but I don't want you to use it as an opportunity to get too close to Anca. I know what men are like, always think with your dicks when you're alone with a sexy, young woman! And I know you think she is a sexy, young woman, no matter what you say. Remind me again, how often did you say men think about sex?"

"Every ninety seconds, they say," he said, laughing, "which means that whilst we have been talking, I have been thinking of sex at least ten times!"

"That much? Maybe you will get lucky later but first we need to finish talking about this bombshell you've dropped on me."

"Oh? What's left to talk about?" he said, putting his hand around her waist.

Adrienne pulled away slightly, just out of his reach. "Flint, wait. Haven't you forgotten something else to tell me about this crazy idea of yours?"

"Oh, what is that?"

"The office, when did you say it is opening up?"

"January. The office needs to be up and running by the beginning of January."

"Wow! That's only three months away. Our baby will only be a few weeks old by then."

"You could come out at the end of January with Anca?"

"Yes, I think I prefer that."

"Great. I had better pass these brochures back to you, then," he said, kissing her.

"How much can I spend?"

"Up to eight million dirham."

"Dirham? Is that the currency of the Emirates? How much is that in euros?"

"I have no idea in euros but in the Queen's currency it is approximately two million pounds. That should get us quite a decent property. But note the areas I have indicated are where foreigners can buy property. We cannot just buy anywhere we fancy, only in designated development areas."

"Wow! That seems a lot of money to be spending to just be there for three years. Then what? Would you sell it?"

"I was thinking of keeping it as an investment. The Emirates is very popular and prices are on the rise and will continue to do so and the advice I have been getting from property experts is that it would be a sound investment for us."

"Us? Is it not just going into the Theodore Blenkinsop pension fund?" she teased.

"Yes, us Kiffy. I was planning to make you joint owner, a half share in it. And any profits that may accrue from renting it out or selling it on at some point in the future, fifty percent of them would go to you."

"Wow! Are you sure you want to do that, Englishman? Are you sure you will not be breaking the terms of the pre-nuptial agreement that you forced me to sign?" she said, relentless in teasing him.

Theo remained unflappable. "Hmm, maybe you are right, Kiffy. Too generous. I change my mind, I am keeping it all to myself!"

"Don't you dare, Flint! Taking away my share already." Theo was laughing heartily.

"How much money are you making out of this, Flint?"

"It will put bread on the table, for sure. As lead counsel, I will be entitled to a bigger share than the others."

"Flint, how much?"

"And as a partner in the firm I also get a cut of the overall deal."

"How much?"

"And I also get a larger proportion of expenses, including accommodation and living expenses.

"How much? Flint, you can stall all you like but you know I am going to keep asking until you tell me," she said, pounding him gently on the chest.

Theo lifted her head up and whispered the amount in her ear.

"Wow!"

"Free of UK tax as we will be living abroad for three years."

"Flint! That is an obscene amount of money. Most people wouldn't earn that in a lifetime, ten lifetimes!"

"Most people are not corporate lawyers with huge responsibilities and doing business in the Persian Gulf. And compared to a footballer or a racing car driver it is quite modest."

"What are you going to do with all that money, Flint? Put it into another one of your Dutch Antilles funds away from prying eyes?"

"I am not going to buy myself a Ferrari or a Lamborghini."

"Of course not. Not *my* husband. Too modest for something as showy as that, hey Flint?" she giggled.

"Or anything stupid like a yacht."

"No, would only make you seasick, right?" she said, kissing him.

"And it would be prudent to put some of it away for a rainy day, would it not Kiffy?"

"Yes, Flint, for a rainy day, in case all the other millions you have tucked away acquire legs and leave you. So, after you've saved for a rainy day, what will you do with the rest? School fund?"

"Already taken care of," he said, kissing her along her neck. "Actually, I was thinking of maybe buying a holiday home for us to retreat to, for instance outside school term."

"Somewhere to spend the summer with the kids?"

"I'll ignore the 's' added on to 'kid' for the time being, but that is the general idea, yes."

"Where did you have in mind?"

"Somewhere warm. I was thinking of somewhere on the Mediterranean."

"Cote D'Azure?"

"Definitely not!"

"Why not?" she said, pulling his shirt.

"Too many French. Not sure I can cope with more than one French person at a time, Kiffy," he laughed. "My child, note singular, could be traumatised seeing all these spoilt, pouty French women, skinny as hell, smoking like chimneys, dragging along their fancily-coiffured poodles. We do not want our daughter to look at them as role models, do we?"

"Hey! You can't just insult my fellow countrymen like that, Englishman! And what about me, I am skinny!"

"And pouty!"

"I'm not!"

"And spoilt!"

"Spoilt? Me? Never! Flint, you can say whatever you like about me but I have never been spoilt and you know that."

"I spoil you, don't I?"

Adrienne giggled and kissed him. "We could have a philosophical discussion about whether what you have done for me can be classed as spoiling me or ensuring happiness in your life."

"Yes, that must be it, ensuring my happiness. Could not have put it better myself," he said, laughing.

"Flint, one last thing. Next year you were supposed to be taking over from your father as the new head of Josiah Hall. How will you do that if you are in Abu Dhabi?"

"I have asked my father if he is willing to act on my behalf whilst I am away and he has agreed."

"And Bertie? Didn't you tell me he was agitating to take over from you? If we are thousands of miles away in Abu Dhabi, won't that give him an extra incentive to do just that?"

"No. I have given him an incentive not to do that."

"Oh? What's that?"

"All the income, every single penny that I am entitled to from the proceeds of Josiah Hall, will go to him whilst I am away. I drew up a document to that effect and got him to sign it. For commercial sensitivity reasons, I could not tell you earlier as you were not yet my wife."

"Thought of everything, haven't you?"

"I try to, Kiffy, even if I do not always succeed. As a lawyer I have to deal in certainty not ambiguity. To do that, one has to first try and identify all the unknowns and then get a measure of them, decide how to deal with them and finally nail them down. That is what makes for a good outcome."

"Have you nailed me down then?" Theo smiled.

"Only when you let me!"

"When have I ever denied you?" she said and started to undo his shirt before sliding it off his shoulders and then lifting off her own t-shirt and pressing herself against him, hugging him tight, loving the feel of his warm skin on hers.

"I love you, hubby," she said.

"Hey, Kiffy, don't go all soft on me, please call me, Flint. It reminds me very much of how we met and it tickles me when I think about it."

"You were such a cold, horrible, stuck up Englishman!" she giggled.

"And now?"

"Still the same, except you are not horrible."

"And not all parts of me are cold, Kiffy."

"True. Not what's in my hand, that's for sure, Flint," she said, as she started to stroke him.

"Kiffy, that reminds me. Did you not say, as you get bigger, doing it face to face becomes, how shall I put it, more challenging, n'est pas?"

"From behind, we can do it from behind. Doggy-style. You like that, Flint, don't you?"

"Yes, I do, I was thinking, perhaps we should get some practice in, just in case I have forgotten how. In a few weeks, at the rate the bump is growing, that is going to be the only option for us."

"Yes, good idea. Let's do that. Practice makes perfect, isn't that what you English say?" said Adrienne and kneeled up on the sofa, her hands resting over the arm.

One of Theo's concerns had been the effect of sex on the unborn child. Although he had read making love did not have any adverse effect on the growing baby, he was unconvinced and he entered her very gently and gingerly.

"Flint, what are you doing?" said Adrienne, trying to push back on him but being prevented by his hands holding her hips.

"Just want to be careful, that's all," he explained.

"I want it now, Flint," said Adrienne, impatiently but he persisted in controlling her thrusts against him so that they were very slow and not at all as deep as she would have liked.

"Flint!"

"Just being careful," he explained.

Adrienne pulled away from him and kneeled up. "I have a better idea, you sit on the sofa and I'll sit on you."

"Won't your bump be in the way?"

"Its fine," she said, pushing Theo onto the sofa and then sitting astride him. "Mmm, that feels great, Flint."

As she rode him, Adrienne leaned forward so that her breasts, which were even more sensitive than usual, brushed up against his mouth sending tingles that transmitted right through her body. It was whilst she had Theo pressed against her breasts that she noticed someone was watching them through the glass doors leading into the room and that someone was Anca. She was holding a glass of water and staring. Adrienne looked straight at Anca and smiled. It was returned in kind. Theo was unaware, wrapped up in his own sensual world, caressing Adrienne's enlarged breasts, feeling her silky wetness on him as she lifted herself up and down. The gentle movement was more to his liking and he put it down to her getting tired from the extra weight of the baby. Little did he know that Adrienne was putting on a show for Anca, finding it thrilling in knowing that another woman was watching her making love.

Abruptly, Adrienne pressed her hands down on his thighs and pushed herself up and off Theo, turning around to whisper in his ear what she wanted, before lying back on the sofa with her legs up and spread wide.

"Shameless," thought Theo but it did not stop him from kneeling in front of her and start to caress her inner thighs, unbeknown to him that Anca was looking on, her eyes flitting between Adrienne and him. She tiptoed a few steps sideways so as to get a better view which elicited a nod of approval from Adrienne. Having Anca share the eroticism of the moment heightened the pleasure she was getting. The exhibitionist in her enjoyed the thrill, the kinkiness of having another woman watch her. It was exquisite and decadent and she loved every minute of it. She did not hold back, this was the main act, caressing her own breasts, looking at Anca, willing her to do the same. Anca remained immovable for what seemed like ages, the alabaster skin tone of her shapely curves making her look like a latter-day statue. Then it started to happen, an almost imperceptible movement of the hand, disappearing under the long t-shirt she was wearing. Adrienne couldn't see exactly what she was doing, as the window frame was partially obscuring her view, but what she couldn't see her imagination filled in and it was enough to send her over the edge, involuntarily clamping her legs, holding Theo's head as she reached her peak, crying out aloud, as much for Anca's ears as for her own sexual relief.

When Adrienne relaxed her legs, Theo sat back on his haunches and smiled. It was the smile of someone who has enjoyed giving pleasure to a loved one.

"Wow! That was a loud one," he commented.

"It's your silky tongue, Flint. Never fails to please," she said, giggling. "I wonder how much practice it has had to be that good."

"I have not had any complaints, so far," he replied. "But my nose feels a bit sore after that. It feels chafed from the bristles. You need to shave down there again, Kiffy."

"I can't do it myself, Flint. You'll have to do it for me."

"Me? No Way! I can just about manage my own chin, let alone attempting to do it down there, a very sensitive area and risk cutting you. I won't even do my own down there which is growing back and very itchy."

Adrienne giggled. "Well, I shall have to ask Anca to do me," she suggested.

"That's fine by me," he shrugged. "Safer than getting me to do it and she will probably do a better job of it."

“You know what happened last time she shaved me,” she said tantalisingly, as she gestured for Theo to stand up in front of her.

“Yes, you told me. If Anca does not mind and you are not putting her under any pressure, then you will get a shave and a sweet release too. Kill two birds with one stone as it were,” he joked and sucked in his breath as she started to stroke him.

“She could shave you clean too, Flint.”

“I would be too embarrassed to ask her do that. Besides, I would prefer to let it grow back, if you don’t mind.”

“Flint, I could ask her for you. I prefer you to be *sans* hair. Better experience for you and most definitely better experience for me,” she said and then proceeded to use her mouth on him, looking across to see whether Anca was still there or had left.

She was still there, observing every movement, totally focused as Adrienne put on a big show of pleasuring her husband, exaggerating her every action for effect.

‘Enjoy Anca: you get to see your own sex show without having to go to some seedy Amsterdam theatre,’ she said for her own ears only.

“Flint, do you remember the pretend Anca doing this for you?” she said.

“Yes, I do. How can I forget?” he said quietly.

“Wouldn’t it be nice if the real Anca did this for you?”

Theo made no comment. He was sure that she was testing him once again. “Wouldn’t you like that?”

Inasmuch as he had fantasised about it, especially in Amsterdam where they were role playing, he was still inclined to not admit as such for fear of engendering some acerbic reaction from Adrienne and he refused to be drawn on it.

“You’re not saying anything because you’re afraid of what I might think. But to put your mind at ease, I don’t mind, Flint. Really, I don’t mind. As long as you remember only these legs ever get to wrap around you, I don’t mind if occasionally you feel like fooling around.”

“What has brought this on all of a sudden?” he said, pulling back.

“I find the idea of it very erotic. Just imagining another woman, doing what I am doing for you now, for instance.” she said provocatively. “I like the idea that you tell me afterwards what you did.”

"You are very kinky, aren't you Kiffy?"

"If having a healthy attitude towards sex is kinky, then yes, I am. I'm not some stuck-up English girl who has been repressed or pretends she doesn't like sex. Sex is to be enjoyed, Flint. And if it gives you pleasure to fool around, then I am saying you can use some of that ninety seconds of thinking about sex to satisfy your needs when I am not around, as long as you remember that this," she said, holding his manhood, "is mine and only ever goes inside me. It is for me to enjoy in our lovemaking and only for me."

"This is weird, Kiffy."

"I want you not to feel so restricted," she said, taking him in hand again, stroking him gently. It was showy and meant for an audience the other side of the glass door and when she could feel him tensing and near the point of no return, she quickened her action until he was about to erupt, at which point she directed him upwards, watching and being watched as her husband's essence pulsed out of him.

There was a smile coming from the other side of the glass and she smiled back. "That was great, Kiffy," said Theo. "You let me come on your…'

"Face."

"Yes. I was surprised — you are normally averse to my doing that. What has changed your mind?"

"I know you like it, Flint, so I let it happen. It was the moment and I was lost in the eroticism of it. Pregnancy does that to a woman," she explained.

"Maybe scientists should find out what causes that eroticism and bottle it. Would make an absolute fortune for the pharmaceutical company that marketed it. Even better than Viagra did for men."

"Flint, you are funny. But don't get used to the idea that I will do it for you all the time. This was a spur of the moment, thing," she warned.

"I am normally averse to spur of the moments as they are unpredictable and unreliable but this one is the exception!" he chuckled.

The following day when Anca came back from one of her clients, Theo raised the prospect of moving to the Persian Gulf for three years. Her face turned to one of concern until Theo assured her that she was in their plans. It made her smile with relief. He waited until that had settled and then added that if she was interested, he would like to help set her up in business, running her own fitness and Pilates studio. She was so delighted with his generosity that she burst into tears of joy and leapt up out of her seat and jumped on Theo, hugging and kissing him.

"Thank you, thank you, Theo. It would be a dream come true for me. I never imagined I would ever be able to do that. You are so kind to me," she said and kissed him again. Only this time it was not on the cheek and it lingered. It may only have been a second or two longer than a peck but it was sensual and left Theo feeling embarrassed, knowing that Adrienne would not have missed that. He gently lifted her off him and left the room to take a phone call from the office and missed out on seeing Anca also thank Adrienne, with an even longer, lingering kiss.

"Thank you," she said.

"For the studio? That was Theo's idea, I can't claim any credit for that. For the show yesterday, that was definitely me!" she giggled.

Anca laughed. "For both. You are very erotic, Adrienne."

"You want me to stop?"

"No, you must do whatever you feel like doing," she replied.

"You're not offended then, Anca?"

"Of course, not. Why should I be? You are only doing what is natural between human beings. Only narrow-minded people would be offended. The only thing is, watching you it was making me feel…" she hesitated and blushed.

"Horny?"

"Yes, you could say that," Anca replied, being circumspect. She could never reveal to Adrienne that what she really meant was that in looking at her with Theo, she was wondering what it would have been like if she had been there instead of her.

After several days of consultations going back and forth between Theo, Gareth and Nicola and Abla in Abu Dhabi, they managed to put together a three-day visit in which to view suitable office and living accommodation, for rent or buy, that would be suitable for a three-year stay. The office booked them flights and hotels for three nights, paid for out of the initial payment from Rashid's department.

Theo was concerned to leave Adrienne alone and his sister Suzy was happy to move in with her temporarily. "If only to sample some of that fine cuisine of yours my brother talks about," she quipped.

On the flight over, Theo was pleased to see that Nicola and Anca were talking and from where he was sitting, it looked warm and friendly and he could shut his eyes on the long flight and rest easy. The dream was another step closer to becoming a reality.

When they landed, Theo phoned Abla to say that they would meet her at the offices of the real estate agents who were handling their accommodation requirements after they had settled in. Theo had rented an apartment for the three day stay with three bedrooms, one each for Nicola and Anca and the main bedroom for himself. Gareth had brought along his wife and they decided to stay in a downtown hotel.

Having worked with them in the past, Abla knew Gareth and Nicola but had not met Bethan, his wife, nor Anca before. When they met up in the overseas offices of a well-known, British, real estate agent they decided to split into two groups, Gareth and his wife wanted to start the search for a suitable house to rent, based on those they had pencilled in from the brochures. They went off in a car with one of the agents, whilst Theo, Anca and Nicola were driven off by Abla to a number of properties on their short-lists.

With each viewing, they showed Adrienne through WhatsApp video and by the end of the day, they had narrowed the search down to just two properties from the ones they had seen. Nicola decided that she wanted to rent near where Theo had his house and it was agreed that a search for her accommodation would be left until afterwards.

When they re-grouped in the early evening, in the lobby of Gareth's hotel, they were all quite weary, the intense heat having taken its toll. Despite the tiredness, Theo was pleased to see that everyone was still chirpy about the experience. Bethan was particularly animated about the house they had earmarked which had its own swimming pool and a landscaped garden and also because the highly respected international school for their children was just a short ten-minute drive away and waterparks and other leisure activities would be enough to keep their interest.

"Day two of the plan then is for Bethan and Gareth to re-visit the property they might want to rent, do some more research on the other items on each of our checklists. I have an appointment for one last property before going back to the first two that we quite liked the look of. We want to make that decision by early afternoon and all being well, proceed with an offer on one of those places. We will then find a place for Nicola, hopefully nearby. On day three, we will home in on a couple of offices that Abla has already looked into for us, that look very promising. We do not need to go mob-handed, so you can have the day off to go down to the beach or just relax."

Back in the apartment, having washed and eaten, Theo had his laptop open at the table and was looking over the contract details of one of the offices that Abla had found for them as being the most promising. Nicola was researching possible apartments to rent which were close by to the properties that Adrienne and Anca had short-listed.

Theo stretched out and then stood up, moving away from the table, going to the far end of the room and then opening the balcony door to sit outside. He had taken the phone with him and rang Adrienne.

"You know that is the first time ever that you've rang me from out there, Flint. Oh my God, what is the world coming to!" she teased.

"Hmm, someone is feeling in a good mood," he said.

"Of course, Suzy and I are doing great. We have a couple of young men here entertaining us, what more could we want?"

He heard his sister shout out, "Hello Brother."

"How's Anca? Is she okay?"

"Yes, she's fine, reading through the property details the two of you liked."

"She's in your room?"

"Yes."

"Alone with you?"

"No, Kiffy, one of my colleagues is also here. We are carrying on with our research. We still need to find a suitable studio for Anca which might take a bit longer."

"Hey Flint, did I tell you that I miss you already?"

"You did in a roundabout sort of way," he joked.

"I wanted to come but was afraid for our baby. It's weird but even though she is not yet borne but I feel quite close to her. I've even given her a name. Three names in fact."

"You have? Do I get say in what they are?"

"No! I get to choose her names!" He thought he heard a giggle.

"Kiffy, my daughter has to have at least one English name and no stupid, made up names, okay. I won't hear it if you want to give her some name of a plant or a bridge or something that's abstract."

"Flint, I have chosen very nice names for her. Do you want to hear them now or wait until you get home?"

"I would prefer to wait until I get back, just in case I am not enamoured with any of them and it makes me cross."

"My sweet husband, so trusting of his wife. Flint, go to sleep and you have nothing to worry about."

"I trust you, Kiffy, at least until I get home," he quipped. "Anyway, bye for now, I've still got a lot of research to do before I hit the sack as they say. And Kiffy, before you tell me off for not saying so, I do miss you!"

When he put the phone down, Theo stretched his arms out and twisted them around to form circles as Anca had taught him when his shoulders were feeling tight, then opened his left arm out and stretched his neck to face to his right before reversing it and repeating it several times.

"I wonder why they call this exercise dumb waiters," he muttered, as he went through the exercises one by one.

Returning to the table, Nicola prompted him to sit next to her as she wanted his opinion on an apartment that she liked the look of.

"Theo, what did you say my budget was for accommodation? I might be able to afford this one which is really cool," she said, showing him a picture of a penthouse apartment with a plunge pool on the balcony.

"Maximum of six thousand a month and three thousand a month to live on. Anything above that comes out of your salary," he said.

"In that case, unless the Pound suddenly takes a dive against the Dirham, I can definitely afford it. Wow! How will I ever want to go back after living in this luxury for three years? And all thanks to you. Really, I am very grateful to you for giving me this great opportunity, Theo. Rest assured I won't let you down."

"Nicola, as I have told you before on many occasions, I am not doing you any favours. You deserve to be here. You have earned that right through your skill and hard work. And if you want to spend three years in a luxury apartment then I am very happy for you."

Nicola leaned over and kissed him on the cheek and whispered, "I'd give you a proper kiss but Anca is only in the kitchen making tea for us, so can't risk it."

"Yes, best not," he said, looking in the direction of the kitchen where he could hear the clatter of cups.

"And how is this?" she said, putting her hand under the table and on to his lap.

"Nicola, stop it. I am a married man now!"

"So? Isn't it supposed to be more fun now that you're married?" she said, starting to run her fingers up and down him until she could feel a response under his shorts. "Hmm something is stirring in there!"

"Nicola, please you must stop doing that. It would be embarrassing if we got caught to say the least," he pleaded but made no attempt to put a stop to her lascivious touching. Adrienne's words were coming back to him, the license to fool around and what Nicola's fingers were doing fell within that boundary. Fortunately for him, he was not fully tested as to how far he was prepared to let Nicola go with her unsolicited caressing as the door opened and Anca walked in with a tray of teas and Nicola removed her hand just in time.

The second day had gone even better than the first and Gareth was sufficiently confident to sign a three-year rental agreement on a fully furnished house, impressed with the minimum of autocracy it had taken, with no references required, just a deposit which he paid for on his credit card. Theo too had found a property, going back to the very first house that Adrienne and Anca had picked out. It had appealed to them on many levels including its privacy, the lush, green, gardens with mature palms, a swimming pool and full air conditioning for the hot summers which could reach over 45C. It was set in a crescent-shaped road, laid out with lawns and lined with trees in a largely European community of expatriates, which made Adrienne feel that she would not be totally isolated culturally. Being an enclosed road, it also made it feel safer, not least because the security was very good with manned gates at the entrance twenty-four hours a day and CCTV cameras around the grounds.

Adrienne gave the house the thumbs up, made even more happy that it was unfurnished so that she could put her own stamp on it. She would be mistress of the house and one she actually owned!

Theo signed over a small deposit to secure the six-bedroomed house. They also visited the apartment that Nicola had her eye on which was conveniently close by, less than a ten-minute walk, although no one envisaged having to walk in the blistering heat of the day, or at night even if the Emirates was one of the safest places for expatriates to live in. Nicola was very enthusiastic about taking it and badgered Theo into putting down a deposit on it to secure the property, hugging and kissing him. She was over the moon when they received confirmation that it had been accepted.

There was even time to join Abla for a tour of the offices that she thought would be the best fit for their requirements and he accepted her recommendation, although he did not sign a short lease for it, despite her pressing him. Theo wanted to wait and return in the morning for a second look in the light of day before agreeing to proceed. He explained to Nicola, who queried the hesitation, that he wanted to see what the morning traffic and noise was like. The offices were in a busy financial district with great views over the Persian Gulf but it was also very close to an arterial road and that would concern him if it was gridlocked with traffic.

In the evening they all went out for a meal, with Abla joining them at a restaurant of her choice, Meylas, one of her favourites with an authentic Emirati taste. She held court, telling everyone amusing stories of past experiences including those in her early life when she had worked together with Theo, occasionally casting a warm smile in his direction. As the conversation flowed to and fro, and the food kept coming, Theo felt a sense of peace and happiness. It was happening. They would be moving out here and his dream was being realised.

Back at the rented apartment when the others had gone to bed, he rang Adrienne, surprised to find that Suzy had answered the phone instead. She told him that Adrienne had worn herself out researching furniture for the house in Abu Dhabi. She had gone to bed tired but contented that she had decided on how she wanted the house to look. "And Monty, I can tell you now, it has none of the traditional look you are so fond of."

Theo chuckled, because he actually agreed with her. Having seen so many houses over-ornately decorated, he had long concluded that a simple, modern, minimalist style was just what was needed.

He had just gone back to his bedroom and jumped into bed when there was a quiet knock on the door and he jumped up, naked.

"What took her so long," he said, expecting Nicola to be at the door. He had been half hoping that Nicola would not have been put off by his protestations and he tiptoed to the door with a grin on his face.

"Anca, it is you," he said in surprise. "Is something wrong?"

"I've come to shave you," she said directly, as she walked inside.

"What? Now?"

"Yes, I could not come earlier as Nicola was still awake," she explained.

"Adrienne asked me to shave you so here I am."

"Erm, okay but if it is something you would rather not do, then please say so. I do not want you to feel obliged or under any pressure, Anca." he said.

"Its fine, Theo. I don't mind at all. I'd like to do it. I shaved Adrienne too before I left. She said to do you too as you complained of a sore nose," she giggled.

"Yes, well it was a bit bristly," he said, sheepishly.

"Not any more, Theo. She is super smooth and your nose is safe," she chuckled.

"Thank God, for small mercies," he joked.

"So now it is your turn. Where shall we do it, here or in your bathroom?"

"Mm, there's nowhere for me to sit in the bathroom, unless I just stand up and you er…" he said, hesitating.

"No, I am not kneeling down, Theo. It is the wrong angle and I might cut you. On the bed it is better. I will fetch a towel from the bathroom and put it on top of your bedsheet so it does not get wet."

Theo did not know what to do with himself as he found the whole thing embarrassing. It was not that Anca was seeing him naked, that happened whenever he had a massage from her, it was the knowledge that in a minute or so she would be working closely around his nether regions, recalling that the one and only time he had been shaved there, in

Amsterdam, he had been unable to maintain a sense of calm and decorum, if that was even possible in such a situation.

"Lie down on the bed, Theo," said Anca, after she laid a towel down for him.

Theo lay on the bed as Anca soaped up her hands and then pushed his legs apart, tensing in expectation of what was about to happen.

"This was not my idea you know," he said.

"Shaving your pubic hair off?"

"Yes."

"I like it shaved. It looks nice and clean and of course from a woman's point of view, it is also better for her when giving her man oral sex. And as a man giving a woman oral sex, you appreciate it too, don't you?"

"Yes, when you put it that way, it seems eminently sensible," he said, trying to keep a normal voice as he felt her fingers working the lather into his skin.

"I shave mine off too," she revealed.

"You do? Ah well, you have the advantage of youth, more flexible. And as a Pilates instructor, you probably have an exercise that shaving ones pubes makes it easier," he joked.

"Theo, you are funny. There is no Pilates exercise for holding a razor and shaving yourself there. You either go to a beautician or get someone to do it for you."

"What did you do, if it is not impolite to ask?"

"I got someone to do it for me. You know I said I shaved Adrienne? Well, she shaved me in return," she said.

Theo winced slightly as he felt the razor glide over his skin.

"Don't worry Theo, I am not about to cut you. Adrienne would never forgive me," she giggled.

"Neither would I. Comes in handy you know," he joked.

Anca then took him in her hand so that she could shave around him and he was pleased with himself for not reacting to her touch.

"She is very good," she said quietly. "Adrienne is very good, very careful. Her fingers are magic."

"Are they?"

Anca nodded. "Made me tingle," she said shyly.

"Fun was it?"

"It's fun when Adrienne and I get together, she is so chatty and open."

"Unlike me," he said.

"That's not what I meant, Theo. It's just two women enjoying each other's company. She makes me smile and I make her smile. She tells me almost everything and anything, you don't have that many secrets from me, I'm afraid, Theo."

"Such as?"

"Maybe I shouldn't say but we talked about the time a few days ago when I watched you making love in the conservatory."

"You did? Really? I was not aware of your presence at all. Adrienne did not let on that you were there," he said.

"Don't move, Theo, we don't want an accident, do we?" she said, feeling him squirm under her hand. "Yes, I watched it all. I didn't mean to, just came down to make some tea and ask you if you wanted any. I was about to come in and stopped. I would have walked away but Adrienne was mouthing for me to stay and watch, so I did."

"I should apologise, we should have been more discrete."

"Nothing to be sorry about, Theo," she assured him. "You weren't harming anyone, just doing what comes naturally. And I can't say that I hated it! I enjoyed watching, if I am honest."

"Your very own sex show, Anca. Did you see it all, right to the end?"

"Yes, sorry I couldn't turn away. It was like you had me in a spell. And, in any case, Adrienne was encouraging me to stay."

"She was doing that, was she? And, for the avoidance of doubt, which was the best part of the show we put on for you?"

"All of it. I loved seeing the look on Adrienne's face and watching you on your knees worshipping Adrienne. And her being shaved down there was better for you, not so? She was so enjoying what you were doing with your mouth, Theo," she said. "And I could see that you were really trying to please her, enjoying what you were doing, too. Not just doing it because she wanted you to do it, as some men seem to do."

"Tried my best," said Theo proudly.

"Adrienne said she gave you nine out of ten," she giggled.

"That high?"

"From where I was standing it looked good, Theo. Shouldn't say that as it will make you more arrogant, but it is true," said Anca, naturally. She could feel him start to harden between her fingers and as much as she wanted to, she resisted doing anything about it. "And it was also exciting hearing Adrienne being loud and totally liberated, looking like she was having so much pleasure. It was thrilling and exciting to watch as it was all genuine."

"Glad, you enjoyed the performance! It was genuine all right, no scripted show. Just two people going at it, at least one of them completely oblivious to an audience, otherwise I think the show might have ended abruptly with my embarrassment!"

"Why? You weren't doing anything that nature did not mean for you to do."

"I was naked."

"So? How many times have I seen you naked when I massage you? And now, are you not naked? Your penis is even getting hard under my hand and I am okay with that, Theo."

"Ah yes, sorry about that. Can't help it."

"Nothing to feel sorry about, Theo. Natural reaction to a woman's touch," she said and then added alluringly, "Do you want me to do what Adrienne was doing when I was watching you. It was just as exciting watching her pleasure you too, Theo."

"Really? You would do that for me?"

"If you want me to. Do you?"

He nodded.

"I will but would I be asking too much if you could do what you did for Adrienne for me?"

"Of course, my pleasure," he said, kindly.

"My pleasure, I hope, Theo!" said, Anca giggling as she stood up.

Theo stood up, facing her and took off his t-shirt and watched as Anca did the same, brazenly staring at her rounded breasts, reminding himself of when he last saw them in the secret garden away from prying eyes.

Anca waited for him to make the next move and she did not have to wait long as he reduced the distance between them until she was pressed up against him, feeling her firm breasts on his chest, her nipples already stiff in expectation of what was to come.

Theo kissed her tenderly and then moved her gently until she was on the bed and then lifted her legs up so he could pull her panties off.

'I suppose I'd better get to work and prove my nine out of ten,' he said to himself. 'Wonder what it would take to get all ten. Have to think about that.'

Being on the receiving end of his caresses was thrilling to Anca; beyond what she could tell him. Up until that point, when she felt him caress her with his mouth, it had been no more than a fantasy, the intimacy that she craved unfulfilled, only able to watch, never the one to receive. Now she was no longer that bystander but the woman who was sharing the most intimate of moments with the one man she most desired to be with. And if it wasn't out of loyalty to her friend, she would not hold back, she would have him completely, in her arms and cradled in her loins. But she loved Adrienne too much to do that to her, playing was all she could do and she was enjoying every moment of it as Theo's tongue was as good as she imagined it to be, in its electrifying effect on her heightened sensitivities. As much as she tried to hold back and prolong the delicious assail of her body, she could not. Barely a minute or two later, she found herself building up to a giant, shuddering, orgasmic spasm. Every muscle and sinew in her body seemed to be at one, like a drug administered to every part of her body from head to toe, lost in a state of shear bliss for those few precious seconds.

Theo continued to kiss her gently there, caressing her inner thighs. Even in the dim light of the side lamp he could see the look of contentment on her face, her hair sticking to her cheeks from the sweat of someone who has just had a pleasurable experience. He rose up from the bed and headed back to the bathroom for his second wash of the night.

When he returned, Anca was turned on her side, facing him with her eyes closed. He smiled as he gently pulled back Anca's hair that had fallen over her face. "One satisfied customer. Never did get to hear my marks out of ten," he said, almost silently and only for his ears, before sliding into bed next to her and reaching out to switch the bedside lamp off. In a few minutes, Anca in her sleep, had unconsciously repositioned herself so that she was tucked up close to Theo, her head next to his, sharing his pillow and her arm resting across his chest.

By the end of the third and last day, after two further visits to the proposed offices, Theo had been sufficiently convinced by Abla's urging and Nicola's checks against their requirements, to sign a three-year lease with an initial deposit. Together with Anca and with Nicola in tow, they also found a disused store house that was of a size that could make it suitable for conversion into a fitness studio. It was also in a prime location close to a cluster of up-market European homes, the sort that have ladies that are full of energy and nothing to expend it on, according to Anca. After making enquiries, they discovered that it had been on the market for over two years with no takers as potential developers had been put off by the stipulation that it could only be used for a business function not for residential purposes. It was, therefore, straightforward to persuade the landlord to take just a minimum deposit and allow them three months to decide if they wanted it or not.

When Anca asked why he would take so little, Theo replied, "Did you see the look of hunger in his eyes? Some money is better than no money. It puts food on the table and keeps his own creditors at bay. It suits us Anca as there is no way we can commit to it until we've done more research, background checks and the like. I would be very happy if you take the lead on that and use Abla to help you with potential builders and how to navigate Emirati laws, to ensure that what we are proposing to do does not infringe any state or local laws."

Despite overtures from Anca, Theo intimated that he was tired and just wanted to relax before their early morning flight back to England. Instead, he accepted a massage from her. Having established a level of intimacy the previous evening, Anca was not at all self-conscious about removing her clothes before she began to knead Theo's aching limbs. Nor was she shy in sitting astride him and leaning down, her breasts touching his back, as she massaged his shoulders. Theo was unfazed by the brazenness of it, just enjoying the soothing touch, lulling him into a warm and comfortable snooze. He was fast asleep and dead to the world, well before Anca cuddled up next to him in bed.

When the plane touched down in Heathrow, Nicola and Anca exited together, satisfied with the progress towards making living in the Persian Gulf a reality. For Nicola, the huge financial rewards were not lost on her parents who managed a friendly smile towards Theo instead of wearing their usual scowl.

"Flint, I've been spending your money furnishing the house," said Adrienne when they got back home. "If I'm going to be marooned thousands of miles away from my home then I can at least decorate it how I like."

"And how is that, Kiffy?"

"Very modern, very Parisian chic. You will love it, Flint."

"Oh dear. Will there be at least one chair or sofa that is remotely comfortable for me to use? French modern furniture seems to be all spindly and angular, all melamine and chrome and sofas without a back for you to rest your head on."

"Hmm, what about your Chesterfield, can hardly rest your head against that, can you? But you still love it!"

Theo leant forward and whispered in her ear, "Yes, but it's good for hanky-panky. You can slide around it. And the height of the cushions is just right."

Adrienne giggled, "You are naughty! Missed me, did you?" Theo nodded.

"Later," she said and kissed him lightly.

Suzy decided not to stay the night. "I'm done with babysitting," she said, teasing Adrienne. "Besides, if I have one more gourmet meal cooked by this lovely wife of yours, Theo, I won't be able to get through my front door! I think I've put on a kilo in the three days you've been gone."

That night in bed, Theo sat up against the headboard watching as Adrienne undressed, noting how her abdomen was looking much larger, even in the short time he had been away. He had thought that he would find it repulsive but in a strange way, he actually found the new curves that Adrienne had acquired much to his liking: sensuous and inviting.

"Flint, you are staring at me," said Adrienne, as she sat at her dressing table applying creams.

Theo could not contain himself any longer and got out of bed and walked around until he was standing next to her. "Let me," he said as he bent down and taking some of the body lotion, started to rub it into her shoulders, gently kneading them.

"That's good, Flint. Keep going, I'm liking this," she said quietly.

Theo moved his hands along her neck and back to her shoulders and with each movement, working lower and lower across her chest, marvelling how in the space of a few weeks, nature had plumped up what otherwise could only have been achieved with silicone implants.

With a squirt of the lotion, he ran his hands around her breasts as he leant down, cupping and gently fondling them. Adrienne closed her eyes as she enjoyed the sensuous touch. He watched the reaction on her face, seeing her furrow her eyebrows and bite her bottom lip when she felt his fingers tease her nipples with the ball of his thumbs, feeling them stiffen to his touch. Slowly, slowly, one hand worked its way downwards. There was no rush in his movement, just inching lower and lower, nearer and nearer. Adrienne willingly opened her legs to make the path his fingers were tracing easier, letting out a barely audible whimper of joy when they brushed over her sensitive spot.

"Let's see if I can improve on that nine out of ten," he whispered and turned her chair around.

"No, Flint, don't. Just your hand, my darling," she said, reaching up and kissing him passionately and hungrily, her moans suppressed as he started to fulfil her wishes.

It did not take long before she was close to her peak, holding his hand as she writhed against it. He marvelled at the beauty and naturalness of the woman who he was being intimate with, who was bearing his child within her body and it gave him nearly as much pleasure in giving her pleasure. She did not hold back, did not try to suppress how she was feeling at that moment, not depriving herself of that exquisite moment in a way that previous lovers had.

Adrienne said, "Mmm, that was a nice end to the day, Flint."

Theo put her hand on him but it remained limp. "Later Flint, I'm tired. You wore me out."

'I seem to satisfy women who cannot stay the distance,' he smiled to himself. 'I think on my epitaph it will say 'later'.'

Stabbing Pains

Adrienne was reading through the manual on all the different warning lights on the Jaguar, pages and pages describing what each one meant, the circumstances when each would be alerted and the action to be taken in the event that it was triggered. As someone who was just an occasional driver, Theo did not have the patience to go through it and between them, Anca and Adrienne had undertaken to do just that and make a short summary for him of the most important ones that might flash up.

"Kiffy, in a few months we'll be gone. I don't see the value in my spending too much time in finding out every conceivable aspect of the car. We paid a king's ransom for this car so it should pretty much drive itself without us having to memorise two inches of pulp in what it does," he had protested.

"Flint, it is important for our safety. And you haven't driven it yet. What if you have to drive me to the hospital in the middle of the night?" she insisted. But it was to no avail.

"It's got a steering wheel, an accelerator and a brake hasn't it? That should be enough knowledge to get me there. What else is there I need to worry about in such a situation? Besides, I'm too old to remember so much information," he said, jokingly.

"Hm, a man who can read a one-thousand-page document, tells me that he can't read a simple car manual and remember it. Okay, Flint, I get it, you are not interested. Anca and I will do it and make a summary for you," she said, blowing him a kiss.

"Right then, who is going to put that new-found knowledge about the car to good use and give me a lift to the station?" asked Theo.

Anca jumped up. "Let's go," she said.

Theo bent down and Adrienne took his hand in hers and kissed it. "Love you, Flint," she shouted after him, as he left with Anca.

"She is right, you know, Theo. You should at least familiarise yourself with the controls just in case I am not around and Adrienne needs you," said Anca, as they approached the station.

"Okay, when I get home today, perhaps you can take me for a spin in the Toothbrush," he said, as she glided the big car to a silent halt.

"Yes, let's do that," said Anca, smiling. "Have a nice day, Theo."

"You are a very caring person, Anca," he said, as he leant across and kissed her. It was something he always did but this time she held him just a little longer.

"It is because I care for you and Adrienne. I love you both."

"And we love you too, Anca, you know that. Now I had better be off and get to the cafe to try and squeeze in a latte before the train pulls in. See you later."

And then the car door closed and he was gone. Anca waited to see him stride up with alacrity onto the platform, listening until she heard his Oyster card click, a sign that the train was running and then started the car again. She was off, the scent of his aftershave wafting into her nostrils never failed to leave her with a warm, comforting feeling.

Adrienne was reading the car manual intently and making notes on her laptop, swearing in French in frustration when she didn't understand some badly written explanation. "Sorry baby, I didn't mean to swear, mama is just annoyed with some of these useless instructions," she said, gently stroking her abdomen. "I should really be singing to you, shouldn't I? Some French song, just to wind up your papa." She was giggling as she started humming, imagining the look of horror on Theo's face were he to see her do that.

When Anca returned, they worked together and after an hour they had read all they needed to digest, about how to drive the car and then neatly summarised it.

"Still too long, Adrienne. Theo once told me that a summary should not exceed one side of A4 paper otherwise no one will want to read it. We need to cut out even more and just put the minimum needed. Like, does he really need to know about lane departure warnings?"

"I'm fed up of this, let's take a break. I need to stretch my legs. No good for my swelling ankles if I just sit here," said Adrienne. "I think I'll go into the gym and walk on the treadmill."

"I'll come too and go on the cross-country trainer and on the weight machines. We can do some Pilates exercise afterwards, it will be good for you, Adrienne. Then I'll finish off by giving you a massage, how does that sound?"

"Brilliant. You look after me so well, Anca," she said and kissed her cheek as they walked towards the stairs. At the bottom of the stairs, they stopped and Adrienne looked up. "Why did Theo have to put the gym up so high on the third floor? So many steps to climb up."

"Good exercise for you, Adrienne. Come on let's go," she said encouragingly, putting an arm around her waist.

After forty-five minutes on the treadmill and a further hour of Pilates, stretching and twisting, exercising glutes and calf muscles, hamstrings and hip flexors, egged on by Anca all the way, Adrienne announced she had had enough and was taking a shower.

"Me too. Feel so sweaty," said Anca.

"Would you like to join me in mine?" Adrienne giggled. "It's massive, plenty of room for two. Sometimes Theo and I take one together. Saves on water. More eco-friendly!"

"Oh, that's the reason, is it?" Anca giggled. "Sure, let's be eco-friendly!"

After showering and drying off, Adrienne lay on her back ready for Anca to massage her. "How are we going to manage this, Anca? I can't lie on my front with this bump in the way?"

"As we've been doing a lot of leg-related exercises today, I was thinking of working on your calf muscles, then quads and hamstrings, and of course your swollen ankles and feet, all of which I can manage with you lying down on your side with pillows keeping you up. I can finish off by doing your shoulders and head with you sitting up."

As Anca was about to put on her t-shirt, Adrienne said, "You don't have to if you don't want to, Anca. It is warm in here and I am comfortable with you staying like that when you massage me, after all, it's not as if I haven't seen you naked."

Anca giggled. "I know, seems silly as we've just taken a shower together but I wasn't sure if you wanted me to put something on."

"No, it's fine. Clothes are not necessary, unless you prefer it that way. You have a lovely figure, Anca and if you don't mind, I love looking at you, reminds me of how I once was before this bump came along. Stops me from getting depressed about my body and how I look," she said.

Anca smiled. "Thank you. But you mustn't think like that about yourself, Adrienne. You are so beautiful, even with this big bump in the way," she said, touching her abdomen.

"Can't wait for her to show herself into this world and for my body to get back to normal," she said. "Everything seems to take me longer to do. I wear big clothes I would not wish for anyone to see me dressed in. Sleeping is not easy, such an effort to turn in bed and I wake myself up. Eating gives me indigestion. Even sex is harder to do. Not so many choices." she said, laughing. "And I can't even play with myself as easily as before. Which is really weird because I feel that I want sex even more now. Nature is weird isn't it? Why make a pregnant woman want more sex."

Anca giggled. "I'm sure Theo takes care of that for you."

"Oh yes he does, as you saw when you were watching me. But he is not always around when I want it," she said and looking straight into Anca's eyes added, "like right now, for instance."

"Need a helping hand, Adrienne?" Anca asked, grinning.

She nodded. "That would be really nice, Anca, if you don't mind."

"Okay, I'll work it into my massage routine for you," she said.

"Thank you, Anca, that would be lovely. Your fingers are wonderful, Anca and you know how to send me over the edge but ever since I woke up and started to feel erotic, I've been thinking about something softer, wondering what it would be like to feel your…" Adrienne hesitated.

"Tongue?"

"Yes."

Anca giggled. "Let me soothe these aching legs first."

"Anca. When you were shaving me in the shower, I'm not embarrassed to say that it was arousing me. Being pregnant, it makes all your hormones so sensitive, the slightest of touches and you want it. At least that's how I feel. I felt like that when I got up and, in the shower, and I have thought about nothing since we got out of the shower."

"It's not just pregnant women, Adrienne. When you were shaving me, I too was getting aroused. Your fingers brushing up against me had that effect. It's nature, I guess."

"What about when you were shaving Theo, did he not get aroused?"

"When we were in Abu Dhabi, I shaved him down there like you asked me to. Of course he got hard, it is only natural."

"Did you give him a happy ending?" Adrienne giggled.

"No but that wasn't my fault. I so wanted to experience what you did the other day when I was watching you. Theo was great but I just fell asleep when he got in the shower and then it didn't work out, the moment was gone. I think Theo was too embarrassed to straight out ask me to give him a happy ending as you put it."

"Hehe, my poor hubby not getting off. But I am glad he was a gentleman and took care of you. I am really happy for you Anca. He has a lovely tongue, doesn't he?"

Anca blushed. "Oh yes, ten out of ten! But I didn't tell him that. In fact, I didn't say anything, we didn't speak about it."

"Ooh, that's nice," said Adrienne as Anca started to plant little kisses along her inner thighs. "So nice. Makes my body shiver."

"I like to please you, Adrienne. I feel very close to you when we are being intimate," she said, as she kissed her way nearer and nearer to where Adrienne wanted her to go, her mouth just a few millimetres above and her breath feeling like the most subtle of touches.

"Anca, when Theo was working his magic on you, did you ever feel that you would have liked it to go further than just that?"

"I won't lie to you, Adrienne. I am a woman and it is a most natural thing to want. But I am also a very loyal person and I would never do that to you and I would never put that temptation in front of Theo for the same reason. You have nothing to worry about."

"Anca, I trust you completely with Theo and I trust him with you. I know you would never do anything like that behind my back," said Adrienne earnestly. "But I am not blind and I can see that you want him and in the right circumstance, I might be willing to let the two of you be together up to a point."

"What do you mean Adrienne?"

"I haven't thought it through but so you know, I have told Theo that I don't mind if he sometimes wants to fool around. But I won't allow Theo to have full sex with anyone, absolutely no one; sorry not even you, Anca. He is mine in that respect and mine only but anything else is okay. So, if you want to have sex with Theo you can but no penetration whatsoever. It is my gift to you for all the kindness and love you've shown me."

"I don't know what to say, Adrienne. Honestly, as much as I have thought about Theo like that, as I said, I couldn't do it behind your back. Before we left to go to Abu Dhabi you told me that you wanted me to experience what you did with Theo. As much as it was lovely, really nice, I felt uncomfortable as you were not there and not knowing what we were doing. And I think Theo felt the same way."

"You wanted me to be there? To be with you for us to share the moment, to share him, together? It would be the ultimate expression of our love between the three of us. I will do that for you, Anca."

"Wow! I never expected that, from you," said Anca, as she caressed where Adrienne wanted her to be.

For Adrienne it felt like an electric shock, to receive such an intimate caress. The decadent sensuality of it always excited her and this time it was no exception, causing her to gasp from the sensation of feeling another woman's tongue on her. It felt even better than the pretend Anca in Amsterdam.

"I've made love to you already once in Amsterdam," said Adrienne, almost in a whisper as Anca's oral caresses sent pulse after pulse of pleasure right through her.

Adrienne revealed how she had booked an Anca lookalike escort and the night of pleasure the three of them had enjoyed until the early hours of the morning.

"Wow, I've never done that, with two other people," said Anca, feeling herself getting wet at the thought that Theo and Adrienne were living out a fantasy that entailed her.

"A ménage à trois? It is not for everyone and only to be done on rare occasions, like in Amsterdam. Not planned and just spur of the moment type of thing."

"What did you enjoy the most Adrienne, the girl that looked like me?"

"It was very nice but what I enjoyed the most, what I found the most erotic, was watching her with Theo," said Adrienne, dropping that on her.

"Really? Why?" she asked and she could feel herself getting wetter and wetter down below, the more Adrienne revealed about her night of passion in Amsterdam.

"Because Anca, I was imagining that Theo was having sex with you and I was watching. That is what made it so erotic. I'm sorry if that seems too weird and kinky for you but I have always believed in being open and honest about sex."

"Its fine, Adrienne. Really, I am comfortable with you telling me this. And if I am being honest and open, it has made me very wet, you telling me that," she said, her face flushed and her own breathing getting as ragged as the person on the receiving end of her stimulation. Adrienne submitted to the tortuous and pleasure-filled all over body experience from her toes which were curling to her engorged breasts and her eyes, sparkling with the excitement and the joy of the attention she was getting from Anca. Hearing Adrienne's deep lustful moans and laboured breathing, Anca let herself go too, whimpering when she felt fingers finding their way down her back, between her buttocks and then between her legs.

"You are wet, very wet, Anca" said Adrienne, in barely a whisper as Anca's moaning became more intense and deeper. Every fibre in Adrienne's body seemed to come alive, made even more pleasurable seeing the effect of her touching was having on Anca. It was enough to tip her over the edge and into a thundering orgasm, feeling, thrashing her legs, holding Anca down and thrusting her hips upwards, her heels digging into the bed. It was short-lived but the high was intense, it was concentrated and the climax was like riding a superfast rocket into an orbit of sheer pleasure. And now she wanted to make Anca feel the same. And she did.

Adrienne was lying in bed relaxing, a respite from carrying her child, not in a hurry to get up, the embers of the pleasure she had felt from the earlier intimacy with Anca still making her tingle. The harsh buzz from the phone on the side table, jolting her from the reverie she was enjoying. It was a message from Theo to say he had had a big lunch with a client and did not feel hungry. It made her smile to think of him.

'My poor husband, I have been neglecting him. Tonight, Flint. I will be all yours to serve you as you please,' she said to herself as she got up and looked at herself in the mirror, touching herself intimately. She threw a robe around her and padded downstairs.

Anca was in the kitchen preparing the evening meal for just the two of them, as Theo had also sent her the same text he had sent Adrienne. As it was a warm day and Adrienne's stomach was still feeling sensitive to anything heavily cooked and rich in sauces, Anca decided that she would make something lighter. She was boiling eggs and French beans, opening up a tin of tuna and pulling out anchovies from a bottle, all to go into a salad Niçoise; something she had wanted to surprise Adrienne with. She was about to add capers and slices of pickled cucumber as her own artistic touch to this classic French dish when the doorbell rang. Looking at her door security phone app, she could see the face of a pretty young lady, with hair tied up in a bun. She was austere and stern-looking, bordering on the sombre. Anca recognised the look.

'Not Jehovah's Witness again,' she told herself, wiping her hands on her apron. She switched the hob off and went to answer the door, ready to tell them to go away. As someone with strong Christian beliefs she had no time for the Jehovah's and Mormons who seemed to plague the area.

The person who stood before her when she opened the door was not what she expected, but furrowed her eyebrows out of curiosity. 'Not them at least, maybe another neighbourhood watch chat,' she thought.

"Mrs Blenkinsop?"

"No but I can get her. What is it in regard to please?"

"I'm afraid I need to speak to Mrs Blenkinsop directly."

"I look after Mrs Blenkinsop. Wait here please," said Anca, after checking the credentials of the policewoman.

"Adrienne, there is a policewoman who wants to speak to you," she said, poking her head into the study where Adrienne was sitting, feet up on a stool, the previous Sunday Times crossword resting on her bump, eyes barely open.

"Policewoman? What does she want? Has there been another robbery?"

Anca helped her up and the two walked together to the door. When Anca opened it, the policewoman was speaking into her phone but stopped when she saw Adrienne. She had not expected to see a pregnant woman.

"Mrs Blenkinsop?"

"Yes, and you are?"

"PC Clare Davies, madam. May I come in, there is something I would like to discuss with you," she said, remaining expressionless, her face giving nothing away as to the nature of her business.

Adrienne led the way into the kitchen and they sat at the refectory table, Anca next to her and the policewoman opposite them.

"What is this about? Has there been more robberies in the area?" asked Adrienne.

"Can I just check, you are the wife of Theodore Blenkinsop?" said the policewoman, ignoring Adrienne's question.

"Yes, I am. Please can you tell me what this is about?" said Adrienne, beginning to get anxious. Anca took her hand into hers, by way of reassurance.

"It concerns your husband, Mrs Blenkinsop. There was an incident on the 1625 train that left Victoria bound for Horsham. Your husband was involved."

"What sort of incident?" said Adrienne, interrupting her.

"There appears to have been an altercation between your husband and another adult male which resulted in your husband being stabbed a number of times. Not fatally, I hasten to add."

"What!" Adrienne shouted, putting her hand on her mouth. "My husband? Are you sure? I don't believe it."

"We identified him from his credit cards and work security pass, Mrs Blenkinsop. Your husband has been admitted to Epsom General hospital and is receiving medical attention."

Adrienne was speechless. Anca put her arm around her, trying to comfort her. "Is he all right?"

"I'm afraid I have no further information on his medical condition, Miss."

"What happened?" asked Anca.

"According to witnesses, there was a violent altercation between a man and a woman on the train around the Sutton area. The man had stabbed the woman once already and was about to do it again when Mr Blenkinsop stepped in to protect her, pulling her away. Evidently, this enraged the man and he turned on Mr Blenkinsop, who managed to fight him off but not before he received several stab wounds with what we believe to be some form of kitchen knife."

"I must go to him. Anca, let's go," said Adrienne, standing up looking as white as a ghost. "Thank you for informing us PC Davies, you will excuse me, I need to go and see my husband. Please can you see yourself out?"

Anca drove them in silence, worried for Adrienne. The shock from the news had left her numb and speechless. There were no tears, she was just clasping the seat belt as if her life depended on it and looking out, staring into space. At that time of day, the commuter traffic was heading home and making progress around the one-way system in Epsom was very slow, almost no faster than a walking pace.

"Don't let him in!" said Adrienne angrily, as a van tried to cut across them, from parking to the outside of the two lanes. "This traffic is ridiculous, why don't they better plan this road? The transport department in Surrey is run by idiots!"

Anca did not react to her friend's rant. She put a sympathetic hand on hers as she let the van go in front of them. Adrienne looked across to her for an explanation.

"Adrienne, we're stuck in traffic, letting one person in will not make any difference," she explained.

The cars were crawling, inching along, bumper to bumper and it took nearly three quarters of an hour before they finally turned into the car park of Epsom General Hospital and parked. They headed for the Accident and Emergency Department, neither inclined to talking and both looking grim-faced. Inside, Adrienne was taken aback with the huge number of people waiting to be seen. Almost the entire waiting room was filled up. People with unseen ailments, people with cuts, some coughing and wheezing, all seats taken, people pressed against walls, some sitting on the floor, all of them looking as if they would rather not be there, but bearing up, resigned to having to wait their turn. Even at the Booking In and Enquiry desk there was a queue and Adrienne was getting irritated and impatient at having to wait her turn. Anca offered to find her a chair to sit down and she would then queue on their behalf. Adrienne would not have it.

"I'll only get sick if I get near these people," she said, pulling a face showing her distaste.

After what seemed an eternity, they were called into one of the cubicles by a frazzled looking junior doctor. The nurse in attendance pulled the curtain closed for privacy. As the doctor started talking, Adrienne kept looking at the curtains and back to him, concerned at the lack of privacy. They could hear everything being said in the cubicle next to theirs: the man was clearly in some distress and if they could hear him, then there was no doubt that he would be able to hear everything that might be said in their cubicle.

Adrienne gestured with her hand for the doctor to stop. "Is there somewhere more private where we can talk?" she said, interrupting him.

"No, this is it I am afraid," he said, matter of factly.

"Please, can we go somewhere else? I am finding it very difficult to cope with this and talking about my husband who has been stabbed, out in the open like this is not helping," she pleaded.

Anca waded in, pointing out to him that as a pregnant woman she was even more vulnerable and stressed and surely, he did not want to risk that. The doctor shrugged his shoulders and agreed to take them to the nurses station, which, although busy with people, at least it was just medical personnel and it was where they could have a more discrete chat about her husband's condition. Having been initially indifferent, the doctor then pulled up two chairs for them to sit down on and fetched Adrienne a cup of water to drink.

The doctor started by saying that her husband was in theatre having his wounds attended to. He had been there for approximately an hour. He was not sure how long he would be in there for but given the nature of his wounds, he estimated another hour or so, before he would then be moved to a recovery room.

"Can I see him then?"

The doctor explained that after being operated on, the standard practice was for patients to be moved to the High Dependency Unit for a duration to be determined by the surgical consultant who was currently operating on her husband.

"Operating? Why is he being operated on? So not just a few stitches then?" Adrienne interrupted.

"Mrs Blenkinsop, you do know that your husband sustained injuries as a result of being stabbed?"

"Yes, but we haven't been told how bad or where. Can someone please be open and tell me what's going on!" she said angrily.

The doctor took a deep breath and looked at Anca for guidance and the slightest of nods was the go-ahead he needed.

"Okay. I was in attendance when your husband was brought in by the ambulance. He had sustained multiple stab wounds to the chest and the abdomen and he has lost a significant amount of blood. He was rushed straight to theatre where he is currently. He is in very capable hands, Mrs Blenkinsop. The duty consultant surgeon is very experienced in dealing with knife wounds."

Adrienne bit her finger. "I can't believe it."

"How was he when he was brought to the hospital, doctor?" asked Anca.

"The paramedics had patched him up to try and staunch the blood loss and he was breathing with the aid of apparatus. His eyes were closed but he was responding with nods when asked questions. That's all I can tell you."

"How long did you say before he is out of the operating theatre?" asked Anca, as Adrienne squeezed her hand so tightly for support, her blood circulation was in danger of being cut off.

"My estimate is for another hour, maybe a little longer but it will be for the consultant to assess how bad the cuts were and the extent to which what damage, if any, was done to any organs. As I said, following theatre, your husband will be wheeled into recovery where he will spend a further thirty minutes to an hour there, before he is then moved to the HDU.

My advice would be to go home and come back in the morning. He will be unconscious for several hours, so you best get some sleep and pop in tomorrow morning, when he should be awake by then. There is nothing for you to do here."

"I want to stay and talk to the consultant when he has finished with my husband," said Adrienne in a determined tone, that told him in no uncertain terms that she was not to be dissuaded.

The doctor decided that it would be better not to add to the distress of a pregnant woman by asking them to return to the waiting room and instead said that they could wait by the nurses station to the side, out of the way of nurses coming and going. And that is where they stayed, hardly a word passed between them, sitting in silence each absorbed in their own thoughts.

Adrienne recalled what the policewoman had told them. "It appears that this is just another case of domestic violence," PC Davies had said blithely. "We get a lot of it. An ex-husband so enraged that his ex-wife was seeing another man and not willing to listen to his futile attempts at his latest attempt at reconciliation, that he was going to kill her."

"Why do people resort to such violence?" she muttered, not particularly for anyone's ears. "My poor husband is on an operating table because this man could not just simply walk away and accept that his ex-wife didn't want him. Why has it become much more common for women to get beaten up and killed nowadays? What is it that is driving men to behave like wild animals of the jungle?"

"I see it in the news every day. In the UK, domestic violence seems to be increasing, women are getting beaten up, knifed and there doesn't seem to be anything that the law can do about it," said Anca.

"I'm ashamed to say, it is not just in England, Anca. In my own country, do you know last year alone over one hundred and fifty women were killed by violent men in so-called domestic disputes? Men are brutes!"

"Not all men, Adrienne. Your man did a very brave thing and stopped another man from killing a woman."

Adrienne nodded and started to cry. "He did, he did. Oh Flint, please don't leave me alone."

"Adrienne! Stop talking like that! The doctors are fixing Theo and he will be with you, with us, soon. Before you know, it he will be back to normal and you can tease his English ways like usual. And in less than three months, he will be the proud father of your baby and this will be just a bad dream," said Anca with a half-smile, trying to sound positive.

"Until I talk to the doctor, I can't relax, Anca. I feel like I am sitting on hot charcoal."

Time seemed to stand still. They waited and waited, standing up, sitting down, pacing up and down within the small confined area of the nurses station, reading all the notices, looking at the bare walls. Finally, nearly two and a half hours later, a nurse in a bright blue uniform introduced herself as Sister Moreton and explained that she was taking them to meet the doctor. The nurse took off and bounded down what seemed like a bewildering maze of corridors, irritated at having to slow her pace and keep looking back, when she realised that they could not keep up with her. At the lift, she waited until Adrienne had caught her breath and then pressed for the second floor. It was then down yet another long corridor, even more squeaky clean and with hardly anyone to be seen before she finally pushed open a door and ushered them into a small room and told them to wait there and the doctor would be coming shortly. They sat down on the two chairs at one side of a large desk that had been put there for them. The other side held another chair and other than posters about cleanliness and a sink with hand sanitisers and a small, locked cupboard, the room was bereft of any furniture or any indication as to what its purpose was for.

The room was eerily silent and with its bright lights overhead and the faint sound of air-conditioning, it had more of a look of a police interrogation room than a place where people go and get mended.

A few minutes later they could hear the sound of muffled voices immediately outside the room, raising their expectations that they were about to be visited by the said doctor, only for the voices to die away leading to disappointment. Anca rolled her eyes and stood up. "I'll go and find out where the doctor is," she said.

Just then, the door opened and the consultant surgeon emerged to speak to them with Sister Moreton in tow. He apologised for keeping them waiting and introduced himself politely as Mr Shah, adding modestly that he was the surgeon in attendance. He seemed well-spoken and a kind-faced man and when he shook hands with Adrienne and started to speak, for the first time that evening she felt comforted and reassured that she was listening to someone in the know. She also had this inner feeling that Theo had been in capable hands and she felt as if an invisible weight had been partially lifted off her shoulders.

"Mrs Blenkinsop, I will go through your husband's medical condition. Stop me at any time to ask questions. First the good news. Mr Blenkinsop is out of theatre and in the recovery room. He is breathing on his own without any mechanical assistance, which is always good news. He is heavily sedated and will not be waking up for a few hours," said Mr Shah and paused, looking from one woman to the other, gauging their reaction before proceeding.

"In theatre, Mr Blenkinsop underwent a significant amount of surgery to patch up the wounds he sustained as a result of multiple injuries from being stabbed with a knife that had a serrated edge, like a kitchen bread knife. The knife penetrated his rib cage resulting in cardiac injuries and lesions, damage to three ribs and trauma to his spleen. The injuries caused significant bleeding and Mr Blenkinsop required quite a few units of blood to replace what he had lost."

"Wait, did you say 'spleen'? What does a spleen do, doctor?" asked Adrienne, softening her tone.

"It plays an important role in fighting off infection from bacteria."

"It was injured you said."

"Yes. It received significant trauma from the blade of the knife but I am confident that we have managed to save it. Time will tell if my prognosis is correct."

"And cardiac injuries? That means his heart, right?"

"Yes, it was pierced at the left ventricle, which is why he has lost so much blood. But he was lucky, ten millimetres to the right and..." said Mr Shah and then checked himself from saying any more. "At any rate, I have managed to close up the wound and it is no longer leaking any blood."

"Poor Flint," said Adrienne and she could not contain herself any longer and she sobbed, tears streaming down her face.

Anca took her in her arms and was doing her best to comfort her. Mr Shah, with a gesture of his head, indicated to the nurse standing alongside him to fetch some water. Between Anca and the nurse, they managed to reduce the sobs to a whimper.

"What happens next, Mr Shah?" asked Adrienne, looking up, desperately searching his eyes for some words of comfort, like someone who has fallen into the sea looking out for someone to throw a lifebelt after them.

"We expect to move your husband to the High Dependency Unit shortly, where he will be closely monitored around the clock. He will stay there for approximately forty-eight hours or until we feel he is out of immediate danger. Then, all being well, he will be moved to a regular ward, or, if you prefer, to his own room in our private medical suite."

"Yes, I would like that please," said Adrienne.

Mr Shah smiled and nodded to the nurse, who made a note of it.

"Is there anything else you would like to ask me?" he asked, unhurried and with a caring tone.

"How long before he is out of hospital?" Anca asked.

"I don't expect him to be there for more than five or six days at the most. It is better for a patient to be back in their own environment as soon as possible. Better for their recovery."

"Really? Isn't that too soon?" asked Adrienne.

Mr Shah smiled. "Mrs Blenkinsop, although your husband has a lot of injuries, we will soon be having him up and about. In fact, the day after he enters the HDU, I am sure the nurses will have him up and helping him to walk about. Walking is good for his circulation; it helps prevent thrombosis and also good for his mental wellbeing. When we move him to his room, we will spend the next few days getting him ready to leave hospital. A physiotherapist will be assigned to him to get him walking and exercising, a few steps a day, building up his fitness. By day four, we will try and get him to climb up and down stairs. When he can do that without any help, usually by day five or six, we will discharge him."

"How long before he will be back to normal?"

"When he gets home, he will need to build up his strength slowly. Within four weeks he should be able to move about comfortably. He will not be able to lift any weight for three months or longer, so he will not be able to put the kettle on and make you a cup of tea."

Adrienne smiled, trying to remember the last time when Theo had offered to make her tea.

"He doesn't do it that often anyway," said Anca, reading her mind.

"Can I just ask you when you are due to give birth, Mrs Blenkinsop?"

"In two and half months."

Mr Shah nodded, "By then he may be able to hold the baby but not lift it up. Maybe after the baby is ten to fifteen days old, by then we can probably say it will be okay for him to do that."

When Mr Shah left them, Adrienne felt a sense of relief that Theo had got over the worst and now it was a matter of supporting him in his recovery. At the same time, until she saw him and held his hand in hers, she could not relax. They sat in silence for a few minutes before Adrienne looked up to see that Anca's head was bowed down and she was staring at the floor. She stood up and trudged over to Anca and put her arm around her.

"He will be back to us soon," said Adrienne, squeezing her friend.

"I miss him," said Anca, tears silently rolling down her face.

"Come on, let's go home, Anca. There's nothing we can do here tonight. We'll be back in the morning," she said and hugged Anca as she stood up. "Sleep in my room tonight, it's not good for either of us to be alone."

"Thank you," uttered Anca, choking with emotion.

Healing

Finding the High Dependency Unit was straightforward as it was on the same floor as the operating theatre. It was also one of the smallest wards and when they peered into it from the window in the door, they could make out only four curtained-off beds. From the outside looking in, it seemed no different to any other ward, calm and peaceful. There was no discernible movement of people except for nurses passing to and fro, silently gliding from one bed to another, disappearing behind curtains, emerging with their computer tablets updated with the patients' vital readings.

"How is he doing?" Adrienne asked one of the nurses.

"Fine. Obviously, he is in a lot of discomfort and we have him on medication for pain relief and liquids to keep him hydrated but otherwise he is doing okay. You will see him attached to a number of drips and a number of monitors. Please don't be alarmed, that is all part of the close monitoring that we do. You may also hear an alarm being sounded from time to time. Usually that arises because a patient has moved around in bed and dislodged one of the monitors. We will come immediately to see what's going on. Now, follow me please and I will take you to him."

Adrienne looked at Anca and they smiled at each other, reassured by the kind and professional voice of the nurse.

They passed two beds before the nurse drew back the curtain of the furthest cubicle on the left slightly and they peered inside. The nurse gestured for them to sit in the two visitor chairs. Adrienne had bitten her lip in anticipation of what she might see but she relaxed when she saw Theo asleep in a semi-prone position, with a blanket around him.

Having expected to see his face bruised and cut from the brutal violence he had received, save for the oxygen feed to his nose, he appeared to all intents and purposes to be his normal self. Having been told that he had been stabbed several times, there was nothing visible to that effect and she was glad of it. The only hint that he had undergone something serious was when she looked further down his body to see that there were three catheters taped to his left hand and one to his right hand all hooked up on to the intravenous fluids pole: two were colourless and one was red with what she assumed was blood. She also noticed, tucked discretely under the bed was a transparent bag. There was a small amount of amber liquid in it.

She looked up at the nurse for an explanation. "That's his pee; we have a catheter set up for that," she whispered.

The nurse then patiently explained what each of the drips was for and also pointed to one which was controlled by the patient. "That one is for pain relief. The patient can press a button when the pain gets too much and it will release a small amount of morphine."

"So Flint will be able to get high," Adrienne giggled.

"You're not the first to say that. The system only releases a measured amount of morphine and at a maximum frequency of seven minutes no matter how many times the patient presses the button. This prevents an accidental overdose or someone getting high."

When the nurse left them, there was silence once again, except for the occasional alarm being set off by one of the other patients resulting in a nurse coming quickly to reset it and look in on the patient. After some thirty minutes, a nurse came by to take Theo's temperature by aiming a device on his forehead and then noting it down. She followed this up by gently lifting his arm to take his blood pressure and a finger clamp that she explained was to measure his oxygen levels.

"Nurse, you recorded that his temperature was 34.8 Celsius, isn't that a bit low? I remember from my school days the temperature should be 37 Celsius?" asked Adrienne.

"It is a little on the low side but nothing to worry about. We often find that patients have fluctuating temperature following operations but it will settle down," she reassured them and then offered to get them some tea, Adrienne saying she preferred coffee.

"Why do the English always offer tea not coffee? They think the whole world loves tea?" she joked.

"Theo once told me that England conquered the world on cups of tea," laughed Anca.

Adrienne giggled. "Probably true! Look at us. A French woman, a Slovakian woman and half the Arab world have all come under his spell!"

Time seemed to stand still, each in their own thoughts as they faced Theo who was lying there propped up on pillows, completely motionless and oblivious to their presence. As Adrienne watched the monitor reading his heartbeat, she recalled how they had first met on that fateful morning on the London-bound train. It had bizarrely been antagonism that had brought them into contact, those initial words of ill-feeling sowing the seeds of a relationship. In spite of the acerbic exchanges, she had felt a connection with him, this haughty Englishman, a bond she had never felt with any other man before him and she was determined to make him hers. And just as she had succeeded, it was antagonism of a different kind, a violent kind, a moment of madness, that had threatened to undermine and destroy that. She had no doubt that Mr Shah and his medical team had done their best for him, but until he opened his eyes and spoke to her, until she held his hand in hers and she saw him smile, she would not be convinced by Mr Shah's kind words that he was indeed on the mend, as he had put it.

Anca was in her own world, recalling the first few weeks of living with him, how scared and in awe of him she had been. But he had never shouted at her or abused her in any way and he had been patient with her poor English, encouraging her learning. He had paid for her to have English lessons, he had helped her get a driving license, and sought out potential customers for her to build up fitness training and Pilates clientele. And slowly, slowly they had established a rapport which had developed with time into a much closer relationship, to the point where he was her confidant and she could trust him to talk about any subject that was of concern to her. She felt warm and safe around him. It felt perfectly natural that she could sit on his lap when she needed a cuddle or comfort. She loved Sunday mornings when they sat reading the papers together or discussed politics. She loved him and it was a very unwelcome jolt when the policewoman told them in a spiritless way, devoid of all feeling, that he had been stabbed suffering serious injury. If it wasn't for her love for Adrienne and the need to remain calm and strong for her, she too would have burst into tears. Only later could she let her feelings come to the fore. As a devout Christian, she had prayed to God for Theo to pull through and now, watching him sleep quietly, it seemed that the Almighty had indeed listened to her.

They hadn't realised it, but in their reverie, they had both fallen asleep, Anca slouched over Theo's bed on one side and Adrienne on the other, her head resting against his arm. There was something comforting about just being able to touch him, feel his body warmth.

The swishing of the curtain as a nurse pulled it back woke them and they sat up. As Theo was still soundly asleep, she suggested that they might want to leave and return later in the evening but neither Adrienne nor Anca were willing to budge except to stretch their legs and go for a short walk, whilst the nurses took his temperature and pressure again.

When they returned, the nurses had gone. Anca pointed to the new unit of liquid that had been replenished and the bag under the bed had been replaced.

"He is sleeping a long time," Adrienne whispered.

"No, he isn't," said Theo groggily, through half-opened eyes.

"Flint! You are awake!" said Adrienne, smiling sweetly to him. She had promised herself that no matter what, no matter how she felt she would not cry. His words were like a soothing ointment and she smiled from ear to ear. "I want to kiss you and hug you but all these tubes and this bump of mine are getting in the way."

"Yes, it would not be a good idea," he said and his voice sounded laboured and tired. He reached out his arm and touched her hand. It felt cold but she was delighted to feel it.

"Nice to hear your voice again, Theo," said Anca, her hand touching his other hand, careful not to dislodge the catheters taped into the veins in his knuckles.

"How are you feeling, Flint. Does it hurt a lot?" said Adrienne, with concern on her face.

"Not a jot, Kiffy. I have so much painkiller pumped into me that actually I am completely numb. It is as if nothing has happened to me. I am sure once it wears off the pain will kick in but for now, I feel nothing. Wide awake, right as rain," he said cheerfully.

"You've been sleeping a long time," said Anca.

"Actually, I was awake earlier but you were both fast asleep and I didn't want to wake you. And when you were talking to the nurses I was trying not to smile and give the game away. Listening to the two of you interrogating the senior nurse about my readings made me chuckle inside. I could tell you were not happy with her explanations and I could tell from the tone of her voice she was not happy either."

"Oh Flint, you don't know how happy I am to hear you talk like normal. I so want to kiss you!" said Adrienne.

"Me too, right now. As part of your, wait was that word you taught me? recuperation!" said Anca.

"Hmm, well as I can't kiss you and as part of my recuperation as Anca put it so well, I've got a better idea," said Theo.

"Oh? What's that, my dear husband? Just ask and we will do it," said Adrienne and Anca willingly nodded her assent.

"I can't kiss each of you so why don't you kiss each other," he joked.

"Flint! You are naughty! You are supposed to be ill not asking us to do naughty things!"

Anca giggled. "We don't want to be getting your blood pressure up, Theo. It will trigger the alarm and then the nurses will come running in."

"Hmm, pathetic excuses. Firstly, I am not ill, just full of holes and staples where they sealed them. Secondly, I thought it wouldn't be a bad idea to check my other vital organs were still working!" he joked.

"That other vital organ can wait a while longer!" Adrienne giggled. "I will take care of it when you are better."

"And I will help Adrienne," said Anca, egged on by her. "Besides, you can't do anything anyway, you do realise you have a catheter attached to you?"

"Really? As I said, I can't feel a thing. Never stopped to think why I haven't been wanting to take a pee. It's weird: I don't feel thirsty or hungry, absolutely nothing."

They chatted about who to let know and Theo asked Anca to let his work know, specifically Graham so that he could continue with preparations for the move to Abu Dhabi and Andy Bedford, a senior partner like himself: they were working together on a number of cases for London-based clients.

"When you come out of here, I have asked them to move you into the private ward where you will have your own room, Flint. Can't have a posh Englishman like you, mixing with the proletariat, can we?" Adrienne teased.

"Quite right. Look what happened to me the last two times I did that.

The first time I got entangled with a fiery French woman who I ended up marrying and the second time I ended up with several holes in me!" he joked.

"And what would your mother think of me when she comes to visit if her loving son was not receiving the best treatment?" she continued.

"That's a point. When do you want us to tell other people, like your mum and dad? asked Anca.

"Not yet," Adrienne cut in before he could reply. "Let's wait until Flint is out of here and in his own room."

"There was something else I was going to say," he said and then his voice trailed off and his eyes closed.

"He is sleeping again. Poor Flint, we wore him out," whispered Adrienne.

"Let's go home and I will make us some lunch," said Anca. "And you need to rest too, Adrienne. It has been very tiring for you being here, physically and emotionally."

The two women left the hospital much happier than when they entered.

When they were in the car and Anca was driving them home, Adrienne giggled. "That Flint, he wakes up and he has sex on his mind."

Anca laughed. "It was funny, wasn't it?"

When they returned in the evening, they saw that all the curtains were pulled right back and each patient had a number of visitors. Adrienne noticed the one nearest the door was an elderly lady looking very weak. She had just the one solitary visitor, an old man who was sitting near her holding her hand, comforting her. It made Adrienne feel sad to see these two people in the twilight of their lives, clinging onto life itself.

Walking towards the far end, they noticed something big sitting on Theo's table at the foot of his bed and opposite him, there was a crowd of visitors surrounding the patient, who was smiling and laughing. She looked in a much better state than Theo who was staring blankly towards the window, his blanket around his waist. When they got to his bed, he looked around and smiled weakly. It was clear that the anaesthetic and painkillers were starting to wear off and he was in much pain.

"Hi," he said limply.

"Hey, Flint, how are you feeling my darling?" said Adrienne, gently lifting his hand to kiss it.

"Just gave myself a dose of what is otherwise a class A prohibited substance. I have been pumping myself up with this, every seven minutes, as the paracetamol drip on its own doesn't do enough. I'm going to end up a junkie by the time I leave," he joked through the pain.

"Poor you," said Adrienne and kissed his hand again. "Here is another kiss to help you get better."

Anca managed to lean across and kiss him on the cheek.

"What's with the hamper of flowers and fruit, Flint? Seems like you and the woman opposite have them. Are they giving them out to patients nowadays?"

"Something like that," he said wincing but did not elaborate.

"It's okay, Flint you don't have to talk. We'll do the talking," said Adrienne.

Anca brought him up to date with communication she'd had with his colleagues and, turning to her notes on her mobile phone, she read off all those who had sent their best wishes and who would visit him once he was out of the HDU.

"Not sure how much of that he actually heard," said Adrienne, seeing that he had closed his eye once again and his head tilted away from them. She was sad to see him like that, in pain and discomfort and she fought back the tears as they left the hospital.

On the following morning, they could see that his bed was empty and Adrienne's heart started racing as she feared he had taken a turn for the worse.

Seeing the worried look on Adrienne's face, the duty nurse assured them that he had gone for a walk with Annie and the other nurse.

"Walk?"

"Yes, we felt Theo and Annie had been in bed too long and needed to start being mobile on the advice of the doctors. Nurse Ross is just walking them along the corridor."

"Who is Annie?" asked Anca.

"Annie? Has Theo not told you? She is the woman whose life he saved. She was admitted at the same time as him. We only have four beds in the HDU and the other two were occupied so we put them opposite each other. Almost poetic don't you think?"

Adrienne smiled. "And those big bunches of flowers on each of their tables, who brought those?"

"Annie's family. They wanted to say thank you to Theo for saving Annie. Her elder brother wanted to hug him but we stopped him in time. Theo's not yet ready for hugs," she said, chuckling.

A few minutes later, Theo and Annie trudged back, each holding their IV pole, walking at a snail's pace, pain written over both their faces, with Nurse Ross warmly encouraging them to take a step at a time. When they were near his bed, Theo looked up when he recognised the perfume. He tried to raise a smile. Try as he might to hide how he was feeling, it was obvious he was in a good deal of pain. Annie was more mobile than him and managed to get herself into bed, whilst Theo needed Nurse Ross to help him.

"Same again tomorrow, Theo?" Annie called out and he nodded.

"I see you have another admirer," Adrienne teased. "Quite good looking too, except for the tattoo on her arm. Why didn't you say that she was the woman who you saved when we came yesterday?"

"It was not within my gift to do that," he said and they both giggled.

"That's my Flint, a lawyer even on his sick bed," she said and then pressed the button to lower his bed so that she could lean over and kiss him.

There was no pressure on his lips, they just felt cold, even though his hands felt warm. It made her swallow hard not to trigger the tears she felt inside.

"Can you take the blanket off me, this place is way too hot," he complained. Anca pulled it down to his thighs.

"More please Anca, completely off me, I'm baking here. I think they keep it that warm for the biddy in the corner who always feels cold even with two blankets on her."

When Anca took the blanket away he hadn't banked on them seeing the blood stains on his hospital gown.

"It's nothing, just a little oozing. The doctors say it's normal," he explained. "I've got so many staples in me it looks like a railway line. Not looking forward to when they take them off."

"How many, Flint?"

"Not sure if the doctor said thirty-eight or forty-eight, something like that. It's amazing they use staples nowadays, just like how you might staple pieces of paper together. Maybe they don't trust the doctors sewing people up."

"The nurse told us it was Annie's relatives who brought you this big hamper, not the hospital providing it, Flint," said Adrienne.

"I didn't say it was the hospital, Kiffy. It was your conjecture."

"You didn't correct me, Flint.'

"Because it…"

"Was not within his gift to do that," Anca finished off and he laughed.

"Exactly," said Theo, spotting a nurse from afar walking speedily towards him.

"Mr Blenkinsop," she said, "can we have the blanket back over your waist please? I know you are warm but we can't have you flashing the woman opposite, can we?"

"Pardon?"

"Without your blanket strategically placed, your gown is wide open down below and your undercarriage is in full view of the lady opposite," she said, laughing as she placed the blanket back on him.

"Really? Has she complained? A woman with a massive injury from a knife wound is well enough or in the frame of mind to peek up my gown and see my undercarriage as you put it? Which by the way is all shrivelled up."

"Of course she hasn't complained, you're her hero, Mr Blenkinsop. But let's keep it under wraps shall we," said the nurse giggling. "Don't you agree with me, Mrs Blenkinsop?"

"Yes, Flint. Stop being such a slut!" Adrienne laughed.

In the evening when they returned, laden with boxes of biscuits and chocolates that he had asked them to bring for the nurses and the hospital orderlies as a thank you for looking after him, they were surprised to see that the curtains were once again drawn around him and there was a doctor and two nurses in attendance talking amongst themselves. When they approached, one of the nurses introduced them and the doctor said that following a review of his condition they had decided to delay sending him up to his room by twenty-four hours. He explained that after the afternoon exercise, Theo's temperature shot up to 40 Celsius and they had had to cool him down and administer another dose of antibiotics as a precautionary measure, in case of infection. Adrienne was not at all assured by the doctor's diagnosis, that it was quite common for patients to pick up a bug and that they soon shift it. She had read and heard of many a horror story about patients getting MRSA in hospital and she was worried that Theo might have the same.

"Hey, Flint, you're my hero," Adrienne whispered in his ear. "You must get better, my darling. You are going to be a papa soon. I can't do this on my own. I need your support."

The nurse had passed Anca a folded piece of paper before the medics left. It had her name written on it and she could tell from the handwriting that it was from him, he that was lying there fast asleep and not aware of their visit.

"What's that, Anca?" asked Adrienne.

"It's a note from Theo," she said, opening it. She read through it a couple of times and then handed it over to Adrienne saying, "Here, you can read it yourself."

"No, you read it for me please, Anca. I am not sure I can read anything that might upset me," she said.

"It's not upsetting Adrienne but I will read it for you. It says 'Dear Anca, tell Kiffy not to cry, I will be okay. It's just a little setback. Tell her she needs to be happy for the baby and to play good English music to her. I want her to listen to The Beatles, the Rolling Stones, the Kinks, Elton John, George Michael and my favourite, David Bowie. I want our baby to be dancing to Jean Genie and Little China Girl.' That's all. He signs it off with a big kiss to you and to me."

Adrienne started to cry but she was smiling at the same time. "Even when he is ill, Flint is thinking about me and about our baby and he is right, I need to be happy for her. Okay, let's go home and put on some Beatles music. Not sure I like David Bowie that much," she laughed.

The infection that had taken hold kept him in bed most of the next day but Theo was not short of visitors. Aside from Adrienne and Anca, Annie sat with him, her IV pole in tow, for a good deal of time. She kept his mind occupied with tales of her life, as chaotic as it was, going from one bad relationship to another finally ending up with the worst of all, married to the man who had tried to kill her and would have succeeded were it not for Theo's brave intervention.

"Did you not have an inkling that he had a violent streak in him?" Theo asked.

"No. That's just it. I married him because he seemed the most normal of my boyfriends. He'd been an army cook for most of his life and was now a chef in a local restaurant, which is how I met him. Seemed okay, always seemed to behave like a gentleman and when he asked me to marry him, I thought why not, at last I had met a normal man. He didn't drink, he didn't do smack or other drugs and on his days off he just wanted to spend time with me. But he started to get jealous, especially when I wasn't home. He wanted to know all my whereabouts and that's when the violence started. My older brother, Caleb, the one you met, said I should leave him but I wanted to hang on to what I had. I wanted to prove to myself that it wasn't me. Having been dumped a few times, I was thinking maybe it was me, maybe it was my fault. I began to think that maybe he was right, maybe I should stay at home and wait for his return. Trouble is chef's do not keep normal hours, they are out most of the night and when he would come home, sometimes not until two or three in the morning smelling of grease and cooking, I just wasn't interested in him and he took that to mean I was having an affair. The violence continued, a slap here, a push there and I kinda got used to it until one day in a rage, he punched me in the stomach. It hurt so much and I doubled over and hit my head. That was it. I had enough and I moved out of his house and back in with my mum. Then I divorced him. I also took out a restraining order as he kept coming after me, wanting to say sorry and get back together again. My mum was frightened to leave the house. The police had to be called out twice to warn him to stay away or risk being taken into custody. And he did stay away and for a while, things returned to normal and I could once again get on with my life. You know even after we split up, I kept thinking it must have been my fault. But life goes on, isn't that what they say? Everything back to normal, right? Yeah right, all normal, that is until he followed me on the train and you know what happened there. The reason why you and I ended up here, in Epsom Hospital."

"Do you know where he is now?" asked Theo.

"He is on remand, awaiting trial."

"Which means he is behind bars in jail? No longer a threat?"

"Oh yes. Behind bars where he belongs. My brother found out which prison he is being kept in. You and I have nothing to fear, Theo. Caleb and his mates are taking care of things," she said, with a knowing smile which chilled him.

"He will be standing trial and you and I will be going to be giving evidence at some point, won't we?" he asked.

"We'll see about that," she grinned. It was a knowing grin with a hint of menace that did nothing but increase his unease about the whole thing. "Anyway, this is my last day here before I get shipped out to the sheep pen, they call a ward, so I guess this is goodbye. You will forever be in my heart, Theo, my hero. You have restored my faith in humanity and you did a kindness to me that nearly cost you your own life. No one has ever put themselves out that much for me and I am very grateful to you. I will be sending you a Christmas card every year for as long as I live. You must give me your address. Maybe we can even meet up in town once a year and have a natter."

"Thank you, Annie. I never saw myself as being anybody's hero. I just did what I thought was the right thing to do. No point giving you my address as, in a few weeks, I am leaving the country."

"Really? Not because of what happened, surely? Don't worry, the fucker will not be in a state to come and get you after…" she stopped herself.

"No, it's not about him or what happened, so please don't do anything precipitous on my account. This was a trip that I have been spending half my lifetime planning and hopefully it is going to be happening soon."

"Anywhere nice?"

"America," he said, instinct telling him that a little white lie was in order. "California, land of opportunity and all that."

"Well, good luck with that. I wish you the best," she said and taking his head in her hands, planted her lips on his.

As she turned to trudge back to her bed, he quickly wiped his mouth with the back of his hand. It was not a welcome kiss and it left him feeling sick in the pit of his stomach. The words that came to mind were 'low life' and he felt ashamed of himself for thinking like that. 'No one deserves to be treated like that. Why do people, men resort to violence?'

The following day, Mr Shah visited him and pronounced Theo well enough to be moved out of the HDU. There was an emotional goodbye with Annie who came back down to visit him one last time and with the nurses that had cared and tended to him night and day. Theo tried to hold back his feelings.

"Oh my God, Flint. I think you are already well. Back to normal!" Adrienne teased.

"Er? What do you mean, Kiffy?" he asked, looking puzzled.

"That stiff upper lip of yours was back, Flint. A normal person would have become emotional and cried but not you, Flint. I thought I saw a slight wobble, the tiniest change in colour on those lovely cheekbones of yours. But nothing else from my proud Englishman," Adrienne chuckled. "You can shed a tear if you want to, Flint. I won't even look if it helps."

"Shut up, Kiffy. We don't all express ourselves by being all blubbery and wailing, something you French are so good at," he joked. "And you for one shed enough for both of us."

Adrienne was holding his hand as the hospital porter wheeled him out of the HDU. It was a relief to her, as the next stage in his recovery was beginning. Leaving the HDU had alleviated a whole bunch of demons that had been circulating in her head, something she had not shared even with Anca.

"Bet you are glad to be out of there and into your own room," said Anca.

Theo recalled the very last conversation he had had with a member of Annie's family. "Don't worry mate, we'll fix him for you so that he will never do that again. Not to you, not to anyone," he had said, with a smile that left him in no doubt that menace was what he was planning for Annie's ex-husband.

The room that had been earmarked for Theo was bright and spacious with its own en suite shower and toilet, his own TV and a choice of menus. The nurses wore a different colour of uniform indicating that they were there to serve private patients. There seemed more of them, fussing over him in numbers, be it to take his vital readings, changing his urine bag or fluffing up his pillows. So much so, that when he wanted to have a wash, a nurse immediately offered her services to help him, holding him as he managed to shuffle out of bed and walk unsteadily into his bathroom. Calmly and efficiently, she removed his hospital gown and then lead him to the sink area. She gestured for him to hold on to the sink so she could sponge wash him. Theo was tense with apprehension, expecting any moment for pain to cut in but the combination of morphine and paracetamol was keeping it at bay. The nurse smiled reassuringly as she began to wash him and he began to relax. He did not even stir when she started to wash him below the waist, around his bottom and in between his legs. But when she started to sponge his manhood, he was startled and pulled back involuntarily.

"It's okay. You don't have to be embarrassed, Theo. I have done this hundreds of times," she said and carried on with her handiwork.

When she knelt down on a towel to soap his feet, he recalled the last time Adrienne had knelt in front of him like that. The memory of that delicious moment had absolutely no effect on the part of him that was now being washed.

Back in bed, he was being visited by the most senior of the nurses, Sister Mary from the Philippines; the mere mention of her name striking the fear of God into the other nurses. Whenever she said anything, the other nurses seemed to jump to order and she was no different with the patients either, as Theo soon came to realise for himself that she was not one to pander to malingering guest patients, as she called them.

"Why are you lying in bed all day?" she said to him.

"Sorry, I forgot my football boots at home otherwise I would be outside having a kickabout," he joked.

Sister Mary would have none of it. "Come on, get up, let's have you walking about the ward. I don't want to see you back in this bed for fifteen minutes, Mr Blenkinsop."

"I'm not sure I can manage a whole fifteen minutes, seems a lot. The most I've walked so far is five minutes," said Theo, as he manoeuvred himself to sit up in bed.

"I have a physiotherapist coming to help you to walk. She will be here in a minute," she said in a clipped tone. Seeing that he was wincing when he tried to sit up, she softened her tone and added, "I know you are trying Mr Blenkinsop, a little a day will help you, trust me."

Theo was struggling to adjust his hospital gown which had become twisted and at the same time take care not to dislodge the catheters attached to the tubes on his IV pole, whilst keeping the pain at bay as the stitches stretched across his belly.

"Oh dear, seem to be leaking a bit," he said, looking down and noticing spots of blood oozing through the long bandages covering the stitches. He pulled the robe to the side to take a closer look and pulled a face when he saw that his abdomen was purple blue from the bruising he had suffered, although he did not know if that was the operation to fix him or the stabbing itself.

'Theo, you've really been through the wars this time, old chap,' he told himself. 'You've been going back and forth to one of the most volatile areas in the world all these years and come back each time without so much as a scratch and here, right on your doorstep, someone in a moment of madness decides to carve you up. What an odd world we live in.'

When a young woman entered his room, Theo attempted to cover himself, thinking that she might have been a visitor for one of the other patients, dressed as she was in just a t-shirt and leggings and was minded to politely ask her to leave. Her unkempt hair, oily, spot-riddled, cheeks and her nervous smile convinced him that she was just a teenager who had got lost on her way to visit someone. There was just the faintest of smiles as she walked up to his bed.

"Excuse me, Miss, I think you may have the wrong room," said Theo. "Who were you hoping to visit?"

The woman pulled a face in puzzlement and then introduced herself as Helen Masters, his physiotherapist. "I believe Sister Mary told you of my forthcoming visit."

"Yes, she did, although she did not say anything about who you were, what your name was, what time you would drop by and not even what you look like. I thought you might be someone's visitor the way…" he stopped himself. "I was expecting someone older I guess."

"Before we start, I just want to check a few of your details," she said, looking down at her computer tablet.

"Before we go into that, can I see some ID of yours, please? I don't know you from Adam or should I say Eve. At any rate, I would be grateful of some proof of who you say you are. This is a hospital with as far as I can tell no security whatsoever, so I wouldn't know if you were just the patient next door!"

She looked irritated but flashed her pass to him which he looked at closely and then handed it back.

"Right then. You are Mr Theodore Blenkinsop?"

"No, Hannibal Lecter," Theo quipped.

"Pardon? I was given to understand that I was seeing Theodore Blenkinsop," she said, looking confused.

"If that's who you thought I was and the plate on the door says I am Theodore Blenkinsop and the clipboard on the end of my bed says the same thing and the whiteboard next to me has today's date and my name inked in and the band around my wrist all say the same thing, then what do you reckon?"

"It's just a standard check, Mr Blenkinsop."

"And before you ask me, if you want to know my other details, like date of birth, then look it up."

"I'm just checking, standard hospital routine, Mr Blenkinsop."

"Let me ask you something; who are you cross-checking with?"

"These notes I have in front of me."

"And where do you think the source of that information came from?" She looked up from her tablet and pointed a pen at him.

"Clever girl, got it in one. You are cross-checking with me that the information supplied by me is correct, so unless you are checking whether the loss of blood was so bad that it affected my memory then this is a pointless exercise. I had the same thing in the HDU and in the CT scanning room, relentlessly being asked to verify details I had provided myself. Pointless questions. As I said, it's all on my wrist tag anyway."

Helen Masters shrugged. "As I said, it's routine."

"Okay, now that we have established I am who I am supposed to be, what are we here to do today? Fireside chat is it? Fancy a game of cards? Perhaps a game of 'I spy with my little eye'?"

"Mr Blenkinsop, I am here to help you get back on your feet, not to entertain you. I can see from your face that you are in some pain. If you want that pain to lessen, then the sooner we have you mobile, the faster your recovery will be and then you can leave the hospital. So, let's get you out of bed and go for a walk. As soon as you can walk to the end of the corridor as fast as me and go up and down those stairs, then it will be time for you to leave. Come on, you know it is in your interest to cooperate with me," she said, good-naturedly.

"Yes, you are right of course. I apologise for my rant. There is still mileage in using pain as an excuse for my rudeness," he said.

She walked around to where he had lowered the bed and seeing him struggle, bent down to put the slippers on his feet and helped him to adjust his gown and then to put a robe on. Theo held on to the arm she offered, as he could not trust himself to stand up unaided. He took a few tentative pigeon steps until he found his balance. They walked together, his arm around hers at a pace that he dictated. They were small steps.

"At this speed, I think I would have missed my train by now," he muttered to himself. "Wonder when I will get back to commuting again?"

They had managed to walk to the first bend in the corridor when Theo felt exhausted from the effort and he leant against the wall to rest. His feet felt leaden and the pull of the stitches was causing him a lot of soreness and discomfort. He looked at his watch despondently, as they had barely walked for five minutes.

"Do you want to stop or shall we go on a little further?" she asked him gently.

"Better go on another few minutes before we turn back. Don't want you reporting back to Sister Mary that I did not achieve fifteen minutes today, she'll skin me alive."

Throughout their walk she remained silent, just acting as his anchor whenever he needed to rest. He could feel his temples throbbing and his heart beating fast from the exertion as they turned around and at the next bend in the corridor, he could see the door to his room. It was close by yet seemed so far as he trudged back, holding her with one hand and the wall with the other one. But what slowed him down the most was that he was thinking about his stitches and what might happen if he missed his footing and slipped. Would they burst open, spilling out all his guts onto the floor and then finding himself wheeled back to the operating room?

When she helped him back into bed and covered him, he let out a sigh of relief and closed his eyes.

"You did well, Mr Blenkinsop. Same again tomorrow? I'll be here at 10 a.m." she said.

"Today the corridor, tomorrow Le Mans," he jested.

"Le Mans? The twenty-four-hour race in France? Ha-ha!"

Theo squeezed her hand and mouthed 'thanks'. He closed his eyes, exhausted from the effort.

Helen left the room having updated her notes. He barely had half an hour's respite before he heard the duty nurse enter and the sound of the tell-tale monitoring device. He was tired and could have done with more sleep but held his arm out without even opening his eyes. She took his pulse and body temperature and checked each of his catheters and the urine bag and then left him to it.

'Ah, the bliss of silence,' he said to himself.

For the next two days, with Helen's help, Theo was managing to walk once completely around the corridor and back taking nearly twenty minutes. It was progress but still very slow. The image of him slipping and his chest opening up that he had created for himself had become etched in his mind and undermined any confidence he may have had, in attempting to walk without holding on to her. Each time Helen tried to encourage him to try, he would say, "Not yet: soon."

He had just returned to his room and Helen had helped him into bed and he was resting when he heard the door open. Thinking that it was the nurse, he held his arm open ready for her to do her measurements and was surprised when a hand took his and entwined it with theirs.

He half-opened his eyes and saw that it was Adrienne.

"Hello, Flint," she said, kissing his limp hand. "How's my darling husband today?"

"Hello, Kiffy," he said weakly. "Sorry, just did my exercise and feeling a bit tired."

Anca sat the other side of him and touched his arm. She did not need to say any more.

"Hey Flint, your daughter has been dancing around inside me to Penny Lane and Strawberry Fields Forever," she said, putting his hand to her abdomen.

Theo took a cursory look, and closed his eyes again. "God you look so fat and…"

"I do, don't I? Your fault, Flint," she said, interrupting him.

"And beautiful," he said, his voice trailing off.

Adrienne smiled, trying not to cry when he uttered those words. She had missed being able to talk to him, to listen to his voice and she felt lonely. Inasmuch as Anca was great company, the nearer she got to giving birth the more acutely she felt the need for him be with her, to hold her and to reassure her. She reached out and gently, put her hand on his forehead and it felt warm. "Shall we call the nurse?" she whispered, looking at Anca.

Anca stood up and touched him and nodded. She pointed to the door and tiptoed quietly out.

"Come on Flint, my darling. Get better soon, I need you. Life is so lonely without you. Please come to me sweetheart, I beg you," she whispered, desperately holding back tears.

The duty nurse came in and took his vital readings again and confirmed that he had a higher-than-normal temperature and that she would get a doctor. In the meantime, they took the bedding off him so that he was left with just his hospital gown. She also sponged his face with warm water, encouraging Anca to continue doing that whilst she went to get the doctor.

The doctor arrived in a few minutes and after checking some of Theo's readings seemed unconcerned, saying keeping him cool was sufficient and put it down to over-exertion, recommending that he stayed in bed the following day until his temperature settled down. He also asked the nurse to replace the liquid paracetamol he was receiving.

The doctor put his hand on Adrienne's shoulder, reassuring her that her husband was doing fine and his recovery was going well.

"Soon be right as rain," he said, before he marched off to attend to another patient.

It took two days before Theo felt sufficiently right as rain to get up and resume walking with Helen. In those two days when he was bed-ridden, he had a string of visitors, his sister Suzy popped in with a box of expensive chocolates — most of which she ate herself, his mother and Arabella drove up for the day and came laden with some of his favourite pies made by Mrs Chalfont and from work, Nicola and Gareth took an early afternoon off to visit him. As much as it was tiring, talking about work was a good way of distracting him from his situation and gave him fortitude to get on with the job of recovering and getting back into the buzz of working on legal matters. Reluctantly, Gareth handed over a contract for him to read over. He did not wish to put Theo under any pressure and gave it to him under duress but for Theo, sitting up and reading it after they had left was the best restorative medicine he could have had.

"Better than any of the stuff they have been injecting into my veins," he told Helen, as he walked around the corridor unaided for the first time.

When he walked for the full fifteen minutes with only once having to hold on to her, Theo was grinning from ear to ear.

"Well done, Theo," she said, as she helped him back into his bed.

"Tomorrow I'd like to take a look at those steps," he said.

"Sure?"

"Yes, I think I'm ready for it," he said.

When Helen, left he did not feel tired nor a need to sleep. Instead, he opened his iPad, typed in the document password to open it and started to read the contract. He stretched his arms out as much as he could and he felt good. For the first time in many days, notwithstanding the tug of the stitches when he turned, he felt that he was on top of his injuries, psychologically as well as physically. He was looking forward to leaving the hospital.

After two days of further exercise culminating in him being able to walk up and down five or six steps of a staircase, it was agreed that he was well enough to be discharged and to go home at the end of the day. In the afternoon, Adrienne and Anca came to take Theo home, but he could not be discharged until one final examination from the duty doctor and they sat waiting in the room.

"It's okay, Kiffy, just have a cup of tea and relax. Won't be long now," he assured her, as she paced around the room impatiently.

"You know I don't much like tea, Flint and the coffee they make here is bad," she said.

Sister Mary wandered into the room and wished him well in his recovery and handed him what she called a bag of goodies for him to take. Theo peered inside to see what looked like medicines, extra bandages and boxes of syringes.

"What are these for?" he asked.

"The medicines are strong painkillers if you find it difficult to manage but use them sparingly. The bandages should be changed every few days. They are waterproof so don't worry about getting them wet in the shower. The other boxes contain syringes with medicine to reduce the risk of blood clotting. You have to inject yourself twice a day for three weeks," she said nonchalantly. "The nurse will be here shortly to show you what to do."

"Wait. Did I hear you right? Inject myself? You're joking? I've never done that before and I'm not sure I can do it," he said.

"The nurse will show you but if you still can't, maybe your wife can do it for you."

Adrienne giggled. "I don't mind sticking a needle in your bum, Flint."

"It's not there you inject him, madam," said Sister Mary and pointed to where it had to go.

"In his stomach? No way! I can't do that," said Adrienne, shaking her head. "Impossible. Can't a nurse come round to do it for him."

"It is possible but you have to arrange it yourself with the district nurse," shrugged Sister Mary. "But it's not a big deal, you can teach a child to do it."

"I can do it if you show me how," Anca volunteered. "I've never done anything like that before but I am willing to try, if Theo trusts me to do it."

Theo nodded and when the nurse came in and took Anca through what was required, his very first injection was administered in the abdomen by her.

"Just remember to always keep the needle perpendicular to the stomach when it goes in and do it quickly. It will be less painful and there will be less bruising if you do that," she advised.

"I need to take forty-two of these. Is that correct?" asked Theo.

"Yes, twice a day, with twelve hours in between, for twenty-one days. You've had one already so forty-one to go. And as it is 2 p.m., the next one is due at 2 a.m., so you will need to wake up in the night to do it. Gradually change the time so you get back to say midday to midnight or 11 a.m. to 11 p.m.," she advised.

The nurse also suggested that it would be better for Theo to sleep in his own bedroom for the time being as it reduced the risk of the stitches being accidently bumped.

"That would be good for me too. I've got used to sleeping without him," joked Adrienne, winking at Theo.

The road back to the house seemed tortuous to Theo. Inasmuch as the suspension of the Jaguar absorbed most of the shocks from the bumps and ruts in the road, even the slightest deviation from a smooth surface jolted his stitches and it felt as if someone was tugging at them. He found himself gritting his teeth and grimacing, beads of sweat forming on his forehead as they progressed through the early evening traffic in town.

Anca glanced at Theo in her rear-view mirror and could see that he was not having a happy time of it. "Sorry Theo, doing my best to go over the smoothest bits of the road. Not long to go now."

"It just shows me how little Surrey County Council has done to maintain our roads. Aside from jazzing up the area around the Epsom clocktower, the rest of the roads are in such a parlous state. Why they had to spend so much money paving the pedestrian area instead of fixing the roads is beyond me," he complained and winced as they went over a rutted stretch of the road heading out of Epsom.

Adrienne looked back and smiled at him. "You know Flint, the only time you show any emotion is when you're in pain. Maybe I should touch your stitches now and again just to see your face change!" she teased.

"Kiffy, I can think of other places you can touch to get a reaction out of me," he replied.

"Flint, you are so naughty! Can't do that my darling, don't want to send you back into hospital with all that exertion!"

"What I had in mind involved no exertion on my part," he said, laughing.

"Quiet you two, you're making me lose concentration on driving," Anca chuckled. When Anca slowed down to turn into the drive and the electric gates silently opened, it felt as good as getting back to his bedroom in the hospital.

"We're home, Flint," said Adrienne.

The words felt comforting. Two weeks earlier as he collapsed on the train, his last thought before passing out had been that he would never again see his home, nor his wife or his family and his dream of a life in the Persian Gulf and all he had thus far achieved, was going to die there with him. Now, by the skill of the surgeons and good fortune, he was gingerly sliding out of his car and taking steps to enter that very home he thought he would never see again. It was choking him but true to form, only he knew that.

When Philip ran up to him and mewed it seemed to make his return home complete.

"Missed you too, old chap," he said, as he wearily trundled into the living room and gently eased himself down into his favourite leather armchair.

"Good to have you home, Flint," said Adrienne, as she brushed his hair back and kissed him. "I've missed my Englishman."

After Effects

At the end of three weeks of being punctured with needles twice a day in the stomach, a milestone had been reached in Theo's recovery. Anca ceremoniously discarded the last syringe into the special box provided after administering the medicine into Theo's stomach for the last time.

"Well done, Flint, all over," said Adrienne, as she applauded.

"If there is such thing as a next life, I am sure I will be coming back as a pin cushion," Theo joked.

By the fourth week back from hospital he was able to visit the surgery for the GP to look at his wounds. Although there were spots of blood here and there indicating that the wounds hadn't totally sealed up, the doctor smiled and assured him that the healing was going to plan and that he could book an appointment with the nurse to have the stitches out for the following week.

The taking of the stitches out was an act of using surgical pliers to remove the staples in turn, one at a time, the nurse explained but assured him she was trained to do that. As Theo lay on the bed, the nurse gently and carefully prized away each staple and dropped it into a metal dish, the clanging sound as it hit the metal an unwelcome reminder for Theo. With each one being pulled off, he tensed up in anticipation of the tugging feeling and some were more resistant than others, making him wince and look away, preferring to face the wall rather than look down at what was happening.

"That makes it twenty-eight, do you want to have a little break and have a glass of water?" asked the kind nurse, as she sat back up and wiped the beads of sweat from his forehead.

"Are there many more to go?" he asked.

She nodded. "'Fraid so. Probably the same again," she said.

Theo swallowed hard and asked that she continue through to the end without stopping. He was counting off each one as he heard the clatter in the metal dish. One clang after the other, getting nearer to the end. When he reached twenty-five, he stopped counting as it was nearing the end or so he thought. But the nurse kept going beyond what he expected and it was five more minutes before she declared it was over.

"Finished! Well done you, so brave. I've pulled out sixty-five staples; the most I have ever done, I think. I'll just clean your wounds and put the fresh bandages on that you brought with you and then send you on your merry way."

The nurse made a couple of trips to the dustbin and Theo noticed the sterile tissue she had discarded was coloured with his blood. He was beyond caring.

'Worst is over, old chap,' he told himself. 'No more rivets holding you together. Just Blenkinsop flesh and sinew doing its job now.'

"Come and see me in a week's time so I can look at those wounds again," said the nurse, as she helped him to put his shirt back on and then to stand up.

In the corridor, Anca was waiting for him and she took his arm and led him out to the car, parked in a doctor's bay as a special dispensation granted by the practice manager, much to the displeasure of the receptionist who was about to give Anca a dressing down, until he stepped in with an assuring nod.

When they got back home, Adrienne was resting on the couch, sleeping quietly. Her countenance suggested whatever she was dreaming about was making her happy. 'Wonder what is making her smile,' Theo thought. He had wanted to kiss those lovely, sensuous lips of hers but aside from not wanting to disturb her sleep, the act of bending down to do that scared him. Inasmuch as he hated the staples, without them he felt vulnerable, as if there was a danger that he could split wide open. He remembered the words of Mr Shah when he warned him not to be in a hurry to do anything, "We don't want to have to wheel you back in to be stitched up again, Mr Blenkinsop. There are only so many staples in my stapler!"

He plodded over to his office, his place of refuge, of calmness and tranquillity and holding on to the side cabinet of books, made his way to his big, leather chair and gently lowered himself into it. Opening up his laptop, he opened up a spreadsheet. It was unlike any other that he had produced. This spreadsheet did not have a single column of financial figures, not a fee rate, nothing on expense and no accounting costs or invoices.

Theo started to read down the column of numbers.

"Not bad progress," he told himself. "You managed just one hundred and forty-two steps on day one, one thousand and sixty-five by the end of the first week, and now, four weeks later you are up to three thousand two hundred and twenty-six steps. Well done me."

The cat had wandered into the room and, after wrapping himself around Theo's legs, hovered next to him, looking up, waiting for the go-ahead to leap onto his master's lap. "Not just yet, Philip. Maybe in a month's time," he said and stroked Philip's head. The purring sound assured him that the recipient of his caress was content for now.

It reminded Theo that he had yet to make provision for Philip for when they departed for the Persian Gulf.

"Can't take you with me, Philip. Way too hot for you and not sure they allow pets into the country. Might have to leave you with Suzy if she'll have you or it's down in the countryside for you with Grannie Trixie looking after you."

Having updated his spreadsheet, the next thing that Theo did was to go online and find his shortcut to a site that he had been visiting frequently in recent times.

'Hmm, what does it say for a woman who is twenty-eight weeks pregnant?' he said to himself as he started reading. 'Wow! Weighs about the same as a bag of sugar. Well, I never! And what about Adrienne, what should I look out for?'

Theo read on, jotting down brief notes on a pad.

When a sleepy-eyed Adrienne wandered in and walked up to him, he put his arm around her waist.

"How are you feeling, Kiffy?" he said. "I realise all the attention has been on me lately so I apologise for not asking about you."

"I'm fine, Flint," she said and kissed him. "Very thoughtful of you to ask."

"Do you feel bloated at all?"

"No, nothing at all."

"Any dizziness or feeling light-headed?"

"No, nothing. I'm fine."

"Stuffy nose? Like can't breathe easily?"

"No Flint. I'm breathing fine" she said, smiling.

"How about bleeding gums? Any sign of that?"

"No, nothing. What's this all about, Flint?" she asked, bemused.

"Just checking you're okay," he said, shrugging.

"I'm really fine, Flint. Just awkward carrying this bump around, nothing else," she said and then she said, "Actually there is something else."

"Oh? What's that?"

Adrienne whispered in his ear and he smiled. "Really?"

"Yes. It is my hormones, makes me super-sensitive down there!"

"Not a lot I can do about that in my position, Kiffy!" he said and then joked, "I don't even know if it's still working!"

"We can find that out easily," she said and reached down to his trousers. Theo put his hand over hers and stopped her progressing any further.

"Let's wait a bit. I've only just had the staples out, wait until the paint is dry," he said in jest.

Adrienne frowned her disappointment until his arm moved under her skirt and his hand managed to snake under the loose panties she was wearing.

"Smooth. Very nice," he said, as he started to caress her.

"Of course! Just for you, awaiting your return," she said and added temptingly, "Whenever you're ready, Flint."

"Had help keeping it that way, have you?" he teased.

"What do you think?" she said, smiling.

Just then, poking her head around the door Anca appeared, wearing just a long bathrobe.

"Hey stop that! Give him a chance to recover, Adrienne!" she giggled, as she entered the room.

"I can't help it. I miss Flint, I miss my husband. I'm feeling horny."

"Haven't I been taking care of you?" she sniggered.

Adrienne nodded and smiled broadly. "Oh yes, you have."

"I was going to say, can we have Chinese tonight? I'm exhausted after my workout in the gym and don't feel like cooking," she said, as she leant against the side cabinet.

"How long will it take for them to come with our order," said

Adrienne.

"Usually thirty to forty-five minutes, depends."

Adrienne smiled. "Plenty of time," she said, taking her hand. "We'll go and lay the table." Anca giggled.

"I somehow think it's not the table that's going to get laid," he said, after they had left the room and he was once again alone. "Not fair! I'm left here, high and dry!"

Later that night after they had gone to bed, Theo could not get comfortable and he was having a restless sleep. Dreams of his stomach opening up like a zip being undone, interspersed with vivid images of Annie's ex-husband repeatedly stabbing him were keeping him awake. It was therefore not unwelcome when he saw a dark figure enter the room, creep under the bedsheets and start to caress his manhood. As much as he was enjoying the feeling of a hand on him, at first, he was very nervous and was worried that he might not be able to react.

'God knows what all these medicines are doing to me,' he thought.

But the gentle and sensual touch began to have the desired effect and his body began to respond. He was holding his breath in anticipation of pain kicking in but it was not sufficient to stop enjoying the treatment he was receiving, especially when something warm and wet had enveloped him. The sensual feeling made him smile. It was exciting but more than anything else it was a relief that he found himself able to react as nature intended. It had been more than a month since the last time he had had sex and within a couple of minutes it showed, as he could not hold back any longer. The figure that had given him so much pleasure disappeared as stealthily as it had appeared.

"Better than a paracetamol or sleeping pill," he muttered to himself, before dozing off.

In the adjacent bedroom, Adrienne whispered, "How did it go?"

"I did as you asked me to," came the voice of the person who was now cuddled up next to her, spooning.

"And?"

"No problem. All working well," she whispered.

"Thank God. I was worried for him. Thank you, Anca. Love you," said Adrienne and kissed her.

Two days later, Theo felt well enough to volunteer to join them for

Adrienne's ante-natal class but they would not have it.

"It's my last hypnotherapy class, Flint. Anca has been coming with me all this time, not you. Coming to the last session won't mean anything to you," said Adrienne.

"What is a hypnotherapy class, Kiffy? Let me guess, someone stands at the front of the class and waves a pendulum clock in front of you and sends you all to sleep! Like stories of French war victories!"

"Very funny, Flint! Hypnotherapy helps women to be more in control, confident and relaxed in getting to child birth."

"And is it working? Can you be more in control or confident than you already are?"

"It is. I was even relaxing, that is before you got yourself knifed!"

"Pardon me for being so inconsiderate. I should have asked my assailant to wait until after your last session," he joked.

Adrienne ignored him. "See you later, my sweet," she said and kissed him. "We normally go for a coffee and a bite to eat after so we won't be back for a couple of hours. Don't do anything stupid, Flint."

"I thought I might go for a run!"

"Flint! Don't even joke about it. I'll kill you if you do that!"

When the door slammed closed, Theo shuffled up to the bottom of the stairs followed by Philip who got impatient waiting for him and ran up ahead, hopping from one step to the other until he was at the top in no time and sitting there, looking back down and waiting for his master to join him.

"Philip, you're showing off again!" he muttered and began the laborious task of climbing up the stairs a step at a time, each one taken with the utmost concentration so as not to pull on where his stitches had been, straining his arms as he gripped the banister to help haul himself up. After every few steps up, he stopped for a breather and opening his robe, he looked under his t-shirt and on the surgical bandages for any sign that might mean that he had not healed. "When there are no more blood spots then I will start to relax," he had told his doctor at the last check-up, not assured that these were only temporary.

Philip had lost patience waiting for his master and tiptoed elegantly away to find a comfortable bed to jump onto and curl up. When Theo finally reached the top of the stairs on the first landing, he was out of breath but felt triumphant and elated as if he had climbed some high, Alpine mountain. Without Anca standing behind him as a precaution in case he should slip and fall, it felt as if he had undertaken a high wire act without the safety line.

"Progress!" he told himself.

Having regained his composure, he walked around the galleried landing, holding on to the banister rail to steady himself until he came to the next set of stairs. He grasped the newel post and hesitated as he remembered the stern words from Adrienne, 'don't do anything stupid'. He looked up and counted the steps off. "Just another twelve more to go," he said out loud.

Theo thought that the second set of steps would prove to be easier but it was far from the case and by the time he had reached his destination he was exhausted and he sat down on the top step. He began to get anxious as he felt he could feel his heart beating fast and he was feeling light-headed. What was going through his mind was that perhaps the internal stitches had come apart and blood was oozing out. His anxiety was exacerbated when he lifted his t-shirt up and the surgical bandages had a few more red spots than at the top of the first set of stairs. "Hmm not, good," he told himself.

Philip looked up from the first-floor landing and then skipped up the steps in seconds before sitting next to his master.

"I think I may have overdone it a bit, Philip," he said, stroking his furry friend. "Let's go and lie down, shall we."

With great effort, Theo lifted himself up and wandered into the gym. The massage bed was too high for him to climb up onto, so he lay on one of the mats, using a half-deflated Pilates ball as a pillow. He fell asleep in no time at all with Philip cuddled up next to him under his arm.

When Adrienne and Anca returned, aside from the hall lights which were programmed to come on at dusk, the rest of the house was in darkness. Other than the buzz of the refrigerators and creaking pipes, as the central heating had only just kicked in, it was also very quiet, almost silent. As Theo had not shown his face nor called out, they expected that he might be resting and whispered between themselves as they off-loaded their purchases and kicked off their shoes.

Anca gave Adrienne a peck on the cheek, thanking her for the clothes that she had bought for her and then ran upstairs to her room to hang them up. She poked her head into each of the bedrooms but Theo was not in any of them.

Adrienne waddled as quietly as she could into each of the rooms but could not see any sign of Theo, and surmised he must have gone to bed to rest. Inasmuch as she enjoyed having lunch and then going shopping with Anca, it had been very tiring with the bump actively reminding her with occasional jolts and kicks that she was transporting two people around, not just herself. She had just sat down on the sofa, propped up with cushions and ready to nod off when the doorbell rang, sounding loud and intrusive in an otherwise quiet house.

Anca looked at her mobile phone and her video doorbell app displayed the face of the same woman who had visited them weeks earlier. She hurriedly pulled on one of her Che Guevara t-shirts and leggings and came down running, jumping two steps at a time. She opened the door just as the visitor was about to ring the doorbell again. "PC Davies, madam. Hello again. I am here to see Mr Blenkinsop. Is he about?"

"I think he is asleep," said Anca. "Is it important? Did you want me to wake him?"

The policewoman was content to wait for Theo to wake and they agreed a time in the evening when she would return to talk to him.

When Anca told Adrienne, she frowned. "I wonder why she wants him? Perhaps it is about having to go to court to testify," she speculated. "By the way, where is my dear husband?"

"He's not upstairs. I looked in all the bedrooms. Is he not around here?"

"No! I've looked and he is not down here," said Adrienne, sitting up. The look of calmness had evaporated in an instant.

"Not in his study?" asked Anca. Adrienne shook her head.

"Perhaps he went into the garden, let me check," said Anca and leapt off her chair. She returned soon after, and added, "The back door is locked: he is not outside."

"Where could he be?" asked Adrienne anxiously. "I hope he didn't try to go for a walk on his own. Ring his mobile please Anca."

They could hear the phone ringing in one of the adjacent rooms.

"Wherever he's gone, it's without his phone," said Anca. She was concerned but put on a brave face for her friend. "Theo's too sensible to go wandering off, Adrienne. Perhaps I didn't search thoroughly upstairs. I'll go and look again."

"Wait, you don't think he went up to the second floor, do you? To the gym?" asked Adrienne, standing up.

"Stay here, Adrienne, let me go and find out quickly," said Anca.

A minute or so later, Anca called down that she had found him and was helping him to walk back down the stairs.

"Flint! Don't do this to me," said Adrienne, hugging him tightly causing him to feel pain and pull her off him. "Where did you hide yourself?"

"I found him in the gym!" Anca giggled. "But don't get upset he was just lying down with Philip."

"Flint, why did you go up on your own so high? You have never been up there on your own. That was very…" before she could finish what she was going to say, Theo kissed her.

"Kiffy, I am fine. But I do have a headache so please don't add to it and also, I am hungry," he said. He took her hand and added, "Let's go to the kitchen, I fancy the best gift England gave to the world after Winston Churchill, Maggie Thatcher, fish and chips and tea."

"And what's that, Flint? English Breakfast? It's evening, Flint."

"That comes close but the next best thing is not that, it is." He paused and looking at Anca added, "do you want to tell her?"

"Cheese and Branston pickle sandwich!" she said, giggling. "I'll get right on to it."

"Nothing you French have invented, not croissants, not crepes, not tapenades, nor saucisson, even remotely comes close, Kiffy!" he teased.

"Hmm!" said Adrienne and then called to Anca, "can I have one too, please Anca?"

Theo squeezed her hand and smiled as they walked together to the kitchen where Anca was preparing the sandwiches.

"Shopping makes me hungry, too," she said.

Adrienne cut up slices of avocadoes, dressing them with pepper and lemon juice and then putting shavings of smoked salmon alongside them in a platter.

"Voila," she said, setting it out on the table, catching Theo's eye and blowing him a kiss. Despite the pain in the stomach and across his chest from over-exerting himself, Theo felt happy, sitting on a stool with the two people he most cared about. It was very comforting and he felt a lump in his throat which he disguised by taking a glass of water to his lips.

'A few millimetres either way, less than the width of the nail on my little finger and I might not be here,' he told himself, as he took another slug of water.

They were about to start eating when the doorbell rang again. Adrienne looked at her watch.

"She's back," said Anca. "We forgot about her."

"Who's back?" asked Theo.

"The policewoman. She came to see you but you were asleep and we told her to come back later," said Adrienne, as Anca went to answer the door.

Anca had shown PC Davies into the hall and asked her to wait there.

"She wants to talk to you in private, Theo," Anca reported. "Shall I show how her into the front living room?"

Theo looked at Adrienne for an explanation but she shrugged ignorance. He walked into the living room and PC Davies rose to shake hands.

"What's this all about officer?" he asked, as he carefully sat down.

The policewoman waited until Anca had left the room and closed the door behind her before taking out her notebook. She proceeded to outline the purpose of her friendly visit and then proceeded to ask him a number of pointed questions reading from her notes. Not surprisingly, they were all related to his attack and subsequent events thereafter. He answered as best he could and was surprised at the forthright tone in her voice. He was irritated by it but to all intents and purposes he was the personification of calmness and that, in turn, seemed to get to her and her questioning started to become more insistent, bordering on hostility.

"Officer Davies, may I ask you a question?" he said innocently.

"Yes, of course, please go ahead," she replied.

"May I ask why are you being aggressive?"

That seemed to throw her and she seemed flustered. "I am not."

"You may not be intentionally but you are being aggressive. Let me remind you that communication is not what you say but how it is received. Any reasonable person listening in would conclude that you are being aggressive towards a victim of a serious crime."

"I apologise if that is how I came across," she said, reddening with embarrassment.

"Have I given you any cause to be aggressive towards me, officer?"

"No, Mr Blenkinsop, you haven't."

"And, for the avoidance of doubt, do you accept that I have answered all your questions without fail?"

"Yes, you have!"

"And do you have any doubts as to the veracity of my answers?"

"None, whatsoever, it's just that…"

"Then I have fully cooperated with your enquiry, have I not?"

"Yes, you have Mr Blenkinsop!"

"Is there anything else you wish to ask me, Officer Davies?" he said, standing up.

"No, that's it, thank you. And I apologise for taking up your time and if I came across too strong earlier," she said, taking the hand that he offered in a handshake.

"What was that all about?" asked Adrienne, after he let the policewoman out.

"I won't have to go to court," said Theo.

"Oh? Why is that? *Habeus corpus* and all that?" asked Adrienne.

"There will not need to be a court case, Kiffy. PC Davies informed me that my assailant has gone to meet his maker," he said calmly.

"Oh my God! Really!"

"Yes. Committed suicide whilst in prison on remand, awaiting trial."

"So, he will not get his rightful reckoning!" said Adrienne.

"*Mors ultima ratio*," said Theo flatly. "Death is the final reckoning, Kiffy."

"You were talking for a long time," Anca noted.

Theo looked at her. "Very observant Anca. PC Davies wanted to ask if I may have had knowledge of the circumstances in which he killed himself," he said. "Of course that is absurd and she was just doing her duty asking me questions. Now let me eat, I am truly starving."

As he munched on his cheese and pickle sandwich, he recalled the comment Annie had made, as they'd said their goodbyes to each other: '*Don't worry, the fucker will not be in a state to come after you*'. He had not volunteered that information to PC Davies and it chilled him to wonder whether the assailant, Annie's ex-husband, may have had help in his demise.

A New Birth

Theo was having his morning coffee in the study. Even though Mr Shah had said he should not lift anything heavy for three months, he had felt well enough to just fill a kettle with sufficient water to make himself a cup of coffee. Adrienne would have frowned at seeing him using instant coffee but she was still in bed asleep. Anca was out with one of her early morning fitness training clients.

As he sipped the hot liquid, Theo was consulting his online guru on the baby's development at thirty-two weeks and was surprised to learn that to all intents and purposes, it was fully formed. He then read through what to look out for in a woman in her thirty-second week of pregnancy and made notes. He told himself that he would not interrogate Adrienne but observe any serious changes such as dizziness.

'Right, let's get back to work,' he told himself and launched Skype, so he could catch up with the regular partners' meeting. It was all smiles and friendly banter but whilst appreciating all the well-wishing and bonhomie, he was under no illusion as to his status. If he had not landed the huge contract in Abu Dhabi, they might have been less kindly disposed towards his enforced convalescence. Money talks and in lining their pockets with their share of that business, he was keeping the vultures of corporate law at bay.

As to his own health, he was still feeling weak and tired, particularly climbing stairs. His GP referred him back to Mr Shah for some tests. She suspected that he might have contracted a minor infection. The blood tests she had commissioned had shown nothing abnormal other than his blood counts were low, indicating the possibility of anaemia. It was nothing to be concerned about she said to assure him but there was merit in getting it checked out. The appointment had been made for the week after Mr Shah got back from his holiday.

Adrienne wandered into the study with a bowl of blueberries and yoghurt. With her belly heavily distended, she looked distinctly uncomfortable.

"Wish this baby would come out soon, I am getting fed up," she said. "I feel horrible, Flint. Look what you've done to my body!"

Theo laughed. "I seem to recall you had a hand in that. In fact, if memory serves me well, it was your idea in the first place."

Adrienne giggled. "I seduced you, didn't I!"

"You most certainly did."

"In the arms of a woman, the British Empire came crashing down. See Flint, we French prefer to use our charms to win not guns!"

"And you most certainly did that, not to mention the use of other devices to achieve your goal," he teased.

"What do you mean, Flint?"

"Like cunning."

"Oh that," she shrugged.

"Deception."

Adrienne wrinkled her nose.

"Guile."

"So?"

"Underhandedness!"

"You complaining, Flint?" she said.

"No, not at all!" he said, smiling. "That is part of the allure, being seduced and hoodwinked by my own French goddess."

"And you still love me."

"I'll let you know when I stop being smitten," he said and bent down to kiss her.

"And you know I love you with all my heart and I am so happy you are getting better, my darling. That really scared me," she said and her eyes welled up. "I so want to make love to you right now, Flint. But with this baby and your stomach we can't do anything."

"'Fraid not yet, Kiffy. I can sort of lean down after a fashion but not sure how to with the bump in the way. Also, it would feel a bit weird putting my head down there."

"What do you mean? What's weird?"

"You know, putting my head, virtually right next to my daughter's head. My research tells me that the baby's head is probably engaged by now which means it is already upside down and its head is right there. It would be weird to put my head there too."

"Don't be crazy, Flint. Of course it would be okay."

Theo was adamant. To divert her, he started to kiss her and let his hand wander downwards until he had found her sensitive spot and that seemed to appease her, rocking back and forth on his fingers until she had reached her peak.

"I always thought women went off sex during pregnancy but I know beyond a shadow of doubt that it is not the case," he said.

"Who told you that? My sexuality has been heightened. I feel I want it even more than before," said Adrienne.

"Yes, I know, you've worn me out!" he joked.

"Not complaining are you, Flint?"

"No, not at all."

As Adrienne pulled him closer to her and started to fumble at his trouser belt, Theo stopped her. "Err, I am okay for now, maybe later."

"Not like you to turn me down, Flint," said Adrienne. "Are you in pain?"

Theo sat on his swivel armchair and wheeled it round until he was facing her.

"Kiffy, I keep meaning to bring up the subject but what with one thing or another I have not got around to it, yet. The subject is names," he said.

"Names? As in our baby's name?"

"Yes. If you recall, when I was out in Abu Dhabi in your call to me, you intimated that you had picked out some names already. It slipped my mind to ask you what these were. In all honesty, I am glad that you did as I would not know where to begin. And, since you are doing nearly all the hard work bringing this baby into the world, it is right and proper and I am sure you will not object, that you get to choose the baby's names." Adrienne chuckled.

"So kind of you, Flint!"

"My only stipulation is that I have got to like the names or to be more accurate, not dislike them. So, without further ado as they say, I would be very pleased to hear what they are. You have chosen names, have you not, Kiffy? Or was that just a tease?" Adrienne grinned.

"Not a tease, Flint. I have chosen beautiful names for our daughter."

"Let me speculate, French?" he said, jokingly.

"French and English, Flint," she said, choosing not to elaborate, savouring the moment.

"And?"

"In keeping with the Blenkinsop tradition, she will have more than one name," she said.

"And?"

"The names I have given her are Eloise Beatrix Madeleine. I have always loved the name Eloise and I promised myself if I have a girl child, that is the name I would give her. Her second name is to honour your mother, who I love and who brought you into this world for me to capture!"

"And that you did," he joked. "And the third name, Madeleine?"

"My grandmother, my mother's mother who brought me up when my mother was too busy helping my father build up the farm."

"Great names, Kiffy. I salute your choice. My mother will be over the moon that you chose her name. But what about your mother, will she not be hurt that you did not choose her name?"

"Cecile? I don't like that name at all," she replied.

"Eloise? I like that name," he said. "Bit of a mouthful for a baby. Is there a shortened version we can use?"

"Ellie. When she is growing up, and between us, she will be called Ellie. When she is out there, setting the world to rights as a lawyer she will be Ms Eloise Blenkinsop!"

"So, she is going to be a lawyer, is she?" he laughed.

"Yes. But not a money-grabbing, corporate lawyer like you, Flint. No offence my darling but I want her to make a contribution to the world. She can start off in a corporation but I want her to work for human rights, to work for justice."

"No money in that, Kiffy. The reason we have such a great lifestyle is not obtained by setting the world to rights. But let's see. She may decide law is not for her and go and become an eye surgeon, work for the civil service or, heaven forbid, become a teacher!" They laughed about it and Adrienne took his hand in hers and he kissed it.

"In two months' time, we get to meet Miss Eloise Beatrix Madeleine Blenkinsop," he said, nodding to himself.

"Excited, Flint? You are going to be a papa."

"It does feel surreal. I never thought at my age I would be contemplating parenthood."

"Flint, I know you and I am one hundred percent certain you will be a good father," she assured him.

A week later, Theo was sitting in the so-called VIP room, sipping on a cup of Earl Grey and reading an old copy of Country Life whilst waiting for the results of his MRI scan to come through. He looked up to see Anca was rummaging through all the different biscuits on offer, to accompany her hot chocolate drink. Looking at some of the properties in the verdant pastures of the Home Counties it reminded him of what he was giving up, at least in the short-term to fulfil his dream of living in the Middle East. In moments of contemplation: when he considered the upheaval, when he thought about taking his wife to live thousands of miles away, in a world she knew little about, when he thought about the challenge of raising a new-born child in a hot and harsh climate, it all seemed madness. Yet, as he thumbed through the magazine, the dream was as real and vivid today as it ever was over twenty-five years earlier, when he was there as a wet-behind-the-ears, young man with adventure and fire in his belly.

"Mr Blenkinsop? Follow me please, Mr Shah is ready for you," said the nurse, holding the door open for him. Anca smiled to him reassuringly as he left her behind.

After they shook hands, Theo sat adjacent to Mr Shah who was busy clicking on the MRI images as he talked.

"I'm just going to show you the images we took of you today, Mr Blenkinsop. The good news is that all the patchwork we undertook is healing nicely. As far as we can tell, everything should be back to normal. Your heart is fine, no leaks, the stitching has held. The spleen is also looking very healthy. Your ribs have healed. Other than a few nicks where the blade touched them, they are completely healed."

"Great but I fear there is a 'but' coming."

Mr Shah looked at him directly. "There is one thing though that has emerged that needs attention. Let me put up the MRI image that shows it off to best effect."

Having flashed up the image on the screen, he explained what the problem was. “Can I just stop you there, Mr Shah? I can barely see what you mean. Are you telling me that the very faint dark line is an indication that I have a hole in my intestine?”

“Not a hole as such Mr Blenkinsop, more of a very minor cut where the edge of the knife must have caught it. It is very tiny but it is oozing blood into your colon. It explains why your iron levels are still low so many weeks after your operation.”

“So, are you going to glue it back?” he said, facetiously.

“Pretty much, although more like fuse it using a new electrical method,” said Mr Shah and then explained the procedure and the risks involved.

When he was back in the car, Anca asked him if everything was okay. He looked across at her and pulled a face. “It looks like I need to go back in.”

“Sorry to hear that Theo. For how long?” she said, reaching for his hand and squeezing it.

“Not long. They’ll be using key-hole surgery which is quicker apparently. Mr Shah is trying to find a slot for next week.”

“How long will they keep you in?”

“Not sure, should be quick then I’ll be up and about well in time for when the baby is due,” he said, as much to reassure himself as anything else.

“You know it is going to scare Adrienne when you tell her.”

Theo nodded and Anca ran her hand over his. “Don’t worry Theo, I’ll look after her.”

Just as they arrived back home, he received a text from Mr Shah’s secretary that he could be fitted in on a Saturday morning in a week’s time and she would be sending him the details of the arrangements in the post.

“I can take a cab there, Anca. No need for you to take me. Better if you stayed with her highness.”

Anca smiled.

When they opened the front door and entered, they could hear rattling and shouting coming from the kitchen and they looked at each other.

“I’m not sure if that is the sound of cooking food or cooking up a storm," said Theo. "Either way, I think I'll disappear into my study. Prefer to be unobtrusive for the time being."

"Theo, how can a man who tackled a knifeman so bravely, act so scared in front of his wife?" Anca laughed.

"That was different. I didn't have to listen to him!"

Calm returned to the house after Anca had helped restore the kitchen back to what it was, picking up and scrubbing off the remnants of Adrienne's first attempt to make a curry.

"I was hungry and wanted to try something different," she said, as they sat down to a meal of grilled fish and vegetables. "I wanted to surprise you, Flint."

"You certainly did that. I could hear your surprise from the moment we walked into the house," he teased. "And I could smell it too! But nice try, Kiffy. We might have to re-paint the wall around the stove with all the turmeric that seems to have spewed onto it." Anca tried to suppress a giggle.

"Flint, you brute! Your poor, heavily-pregnant wife tries to cook you a meal and what do you do? Laugh in my face! Not nice," she pouted.

"I'm not laughing, I just prefer to see my dinner on a plate, not on the wall, or all over the sides and on the kitchen floor!"

Adrienne was about to answer him back in no uncertain terms and Theo was prepared to be on the receiving end of her Gallic temper when instead, she burst out laughing. "It was funny, wasn't it? It looked like someone had planted a bomb in the kitchen. Not my fault, this baby is impatient to come out and kept kicking me so I lost concentration and maybe missed a few steps in the recipe."

After the laughter had died down and the plates were cleared away, Anca left the house to meet up with her friend Lenka in a local pub, taking the Micra with her with a promise not to drink.

Adrienne and Theo were alone, each on their own sofa, stretched out and reading. Theo was going through a progress report from Abla on the office set up and on the status of the accommodation they had signed up for. It seemed to be going fine and on schedule for the office to be active by the first week of January. Their accommodation, including the furniture that Adrienne had ordered had arrived. Workmen had delivered it and it was already in each of the rooms as per her instructions.

Theo smiled. He was pleased that despite his mishap, the plan remained on schedule. He started to type out a response when out of the corner of his eye he caught Adrienne looking in his direction.

"You all right, Kiffy?"

"Just thinking, Flint," she mused.

"Anything you care to share?"

"Just thinking how lucky I am to have you, Englishman," she smiled. "Even though you were obnoxious to me, there was some connection that was impossible for me to ignore. Now we are married and expecting our first child. Thank you, Flint."

"For what?"

"Being you."

"For being obnoxious to you?"

"Not anymore, only then."

"And cold towards you?"

"Maybe still a little but you can't help that, it is in your genes. All middle-class English people are like that," she said, ribbing him.

"And I am delighted my little French siren ensnared me," he joked. "Not a dull moment that's for sure!"

"And the best sex you ever had!"

"That too."

They laughed together and she shifted herself off the sofa with effort and waddled over to him and moved his legs so she could sit next to him.

"You know, you haven't asked me about my birth plan, Flint," she said.

"There is a plan for how to give birth? Surely all you do is push and then you do a lot of shouting with a few colourful epithets, probably in French, culminating in a crescendo of expletives and then you squirt the baby out and this blood and muck-covered little creature emerges, is unceremoniously held up by the midwife, screams its little head off and they hand it to you and say 'well done'? Is there more than that?" he joked.

"Flint! You have no idea! You have to consider everything," she said. "Like what position you want to do it in."

"There is more than one? So, it's like sex, is it? You can choose to have missionary, rear entry or in this case rear exit, sitting up, cowgirl style, even on your side? Hmm, it would be somewhat poetic if the position Eloise pops out in, is also the position she was conceived in. Do you know what position we were doing it when it happened, Kiffy?"

"Don't be silly, Flint! Birthing position is important. I haven't made up my mind but I was thinking of either sitting up or kneeling. It is supposed to make it easier, less stress on the spine," she explained.

"Really? Perhaps you should watch some of those David Attenborough documentaries to help you decide," he suggested, frivolously.

"How will that help? I don't see the connection, Flint."

"Well, they show you how nature does it. Some animals do it lying down, others standing up. You never know, might give you some ideas."

Adrienne giggled. "If I have it standing up, you will need to be there underneath ready to catch her, Flint. We don't want her bumping her head as her first introduction to this world."

"Hmm, maybe rule out the standing up position. At the end of the day, Kiffy, five million years of human existence has probably worked out the optimum position and billions of women around the world don't get the choice, so I wouldn't get too stressed about it. If it was about risk mitigation, then maybe ask the midwives who will be attending you what is their preference, what it is they are most used to."

"Actually, I was thinking of something completely different altogether, Flint," she said.

"Oh, you are? Let me guess, you're going to get someone else to do it for you? Have you asked Anca?"

"Flint! I'm trying to be serious and you are making fun of me."

"Sorry, I didn't realise that there was more to it than just letting nature take its course. So what is this other way of giving birth you are considering?"

"A C-sect."

"Pardon?"

"Caesarean."

"I have heard of the term but you'll have to pardon my ignorance, what exactly is a caesarean birthing method."

"Instead of giving birth naturally, they cut it out."

"What! That sounds horrendous, how do they do that?" he asked, with images of the sort of knife that he had been stabbed with coming to the fore.

"I'm not sure of all the details, I'm still reading up about it. I think when the baby is due, I go into hospital and they make an incision down below, exactly where I don't know and then they take the baby out."

"Sounds really painful. Are you sure you want to do that, Kiffy?"

"Flint, I've been told that it is not painful at all. If anything, I won't feel a thing as they numb me with pain killers."

"Kiffy, if they numb you with painkillers might that be transmitted through your bloodstream into the baby's? Might it be dangerous for the baby?"

"Not sure but good question, Flint. I will talk to the midwife about it."

"And what is the supposed advantage of this over normal childbirth? I get that you will be on painkillers but will you not miss out on the very joy of bringing the child into this world; this creature that you have been carrying all these months? If you are numb from the pain killers will you even be awake or able to hold her?"

"All good points, Flint and I will find out about it."

"Thank you!" he said, relieved. "I've had enough of knives recently, I'd rather not see you cut up too, Kiffy."

"It is better for you, Flint, if you think about it."

"You being carved open is better for me? How so?" he said, through furrowed eyebrows.

"Better for sex. Just imagine the baby's head and body has to come out of that small opening. Imagine how much that is going to stretch my vagina and from what I've read, some women even tear down there."

"Ouch!"

"And what if I don't return to normal? You might not like to have sex with me anymore. You will be chasing all those Arab women instead."

"Hmm, I see your point. Still, your welfare trumps any impact on my, our sex life, don't you think? It is, of course, your decision Kiffy but in my view, surgery, when you have a tried and tested method with mother nature's blessing available, should be a last resort. If it was a choice between natural birth and surgery, for the sake of our sex life, I vote for natural birth."

"I love you even more for saying that Flint," she said, her eyes welling up.

When the post arrived a day later, Anca was not about, being in the gym with Theo working on his rehabilitation and Adrienne decided to get it herself, hoping it would include a response from the hospital. She was waiting to hear from Queen Charlotte's Hospital as to whether she had secured a private room that she had requested to recover in, after the birth of the baby. Aside from all the junk mail, there were two large envelopes and she took these with her to the kitchen. Looking on the reverse of the first, she was pleased to see that it was from Queen Charlotte's Hospital and she broke open the seal to find an information pack inside. Adrienne grinned when she read that she had indeed been successful in securing a private bedroom in the Lindo Wing and that she had been allocated this room for five days, after which she was expected to go home.

"Eloise, my little one, you will be born in the same hospital as your papa," she said softly.

She got up to tell Theo the good news when she dropped the other envelope. On bending to pick it up, she saw it was addressed to Theo, and on the reverse it indicated it was from Epsom Hospital. The letter had been marked 'Private and Confidential' and although she was very curious as to its contents, she could not bring herself round to opening it. She opted for the next best thing which was to walk up the two flights of stairs and take it to Theo. In concentrating on herself and giving birth, she felt guilty for not asking about his medical appointment and she was going to put that right there and then, apologising to him for her thoughtlessness.

When she entered the gym, Theo was lying on his back with his leg up, pressed against Anca's thigh. She was standing over him, gently pushing his leg further towards him, getting him to stretch.

"Is that a new sex position I can see?" Adrienne said smiling.

"Just giving his hamstrings a stretch," Anca explained. "They are very tight from the lack of use recently."

As she bent over to lower his leg back down gently, Adrienne could see that beneath her t-shirt Anca was bra-less and she could see that Theo had noticed it too.

"Theo, stop staring at her breasts!" she giggled.

"It's part of my exercise routine. Doctor said I need to make sure I can see properly," he joked.

Anca laughed. "You two are so funny," she said and helped Theo to get back on his feet. "I'm going to go and take a shower now and leave you two in peace."

"Speaking of doctors, Flint, I am really sorry. I have been so pre-occupied about getting ready for birth I forgot to ask you about your appointment. How did it go?"

Theo shrugged. "Nothing to worry about."

"This came for you," she said and handed him the big envelope.

Theo took it and put it under his arm and headed for the door. "I need a shower too, I'll read it later."

"Why not read it now?" she asked, suspiciously.

"No need. You know what they say, 'good news can wait' and all that," he replied. As he attempted to walk past her, Adrienne took the envelope from under his arm.

"Open it Flint. If you don't, I will."

Theo looked at her and said, "I know what it is about. I have to go in for a little procedure."

Try as she might, as Theo explained what needed to be done, Adrienne could not hold back the tears.

"That bastard may have died but his victim is still hurting. Even from the grave, he is hurting his victim. I hate him, I hate him," she sobbed, as Theo hugged her.

"It will be fine, Kiffy. And I am here standing, am I not? I'm on the mend and in a few weeks' time I will be holding Eloise on my lap and all this will be forgotten about."

"I'm not sure she is going to wait that long, Flint. I am getting these weird contractions. I'm not sure if it means she is on her way or just my body practicing; I am going to see the midwife tomorrow. Oh, and by the way, I have my bed. Queen Charlotte's confirmed it today."

"Great news. All looking good, Kiffy. And you do look so sexy as you are. And I was going to suggest that you could jump in the shower with me? I'll soap your back and you can soap my…" he said, looking down as he kissed her.

"That would be fun but I am worried about slipping in the shower with both of us in it. Me, with my big belly in the way and you held together with glue and still having problems with your stomach. I don't want to take the risk of hurting you. Not a good idea for us to be showering together until after the baby is born and you get better. Anca will help you."

"Help me to wash?"

"Yes, Flint. Soap you down. And if you want and if she is willing, anything else too!"

"What do you mean by anything else, Kiffy?"

"You want to fuck her, Flint?" she whispered.

Theo was silent. 'Whatever I say will be the wrong answer so best say nothing. As someone once noted, you can never be misquoted if you do not say anything,' he said to himself.

"It's okay, Flint. I give you permission," she said.

"Not that again. Why? What has brought this on all of a sudden. I thought we had consigned that to the past?"

"Because I know you want to and I know she wants to and I love both of you. And I would rather you did it with me knowing about it rather than doing it behind my back."

"You and I can still do it, Kiffy. Okay, I agree not in the shower but you know, practice your birth position, from behind, like two animals on heat," he joked. "You've always liked it from behind."

"True and I do want to," she hesitated and then added, "but I want to watch you do it even more."

"With Anca? She may not like to be watched."

"We've talked about it already and she likes the idea of doing it as much as I do."

"Not one to turn down such an offer, Kiffy, but how about after the baby is born when you are back to normal and I have fully recovered? That would be better all round, would it not?" he suggested.

"Maybe," she shrugged. "On the other hand, it could be more fun watching you now with my super sensitive hormones. Who knows, after I give birth I may be worn out. I may suffer from post-natal depression, I may not even like sex, God forbid. I have read about these things and who knows, what is that English phrase? 'Strike whilst the iron is hot'." Theo laughed.

"And I can see your iron is getting hot, Flint," she giggled, as she helped him to take his t-shirt and shorts off.

"You know I can probably manage by myself in the shower," he said.

"No, Flint. I have been in there with you every day since you came home and it may be still a little too early to be on your own. I'm too scared to let you go in the shower on your own, with nothing to grab on to. I'll call Anca to come."

Theo turned the shower on and when the blue light stopped flashing, he stuck out a tentative foot. It was a walk-in shower, tiled ahead and to his right with a huge, floor-to-ceiling glass screen to his left. Ordinarily, he would have marched straight in and not given it a second thought. But now, with Adrienne nor Anca being there with him, he felt vulnerable. There was nothing to hold on to once he stepped into the shower and he was only too conscious of the possible effect on his healing scars and his still yet to be repaired, internal wound, in the event that he slipped. Until now, he hadn't really thought about how much he had relied on Adrienne being with him in the shower, ready to offer an arm that he could reach out for, or at least get help for him. But she was right, why take a chance? The last thing he wanted was to add to the repair work that Mr Shah was shortly to undertake. He stayed by the edge of the shower where he could at least hold on to the edge of the glass screen and decided he would wait for Anca.

He heard chuckling outside and then Adrienne entered with Anca both smiling.

"Poor baby, standing there waiting for us," Adrienne teased. "Well, the wait is over, Flint, Anca is here to help you. I will leave you to it. I shall be in the bedroom when you are a clean boy," she laughed and left.

Theo switched the shower back on once again and was about to enter when Anca took his hand. "Just a second, Theo," she said and then removed her towel. "Right, let's get you in."

He clung on to Anca as the water cascaded down on him until he had reached the shower head wall and he could hold on to the second, hand held shower.

"Not so bad, after all," he said, through the sound of the rushing water as he looked at the wall. He had wanted to turn around so he could admire her naked form but he was scared of letting go. There was also another reason he was uncomfortable at the idea of seeing Anca. He knew it was absurd; after all, they had spent a night together in Abu Dhabi but that was that and in his own house nothing of the sort had ever happened. It was as if it was okay to do it over there, out of sight and well away but never here and it was disconcerting.

When Anca started to gently wash him, her first touch made him jump slightly and he clung on to the up and down pole of the hand-held shower like it was a life raft. But that soon changed as her warm hands, lubricated by the lather of the shower gel, made their way over and around his back. And then it happened, the touch of her body against his. It seemed that it could have been accidental that first time but it happened again and again and it was having the desired effect as it was arousing him. Even though he was facing away from her, he knew that she knew what was happening to him. Anca started to press herself against him. Her breasts touching his back.

"Relax," she said but he could not hear her above the rush of the steaming water. All he could discern was the touch of her body against his.

Theo could stand it no more and turned around. Anca could see his excitement and smiled and she closed the space between them feeling him against her.

"I love you," she said but her voice was lost in the jets of water that rained down on them.

Adrienne and Anca had left for the hospital after the morning rush hour and Theo was delighted to have his personal time to do as he pleased. Working from home was not something he cared too much for and even if they were only going to be away for a few hours, as far as he was concerned it was a welcome respite. He was under strict instructions not to do anything too physical.

"No chance of that," he had responded, as they left. Instead, he occupied himself with his favourite pastime: legal matters. He had reviewed a paper that had been sent to him, made a few tracked changes and emailed the document back to his office. Nicola had sent him a sweet email wishing him a speedy recovery and a little personal message that was disguised as being on behalf of the team to say that he had been missed. It made him smile. Most of the morning was taken up with reviewing papers and answering and sending emails, including a dialogue with Abla, going through progress on the preparations for establishing the office. He had not moved for a while and he felt thirsty and cold.

"What do you think Philip? About time we had a drink," he said, stroking his cat who was perched serenely on the printer next to his table, looking down on his master.

Taking his empty coffee cup with him and Philip following his every movement with just the slightest movement of his head, Theo padded to the kitchen. He was about to lift up the kettle and fill it with water when he remembered Mr Shah's words and instead filled two cups of water and poured then into it.

"More than one way of skinning a cat," he said, smugly.

The kitchen was vast and with porcelain tiles on the floor and ceramic tiles on all the walls, the room felt cold. The heating had gone off and he would have liked it on but he realised that he did not know how to override the timer and he didn't want to switch it off altogether for when the girls came back home.

'Oh well, just need to put on another jumper,' he told himself, then changed his mind once he realised that he would have to walk up the stairs to get one. "Good exercise it might be Anca but I just don't feel like traipsing up those stairs until I have to," he muttered. The water had just boiled and he was figuring how to pour the hot water into his cup without lifting the kettle up when a WhatsApp message came through. It was from Anca with an update.

"Keeping Adrienne in for tonight. Not to worry just for observation. Can you bring her nightie? xx."

When Theo put his mobile phone down, the first thing that came to mind was if there was nothing to worry about then why the need to keep her in.

'Not to worry? Observation?' he asked himself. 'There must be something. Could it be the baby is stressed? Could it be Kiffy? Could even be both. Whatever it is, it is not nothing. But no time to cogitate on what it might be, need to hot-foot it out of here.'

He would have liked to run up the stairs, but his current health meant he had to take it slowly and methodically, holding on to the banister. "Last thing we need is to rush and slip and end up in hospital too," he muttered.

At the top of the stairs, he stopped to catch his breath. Walking slowly had enabled him to think ahead and plan what he needed to do. "Nightie, maybe the black one and she will need socks, as she's always complaining her feet are cold. And taxi. I'm not fit to drive so I need a taxi. And the hospital, Queen Charlotte's. Not exactly down the road and in the traffic, it could easily take an hour. I'd better take some pain killers with me just in case. Also, a bottle of water for Kiffy, she will not like hospital water. Should I take some fruit too? See what we have in the fridge."

Cutting across west London in the afternoon it was almost a certainty that progress would be slow and they hit traffic. The cab driver was none-too-pleased as it was holding up his next job. It took the best part of two hours from when he took the message before Theo gingerly stepped out from the taxi at the entrance to Queen Charlotte's.

'Good to see you once again. Last time I was here, I was flat on my back,' he mused. Walking down the quiet corridor of the Lindo Wing he thought he recognised the chatter and giggles ahead. 'A good bet if I follow the noise, I will get to Kiffy!' he told himself, smiling at the nurses going to and fro effortlessly, whilst every step he took was slow and ponderous, measured and heel to toe as Anca had instructed him to do so as to build up his core muscles.

"At this rate of progress, I shall also need a bed for the night myself," he muttered.

A nurse smiled at him and seeing his laboured walking, asked him if he was all right and offered him a seat to take a breather. The last few yards seem to take a lifetime to get there but eventually, he was standing in the open doorway of a private room and the love of his life was already in bed and chatting away merrily to Anca, who had her back turned to him.

"Flint! You're here," said Adrienne, smiling sweetly. "You found me then?"

"Well, if the person I am looking at is not you, I am in serious trouble as there is someone who looks remarkably like you," he joked, as he entered the room. "How are you, Kiffy? Come to check out your private room I see."

Theo leant over and kissed her, eliciting arms around his neck. "The nipper giving you trouble?"

"The nipper? Oh, you mean the baby. Yes. Seems like she is in a hurry to see what the world looks like. Those contractions I was feeling, they weren't my imagination, they were real. Midwife would prefer if baby stayed inside a bit longer so being here is to see how it goes. Nice, calm environment. Less stressful they say."

"Hmm, the implication being life at home is stressful, is it?"

"Yes, it is, Flint! You stress me out. If you're not planning on dragging me to the other side of the world, you're getting yourself stabbed," she said giggling. "I should have married a Frenchman. Not really my darling, wouldn't swap you. Not for all the tea in China."

"I've never really understood that phrase, I always understood that most tea is produced in India. Anyway, glad to see you are in high spirits, Kiffy."

"It's because I have my dearest friend keeping me company," she said, looking at Anca and squeezing her hand. "This girl has been brilliant for me, Flint. You look after her whilst I am in here."

"Currently, even looking after myself is challenging enough, let alone anyone else. I had to cab it here as I am not deemed to be fit to drive."

"That reminds me, did you remember to bring my nightie, Flint?"

Theo proudly handed over a hessian bag. "Yes, and other goodies you might need," he said.

"You walked through the ward carrying my things in a carrier bag?" she asked, incredulously holding it up with disgust.

"I'm not sure I understand, Kiffy," he frowned. "What is the problem with doing that?"

Anca giggled. "At least it's from Waitrose and not Tesco's. Adrienne," she said.

"And it is made of hessian and not plastic so you can show off your eco-friendly credentials, Kiffy," he teased.

"Flint, when you were in hospital what did I bring for you?" asked

Adrienne.

Theo shrugged his shoulders and held his arms out. "I can't say I noticed," he confessed. "Anyway, Miss shopping snob, I brought you something which you never asked for but I know you will want."

Adrienne felt something hard and pulled it out. "The Hound of the Baskervilles," she said, reading the title. "You brought me a murder mystery?"

"A classic English story set in classic English countryside, written by Sir Arthur Conan Doyle, an English gentleman and with the main character being the world's most famous detective who is…" he said, turning to Anca.

"Sherlock Holmes!" she said laughing.

"Spot on, Anca. Sherlock Holmes — the best detective in the world and he is English," he said. "Oh, and he has a stiff upper lip too, Kiffy."

"No, he hasn't. He smokes a pipe. If he had a stiff upper lip, the pipe would fall out of his mouth," she joked.

"Anyway, if baby is distracting you, or if like me you find the room is too hot, then have a good read, the story will chill you to the bones!"

"Actually, I find my bed is cold, Flint. My feet are freezing!"

"Well, look no further than that carrier bag you turned your nose up at for a solution to your problem."

Adrienne rummaged and pulled out the socks.

"My alpaca, woolly, walking socks! You know me, Englishman. Flint that was really thoughtful. Thank you, my darling."

"I think he deserves another kiss for that, don't you think?" said Anca. Adrienne gestured for him to stand up and approach.

"Can we do it later, Kiffy? I've just sat down and I'm feeling a bit weary."

"Anca, you give him a kiss on my behalf," said Adrienne.

Anca blushed and walked around the bed and pecked his cheek. "Very thoughtful, Theo."

When visiting time was over, Theo and Anca walked together back to the car park, arms locked. For Theo, it was a relief that he had the assurance that if he was to slip or trip, she'd be there by his side and rescue him. For Anca, it was the enjoyment and intimacy of having him close by.

The following day, Anca went to the hospital on her own, Adrienne insisting that it was too tiring for Theo to make the long journey. After getting an update from the midwife attending Adrienne, Anca phoned Theo to say that she had had a bad night with irregular contractions coming and going and they wanted to keep her in longer. Adrienne was exhausted and was sleeping.

"Did they say if the baby is likely to pop out at any moment?" he asked.

"The senior midwife says there is a possibility that by Sunday, Eloise might come out but they are hoping it will be a little longer to give her more time to develop. 'More time in the womb means less time in an incubator', is what one of them said."

"And how is Kiffy, health wise? What did they say about that?"

"They said she is doing well, very chatty and starting to boss them around a bit; you know what she is like."

Theo smiled to himself. "At least she is all right." He sighed. "Being in a relationship with someone is really tough on one's nerves. Forgotten what it was like!"

On her return, he could see that Anca was tired from the driving and he offered for them to have either a takeaway or if she was minded to, they could eat out in a local restaurant. However tired Anca was, she could not pass up the chance of going out with Theo and she said she wanted to eat out but that the choice was his. He was minded on Indian, his favourite type of cuisine but knowing it was not to her liking he settled on Italian in Banstead village. He also insisted that they would go by cab as she had done a lot of driving. Anca raced up the stairs to have a shower and get changed and when she bounded down the stairs she had been transformed. Out went the ubiquitous leggings, in came a skirt that he recognised as being one of Adrienne's and she had on an elegant blouse. She had also put on some make-up and perfume.

"Wow! You look lovely," he said. "I didn't realise you had legs!"

Anca blushed and did a twirl. "Theo, you've seen me naked, how can you say that?"

"That is entirely different. I've never seen you in a skirt, except when you are going out clubbing with Lenka and I'm not sure that qualifies as a skirt or just a swimming costume," he teased. "At any rate, you look lovely."

Aside from the initial sideways looks when they entered after they had sat down and ordered, they were largely ignored, to Theo's relief as he wanted to protect Anca from any whispers regarding her status with him.

"Did you see those looks?" Anca said quietly.

"People are naturally curious. I wouldn't worry about it, Anca," he assured her.

"It's not for me I worry about, it's for you," she said and touched his hand.

"Because I am so much older than you? I could be your father or an uncle, or even a colleague."

"Or my sugar daddy?"

"Well, I am not that am I!"

Anca giggled. "I don't know, maybe you are that, Theo. You keep me in house and home, you give me a pay that is very generous, buy me clothes, I get to drive your car more than you do, and…" she paused and then lowering her voice, "you see me naked and we've had sex, maybe not all the way but we've had that too! Does all that not count as being a sugar daddy?"

"See your point. Does Adrienne then qualify as your sugar mummy as she has done all of that with you?" he laughed.

Midway through the pasta course, Theo felt his phone vibrate and he excused himself to read it as he was concerned it might be about Adrienne. He read the message and frowned.

"Is she okay?" asked Anca.

"Oh, it is not from her or about her. It is just Mr Shah's secretary. She has made me an appointment for me to see him tomorrow morning at Ashtead. He wants to see me to talk about the forthcoming procedure. I wonder why she messaged me this late. Private health for you; no rest. Probably nothing."

That night in bed, Theo could not sleep. He was restless, worried about Adrienne, worried about the baby and more than curious as to what Mr Shah had to say that needed him to attend his clinic first thing in the morning. He was tossing and turning, blowing between hot and cold. He tried to obliterate from his mind, horrible images of Adrienne writhing in pain, the baby not breathing, the midwife trying desperately to revive her, interspersed with images of the knife as it plunged into him and the look of pure venom in his assailant's eyes. It was tiring him but he was wide awake and he hauled himself up to a sitting position, reaching out for his water bottle and dropping it, the metal hitting the wooden floor making a harsh clatter in the stillness of the night. He was about to lean down to pick it up, when a shaft of light from the door distracted him. "I'll get that for you, Theo," Anca said quietly.

"I seem unable to sleep for some reason," he said, as he downed the water. "Sorry if I woke you up."

"I can't sleep, either," she said and ran her hand through his hair. "Come, let's get you back into bed."

Anca helped him back into bed. "Want me to stay?"

Theo nodded and she climbed into bed next to him and she cuddled him until he was fast asleep, his even breathing being the sedative she needed to fall asleep too.

Mr Shah was waiting for him in the VIP reception area at Ashtead Hospital and walked with him to the consultancy room he had been allocated for that day and greeted him in that same affable patient-friendly manner that had the effect of easing ones anxieties. "Mr Blenkinsop, the reason I called you in rather than do it by phone is to explain a slight change to the procedure we will be carrying out this Saturday and to give you an opportunity to ask questions."

"Change? What change is that, Mr Shah?"

"I have reviewed the scans we took and aside from the small leak which we are going to seal, I noticed two or three other dark areas which looked suspiciously like polyps. I consulted my colleagues, including an expert in imaging photography and they agree with my analysis."

"Polyps? As in bumps?"

"Yes, like that. It is tissue which has developed into small projections, like nodules. Normally, the body flushes these out and you are not aware of it. But sometimes they persist. I believe you have two or three of these and they need to be cut out. As I am going to be working in that area, it seems sensible to me to do this at the same time as plugging your little leak."

"Is that the change then, cutting these out?"

"Yes, that is the objective but the method also changes slightly. You will now be having what we call a combined endoscopic and laparoscopic procedure."

Mr Shah then explained the procedure in detail, assuring Theo that as he would be under general anaesthetic, he would not feel a thing as the endoscope entered his back passage and there would be a small cut in his belly to enable the instruments and camera to be inserted. Theo nodded that he understood the process and the risks associated and it all seemed reasonable.

"You said these polyps are tested after you cut them out Mr Shah. What are they tested for?" he asked.

"To see if they are malignant, if they are cancerous."

"And if they are?"

"You don't need to worry about that, Mr Blenkinsop. You are far too young to have cancer but we check them as a matter of precaution. Don't worry about it," said Mr Shah, putting a hand on his shoulder.

As the taxi weaved its way through the morning Epsom traffic, Theo was recalling his conversation with Mr Shah. 'Don't worry about it' he had said but until he had the operation and the results were back and deemed to be clear, he would be doing just that.

'Perhaps it was not meant to be for me to be living and working out in the Persian Gulf. Maybe my dream is just that, never to become a reality,' he said to himself.

It was Saturday morning and the day of his procedure. Taking his watch off he noticed it was seven o'clock, the sun hadn't even showed its head over the horizon. In the little room he had been afforded, Theo had stripped off and was fumbling with the hospital gown when a text came through from Anca.

"Eloise, could not wait any longer. Adrienne gave birth to her. All went well. Eloise is big; Adrienne says she has your feet. Congrats Theo, you are now officially a dad. Xxx."

In the privacy of the room, Theo clutched his phone tightly and bit his hand in trying to stop himself from crying. A nurse opened the door unceremoniously and told him off for dawdling, manhandling him until the gown was on. She collected his clothes and put them under the wheeled-bed before helping him get on it.

Mr Shah came to see him in the pre-operational room, smiling as ever, putting an assuring hand on his bed.

"I have just been informed that my wife has given birth. I am now a father, Mr Shah. Please keep me alive long enough to see my wife and daughter," he said, a tear running down the side of his face.

At 7.25 a.m., the cold anaesthetic that entered his bloodstream sent Theo into a dark and deep sleep by the time he entered the operating theatre, where a number of medical professionals waited for him behind surgical masks. When he awoke in a groggy, half-asleep half-awake state, he recognised that he was back in the High Dependency Unit and for a brief moment, his foggy mind imagined that he had dreamt the last few weeks. With a good deal of effort, he looked up to see who was opposite him but the curtain was drawn, he could not tell if Annie was still there. As much as he didn't want to know, he mustered up sufficient courage to move his hand gingerly over his abdomen in search of corroborating evidence and the moment his fingertips made contact with the edge of a bandage he pulled it back.

"Surely not," he muttered. "Did I dream all this? Where's Annie, where's the nurse?"

He was not so weak that he could not press the help button next to him if he wanted to but he was unsure as to whether he wanted to know and instead, he breathed out and willed himself to relax and fall back to sleep.

Sometime later, he didn't know when, he could hear voices talking, familiar voices but he was disinclined to open his eyes for fear of confirming that his nightmare was indeed for real and that he was still recovering from being stabbed and sliced open.

"He should be awake by now," the voice said.

"I don't want to wake him, just wondered if he got the message I sent him, about becoming a father," the other voice said.

Theo grinned. He was relieved. "He did get the message," he said smiling but not opening his eyes.

"Theo!" said Anca and rushed over to his side, bending down and kissed him. "Congratulations daddy!"

"Thank you, Anca," he said and reached up to hug her as much as the IV connections would allow him. "How is Adrienne? How is the baby?"

"Adrienne is fine. She is loving all the attention. Oh, and before I forget," she said and looked round to see if anyone was about: Mr Shah had discretely made himself scarce and there was no nurse in sight. "This is from her and a message to get well soon." Anca leaned over once again and kissed Theo deeply.

"Nice. I am not sure I got the message correct, can you repeat it?" he joked and Anca kissed him again.

"And the baby, how is she doing? I read somewhere that premature babies can have problems," asked Theo, feeling slightly anxious.

"Eloise is fine. She is breathing okay and feeding. Adrienne is proudly breast feeding her. She gets put in an incubator because the doctors say she doesn't have enough fat on her and she feels the cold more."

"Slim, like her mother," he said, smiling. "But otherwise, Eloise is fine?"

"Yes, nothing to worry about Theo, doctors are really happy with her progress," Anca assured him. "Adrienne says she is quiet, like you! Hardly cries, except when she is hungry."

"When will I get to see them?"

"Depends on who comes out of hospital first. Adrienne will need to be there for a few more days the doctors say. Mr Shah told me that your operation was a success but didn't say how long will you be staying in here."

Theo shrugged. "Supposedly with this type of surgery, recovery is quicker but I have to speak to Mr Shah. When you do see Adrienne, tell her I miss her but cannot come to the hospital. I expect I will be back at home before her."

Anca touched his arm to reassure him and stayed a little longer with him before saying she had to get back to the house and then back to Adrienne.

Before she left, Theo asked about who had been informed and was told Adrienne had told all his family and his mother was delighted that she had a grandchild named after her and suggested a christening party down in Josiah's Hall.

Later that day, he was visited by Mr Shah who went over the

operation with Theo, stating that the cut had been sealed and he had also removed five polyps but the good news was that none of them were malignant and as far as he was concerned, as soon as Theo was well enough, he could leave the hospital. Two days later, Theo did exactly that and was back home. Anca was going back and forth spending time between Adrienne and Theo, relaying messages between them. Mr Shah had strongly advised against any travel for at least a couple of weeks after he returned home, to reduce the risk of infection and to give the wounds a chance to heal properly. Theo had wanted to phone but he feared Adrienne would get too emotional and start to cry or that he might be guilty of that himself. The first few days at home, he was inclined just to sleep or sit up reading but carrying out Mr Shah's instructions, Anca encouraged him to walk a few steps each day, building up the number and duration, holding him up with her arm when he felt unsteady.

Time seemed to stand still as he waited for Adrienne's return. At first, he was counting off the hours convinced that she would be back at any moment and that he would hear the sound of the baby crying. But hours turned to days as Anca reported that a combination of Adrienne feeling weak and Eloise needing to spend a little longer in the incubator delayed her discharge. One day, two days, three days passed and they were still in the hospital. He stopped asking Anca for a report as the next day seemed to be the same as the previous day. Lethargy had set in and he was even disinclined to think about work, not even logging in to his laptop computer to check for messages and updates. He could not be bothered to read the cards of congratulations that had been sent, except for the communal one from his office and one from Abla which was sent with a box of his favourite, fresh, medjool dates. Nor did he wish to take phone calls from anyone, using recovering from an operation as a perfect excuse. He just wanted to close his eyes and not think about anyone nor anything; not about becoming a husband, nor about becoming a father and certainly wished not to be having thoughts about being knifed by a bitter husband who then killed himself. But the shiny knife already covered in Annie's blood and the look on his face lingered. The new stitches in his belly were a constant reminder and would not allow him to forget those images any time soon.

He looked at his watch and realised that he had not moved for two hours, having been engrossed in his book on the history of the Sumerians. Anca had left for the morning and as part of his exercise regime, he got up off the sofa and walked to the front of the house and then to the back, with Philip watching his every step. When Theo reached the kitchen, he ran ahead of his master in expectation that he would be fed. And in case the message didn't get through, he tapped the cupboard where he knew his food was kept with a stretch of his paw.

"Ah, Philip, a man of few words but still speaking volumes. A man after my own heart. Okay old chap, be patient and this human old man will do your bidding," said Theo, as he bent down to pick up the cat's bowl. As he took it to the sink to wash out, he felt the stitches pulling. He lifted up his t-shirt but was pleased to find that there were no new spots of blood.

"Cat fed, two hundred and fifty steps completed and coffee made. Enough physical activity for this morning. Time to get back to the Sumerians and a bit of rest and relaxation," he said aloud, as he sauntered into the living room, coffee in hand. He had barely lowered himself back into the sumptuous leather sofa when he closed his eyes. He managed just one sip of the coffee before tiredness overcame him and he fell asleep, the coffee left untouched on the side.

When the car silently pulled into the drive, only the opening and closing of the doors could be heard. And it was only Philip who heard them and jumped down from the sofa where he had been sleeping, curled up next to his master who was oblivious to the faint and distant noise.

"It's good to be home again," said Adrienne, holding the baby in her arms as she stepped over the threshold. She sighed and shed a tear but it was one of happiness, glad to be back to familiar surroundings and her husband. Ten days she had been away, nine of those without seeing Theo and she so wanted to be held and cuddled by him. She was about to call him when Anca gestured not to do that.

"He might be sleeping," she whispered.

They walked inside silently, Anca showing Adrienne where she had placed the baby's cot, in one of the spare living rooms with a baby monitor ready to be switched on.

"I think I'll keep her on me for now, Anca. Don't want to disturb her," she said, kicking off her shoes and walking into the kitchen. Philip followed her, curious as to what she was holding against her chest.

After drinking a satisfying glass of water, Adrienne wandered from room to room, kissing the baby's head with the finest of touches. When she came to the living room, she couldn't help smiling and then fought back tears seeing Theo propped up with pillows, looking peaceful in his sleep.

"I missed you, Flint," she said quietly, as she sat down next to him. She leant against him, putting her feet up next to his on the pouf. Before long, her eyes felt heavy and she too fell asleep.

Anca had come into the room to offer to make Adrienne a proper cup of coffee as she called it but seeing them contentedly asleep, she decided not to disturb them. Instead, she opened her phone and took several pictures of the three people who were in her care.

Theo thought he could hear a quiet, whimpering noise. He wasn't sure whether that was real or in his sleep and half-opened his eyes. The clock on the mantle was showing early afternoon.

"Flint, are you awake?" said a voice and looking to his left, she was there.

"Kiffy! You are back, and oh my God, it's…" he was lost for words.

"Yes, that's right, Flint. Mister Theodore Blenkinsop, let me introduce you to your daughter, Eloise Beatrix Madeleine Blenkinsop. She's sorry she can't talk right now but she is busy feeding," she giggled, as the baby suckled on her breast.

"I can't believe it, I finally get to meet her," he said, excitedly casting away his normal reserve.

"So glad to be home, Flint. Queen Charlotte's have been brilliant looking after me and Eloise but I couldn't wait to come home, sleep in my own bed, with my hubby next to me," she said and started to cry. "I am so happy, Flint. Really happy. I couldn't be happier. I have the man of my dreams and I have the most delightful gift of a baby you have given me. I can't be any happier."

"Glad you are back too, Kiffy. The house feels empty without you here, and I missed you. I think I even missed you shouting at me!" he joked.

"No more of that, we don't want to give Eloise the wrong impression about mama and papa, do we?"

"She is so small," he whispered, trying to turn and peer at the baby.

"She is six or seven weeks early, Flint, what do you expect? But she is going to be tall, the midwife told me. Even though she was born premature, she is very long for her age. She will take after her father, no doubt."

Theo watched intently as the baby suckled instinctively.

"Hey Flint, don't look. These are off limits for the next year or so. From now on they are just for Eloise, her food not for your entertainment," she said, giggling.

"That's fine, Kiffy, I never expected anything else. I read about how important it is for the baby to have breast milk, most nutritional meal it can get. So, no problem with that."

"And also, I'm sore down below so that's off limits for a while," she said.

"So you had a natural birth in the end not by c section or whatever you call it?"

"No, I chickened out. The more I read about it the less sure I was that it was the right thing to do. Besides, Eloise was in a hurry to come out and being born early she was not as big as some babies, just 2.1 kilos. Still, it is a big thing to come out of that narrow opening and I tore a bit; I needed two stitches. So, nothing for you for a while, I'm afraid, at least not from me."

Theo pulled a face. "It is not a problem, Kiffy. I understand. I am not exactly in a fit state myself."

"Oh my God, I'm so selfish. I completely forgot to ask about how you are. Oh Flint, please forgive me, my darling. This baby has so preoccupied me I forget about the people around me. How did your operation go? Anca told me Mr Shah said it was fine but how do you feel?"

"I really am fine," he said, touching her arm by way of assurance. "I just need to take it easy, that's all. By the way, Mr Shah said I cannot lift anything heavy so, as much as I want to, I will not be able to help with the nappy changes I'm afraid."

"As if you would!" she laughed.

Leaving

“So now you’ve told me that since we went our separate ways you’ve got married and you also have a child by your old man, and now you come to see me to say goodbye, after all this time, Adrienne?” he said, in a tone with a hint of disbelief.

“No, yes, not exactly,” she said, distracted by the breathing noise in the pram. She peered in and was assured all was well. “I came to make peace and leave on a good note between us, Jonas. When we broke up, if you remember, there was a lot of shouting and bad words said. We both said horrible things and I’ve never felt good about that, maybe even a little ashamed and I wanted to apologise for my part in it. I am sure you had your reasons for doing what you did and I didn’t give you a chance to explain yourself.”

“No, you didn’t but it doesn’t matter now. I am in a new relationship as you are, so we each got what we wanted in the end. Not sure I would go so far as getting married and having a kid, as you have. That’s definitely not me but we’ve made a life together.”

“The girl I caught you fucking on our bed?” she said, caustically.

“Jane? No, that didn’t last. I have moved on, found someone else,” he said, without elaborating.

“You know she, Jane that is, did us a massive favour, Jonas. We weren’t going anywhere, just drifting, like two sticks of wood down a stream. Sooner or later, we were going to break up. We were too comfortable, not really trying. In a nothing state which seemed to suit both of us. I guess I wanted something more out of life and Jane was the push that I needed, to get up off my ass and do something.”

“You certainly did, Adrienne. In less than a year you met someone, you got married and had a child. And not just an ordinary man, a very wealthy, corporate lawyer, no less, who introduced you to a lifestyle that you could only dream of. You certainly landed on your feet, as the English say,” he said, mockingly.

“Yes, Jonas, you are right. Up to a point. You see, I knew I could make that dream come true, with the right man, but just not…" she stopped herself.

"Just not me," he said, finishing her sentence. "I'm just a car salesman."

"You said it, Jonas. I'm afraid I outgrew you. I wanted more than that."

"You always were a snob, Adrienne. We bought an overpriced apartment in Putney overlooking the river because you wanted to live somewhere trendy."

"What's wrong with that? I wanted the best," she defended.

"And you didn't find that in me. I get it," he said and then added, "And this guy, Theo, he's the best, is he?"

"Yes! The very best." she said proudly.

"Good in bed, is he?"

"The best!"

"You love him?"

"With all my heart."

"Not just because he is rich, very rich and keeps you in a luxurious lifestyle?" he taunted.

"You can laugh at me, call me shallow or whatever you like, Jonas but that lifestyle is important to me. Isn't easy living what most people want, even you, Jonas? But even if he wasn't rich, he would still be the one for me. He and I click on so many levels, not just in bed. He stimulates my mind, challenges me, makes me laugh, makes me cry, we laugh a lot, we fight…"

"You fight? You and I never had a fight," he pointed out.

"Yes Jonas, you and I never had a fight because there was no passion between us; we never argued about anything. If I said something and you didn't agree or disliked it, you politely kept quiet and if you said something I didn't agree with or didn't like, I didn't say anything to you about it. It was like we were two friends and too polite to challenge each other. But with Theo, he is my soulmate as well as my lover and we argue; not in a horrible way but we talk about anything and everything and neither of us holds back if they disagree. That is the big difference; when you are close to someone you can do that. You and I were…"

"Never that close. I know, that. You are right, Adrienne. I may be just a car salesman but not such a clunk-head that I couldn't see that we were miles apart. I just didn't know what to do about it," he sighed. "So what now for you?"

"Theo is in Abu Dhabi already. He has started working there since the beginning of January. He was over the moon when his business opened up on time. He is doing what he loves, being a lawyer in the Middle East, his lifelong dream is being fulfilled.

"We have said our goodbyes to everyone. We went down to his family home and they had a big party to welcome our new baby. We had a christening and a leaving party and celebrated Christmas too, all rolled into one."

"Christening? I thought you were against all that?" he quizzed her.

"Yes, but Theo wanted it and his family wanted it. Why wouldn't I agree? That would be very selfish of me!"

"Hmm, maybe this guy has been good for you after all, Adrienne. You used to be so selfish when you lived with me," he laughed.

"Yes, Jonas, he has been good for me. He is everything I want in a man and he brings out the best in me, for sure. I even like a bacon sandwich although I always kick up a fuss when he suggests it," she chuckled.

"All set to go then? Everything sorted and shipped out?"

"Pretty much. The house is being looked after by Theo's sister. We still need a base in London and Theo didn't want to rent it to strangers and I agree with him. The electric family car went to his father, even if he doesn't like it. Quite funny because he said it was weird driving a battery-driven car, which is exactly what Theo said. Like father, like son, hey? Everything else is taken care of. Anca is still here and she will be flying out with me, to live with us and hopefully start a fitness business out there. I am also looking to start French classes once the baby is a little older and I get into some sort of routine."

"You're going to work? A rich woman like you? Why would you want to do that and in a strange country? If you were my wife, I wouldn't want you to work," he said, reprovingly.

"That's one of the differences between you and him, Jonas. He encourages me to do what I want to do, doesn't try to put me off or set limits as to what I can or cannot do."

"No limits? He's brave, isn't he? Being an old man," he said and paused to see any change in her reaction, "is he not nervous that you might meet a young, handsome, Arab who will whisk you away from him? You know what you're like, Adrienne. You're never going to be content with what you have. You're a free spirit as you once told me; restless. Not the settling down type and I don't see you doing that for long and certainly not with a man old enough to be your father."

"You're wrong, Jonas. That may have been true of me in the past. But now I have found everything I want in my life. The restlessness has gone and with this man, my spirit is even more free than it ever was. And as for his age, I have never felt it. I don't need a younger man, be it an Arab or any other man."

"Not even in bed? You were always very passionate, very demanding in bed," he said.

"Jonas, I don't want to hurt your feelings but he satisfies me in ways you could not. And in two days' time, I will be flying out there to join him and start the next part of my life. A new and exciting life with my husband and my daughter."

Jonas was silent.

"Anyway, I just came to say goodbye, Jonas. To wish you well in the future. With your new girlfriend. I hope it works out for you, this time. Work at it. You have the looks: classic, German, tall, handsome-type that I fell for what seems like a long, long time ago. You just need to work on the rest and I am sure it will turn out good for you."

Jonas managed a smile. "Friends?"

"Friends," she said and opened her arms out for a hug.

"Can I visit? I've never been to Abu Dhabi?"

Adrienne shrugged. "Sure, why not? But only with your partner, not on your own. When you have a full-time girlfriend, Jonas, you will be welcome to come and visit us."

Jonas chuckled.

Two days later, Adrienne, with Eloise sleeping against her chest, followed Anca into the first-class compartment of the Airbus A380 airplane that was taking them to the start of a new life.

"I'm really excited," said Anca, as she settled into her luxurious seat.

"Me too," said Adrienne. As for Eloise, she was blissfully unaware that eight hours later, a new life would be awaiting her in the Persian Gulf.